It is true, writing is a solitary endeavor. It is equally true, the work would not be complete without the help and input from countless others. This is certainly the case with "Jenny." While it is impossible to name all to whom I am very grateful, there are a few who have journeyed with me much of way. I am most grateful for my wife, Diane's, patience during my endless hours at the computer. I can never thank the unknown Arizona Highway Patrolman who stopped me for speeding while Jenny was in its infancy and provided great insight into illegal immigration and the work of the "Coyote." I am thankful of my twin brother, Rollie, for his taunting to get with it and finish the work. I am thankful for my many friends, who like Jim and Linda Ring encouraged me emotionally and financially throughout the writing process. I owe much thanks to my friend Ron Hughes, whose editor's eye and sense of word usage provided a final critical edit for the work's completion. Lastly, I thank you the reader, for joining Jenny's journey. I pray you enjoy the story as much as I enjoyed bringing Jenny to life.

Prologue

Boston, *August 1994*

"Forgive me, Father, for I have sinned," said the effeminate voice.

The dark confessional booth smelled of old wood and burning wax from rows of candles flickering on the altar beyond the narrow wood entrance to the little cell. Dust particles floated along a thin shaft of light penetrating the space through a cracked hinge.

The aged priest recognized the pleading. "Speak to me, my son," he beckoned timeless words spoken to hopeless, nameless souls seeking forgiveness and release from their burdensome deeds, thoughts, and fears. "The Lord is merciful beyond measure. His mercy endures forever." The priest asked no questions, made no demands. He simply reflected the love of Jesus and granted forgiveness, for all have sinned.

Outside, a new Mercedes sedan, its lights on, moved slowly through Boston's narrow streets toward the old gray-stone church on the fringe of the city's red-light district. An early-August heat wave was taking its toll on city residents. The misty air smelled of two-week old garbage that would not be collected until the demands of the local garbage haulers' union were met without exception. Godsent was the occasional coastal breeze that refreshed the air with a saltiness one could taste. Streetlights had been lit for at least thirty minutes, illuminating tenements in a dim cast. Eeriness rode the stench of this still-humid night.

At the church, the sedan pulled to the curb. Its lights blinked off. Its engine purred at idle. The car's thermostat registered in the blue; everything was cool. The dark-skinned driver, young, in his late twenties or early thirties, lit a cigarette and settled back into the elegant leather seat. Savoring his inhale, he surveyed the eight century-worn stone steps rising from the sidewalk to two gigantic doors he knew would soon open. He looked at his watch.

A distant horn sounded. As on cue, the driver snapped on the dome light that reflected off his jet-black hair, subdued with fragrant sweet-smelling oil. A small gold cross shimmered at the end of a delicate gold chain adorning one ear. On the passenger's seat sat a small leather compact disc case and a stone-black pistol, an automatic with a silencer. The driver wore surgical gloves on both hands that now opened the CD case and selected a reggae album—a remembrance from home—and inserted it into the car's dashboard player. Instantly, the interior filled with a delightfully happy tune. He switched off the light, exhaled, and settled back to wait. Everything remained cool.

"Go in God's peace and sin no more," offered the priest to his restless parishioner.

"Thank you, Father," acknowledged the young man. Then he pushed open the door and stepped with expensive Italian shoes onto the sanctuary's worn stone floor. Pausing briefly at the altar, he produced a small gold lighter, found a candle, and lit it. Placing it with the others, he crossed himself and walked up the aisle.

Sprinkled in the old worn pews were parishioners kneeling in prayer. A young couple holding hands stepped to one side and smiled as he passed. Beyond the narthex, he pushed open one large door and paused for a moment on the wide top step to survey the dimly lit street.

JENNY

The familiar car waiting at the curb brought a smile. He breathed deeply, tucked his shirt into skin-tight jeans, and slowly unbuttoned the top three buttons of his billowing silk shirt to reveal half a dozen gold chains cascading down his baby-smooth chest. Ready, he thrust back his head and shoulders and pranced lightly toward the waiting car, its passenger window slowly receding into the door panel. Smiling, he bent to look inside. "You've come alone? No matter, tonight will be a night to remember."

The driver's deep voice resonated, "One you will remember for eternity. The senator sends his love." Then quickly, he raised his pistol to the forehead of the grinning face and fired. There was a poking sound of muffled air as a small round hole appeared between the young man's eyes, suddenly opened wide in disbelief.

The body fell backward onto the church steps where a dark pool quickly formed beneath the lifeless addition to the city's garbage. The car's headlights blinked on. The sound of reggae disappeared into the swirling mist of the car's wake. Inside, everything remained cool.

Chapter 1

Honking Canada geese shattered the predawn silence, swooping low over the placid channel beyond Jennifer Poole's bedroom balcony. She stirred under the cotton blanket, partially covering her slim summer-tanned body. She could almost hear the flapping of their wings through the open sliding glass door as the nocturnal fog gave way to the reality of a new day.

She loved the call of the geese announcing their return early spring each year, as the lake's black ice turned honeycomb and magically disappeared. In fact, spring was Jenny's favorite season, a time of renewed hope, filled with anticipation. She and Christopher had married in the spring. It was spring, five years earlier, when they bought their town house on Lake Minnetonka. Her son Jason was five then; the spring she landed her marketing position at WYCO Toys, one of the nation's largest international toy companies.

But spring had passed; it was now summer, and the noisy honking was annoying. As the big birds made another pass, she buried her head under her pillow to mute the sound. Then she remembered, today was Thursday. She raised a corner of the pillow to focus one eye on her clock blinking 5:43 a.m. She was ahead of schedule. *Good*, she sighed. This was not just another Thursday; it was a day of celebration.

Her employer WYCO Toys, the abbreviated name of Wayzata Toy Company, had opened their large and very successful retail store at Minnesota's Mall of America the previous year. She had no small role in that success. The store's name, House of Toys, had been her submission in a company-wide contest and had been personally selected by Virginia Leonard, wife of CEO Creighton Leonard, the company's new majority shareholder. Today marked the kickoff of a new marketing campaign, also her idea. Later at the store, on national television, she would be recognized for her career achievements, her contributions to the success of the famed Wayzata Toy Company, a name she had grown up with, living on Minnesota's Lake Minnetonka.

She knew she was just added dressing to a far bigger show. She would join Creighton Leonard at the podium. Beside him would be visiting Japanese dignitaries, more dressing to show support for the controversial Latin America Industrial Partnership Treaty, known by its acronym LAIPT. The treaty was unprecedented but expected to soon get congressional approval. Massachusetts Senator Malovich, controversial chairman of the Senate committee sponsoring the treaty, would be in attendance to present a bronze plaque to Creighton Leonard, honoring WYCO's contribution to his Senate committee, a vital element of the bill's successful passage. That is if he could leave Washington during the Senate's own investigation into his personal ethics and conduct.

Nonetheless, today would begin like all nice-weather Thursdays during Minnesota's short summers with a boat ride and a breakfast at Milly's, her son Jason's favorite restaurant at the east end of Water Street in the lake-town of Excelsior. It had become their summer tradition, especially welcome with Chris traveling much of the time. A busy schedule, but somehow, she'd squeeze it all in. She always did.

After breakfast, she'd drop Jason at Sue Webster's lakeshore home in Woodland at the lake's east end, where he'd spend the day with his buddy Peter. She'd push *Little Red* to full throttle for the five-mile return home and a change of clothes. At seventy miles per hour, she'd have plenty of time. Christian had promised to catch an early flight home and share her moment of honor. It was a *perfect* August day—the weather, delightful, and the lake, glass calm. *Perfection*, she said to herself as her feet touched the floor.

"Jason. Time to get going," Jenny shouted as she passed Jason's bedroom on her way to her morning coffee, her bare feet barely touching the steps to the first-floor kitchen. Like her bedroom, the kitchen viewed the backyard and the channel beyond. The morning sun gave the sky a crimson cast. A dozen ducks floated half-submerged, bottoms up, bottom feeding close to shore.

She checked the calendar on the kitchen counter, tore off yesterday's verse, and read the verse for the day: "This is a day that the Lord has made. Rejoice and be glad in it." "I can do that," she said to no one in particular and turned to the sputtering coffee maker. For an instant, she sniffed the air, savored the aroma, finding it almost… sensual. "Jason, it's time. Let's get going," she yelled again as she looked at her watch. No time to waste. Not today.

"I know," came a response.

Well, at least he's awake.

A moment later, she felt Jason's arms reach around her waist as he snuggled in behind her, resting his head against the curve of her slim hips. "Good morning, sir," she said. "I didn't hear you come down." She turned, leaned back against the counter, and ran her fingers through his satiny brown hair. Jason stood silently in his pajamas, still half-asleep.

She loved his affection, his gentle hugs, felt blessed; needed it with Christian off in some faraway place. Jason so resembled his father. In childhood photos, they appeared identical. They laughed the same, shared the same quiet, often mischievous, temperament. "Let's see if your father called."

She dragged Jason, still in hug mode, across the room to the telephone. She had not heard it ring during the night, but its message light was blinking. Her finger found the retrieve button. "Good morning," boomed Chris's singsong greeting. She pushed "speaker" so Jason could hear. "I'm in New York City. Got in late, twelve-thirty here…thunderstorms…same bad weather that messed up our weekend on the lake."

Jenny's body tensed, sensing what was coming. "I'll be here through Saturday. Bad news, I know. Jen, I'm truly sorry. I'm sick that I can't be there today. You know how it is. I just can't break away." Jenny shook her head. She knew; boy did she know. Now he addressed Jason, "Mind your mom and take good care of her. You're the man of the house when I'm gone, remember."

Jenny watched a smile form on Jason's face. Her face flushed with anger. She wanted to throw the answering machine against the wall. *When will it end? When he becomes a full partner?* That was always her husband's answer.

"Jen, I really am sorry. Believe it, please. It can't be helped. Honest. I love you."

She hid her anger as the message ended, and she turned to Jason. "So, man-of-the-house, are you ready for pancakes at Milly's? The lake is like glass, and there's not a cloud in the sky."

Jason cocked his head and smiled. "Can I drive? Like, I mean, really drive? From here to Excelsior. You can still dock it. Mom, can I?"

She smiled and barked, "Upstairs," and pushed Jason toward the stairs, with a swat to his muscular behind, the butt of a hockey player, another quality Jason shared with his father.

She watched him disappear and refilled her cup, then turned to the window, and the high-performance bass boat tethered at the dock. Jason would soon want to take it out himself. But not today, she resolved, way too dangerous, then she turned to reset the answering machine, pushed rewind, and then pushed play in case she had missed a call.

She had missed a call. "Jenny, it's Sharon, Wednesday afternoon, five-fifteen, working late." The voice was Sharon Miller's, her assistant. Jenny smiled. Sharon was as dedicated as any one person could be, loved working late and loved to rub it in. "Have you seen Jennifer Stewart, the new girl? She's supposed to be helping me get ready for tomorrow. Seems she's disappeared. Started…a week ago, recently anyway, 'gofer' status, but has not been seen since. If you see her, tell her I'm expecting her at the store tomorrow, early." Jenny was aware a new girl had been assigned to her department, but they had not met. *So her name is Jenny Stewart.* Sharon continued, "Oh, and if I don't see you before your performance, break a leg, or whatever it is you're supposed to do for good luck."

Jenny rewound the tape, swallowed a final gulp of coffee, dropped the cup in the sink, and turned to go upstairs when the phone rang. Expecting it to be Chris calling to wish her well, she lifted the receiver and snapped playfully, "Yes, and what do you want?"

"Is this Jennifer?" asked a strange voice.

"Yes it is. This is Jennifer Poole," she answered pleasantly. "Can I help you?"

"Oh! I'm sorry. This isn't Jennifer Stewart?"

"No. You have the wrong number. This is Jennifer Poole." Before Jenny could finish, the line clicked dead.

Jennifer Stewart. The new girl. Odd, she thought as she slowly placed the phone back on its cradle. *Her name twice in as many minutes? Why would someone call my number, my home, looking for… Jennifer Stewart? Same first name? Same employer? Happenstance,* she concluded and sprinted up the stairs, taking two at a time for exercise.

It took ten minutes to shower, dress in jeans—tighter than she remembered—and crawl into an old Harvard Business School sweatshirt that she had liberated from her father's closet. Finally, she grabbed a towel and formed a turban on her head. "Jason, time to go," she yelled one last time and light-footed it down the stairs.

The back door stood wide open. On the dock, Jason was releasing the mooring lines on *Little Red*. *This is a day to rejoice,* Jenny reflected.

She released the last line, threw it on the deck, and jumped aboard. Jason was already behind the wheel grinning like the Cheshire cat. They moved slowly up the channel to the open lake. Red-winged blackbirds bobbed atop cattails responding to *Little Red*'s minimal wake. In open water, Jason gingerly pushed the throttle to bring the boat up on plane for the mile run to Excelsior.

Chapter 2

*C**lap-clap.* The screen doors slamming shut caused Jenny to smile as Jason bolted from Milly's into the humid August air. She'd catch up with him across the street at the city dock *Little Red* was tied and ready for the seven-mile run to Peter's dock. On the ride to Excelsior, Jenny had promised Jason he could take the wheel again the entire way to Peter's dock, even speed it up a notch. That's all Jason needed; he could barely take time to swallow. Breakfast had been a whirlwind. She understood his excitement. He'd be anticipating Peter standing at his dock, watching him skipper *Little Red* and dock it unattended.

"Whew! That boy's in some hurry," observed Milly as she milked her fingers dry on her green flowered apron, a look of concern on her face. She wore a scarf wrapped around her head of dark curly hair, tied off just above her forehead by two small knots giving her a mischievous pixy look. "Couldn't help notice, you two looked awful serious this morning. Everything's okay? I don't mean to pry."

Jenny handed Millie a twenty, accepted change, and stepped back from the counter as Milly nudged the cash register drawer closed and considered her response. She liked Milly, considered her to be a sincere and compassionate friend.

"Everything is fine. Jason just misses his dad."

"Still traveling a lot, is he?"

"Until he makes partner." Jenny grimaced in a pout. "It's complicated. His best friend's parents are getting a divorce. A dad that is never home. Jason…You know, he's comparing that to his own dad's traveling…It's complicated."

"Boys need their dads. That's for sure," Milly said sympathetically, changing the subject. "Say, isn't this your big day? You know a salute to your illustrious career, womanhood and all that? And did I hear some senator is in town for the occasion?" Milly—forty-something—twanged like a Texan who had been living in the North for a while, but not long enough to sound Minnesotan with its clearly defined and enunciated vowels.

"Senator Malovich. He's not coming for me. He's a friend of our CEO Creighton Leonard. And then there's this treaty thing. How did you know?"

"You're a celebrity. It's been all over the news," declared Milly, somewhat gleefully.

"I guess. It's a job…And a good one. I do like it, but often I prefer being just a wife and a mother. Besides, they make it sound like it was all me. It was a team effort. I worked hard, but others did too," she said humbly. "I'm pleased, really. Honored is a better word. What can I say?"

"Well, darlin', accept it. A little recognition should do your heart good. Some people work a lifetime and never get a speck of notice."

"As Chris keeps reminding me."

"He's coming home for this, I bet." It was more of a question than a statement.

"No, unfortunately. He's stuck in New York. Again. It's his job. That's what's so tough on Jason. He sees me upset, and…he gets concerned. Guess I'm not hiding it well this time."

"It'll get better, hon. It surely will."

"I know. I really believe that. I do. I live with that hope." She pushed the change into her pocket. "It'll be televised. Scheduled to air at noon."

"No television here. But you can tell me all about it next Thursday. Besides, I'll catch it on the late news."

JENNY

Jenny smiled, pushed open the double doors, heard the friendly *clap-clap* behind her, and surveyed the parking lot for Jason. No Jason. She sprinted toward the city docks.

Long gone were Abel Catering's trademark stainless steel delivery vans that had been parked at the curb when Jenny and Jason docked. Visible were the stately tour boats that plied the waters of Lake Minnetonka during the lake's short summer season. They waited quietly at their moorings, their crews inside preparing for the day's charters, restocking galleys with hot meals and coffee delivered dockside by Abel Catering.

At the city dock, *Little Red*'s bright-red hull reflected off glass-smooth water, ropes still attached. No sign of Jason. "Jason!" she yelled, quickening her pace. She expected to see him sitting behind the steering wheel. "Jason. Where…?" She yelled again, closing the distance to *Little Red*.

Visiting at one of the charters, she thought and glanced about to see if Captain Hank and his boat, *Drift Away*, was docked nearby. Jason loved Captain Hank, often easily sidetracked by this seasoned skipper and his stories of the lake, its boats and the people who owned and drove them. *Of course. Jason would want Hank to know his own day of passage had arrived.*

She stepped off the dock onto the walkway that meandered along the shoreline. There were several large sturdy docks, built strong to withstand Minnesota's winters and the spring ice flow. Viewing the many boats, *Drift Away* was not one. But Jason could be on any one; he loved the big boats. Their crews consisted mostly of college kids, many with younger brothers and sisters. They enjoyed Jason's visits, his knowledge of the lake, and Jason was always careful to stay out of their way. She walked slowly along the line of boats. No Jason. It wasn't like Jason to go inside without telling her.

A rusty brown van with its back doors open was parked beside the path leading to one of the large boats. A young man, coveralls black with grease, rummaged through a toolbox. Parts scattered about said he'd been there awhile. She started toward him.

Further on at the intersection, a green sports car pulled to a stop. Its driver rolled down his window, his eyes fixed on Jenny. Sensing his stare, she glanced in his direction. For an instant, their eyes connected. *Was that a look of surprise*, she wondered. But his long thin face was not one she recognized. Yet, there was something…something familiar sparking deep in her memory. She ignored the distraction, quickened her pace toward the dirty mechanic. The green car's driver struggled for a final look and drove off.

Hearing Jenny's footsteps, the mechanic turned to face her when suddenly an object floating near the dock caught her attention. She did an abrupt about-face. Registering his confusion, the mechanic shook his head while his eyes followed her running toward the object.

Cautiously she approached the shore and the object floating half-submerged ten feet beyond, encased in a mass of lake weeds. Suddenly gripped by fear, her eyes probed the surface. *Could he have lost his balance, fallen into the lake unable to call for help? God, no*, she prayed silently. For three agonizing seconds, her breathing stopped until she recognized a soggy beer case and sighed thankfully. *Thank heaven. What am I thinking?* Now fear turned to anger. She'd allowed fear to create an image so real, so vivid—Jason floating facedown in the weeds.

She shrugged and returned her attention to the mechanic who had not taken his eyes off her but stood mesmerized, gripping a part for something in his hand as she walked toward him. "Did you see a boy? Brown hair, about this tall?" she asked, stopping three feet from him, holding a hand at midchest to indicate his height. But he was speechless standing there, his smudged face contorted, his mouth moving, but with no audible words.

"He's wearing a…a striped T-shirt and Levi's," she added.

"No. I…I'm sorry," he stuttered finally. "I haven't seen… seen anyone. This engine…I've…" His words stopped. His mouth dropped open. What could he say? He wasn't good with words. His eyes, though, said he cared.

"Thanks," said Jenny, forcing a smile before darting back toward Milly's.

Chapter 3

Some called him Mike. To others, he was Old Mike, pushing sixty-something. Mentally challenged since birth, he captured the hearts of the residents and was now a ward of the town. He'd been cared for by his mother in a clapboard house, back on Third Street, until she began to fail. Then it was time for Mike to care for her, which he did against all odds, until her last breath. That's when Excelsior more or less adopted him, and he became an unofficial ward of the town.

The previous summer, Jason and Mike had met on the Excelsior Commons, a large park bordering Lake Minnetonka's Excelsior Bay, where both had stopped to admire the hundreds of geese that had come ashore. They had bonded instantly. Their bodies were of different generations, but their minds were of the same—kids in mind and in heart. Jason considered Mike simply as a kid trapped in a sixty-year-old body. They were pals.

He appeared now from nowhere. Jenny almost ran past him but was halted by his soft baritone voice. All five-foot-five of him stood on the sidewalk across the street from the mechanic, shirt tails hanging out, a short, soggy cigar clenched between coffee- and tobacco-stained teeth, while he carried on a conversation with someone seen only by him.

Jenny stopped to face him and asked, "What? What did you say?"

Much the gentleman, Old Mike tipped his tattered hat. A well-chewed cigar dangled loosely in his hand. "Looking for your boy?" He didn't give Jenny time to answer. "I saw him."

"You saw my son Jason? Where?"

"Here."

"Mike, how long ago did you see him?"

"Not long." He tugged at a chain tied to his belt loop to retrieve a large pocket watch, mumbled something, and returned it to his pocket. "He ran out the door…Milly's. A man in one of the trucks grabbed him. Took him and drove away."

"Someone…took Jason? You saw someone take him?" Jenny was incredulous.

"From one of the food trucks. A man in white…Not a nice man. Not like the others. Wouldn't give me coffee. Came up behind Jason. Covered Jason's nose. Jason tried to get away, but another man got out and put him inside. It happened fast. He couldn't—"

"Where'd they go?" she asked, horrified.

"Don't know…They left."

"Which way? Did you see?"

Mike pointed east, out of town, beyond the municipal liquor store.

"Please wait here! Please, don't go!" Jenny started toward Milly's but returned after a few steps, placed her hands on Mike's shoulders, and looked him squarely in the eyes.

Mike pulled away, startled, but Jenny held on. "Mike, I'm sorry…please," she pleaded, her eyes focused on his. "You are sure?" she asked resolutely, slowly enunciating each word. "You saw a man from one of the food trucks grab Jason and drive away?" It was too impossible to believe. She released Mike's shoulders and cradled her face in her hands. It was more than she could comprehend. She wanted to scream at the top of her lungs. She wanted to cry.

"Yes, ma'am"—he pointed toward the Commons—"back there." In a few words, Mike explained what he had seen. His eyes darted from side to side as he spoke excitedly. Each word intensifying Jenny's anxiety. When his eyes again fixed on Jenny, he became silent.

"Okay, Mike. I'll be right back. Please…please stay here."

JENNY

Mike smiled, returned the wrinkled hat to his head, and watched Jenny run to Milly's and explode through her double doors.

The cafe was empty except for Milly wiping tables with a damp cloth. She leaned over the table where minutes earlier Jenny and Jason had enjoyed breakfast and talked of Peter Webster and his parent's divorce. Sweeping crumbs into cupped hand, she turned at the sound of the door, nearly losing her balance. "Jenny?" Milly gasped.

"Milly, where's your phone? Call 911! Call the police!"

Milly dropped the damp cloth and sprang toward the kitchen and the phone hanging on the doorframe. She wrung her hands in her apron as she ran. "Jenny, what's wrong? Was there an accident?" she questioned as she put the receiver to her ear.

"It's Jason. Milly, he's been kidnapped. He's gone. A man from one of those food trucks took him. Please, Milly, call 911. Now! Milly!"

Milly's eyes followed her until the doors clapped shut. Milly poked at the phone in her hand, took a breath, and poked again at the keypad and waited for a voice on the other end of the line.

Mike had not moved. He removed the drooping cigar from his mouth. His eyes glued on Jenny as she ran toward him from the parking lot. A siren whined in the distance.

Chapter 4

A white police car screamed into the parking lot and stopped abruptly at the curb in front of Milly's double doors, its flashing red lights casting an eerie, animated glow on Milly's windows and those of neighboring shops. The electronic siren slowly died like a balloon losing its last bit of air. But not before all of Excelsior knew something was amiss at Milly's.

Milly was waiting outside and loosed her hands from her apron to direct the officer to Jenny, deep in conversation with Old Mike, whose bulbous belly protruded beneath his brightly checkered shirt with half its buttons missing. Beneath Mike's dent-pocked hat, dark-brown eyes darted from Jenny to the flashing lights and back again. On the ground beside Mike's new blue sneakers lay one very soggy, well-chewed cigar.

The officer spoke into his microphone, grabbed his clipboard from the front seat of his cruiser, and marched toward Jenny and Old Mike. Mike's eyes exploded like saucers. "I'm Officer Larry Randall. We received a 911 call…abduction of a young boy," said Randall, his manner trained, disciplined, and official.

"My son, Jason Poole. He's ten." Her voice faltered as she fought back tears. "We just finished breakfast. Minutes ago. We came by boat." Jenny pointed to the city docks. "He left before me to get the boat ready. When I came out, he was gone. Someone took him! Why? Tell me this isn't happening." Sobbing engulfed her.

Randall let her cry for a moment then asked apologetically, "I know this is difficult, but are you sure he was abducted? Did you see someone take him?"

"No. I was inside Milly's." She pointed to Mike. "But Mike saw the whole—"

Randall looked questioningly at Mike. "Who beside Mike witnessed the abduction?" interrupted Randall.

"I don't know. Possibly someone on the boats. Look, Mike did see it. He's the one who told me Jason was kidnapped. He was on his way back from the Commons and saw them," explained Jenny, frustration sounding in her voice. *Why doesn't he believe me?* "Look, Mike saw it. We're all that's here," she said and waived her arm in a big circle for emphasis.

Randall nodded toward the mechanic at his van. "How about him? Did he see anything?"

"I asked, and he didn't see anything," said Jenny, a slow anger replacing her tears. "Officer Randall, Mike is the only one who saw anything." After Randall made a notation on his clipboard, she added, "Oh…there was a green sports car at the stop sign. I sensed it had been there awhile. I don't know…He could have seen something. Long gone as you can see."

A few early risers had stopped on the sidewalk, wondering at the commotion. A distracted jogger ran into the back of a parked car and limped off, embarrassed and in obvious pain.

Randall switched to his most reassuring voice. "Miss?"

"I'm Jennifer Poole. Please call me Jenny."

"Jenny, I'd like you to step over to my car, please." Randall then motioned to Mike, whose lips moved but made no sound. "You too, Mike. It'll be okay. I have just a few questions. Mike, you saw what happened?" he asked. Mike nodded.

Randall opened both passenger doors. Jenny squeezed into the front next to Randall's computer. Mike hesitantly eyed the back seat behind the squad's bulletproof divider, reached inside his sweater, extracted a slightly used cigar from his shirt pocket, jammed it into his mouth, rolled it a quarter turn, bit down, then repeated the process several times, unable to make himself move. His eyes darted from Officer Randall to the car and back.

After an awkward silence, Randall addressed Old Mike, "It's okay, Mike. We can talk later. How'd you like a cup of Milly's coffee? I bet she's got a fresh pot."

Milly had been watching and understood. "Mike," she beckoned and opened a door for Mike to enter. He walked up the few stairs to Milly's entrance, removed his hat, stepped inside, and placed the cigar bank in his shirt pocket.

Randall climbed in behind the wheel, turned off his flashing lights, and turned to face Jenny. "Mrs. Poole…Jenny," he corrected himself, "we'll do everything in our power to find your son." He assured with a voice official yet friendly. "Our chief is one of the best there is. He'll bring in all the resources we need. But we must act quickly. You understand that?"

Jenny nodded, extracted her billfold from her purse and fumbled to produce a small photograph of Jason. For several seconds, she savored a final look then handed it to Randall. "This was taken six months ago. He's grown a little, but he looks the same. He's ten years old, dark-brown hair, brown eyes, dark complexion, about four feet ten inches tall. Firm build, he plays hockey. He's wearing Levi's and a striped Polo T-shirt with a yellow emblem."

"Any birthmarks? Scars or anything that can help identify him?"

"A scar from a skate cut on his left leg."

Randall jotted a few notes. "Now what did Mike see?"

Jenny sighed and took a breath. "Mike was returning from the Commons, maybe half a block away. He watched Jason leave the restaurant, cross the parking lot, and stop at the curb. Then a man in a white uniform got out of the truck, came up behind him, put his hand over Jason's mouth and nose. Jason struggled, but could not get away. A second man was waiting on the passenger side with his door open. This man picked up Jason and put him inside."

"Did he describe the men?"

"Mike said the men were dark complected. Both had black hair. The driver's hair was wavy, not short, but not long either. Both wore white and came from one of those stainless vans."

"An Abel Food Services van. They're a large catering company out of Eden Prairie and service most of the charters operating here, as well as the airlines and many businesses. Their trucks are one of a kind. Please continue."

Jenny slowly recalled all that Mike had told her. "Mike thought the driver might be religious. He wore an earring with a small gold cross dangling from a chain. These men weren't the regulars Mike knew. They wouldn't give him free coffee and a roll. The driver told him to get lost."

"Mike spoke to them?"

"Earlier…on his way to the Commons. When we arrived, there were two trucks, one large, one small. We walked between them to Milly's. The small truck was on our right. The driver was a woman. I remember the smell of fresh coffee. She was moving large urns to the boats."

"And the second truck?"

"Shiny and bigger. That's all I remember."

Randall squirmed in his seat and spoke as he jotted more notes, "You're married?"

"Christian Poole is my husband."

"Happily married?"

"Y…e…s," she answered, dragging out the word, feeling slightly insulted.

"Your husband, where is he now?"

"He's an attorney with Johnson, Carlson, Shapiro and Nord on assignment in New York. He's a labor relations specialist, leading contract negotiations for an East Coast manufacturing firm following a merger." She paused then added, "The firm's clients are everywhere but here."

"And you are sure he really is in New York?"

"Of course. What are you implying?"

"Is there any reason to believe he's involved with your son's abduction? It happens all the time. Every day children are abducted by someone they know, a spouse, parent."

"Not this time. Even the thought is absurd. My husband loves his son more than his own life." A tear formed on Jenny's cheek, sending her rummaging through her purse for a tissue.

Randall persisted, "And you and your son have a good relationship?"

"What are you asking? Of course, we do. I'm his mother. We're a very close family. That includes his father…my husband…and me."

Silence again. Jenny turned to look out her window.

Randall persisted, "Can you think of anyone who would want to kidnap Jason? Possibly someone from work. Or someone who might want to get at you or your husband? Get even? Revenge?"

"No. I'm a marketing director at WYCO Toys. Someone could be jealous, I suppose. But I'm the least political in the organization. I can't imagine anyone sick enough to do this. And why? And Christian doesn't have any enemies. Not here anyway. The guy is never home. If he has enemies they're someplace out there." She waved her arms over her head for emphasis. "Some place out there." Tears became visible on her cheeks.

Feeling awkward because of Jenny's tears, Randall decided on another approach. "WYCO Toys? Jordan Green is your head of plant security. Do you know him?"

"Know of him. We office at different locations. Why do you ask?"

"He lives here in Excelsior. He was an MP in Vietnam and never got police work out of his system. He frequently stops at the station on his way home. He'll be calling when he catches wind of this. You can count on it. He'll offer to help any way he can."

Jenny could care less. But the tears stopped.

"I don't have any more questions," said Randall as he tucked his clipboard beside his seat. "You said you came by boat, but can I drive you home? We can have someone return your boat. It's important you remain near your phone."

"No. I'm fine."

"The chief will want to put surveillance on your phone in case someone contacts you for ransom. What is the best number to reach you?"

Jenny recited the list of telephone numbers she gave to sitters, but I'll be home.

"You do understand the importance of staying near a phone?" Randall asked, extracting a business card from his shirt pocket.

Jenny nodded, more tears on the way.

"Sure I can't drive you home?" Randall asked as he reached across and opened her door.

"No. I'm fine." Operating in a fog, she needed time to work through it. *Little Red* was her quiet place, a place to pray. Prayer had protected and preserved her marriage to Chris, kept them together during those difficult lean years when she waited tables so Chris could devote himself to his studies.

Her prayers, their mutual faith was the glue that held their marriage together at a time when one of every two marriages failed. She needed strength, wisdom, answers…and direction. Jason needed divine protection. Her mind was racing, *Jason kidnapped? How could it be? Why?* The whirlwind in her mind intensified. Her God was her strength.

"Jenny, we'll find him," assured Randall. Jenny forced a smile and closed the cruiser's door.

Chapter 5

Dan Sheridan ignored the phone ringing on his desk. If it were important, the caller would call again. Two more rings, then silence. He looked at his watch. Time was running out.

Minutes earlier, the governor's office had called. It was a staffer he'd often spoken with during the past two weeks. He seemed more agitated than usual, checking on the readiness of Dan's security team to protect Massachusetts' Senator Malovich. In a last-minute change, the senator had decided to leave Washington and the investigation into his personal affairs for a photo op, better publicity, and an opportunity to promote his committee's pending legislation. The director of security for Mall of America's was as ready as he could be.

Two weeks had been more than enough time to get ready for the news conference and honors ceremony that had been scheduled months earlier. At the time, Malovich's staff had declared the senator far too busy to participate. "We'll see," Dan remembers thinking and immediately began making plans for the senator's inevitable visit.

Visiting Japanese dignitaries were also scheduled to attend, but that was no big deal. In fact, such a visit to the nation's largest mall by foreign dignitaries was a common occurrence. What was important was the senator's enemies. While popular in his home state of Massachusetts, Malovich was not well-liked elsewhere, particularly in Minnesota, where a few major players in the state's economy were threatening to move production to Mexico once the senator's LAIPT trade bill became law. Dan and his team prepared for the worst.

Another ring. He picked up the phone. It was the aid calling back to add a new worrisome dimension. The governor's office had received an anonymous tip that an assassination attempt would be made on the life of someone in the delegation. No target had been named, but the senator was the presumed target. And he added, "Dan, it's an insider, one of your own."

Dan knew each member of his handpicked team and asked with a hint of sarcasm, "Now that's according to an anonymous caller?"

"That's right. We don't have a name. We're trying to track the call, but not much luck there. The governor wants to take every precaution. He believes it's serious. Better check your files."

Any one of Dan's team could pull the trigger if necessary, but none was a killer. These were trained agents, professionals screened by him personally. Most of his inner circle had seen death close up and ugly, just like him, while in service to their country. Some had taken life, the life of an enemy. But he was certain that an assassin was not in his inner circle. A rent-a-cop, contract security staff, maybe—but unlikely. These were light-duty mall walkers, and they would be nowhere near the news conference.

Then there was Fredrick Bartlett, the young man whose life was detailed somewhere in papers piled on his desk. He had applied for a position but wasn't hired. Bartlett talked the talk and showed credentials: ex-military, special forces, behind-enemy-lines kind of agent, a loner. Or so he said. But Dan felt uneasy about him. Bartlett was an angry young man, too angry for his team. Relying on his gut, Dan had passed him over.

Bartlett eventually found employment at the mall as a bouncer at a glitzy upscale nightclub where he worked without incident. Dan thought the job was a good temporary fit while Bartlett looked for something more befitting his skill. But Bartlett stayed on. A fact Dan thought was a bit peculiar. The club was frequented by Hollywood celebrities and recording artists visiting the Twin Cities, hence its name, Stars' Host. The celebrity angle could be Bartlett's interest, perhaps hired out as a bodyguard for someone rich and famous. But a hired assassin? If that were the case, Malovich could provide opportunity. But that seemed a stretch. Still the governor's concern warranted taking every precaution. And then there was his gut feeling that Bartlett was a concern. Dan would keep an eye out for him.

Chapter 6

Leaving Officer Randall, Jenny scanned the street one last time, hoping somehow Jason would appear. *This can't be happening.* She felt so helpless, useless.

The rusty brown van's doors were shut; the mechanic probably off working on one of the boats. *If only he had been more observant.* As she moved toward *Little Red*, each step brought more questions.

Was Jason okay? He had to be. God was faithful. She'd cling to that hope. *Things happen for a reason. God would watch over him.* She believed that with all her heart. "God!" she shouted with a voice deep inside, "protect him."

Officer Randall seemed so confident. The police would find Jason. She'd get the call. She'd be ready. She needed to get home.

Her final glance toward Milly's caught Officer Randall's attention. He offered a friendly salute and disappeared inside. What would he learn from Old Mike? Could Mike say anything to help? Mike was always seeing things unseen by others. Was this any different?

At the dock, she dropped down onto *Little Red's* fishing platform, found the keys in her handbag along with her cell phone, and moved behind the wheel. She looked at her watch. It read 9:30 a.m. New York time. Christian would already be in meetings. She punched in his office voice mail and waited. "Christian! I need you," she pleaded into the phone. "Come on, retrieve this message."

Hearing Christian's recorded greeting, she didn't know what to say. How could she tell her husband their son had been kidnapped? Finally, she simply exploded, "Chris, come home, you're needed here!

Jason has been kidnapped!" Her words sounded so foreign, so someone else's. "Yes! I said kidnapped. He was outside Milly's. Two men took him. I've talked with the police. The police want me to stay by a phone. I'm taking the boat home. Call me."

Next she punched in the law firm's switchboard and asked to speak to Renee (Nicki) Nichols. Chris's secretary could reach him if anyone could. It could be hours before Chris retrieved his messages.

"Nicki, this is Jenny Poole. Can you locate Chris? It's an emergency. He needs to come home!" she spoke fast, her voice faltering. She felt a knot in her stomach.

"Jenny? What's wrong? Yes, we can reach Chris. He's in New York—"

"I know he's in New York," interrupted Jenny. "He needs to be here. Now! I can't reach him."

"Jenny, I can reach him. I won't give up until I do. He'll catch the next flight home if he needs to. What's the emergency, Jenny?"

Nicki's composure had a calming effect. "I need him! Nicki, someone took Jason. He's been kidnapped." Jenny quickly recited what had happened, doing her best to control her emotions.

When Nicki recovered from shock, she asked. "Why would someone kidnap Jason?"

"I don't know. There was an eyewitness, who saw it." Then it dawned on her. "What kind of case is Christian working on, anyway?"

"Nothing out of the ordinary. Jenny, there must be an explanation. You're sure someone took him?"

"Nicki, I'm sure. Please…locate Chris. I left a message on his voice mail. I'm taking the boat home. I've already talked with the police."

"Jenny, they'll find Jason," assured Nicki. "I'll call Chris. He'll be on the next possible flight." Then she remembered. "His car. Is his car at the airport?"

"No. I was going to pick him up on Sunday."

"Okay, I'll meet him, Jenny. He'll be home as soon as he can. I promise." Suddenly, Nicki's voice faltered. Her boss, Christian, and his family were as much her family too more than she cared to admit.

"Thanks, Nicki."

The next call was to her mother, D' Ward. She answered on the fourth ring. They were more than mother-daughter, they were best friends. No one loved Jason more than his grandmother. D' listened and struggled to contain her emotions. She needed to be strong for Jenny's sake.

She couldn't show her own fear for Jason. Jason kidnapped? Jennifer and Christian had no money for a ransom. But the Ward's finances were beyond speculation. He was numbered in Minnesota's one hundred most wealthy. If money was the reason, they'd do what was necessary. Her heart ached for her daughter, the hardships she'd endured, all for her husband's career. Now this. If ever a daughter needed a mother, it was now. "Jenny, remain where you are. I'll be right there," she said at last.

"No, Mom. I'm in the boat. I've got to get the boat home. Christian—"

"Honey, forget the boat. Someone can get the boat later. I'll be right there."

"Mom! No! I need to get the boat home. Meet me at home. I'm okay. At home."

Chapter 7

Conditioned by years of living on the water, Jenny was now in her element, her moves automatic. She had learned early in life to handle with perfection any boat that suited her father's spirited lifestyle. *Little Red* was proof of that. It was her escape from what troubled her. Water, high-tech boat, and speed were her quiet place.

Releasing the lines, she remembered the press conference and made one last call to her assistant. Sharon could handle it. It would take place as scheduled. To her relief, Sharon didn't answer to ask questions for which she had no answers. Jenny summarized the morning's highlights, told Sharon she'd call her again from home, shut off her phone, and stuffed it in her purse.

She felt a surge of adrenalin as she raised the choke lever and turned the key. *Little Red's* 225 horses responded with a roar and plumes of exhaust. She let the engine rev until its cold throb resonated as an exciting purr and then slammed the throttle lever into reverse.

The metallic red fiberglass hull streaked backward out of the slip. Clear of the dock, she cranked the wheel to the left and thrust the throttle forward to full speed. The engine roared, but *Little Red* remained still, its propeller cavitating, spinning uselessly in a pocket of air caused by the props' sudden rotation. She pulled back on the throttle until the propeller caught, then pushed it full forward. *Little Red* instantly pitched upward, rocketing out of the water, then quickly leveled down on plane. Within seconds, the speedometer arced past sixty-five. *Little Red* shrieked into the open water of Excelsior Bay, leaving a sixty-foot rooster tail to disturb the otherwise calm lake surface.

The rush of humid lake air refreshed her spirit. It also made her eyes water, and for a moment at least, Jenny forgot the staggering events of the morning. The speed, as invigorating as it was, demanded her concentration. Only inches of the boat's hull maintained contact with the lake's mirror-still surface. Its unique aerodynamic design caused *Little Red* to rock gently from side to side as it rode on tunnels of cushioned air. The scream of its high-pitched engine could be heard over the calm water as far away as Jenny's mother's home five miles to the east.

Bad things happen! Even to good people. How often had she consoled friends with such a pronouncement? Mere words that now seemed so shallow. She had never experienced anything as bad as this. Where was solace now? Her mind whirled with conflicting thoughts, taunting her, mocking her like some rude parrot.

No. There's a cause, she reasoned. *Always a reason. Bad things don't just happen. There is always some divine plan: to build character, right a wrong, or to bring about a higher good. Life is built on problems. Always has been; always will be. There is no escaping life's problems. They come unexpectedly, disrupting one's life. But in an orderly universe, there's always a reason. Most often known only to God; a secret God keeps to himself maybe never to be revealed. Like now. Just like now. Even if I can't understand it.* Her faith sought a greater purpose, demanded it. There was a reason for Jason's abduction. Could she dare imagine herself immune from tragedy?

Suddenly, a wave from a passing boat brought Jenny back to reality. The sudden lift of the wave dangerously increased the air under *Little Red's* hull, nearly flipping it backward. She knew better than to allow that. *Lack of attention!* She realized that while her mind wandered, she had allowed the torque of the boat's propeller's to turn the boat to the open water of Lower Lake Minnetonka, not toward home. Propelled by the near seventy-mile-per-hour wind, tears streamed across her temples. Big Island passed in a blur. She could see Woodland's shoreline in the distance. She could see the Gordon's dock.

But she was out of control. As if awakening from a dream, she struggled to collect her thoughts. "Why is this happening to me? Why?" she yelled finally in anguish and began pounding the steering wheel. "For what good, God? What good can come of this? Show me the good. Show me the reason," she screamed her demands until her voice grew weak.

Because "bad" happens! Consoling words she has used so often assaulted her now like neon lights at the end of a tunnel. Then suddenly the engine stopped. Her erratic arm movements had pulled the kill cord attached to her wrist, and instantly, the sudden loss of momentum propelled Jenny forward over the windshield that caught her at her waist.

For twenty minutes, *Little Red* bobbed gently on the lake's glassy surface, and Jenny's body writhed with sobbing.

Chapter 8

Officer Stella Kraemer tore the report from her printer, grabbed a steaming cup of coffee from the corner of her desk, and stomped briskly into Chief Nick Carlson's tidy office, her masculine, official issue shoes resounded throughout the orderly station house.

Much a lady out of uniform, Stella was one of the boys in uniform with one noticeable difference: the bulges in her uniform that was now two sizes too small and on the verge of bursting at every button and seam. She refused to acknowledge defeat in a losing war with obesity, a very private battle that began eleven months earlier, the day the city council declared the station house smoke-free. She had smoked since high school and was determined to quit the coffin nails, as her boyfriend called them. Besides, she didn't like standing alone outside to satisfy a bad habit, particularly during January and February when the temperature outside could dip to twenty degrees below zero. So she complied and replaced one habit with another.

"Your coffee, sir," she said with a smile, entering her chief's office. Servitude was not a requirement of her position, but it was a role she had adopted since quitting smoking. As the official coffee maker, she was responsible for making six pots of coffee daily and for procuring all related supplies. Those supplies included sweet rolls and doughnuts from the local bakery. The chief had an insatiable taste for fresh coffee. She preferred the rolls.

"This just came in." She set the coffee and the report in front of Chief Nick, walked around Nick's chair, and looked over his shoulder as he read. "It's the 911. Larry Randall's response," she added.

"The abduction," confirmed the chief.

"Have we ever had a kidnapping in Excelsior, Chief?"

He responded with a grunting sound, his mind already seeking answers.

She continued, "Right outside Milly's. In broad daylight. Jason Poole, ten years old. Mother…is…Jennifer Ward Poole."

"Oh, God!" Stella shouted at a sudden revelation. "Chief, I know the mother. She's Jenny Ward or was before she married. A couple years ahead of me in school. Your daughter, Anne, would know her. They would have been in high school together."

"Oh?" he responded, his brows arching upward to a growing excitement.

"She must be just sick. Just sick. My God! I can't believe it. I haven't thought about her in years. Chief, we've got to find her son." The chief looked up, annoyed. Stella continued in the same breath, "I put the report out on the 'net'."

Chief wanted to tell her to stop breathing over his shoulder but, pleased with her thoroughness, smiled, shook his head, and returned to the report, which Stella continued to summarize.

"Perpetrator's vehicle is a caterer's truck, stainless steel or shiny, that would be Abel Food Service," she exclaimed with great certainty. "They service most of the excursion boats at the docks. I pulled their number for you. Thought you might want to give them a call." She pointed to her neatly penned notes at the bottom of the report before returning to her glass partition beyond the security door where she scrutinized all visitors before buzzing them in. A smile graced her face, pleased with her thoroughness and her contribution.

Nick grabbed his phone and punched in the number Stella had provided. A businesslike but unusually sensual voice responded after two rings, "Abel Food Services and Gourmet Catering. How may we be of service?"

"I'd like to speak with whoever is in charge of your security plea—"

"Hold the line please." The veteran police chief was cut off, left to four bars of Vivaldi's *Four Seasons* before the voice returned. "I'm sorry you were holding for?"

Irritated, Nick stirred in his chair. "This is Chief Nick Carlson, Lake Minnetonka Community Police. I would like to speak with your head of security. This is an emergency."

"I will transfer your call to Stanley Girard. His direct line is extension 6868."

Two clicks later, a voice said, "Stan Girard. May I help you?"

"Stan, this is Police Chief Nick Carlson, Lake Minnetonka Community Police. We have reason to believe one of your delivery trucks was involved in the abduction of a juvenile at approximately 8:35 a.m., here in Excelsior. Can you help us? Are all your vehicles accounted for?"

"Chief, I have no reports of any missing vehicles. You're certain it's one of ours?" asked Stan defensively.

"We have an eyewitness, and we have the victim's mother."

Girard's voice became more civil, "Chief, we have two hundred trucks on the road any given morning. Our security is very tight around here. If one of our vehicles is missing and I've got a real problem, I'll find it. Give me a couple minutes. I'll get back to you. What's your number? You said a kidnapping?"

"You heard correctly. A young boy has been kidnapped. Moments ago. No more details at this time. I don't have to say, timing is critical…You'll get right on it?" Chief Nick Carlson recited his telephone number.

"I'm on it. I have two kids of my own."

"I appreciate your help," said Nick, slowly replacing the receiver to its carriage while considering what to do next. He leaned back in his armchair, pushed back as far as the springs would allow, feeling the soothing warmth of the coffee cupped in both hands.

He knew of a Matthew Ward. Their daughters were the same age and had shared classes at Minnetonka High School. The kidnapped boy would be Ward's grandson. Ward was a successful businessman who lived out of his jurisdiction in affluent Woodland, a likely target for a kidnapping if money was the motive.

He punched Stella's extension. "Has the bureau been notified?"

"Yes, Chief. They have the same report we broadcast on the 'net'. And I faxed a copy to Minneapolis."

"Sadler is special agent in charge. Gary Sadler. He'll be calling. Patch him through when he does."

"Done, Chief," asserted Stella Kraemer.

At age fifty-two, Nicholas Carlson had enjoyed thirty-plus years in public service on some police force or another. The past six of those years were as chief of Minnetonka Community Police, a service located in the small town of Excelsior, serving several smaller communities that dotted Lake Minnetonka's south shore. In all his years, he had not dealt with an actual kidnapping. People had disappeared on his watch but were found later, or their disappearance had been voluntary. Many prominent families lived around the lake. He counted some as friends. *This is big,* he reflected, *big enough to be picked up by the national media. They'd be calling soon.*

"Stella!" He shouted, ignoring the intercom. "No press! No reporters! No comment! Keep a lid on it! The boy's life is at stake!"

"Yes, sir!" Stella shouted from behind her desk thirty feet away.

Nick relaxed in the comfort of his special chair—a birthday gift from his team—sipped his coffee, and waited for his phone to ring. It would be either Abel's Girard or the bureau's Sadler. *A kidnapping on the streets of Excelsior....No place is really safe anymore, not really safe,* he reflected. *We saw that with Jacob Wetterling, abducted from a quiet road in rural Minnesota. Still not found. Now, here in Excelsior?*

Nick loved kids. His daughter Anne was the single most important person in his life beyond any doubt. Even his wife knew that. More than once he'd said life wouldn't be worth living if anything ever happened to his Anne. He'd had his fears for Anne. His jobs had exposed him to the worst life could dish out: child abuse, pornography, cruelty and neglect; so much evil inflicted upon innocents. Thank God she was now an adult, the danger years behind her, behind them. Now there were her children to worry about. His grandchildren. The world was not a safe place anymore.

Without thinking, he reached for his phone and punched in the number for his daughter, Anne Graham. She lived in Las Vegas—two hours earlier there. He looked at his watch, Anne would be packing her kids off to the daytime sitter. Hearing the busy signal, he lowered the phone. He needed to hear her voice. Ten seconds later, he picked up the phone and pushed redial. Oh, he missed his Anne.

Busy. And no call from Sadler or Girard. *What if this were one of Anne's kids? Thank God it wasn't.* He glared at the phone, daring it to ring. *So Anne had gone to school with Jennifer Ward.* He remembered now. Matthew Ward's daughter Jennifer and his Anne had been friends. He tried to recall an image of her, but nothing appeared. He poked redial.

"Hello." Anne's voice was too gratifying for words. No one could ever miss another more!

As Anne caught him up on his grandkids, a picture of Jennifer Ward emerged in his mind. *Rich kid. Religious too.* His second line blinked. *Smart. Anne always said Jenny Ward was smart. Even wished she could be like her.* His second line blinked again. "Gotta go, honey. Got a call coming. Remember Jennifer Ward?" he asked in parting.

"Sure, Dad. What's up?"

"I'll call you later. Gotta go." He pushed the button for his second line, picturing his only child, his beautiful daughter, dressed for work. She was always a good dresser. She'd probably wear one of those cute hostess dresses. Oh how he missed her.

A click on the line brought Nick back to the present; incoming call, then a dial tone. Angry with himself, he slammed the phone down, disgusted with himself. He knew better. He had wasted precious time. He swore audibly. He missed his Anne.

He found the number for Abel Food Service on Stella's report and punched it in, adding Girard's extension. The same sensual voice answered.

"This is Police Chief Nick Carlson. Would you please page Stan Girard?" He ordered. "I just missed his call."

"One moment please." The chief listened to ten rings. "I'm sorry, Mr. Girard does not answer his page. Would you like his voice mail?"

Before he could reply, she made the transfer. "Stan, Chief Carlson here," he said to the machine. "Sorry, I was on another call." He looked at his watch. "It's 9:07. We need to talk. I'll wait for your call." He returned the phone in its cradle, picked up his cup of coffee, pushed back into his chair, and placed the cup to his lips. It was cold. "Stella!" he shouted. She appeared instantly, a pot of coffee in one hand and a sweet roll in the other, a bite missing.

Girard's call came at 9:17. "Sorry, Chief, I couldn't stay on the line."

"I'm the one who's sorry," Nick confessed. "Found anything?"

"Maybe. Maybe not. We're still digging. We have no formal report of a missing vehicle or anything else out of the ordinary. But personnel claims that one of our drivers called in sick at 8:30 this morning."

Nick sipped his coffee, wedged his phone between his right shoulder and his ear, and grabbed a pencil and paper.

"With five hundred employees at this location, someone is always calling in sick. But…now this is interesting. This driver's truck should be parked in stall 19. Well, it isn't. It's gone. Reportedly, the truck went out on delivery as scheduled shortly after 6:00 a.m. We're attempting to confirm his stops. At 9:15, it should have made two stops." He paused briefly. "This may be of interest. This route usually goes through Excelsior."

Girard's secretary handed him a slip of paper. He paraphrased its content, "First stop was a special order for WYCO Toys, a special meeting they couldn't handle in-house. Gourmet entrees for some visiting dignitaries. WYCO confirmed they have their delivery. That's it. Nothing out of the ordinary. Now the second stop should have been Carson Industries scheduled for 9:00. That delivery hasn't arrived. Too soon, though, to read anything into that. The driver could be running late. Haven't been able to reach the driver."

"Off fishing?" the chief guessed. "A friend took his route for the day." After a brief pause, "Is this the vehicle whose driver called in sick at 8:30?"

"It is. And, it's still out. It should be in 19. No record of a sub taking over, but we wouldn't be the wiser unless a no-show had been called in. But as I said, the WYCO stop was on schedule."

"You don't have radios in your trucks?" asked the chief.

"Some, but not all."

"Any identifying markings we can spot from the air? There's not enough available manpower to stop all two hundred of your trucks. Our witness didn't say anything special about the one he saw. Your trucks are numbered, right?"

Stella had been listening and handed her boss a note. "Just got this. Witness said the truck had the numbers 622." He didn't add the witness was mentally impaired.

"Could be it. Like I said, I'll have to check it out and get back to you. Numbers are located on the side, back, and big numbers on the top. For quality control purposes, every delivery can be tracked through the truck's number. Our trucks swarm airport runways and gateways like bees. Traffic control needs to be able to spot them from the tower. Quick location and identification is designed into our tracking system. All airport delivery trucks are equipped with radios. Unfortunately, not the case with 622. It doesn't have a radio."

"If 622 were stolen, the driver wouldn't answer anyway," observed the chief. He thanked Girard, suggested the FBI would probably contact him, and promised he'd keep him in the loop.

Officer Kraemer appeared again at Nick's door, waited without interrupting until her chief replaced the receiver. "Sadler is holding on two."

Nick punched line two. "Gary. Nick. Thanks for the call."

Following thirty seconds of small talk, Sadler cut to the chase. "You've got a child missing? Your message presumed kidnapping? What else?"

"This may be more than just a simple abduction. This is the grandson of Matthew Ward. You know the name?"

"I do. And no abduction is simple."

"Money is a plausible motive, first blush. From what I know, this is a close family, and Grandpa has significant funds. A witness identified the kidnap vehicle, a truck belonging to Abel Catering, unit 622. Obviously, stolen." Nick explained what he knew. "The truck's number is painted on the roof of the unit. They're large numbers, clearly visible, designed to be spotted from the air."

"We're already on it. A chopper, one of our own is standing by at Twin Cities International. We've also made a request to local television. They've been calling. Anyone with a scanner is picking up the activity. We've asked the media to keep a lid on for now. Channel 6 has offered their "Eye in the Sky" to assist. It's standing by. We don't have much time. We're accepting all help. Be in touch." The phone went dead. Both professionals had work to do.

Sadler scribbled 622 onto a notepad, added "top of truck," and handed it to Shirley Jones, his young and excitedly eager assistant. She had taken in every word. Her flesh tingled with excitement for her first assignment. What a break. She had read the report, had no knowledge of any Matthew Ward. But from her boss's reaction, Ward was important. This was big. It's what she dreamed of when joining the bureau.

Within minutes, two helicopters became airborne. The bureau's bird departed Twin Cities International to cover the southern sector, working its way westward, following Interstate 494. Onboard spotters were equipped with powerful binoculars.

Channel 6's bird, with anchor Donald Stone, his cameraman and a hastily assembled cadre of volunteers, lifted off from the station's downtown heliport. They'd concentrate on the interstate and major roadways entering the downtown area from the west. Both helicopters reported in the air at 9:29 a.m.

At 9:40, Sadler was on secure line to both pilots. "Don't keep me in suspense. Anything yet? Report in," ordered Sadler.

"Yes, sir." The bureau's pilot was first to respond. "Several Abel type vans in and around the airport. None with 622 on top. Sun's at a good angle of reflection too. They're easy to spot. We've circled the southbound exit twice. If 622 was here, we'd have seen it. We'll move west along the interstate."

"You're close to Mall of America?"

"Yes, sir. Just ahead and a little south."

"Check it out," Sadler instructed, heeding some inner voice.

"Sir? You're telling me to leave the grid?" asked the pilot, seeking confirmation to deviate from their prearranged pattern.

"Check it out. Circle it a couple of times. It's just a feeling. Maybe nothing, but there's a press conference scheduled there at noon today. It's a long shot. There could be a connection. Just check it out. Okay?"

"Roger that," said the pilot and banked left.

A minute passed. In the distance, the bureau pilot caught a bright reflection, one of many, lasting only an instant, an Abel delivery moving in traffic toward the mall. His gut working too, he locked on and headed straight for it.

Approaching from the north, spotters on board scanned the roadways, moving slowly, deliberately, anticipating another brilliant flash. Every eye strained to see the slightest sign of truck 622, but there was nothing, not a sign. The truck had disappeared, probably under cover of the parking ramp or bridge. The chopper hovered briefly then passed over the mall.

"Thought we had something," he reported. "Making another circle, then we're back on grid."

Chapter 9

Dan found nothing new in Bartlett's file, but a call to a friend at the bureau added insight. Bartlett had been a Navy Seal, black ops, highly skilled, deadly, and fiercely loyal to country and all things good. Left the service for personal reasons. He apparently had a wife and a son in Columbia, both deceased, killed by probable child traffickers under investigation—a warning. He left the service for the same reason as Dan's: too much harm to those you loved most, duty over life. So what brought him to the Twin Cities and Mall of America? Probably the same motivation as Dan's—a new beginning. He deserved benefit of the doubt.

But anger is a good motivator. *Would Bartlett turn and do something sinister. It didn't fit.* It was Bartlett's anger that had ended the interview. *Who or what was the object of his anger? The senator from Massachusetts?* It was the senator's last-minute decision to attend today's press conference that was the focus of the governor's concern? *Could Bartlett be the inside threat? What was the connection?*

The senator would come with his own protection, provided by the government as well as hired guns. Dan's troops would provide backup, professional and exceptional. The warning "one of your own" was bothersome—someone on the inside. Did it matter that Bartlett's arrival predated any talk of a press conference, let alone Senator Malovich's sudden change of heart, his attendance?

Dan didn't believe in coincidence. He couldn't give a reason why some things happened, but coincidence was not one. Bartlett coming to mind after the governor's call was not coincidence. But it didn't make sense yet. No puzzle made sense when first dropped out of the box.

The House of Toys, the senator from Massachusetts, the press conference, security was as tight as possible. Dan was ready. Protection was as impenetrable as Dan could make it.

His phone blinked. He picked it up, "Sheridan, mall security."

"A boy needs help, second level men's restroom, west ramp. Immediate help! His name is Jason." The voice was deep and muffled, obviously disguised, but obviously a man's. Then it was gone.

Prank calls were not uncommon. But seldom did they raise the hair on his neck, as was the case now. He considered the caller's words, pushed his secretary's call button. "Did you get any of that?"

"Not his conversation with you. But what I heard, the caller sounded irritated, maybe angry. I transferred it right in. Said he had called moments earlier but got your voice mail. You must have been…busy? Strange voice."

"Disguised."

He paused, then ordered, "Send C team to the men's restroom, number 2, west. Have them stand by outside until I get there. Sounds like we have an abandoned child. Or worse, God forbid. A boy named Jason. And locate Lilly Turner. She's good with kids. Have her meet me there. And… call Gary Sadler at the FBI. See what they have on the disappearance of a young boy named Jason. Patch him through to my handheld."

Dan's footsteps echoed down the long mall corridor as he hurried to the west skyway entrance connecting the mall to one of the large parking ramps. Restrooms were located immediately inside the skyway entrance. Ahead on his left, he counted four of his security team, three men and one woman, waiting outside. Their eyes locked as he approached.

Behind him, he heard a woman running in heels. That would be Lilly. Lilly held a master's degree in psychology and before joining Dan's team had served as detective lieutenant with the Minneapolis police force, an accomplished investigator. Her status in Dan's little army was not much different, but her pay significantly improved. She had enjoyed the Minneapolis force, but it had cost her a marriage. With Dan, her work hours decreased, pay increased. She was a devoted mother of four, had a loving way with kids, and was frequently called in to assist with distressed children.

A handful of people milled about waiting for the roll-up storefronts to open at 10:00 a.m. Dan's watch read 9:54. A man and a woman, in their late sixties, dressed in sweat clothes and sneakers, members of one of the mall's many walker clubs, moved grudgingly to one side as Dan and Lilly approached. They shook their heads in unison, visibly annoyed by the intrusion into their space.

"Been inside?" Dan gasped, out of breath, reining in a few feet from C team who had formed a line in front of the restroom area to stop anyone from coming or going.

"No. Your orders…" reminded one of the four, sounding confused.

Dan let it pass. "Observations?"

"Nothing. Just walkers. People waiting for the stores to open."

"Okay. I received a phone call. Caller could have called from a phone close by. How about the phones?" He pointed to the bank of telephones located directly across the corridor. "The caller sounded concerned enough to stick around to make sure we found the boy."

"No one," said one of the team with the others nodding agreement.

"Close off the area. No one is to enter the area until I give the okay. Call maintenance. And tape off the phones. Don't touch anything, they may have prints."

Dan turned to Lilly. "I'll go in. Let's see what we've got here. I'll call you if I need you. Keep the public away."

Dan stepped inside apprehensively, his words echoed off the tiled walls. "Jason."

The caller had said, "A boy needs attention."

What would that mean? He rounded a partition and surveyed the room. Empty. No sign of a boy named Jason. No sign of violence.

On his right were sinks, mirrors, and a couple of hand dryers. To his left were three closed toilet stalls.

"Jason?" he said again, his voice reassuring as he bent down to look under the stall partitions. Tennis shoes. There he was. "Jason," he said again. "Jason, are you in here? My name is Dan Sheridan. I'm here to take you home, son. Are you all right?" he asked and waited.

"Yes. I'm in here," answered a quiet but strong voice.

Dan gently pushed open the door and found Jason sitting on the edge of the toilet. Dan guessed him to be ten or eleven years old. His bright-brown eyes locked on Dan's. For a moment, each surveyed the other until Dan broke the silence, "You are Jason?"

Jason nodded.

"Jason, do you know where you are? Or who brought you here?"

"No," Jason answered after a brief silence, adding, "I mean, not really. A man brought me here. He told me to stay here until someone came to get me."

"Was that man your father? A brother? A friend?"

"I don't have a brother, and my dad is traveling…in New York. I was with my mother in Excelsior. We were at Milly's."

"Milly's?"

"It's a restaurant. We go there for breakfast. On Thursdays. By boat mostly. I left Milly's before Mom to get the boat ready. Someone grabbed me. And…then a man told me to stay here. And…that's all I remember. Then I heard you say my name."

"But you remember a man brought you here?"

"Sort of. It's like looking through a cloud."

"You feel okay?"

"I think so."

Dan reached into his pocket, retrieved a small flashlight and shined it into Jason's eyes. They appeared slightly dilated, otherwise clear and alert. "Jason, I'm going to take you to your mother. Would you like that?" Jason's smile was answer enough. There would be time later for more questions.

"Dan," said Helen's voice on Dan's handheld.

"What's up?" he asked, his eyes fixed on Jason.

"It's Sadler. I'll patch him through."

A few clicks later, Gary Sadler's voice came through the speaker. Jason, sitting uncomfortably on the edge of the toilet seat, kept his eye glued on Dan.

"This is Gary Sadler. I understand you have found Jason Poole?"

"I have found a boy named Jason. You say his last name is Poole?" Dan smiled at Jason and asked, "Are you Jason Poole?" Jason smiled and nodded. "It's him. He appears to be fine. Says a man brought him here to a men's restroom. What do you have?" Dan waited for Sadler's response.

"His name is Jason Poole. Age ten, abducted this morning at approximately 8:30 a.m. outside a restaurant in Excelsior."

"Milly's," supplied Dan.

"Yeah, right. His mother...a Jennifer Pool. They had just finished breakfast. Apparently, the boy left the restaurant ahead of his mother. Outside someone grabbed him."

"Well, he's safe now. He doesn't know how he got here. But he seems fine. I'm with him now. We're still in the restroom where I found him. Gary, can I call you back from my office. We're on our way there. You're in touch with the boy's parents?"

He smiled to Jason and motioned for him to follow.

"We are. Boy's father is out of town. We believe his mother is standing by a phone."

"You can tell them their son is fine. No sign of injury or abuse. But we should have a doctor take a look at him. I suspect he was drugged. His eyes are slightly dilated, and he appears confused, memory impaired. Sooner is better than later. We've got a good clinic here. We'll need a blood sample if you want to determine the drug. Can you get the parent's consent?"

"We'll ask. We're calling off the search. We've got two helicopters in the air looking for him. I'll fill you in later. One more thing. I understand you were bureau. Is that right?"

"Still have my blue suit and tie," quipped Dan.

"But does it fit? Your new posh life and all," Sadler chided. "I'll wait for your call from your office."

"Right," said Dan. "Oh!" The afterthought came as a revelation. "You said the mother is Jennifer Poole. The same Jennifer Poole who's scheduled to be honored today at a press conference at WYCO Toys's Jennifer Poole?" Sadler had already rung off. *No such thing as coincidence.*

Sadler had not met Sheridan and knew little about him: former FBI, distinguished record. Resigned in March 1993 for personal reasons. He'd like to know more. A smile crossed his face, and he pushed several extensions on his phone to locate Special Agent Shirley Jones in the communications room where she had been monitoring radio contact with the hastily assembled helicopter search team. "Call off the search. Jones, the boy, has been found. You'll be working with me on the follow-up. Please come to my office."

Seconds later, Shirley Jones entered Sadler's austere office and unloaded quickly. "Sir, Donald Stone, Channel 6, wants to know where the boy is. He says we owe him the story."

"We owe him nothing," barked Sadler matter-of-factly. "But we'll give him the story. I appreciate their help. Tell him…" He thought for a moment. "Tell him to pick me up here. We'll meet him on the roof. He's in his chopper. He can drive. That's the way he'll get his story. But…don't say it that way. You know what I mean."

Jones turned on her heels. Sadler watched her leave, then placed a call to Chief Nick Carlson, and filled him in. No state lines were crossed. Much of the discovery would now be up to Nick and the Bureau of Criminal Apprehension. Gary would help where he could, but his plate was already full.

Next, he placed a call to Jennifer Poole's home phone and got the answering machine after four rings. "Mrs. Poole, this is Gary Sadler, special agent in charge, Minneapolis office of the FBI. We have found your son, Jason. He is unharmed and doing just fine. I'm on my way to him now. Please stay by your phone. I repeat, Jason has been found unharmed and doing fine. Stay by your phone."

Jones appeared at his door as his phone hit its cradle. "Sir, Donald Stone is delighted to be of service. He'll be up top when you're ready."

"Thank you, Jones—"

"It's Shirley, sir. It's all right for you to use my first name. It's Shirley."

"Thank you, Shirley. Hard to know just how to address a woman these days. Know what I mean? Too many harassment suits."

Shirley smiled at her boss. "Sir, please call me Shirley."

"Shirley, Jason Poole has been found."

"That was fast, sir. He's okay?"

"Yes, according to Dan Sheridan, director of security for Mall of America. Good man, I'm told. Former FBI, good record in DC. Also, some CIA. Transferred out at his request. Anyway, he should know his stuff. Found the boy in a men's room. I'm waiting for his call and more details. We'll wait for a few more minutes, then we go. We'll also check out the news conference. Senator Malovich is putting in a last-minute appearance. "Could be trouble," he said without knowing why. *Mmm…any connection?*

"The mother?" inquired Shirley.

"I've left a message on her home machine. You can call her again when we know more."

"Sir, I see the mother is Jennifer Poole. That's a name listed as a participant at the press conference. One and the same? Wasn't she to be honored there today?"

"Yeah" seemed to roll from his mouth as he considered something, a thought bubbling to the surface. "And, no, I don't know what it means. But I don't think she'll be attending. Apparently, she's returning a boat to her home." Shirley changed her stance. "And don't ask," he said to Shirley's raised brow. "We'll learn more momentarily," he said and started toward the door.

"The call, sir? Dan Sheridan?" she reminded hesitantly.

"We've waited long enough. Let's meet this man-of-the-hour in person."

JENNY

Shirley trailed Sadler as he walked out the door, asking, "Sir, isn't this all peculiar? I mean kidnap someone only to release that someone a couple hours later? And at Mall of America. Why there?"

"That's for us to discover," responded Sadler.

Chapter 10

Dan took Jason's hand and led him to Lilly Turner who was waiting with the small security team outside the lavatory's entrance. "This is Mr. Jason Poole," he said. Jason, somewhat bewildered, extended his hand to each in turn, while he stole glances at his surroundings.

"This is Mall of America, right?" Suddenly aware of his surroundings, he peered through the ring of adults. "How did I get here? Where's my mom?"

Dan bent down to Jason's level and placed his hands on Jason's shoulders. "Welcome, Jason, to Mall of America." He looked squarely into Jason's eyes. "I don't know how you got here. In fact, that's a question I hope you can help us answer. We're locating your mother now. If I'm not mistaken, she was to be here today." Dan resumed standing. "Do you know anything about that, Jason?"

Jason shook his head slowly, thinking, and said finally, "No."

Two maintenance workers in gray coveralls sauntered up with Mall of America logos embroidered on their left breast pockets. Each carried two knee-high folding signs that read OUT OF SERVICE and stood them in the entrances to both the men's and the women's restrooms, glanced at the security team hovering over Jason, walked to the bank of telephones across the corridor, and stretched yellow tape across the phones and headed back in the direction they came from.

Dan stationed Ken, one of his uniformed team, outside the restrooms. "Keep an eye on things. No one gets near without my authorization. The FBI will get here soon. For now this is their crime scene. They'll want prints. Report anything out of the ordinary to me."

"Excuse me, sir," interjected the new female member of the team. "What kind of authorization? How will we know you authorized… anyone…?"

Dan held out his "handheld." "My personal okay. You got a question, you call me. That's how!" he ordered and turned to Lilly. "Come with us, please, Lilly."

Ken rocked back onto his heels, a smile on his face, and watched his boss disappear down the wide corridor hand in hand with Jason and Lilly at his side. *This is what it's like being a cop*, he mused, a new self-image forming in his mind. *A real cop, just like on TV.*

"Been here before, Jason, or is this your first visit?" asked Dan as they began down the corridor. Jason gave Dan a weird look but didn't answer. Dumb question; this wasn't exactly a planned visit. His expression was not lost on Dan, who smiled down at his young charge.

They followed the west entry corridor to the escalators to the mall's third level. He felt the warmth of Jason's hand in his. Immediately attracted to Jason, Dan was relieved, even a little surprised, that Jason wasn't frightened. His own son would be the same age as Jason, had he lived; had Cory not been struck and killed by a runaway car.

For a moment, memories long buried bubbled to the surface only to be quickly dismissed. That life had passed. *Who would hurt a child?* he wondered now, forcing the thought to clear his mind of the past. *Was Jason's abduction a quirky twist in the alleged assignation plot that had so ignited the governor's concern? What was so important about a WYCO Toy's employee Jennifer Poole, Jason's mother?* Nothing made sense. Nothing time would not reveal.

"I come here a lot. Neat place," Jason said as they crossed one of the mall's main interior bridges. "But this is too weird," he said casually and looked up at Dan, studying the man who had come to his rescue. He was tall like his dad. His grip was strong but gentle, like his dad's. "Weird," he said again. Jason was enjoying being the center of attention. Whoever Dan Sheridan was, he seemed nice enough, and he was taking him to his mother…somehow. He liked adventure and was content for his adventure to continue.

Dan was enjoying it too, pleased that Jason was loosening up. And Jason's memory seemed to be improving—a good sign.

"I understand you live near Lake Minnetonka. Excelsior, isn't it?"

"Yeah, sort of. Tonka Bay, really. It's close. We live on the lake. Well, not on it. On the shore, actually." Jason smiled at his joke that had not gone unnoticed by Dan and Lilly, both smiling. "And we have a boat. Really cool, really fast."

Large stores, shops, and restaurants lined the mall's perimeter with wide hallways that bound a large fun park comprising the mall's vaulted center area. The theme park stretched upward, offering several exciting amusement park rides. It was surrounded by three levels of stores, layered on balconies along either side with wide bridged walkways at intervals connecting the sides. At the four corners of the mall complex, appended like satellites to the large rectangular building, were anchor stores, large big box department stores each with its own three levels of shopping.

"The House of Toys is down there, right?" Jason asked Dan as they stepped onto the escalator on the building's west side.

"Looking familiar?" Dan asked, knowing the answer. One piece of the puzzle was falling into place. "It's quite a store?" he prompted.

"Yeah. My mom works at WYCO. She helped start the store. I come here a lot with her."

"We haven't been able to reach your mother by telephone. Maybe she's here, at the store."

"I don't know." Jason shook his head, bewildered. "I really don't have any idea how I got here. We were in Excelsior. We had breakfast at Milly's. That's a restaurant. I drove the boat there. I don't know…" His voice trailed off. It was all too confusing, like fish swimming upside down in an aquarium. He preferred to let adults sort it all out. That's what adults did.

Dan led Jason to the second-floor entrance of the House of Toys. Lilly Turner followed. They walked past a large display of miniature tractors, earthmovers, graders, cars, and building equipment in work settings resembling the real world common to each machine. "This stuff is very realistic. I understand your mother designed these displays," commented Dan. Their pace slowed to take it all in.

"Yeah," answered Jason with pride, obviously admiring his mother's creative genius.

The large store housed three floors of displays and shelf space interspersed with extensive play areas for children and their parents to experience hands-on play with the world's best toys. Just visiting the store was a captivating experience. There was no denying the originality of such lavish product presentation. Dan was beginning to understand the success behind Jason's mother's popularity. Jason's mother was someone he would like very much to meet.

Along the outer wall on each floor were offices and conference areas with large windows overlooking the theme park, Camp Snoopy. It was in these well-appointed spaces that visitors and corporate clients from around the world were fed, entertained, and royally schmoozed. There was no better place on earth for WYCO Toys to cement a deal than at the House of Toys at Mall of America. Dan agreed, it was a fitting setting for a press conference.

Excitement energized everything inside the store. Dan felt it immediately as he entered. Since taking the head of security position at the nation's biggest mall, he had whiled away a lunch hour or two wandering through the large displays as kids and adults lost themselves in a world of make-believe, a world that for them became very real.

On one such occasion, he had actually filled miniature dump trucks with buckets of real dirt and sand. He had squeezed the lifelike animals to hear them squeal and growl. He had exercised his own imagination in WYCO's world of make-believe. Seeing it again with

Jason, he was even more awestruck, wowed by the fruits of Jenny Poole's hard work. She possessed a unique and creative talent, an energy fueled by a mother's insights, probably captured while watching Jason at play. He looked forward to meeting Jason's mother.

They strolled through one elaborate display after another. Dan almost forgot his purpose for being there in such a happy place. He felt buoyant, uplifted, almost giddy inside. It took a gifted person to create such a warm environment, so carefree? That gifted person's son was their guide, leading them along the whimsical path winding through the store. Jason's hand still clutching his.

His thoughts again turned to his son Cory and his wife, ex-wife, Gale. *Where was she now? Could he ever have tasted such joy in real life,* he wondered? *It wasn't to be. It just wasn't to be.* His life had too many *ifs*. If he had been able to leave his surveillance assignment eight years earlier, if he would have been home with Gale and eighteen-month-old Cory that day on his walk with Mom. If the old lady had not picked that day to go shopping. If she had not decided to drive herself, knowing her frail condition. If the old lady hadn't then had a stroke. If timing had just been minutes different. If… Then Cory might not have stepped into harm's way. If only… Then…he could now be strolling through the House of Toys with Cory and Gale.

But it was Lilly who stood beside him, not Gale. Lilly was attractive, but in a matronly way. She and Gale would be about the same age and stature. But she was not the raving beauty that was Gale. Definitely not the beauty that Gale had been. Before the accident, Gale had been the sexiest, most beautiful girl in the world. Her long *blonde* hair, her well-defined figure, her graceful saunter turned heads when she entered a room. But that had changed. He had not thought about Gale in two years. He'd torn that chapter from his life, or so he thought. Where was she? He didn't know. Didn't want to know. He didn't want to think of her now.

He looked at his watch: 10:25. By now, Sadler should have received permission for the blood test. Any minute he'd be calling, needed to call; the press conference was scheduled for noon. Time was short. They passed a large jungle display of toy animals, monkeys swinging from trees, water buffalo nibbling grass, giraffes munching the silk leaves from trees, lairs of lions lounging in tall silk grass. In one lifelike display, a child played with a full-maned lion. *Too real.*

Jason led the way across a small wooden bridge, stopping short of an escalator to wait for Lilly to catch up. Dan stepped on first and looked back at Jason; his wide grin said it all—he was in the moment and loving it. *Cory would love it too. If only…Cory*, he thought. Seconds later, he stepped off at level three.

It was abuzz with activity: technicians, press, governor's staff, you name it, everyone scrambling with last-minute preparation. Whatever would happen would happen in the next one 120 minutes. Beyond, a large inflatable Snoopy bobbled in front of a large window overlooking Camp Snoopy. And it would happen here.

"May I help you?" The voice came from an attractive woman, midthirties, maybe. She approached Dan from behind. In heels, they stood eye to eye. She had light-brown hair, accented by a *blonde* streak, pulled tightly back over her ears, terminating in a bun. She obviously spent time in the sun and wore just enough makeup to make her look wholesome and *all-business.*

She clutched a clipboard close against her breasts and peered over large circular glasses, perched slightly off the bridge of her nose, which Dan noted was offensively pointed upward, although necessary for her to see into the distance. Her scowled expression said Dan was interrupting her party. And she didn't like that. Despite that, Dan liked what he saw.

"We're looking for Jennifer Poole. Is she here?" asked Dan.

"I'm sorry, she's not here. Is she expecting you?" she asked in a voice not at all friendly. Dan looked around to see if someone other than him could be setting her off.

"No. Jason here." Dan began.

At the mention of Jason's name, the woman's scowl softened; she recognized the boy standing beside Dan.

"Jason? Jason Poole?" she shouted and bent toward him as though to plant a kiss on his forehead but caught herself and pulled back. "Jason, it's me, Sharon. You remember? I work with your mom, for her actually." Jason smiled. "You're here…? Your mom left me a message…You were kidnapped?" She glanced questioningly at Dan then back at Jason. "Your mom is sitting by her phone…waiting for some…message about you. Does she know you're here?"

"Ah….It's a long story—" Jason began when Dan came to his rescue.

"It is a long story. Someone did take Jason and then brought him here. We don't know why. We've been trying to reach his mother, leaving messages. Hopefully, by now she knows that he's been found safe."

There was an awkward pause as each adult considered what to say next. Jason was not about to interfere. Finally, "It's Sharon?" Dan asked.

"It's Ms. Miller!" she corrected. "And you are?"

"Sharon is friendlier," he chided. "I'm Dan Sheridan. I direct mall security. I need to speak with Jason's mother. It's very important."

"As I said, she's not here. As much as I wish she was. There's a lot happening here today, and Mrs. Poole was to be very much a part of it."

Dan found a business card in his shirt pocket and handed it to Sharon and tugged Jason's arm. "Let's go, bud," he said and started toward the exit, turned and said to Ms. Miller, "If his mother calls or shows up, please have her contact me immediately."

Glancing quickly at the card, Sharon bolted after him; now well ahead of her, Jason's hand in his. "Wait!" she yelled. Dan didn't stop. Now she ran. When she reached him, she grabbed at his shoulder and shouted, "Where are you going with Jason? Where are you taking him? What's going on here, Dan?… Mr. Security?"

Dan stopped short. The FBI was waiting. "Ms. Miller, I'm not sure what is going on," he answered with intended firmness. "That's why I need to speak with Jason's mother. The person or persons who grabbed Jason this morning gave him a drug to inhibit his memory. We need her permission to administer a blood test to determine the nature of that drug."

"A drug? Blood test?" she echoed.

"Yes. Now I'm taking him to my office until we locate his—"

"Look, Mr. Sheridan, I'm sorry. I…uh, didn't mean…I'm…I'm…just sorry." Dan could see concern on her face. "Jason is welcome to stay here. Really, he'll be safe. He certainly knows the store. His mother designed all the displays for God's sake. I'm sorry," she said, catching herself. "Jason's been here a lot. More than me, actually."

Dan thought for a moment, looked about at people streaming into the large open area. "Ms. Miller," he began.

"Please call me Sharon," she corrected with a warm smile.

"Sharon, you said Jason could stay here. Lilly can remain here with him. You have other things to attend to." Dan turned and nodded to Lilly, introduced her to Sharon. "If his mother doesn't show up here, I will personally take Jason home. For now, I've got the FBI standing by. I need to get to my office. It shouldn't take long."

Dan's watch read 10:32. He left Lilly, Jason, and Sharon looking after him as he turned, headed toward his office with his handheld to his mouth when Helen answered, "It's Dan. I'm at the House of Toys. Would you call Sadler, FBI, and patch him through? He's waiting for my call."

"He's not waiting anymore," corrected Helen. "He's here in your office. Channel 6 is with him, Donald Stone and a cameraman, and agent Shirley Jones."

"Who called the media?" he asked, more a reflex than an actual question. He knew they'd show up. It was just a matter of time. He just didn't like it.

"No one. Their helicopter brought Sadler here. Channel 6 was part of the air search team, I guess."

"Okay. But no one wants them over here, not yet, anyway. Have them wait there. I'll be right over. Jason is with Lilly here at the store.

His mother, Jennifer, was to be part of the news conference scheduled here at noon. I don't think she'll make it. Don't tell Stone that Jason is here."

A final glance over his shoulder saw Lilly and Sharon hovering over Jason. Dan and Jason made eye contact; Jason's eyes said he'd had enough fondling.

Chapter 11

Gravel and dust swirled behind the aged Honda traveling a country road twenty miles outside Hastings, Nebraska. The driver watched her mirrors as much as the road in front of her. It ran south for as far as the eye could see, intersected every few miles by more gravel running east and west.

Her heading was generally southeast, driving south for a few miles, then east for a few, then south, and so on. At each turn, she could see anyone following her. At one point, seeing a plume of dust closing behind her, she turned right, made two more right turns, as the terrain allowed to bring her up behind her pursuer, only to discover the vehicle long gone, caught in a dust trail miles ahead.

At the town of Fairfield, she turned east for a few miles, then north to her brother's farm, actually her childhood home, the Stewart family farmstead, Stewart's Hogs, run by her brother Jim, since their father's death a few years back.

Jennifer Stewart had been home for a week, and today was her first day off the farm, only because Jim had insisted. She had arrived early one morning, tired and shaky from her ordeal and hasty departure from Minnesota. Jim sat through her long explanation of her return home with few interruptions, seeking only an occasional clarification. She knew he believed her story, but he wasn't as concerned, nor as worried, as she was that her pursuers would find her, whoever they might be.

In the time since her fearful flight, she'd lie awake at night desperately attempting to connect the dots, trying to recall exactly what she had seen at her employer's corporate offices. What could be so important to cause someone to chase her, maybe even want her dead to keep her quiet? She feared it was only a matter of time before they'd find her.

She had been enjoying her second week at The Wayzata Toy Company, one of the nation's largest and most-loved toy manufacturers, whose facilities were located a few miles west of Minneapolis, Minnesota, on the shores of Lake Minnetonka; she was a proud new employee having found her dream job. She relished the realization that in her late twenties, she was young to be so well-established, a low-level position to be sure, but a starting position as a department assistant, a "gofer."

The company's executive offices had recently moved to new and opulent corporate digs at the Carlson Towers, a newly constructed office complex, just off the interstate in the Lake Minnetonka community of Wayzata, five miles to the east of the original corporate headquarters, where production and marketing remained. Since the opening of the House of Toys at Mall of America, the company's hallmark store, marketing, and merchandising had grown quickly and merged operations to absorb the vacated space.

One afternoon, Jennifer Stewart found herself working late to complete an assignment and wandered onto the floor previously occupied by the board of directors. Still lavish with executive apartments and offices for staff assisting whoever was in residence, the space was in constant use by visiting dignitaries and management in town for meetings.

Attracted by the allure of bright lights, she had walked down a long corridor to what appeared to be some kind of promotional filming underway in the elaborate corporate suite. Behind double-glass paneled doors stood lighting systems, cameras, and miscellaneous equipment, all unattended and at the ready, and separated from the actual filming, which she surmised was in progress behind another set of large paneled doors. With no one to whom she could inquire about the activity, she cautiously pushed open one of the doors and entered for a better look. The scene before her took a moment to register. She was aghast, couldn't believe her eyes. Before her was a scene she had not intended to see. She began to back out when her foot hit a table leg, sending a lamp crashing. Suddenly, all eyes were upon her.

Pandemonium broke loose. It had happened quickly. Two men and a teenage boy were in varied stages of undress, performing what she could only guess under very bright lights. Closest to her was the boy who turned her way with deep-set dark eyes, lifeless eyes, as though he had been drugged.

A middle-aged man with no clothes followed the boy's look, his face showing total surprise, but no shame. Somewhere she had seen that face before. Now that face had seen her. Others in the room couldn't see her because of the lights.

Suddenly, a figure emerged from the shadows. A man knocking over a chair as he charged toward her. She turned and ran down the partially lit hall toward the back stairs, looking back only when she reached the stairway entrance. A couple hundred feet behind her, moving quickly, was a tall silhouette in pursuit. The faster of the two, she flew down eight flights of stairs, taking four at a time, wondering what it was she had seen in his hand. *Was it a gun? Why would it be?*

Exploding out the back door onto the parking, she saw her car where she had left it earlier that morning; for some reason, she had not parked in her usual spot in front. She ran to it under a lamp pole, the lamp now extinguished, climbed in, and turned the key. It popped first try.

The parking lot exited through an ally that ran the length of the building. On the street, she had options: head west toward Mound or east in the direction that gave her the choice of Excelsior or Wayzata, either the south side or north side of Lake Minnetonka. She chose east and managed to make the turn as her pursuer threw open the door and bolted onto the lot. She could see him in her rearview mirror. Yes, it was a gun. She was certain.

Reacting quickly, she had an idea; she wanted him to see her vanish eastward and follow her through a maze of twisting and turning streets, any one of which would lead him in endless circles where she could lose him.

She turned east for one block, down a side street for two blocks, then another turn, a straight away, then two more turns. When her pursuer was no longer visible in her mirror she took a shortcut to Excelsior and her apartment. No one followed.

Since moving to Minnesota and her dream job, her home was a tidy one-bedroom apartment on the building's second floor—one of four in an old brick structure she'd been told once housed Excelsior's fire department before the consolidation of several neighboring villages into the South Lake Community. Working quickly in the ambient light of the disappearing sun, she grabbed clothes, money, and a couple photos of her, removing as much evidence of her identity as possible and threw it onto the back seat of her Honda. With a nearly empty gas tank, she filled at the local Standard, and moments later accelerated down the ramp to eastbound seven.

She drove straight through to Hastings, Nebraska, making only a couple of stops for fuel and food and to relieve a cramped bottom. Twice she tried to call her brother Jim but only got the answering machine. Her only message, "It's Jenny. Coming home." The hour was late, and he was early to bed and early to rise. He'd be up by the time she got there.

She was still shaking when she arrived ten hours later and found Jim in one of the big hog barns, one of several that housed several thousand hogs, the product of the family business. He'd been expecting her and embraced her lovingly but was unable to mask his surprise at her sudden change of plans. She tried to explain what had happened as Jim listened attentively and patiently while she broke down several times engulfed in tears.

For the next few days, they spoke little about her ordeal. Finally, he asked, "Are you absolutely sure?" Jim wanted to believe her story, but it was so out there, off the charts as he saw it, living isolated on a couple thousand acres of prairie country. Then today he insisted, "Sis, you gotta get on with life. Go to Hastings, do some shopping."

And she did.

Chapter 12

Dan's secretary had already offered coffee and soft drinks to the four people seated in Dan's gracious reception area. Sadler accepted a Coke and sipped it as he eyed Dan. While the two had never met personally, Dan recognized him as the special agent in charge. He simply looked the part, although his suit was dark brown, not blue.

The foursome stood as Dan drew near. The red light on the top of the camera remained dark, not yet recording but ready and trained directly on Dan.

"Mr. Sheridan, I'm Gary Sadler with the FBI. I've been looking forward to meeting you," said Sadler, extending his hand. Dan accepted and smiled at the firmness of Sadler's grip.

Next he introduced Special Agent Shirley Jones. Then turning to Stone, he said, "I believe you know Donald Stone, Channel 6 News. He offered the use of their helicopter to assist in the air search for the van believed to have been used by Jason Poole's abductors. The van, by the way, has been located in your ramp, just outside the west entrance to level 2, less than 100 yards from the restroom where you found Jason."

Dan remembered Donald Stone. "Stone Cold Donald Stone," an aggressive, narcissist glory-seeker with little regard for the people whose story he covered or those who stood in his way in his pursuit of a story. Granite hard, immovable, and often ruthless—trademarks he carried with pride.

There was friction between the two from the beginning. He had ridiculed Dan for being overly cautious in his approach to mall security, hiring what amounted to a private swat team to patrol the mall to discourage the growing number of street gangs calling the mall their turf. During a widely publicized newscast, he had referred to Dan as a "macho, glory-seeking Wyatt Earp."

Dan accepted Stone's outstretched hand, gripped it harder than necessary. "Just call me, Wyatt," he suggested politely. Sadler raised one eyebrow and nodded to agent Jones with an expression that suggested *I guess we needed to be there*. Stone simply smiled.

Breaking the ice, Sadler addressed Dan, "So we have a kidnapping with a happy ending"—a statement seeking confirmation. "Jason Poole, found unharmed and in good condition? Right?" A puzzled look crossed his face. "By the way, where is he? I thought he was with you."

Stone had his spiral notepad at the ready as he thrust the microphone in Dan's face and nodded to the cameraman whose red light blinked on.

"Yes, Jason Poole is safe and in good condition. Currently with one of my staff," confirmed Dan. With measured words, Dan replayed how he had received an anonymous call that led him to the restroom where he found the boy the caller had referred to as Jason. "I immediately went to the restroom, found a young boy inside one of the stalls sitting on the edge of a toilet. I identified myself, spoke his name, and Jason responded. He was alert, did not appear to be harmed in any way and had no knowledge of how he came to be in the restroom other than a vague recollection of a man's voice instructing him to remain there until someone came for him. It appears it was that caller's intention that Jason be found quickly. He called and asked to speak to me personally."

"Has his medical condition been confirmed?" inquired Stone.

"We are seeking parental consent as we speak."

"And the boy is—?"

"With my agent, Lilly Turner, at the House of Toys," interrupted Dan. "Jason Poole is the son of Jennifer Poole, a WYCO Toys employee with management responsibility here at the House of Toys. They are accompanied by Sharon Miller, Mrs. Poole's close friend and administrative manager."

"And Mrs. Poole was to be honored at that press conference, moments from now, at the House of Toys?"

"And Massachusetts's Senator Malovich is scheduled to attend."

"Yes," answered Dan, guessing what was coming next.

"Mr. Sheridan, do you see any connection between today's abduction of Jason Poole, the son of a WYCO Toys marketing manager, this nationally televised press conference, and the attendance of the controversial Senator Malovich?"

"No," answered Dan. "There is no apparent connection with Jennifer Poole, her son Jason, and today's conference, and certainly no connection to Malovich. We view the two incidents as unrelated. It's not my job to speculate. That is better left to the FBI."

Stone spoke to the camera and turned to Sadler. "Mr. Gary Sadler, special agent in charge of the FBI is here. Is this an FBI matter? Are the Bloomington police involved in the investigation? Isn't this their jurisdiction?" Stone shifted his mic to Sadler; the camera followed.

Sadler moved to Dan's side as the cameraman adjusted his lens to bring both into view. "This case involves the abduction of a juvenile, a crime of great interest to the FBI. The first minutes and hours of the investigation are the most critical. As an agency of the federal government, the Federal Bureau of Investigation has the greatest resources to bring into the investigation during this very critical period." There was a brief silence. "And, of course, Malovich is a United States senator, an obvious person of national interest as well.

"We were brought into the case early on by police chief Nicholas Carlson of the Lake Minnetonka Community Police. The abduction took place in his jurisdiction in the town of Excelsior. His officers responded immediately to the 911 call at approximately 8:45 this morning. Within minutes of the incident, the resources of the federal government were placed into service. When I received the call from Mr. Sheridan notifying me that the boy had been located in Mall of America, I immediately notified the Bloomington police. They are assisting the bureau in the ongoing investigation."

"Do you have any knowledge of the identity of the perpetrators?" asked Stone.

"Not specifically. However, on that point, we are very grateful for the quick thinking of Dan Sheridan. Before Dan's appointment as head of security for Mall of America, Dan was an investigator for the FBI, one of our finest, I might add. His actions to immediately isolate all areas pertinent to the case are enabling a thorough investigation."

"But you don't know the identity of the perpetrators?" Stone persisted.

"No. Not at this time. We're in the initial phase of evaluating the evidence. We are optimistic. Thanks to Dan, we have good crime scene. But it takes time."

Stone sensed a warning in Sadler's tone and changed his tact. "Mr. Sadler, the vehicle believed to have been used in the abduction of Jason has been located here at the mall. Is that correct? Can you tell the public more?"

"We can confirm that we have located a vehicle, which, evidence indicates, was used in the abduction and was the vehicle used to bring Jason to the mall."

"Could you tell us what evidence?" pressed Stone.

Sadler looked at Dan then answered, "I'm not at liberty to discuss further facts concerning this case. We do not in any way want to compromise the investigation or the well-being of the victim, Jason Poole. We are gratified that Jason will soon be reunited with his family. But this case is far from over. The investigation has just begun."

Donald Stone accepted Sadler's conclusion and stepped quickly before the camera, leaving Dan and Gary in the background while he addressed his unseen audience. "As you have seen, the kidnapping of Jason Poole has a happy ending. Jason has been found unharmed and will soon be reunited with his family. The drama that began at 8:30 this very morning on the quiet streets of Excelsior, on the peaceful shores of Lake Minnetonka, has ended here at Mall of America. You saw it first here on Channel 6. While Jason's ordeal is over, and he soon will be reunited with his family, there remains significant evidence for the experts to evaluate. The investigation phase is expected to continue for many weeks. As it continues, and as more facts become known, we will update you here on Channel 6. This is Donald Stone reporting live. Now back to the studio."

The red light atop the camera blinked off as Stone barked to his cameraman, "John, we're off to the House of Toys. Run down there. On your way get this tape to a courier and back to the station. Our crews should be setting up. I want it ready for Janet's Noon News. Leave your gear here for now." He looked at Dan; Dan looked at Helen. They both shrugged. Stone continued, "Tell Janet I want in on the conference. I'm senior here, and I believe there's a connection. I know she's scheduled solo, but you tell the princess that I want in. I'll be down in a couple of minutes."

Carefully setting down his expensive equipment, the cameraman rushed out the door. Stone then turned to address Dan and Gary as the phone rang. Dan had his fill of Donald Stone and turned toward Helen, who had picked up the phone after one ring. She whispered to Dan, "It's for you. I'll send it to your office." From the tone in Helen's voice, he knew he had better take the call and without excusing himself stepped from the reception area into his large office and closed the door behind him.

He walked contemplatively to the far side of his desk and deposited himself in his comfortable leather chair, pushed the Bartlett file aside, took a deep breath, and reached for the phone.

Chapter 13

The aroma of freshly brewed coffee filled Jennifer's lakeside townhome. *Little Red* again floated peacefully, tethered beside the dock, fifty feet beyond the kitchen window.

Jennifer's mother, D' Ward, arrived at Jenny's thirty minutes ahead of her daughter, a wait sufficiently long for her to worry something terrible could also have happened to Jenny. Relief came when Jenny's red boat entered the channel. D' was ready when the boat came alongside the dock and grabbed and secured the bowline while Jenny secured the stern.

Normally stoic, she struggled to hold back tears and watched for any sign of Jenny's emotional state, always emotionally strong, buoyed by a deep faith. They drew close. D' opened her arms and hugged her daughter tightly, quietly, gently rocked her as love, courage, and hope flowed electrically between them—a communion only a mother and daughter could know.

They rocked quietly for a few minutes. Jenny's well of tears gone dry and no desire to talk. Biting her bottom lip, D' waited. The answers to her unasked questions would come when Jenny was ready.

Jennifer turned to go inside and went straight to the answering machine. Peter had called for Jason; they had planned their own adventure for the day. A lost tear found its way to Jenny's cheek. Christian had called, distraught, angry, scared for Jason, said he would hijack a plane if necessary to get home. The third call was from Nicki, Christian's secretary, confirming Christian caught a flight arriving in Minneapolis by 4:15 p.m. She'd pick him up and bring him home by 5:00 p.m. Then, as though blessed with divine wisdom, she assured Jenny all would be well. Another tear ran down Jenny's cheek.

The fourth call was a total surprise. Jenny and her mother listened expectantly with fists clenched under their chins, listening to words that brought tears to both amidst conflicting emotions of delight and disbelief.

The caller identified himself as Gary Sadler, FBI special agent in charge. Jason was found safe and unharmed at Mall of America. Of all places. Could it be true? Of course, it could! Faith had already declared it so. It must be true? But where was Jason? She rewound the tape, pushed play, listened. Rewound it once more, pushed play, and strained to hear mention of where she could find her son. Sadler wasn't saying but instructed Jenny to remain by her telephone. He would call again soon. Both women turned to face one another and embraced excitedly. Jason was safe!

The next caller was Police Chief Nick Carlson, confirming Jason had been found, adding that the FBI had the case and would be contacting her soon. Then he consoled, "The worst is over. Please remain by your phone."

No mention of Jason's location. D' walked to the television and turned it on in time to catch a news flash on Channel 6. *More than luck*, she said to herself. "Good morning, I'm Janet Spalding. This from our Channel 6 news room. We have just received word that Jason Poole, the son of Jennifer Poole, an executive with WYCO Toys, has been kidnapped, taken this morning at approximately 8:30, after having breakfast with his mother in the west suburban town of Excelsior. Now just in, moments ago, Jason Poole has been found unharmed at Mall of America where WYCO Toys operates their large superstore, House of Toys." She paused, suddenly charged with emotion, her eyes visibly moistened, took one deep breath, and continued, "Shortly after noon today, Channel 6 will bring you a live telecast of the previously scheduled WYCO Toys press conference from the House of Toys, and will report up-to-the-minute details of young Jason's abduction and rescue."

Irritation crossed her face as she quietly read a note handed to her from someone off camera. With the camera still shooting, she mouthed, "Stone is doing it?" The look of irritation turned to rage as her face turned red. Catching herself, she turned back to the camera. "We confirm the press conference is scheduled for noon today amidst speculation that the two events, the kidnapping of the son of a WYCO executive and the press conference, could be, in some way, related. You'll learn the whole story on our News at Noon. This is Janet Spalding. Now back to our program in progress."

Jenny walked to the television and turned it off. So Jason was at Mall of America. She found her phone and quickly punched in the number for information, got the number for Mall of America, and placed the call. When a pleasant voice answered, she asked to speak to the person in charge of mall security and was transferred to Dan Sheridan.

"Dan Sheridan," said Dan into the phone with his most pleasant voice.

"This is Jennifer Poole. I just saw on the news you have my son Jason. Is it true? Is he really all right? I'm coming right down." She was excited, agitated, and forceful.

"Jason's mother? I hoped you would call."

"Yes. I'm Jason's mother. I received a message from a Gary Sadler, FBI. He said Jason had been found and instructed me to remain by a telephone. He didn't give any details, and he has not called back to tell me where I can find my son. According to the news, he is with you."

"Yes. Actually, Mrs. Poole, Jason is at your House of Toys with one of my senior people, a mother with four children of her own, and your assistant, Sharon Miller."

He paused to think, searching for words to calm her, and then continued, "You have quite a boy, Mrs. Poole. He is alert, and he has not been harmed—"

"Thank you," interrupted Jenny. "Mr. Sheridan, I am with my mother. We're on our way down. Where can I find my son?" she said quickly, not willing to be put off.

"Mrs. Poole, I believe your son is having the time of his life. As I said, he is unharmed and has no recollection of the incident. He only knows that suddenly he's receiving a lot of attention at Mall of America. I would be honored to bring him to you personally right after the press conference. Besides, I would like to protect him from the media. Right now, they are all over the place. If you were to come down here, the press would besiege you. I don't think you want that."

Oh my! The news conference! she thought for a moment. "You're right. I just want to get Jason home. You've met my assistant Sharon. She can handle it. Well, most of it. I'll call her."

"I understand you were to take part in the press conference here today. I believe it best if you stay away." The governor's concern flashed through his mind. *Could she be the target?* "I can keep Jason isolated from the press. After the press conference, I'll personally return him to you, a couple of hours, if that's all right?" Resolute, he waited for her response.

"Mr. Sheridan, he's my son! I should be with him."

"Mrs. Poole, he really is doing very well. He'll be fine."

Following a moment of silence, she answered, "You're right. I couldn't take the press right now. Jason doesn't need them either, although he probably would enjoy every minute. I expect there'll be more opportunity for that."

"Yes, there will. The press does not give up easily," confirmed Dan.

"Okay. Do you know where we live?"

"Tonka Bay. Jason can direct me." He paused briefly. "Mrs. Poole, there is something else. It's most unusual that Jason has no recollection of what happened to him. I believe he was given something to block his memory. A drug."

"Drug! What kind of drug?" Gasped Jenny.

"We'll need lab work to know for sure. He shows no visible effects of any drugs, Mrs. Poole, but his memory loss is unusual. I would like to have our qualified physician draw a sample of Jason's blood to send to the FBI labs in Washington, DC, for analysis. It could provide a lead, Mrs. Poole. Do I have your consent to draw a small blood sample from Jason's arm?"

Dan's watch read 11:03. He knew some traces of drugs in Jason's system would have dissipated. What he proposed was a long shot. He waited. The truth had to be known. He hoped Jenny Poole and Gary Sadler saw it the same way.

"Mrs. Poole?" Dan persisted.

"Is it necessary?"

"We need to unravel this mystery. Who did this, and why."

"Jason doesn't like needles."

"Dr. Jim Clark is a skilled physician. It won't hurt Jason. How about if we let Jason decide? If he says no, it's a dead issue."

"I just want this entire incident to be over."

"Mrs. Poole, I know how you feel, but this is not just an incident. Jason was kidnapped. He was lucky, he could have been harmed…killed. Whoever did this must be stopped before they do it again. And it could happen again, Mrs. Poole, maybe not to Jason, but to some other child. No one knows why he was taken or who took him. Maybe it has something to do with the press conference. It's possible Jason could remain someone's target." Dan really didn't want to play on her fear to manipulate her, but Jason could still be in harm's way.

"You're saying you don't think it's over, is that it?"

Dan remained silent.

"Okay, Mr. Sheridan. I agree, let Jason decide. But I want your promise."

"What promise, Mrs. Poole?"

"That you'll keep him safe."

"Jenny, I will protect him with my life. I lost a son who would be the same age as Jason," he said seriously.

"Thank you, Mr. Sheridan. You said you'd be here by 2:00. We're waiting."

Dan thought for a moment, shook his head as he considered what he was about to say. "Tell you what, Jenny. Once he meets with our doctor, I'll bring him home. I've got staff who can handle everything here. We'll get him home as soon as we can."

"Thank you, Mr. Sheridan."

Gary Sadler had partially opened Dan's office door and now stood half inside and half out. Dan wasn't sure how much Gary had overheard.

"Come in, Gary. Thanks for the support. With Stone, I mean."

Sadler approached Dan's big executive desk and was directed to a comfortable chair at his coffee table. Dan followed him across the room, taking a seat across the table.

"Very nice! Nice indeed!" Sadler's envy was obvious as he lowered himself into the chair. Dan smiled but didn't answer.

"What's with you two? That thing with Stone? He took to you like a hound to a raccoon. I mean he was ready to bite."

"It's a long story."

Sadler looked at his watch, a nervous habit, but didn't notice the time. "Well?"

"Later."

"I meant what I said back there. All that I have learned about you so far has been very good. The company. The bureau. You were head of your class. This"—he waved his arm about the room—"I'm proud to know you were on the team. What happened? The report isn't too clear."

"Another time, Gary."

Gary let it drop for the present. "Well, you've been well-trained. It shows. You've left a lot for our guys to piece this together. I do appreciate that. Someone else could have—"

"So what will they do with it? What will you do, Gary?"

"You know the routine. The boy has been returned. He's unharmed. He was lucky, of course. There's no longer urgency in the case that we're aware of. We're dusting the men's room. Taking apart the van. Abel Food Service is not too happy with us. Their van will be out of commission until we're through, could be weeks. They run a tight ship. I'm sure they're busy trying to find out who breached their security." His eyes began to wander around the room as he fell silent. Beyond Dan's office window, he could see the superstructure for the park's roller coaster.

"Dan, we'll do what we can. Okay?" he added after collecting his thoughts. "You got out at the right time, you know. Good thing you're young. Not much use for us used trench coat types." Gary placed his hands on his knees, rubbed them like an old wound. "I'm fifty-five, soon to be fifty-six. One more year, and I'm out of here. That's whether I want it or not. You know that."

"It's been your life, and you don't want to leave. Good or bad, you love it."

Sadler shrugged. The bureau was his life. "So to the question at hand. What can I do?" He continued, "Budgets are being pared back...staff reductions. There's only so much I can do. Now with the boy back home, there'll be more pressing cases than his. You know that."

"He should have been killed then? Is that what you're saying? So the investigation could continue in earnest?"

"If he had been, the president himself would fund the investigation. Kids and crime are politically correct."

Dan understood the truth in Sadler's words. "Who do you think did this?" he asked, getting back on track.

"Couldn't say at this point. Two men stole a food van, drove it to Excelsior after making one scheduled delivery—now that doesn't make any sense—waited for Jason, and took him while his mother was inside paying for breakfast. They drive around for half an hour and drop him off at Mall of America. Not everyone goes to Disney World, I guess. There is no motive, none apparent, anyway. Seems like a lot of risk for a nonevent. I mean it's a federal offense. Prison if caught. That's a lot of risk for nothing."

"A lot of risk if the investigation continues, and they get caught. Sounds like that may not happen here. It being a nonevent."

"Touché. But you know that's not what I meant. I said we'd do what we can. I just can't make any promises."

Dan looked at his watch. It was 11:20. "Can we talk more later? You may have overheard that I have the mother's consent to take a blood sample. Can you run it? The works, drugs, anything you can find."

"Sure, but no promises. I'll let you know. I also heard you're bailing on the news conference."

"Call it payment to Jason's mom for the blood sample. I've got a great team here. Any one of them can handle the conference. Helen can arrange for anything you may need. You're staying, right?"

"I am. We'll work with your guys. You go. We can handle things here. And I'm calling in my full team. Malovich has me concerned. More than a little."

"Thanks, Gary." Dan held out his hand. Gary accepted, squeezed it thoughtfully. "I'm on the outside now, but I'd like to keep current on this one, personally. Will you help?" Dan added almost as an afterthought.

Sadler nodded as Dan walked him to the door. "No promises," repeated Sadler while the door closed behind him. Dan returned to the file on his desk. The index tab read Frederick C. Bartlett. It contained only a few papers. Thumbing through pages of facts he'd already read, he stopped on a page titled *family*. Yes, Bartlett had a wife, or did have a wife and a son, now deceased. No reason given. Killed in Columbia where Bartlett had been assigned.

His phone rang. It was Helen. "Just got word the press conference is running late. The senator's plane is delayed. Half an hour to an hour." He stood, glanced at his watch, relieved to have more time; he didn't want to be anywhere near the press conference where something could delay Jason's return home. On his way out, he passed Helen's desk. "Locate Lilly, have her bring Jason to Doctor Clark to have blood drawn. Get the sample to Sadler. Right away. I'm bringing him home."

"The press conference?" quizzed Helen.

Dan shrugged. "I know." He paused. "This is something I just have to do. Call it personal. With the delay, I should be okay. Sadler will be here with his entire team. Give him whatever he needs. Tell our guys to be as helpful as they can. I've got a confused boy I need to reunite with his mother. If you need me, call."

Dan jogged the entire distance to the House of Toys, entering the store on the third level and went directly to the area of greatest activity where Sharon Miller was talking with a Channel 6 guy. She smiled as he approached, a new friendliness not lost on Dan. "Jason is with Lilly, off to the clinic," she said, adding, "for a blood test?"

"Yes, with his mother's approval."

"She called. I guess I'm on my own here."

"You'll do fine," assured Dan.

"Thanks for your confidence."

Creighton Leonard, Massachusetts's Senator Malovich, and the delegation of Japanese businessmen and their wives had not yet arrived. Stone and Spalding were hot at it in one corner of the room, sparks flying. Dan watched amused. Suddenly, without warning, Janet raised her hand and slapped Stone across the face, the noise of the impact clearly audible over the din of a hundred voices. Stone brought his hand to his reddening face, grimacing in total disbelief and watched Janet storm out of the display area. Eyes turned to look at Stone but only for an instant; there was much to do in too little time, and Stone/Spalding power spats were nearly a daily occurrence.

"Couldn't happen to a nicer guy," said Dan, causing Sharon to shake her head in amusement.

"Jason's mother told you I'll be taking Jason home? From the clinic."

"She did. When you see her, tell her I've got everything under control here," suggested Sharon, smiling confidently.

"No doubt. And, yes, I'll tell her," replied Dan as he turned to track down Jason.

Dan found Jason and Lilly at the clinic. The doc saw him coming. "We're all set. Jason is a brave young man, didn't even flinch. He is in excellent condition as far as I can tell. Other than a possible residual effect of a drug, which does not appear to be the case, no damage done. Good to go."

Dan turned to Jason. "What do you say, Jason? Ready to go home? See your mom?"

Jason, slow to answer, cocked his head demurely. "Yeah…Can I go on a ride first? Like on the way out."

Dan couldn't resist laughing. "Well…Not this time. Your mom is waiting. I promised I'd bring you right home. We'll do it another day, I promise. Besides, there's a lot going on around here today."

Jason thought for a moment, *Okay*.

Dan stepped toward the reception area entrance but stopped suddenly. Turning a corner still a good distance away, Dan Stone was moving fast in their direction, his cameraman in tow. "Is there another way out? Channel 6 is on their way."

"The emergency exit, down that hall," responded the doc, pointing back over his shoulder.

"Good," Dan said and placed his hand on Jason's shoulder to nudge him toward the exit.

"It's 6's man, Stone. Stall him as long as you can. If he asks, you can tell him Jason is fine, but no more, doctor-patient privilege."

They walked quickly and quietly down the exit stairs to the garage and Dan's unmarked car, concealed lights, siren, the works. Jason took it all in as he entered the passenger side and buckled up.

On the move, a few quick turns brought them to the mall exit, northbound to Highway 77 where Dan hit the gas and his lights. Not quite legal, but he was in a hurry. The news conference would start within the hour, and he wanted to have Jason home by then. He was probably in the clear and wouldn't be missed until it started. His team knew what to do, and wishfully, he couldn't imagine anything happening before it began. After that, bets were off. They had his number, and he was sure someone would use it.

The turn to westbound 494 came suddenly. Running a little fast, his tires squealed as he made the turn. Jason hung on in the passenger seat, smiling from ear to ear. They merged onto 494, and Dan hit his cruise button at sixty-five, a fast but safe speed at five over the limit in light traffic. Through the "bud" in his ear, his police radio would warn him if any locals picked him up.

"You've had quite a day, Jason," said Dan, glancing at Jason.

"Yeah," Jason answered and returned to his thoughts, images of the day's events dancing through his mind.

Dan was pleased to see evidence of Jason's mind working and let him collect his thoughts. But as Highway 494 turned north toward Highway 7, still several miles ahead, he had to ask, "Remember anything about this morning?"

Jason took a few seconds to respond. "Not really."

"I understand you had breakfast in Excelsior with your mom."

"At Milly's restaurant. Every Thursday if the weather's nice. We go by boat."

"By boat?"

"Yeah, a high-performance bass boat. Really cool. Really fast. And my dad says really dangerous." A smile crossed Jason's face, recalling the morning's ride. "Today, I got to drive it by myself. Not alone, but without mom helping. I even docked it. I remember that. It was cool."

"A tournament boat? Do your mom or dad fish?"

"Not really. Off the dock maybe to keep me company. It's really my mom's boat, *Little Red*. She's really good with boats. Bought it off the floor at a sports show. My dad travels a lot so he doesn't get to use it often."

Dan caught the exit to westbound Highway 7, looked at his watch, turned off his lights, and merged into light traffic. Ten quiet minutes later, they had made all the stoplights the entire way to Excelsior. Following the sign to downtown Excelsior, he took a shallow right turn over a bridge to an intersection offering several options.

"Which way to Milly's?" he asked.

"Take a right and follow the shoreline," answered Jason, coming out of his muse that Dan hoped would reveal more information in the more familiar surroundings.

"There's the city dock where I docked *Little Red*," Jason exclaimed excitedly, pointing to the sturdy pier that welcomed Excelsior's visitors arriving by boat. Then turning in his seat, he pointed across the street to a row of small shops facing the shore and fronted by a boardwalk with three steps to a small street side parking lot. "That's Milly's in the center."

At the stop sign, Dan turned up Water Street, found an empty parking space where he could see Milly's, and pulled in. *Would Jason remember anything?* he wondered and waited quietly for Jason to say something. Only when a disheveled man with a cigar in his mouth sauntered by did he speak.

"That's Old Mike. He's really cool. We're friends…kinda. You want to know what's going on in Excelsior, just ask Old Mike. He talks a lot to people, most of them imaginary, people others can't see, but he sees everything. And, wow, does he have a memory. He remembers everything."

"How about your memory? Do you remember anything about this morning after breakfast?"

Jason thought for a few minutes and answered, "I remember thinking about driving *Little Red* again. That's about it."

Dan pulled away from the curb and proceeded up Water Street. At the stoplight, he turned onto County Road 19. Next stop, Jason's home. A smile crossed his face as he anticipated meeting Jason's mom.

The road meandered through Tonka Bay toward the Narrows, separating upper and lower Lake Minnetonka. "There's where I live," Jason said, pointing to a small cluster of townhomes dotting a quiet channel that emptied into the lower lake.

As they approached the road leading to the townhomes, Dan could see upper Lake Minnetonka to his left, a mirror-like surface stretching westward a couple miles before giving way to more small channels and islands that marked the west end of the lake. Dan noticed tall cumulous clouds marching eastward, barely visible on the western horizon. The calm before the storm the weatherman had warned.

Dan entered the private drive to Jason's townhome and parked beside a baby blue Mercedes in Jason's driveway. "My grandma is here. That's her car," said Jason excitedly as he opened his door and jumped out. "Come on. I'll show you *Little Red*." His door slammed, and his voice trailed off as he disappeared around the corner of the town house.

The front door seemed a better idea, but Dan obediently followed. Rounding the corner, he saw a large dock and Jason pointing to one of the half-dozen boat slips.

"Come on, Dan. This is *Little Red*," Jason shouted and jumped from the dock to the front platform of a metallic red bass boat.

Stepping toward the dock, Dan heard a sliding patio door open behind him. "Jason! Jason!" Jason's mother shouted and excitedly ran past Dan, ignoring him completely, to be reunited with her son.

"Mom!" shouted Jason and ran to his mother's waiting arms.

While they embraced, Dan's attention drifted toward the patio door to an attractive woman who could easily be mistaken as a sister, who stopped to watch the joyful reunion. *This must be grandma?* Dan realized. Like her daughter, she was wearing jeans and wore them very well. She wasn't as tan as her daughter, but maturity gave her an added measure of grace. She looked at Dan and walked toward him in a graceful stride across the manicured lawn to extend her hand. Up close, he realized he was addressing a beautiful woman in her fifties who had found the fountain of youth.

"You must be Dan Sheridan. I'm D' Ward, Jason's grandmother."

"Yes," he answered, extending his hand. "I've enjoyed getting to know your grandson. He's quite a boy."

"I understand it was you who found him. Thank you for taking such good care of him and for taking time to bring him home. Today is a big day at the mall."

"I have an excellent professional staff to handle the activity there so that I could bring Jason home and meet his family."

Jason released himself from his mother's grip and headed back toward the dock and shouted, "Come on, Dan, come see *Little Red*." His mother gave him *that* look that mothers are known for, sending him toward the dock alone. He jumped onto *Little Red*, moved behind the controls, and sat there looking very unhappy.

To break the awkward silence that followed, D' Ward smiled and offered, "Would anyone like something to drink, iced tea, beer, maybe something stronger?"

"Lemonade is fine, Mrs. Ward. I'm still working. Before the day is over, I'll go to something stronger."

"That's good," interjected Jenny. "We don't have anything stronger than lemonade or tea."

Jenny motioned for Dan to go to the deck and a cluster of comfortable rocker-style patio chairs. After a few minutes, D' returned with refreshments and set them on a small table before seating herself. They were ready.

Jenny began, looking Dan squarely in the eyes, "Mr. Sheridan, is Jason safe? Is this over for him? On the phone, you intimated there could be more."

Dan thought for a moment before answering, "Right now, he's safe at home with you. Is it over?" He paused. "I can't answer that. There are too many unanswered questions: why was he taken, by whom, why was he suddenly released, released at Mall of America, where you were the subject of a presentation and a press conference at a store you helped establish? Then there's the issue of the good senator from Massachusetts. Many questions.

"I can tell you, the FBI, my office, the Bloomington police, and your local police are all seeking the answers to those questions with your family very much in mind. We will all do what we can to keep your family safe."

Jenny changed the subject. "The local television networks have called. Channel 6's earlier story of the kidnapping and rescue has created a lot of attention. And because I'm not attending today's news conference, they want to come out and interview us live here tonight."

Dan nodded, a concerned look on his face. "Excuse me, but are you willing to subject yourself to an invasion of your privacy by a very nosy media? I brought him home so you could avoid that kind of scrutiny."

"And for that, we're very grateful. It's just that…I've had time to think about it, pray about it." She paused a minute before continuing, "I'm a Christian. And I believe God is in charge, and all things happen for a reason. Now, I don't have any idea what is the reason for what has happened today. And that's my concern. I believe I am supposed to discover that reason."

Dan smiled and nodded thoughtfully. "Who and how many?"

"Channels 6 and 3. I tried to say no, but they were insistent… actually pushy and disrespectful. They should start arriving about 4:30."

"And they both want to interview Jason. Right?" Dan knew the drill.

"Can we prevent it?"

"You could. You could change your mind and refuse. You're his mother. Or you could send him home with your mother."

"Should I have said no?"

Before Dan could answer, D' spoke, "Jason can certainly come home with me. But Christian would be awfully disappointed coming home and not finding Jason here."

"He'll arrive at news time. I'm sure he'll understand. That might be what he would want as well," said Jenny, concerned and disappointed she had not considered the possible danger.

"Mom!" said Jason from out of nowhere. Jason had quietly returned from the dock and had been listening. He didn't like the way the adults were solving the problem without giving him any say in the matter.

Dan spoke first, "If you stay here, the reporters will ask you all kinds of questions about the people who took you. You could say something that could put you in danger."

"What if I don't tell them anything?"

"Well, that's exactly what you must do. It's very important that you tell them you do not remember anything. Anything at all. Do you understand? They may try to trick you into saying something you shouldn't, to see if you're telling the truth. It might be better for you to go with your grandmother."

"I can handle it. I'll tell them I don't remember anything."

Dan looked to Jenny and her mother. "This is very important, Jason. You don't want to put you and your mother in danger."

Jenny now looked fearful as she turned to Jason. "Jason, would you please go to the kitchen and bring more ice cubes and some sweetener."

Jason frowned but did as he was told. After Jason passed through the patio door, Jenny spoke, "Look, if he acts stupid, like he can't remember, will everyone leave him alone?" Jenny needed to know the truth.

Dan answered quickly before Jason would return. "Mrs. Poole, Mrs. Ward, I can't give you a good answer to that question. I believe the people who took Jason are confident they are safe. I'm convinced they gave him some kind of a drug to block his memory. The fact that they let him go leads me to believe they're certain Jason won't remember anything."

"And if they're wrong. If Jason does begin to remember, what then?"

"That creates a big problem for them, and for you. We don't know who took him or why or why they returned him as they did. I do know these are dangerous people." Dan had been fearful Jason's quick return would give the family a false sense of security; he was pleased to see that begin to unravel.

"And is Jason beginning to remember?" asked Jenny.

"Nothing so far. But little by little, he could. It's impossible to say how much he will remember, or if he will remember anything at all. Regardless, we want the world to believe that he has no memory. We need his abductors to feel secure, and we don't want to give them any cause to worry."

"Well then, we need to convince everyone that he really can't remember?"

"You mean let the media interview him?" Dan speculated. "That's risky."

"Mr. Sheridan. I can't see us living the rest of our lives in fear. Jason can pull it off. If whoever did this is so sure of themselves, let's erase any doubt."

In his mind, Dan weighed the dangers. "It could work. But it is risky. You have to know that. It's your call. And I'd suggest Jason's."

Jenny had another question. "What's the likelihood they'll get caught? Can any of us really be safe until they are?"

"You're safe until they get spooked and become nervous."

D' raised an eyebrow but remained silent as Jason appeared at the patio door, a bowl of fresh ice in one hand and a sugar bowl in the other. He walked expectantly to the table and asked, "Well?"

Jenny nodded to Dan, who answered, "Well, Agent Jason, we've got some planning to do. Please sit down."

Jason's delight was visible as he sat down beside Dan and for several minutes listened to instructions that could keep him and his family safe a little longer. He glanced at his mother and grandmother sitting quietly with their eyes closed and knew they were praying through the details.

"I can do that," said Jason, confidently, when Dan finished.

"Okay, Jason, we're depending on you."

Sensing that Dan was about to leave, D' Ward asked, "How much help can we expect from the police and the FBI?"

Dan thought for a moment. "Gary Sadler is the FBI's special agent in charge. We've met, I know of him by reputation. He's good, seasoned, and gave me his word that he'll do whatever he can.

Kidnapping is a serious crime, and child abduction is a sensitive issue right now. His team is highly trained and know what they're doing. As far as the police is concerned, the Bloomington police will have their hands full. The mall is their jurisdiction, and they're motivated to eliminate any bad publicity. I suspect they'll defer to the FBI. I don't know the Minnetonka Community Police, but I understand their Chief Nichols is a good cop. I expect he'll assist and do everything he can."

Dan looked at his watch and thought of the news conference taking place at his mall. To the west, the small puffy clouds he had seen on the horizon had grown. Not yet visible was the dark leading edge of a massive frontal system marching slowly eastward, increasing in intensity each mile of the way, fueled by the hot August sun.

Suddenly, his cell phone rang. He picked up immediately. "It's Dan," he said.

While he listened, he looked at Jenny and D'. His expression showing surprise followed by concern that grew more evident each second. A minute passed, then two, and he said, "I'm on my way. Twenty minutes," and returned his phone to his pocket.

Seeing the concerned expressions on Jenny and D', he summarized the call. "That was Sadler, FBI at the House of Toys. There's been a shooting. Preparations were underway for the news conference with people gathering on stage when an agent spotted a man in the audience pull a gun. He acted quickly and got to him before the gunman could pull the trigger. There was a scuffle, and the gun went off hitting the gunman. He is alive but unconscious on his way to HCMC. No one else was injured. They don't know who may have been the intended target."

"Senator Malovich," suggested Jenny.

"Anyone's guess. Another mystery," he spoke as he turned to leave, addressing Jenny. "What you're about to do, be very careful. This is becoming more dangerous than it seems. I'll do what I can to help and will keep you informed. Be safe!"

JENNY

The head of security for Mall of America excused himself to return to where duty called, a duty that now included a self-imposed assignment: protecting a family who couldn't possibly understand what they may be getting into.

Its Bartlett, he thought as he turned his ignition, shifted into gear, turned on his concealed flashing lights while screeching tires left marks on the county road.

Chapter 14

A green sports car entered the Wayzata Towers parking ramp and parked close to the elevators in a stall marked "Reserved." The driver opened his door, unfolded his lanky body, stood beside his car while he fumbled with his key-fob until his horn honked and his lights blinked, then turned and walked quickly to the bank of elevators. In his thirties, he was dressed fashionably in a double-breasted suit, mirror-black shoes, and an angry demeanor.

Inside the brass and glass elevator, he pushed the button marked "Penthouse," the home of the Wayzata Toy Company known to the world as WYCO Toys. The elevator stopped at "8" where a young woman, blonde and very attractive stepped in carrying a tray of food. Single, reasonably good-looking and rich, six-foot-six, JB (Jeb) Barons considered introducing himself but, instead, only smiled and barely noticed when the car stopped on 18, where she exited.

When the door opened again, Jeb Barons stepped into a luxurious, semicircular reception area with a scattering of comfortable chairs and small writing tables positioned on a well-polished, rust-and-white marble floor.

Against the back wall, an attractive brunette in her early thirties greeted all visitors from a semicircular marble desk. Behind her were the company's executive offices and conference rooms, far grander than the older office on the shores of Lake Minnetonka.

JB strode past the receptionist. She smiled. He smiled and proceeded down a corridor opening to another reception area, smaller but even more luxurious than the one he had just passed through. At a massive walnut desk in the center of the paneled room, he was greeted by Kathleen Warren, Creighton Leonard's administrative secretary and his own personal assistant—when her time allowed. On her desk were the usual telephones, computer screen, keyboard, and laser printer. She wore a headset with a microphone plugged to a small console arrayed with many flashing lights—Creighton's private lines to kings, politicians, presidents, and dignitaries from around the world.

"I still can't believe it," she said as though continuing an ongoing conversation.

"Well, believe it. It's a mess. This entire day…Well…It just should not have happened."

A light on her console lit up. "The phone's been ringing off the hook." She pushed a button and spoke into her microphone, quickly dismissing the caller, "I'm sorry, Mr. Leonard is not available."

"The whole world, it seems, wants to speak with Creighton," she said. "Is he all right, Creighton? Was he the target? They have the shooter, right? Do we know who he is? Or why he did it?"

"Why, we don't know. Until the shooter regains consciousness, if he ever does, we probably won't know his motivation. The authorities are working on the *who*. The police don't think he was after Creighton. He apparently works at the mall, and they feel he's had other opportunities to hit Creighton if he was a target."

"Where's Creighton now. He hasn't called."

"With the governor."

"Doing okay?"

"They're at the capitol doing damage control. The gov's upset. He's convinced this was planned just to make him look bad, blaming both the Republicans and the Democrats."

"And the senator?"

"On his way back to DC, shaking in his boots. He believes he was the target. The authorities seem to agree. From what I know of Malovich, he probably deserves it."

"And how is Jennifer Poole? The attempted shooting really overshadowed her son's kidnapping. The poor girl. Thank God, her son is unharmed. I understand he's safe at home."

Jeb's face reddened at the mention of Jennifer's name. "Know her?" he asked.

"Not really. She's not been up here as long as I've been here. What…six months since Creighton brought me here."

"Well, we've never met." Jeb lied. "So, tell me, what do you know about her?"

"She's liked, respected by marketing and the people who know her, and mostly admired by others—no reason not to be. Some say she's prudish. I guess because she's a person of faith. Some want her job, but none have her kind of talent. I hear what I hear but try not to get involved. She's at plant 1, and the old offices are a different world. I've never been there. Sometimes I wonder if they're apart of us here?"

Surprised by her statement, Jeb said, "Seems to me those people are why we're here. We could use a thousand Jennifer Pooles. What they do over there is what keeps us employed."

"My, my. Sounds like you do know about our Jennifer Poole?"

JB placed his hands on Kathleen's desk deliberately towering over her. "Look, I know we're fortunate to have her here. The rest of those at plant 1, I don't know. Now just who is in charge of the conference area over there?"

"JB, I'm sorry. I really didn't mean anything by that."

"I'm sorry too, it's been a tough day." He apologized in a softer tone.

Kathleen sighed. "For me too. Now, does anyone know anything about the abduction? Callers keep asking. Are the two related, the abduction and the conference? Like, what's her son got to do with anything?"

Waiting for an answer, she searched her company directory and didn't notice Jeb's complexion become redder.

"It's possible the events are related," said JB. "The media certainly thinks so." Impatiently he jingled loose change in his pant's pocket. "A name?"

"Mildred Knowles. I call her when we need their conference center. She's been around forever, knows the ropes. Come to think of it, I've been calling her a lot lately. She schedules everything and keeps the log. Mildred Knowles."

"A log? That's what I need."

"Nothing after-hours. She leaves at 4:30 usually. Visiting guests are housed there and could use the conference area after hours, and Mildred wouldn't know."

"Get her for me," ordered Jeb, then turned to his office but paused and added in a softer tone, "Please."

Entering his beautifully paneled office, he closed his door, grimaced in pain as he sat, and his knees hit the underside of his desk. It was mahogany, big and clear of papers and projects that Kathleen had found time to file. On one side was his telephone, blinking. It would be Mrs. Knowles. He picked it up.

"Mrs. Knowles. This is JB Barons. I know we've not yet met," he said politely.

"You're Mr. Creighton's assistant. What can I do for you, Mr. Barons?"

"I've misplaced my planner and could use your help."

"Certainly."

"Last Thursday, we entertained a Mexican consulting group. A plant tour, that sort of thing. Did they use the suite? I'm retracing our time with them."

"Yes, the Martinez Group. They were still here when I left at 4:30. Scheduled out at 5:15."

"Anyone working late that night?"

"Kohl asked the same question last Friday."

JB was aware of Kohl's inquiry. Kohl was director of personnel and had insisted the only person working late in the executive area was Jennifer Poole.

"What did you tell him, Mrs. Knowles?"

"I told him I couldn't be sure. You know, several managers have keys. Someone is always coming in to work late."

"Did you give Kohl a name?"

"I told him Jennifer Poole frequently works late."

Then Kohl was right, thought JB, not wanting to believe it.

"She's a hard worker," continued Mrs. Knowles. "Her husband is an attorney and travels a lot. She lives close by and sometime comes in after hours to get caught up. She has a ten-year-old son, Jason. Doesn't give her much free time. I know she was preparing for the press conference. By the way, how did it go? Were you there?"

"You haven't heard the news?" he asked in amazement. *How could anyone not be aware of that fiasco?* "I was." *Talk about isolation!* "Can't get into that now. Watch the news tonight. Channel 6 probably has the best coverage," he advised.

"Was Mrs. Poole the only person working late when the Martinez Group was there?"

"Well, actually, I don't believe so. Kohl rang off before I could tell him. Jennifer Stewart is, or was, the new *gofer* here. She was trying really hard to make a good impression. Her first big corporate job—big to her. Nice girl, trying to learn the ropes. I believe she worked late that night. Come to think of it, she hasn't been here since."

"Jennifer Stewart? On vacation, possibly?"

"She hasn't been here long enough. Homesick, maybe. She doesn't report to me. I can't keep track of everyone. Personnel would know, check with them."

"That'd be Kohl?" he asked.

"It would be."

"I'll check. Please call me if Stewart calls in? I'd like to speak with her. And…Thanks."

"I certainly will. And you're welcome, Mr. Barons. I hope you find your planner."

"Oh, one more thing. Jennifer Stewart is a chubby woman with glasses, right?" he asked, knowing the answer. He'd guess the two

Jennys not only shared the same name but looks as well. Mistaken identity had to have played a role in today's debacle. It had to be Jennifer Stewart who was in the wrong place at the wrong time. *That imbecile Kohl!*

"Goodness, no. Nothing chubby about her! She's a beautiful girl. Actually, she and Jennifer Poole look a lot alike. Could mistake them at a distance," confirmed Mildred Knowles.

"Thanks again, Mrs. Knowles." His voice trailed off as he placed the phone back on its cradle. *What to do?* He rang Kathleen's direct line. "Get me the Martinez Group, Alverez." Then, still holding the phone, he looked at his watch and redialed Kathleen. "Cancel that call. I'll try later." Alverez would not yet have arrived in Miami.

JB pushed his chair back from his desk and swung it around to stare out his large window. His office was smaller than Creighton's but grander than most and appropriately sized for the personal assistant to the president and CEO. He enjoyed the prestige, the power accorded his position and was willing to put up with the problems inherent in his position, like cleaning up the mistakes of others that would detract from the company's unmarred reputation and meticulously ensuring to make none himself.

Looking east beyond his rooftop patio sprawled the skyline of Minneapolis, mountains of glass reflecting the midday sun like glistening gem stones. He smiled as he took it all in. He had never seen it quite that way before. On the ground below was a large tranquil pond bordered on one side by woods. Both teemed with geese and ducks, an occasional deer and fox. Around the perimeter was a walking path that one day he would walk for the exercise. After things settled down, the six months since he and Creighton Leonard had taken control of WYCO Toys in a hostile takeover had allowed JB little time for personal matters.

Today's events would only worsen matters well into the future, a future that had nearly ended at noon. He much preferred having a future with problems than have no future at all.

He ran his fingers through his hair and surveyed the horizon ten miles to his east. It was not the horizon he knew fifteen years ago when he left to find his own pot of gold. He was not who he had been fifteen years ago. Then his innocence had been a virtue, and success but a dream; pie in the sky, his motivation.

Fifteen years had matured him and brought him position, prestige, and power. As to virtue? He was not so naïve. His activities had never been illegal, but only because he was meticulously careful. His crowning achievement was helping propel Creighton Leonard to the helm of WYCO Toys and himself along with him. Being careful had been his hallmark until now.

He wondered what his Minnetonka High School graduating class would think of him now if they only knew. He doubted any would remember his name. He had not been a popular kid, tall for his age, gangly and awkward, new to the area with a bit of a southern drawl. A curiosity more than a friend. It had been his classmates who had nicknamed him Jeb, after the dopey lead character in *The Beverly Hillbillies*, the popular television show back then. *Wasn't it Jennifer Ward's class that named me?* He didn't mind. He liked the show, liked the character, and he liked Jennifer Ward. And it was a form of recognition.

What would Jennifer Ward think of me now? It had been Jennifer Ward he had seen crossing that street corner in Excelsior. He could never forget that face, as brief a glimpse as it was, and after so many years. But it had to be her. The media identified her as Jennifer Poole. She had married and had a new name. How he had loved her once, but she had never known.

Yes, much had changed in fifteen years. He could never have imagined that the girl of his dreams would become a marketing executive with the very company he now assisted in running? There was no way on earth he could have known. But here she was. A serious complication. If only he had known. He felt responsible for her troubles today, and rightly so. But he was not entirely to blame. The blame rested with that dolt, Kohl. It was Kohl's mistake. Now he

JENNY

had to fix it. *Oh, Jenny! Jenny! Jenny!* He sighed and buried his head in his hands while his heart waged war with yesterday's passion that suddenly was taking on new relevance.

Chapter 15

Getting home was a greater ordeal than Christian Poole could have imagined. Before boarding his plane in New York, he received a page informing him Jason had been found unharmed and would be returned home by 2:00 p.m. Little else was known, but it was sufficient to relieve his fear. Still, he could not quiet his mind and turn off the questions that nagged him. *Why? Why would anyone target his family? Why? Why would someone take Jason? There had been no demands. Had it been for financial gain? Maybe Jenny's father's wealth, but certainly not his. Was it client-related?*

Why didn't really matter. Jason was safe—that mattered.

His plane landed in Detroit on schedule. With his one carry-on, he ran down the concourse to his next flight. It was canceled due to a mechanical failure, or so they said. A look around the departure lounge and lack of passengers in the boarding suggested a different reason.

The gate attendant apologized with a smile and advised him the next flight would leave Detroit for Minneapolis at 6:00 p.m., getting him to Minneapolis a little after seven. It would be 8:30 before he could hold his wife and hug his son. That just would not do.

Seeing Chris's obvious disappointment, the attendant punched his computer and booked a seat on a competing airline, giving Chris a new Minneapolis arrival only forty-five minutes late.

"Thank you," he said, sighing relief and walked to the nearest bank of phones where he called his office and left a message on Nicki's voice mail informing her of his new arrival time. Nicki would

JENNY

call Jenny to give her the schedule change. Then he walked to the next concourse with time to spare.

Five minutes before departure, he found a phone and punched in his home number. The line was busy. His watch said 1:45. In fifteen minutes, Jenny would be reunited with Jason, and he'd be in the air.

He returned to a seat in front of the TV where a CNN commentator was summarizing the day's top stories: "Today, Massachusetts's senator, Willard Malovich, denied allegations that he had engaged in homosexual activity with a teenage male prostitute. Republicans demand a full senate inquiry. In other news, WYCO Toys, acclaimed the world's largest toy manufacturer, came under siege today, the target of two separate acts of violence." Chris looked at his watch. Boarding would begin in minutes. He'd miss the segment, and he knew one of those acts of violence involved his wife and his son.

When a distant loudspeaker announced his flight, he stood and strained to hear the CNN commentator, "Jason Poole, son of WYCO Toys executive Jennifer Poole, was kidnapped this morning in the suburban Minneapolis town of Excelsior only to be returned unharmed a short time later to Mall of America, where Jennifer Poole was to be honored at a press conference at the company's signature store, House of Toys."

The picture changed to the House of Toys just as Chris heard the final call for his flight. But he couldn't move; he was mesmerized as the picture centered on two men in the crowd tussling as a gun went off, sending frightened onlookers scurrying. What's that all about?

"Sir," said a voice from behind him. He turned to see an attendant glaring at him, waiting to close the jet-way door. He entered and stepped aboard. Nicki had booked him in first class, but in spite of the great accommodations, he struggled to relax. He settled into his seat and extended his legs out as far as possible, but restlessness persisted.

Flight 713 from Detroit was on schedule. Its vectored path brought it several miles southeast of the Twin Cities where it began its approach to runway 27 into the approaching storm.

Over the past five years, he had flown in all kinds of weather, easily logging more than one hundred thousand air miles per year. Flying had become routine. He had great confidence in the pilots who piloted their multimillion-dollar aircraft with their trusting cargoes of men, women, and children. But despite his respect for the pilots and crew, he didn't like flying in adverse conditions when the outcome was more in God's hands than in the pilots.

He was glad their approach was from the east as he watched out his port side window of the wide body 737. He had been watching the approaching storm for the past twenty minutes as it raged behind a black frontal line stretching from Oklahoma City to Fargo. It was an awesome and strangely exhilarating sight, an impenetrable wall of cumulous-nimbus clouds towering beyond forty-five thousand feet, filled with rain, ice, hail, cyclone winds, and several tornadoes that had caused serious destruction along the storm's path according to the pilot.

The approach pattern brought the flight west of the Twin Cities and over Lake Minnetonka and his townhome where Jenny and Jason were waiting. He waved symbolically. At 3:58 p.m., the front remained several miles west of Minneapolis but was sure to overrun Lake Minnetonka by the time he arrived home. In the distance, lightning flashed continuously like cannon fire dividing east from west, from the north to south for as far as the eye could see.

He hoped he would be home by 5:00. He couldn't wait. *Thank God, Jason is safe.* In spite of the weather, the final leg of the flight had a calming effect. Jenny's morning message seemed a bad dream from which he was very much awake. *But the struggle for the gun and the shot fired, what was that?* He shook his head to dislodge that grim thought for the moment and waited for the stewardess to gather his spent can of soda.

Chapter 16

The bile in Bill Wilson's gut had bubbled all day. Anxious and depressed and unable to continue his work, he left two hours early and headed directly home.

Home was a modest wood frame Victorian farmhouse that he had remodeled little by little over the years. Nestled among tall oaks and maples two miles west of Excelsior on a quiet tree-lined road, he lived conveniently less than seven miles from WYCO Toys plant 1 where he worked in the company's kitchens as food service supervisor.

He drove to the end of his gravel drive where he parked and with lunch box in hand climbed out of his *beater* of a car and slammed its door. Suddenly aware of the weather, he looked to the west to see a massive wall of ominous gray clouds and watched for a moment as it moved ever closer. He had not concerned himself with the weather all day and, with other things on his mind, had not turned on his radio at work. Besides, he did not want to be reminded of his stupidity, his participation in the theft of a caterer's van earlier in the day that would have made the news. Jordan had insisted his help was necessary for the good of his company, maybe his job, and he had believed him. He hung his head and quietly cursed himself.

Profanity was not common to Bill's vocabulary, but vulgar expletives had obsessed him the entire day. *How could he be so dumb?* His mood was as dark and morose as the clouds that would soon descend upon him. It had not been a good day. Not good at all.

When he had finally turned on the news, what he heard sent chills up his spine; he was now a criminal. The van he helped "borrow" was used to kidnap a boy, the son of a WYCO employee. What would Martha say?

He stepped onto his screen porch through an opening needing a screen door and opened the door to his wife's tidy, and now quite dark, kitchen.

"Bill! That you? You're home early." Martha's voice came from the basement where she was finishing the week's ironing accompanied by the smell of aromatic fabric softener drifting up the stairs on warm humid air and the sound of light pop music from a small boom box Martha kept at her side during the day.

"It's me," he yelled back.

He went to the refrigerator and removed a cold one; a dark ale suited his mood. Then finding nothing good to eat, slammed the door shut. The low constant rumble of thunder in the distance brought him back to the screen porch. The sky had become darker, and the clouds had a greenish hue. *Not a good sign.* Remembering his open car windows, he walked to the car and one by one opened the doors and cranked the windows closed. Satisfied, he returned to the screen porch and sat down on the top step with his beer in hand and waited.

He had grown up with Martha's brother, Jordan Green. They had attended Excelsior Elementary School together and had been buddies ever since. They did everything together: hunted and fished for bass and crappie winter and summer; drank beer; played poker; watched football; everything. Jordan had graduated from high school one year ahead of Bill. Because the military draft had been eliminated, Jordan worked for one year at a local car wash, so when Bill graduated, they could enlist in the army together. Vietnam was not a popular war, but *what the hell.*

They arrived in Vietnam as the war was winding down. Bill was assigned to the motor pool; Jordan joined the MPs. Through some fluke, Bill ended up driving a truck for the base commissary and developed a friendship with the chief in charge, who was short-handed one day and engineered Bill's transfer to food services.

Neither Jordan nor Bill had career goals when they entered the service and found it opportune, if not prudent, to utilize their training upon their release. Jordan found a job with a local Minneapolis security firm. Bill knocked around as a short-order cook, night chef, grocery chain produce handler, and driver for Abel Food Services. Eventually, Jordan took a full-time security position with WYCO Toys and soon found Bill a job in the company's kitchens. Jordan had always looked after Bill, even set Bill up on his first date with his sister Martha. It was Jordan who convinced Martha that she could not go wrong with someone as steady as Bill.

Bill and Jordan were closer than brothers, but now *Bill* felt betrayed. Oh, Jordan had gotten him into trouble before, but nothing too serious. Nothing like this. Jordan had insisted he help because, as he put it, he knew the *ins* and *outs* of Abel Food Service where he had been employed there years earlier. Even now as a WYCO employee, he was often picking up special orders when "out-of-towners" came to tour the plant and to use the conference suite. If he were seen at Abel, no one would have reason for concern.

Never should have done it. He swore at himself. *Jordan had deceived him.* He had believed Jordan when he said they were dealing with a matter of company security. He believed him when he said it was his duty as a WYCO employee. He didn't have to drive. He just needed to be there. They just needed to borrow a truck for a while. "A few hours," is what Jordan had said. There wasn't time to go through channels, and the company didn't want anyone to know they had a problem with security. Arrangements had been made. An Abel driver would call in sick after he had left the truck's keys under the floor mat. *Likely story.*

Bill raised the beer can to his lips. Finding it empty prompted another trip to the fridge and another cold one from a six pack on the bottom shelf. Then he returned to his perch on the top step of the porch.

Bad decision! Guilt and fear of the consequences of his actions were tightening their grip. He'd have to live with it. *Forever.* He was beginning to shake. *My God, I could go to jail. What would Martha do?* At the thought of jail, he raised the can, took a too-big gulp and began coughing uncontrollably, oblivious to the approaching storm.

The once-low rumble of distant thunder had become a roar, and the constant flashes of lightning created a flickering glow in the approaching devilish clouds. Rolling toward him, the frontal clouds surged with vicious straight-line winds. As though enjoying a death wish, Bill ignored it all. His face cupped in his hands when suddenly a large limb from a towering oak tree cracked and fell with a *thunk* to the soft ground.

Then, as though heaven could no longer hold its payload, the clouds burst open and pummeled the earth with a zillion two-inch balls of ice, covering his yard with three inches of hail. The first hailstone drove Bill under the porch roof for protection. In the near-zero visibility, he caught a glimpse of his car, his only car, and couldn't believe what was happening to his poor old beater. His insurance only covered liability. There was no way he could afford to have the body repaired. He watched helplessly as the hail left hundreds of craters in his car's metal skin.

Crying to himself, he returned to the refrigerator for another cold one and downed half the can before grabbing the remaining six-pack and walked to the family room and his favorite chair. God was dealing with him, he knew. He was being punished for being so stupid and so gullible. He had no right to complain. It was just punishment. God kept score and was now getting even. He deserved it. *Stupid! Just plain stupid,* he cursed again.

He found the TV's remote and pushed "On." Displayed was a radar screen with a large area of green and red superimposed over a map of the Minneapolis area. He spotted Lake Minnetonka when a loud crack shook the house and returned the TV screen to black.

Within a couple minutes, a small light entered the room and marched toward him. "It's a good one, an honest-to-goodness storm. For once, the weatherman was right," Martha said and directed the light in Bill's direction. She smiled and seated herself next to her husband and turned off her flashlight. "Can't iron without electricity," she said in the dark.

Bill could hear her chuckling quietly; the irony of there being so much electricity in the air when her electric iron had none struck her as funny. Bill loved Martha, blessed with a quiet countenance some folks mistook for ignorance. But deep inside, she possessed a resilient, witty spirit that never tired of giving. She was the perfect mate for Bill, who was occasionally given to brooding. She had loved him from the moment her brother Jordan suggested she date his best friend for the very kind person he was. It seemed like yesterday when Bill was a junior at Minnetonka High School, and she was a sophomore.

She listened to Bill's breathing, shallow and barely noticeable, and sensed his brooding. She sought his face, momentarily frozen in the intermittent flashes of lightning, and could feel his torment as though it were hers. *Just what could have so disturbed her Bill? He seems so undone.* "How 'bout a beer, Billy?" she asked affectionately. "You got an extra? Or are you gonna get wasted all by yourself?" Her attempt at levity seemed to go nowhere when out of the flashes of the lightning came Bill's hand and in it an opened cold one.

She would drink a beer only occasionally. This was one of those occasions. And as Bill would say "what the hell," she couldn't iron without electricity.

A moment passed, and in the darkness, she got up and sat down again on Bill's lap. For the moment while the wind blew, the lightning flashed, and thunder rumbled, she ran her fingers through his short hair, and there was comfort and communion as they sipped their cold ones.

Chapter 17

With just his carry-on, Chris walked directly through the terminal to Nicki's waiting car. Reaching for the passenger door handle, he looked to the west at the approaching storm that looked even more ominous viewed from the ground. A menacing black wall cloud stretched across the horizon blanketing the western suburbs. The rain had not begun to fall, but overhead, the constant rumble of thunder could be heard over the sound of jets coming and going. He doubted they could make it home before feeling the storm's full fury.

"Weather really looks bad, Nicki. Could get a little hairy before we reach the house. Want me to drive?"

"Would you mind? We'd get there faster if you do." Nicki crawled over the center console into the passenger seat while Chris moved around the back of the car to take Nicki's place behind the wheel. They wasted no time, buckled in and pulled away from the curb.

With each minute, the sky darkened and, as if on signal headlights, began popping on as drivers prepared for nature's onslaught. At 4:20 p.m., they exited the airport drive and merged onto Interstate 494 during rush hour traffic that was lighter than Chris had expected. Under normal driving conditions, the drive home would take forty-five minutes, give or take, so Chris calculated with luck he'd be home by 5:00.

Neither spoke until they approached the exit sign for Mall of America. As Chris glanced at the nation's largest mall looming on his left, he asked, "Did Jason make it home?"

JENNY

"Yes. He made it all right. The mall's head of security drove him home personally."

"CNN was carrying the news conference at the House of Toys. I didn't catch it all. My flight was boarding. The last I saw, two men were struggling on the floor, I think at the House of Toys, and a shot rang out. What was that all about?"

"Apparently, one of Senator Malovich's security team saw a man in the audience draw a gun and tackled him before he could shoot. In the struggle, a shot was fired, hitting the shooter."

"Kill him?" asked Chris.

"I don't know. He was sent to the hospital. I believe in critical condition."

"Do they know his target?"

"Not for sure. The senator seems to be the popular choice because of his pending legislation."

They continued for several miles in silence before Chris spoke, "It's a miracle Jenny wasn't there. She would have been up there at the podium. I mean, this may sound weird, but Jason being kidnapped, causing her to remain home, could have been a Godsend, keeping her out of harm's way."

"I've spoken with Jenny, and she feels the same. By the way, she wants you to wear your best smile. Channels 3, 6, and 7 will interview Jenny, Jason, and probably you, live, from your living room on the 5:00 p.m. news."

"What!" Chris shouted, incredulous.

Nicki looked at him, surprised. Seldom had she seen her boss look so angry.

A few seconds later, he had calmed. "I don't know why, but I guess I'm not surprised. But how'd Jenny come to allow that? Interview Jason?"

"She tried to refuse, but the networks weren't listening. Finally, she gave in to get it over with. And she said she feels led to find out why this happened. Things happen for a reason. The interview might provide some answers."

Christian shook his head at the black horizon and warned, "I doubt we'll make the 5:00 p.m. This storm could change things. It will be the Jenny and Jason show."

He looked at Nicki. "Where will she put all the people? They'll destroy the place," he asked, not expecting an answer and gripped the steering wheel with greater determination.

Cars were pulling to the side of the road; drivers hurrying to hunker down on the shoulder ahead of the wall of wind, water, and hail now only minutes away. With the town of Excelsior only a few miles ahead, Christian pushed his speed to seventy-five hoping to find better cover among the town's building and didn't notice the color leave Nicki's face as she grabbed the armrest.

Seconds later, Christian knew it was time to stop. Less than one mile west, a solid wall of water and hail was advancing toward them, probably less than thirty seconds away. Suddenly, the car lurched to the right as straight-line winds moved it several feet sideways. It was suicidal to continue, and with only seconds to think, he pulled to the side of the road. *God, help us!*

It struck with the fury of machine gun fire bouncing off armor plate and sounded even worse. Through gray-green clouds, chunks of ice ricocheted and shattered off the windshield and left craters in the thin metal skin of Nicki's one-year-old Mazda sedan. It seemed, at any moment, the wind would pick them up and move them back to Minneapolis, Wisconsin, or Maine, but the car held secure on the roadside, jerking in pain at the staccato pummeling.

Chapter 18

At 4:05, Jenny and Jason looked to the western sky and walked to the dock to secure *Little Red* from the approaching storm. Channel 6 news reported the storm had already caused moderate damage a few miles to their west in Carver and McCloud Counties. Funnel clouds had been reported in the air, but so far, none were reported on the ground. They had also called to say the rain would not keep them away; the telecast would go on as scheduled.

D' Ward left twenty minutes earlier, hoping to get home and close windows before the rain. But before she left, she, Jenny, and Jason had role-played to prepare Jason for his interrogation by the media. While they pretended it was a game, each knew the seriousness of the televised question-and-answer session. Jason had to be convincing. There could be no doubt that Jason had no recollection of his abductors. None whatsoever.

Ten minutes later, the television crews arrived ahead of schedule; they didn't want their delicate equipment to get wet. Lights were set up in the living room directed toward the fireplace, which would serve as a background for the interview. A large portable generator on a trailer sat on their driveway apron to power the vast array of electronic equipment. It was more of a production than Jenny had bargained for.

The networks negotiated amongst themselves and somehow determined Channel 6 would broadcast live at 5:00 p.m., as if there had ever been any doubt. The other channels would tape their interviews for their own 6:00 p.m. telecasts.

At 4:30, Police Chief Nick Carlson backed his black and white to a stop near the end of the drive, maneuvered so that he could exit quickly if necessary. Jason came to the partially opened door at the sound of the bell and, with his mother close behind, carefully stepped over the heavy-duty power cord holding the door open.

Accompanying the chief was a portly woman in uniform, vaguely familiar to Jenny. "Mrs. Poole, I'm Chief Nick Carlson of the Minnetonka Area Police. It was one of my officers who responded to the 911 call this morning."

"Please come in. There's always room for more, I think. The media plans to telecast live from here in just a few minutes. Is everything all right?" Jenny craned her neck to look outside as the two officers entered. The chief politely gave way to the other officer but didn't introduce her.

"Yes. They called us," said Chief Nick. "We knew they were coming, but I wanted to stop by personally to see that you and Jason were okay. We're all very relieved that Jason was found so quickly."

Jason stood behind his mother at the door and at the mention of his name stepped beside her to be seen more clearly by the uniformed officers. "You're Jason. I recognize you from your pictures. You're a very fortunate young man. I have a grandson in Nevada your age. Ten, isn't it?"

Jason nodded.

A young woman dressed in jeans, touting a clipboard came up behind Jenny and tapped her shoulder. "Mrs. Poole, I'm Linda with Channel 6. We're ready to begin. Everyone would like to get started a little early if possible. Our weather people advise we're in for a massive storm. We may not be able to go live, and we'd like to tape a portion early, just in case. If that's all right?"

The sooner the better, thought Jenny, *but where was Christian?* The small-town house was bursting with people. Had the fire marshal been called, he would have demanded that half the people vacate immediately. That thought had also crossed the chief's mind, but he let it pass. In a few minutes, the out-of-doors would not be a good place for anyone.

Jenny walked back to the living room and took her place with Jason at her side in front of the large fireplace. The furniture had been carefully moved to the walls. Outside the sky was black and gray-green. Rain had not yet begun to fall in earnest, but large drops splatting on the wood deck were an ominous prelude of what would shortly follow. Lightning flashes were nearly constant, and the thunder was a steady rumble clearly audible over the din of voices.

The various television news personalities, who had earlier assembled in the second-floor bedrooms to get out the way during setup, came downstairs when Jenny greeted Chief Nick at the door.

Tension, thick as oatmeal, filled the room. People went about their tasks without thinking, fearful of the impending storm and potential danger of working around high-voltage equipment in an electrically charged atmosphere. Yet no one was consciously willing to pull the plug and call it quits.

Janet Spalding stepped from the throng of media people and approached Jenny, boom microphone rising in her wake. Red lights on top of the network video cameras snapped on. Everyone was ready.

After a brief introduction, Janet addressed Jason. "Jason, the entire nation has learned of your experience this morning, and we're all very relieved that you are now safe at home. The question we all have is what really happened to you today and why. Do you remember anything at all of what happened to you? The people who took you?" She tipped her microphone low so Jason could respond.

"I don't remember anything at all," he answered confidently.

Not satisfied with the answer, the seasoned reporter decided on a different tact. "It must have been a horrifying experience to be kidnapped within sight of your mother, in front of the restaurant, where you had just had breakfast. Were you frightened? We understand you then spent several hours with your captors. Did they threaten you? Anything come to mind?"

Jason was glad he had rehearsed this moment with his mother. His response was convincing. It was also true. "It all happened so fast. One minute I was having breakfast with my mother. I left Milly's, that's the restaurant, to go to the docks where our boat was tied. The next I remember, I was at Mall of America. Nothing in between."

Something drew Jenny's attention to her patio door. In the flashes of lightning that punctuated the blackness, she saw the wind blowing the small patio trees nearly horizontal and the deck chairs and table had blown over. She was grateful Jason had removed the umbrella.

Suddenly, a brilliant flash lit the sky, followed by an ear-shattering *crack*! Jenny froze, unable to believe her eyes. Illuminated by the flash was a man standing on the deck in the downpour, water drenching him as he watched through the patio door. He was tall, very slender; his hair and suit coat billowed in the wind, and his tie was wrapped around his neck. Darkness returned, followed an instant later by another brilliant flash and an immediate resounding *boom!* But he was gone. There was no one. She waited for another flash. *Was it her imagination?*

She looked about the room. *Had anyone else seen that man?* Suddenly, lights flickered, and darkness filled the room. Someone yelled. Lightning must have struck close enough to blow the area transformer. Either that or a tree had downed the power line. People scurried away from the electrical equipment. Sparks jumped and sputtered from two lamps powered by the portable transformer, creating an eerie flicker inside that mimicked the lightning outside. Jenny grasped Jason's hand, and the room again fell into total darkness.

In the eerie silence, the only sound was the roaring wind and the constant rumble of thunder as the storm passed over. With no place to go in the darkness, everyone stood in place, wondering what would happen next and hoping the storm's fury would soon be spent.

A flashlight beam pierced the darkness. It was Chief Nick. He opened the door, entered the quiet room, and announced he had turned off the powerful generator as a safety precaution. He apologized. No one spoke. Everyone seemed relieved; someone had taken sensible action.

As he held his light, people moved to the chairs on the perimeter of the room. Some joined Jenny, Jason, and Janet Spalding as they sat on the floor, waiting. "The storm shouldn't last much longer. Streetslights are off. There's no power. When the storm passes, you can safely plug in the generators again," instructed the chief. Then he opened the door and disappeared into the night.

Chapter 19

It was 4:30 when Jordan Green pulled to a stop in the parking lot of the Minnetonka Area Police headquarters on the east edge of Excelsior, part of his daily routine on his way home to stop and chat with whoever might be on duty. It was always a welcome end of the day and the tension of his job at the Wayzata Towers where he directed security for WYCO Toys at all five suburban plants, plus the corporate offices. He lived in Excelsior, and the station house was his last stop of the day.

He had hoped to arrive home before the storm reached Excelsior and had considered not stopping. But today he had a purpose. Confident he had not been implicated in the abduction of Jason Poole, he needed confirmation and hoped to learn firsthand where the investigation was leading.

Somewhat of a hero to the force stationed there, Jordan was always welcomed and greatly respected for lobbying his employer to assist with nonbudgeted station needs. Historically, WYCO Toys was known for its strong commitment to civic affairs and its willingness to help fund important community projects. Jordan was the link to those funds. Two of the department's blue and whites were direct donations from WYCO, as was much of the new electronic equipment found in the station.

As an expression of gratitude, Jordan was made an ex-officio honorary member of the force, a position he had worked hard for, cherished greatly, and one for which his company paid dearly. Jordan had argued WYCO's contribution was good press and meant far more to the community than a country club membership for some official.

Before WYCO's move to the posh Towers headquarters, Jordan had officed at WYCO plant l, where he could lunch daily with his brother-in-law, Bill Wilson. Even today, he much preferred that older location on the quiet shores of Lake Minnetonka where he could feel—as he put it—the real pulse of the company. He was a man who knew his limitations. An executive, he wasn't, and found it, difficult to relate to people in business suits with college degrees, and he felt woefully out of place on the thirty-first floor surrounded by reminders of his peasantry while willingly enjoying the benefits associated with being considered "corporate."

Jordan reported directly to Wendell Moore, the VP of operations, a skilled production engineer who had been recruited from the auto industry to diversify the company's production. Wendell's office was with the "elite" on the penthouse level of the office tower. His passion was production, building things, not police work. If a problem couldn't be solved with an equation and a stopwatch, or be diagrammed in a flowchart, it was someone else's responsibility.

Consequently, company security was Jordan Green's responsibility, and Wendell gave him free reign to handle *his responsibility* with little interference from upper management as long as he kept Wendell Moore informed, if for no other reason than when kudos were handed out, Moore could be first in line. Nonetheless, Jordan took his job seriously and did whatever was necessary to protect his company's shareholders' interests.

He had been surprised one week earlier when JB Barons, the personal assistant to the new owner and CEO, called him directly and requested to see him immediately about an urgent security problem. To most employees, JB was a mystery. What was commonly known was that he worked behind the scenes at the personal bidding of the CEO, Creighton Leonard, a fact Jordan now found intriguing.

Waiting for the elevator, he saw his reflection in the polished brass doors and wondered if he was dressed properly for a high-level meeting. But he was who he was and what he was and quickly dismissed the concern.

At the penthouse level, an attractive receptionist directed him to JB's elegant office, its door welcomingly open. Standing before his east-facing window was a very tall, well-dressed man in his early thirties, dark hair, and *skinny*, thought Jordan. Jordan cleared his throat and waited for the words, "Come in, please. Be seated," before seating himself in an expensive leather chair in front of JB's desk.

"Jordan, we've not met," said JB, his gaze still fixed somewhere in space over the Minneapolis skyline. "I appreciate your running right up."

"No problem, sir." The "sir" was a carryover from his military service. He felt awkward giving that title to someone maybe half his age. He had a similar problem with young lieutenants.

"I appreciate the *sir*, but you can call me JB." JB was not completely honest; he rather enjoyed "sir." However, trust was the issue here, not his ego. "Jordan, do you know who I am?"

Of course, Jordan knew and found the question strange. "I'm not sure I understand your question, JB." The sound of using JB's initials made him smile and wonder how many WYCO employees were privileged to call the CEO's personal assistant by his initials. That would not have happened if Wendell Moore were in town. "I know you as JB Barons. You joined WYCO approximately six months ago when Mr. Leonard became president of the company. You're a member of his personal staff," he answered honestly.

JB turned, found his chair, sat, and leaned back. His hands on his chest with his finger crossed, steeple fashion. "You're right, of course, but there's more to it." He paused. "I am Creighton Leonard's personal representative." He paused again to let his words sink in. "Let me get to the point." He continued, "The company needs your help. Creighton Leonard needs your help. You might say your company's future depends on your cooperation. That's why I asked you here."

The security chief felt his heart beat faster. *Was he getting the recognition he deserved?* He focused on the bridge of JB's nose to give him his undivided attention.

JB continued, "Mr. Leonard knows we're meeting today. What I am about to share with you is extremely sensitive and highly confidential. Can you handle that?"

Do I have any choice? Jordan wondered.

JB caught Jordan's hesitation. "If you'd rather not be involved, the decision is yours. Don't worry about your job. Your job is secure, regardless."

For some reason, Jordan believed otherwise. This was like a combat field position; you volunteer, but if you messed up, it's back to the front. Like it or not, here was opportunity. "Yeah, I'm okay. I'm willing to serve wherever I can to the best of my abilities." *For now.*

Chapter 20

A sharp rap on Jordan's window brought Jordan back to the moment. Exactly what Officer Larry Randall intended. Trying to appear normal, Jordan rolled down his window.

"You okay, Jordan?" asked Randall while his eyes surveyed the interior of Jordan's Explorer, as though he had pulled him over on a drug bust. *Habit.* "I was about to leave. Saw you sitting out here. You're all right?" he asked again, concern in his voice.

"I'm fine. It's been one of those days, a real tough one," babbled Jordan, waiting for his heartbeat to normalize.

"Interesting to say the least. Not every day does someone kidnaps one of your executive's kids, or there's an attempted assassination at your nationally televised press conference." He paused and then added, "You're aware that I'm the officer who got the call about the boy?"

"No. I'm not." Jordan's face showed his surprise. "I've been too busy to turn on my radio. Internal things. What's up?"

Before Randall answered, he looked to the sky, and the ominous bubble-bottomed clouds suspended overhead. "There's a real storm coming, if you haven't heard."

"Yeah, I know. I was thinking, maybe I should just beat it on home."

"Doubt you'd make it. Look, Chief's gone. There's an open stall in the garage. You might as well duck in there and wait out the bad part." He patted Jordan's car roof. "I'd hate to see this go to the shop for hail dings. They're never the same."

Before Jordan could get a word out, Randall walked back into the station house, opened the large overhead garage door, and motioned for Jordan to enter. As he did, a sense of pride swept over him, and he parked beside the department's newest blue and white.

Suddenly, the lights inside flickered. "Don't worry. We're already on standby power. This is one heavy mother coming in. Could be another all-nighter." Randall led the way back into the station. "Tornado warnings. Unconfirmed sightings. Three touched down east of Young America. These *unconfirmed* twisters just blew a couple barns to hell and gone."

They had entered a large square room that shouted *order*, gray metal desks, uncomfortable chairs, and filing cabinets that symmetrically filled the room and allowed only one person at a time to maneuver around the rectangular table where Randall pulled up a chair and offered it to Jordan. "Too busy working? I would have thought you'd be the first to be notified," probed Randall.

Behind a wall of protective glass at the far end, a young woman in uniform sat at a large control panel attached to a headset that covered one ear. She nodded to Randall, who stepped to the coffee station and looked disparagingly at a half-full pot. Jordan shook his head to decline a cup and watched Randall swirl the dark brew, sniff at it, and place his cup back on its rack.

Jordan had spent the entire day out of the way at plant 2 to avoid the radio and the news or anything that might cause him to act suspiciously. He knew the Poole kid was to be taken. That much JB had confided in him. He had been assured the intent was to make the mother—a company employee—aware of her vulnerability after she had allegedly sold some company secrets. No one was to be harmed in any way. It seemed innocent enough.

But an assassination attempt? Was that something he had not been told about? *Was that part of the plan all along? Who was the target? Why wasn't I told! What have I been party to?* Questions exploded in his mind, and he struggled to appear normal.

"I heard talk that a kid belonging to one of our people was kidnapped today. Didn't take it too seriously though," Jordan said at last.

But he wasn't thinking the company cop should have some knowledge of the incident. "My pager was off, and I missed the noon news." He lied. "But I did make a phone call and learned the kid had been found. Safe and unharmed." He was guessing and prayed he was correct. Drops of sweat appeared on his brow. It was dumb not to have listened to the radio. Well—he'd had it on but tuned to MnDOT's jazz station for road conditions and news of the pending storm.

"Found at Mall of America," confirmed Randall. "Should be home by now. The chief and Stella are on their way over to the Poole's to see how he's doing."

Jordan felt relieved, safe, and free from suspicion. "What about this assassination attempt? Haven't heard about that." He was more than curious.

Randall pulled up a chair across the table from Jordan, whose stomach was queasy from sitting too close to the rank coffee. But before sitting, he gave the pot another sniff and moved it off the burner.

"Jordan, how long have you lived here? All your life, right? Have you ever known of anyone being kidnapped in sleepy Excelsior?" Jordan wished Larry would drop the subject and wondered, *Is this an interrogation?* But Randall continued with no apparent interest in a response from Jordan. "I had just come on duty when the 911 came in. I responded. Jason Poole had been plucked from the sidewalk in front of Milly's. I say plucked, grabbed from behind, taken before his mother, Jennifer, your employee, paid for breakfast. Old Mike was a witness. He saw it all. Too bad he was the only one. A man from an Abel catering truck dressed in white grabbed Jason and put him inside. The FBI has the truck, obviously stolen, discovered at Mall of America."

"How'd they locate the boy so soon?" asked Jordan. He had not been told that part of plan.

JENNY

"Anonymous telephone call."

"Any suspects?" Jordan asked, trying not to betray his increased heart rate banging like a judge's gavel announcing his guilt.

"Nothing concrete, last I heard. Mike said the man was dark. He didn't recognize either the driver or the man who grabbed Jason. Said they weren't regulars."

"Nick will find 'em," assured Jordan, wanting to sound confident.

"You mean the feds. FBI has the case. Kidnapping is serious business. We'll assist, of course, but they've got the resources. Some we couldn't imagine."

New sweat formed on his brow. To hide it, he forced a belch like he'd do as a kid to tease his sister Martha. "Sorry, lunch I guess. Something Mexican," he said and wiped his brow.

"Stuff gets to me too. Anyway," continued Randall, "the feds are tearing the truck apart and checking the surveillance tapes from Abel's plant. Whoever stole the truck had to have walked past one of their cameras." Jordan prayed Bill had been smart enough to cover his face and then forced another belch so he could wipe away the new sweat on his brow.

"Say, you could help with something. We tried to reach your brother-in-law, Bill. He still works food services at the company?" Jordan nodded agreement. "The stolen van made one stop. At your plant 1. Maybe Bill could ID the guys in the van. Bill was out when we called. Left early with an upset stomach. You two share the same lunch or something?"

Jordan couldn't raise another belch but wiped his brow again. "He's been fighting an ulcer…or indigestion." *If he isn't now, he certainly will be,* thought Jordan. They had not spoken since Bill and that guy from the Martinez Group stepped out of his Explorer in Abel's parking lot to commandeer the delivery van. "I'll be talking with him. I'll tell him to expect your call." Jordan wanted to leave in the worst way. Leaving the country crossed his mind. "Anything else?"

"You asked about the assassination attempt?"

"Yeah. What can you tell me?" Jordan patted his brow with his handkerchief.

"At the news conference, some guy pulls a gun. A security agent sees it, they struggle, gun goes off, sends the shooter to the hospital unconscious and critical. The media is making a big thing about it, claiming the kidnapping and the shooting are related. No one can confirm that theory. No one's denying it either. Made the network news. Isn't that what it's all about these days, publicity for the cause?"

"What cause?" asked Jordan, wondering if corporate espionage had any part at all in what was happening around him.

"Doesn't matter really. Someone will think of one," quipped Randall.

Feeling that his world was spinning out of control, like he was in Nam all over again and sent to the front, put on point, danger everywhere caused an uncontrollable queasiness. He took a deep breath, stood, and as casually as possible strolled to a west-facing window and peered out through tinted glass at the storm raging outside and watched in silence for a few minutes, praying the storm would end soon. Then calmed, he strolled slowly back to the table and Officer Larry Randall.

"Your people ought to be concerned, Jordan. If the media is right, WYCO is a target. Talk that your company is moving its production to Mexico doesn't set well. Here or elsewhere."

"No way!" said Jordan angrily. He had hushed such rumors before. But he was in no mood to argue. And he knew what Randall was suggesting was true, whether or not he agreed, so he kept his eyes on Randall and listened.

"Think about it, Jordan. The two men who took the truck and the kid are allegedly Latinos, Spanish, Mexicans, or Cuban. Who knows from where? The victim is the son of a marketing executive for WYCO. Japanese business leaders come to town to visit the biggest shopping center in the world, and they don't much like the competition south of our borders. The Mexican economy is going down the tubes, so they'd like to see us dump the Japanese. Sounds like the makings of an international conspiracy to me. And your company could be right in the middle of it."

"You watch too much television," commented Jordan as he stood to leave; he'd had enough. Rain or sun, he was leaving. Randall's eyes followed him as he put his hands into his back pockets, arched his back to relieve the tension that nagged him during times of stress, and proceeded to the garage door.

The western sky was quiet; the storm would soon pass. "I'll speak with Bill, see what he knows," Jordan promised and headed for the door.

Randall followed him out and opened the large overhead door. Jordan climbed into his Explorer, started the engine, and hit reverse. *Randall is probably more right than wrong*, Jordan thought, as he exited and headed home. *No different than Nam*, he thought, *no one gives you the big picture. Just use you. Always use you, a pawn in someone else's game—used, screwed, and tossed aside.*

He'd been used by his own company, no less. The promise of two thousand dollars was little comfort, and that was probably a lie. And even that scant amount would be shared with Bill. He had promised Bill $500, keeping $1500 for himself. Seemed generous at the time, but not so now; Bill had taken the risk after all. *What was I thinking?* They were more than friends; they were family. *He'd make it fifty-fifty.*

Chapter 21

Christian and Nicki waited on the shoulder of Highway 7 for twenty minutes before the storm relented sufficiently for them to drive slowly westward. The hail had stopped, but the wind intensified blowing the rain horizontal, cascading sheets of water as though flung by some invisible giant lurking in the angry dark clouds.

They didn't speak. Christian felt terrible. His lawyer's mind assessing the possible damage. He had endangered Nicki, and he was certain the hail had destroyed her car. Although insurance would repair the hail damage, it would never be quite the same, and the repair would take time and be an inconvenience for her. It didn't seem fair that her good deed was repaid with the destruction of her car. Finally, he spoke up, "I know a mediocre attorney if you need one." Nicki forced a smile; her boss was far from mediocre.

The rain was still heavy as they turned north on County Road 19 that divided upper and lower Lake Minnetonka. Progress was slow as they maneuvered around branches and fallen trees that littered the roadway. Twice Christian had to venture out into the downpour to move tree limbs off the road. No streetlamps were visible, and most houses were dark. Those few that weren't probably had power generators for just such an occasion. It was dark as night, and sunset was still a couple hours away.

They had seen only one other car since leaving Excelsior but had passed three utility trucks already moving through the area to restore power. As they neared Christian's town house, they had a clear view of the open water to the west and a strip of lighter sky growing on the horizon. To the east, the storm's fury could still be seen moving over Minneapolis toward St. Paul in a spectacular display of lightning. But the worst was over for them. They entered Christian's lane to darkened homes, all except Christian's end unit.

Cars and small vans lined the narrow asphalt drive. In the dim light, Christian could read the logos on several of the vehicles identifying the three major television channels. *It must have been quite a production*, he thought. The car's digital clock read 5:43. With his driveway full, he parked at a neighbor's to allow room for anyone wanting to leave.

Reaching toward the ignition, he looked at Nicki sitting with her hands folded in her lap with her eyes closed. *Was she mad, praying, relieved? What could he say?* "Nicki, I'm sorry," he said, and she turned toward him. "I'm truly sorry. Your car…I'm sorry I got you into this." He paused. "Nothing I can say seems adequate. Thanks for your help."

"It wasn't your fault. I'm grateful you were driving. I might… We might be sitting in a ditch somewhere. Or worse."

Nicki opened her car door. In the dome light, he could see her face had paled. She had been frightened beyond words. "Are you okay?" he asked.

She smiled over the top of the car as Christian got out and stood beside his open door. "I will be," she answered. "I'll be fine. I've never been so frightened in my life."

They looked at each other for several seconds without speaking, then looked toward the glowing town house and walked around a large power generator humming away on a trailer at the end of their drive, revealing why Jenny's lights were the only lights on. The wind had subsided, and the rain had all but ceased, leaving large puddles covering the drive and blocking their way. They picked their way over small branches and leaves covering the drive until Nicki stopped. "Icky," said Nicki, grimacing and looking down at thousands of night crawlers that had been forced from their earthen domain by the deluge—slippery worms underfoot now flattened by her weight.

They followed the glow to the open double-wide garage door. Inside the scene could have been taken from a science-fiction movie. Workers silhouetted by the brilliance from three quartz studio lamps were moving about the open area engaged in packing and stowing equipment, staging it inside the garage before moving it into waiting vans. Several nodded at them as they stepped around large black cases and rolled up electrical cords.

"Dad! Dad!" came an excited voice from somewhere in the dark, and soon Christian felt Jason's arms around his midsection.

He dropped his carry-on, gave Jason a long embrace and, kneeling down, looked into his son's smiling face. "Big day, huh, Jason," he said as a tear rolled down his cheek.

"Humongous!" responded Jason. "I drove the boat…half throttle."

Christian smiled; his son had his own list of priorities, and he loved him for it.

Only technical crews remained by the time Chris and Nicki arrived. Earlier, Janet Spalding had pleaded with Jenny to allow a live telecast at six or allow them to complete the taped segment that had been cut short by the storm. But Jenny had refused and this time held firm before she grabbed Jason and slipped away. She now stepped from the shadows, threw her arms around Christian's neck, and nuzzled her nose just under his left ear. "Honey, I'm so glad you're home." She need say no more.

"Me too. Thank God, you're safe. And Jason. I felt so helpless. You're okay?" He gave his wife a big squeeze and felt her nod as she pressed her nose further into the curve of his muscular neck.

When she opened her eyes, she noticed Nicki had followed Christian in. "Hi, Nicki. Thank you for bringing him home. I owe you."

"Well," said Christian, "we could start by getting her a new car."

"That's what insurance is for," admonished Nicki quickly, not wanting to cast blame.

Surprised, Jenny stepped back and looked at Nicki. "What happened? Did you have an accident getting here?" Jenny asked, concerned.

"Not really," Christian answered. "We got caught on the open highway. Hail the size of golf balls destroyed her car, I'm afraid."

"I'm sorry!" Jenny said as sincerely as she could.

Technicians stood patiently with their hands full waiting for the foyer to clear so they could continue loading their equipment. Jenny smiled apologetically at the first in line, reached for Christian's hand, and motioned for Jason and Nicki to follow her back into the shadows. As work continued, they would share their stories, and when the crews were gone and the power restored, life would return to normal.

Chapter 22

A large limb had fallen across the street blocking Jordan's progress. He had driven several blocks with no memory of leaving the station. Realizing he was not going toward home, he put the Explorer into reverse and backed around the nearest corner. Two more turns brought him within sight of the Excelsior Commons. With his mind churning the events of the past couple of days, he turned toward the park and pulled to the curb, viewing the length of the lower lake and the town of Wayzata on the eastern horizon where the storm still raged.

He released his seat belt, slumped into the leather seat, and gripped the steering wheel tightly with both hands to relieve his growing anxiety. All he had wanted was to help his company, help his friends, and help save a young mother being used by someone to steal corporate secrets. *Used. Lied to. Was she being paid?* he wondered. Probably, and most likely, more than a measly few thousand dollars. How much did JB know? Had he been duped too? The company's secrets? What were they worth to anyone? Some serious money, maybe.

He wished he could turn back time before that meeting with JB. "The company needs your help." *That's what got me.*

"You've worked here for what...fifteen years?"

"Going on sixteen years, come January," corrected Jordan.

"You may not know that I graduated from Minnetonka High School. I moved here as a teenager and grew up in the shadow of WYCO Toys. It made me proud."

"For three generations, our company has dominated the world's toy industry. No other company comes close. WYCO is the John Deere, the Caterpillar, the General Motors of its industry.

"But recently, WYCO has had difficulty capturing the hearts and minds of a new generation with its space-age technology and computerized gadgetry."

Jordan took exception to JB's comments. After all, he was a spokesman for the rank and file and couldn't listen any longer without speaking up. "The boys at number 2 say they're working double shifts, seven days a week, making those new gym sets and playground equipment and the like, going great guns. And at number 3, production is taking off. They're hiring."

"You're right, Jordan. For the present, we're doing well. That's now. But for how long? The company's cornerstone products are losing popularity at the retail level. Stock analysts are expressing concern that the company is in decline."

"I can't speak to those things. We've got a bunch of hardworking people doing the best they can. And if that isn't enough, well, I don't know what is," said Jordan in defense of his crew.

Jordan could not see what this had to do with him. What could he do about it? He wondered.

"You're wondering what this has to do with you." Jordan nodded. "Here it is, clear and simple, and it's why your company is turning to you for help. There is a spy in our midst."

Jordan's mouth dropped, a minute passed before he responded. "JB, I don't know. Corporate espionage is a little out of my league," he said honestly, knowing the wrong response could mean his job.

"Let me finish. Please. This has been going on for some time. We really don't know how long."

Jordan shook his head in disbelief.

"Someone in management, respected, on the inside with a sense of the company's pulse, is selling the company's future to the highest bidder."

"I'm sorry. Am I missing something? What does this have to do with me? Security is one thing. Corporate espionage is out of my league. If this means my job, so be it." Jordan couldn't believe his own words, but he might just as well face the music up front.

"Mr. Leonard would like to keep this as quiet as possible. If this became public knowledge, our stock would be downgraded. This kind of news would not sit well with the analysts. We just can't afford a downgrade. He wants to keep it quiet. This is why we need you. No one but you can know about this. You can take care of the problem in house."

"I don't understand," insisted Jordan.

"We know who the spy is," said JB. "At least we have a good suspect. We really don't know for sure. But the evidence points only one way."

Jordan felt renewed hope.

Both were quiet for a moment as Jordan considered JB's words. He could be a hero.

"Who?" Jordan asked finally.

"Jennifer Poole," answered JB and then went silent to allow the name to sink in, hard as it might be for Jordan to believe.

Jordan began shaking his head. He didn't know the woman personally but knew of her, and what he knew was only good. She was respected, a true company asset, in many ways she was plant 1. "That just can't be," he said. Jordan was incredulous. "You're sure?"

"Like I said, no. We're not sure. But Creighton feels sure enough, and that's sufficient for our board. And they want action. Creighton thinks he can turn her, even save her. He wants to put the *fear of God* in her. Scare her. Let her know she's meddling where she doesn't belong. Espionage is a dangerous world."

"Now, run this by me again, please." This was messing with his rank and file; her success had brought them considerable work, and to hurt her would hurt them.

"She's a second-level marketing manager. She was identified one evening lurking outside plant 1's management conference center during a strategy meeting with the Martinez Group, a consulting firm from Mexico. It was a very secret meeting."

"You are aware that she works there, plant 1, same floor?"

"Yes, and that gives her deniability. This is a tough part. Say anything, it'll be denied. The Martinez Group is an evaluation team here to assist management's plan to expand production into government-subsidized plants in Mexico. As you can appreciate, that's a very sensitive issue."

Jordan winced. It was more than sensitive with him; such a move would be ruinous for him, for Bill, for his rank and file.

"We're aware of your feelings on the matter, Jordan. I warned you, this is difficult information. Jennifer Poole was someone no one could have suspected. Creighton was stunned. She's not *inner circle* but reports to someone who is VP of marketing, Burton Lehr. The House of Toys is her success story. In one week, she'll receive public recognition for that achievement at the House of Toys at a major news conference. You see, that's why we must act fast. Her success is the reason she wasn't suspected."

"Jordan, her complicity is undeniable. The evidence, irrefutable. According to human resources, Jennifer Poole was caught spying on the Martinez meeting. Nearly caught, but she managed to flee the building. She was the only woman working late that evening, a fact confirmed by Mildred Knowles. They got a good look at her. Jennifer fits the description."

"You've checked that out? You're sure?"

"Yes," he said hesitantly and added, "not by me but Kohl."

"And he's some bright and shining star," said Jordan, intentionally sarcastic.

JB ignored the remark. "Creighton believes she's been duped, used by someone. We don't know whom. And she's in over her head. That's why we believe she can be saved. We don't want her or anyone hurt. We want her to be scared. Scared right out of the spy business!"

"You've considered confronting her?" Jordan asked condescendingly.

"You're the cop here, Jordan. Tell me what you think she'd do."

"Well...Probably—" began Jordan only to be interrupted by JB.

"The evidence is circumstantial. Look, she'd deny everything. Then she'd lay low for a while. But we'd never know if we could trust her. Now can't you see it, Jordan, we want to save her? She's good. She's very good for the company. She's got a following here. Creighton Leonard respects her talent. He is a gracious and forgiving man. There you have it. That's the way it is. You can help save her and your company."

"I'm having trouble believing this. And...I don't see where I fit in. I like the idea of saving someone for the good of the company. I wouldn't want anyone hurt. I mean, I couldn't...How does the news conference fit in? Why the urgency?"

"Timing. We're working on a plan. We don't know who's using Jennifer Poole. We believe she will then rethink what it is she's doing and get out of the corporate espionage business. The magnitude of the presentation, the news conference, the Japanese delegation, and a visiting senator will impress upon her the importance and severity of her actions. She probably will not totally grasp what's happening, but she won't know whom to trust in the future."

Jordan stared into space for a long few seconds and asked, "Just what do you have planned?"

"Later. I'm not at liberty to disclose that today. We're working out the details." JB looked at his watch. "Look. Got a meeting to attend. Now you've got a friend who used to work at Abel Catering, right?"

"My brother-in-law. He's our food service supervisor at plant 1. Good man too."

"Thanks to you, I suspect." JB smiled as though he shared some close secret, a smile that bothered Jordan for a reason he couldn't identify.

"We're close. I helped him get the interview. He's the best at what he does."

"Look. I didn't mean anything." JB feigned a look of remorse. "Can he be trusted with our secret? Can he be brought in? We need someone who knows the inside of Abel Catering. He'd be perfect for what we have in mind. So, can he be trusted?"

"With my life," confessed Jordan unequivocally. "He's my brother-in-law because he was first my best friend."

"There'll be a bonus, of course. Maybe a thousand apiece." JB looked again at his watch. "Talk to him. Tell him the company needs his help on a little project. Don't say a word about Jennifer and this security business. That's our secret. And the bonus, that's between you and…?"

"Bill Wilson. His name is Bill," said Jordan, contemptuously filling in the blank.

"What you work out with Bill Wilson is between the two of you. I don't even want to know."

Reality returned to Jordan with a sudden clap of thunder overhead as the last of the storm moved eastward. Jordan watched as a sailboat moved into sight, taking advantage of the lingering wind. *What have I done?* He ruminated, turned the key, and continued toward home.

Chapter 23

At 6:45, the last of the television technicians slammed the door of his van and drove out the dark lane. With Nicki's help and working by candlelight, Jenny, Christian, and Jason shoved their home back into order. While no one raised the topic, each was disappointed that the power had not been restored in time to catch the 6:00 p.m. news. With luck, they'd catch the ten o'clock. They had made history and were eager to see it play out on the networks, especially Jason, who felt he should get an Emmy for his taped interview.

At seven, the lights flickered momentarily. "Let there be light!" shouted Christian from somewhere in the house. Fifteen minutes later, they lit again and remained on.

"Oh no!" Christian heard Jenny's shout from their bedroom and quickly ran downstairs to see what was wrong. He found Jenny standing in the center of their living room, showing her aggravation with arms extended downward, palms up and fingers splayed. "Where's that good-for-nothing attorney boss of yours, Nicki? We need a new carpet." Nicki and Jason had entered the room shaking their head as they looked at the once-plush carpet littered with footprints, leaves, and squished worms that had not been visible by candlelight. Emotionally strung, Jenny disappeared into the kitchen holding back tears and swore at the oven clock flashing *NOON… NOON…NOON*.

Seconds later, she felt Chris patting her butt as he came up beside her. "Can I help?" he asked timidly. She gave him *that* look, found a large bucket and a bottle of carpet cleaner in the utility closet—along with some rags—put them in Chris's hands, and then turned him around with an affectionate shove. Nicki and Jason had stepped onto the back patio to survey the debris-strewn backyard and dock.

Dark clouds coursed overhead as clear skies approached the western end of the lake in a spectacular display of patterned light rays that turned the base of the clouds to a fiery red glow. Nicki retrieved three plastic patio chairs from the edge of the yard, putting them in their place on the deck. Jason dashed to the boat, surprisingly secure under a now-torn and battered canopy.

"We could do burgers on the grill if anyone is hungry." No one had eaten, and Jenny was feeling the pangs of hunger. "Nicki, can you stay?" Jenny asked.

"Thanks, Jenny. I really should be going. No telling what the roads will be like. I'll take a rain check," responded Nicki, adding, "sorry, no pun intended."

Suddenly, the sun broke out and reflected off an object lodged between the deck boards at Nicki's feet. "What have we here?" she asked and bent over to pry it free with one of her long fingernails. "Looks expensive!" When she stood, she held in her fingertips a weighty diamond-tipped tiepin, which she turned in the sunlight, examining it more closely. "Know anyone who could afford this? The price would cover my car repairs. I'm sure." She moved slowly toward Jenny, standing a few feet away. "Look at this, will you!" she said excitedly. "Somebody will miss this for sure."

Christian heard Nicki, wiped his hands, stepped onto the deck, and carefully plucked the tiepin from Nicki's open hand. "Jen, could this be your father's?" he said, turning it slowly inches from his eyes. "It's a tiepin. A very expensive tiepin. Your parents were here a couple of weeks ago?" Jenny poked her head closer. "No one else has been here who could afford something like this," observed Chris.

"He wasn't wearing a tie," reminded Jenny. "Could have happened earlier, but mother was here today and didn't mention it."

Suddenly, her eyes lit up. "Wait just a minute. Nicki, where exactly did you find it?" Nicki pointed to the spot on the deck where she had pried it out from between two boards.

Suddenly, Jenny sprinted breathlessly toward the living room, instructing Nicki on the way, "Stand right where you found it." Nicki placed her foot on the location. In the living room, Jenny retraced her steps to where she was standing before the lights went out.

"Jenny, what are you doing?" shouted Chris.

Jenny headed in his direction. "You're not going to believe this."

Suddenly, Jason jumped to the deck behind his dad. "Canvas is history," he reported, interrupting his parents' excitement. When he realized his dad wasn't listening but standing with a dumb expression on his face and holding his hand high like Lady Liberty, he asked, "What do you have, Dad?" Chris lowered his arm so Jason could see the pin perched in his fingertips while he looked at Jenny inquiringly.

"So what is it we will not believe?" he asked Jenny. "We're ready, tell us. It's been a long day." He spoke a little too sarcastically and then having said what he said the way he said it made him feel ashamed. Jenny was offended but, seeing a glint of remorse in Christian's eyes, moved on and took the pin from Christian.

"I know whose pin this is."

"Yes," Chris prodded again.

"When the storm was at its absolute worst, I saw a man standing here on the deck, exactly where Nicki found the pin. Whoever that was is the owner of the pin."

Chris was incredulous. "You're telling us, when everyone was inside, out of the storm there was a man standing out here in the storm? And the pin belongs to him?"

"I'm telling you that, yes. A man, his suit coat drenched and nearly blowing off him, his tie blowing so hard it wrapped tight around his neck, was standing out here in the rain watching me." Jenny's voice began to squeak with emotion. "I know it sounds stupid. His tie was wrapped around his neck because he lost his tiepin. Get it? No one else saw him. I can't prove a thing." She wrapped an arm around her husband's waist and dropped her head onto his shoulder. "I know what I saw. I know what I saw. And that…that pin belongs to…to him." She was quiet for a moment, her emotions spent, then in a calmer voice continued. "You know what? I'm ready for this day to end…just end. Does anyone want a hamburger?" She sniffed and ran the backs of her hands across tear-soaked cheeks and pushed back from Christian. He resisted, pulled her close again, and began rocking her slowly.

They continued for several minutes; his head resting on hers swaying with her, his mouth whispering in her hair, "I'm sorry, Jen. I'm so very sorry. So very sorry." He loved her so much. And amidst that love, he felt guilt. He should have been home for her as he had promised. He should have called her more often to show how concerned he really was. He was sorry he had not given her an easier life. She deserved so much better. He was sorry he was such a jerk.

"I really should be going," said Nicki from across the room and turned to address Jason, who was quietly watching his father and mother embrace. She could see a small tear on his cheek.

She was ignorant of the conversation he'd had with his mother at Milly's that morning, the fear that like his friend Peter's parents, his parent's love for one another could end somehow. Nicki walked to him, ran her fingers through his hair, and looking closely, saw he was smiling. Whatever was coursing through his mind was somehow okay. Then without speaking, she smiled down at him, turned, walked into the living room and out the front door.

Jenny closed the patio door and walked to the kitchen carrying dirty dishes. "Isn't there anything you can do?" she asked.

"You mean about her car? Not really, nothing short of getting her a new one. Pay for her repair, but her insurance should cover that."

"You're right. It just doesn't seem fair." She thought for a moment and added, "Christian, if no one claims that diamond pin, I want you to use it as down payment on a new car for Nicki. Will you promise me that?"

"Jenny, it's not ours to give. Don't ask the impossible."

"It's not impossible. What if we can't find the owner?"

"We have to try," Christian responded and quietly left to join Jason on the dock, admiring *Little Red* and reliving his morning at the controls.

Through the kitchen window, Jenny watched father and son in excited conversation. Life was good, as it should be. She thanked God for the day's outcome, for answered prayer and asked the question that nagged her, "Why? If all things have a reason or purpose, what possibly can be the purpose of today?"

Chapter 24

"Dad, can I stay up to watch the news?" Jason lay sprawled at the foot of his parents' bed while his dad unpacked his suitcase.

"You know what I need? Two of everything. Then I'd always have a bag packed ready to hit the road."

"Dad! You're not listening. The news? Can I watch with you and Mom?" Jason asked again.

"Sure. Get ready for bed first. You're one of the stars!" he answered and looked at his watch. "You've got fifteen minutes."

Jason sprang up and ran excitedly down the hall and into his mother, who had just shut down the house for the evening. "Where are you going in such a hurry?" she asked as though she didn't know.

"Mom, it's the news. I'm a star. Just a few more minutes," he reminded his mother, tearing off his clothes as he continued to his room.

"Shower first, young man," Jenny reminded.

"Oh, Mom," he whined once-over with a washcloth seemed sufficient.

Jenny found Christian emptying his shaving kit onto the bathroom vanity. "You know, you need two of everything, then you'd always be ready to get out of town again," she said as she came up close behind him and placed her arms around his waist.

Beautiful, innocent Jenny, he thought, catching her reflection in the mirror. He turned around slowly and kissed her forehead. *Why was it,* he wondered, *he seemed to love her most when she seemed most vulnerable?*

"I'm so glad your home," she said, looking up at him.

"Me too," he said softly. "You know, Jen, what I said out there on the deck, I really meant it. I'm sorrier than words can say, sorry that I wasn't here for all this. And you know—"

"When you become a partner, it'll be different." She completed his overworked phrase and dropped her head to his shoulders. He drew her near and felt her heart beating. *She's more than I deserve.*

As they embraced, she said, "I've never felt so helpless. You know, we're…just so sheltered."

"It's over, Jen. Over. You're safe. Jason is safe. It's over."

"It's like a bad dream. A nightmare, actually," she corrected.

"And you'll see it again in just a few minutes. Are you up to that?" he declared, thinking of the news.

"Yes. It's Jason's big moment. This has been an exciting day for him. He can't remember any of the bad. Just the fun stuff. Besides, we said he could…"

"I know."

They looked into each other's eyes for several seconds. "Honey, I know it seems over to you," said Jenny. "Maybe it's because you weren't here."

Chris took the rebuke and started to mumble something, but Jenny placed her hand over his mouth. "I know," she assured. "Today is over, and I know that's your perspective. But Dan Sheridan doesn't believe it's over, maybe just the beginning."

"Sheridan? The guy who found him and brought him home? He's an expert in such things?"

"Christian, why are you being sarcastic when this man rescued our son and is trying to help?"

"Because, Jenny, it's over. Look! Jason is home with us now. He's safe here. What else is important?"

"Yes, Jason is safe, but only because his kidnappers feel they are safe for now. They're safe only as long as Jason doesn't remember what they did to him. Don't you see?"

JENNY

"Let's talk after the news," said Chris. "This is how you decided to convince the world that Jason can't remember. Our son is a good actor. I know that. Let's watch, see for ourselves, then maybe we can forget the whole affair."

Jenny pulled away. "You're the attorney…I don't understand you. You can't be serious. Chris, I'm scared. Scared for Jason. Scared for us," she said angrily.

"I know, honey, I'm sorry. But after the news. Okay?"

"You know? I don't think you do know, Christian!" she said firmly. "It doesn't matter what Jason remembers. What matters is what these bad people think he remembers. They could have a bad hair day, and we're in real trouble."

"Jenny, that won't happen. I won't let anything happen to Jason. Or to you. I promise."

"You promise? You can't keep that promise, and you know it. You can't protect him…or me. Not all the time. You're never even here. You're…you're gone most of the time."

That truth hurt.

Suddenly, Jason appeared in his pajamas, smelling of shampoo. Jenny turned to walk with him into the bedroom. With his mind already on other things, Chris gave Jenny a playful pat on the butt and shoved her gently on her way. "After the news, Jen?"

Jenny knew what was on his mind and shook her head as she pushed Jason down the hall. "Just think, you're gonna be one of them," she said to Jason, who looked back at her wondering what she meant. In the bedroom, she picked up two remotes from the bedside; one lit the gas fireplace, the other turned on the large television against the opposing wall. She clicked channels until Channel 6 appeared, just in time.

"It's on," she shouted to Chris, who appeared dripping wet, a towel wrapped around his waist.

"The House of Toys, a house under siege," began the dramatic story from the lips of Donald Stone. "Tonight's lead story began at eight-thirty this morning in the Lake Minnetonka town of Excelsior, where ten-year-old Jason Poole was kidnapped. Today, Janet Spalding visited the Poole family at their home for this story. Janet," said Stone as he passed the baton to his coanchor.

"Thank you, Don," began Janet as she looked toward Donald Stone like they were best of friends, a fact that could not be further from reality. Christian looked down at Jason and began gently rubbing his son's back. A star was about to be born. "Today I had the privilege of visiting the Poole family at their Lake Minnetonka home. And I am delighted to report, Jason is safe at home in very good health. Unfortunately, the storms that swept through our area at dinnertime prevented completion of the interview we had planned. To our audience, we extend our regrets. To the delightful Jason Poole and his family, we express our thanks for their allowing the media to invade their home."

Jason looked up at this mother. "Mom! Aren't they going to show us on TV?" asked Jason, obviously disappointed. "They got my statement before the power went off."

"I don't know, Jason. Maybe it didn't turn out. Maybe they just don't have time. Who knows? Maybe it's a good thing. There's a reason for everything." Jenny smiled at her son, his face contorted in frustration.

"Oh, Mom!" Jason said with resignation, his chin nestled once again into the palms of his hands to watch the balance of the telecast.

Janet's tone was scripted and serious. The camera zoomed to a full view of her attractive pixy face. Small diamond earrings sparkled on her ears, just visible under her short cropped blonde hair. She detailed the abduction of Jason Poole as documented for her by Donald Stone. Because of time constraints, they did not show Stone's interview with Sheridan and Gary Sadler of the FBI.

Finally, concluding her segment, Janet summarized facts she thought of interest to her audience, as interesting for them as they were for her. "As we have stated, the mother of ten-year-old Jason Poole is Jennifer Poole, daughter of respected Minnesota businessman, Matthew Ward, and a highly respected marketing executive for

WYCO Toys. But Jennifer Poole is perhaps best known for her role in the success of the famed toy store, House of Toys, and is the person most often credited with that store's success, every child's favorite store at Mall of America."

"Wow, Mom, you're famous," exclaimed Jason, his eyes glued to the television.

"It is for that success," Spalding continued, "that Jennifer Poole was to be recognized and awarded an honor today at a nationally televised news conference at the House of Toys. For obvious reasons, Jennifer did not attend today's news conference. However, Donald Stone did attend, and we turn to him now for his report. Don." The baton again changed hands.

"Sorry you couldn't have been there, Hon," said Christian as he watched. "But thanks to Janet Spalding, people will know how talented you are. I couldn't be more proud." He gave Jason a swat on his butt. "Thank you, Lord, my family is safe."

Jennifer gave him "that" look. *For the moment*, she thought, *for the moment*.

When the commercials came on, Christian returned to the bathroom to complete his shower.

"Mom, they could have shown my interview. Why didn't they?" asked Jason, rolling beside her on the bed.

"I don't know, Jason. I'll call the station tomorrow. Maybe we can get a copy of the interview. Even if they didn't air it, they may have it on tape." Jenny also wondered why Jason's interview had been cut. His declaration of having no memory of his abduction had been the purpose of allowing the media in. Now all they had to show for it was a destroyed carpet and a diamond tiepin. "Brush your teeth, Jason, you've got a couple of minutes before they show Dan Sheridan." She smiled, swatted Jason's firm butt, and sent him running down the hall.

She'd jump into the shower after the news, while Christian put Jason to bed. In the meanwhile, she quickly undressed and threw on a conservative bathrobe. Dispelling earlier thoughts of a back rub in the tub, she returned to the foot of her bed and the TV as Donald Stone reappeared and Jason resumed his earlier position after a flying leap onto the bed.

"Chris!" she shouted. He quickly reappeared, dry and wearing only a towel wrapped around his waist.

Donald Stone began, "Today, the House of Toys, WYCO Toys' anchor store at Mall of America, where the nationally televised news conference, mentioned earlier, had just begun, nearly became a murder scene. The intended victim? We don't know. It could be one or all: Creighton Leonard, CEO of WYCO Toys, or Yoshi Mikado, leader of a Japanese delegation visiting the mall, or Senator Willard Malovich from Massachusetts, dignitaries standing on the podium, when a man in the audience drew a gun. One shot was fired as security struggled with the would-be shooter, hitting the shooter and sending him to the hospital, unconscious and in critical condition."

In the background, the camera replayed the events as they unfolded. When the camera swept over the panicked audience, Jenny let out a scream nearly causing similar panic in the Poole's bedroom. "It's him. It's him. Look, it's him."

"It's who, Mom?" asked Jason before Christian, surprised and out of breath, could ask the same question.

"The man on our deck during the storm. It's him. He attended the press conference today. He's there in the audience." The camera now showed men in suits towering over two men on the floor.

Jenny was ready for the camera to switch back to the audience. "There he is...there he is. See him? That tall man in the crowd? It has to be him. Honey, it's him. That long face. The man I saw on the deck during the storm. I'm not losing my mind, Chris," squealed Jenny. She turned to Chris. "You saw him. Tell me you did," she pleaded. "It was him. I know it was him, Christian." She used his given name for emphasis.

Christian shook his head as Janet Spalding reappeared. "No. Sorry," he said. "I missed him." Jenny couldn't believe it. The mysterious man Jenny saw on their deck during the worst storms of the summer had eluded him. "Sorry," he said again slowly, not doubting what Jenny believed she saw, but forming new questions in his attorney's mind.

Spalding concluded the segment by identifying the would-be assassin as Frederick Bartlett, a mall employee. "Don, back to you."

"Thank you, Janet," said Stone. "We will return with more on the follies of Willard Malovich, Massachusetts's senator, whose future may still be determined by a full senate investigation into his alleged involvement with young male prostitutes. Was he the intended target at the House of Toys? Please stay tuned."

Jenny hit the remote, turning off the television and addressed Jason. "You must have seen him, that tall man in the crowd? Say you did. Surely one of you…"

"Sorry, Mom," answered Jason. Then in a softer voice, he added, "I didn't see anyone on the deck, either." He crawled over to her on the bed and threw his arms around her neck. "And they didn't show me either. Bummer," he said. She kissed the top of his head. Christian had gone to the closet for a robe. He returned and placed his hand on Jason's shoulder.

"Bedtime," he instructed. Tired, Jason stood, grabbed his father's hand, and led him down the hall to his bedroom.

Halfway down the hall, Jenny heard him ask his father, "Can you stay home tomorrow? Can we go out in the boat?"

"Let's see what tomorrow brings…tomorrow," Christian answered.

When he returned to the bedroom, Jenny was ready for him. "He needs you, Chris. The firm can wait for a day. Think of what he's been through today. Think of what I've been through today. Try thinking of something besides that firm, will you?" With that, she disappeared into the closet where she replaced her robe with pajamas. She really wasn't in the mood for a shower or, more specifically, what she was certain would follow.

When she returned, she stood before her husband and said, "You better have more than just a few minutes for our son tomorrow." Her intended tone confused Chris who slowly dropped to the edge of the bed with a bewildered look on his face. But she wasn't through with him yet. "Somehow, miraculously, Jason survived today, unscathed. And for all that happened to him, he remembers nothing. But what is most important to him, what he does remember, is his boat ride to Milly's. He cares less that he didn't make it on television, except by name. Chris, he drove the boat himself really fast. He had the controls all by himself. He wants you to be a part of that. He wants you to be proud of his manliness. Give our son a break!"

"I'm sorry, Jen." He repeated his earlier confession, wondering when he would have enough humble pie. "You're right. I'm sorry."

"Yes, you said that. So?"

"I'll spend the entire day with him tomorrow. The office can wait. I'll spend whatever time he needs. Tomorrow."

Satisfied, Jenny moved close to him, slipped his robe off his muscular shoulders, and gave him her most sensuous smile. He stood, and his robe became a pile of terry cloth at his feet. Then, without success, he tried not to grin as she reached her arms around him and gently squeezed each bare cheek. "There's room in the shower for two," she whispered in his ear and slipped off her pajamas on her way to the shower.

Chapter 25

The phone beside the bed was ringing. Both Christian and Jenny had drifted off to sleep within minutes after making love. But Jenny soon awoke. She had been dreaming. In her dream, Jason had stared at her with hollow eyes from inside a large cage, his arms outstretched as he shook the black steel bars in a desperate plea for help while the cage slowly receded, pulled by an invisible force.

Chilled from fear and drenched in perspiration, she pulled herself upright and slowly brought the phone to her ear. Christian lay beside her, facing the other direction, deep in sleep. The clock beside the phone said it was 1:35 a.m.

"Hello?" she questioned quietly. There was no response. "Hello. Who is this?" she asked again. Still there was no answer. But she heard breathing. Hard breathing in fact. Was someone crying? "Who is this?" she asked again, this time loud enough to stir Chris. "Answer me. Don't you know what time it is?" The heavy breathing continued, but there was no response.

She started to hang up but again brought the phone to her ear and listened. She heard music and someone singing, voices in the background, muffled talking. She strained to hear more and in the quiet heard the sounds of an August night from the marshy channel below her bedroom window and covered her ear.

Definitely voices, unintelligible words, muffled laughter, a woman's laugh in the quiet before the music returned, country western and very distant. A minute passed, and then there was silence.

"Who is this calling?" she asked again. "If you have something to say, say it! I'm going to hang up!" She demanded loud and angry. Christian stirred and rolled toward her.

"Jenny. What's wrong? Who are you talking to?" Jenny didn't answer.

Finally, the voice asked, "Is this Jennifer Poole?" It sounded more like a woman than a man, but she wasn't sure.

"It is. Now who are you? Why are you calling in the middle of the night?"

"I must know, is Jason safe?"

The mention of Jason's name tied a knot in her stomach and sent a shiver through her body.

"Why do you want to know? Why are you calling? Who are you?" She yelled into the phone. The only response was the wail of a lovesick cowboy and the twang of a guitar before the line went dead and the dial tone echoed in her ear.

She slowly lowered the phone, cradling it in her lap as she sat shaking on the edge of her bed and stared into the star-filled night beyond her balcony door. "What is it?" asked Christian, raising himself on one elbow. Even in the darkness, Jenny's face seemed drained of color. "Who called?"

"No…name," she said quietly. A few seconds later she added, "Sounded like someone calling from a bar. There was country music in the background, some voices. I think it was a woman. She knew my name. She asked about Jason."

"A woman?" asked Chris.

"I think so. Whispers…I just sensed it was a woman." Jenny's voice quivered slightly. She turned to face Christian who was now sitting beside her on the edge of the bed. "Why…Why would someone call in the middle of the night and ask about Jason? What's happening here? He's home. He's safe. Chris, what's going on? Why can't this all just end?"

"It's probably just a crank call." Comforted Chris. "Your name's been all over national TV. Jason's too. It's easy enough to find our number. We're in the book." He draped his arm over her shoulder and gently pulled her toward him. "There're all kinds of kooks out there. One wouldn't have to be too bright to locate us." He squeezed her gently and stroked her hair.

"That's what frightens me. We are so easy to locate. It was so easy for someone to just take Jason. And for what reason? Why. He was returned, and thank God for that. But why? Why does a strange man suddenly appear on our deck during a thunderstorm?" Overcome by emotion, she began to sob quietly. "Honey, why is all this happening? Why is all this happening to us?" She rested her head on her husband's bare muscular shoulder and seemed to choke on her own words, "I'm really frightened, Chris. None of this makes any sense. No sense at all."

"It's been a long and frightening day. Bad things seem their worst when we're tired. Maybe it's too soon and too late to make any sense out of it. Tomorrow will be better. Tomorrow will bring some answers."

"It had better," said Jenny with sudden resolve, resolve that was not lost on Christian.

"What do you mean by that? Jenny, please promise me you will let the authorities handle this. This is not some dispute over one of Jason's hockey games, something you can fix and make better."

"It's Jason we're talking about. You know, our son." She stood beside the bed and looked down at Christian. He pulled the light summer blanket over his lap as he listened to his wife. "Don't you see? Someone is pulling our chain. For whatever distorted reason, someone has set us up. We can't let this continue."

"Jenny, there's nothing we can do."

"I don't know that. I don't know what we can do, but we must do something. We're in the middle of something…Something that seems…very sinister. Not by our choosing, but we're here. I'm not going to sit idly by and let the devil have his way."

"Jenny, then let it be us. And I'm a part of us. Don't exclude me, Jen. I need to know what you're up to." He reached for her hand

and fondled the wedding band on her ring finger. "Honey, this is the kind of thing that could destroy us. If we're not careful, fear, anger, hurt feelings, jealousy—that can destroy us. That's really what the devil wants. We can't let that happen. We have to do this together. Whatever you do, we have to agree to never stop talking with each other. You do what you can. I do what I can. But we do it together."

"You agree? There is something more to this? We need to fight it! You agree? Right?"

"I don't know that I agree. Not totally. Let's just say there could be." He looked into her eyes. "Look…I agree with this," he said. "You have good instincts, the best. You follow those instincts, just as long as you keep me informed, and you don't do anything foolish." He paused, adding, "Or dangerous. We'll find the answers…Tomorrow. We'll begin…tomorrow, Jenny. Okay? Tomorrow?"

"Okay, tomorrow," agreed Jenny. Chris tugged at her hand and pulled her down beside him. Soon he felt her muscles relax, and before long, she snuggled beside him, her head on his shoulder. "Thanks. I think I can sleep now." Her voice trailed, and sleep came to her.

He leaned over her and kissed her forehead. She was all he had ever hoped for, all he had ever prayed for in a wife, the mother of his children, his partner for eternity. Looking at her, he wondered, was he protecting her, or was she protecting him? He also wondered if the authorities could do a better job.

Chapter 26

Sun flooded Creighton Leonard's lavish penthouse office in a golden hue. Small rainbows danced along the elegant paneled walls, light refracted through a crystal decanter on the small table beside his desk. The aroma of strong, fresh coffee filled the room from two steaming cups JB Barons carried into the office on a silver tray.

Placing the tray on a low coffee table, he walked to the large sliding glass doors opening to the penthouse balcony and slid one open to the fresh morning air. The distant expressway roared with traffic—eastbound bumper-to-bumper delayed by an accident miles ahead; westbound streaming out of town.

As usual, JB would spend this weekend in the service of Creighton Leonard, ready to go anywhere, do anything—almost anything—necessary to ensure his mentor's continued success in the highest level of corporate society where money and power brought life's most treasured rewards. Yesterday was one example of his commitment to Creighton Leonard's future—and his—if he could avoid screwups, like yesterday's.

JB now knew the screwup had been Kohl's, but he needed to be careful exposing that source to Creighton, who demanded perfection from himself and others, with no time for incompetence and meaningless accusation and innuendoes.

It had been Creighton who first mentioned Jennifer Poole as a rogue employee. But the reference had originated in human resources from Kohl, the result of Kohl's lack of thoroughness. But Kohl was

Creighton's man, inherited from a previous regime, but Creighton's nonetheless.

JB walked past Creighton who stood admiring his trophy wall, as he called it. On a glass table in front of the wall sat mementos of Creighton's corporate battles, won and lost—mostly won. Creighton abhorred losing and did not like being reminded of losses.

One prize was a pair of bronze trophies honoring his rugby days at Harvard. Another, a bronzed stock certificate for Inco Corporation, the first company he had brought public after leaving college. That had gained him a tidy five million dollars and some lifelong enemies. Inco had been a small, closely held company, but Creighton's clandestine stock purchases behind the scenes soon earned him control. There had been a heated proxy fight when he liquidated its assets; the company caught in a dead-end industry. His vision brought a way out, and the shareholders came out winners in the end with no cause to complain.

Most cherished were gold-plated keys to a classic 150 XKE Jaguar and its replica encased in acrylic—winnings from its driver in a race against Creighton's newer Porsche. The driver had been his friend. They had been drinking when the wager was made but sober when he won and claimed his prize. Creighton cherished the trophy more than the friendship, and they had not spoken in years.

There was a small stone carving of a wolf given to him by his childhood friend Miguel Alverez the day the two were separated, and Creighton, at the insistence of Raymond and Ann Leonard, left primitive New Mexico for a better education in the East. The boys were fourteen years old at the time. Since then, Miguel had become known by those who loved him and those who feared him as *el Lobo*, the Wolf.

On the wall hung a portrait of Senator Willard Malovich, one which JB thought would soon lose its place on the wall. His friendship was becoming a liability.

Hung in beautifully gilded frames at opposing ends of the wall were portraits of Raymond and Ann Leonard, Creighton's parents.

Creighton's secretary, Kathleen Warren, never understood why they were not displayed together as the happy couple Creighton claimed them to be. She also found peculiar the symbol of each subject's faith displayed on the lower right-hand corner of each portrait. Raymond's was the Star of David; Ann's, the crucifix of Catholicism.

Creighton held his parents in high esteem and considered their influence in his life significant yet outside his corporate life. Their representation on the wall was symbolic, opposing faiths that contributed uniquely to his development and made him who he was, the product of his parents' teaching, or lack thereof. And he was their son, whether or not they wanted to admit it.

He had not ignored JB when JB had entered with the morning coffee. Such meetings were routine, his way of preparing for the day. "Did you catch the opening prices this morning?" he asked, his eyes fixated on the wall.

"No, as a matter of fact." JB turned to face Creighton as he answered.

"We opened up three points this morning. Yesterday's incident had no impact. Frankly, I would not have considered that outcome. Who really understands Wall Street anyway? I'm up three million dollars with WYCO alone. On paper, at least. You've made a good amount too. You should feel good about that."

"I really wasn't aware," JB said, pausing. "As for yesterday, it has left me a little depressed."

"According to one analyst, WYCO is a sure bet for increased profits, thanks to our improved access to both Mexico and Japan." Creighton continued as though speaking to the pictures on the wall, "That same analyst downgraded us last week, thanks to our friend, Malovich. Another analyst sees us as a takeover candidate because of increased vulnerability, a target of some international conspiracy inspired by yesterday's incident." Another pause. "But I don't think so. Virginia has no thoughts of bailing. She's in for the long haul, has been since the beginning. No matter. Either way, it's good for you and me and for the rest of the shareholders. Virginia should be happy."

With his mention of his wife's name, he walked to a small framed picture at the end of the glass table and admiringly picked it up. It pictured him with Virginia on a sailing yacht in St. Thomas, Virgin Islands. "Yes, we need her to be happy. We need her good will. And after the agreements are signed, she'll be even more the wealthier."

Creighton turned to JB and motioned for him to be seated. "Do you believe it, she really doesn't care about the money? Oh, she likes the benefits the money provides when she thinks it through. But she really doesn't care." It was a statement that brought a bewildered look to his tanned face; a quirkiness he never understood about Virginia.

"You were lucky, Crey. Really lucky," JB declared cautiously, changing the subject.

Creighton smiled but said nothing.

JB was one of the few people in the world whom Creighton allowed to call him by his nickname, a natural thing for him to do because of their long association that began years earlier when they met at Harvard. Then, JB was a promising, yet brash graduate student; Creighton was an alumnus attending a conference at the Harvard Business School. Their chance meeting had occurred inside a bar in Boston's combat zone where they had a few drinks and later did the town together.

While their meeting in the bar had been coincidental, it was also fortuitous. And unbeknownst to JB, it had been Creighton's intention all along to locate JB during the Harvard conference to seek the help he needed to advance his corporate career.

Years earlier, Creighton and Virginia Leonard had purchased controlling interest in a small electronics firm in Lexington, Kentucky, a company under the control of JB's father, Lester Barons. The take-over had been friendly—Lester Barons had wanted out. After the acquisition, Lester stayed on for one year to help the transition before moving his family to Minnesota, drawn by the state's educational system, reportedly the best in the nation. While the Barons could easily afford a private education, they preferred that JB be educated in a *normal* social environment.

They purchased a modest home near Lake Minnetonka, and Lester enjoyed a second career as a consultant to the computer industry. When his only son, JB, graduated top-of-class from their local high school and earned his MBA from Harvard, the Barons retired to semiluxury in Florida—their life's work completed.

A good judge of people, Creighton was honestly disappointed by Lester's decision to get out of the business. Lester was older than Creighton by more than a few years, and Creighton admired him for having built his business from scratch. Lester's staying on had not been a requirement of the purchase, and Creighton sincerely appreciated Lester's going the extra mile once the acquisition had been completed.

Virginia Leonard's money had financed the acquisition, and placing Virginia's capital at risk early in the Leonard's marriage required considerable finesse on Creighton's part. And because Lester had been so forthright and had stayed on to help secure Virginia's investment, Creighton felt he owed more than money to Lester Barons: an investment in Lester's son, a Harvard education. It was an investment that would benefit everyone and, if he was correct about the young Barons, would benefit Creighton Leonard most of all.

While Creighton couldn't have Lester, he could possibly own Lester's son. So he worked discreetly behind the scenes to ensure JB would have his place at Harvard, and once accepted, partially subsidized the tuition through a private, anonymous scholarship. Only Virginia Leonard knew of Creighton's efforts, which she rightfully believed was motivated by her husband's sincere gratitude for Lester Barons's integrity and loyalty, a gesture she approved because she also held him in high regard.

Creighton's appraisal of JB proved accurate. JB excelled at Harvard, graduating in the top five percent of his class. After a summer internship on Wall Street, a position manipulated and paid for by Creighton, JB entered the business school, where he continued to excel; this despite his forays into the "combat zone," then Boston's center of lasciviousness. He had fallen deeply in love once, in high school, but that love of his life had eluded him. The combat zone was balm on that wound, his show-and-tell. The girls would show all, and he'd tell himself he was getting over Jennifer Ward, the one who got away.

It was on such a foray that JB had his chance encounter with the man who now owned the company his father had built. It didn't take long for an honest, reciprocal friendship to bloom in full, and for the fondness Creighton had felt for Lester Barons to soon transfer to Lester's son, with one significant difference: Creighton was now the mentor in a world he had learned to manipulate and control. It was only a matter of time before JB accepted a position as Creighton's personal assistant, exposing him to all the Leonard's holdings, exactly where Creighton could best use his talents.

To his delight, Creighton soon learned those talents extended well beyond the world of corporate finance. JB was also a gifted strategist. He shared his father's proclivity for building a business from nothing, with a true commitment to the cause and an eagerness to do anything for Creighton Leonard, a quality Creighton could easily exploit, although he would never use that word.

JB had completed his high school education at Minnetonka High School in the shadow of WYCO toys, a large local manufacturer that employed many of his classmates' parents and began an early fascination that blossomed as JB's technical training continued.

JB encouraged Creighton's investment in the Wayzata Toy Company and later engineered Creighton's discreet stock acquisitions and the Leonard's eventual control of the company, a scheme that rewarded JB's burgeoning imagination. At WYCO, their combined skills quickly turned the company around and made millions for Creighton and Ann Leonard. At least on paper.

JB had not previously worked with Creighton in a corporate environment and soon came to admire Creighton's skill as he assumed leadership and exercised total control of WYCO while keeping management in place, despite its shortcomings.

With Creighton at the helm, JB continued as an advisor to corporate staff and now, at a very young age, was a wealthy man with much to lose should disaster strike, as could have been the case yesterday. JB had many reasons to be concerned. As he stood in Creighton's office, his admiration for Creighton was genuine but waning.

"Please sit." Creighton instructed. "The shooter wasn't after me," said Creighton. "Most probably, Malovich was his target." He paused and added, "You seem unusually uptight."

"As I said, you were lucky yesterday. We don't know who the intended target was. You're well liked, but you're not everyone's favorite CEO," he said as he sat.

"I'm not?" Creighton feigned surprise. "I've made fortunes for many people. And it's not been all bad for the employees either."

Preferring not to discuss his likability, he changed the subject. "So why so downcast?" he pressed, topping off his cup of coffee.

"Kohl gave you the wrong name and could have destroyed the career of someone this company desperately needs, Jennifer Poole." Creighton was listening. "The SOB didn't have all the facts. He made wrong assumptions that could have ruined us. Should have asked more questions, but he didn't, jumped to his own conclusions," continued JB, his face red with anger.

"Such language!" scolded Creighton. "Is that a fair commentary on one of our officers?" His tongue-in-cheek rebuke was expected; Creighton could not tolerate profanity, an interesting contrast to his often indiscriminate use of power to gain what he wanted at the expense of others. To Creighton, vulgarity was a sign of gross ignorance, an intolerable weakness. Those who used it had no place in his inner circle.

"Yes…well. There's too much at stake to rely on imbeciles like Kohl."

"But he has the ear of our plant personnel." JB doubted Creighton believed his own words.

"Then the man is deaf. We could have a mutiny on our hands, and he couldn't see it," said JB. "He's one of the reasons we have morale problems." JB related Jordan Green's comments, concern with overindulged executives. "He has no business being here. I suggest you dump him."

"And replace him with whom?"

"Someone from the ranks. Someone capable of keeping the peace with our employees. At least until we shift production to Mexico. Ask your own employees to provide a candidate. Our fortunes exist only on paper! We can't afford problems at home! Not now."

They looked at each other for several minutes before Creighton brought them back on track. "So Jennifer Poole is not the right person? Is that what you started to say?"

"Had Kohl listened, he would have learned that Jennifer Stewart also had worked late the night of the meeting."

"Stewart?"

"A new girl, a secretary. Trying hard to make a name for herself. She was signed in that night. Kohl hung up before Mildred Knowles could give him the name. We scared the wrong Jennifer."

"And just where is Jennifer Stewart?"

"We don't know. She's not reported back for work." JB poured himself another cup of coffee. "It's logical. She gets chased out of the office, scared to death, leaves town."

"Well?" Creighton asked disdainfully.

"We'll find her. She has some pay coming. When she calls in, we'll find her."

"And Jennifer Poole? How about her? What does she know?"

"Nothing! Nothing we're aware of. She's a victim of circumstance. Probably wondering what happened. But with her son safe at home, she'll most likely let it go and get on with life."

JB turned again toward the patio door. An image of Jennifer Poole filled his mind. She was then Jennifer Ward, a schoolmate, one grade ahead of him, and the most beautiful girl he had ever known. An image of her performing with the Minnetonka High School dance line filled his musing, a snap shot forever preserved in

JENNY

his mind. He'd never forgotten her. He recalled placing anonymous notes—two that he could remember—inside her locker, puppy love remarks, dropping them through the locker vents. He soon gave that up as too kinky. Then he had written very private words in her yearbook before graduation. But she was an upperclassman and didn't know he existed. She was the most beautiful girl he knew. Finding her again, a twist of fate after so long, was beyond explanation. He had to protect her.

Creighton brought him back to the moment. "What now? What do you suggest?"

"We wait. If the shooter regains consciousness, find out who the shooter's target was. As far as the Stewart girl, she's nowhere to be found. And that's good. Scared and long gone. By the way, the senator called," said JB, changing the subject.

"Malovich."

"Called yesterday. He tried but couldn't reach you. He left a message on my voice mail."

"And?"

"What you'd expect. He needs more money."

"Anything else?"

"Nothing more. He sounded worried about the allegations."

"Tell him not to worry any longer. The problem has been fixed." Creighton confided with finality.

"What does that mean?" inquired JB.

"He'll understand. If he doesn't? Then he doesn't deserve our support."

"Anything else?"

"Send him another fifty-thousand. That should keep him happy."

"Oh, there's one more thing," said JB, standing face-to-face with Creighton. "I spoke with our head of security, promised him a two-thousand-dollar bonus for his efforts."

"Well, pay him! That's cheap. Do we have a problem?"

"No longer cheap. He wants more. He suspects there's more going on than he understands. He's groping. But he won't betray us. He wants a reward to match the risk."

"What does he want?"

"He hasn't said. Not yet. He feels his career has been compromised."

"Okay, he's your man. You said he could be trusted. Give him what he wants." Creighton turned and walked back to his desk, adding as he sat down, "Within reason, that is. You did say he was a reasonable man. Also, 'small-minded,' I think you said."

He leaned back in his chair and for a moment stared at his protégé. "And you better be right about Jennifer Poole! I don't question her value to the company, but I don't want more complications. You find out how much she knows," he warned and began paging through a pile of reports Kathleen Warren had placed on his desk.

When JB reached the double doors, he turned to answer Creighton. "She couldn't know anything. What's there to suspect? Her son's been returned. Their life continues as before. She'll soon forget anything ever happened. It's over, Crey." He hoped he wasn't sounding defensive. "We need Jennifer Poole in this company. She's the best this company has," he said with great conviction. "The special recognition she has yet to receive is real, earned, and deserved. The House of Toys would not have happened without her. She's a victim of circumstance. Kohl dragged her into this because her name happened to be Jennifer. We'll find the real Jennifer. Jennifer Stewart. Kohl's a risk. Get rid of Kohl!" He waited for Creighton's response. When none came, he exited toward his own office.

Chapter 27

Noise from the grounds crew tugged Jenny from a deep sleep. Her first thoughts were her memory of last night's anonymous caller, voices and western music in the background, and a woman's voice asking about Jason. But Christian's nonchalant reaction had a calming effect, and sleep had been deep and restful, and she dismissed her thoughts. She was glad he was home.

She turned under her light summer blanket and reached for him. In the indent on his pillow was a large piece of paper, and she smiled as she picked it up; he had allowed her to sleep late. But where had he gone? She wondered.

Pulling herself up, she sat on the edge of the bed, rubbed her eyes, and focused on large black-marked letters that read: "Gone fishing. Hope you're able to sleep the morning away. Don't worry about us; we'll fend for ourselves. If it's a good day, we'll have fish for dinner." It was signed "One loving husband."

So father and son were going to spend the day together. She smiled, stood, stretched, and walked slowly to the balcony screen door and slid it open. Beyond the patio, the yard boy was making one last pass with his mower and waved. She waved back, rested both hands on the wood railing, and filled her lungs with the morning air.

For the first time, she noticed the big tear in the canopy covering the empty boat slip. *So yesterday did happen*, she thought. *Jason kidnapped; his return. The storm really did happen.* It seemed too much to believe. She took another deep breath. *There's more to all this than we know or that Christian is willing to admit.* Her eyes moved to where

Nicki had found the diamond tiepin, on the deck where the stranger had stood. In her mind, she saw him again, tall, thin, windblown, and dripping wet. *Christian was right.* Yesterday was less frightening in the light of a new day. There was a reason for yesterday, there had to be, and it was up to her to find it. If the events of yesterday meant nothing, confirmation would be quick and easy. And, as she had promised Christian, she'd check in with him along the way. She had no visions of being a lone ranger.

She showered quickly, stepped into a clean pair of jeans, threw on a fresh blouse, straightened the bed, and walked lazily downstairs to a fresh pot of coffee Christian had prepared for her. She sniffed it, poured a cup, stepped to the phone, and pushed quick dial for her assistant, Sharon Miller. She got the answering machine and left a message, "Sharon, I won't be in today. Cover for me! Running errands this morning and hope to be back here midday."

The good night's sleep had done wonders for her, and the crisp morning air charged her system. She felt alert, her mind surprisingly clear. That had not been the case yesterday when she met the local chief of police at her front door. There were questions she could have asked but didn't. He was first on her list.

Sipping her coffee, she remembered his name was Chief Nick Carlson and reached for the phone. She pushed "Police" on speed dial, and three rings later, a pleasant voice announced, "Minnetonka Area Police. May I direct your call?"

"This is Jennifer Poole. Is the chief available?"

"I'm sorry. The chief has not reported in. He's expected within the hour. Would you care to leave a message?"

"No, thank you," said Jenny, thinking through her day. "I've got errands to run." That wasn't completely true; meeting the chief was her only errand. The rest of the day would follow due course. "I will be in Excelsior in thirty minutes, and I'd like to stop by and speak with him for a few moments. If that's all right."

"Oh, it's all right, Jenny. I'll hold him here if he comes in before you get here."

"Thank you," said Jenny automatically, surprised by the sudden familiarity of the woman on the line. *Odd*, she thought.

After a final sip of coffee, she retrieved Christian's fish scaling board from the garage and the yellow legal pad Christian had used earlier. On it she wrote, "I like my fish cleaned, Thank You. Gone looking for some answers. Be back midday." Next, she located Dan Sheridan's business card and dialed his office at Mall of America. *Funny,* she thought, *they both worked at Mall of America but had not met before he came to Jason's rescue.*

She got his voicemail. "Mr. Sheridan, this is Jennifer Poole. It's Friday morning. I'd like to thank you again for all your help yesterday. Jason did just fine during the interview before the power went off here. Channel 6 didn't include any of what they had taped. I was wondering if you could obtain a video copy of their newscasts. You might have more influence than me. If possible, I'd like to obtain copies of both the news conference and the assassination attempt. Sorry to bother you. You can see I'm taking you up on your offer to help. I'll call back later. Thanks." She hung up the phone and headed back to the garage, but remembering the tiepin, she returned to the kitchen, retrieved it, and returned Sheridan's card to the small directory. The pin was the only evidence of the mysterious man's presence, in case she needed it.

Chapter 28

Officer Stella Kraemer was delighted when Jenny appeared at the glass partition in the station house reception area. They had not been introduced yesterday at Jenny's front door. After a final bite of a sweet roll, she released the security lock on the reception area door and motioned for Jenny to enter.

"Hello, Jenny. I'm Stella Kraemer," she said, adding, "I was two years behind you at Minnetonka High School." That said, she smiled and extended her right hand. "The chief just called. He's on his way in. I told him you were on your way here, so he's expecting to see you first thing. Would you like a cup of coffee while you wait? Maybe a sweet roll?"

Jenny declined.

"No wonder you stay so trim. You look as good as you did your senior year." She paused for a moment. "Wish I could say no. To these I mean," she said, holding up a sweet roll. "I quit smoking. I seem to have replaced one vice for another. But I'm working on it." Jenny sensed Stella's weight was a big concern for her, but she was not there to comfort Stella.

Stella continued, "I was just sick yesterday when we got the call about Jason. Took a while before it registered with me that he was your son and all." She motioned for Jenny to sit down at the chair beside her desk. "The chief and I were so relieved to see him safe at home. Boy, that was some storm that came through. If it's not one thing, it's another."

JENNY

Behind Stella's delightful smile was a pretty face, and that now seemed vaguely familiar, but Jenny couldn't place her. "The chief," Stella continued, "he can't remember anyone ever being kidnapped from Excelsior. None of us can. Do you have any idea, Jenny, who would want to do such a thing?"

"None. I was hoping to ask the chief the same question."

"We're all a blank here. The chief is the best there is, and he's stumped. He's in contact with the FBI, the lead on the case. They've not been able to ID the men in the truck. But, then, I'm sure Nick will tell you that himself." Stella looked down at her watch. "The chief had a late night last night. You know, with the storm. He should be here any minute." She took a deep breath. "Green was in yesterday."

"Green?" asked Jenny.

"Jordan Green, he's your chief of company security. He's in here a lot. Met with Officer Randall. Larry told me about it. They talked about this conspiracy thing. That's what the press is calling it—an international conspiracy."

Jenny knew Jordan Green, but not well. They've met at company functions, and she'd seen him in her plant's production areas. Respected by the rank. She had not seen him since his move to the Wayzata office tower.

Stella glanced up at a security monitor. "Here he is, coming from the garage."

Both Stella and Jennifer stood as the chief approached. "Chief, you remember Jennifer Poole. We've been getting reacquainted. I think I mentioned we attended Minnetonka High School together."

Jenny extended her hand. "It's good to see you again when I'm more together. Yesterday was not a day I wish to relive. And last night was not much fun either. Thanks for stopping by."

"Let's hope we never have another day like it," agreed the chief. "Last night you were under a lot of stress. We're relieved it had a happy ending. What can I do for you, Mrs. Poole?" As he spoke, he motioned for Jenny to precede him to his office. He followed her in and closed the door. "Please have a seat, Mrs. Poole."

Jenny seated herself in a comfortable chair in front of the chief and waited while he pulled back his big chair and seated himself. His desk was neat and tidy, obviously Stella's handiwork before Jenny arrived. He was about to speak when Stella knocked twice and entered carrying a small tray with a steaming cup of coffee and a sweet roll. She placed it on the desk in front of her chief and quickly retreated, closing the door behind her.

The chief began again. "I'm glad you've come in. I'm sure we both have questions for each other. If you don't mind, I'd like to ask mine first. They may help me answer yours."

Jenny nodded. "Fair enough."

"I know you told our Officer Randall that you had no knowledge of who would want to harm your son or possibly get to you through him, possibly to even a score. Do you hold to that answer now that you've had time to reflect on what happened yesterday?"

"Chief, I don't have even the remotest idea of who would want to harm me or my family. That's why I'm here to ask you the same question."

"Mrs. Poole, your father is Matthew Ward?"

"Yes. He's my father."

"Your family is close, are you not?"

"Very," Jenny confirmed.

"Well, you become a candidate for anyone seeking revenge on him, someone unable to harm your father any other way. Can you think of anyone who may want to get at him? His money? He is a wealthy man. Jason is his only grandson."

"There are many men wealthier than my father, Chief. Yes, he has been successful. But I just don't think so. I really don't."

"How about your work, Mrs. Poole? I'm told you are a very popular person at WYCO Toys. Can you think of anyone who may have a grudge of some sort? You've passed by other qualified people, I'm sure, to get to where you are today."

"By working harder, Chief," she responded with some agitation in her voice. "No. I can't believe I've hurt anyone in my career."

"The media is playing the idea of an international conspiracy. I understand you played an important role in the negotiations with both the Japanese and the Mexicans. That could offend someone, wouldn't you say?"

"Chief, I'd like to think I was that important. The truth is I'm just a person doing a job. I'm one marketing manager for one marketing group. In that role, I helped develop a manufacturing protocol that could benefit my company, as well as our Japanese and Mexican counterparts."

"At whose expense?" The chief leaned forward on his desk. "A disgruntled employee?"

"A very remote possibility. But again, I just wasn't all that important."

"I respect your humility, Mrs. Poole. Still your reputation is widely known."

"I hope what is known is the truth."

"You said your protocol would help your Japanese counterparts, but could they not be greatly offended. After all, they could be hurt by the treaty. Implementation could happen soon, I'm told, once Congress enacts a new treaty. Is that correct?"

"Out of my league, Chief. I'm aware of negotiations certainly, but until something is formalized, it's out of my department. That cannot concern me yet."

"I see." The chief smiled and paused momentarily. "I'm sorry, Mrs. Poole. I know very little about business. I'm simply voicing common speculation. It's your turn, Mrs. Poole."

Jenny wished she had made a list and didn't know where to begin. She'd speak from the heart.

"Chief, we've really been caught off guard by what happened yesterday. That's why I'm here. Jason is safe now at home. But I can't shake this fear that it's not over. I need to know. Do I need to be on guard? You're the police, the experts, and have access to more experts, someone who can find the people responsible and put them away. I'm concerned for the well-being of my family, my husband, and my son Jason. Do you, the experts, believe the people responsible for this will strike again?"

"Mrs. Poole, if it would help you sleep better, we can put your home on our regular patrol, place it under surveillance. We can stop when we're in the area just to make sure nothing happens."

"I'd appreciate that, Chief. I would sleep better. My husband's job keeps him on the road. We're alone much of the time."

"And to answer your question, I believe this was an isolated incident. I don't think you are in any further danger."

"Chief. I'd still feel better if you kept us under your watchful eye. I think someone is watching my home. Watching me, my family, I'm not sure."

"What makes you think that?"

"Yesterday during the storm, in a flash of lightning, I saw a man standing on the deck. He was watching me. I saw him for just an instant, just as the power went out."

"I'm the one who pulled the plug, remember? I was outside. We didn't see anyone else."

"You weren't on the back deck. And you left shortly after that. Whoever it was could have waited for you to leave." Jenny straightened one leg and extracted the large diamond tiepin from her pocket. "After the storm, we found this."

"And you believe that belongs to your visitor?"

"It may belong to my father. It may also be just coincidence," said Jenny as she quickly tucked it back into her pocket. "I'd like to locate the rightful owner."

"And if that owner is the man you saw on your deck, then what, Mrs. Poole?" the chief asked in a serious voice.

"I don't know. That's why I'll sleep, better knowing your department is watching out for us."

"Mrs. Poole, let us do the investigating," scolded Chief Nick.

"You said you thought it was an isolated incident. You're the expert. I don't doubt your right. The pin probably belongs to my father who doesn't even know it's gone."

"That was a big stone. If your father lost it, don't you think he'd know?"

"Like you said, he's a wealthy man." Jenny was angry with herself for becoming sarcastic to the chief. "I'm sorry, Chief. I didn't really mean anything by that."

"That's all right, Jennifer. Just remember, we're here to help."

"Thank you, Chief. I will remember that," she said as she rose and let herself out of the chief's office.

She smiled at Stella as she walked past her. The sweet roll that had been on her desk had disappeared. "It was nice to meet you, Stella. It's been a long time since high school. Wish you well with the diet."

Outside, Jenny walked directly to her car and reached inside for her cellular phone. She felt the chief had been honest with her, and that thought was reassuring. The chief's belief that Jason's kidnapping was likely an isolated incident brought further relief. Maybe Christian was right: they were in no real danger. *Unless,* she thought again, *Jason began to remember what had happened, as Dan Sheridan had suggested.*

She'd check with Christian after his day with Jason. He'd detect if Jason was remembering any of his ordeal. So far, he seemed unusually detached from yesterday's events. *It must be the drug they gave him, although drugs had not been proven. But his memory seemed to be totally blocked.* Suddenly she wished he would never remember. She wanted to be done with it.

Jenny looked at approaching clear sky and dialed her mother's number. It rang several times, the answering machine apparently turned off.

Jenny was about to give up when D' Ward answered, "Hello."

"Mom, it's Jenny."

"I was out in the garden. A real mess from the storm. Didn't see you on the ten o'clock news. Did the news crews come out last night?"

"Yes," Jenny answered. "At least they tried. Jason said his part. He did well. Then the power went off. That was that. Christian arrived home as they were packing up. We watched the news at ten and didn't see *us*, either. 6 didn't play the segment. Don't know if the other stations did. No one has said."

She took a deep breath and continued, "The reason I'm calling is to offer some good news. I'm at the police station."

"You're at the police station, that's good news? What's wrong now?"

"Nothing, Mother! I stopped by to see the chief, to see if they knew something we didn't. As if they'd tell me, right?"

"Well?"

"He asked if someone could have tried to get at Dad through his grandson."

"That's absurd! I think," asserted D'.

"Well, you know, check all the angles. I don't believe they suspect any connection. Actually, the chief said he believed it was probably an isolated incident and doubted we were in any further danger."

"Unless Jason—"

"I know." Jenny cut her mother short. "I really don't believe he will remember anything. Christian and Jason are together now, fishing. I know Christian will try to see if Jason's memory is improving. Brings me to the real reason I'm calling. What's good with fish? I think we're having fish for dinner. Thought I'd run to the store."

D' Ward didn't like fish, but she was a good cook. She shared her knowledge of cooking fish with her daughter just as the call-waiting tone sounded in Jenny's ear. "Call coming. One quick question: does dad own a diamond tiepin?"

"Never has. Why?" answered D'.

"Later. Thanks. Got another call. Bye." Jenny disconnected with her mother. The new voice was that of her assistant, Sharon Miller.

"Sorry to bother you. I figured you'd like the entire day off. We have some documents that need your signature or the plant shuts down. Can you stop by? Are you close?"

"You can sign my name." Jenny's response was a reflex; she didn't want to go to the office. Finally, "Never mind. I'll come. So much for a good fish dinner. If there is such a thing."

JENNY

"What?" asked Sharon, totally confused.

"Never mind. Ten minutes."

"Dan Sheridan returned your call. Would like you to call him?" Sharon thought for a moment. "Would you like me to call him for you?" she asked hopeful. She had seen his performance on the news, and suddenly his celebrity status appealed to her.

"No. I need to talk with him. I'll call him from the office," Jenny responded, failing to grasp Sharon's sudden interest in the mall's head of security.

Ten minutes later, Jenny pulled into the parking lot between a green Ford Explorer and an older model car, which, like Nicki's, was seriously pockmarked from yesterday's storm.

She closed her door and walked alongside the building, passed the scrutinizing eye of the production crew, men and women enjoying their morning break as they stood at the streetside loading doors. A wolf whistle acknowledged their failure to recognize the executive in her jeans.

"New outfit?" asked the receptionist as Jenny entered and signed in to receive her ID. Jenny seldom wore jeans but had forgotten what she was wearing when she agreed to sign documents.

A small office elevator took her to the fourth floor, home for several second-level managers and a conference area for visiting dignitaries.

Mildred Knowles smiled as Jenny approached her reception desk. "We're all glad everything is okay, honey," she said with obvious sincerity. "We were glued to our televisions last night. Still can't believe such a thing could happen way out here so far from the city!" Mildred and her husband had moved to "the lake" in the '50s to get away from the city's ever-growing crime. "Thank God Jason is safe."

"Thank you, Mildred. Could you call a courier? I'll have a package for corporate. Say, thirty minutes."

"Sure thing, Mrs. Poole." Mildred's words trailed after Jenny moving quickly down the corridor.

Sharon Miller greeted her as she entered the manager's wing. Together they walked through a large work area, men and women working at computer terminals and word processors and were mostly ignored.

"I won't even ask about what happened," said Sharon. "You must be sick of questions." Jenny nodded. "But I'm dying to hear it all firsthand," Sharon continued. "I had no idea where you were or what had become of you until Dan Sheridan showed up in the store's conference area with Jason by his side. I didn't even recognize Jason at first."

They turned several heads as they passed a telemarketing session in progress. One man winked at Sharon and let his eyes settle on her associate, the brunette in tight fitting jeans. He was new and would later find himself the object of some banter when he learned who the shapely brunette really was.

Jenny headed straight for her desk and the pile of documents prepared for her signature, intending to stay only long enough to keep production running.

"He's some man! Sheridan is," Sharon declared, evoking a questioning look from Jenny. "At first, I thought he was just some arrogant, pretend kind of cop. You know that Saturday-night-bar kind of cop. Hired security."

"I wouldn't know," chided Jenny.

"He told Jason he was CIA and FBI, both. But I didn't believe him. Then later I saw him interviewed on television. I can't believe I was really there. I can't believe it happened. Someone could have been killed.

"I understand he personally drove Jason home. What did you think of him?"

Jenny looked up from her papers. "He's a nice guy. Showed honest and sincere concern for Jason. Seems to know his business. And Jason really likes him," answered Jenny, resuming her signing.

Halfway through the fourth file folder, they heard a knock on the open office door. In the doorway stood a man with short cropped

JENNY

hair, dressed in a white, kitchen uniform. When their eyes met, he took one step closer.

"Excuse me. Would you have a moment, Mrs. Poole?" he asked politely, apologetically.

"Yes, I have one minute. Please come in." Sharon caught the signal in Jenny's look and excused herself but left open the door separating their two offices.

"You're Bill? Bill Wilson from Food Services. Please come in." Observed Jenny in tone that was both cordial and inviting.

The chef's cap that he had been nervously rolling in his hands he now tucked into his belt. He entered slowly and seated himself tentatively on the edge of a high-backed chair in the front of Jenny's desk. "Lake sure looks inviting. You have a great view from up here," he said as he surveyed the view of Lake Minnetonka from Jenny's office window. "All I see is the parking lot and railroad tracks."

Jenny straightened herself. "What can I do for you, Bill?" she asked, causing Bill to shift in his chair.

"I'm sorry, Mrs. Poole. The girl at the front said you'd come in. And I didn't come to take your time, or talk about the weather, or the view," Bill said sincerely. "My wife and I watched the late news last night. Power was out for the six o'clock. We saw what happened to your son, Jason. I just wanted to stop by to say how grateful we are that he's now safe with you at home. No one deserves to have such a thing happen to their family."

Jenny smiled from across the desk. "Thank you for your concern."

Bill continued, "We…my wife and I, have one son. He graduated from Minnetonka High School last year and left us empty nesters, so to speak. We miss him a lot. Don't know what we'd do if we ever lost him." Bill looked down at his hands shaking in his lap. Jenny sensed his nervousness and waited for him to continue. "Well…We felt for you, Mrs. Poole. We're happy everything turned out all right."

"Thank you, Bill. And thank your wife—"

"Martha's her name," supplied Bill.

"And thank, Martha. I appreciate your concern very much. We're very grateful as well."

Having said his piece, Bill nodded sheepishly and stood. "I better be going," he said, turned, and walked toward the door. Inside the doorway, he turned and asked, "Any word on who did it? The news said the police have the truck that was used."

"Yes, an Abel catering truck. Beyond that, nothing. The police believe it's an isolated incident."

"Maybe it was just one big mistake, Mrs. Poole."

"Mistake?" asked Jenny, finding the statement unusual.

"I was thinking the way he was returned so quickly. Maybe it was just a big mistake in the first place."

"That's interesting. You mean mistake as in mistaken identity?"

"Something like that."

"We may never know," Jenny repeated and returned to the files on her desk. When she glanced up again, she saw Bill exit down the stairway to the main floor.

"That was nice of him," said Sharon upon reentering Jenny's office. "I suppose everyone in the company knows what happened. He's the only person who has said anything." Sharon paused reflectively. "It's nice to know someone is concerned and is willing to say so."

Sharon gathered the pile of file folders and headed for the door. "Don't forget Dan Sheridan. He's expecting your call," she reminded, adding, "I don't think I can. Forget him, I mean. I was a real"—she stopped as she considered an accurate expletive—"a jerk. No, I was worse. I was a real bitch to him."

Jenny gave her a disapproving sneer. Her assistant was very good at what she was hired to do but difficult to reform.

Sharon wasn't through and continued, "I didn't know who he was. Then I didn't believe him when he told me. Please let me know if he ever comes out here. I'd like to apologize. I mean, I totally owe the guy that."

"Why don't you look him up at the mall or call him?" suggested Jenny, reaching for the telephone.

JENNY

"I wouldn't want to be too forward. What do you think? You'll find Dan's number on a Post-it by the phone under the word *hunk*," answered Sharon as she smiled and wiggled her way out of the office.

Smiling and shaking her head, Jenny punched Hunk's number into the phone and waited.

"Dan Sheridan, mall security, can I help you?" The response came after only three rings.

"Mr. Sheridan, this is Jenny Poole. I'm sorry I wasn't available when you returned my call. Sharon said that you had called."

"Yes, Sharon? That pretty lady. Wears her glasses on her nose."

"You're right about pretty and the glasses. Did you get my message about the telecasts? I was going to call the stations but thought you might have more pull. I hope you don't mind."

"Yesterday you said I should call you, Jenny. Is that offer still open?"

"Of course, it is," came a quick response.

"Then I want you to call me Dan. Are you okay with that?"

"Yes, Dan," answered Jenny. Her barriers down.

"I've placed a call to Donald Stone." Dan's tone became suddenly serious, businesslike. "So far, he hasn't returned my call. He and I don't get along all that well, but he will call sooner or later. He may think I've got another story for him. He'll get us the copies. Maybe reluctantly, but he'll deliver."

"I suppose if he doesn't, I could call Janet Spalding. She seemed willing to help."

"If you promise her another story. Jenny, that's their business. They're all the same. They'll do anything for a story." He spoke somewhat fatherly. "Jenny, it's Friday. I may not hear from Stone before Monday."

"That's all right. I'm taking the weekend off. The weatherman has promised a couple of nice days. Chris is in town for a change. And Jason is eager to show off his boatmanship."

"Your family deserves a good weekend. I hope the weatherman is right. In my world, we control the weather. It's the same every day."

"This weekend, I'll settle for the real thing."

Dan felt a strange loneliness sweep over him and changed the subject. "Jenny, tell me. What are the tapes for? Are you saving them for posterity, or are you looking for something specific?" He sounded very much the cop.

Jenny hesitated and decided to be honest, even if he thought her to be slightly crazy. He couldn't be of much help if he didn't know what she was up to. "Yes to both. Right now, we'd prefer to forget yesterday, but I know in the future we'll look back and question what really happened. Then it will be nice to have the taped record part of our history."

"So much for posterity. Now what are you looking for?" asked Dan.

"It may be nothing?"

"We'll see. What may be nothing?" Dan persisted.

"A man." Jenny took a deep breath. She was following the only lead she had and was wary of everyone taking her concern too lightly. "During the six o'clock news interview, at the height of the storm, a man appeared on our deck. I saw him briefly when lightning flashed. He was watching me. At least that's the impression I had. It was eerie, one of those strange sensations people talk about and can never explain because no one can believe it." Jenny paused, waiting for a negative comment she was sure would come.

"Please, Jenny, go on," urged Dan.

"Well, later, on the ten o'clock news, as we watched the telecast of the assassination attempt, that same man appeared in the audience. He was one of the spectators during the news conference."

"Are you sure?"

"Sure as I can be. It only lasted for an instant. That's why I want to review the tapes. I need to know if it's the same person."

"And if it is, Jenny? Then what? What does it prove?" asked Dan, adding a dose of reality to the conversation.

"I really don't know, Dan. I don't know," she answered honestly.

"It will take a couple of days to get the tapes. Do you want me to deliver them? I could. Besides, I'd like to say hi to that son of yours. Or would you like to pick them up at the mall?"

"Please call me when you get them. I'll decide then. I'm not often at the store. In fact, these days I'm seldom there. It might be easier if you could bring them out to my home or to my lake office. If you don't mind."

"I don't mind. And I would enjoy seeing Jason again." Dan found himself biting his tongue. He was attracted to her and wanted to say he would like to see her as well. He had no desire to create a conflict; he simply wanted Jenny as a friend. But deep within his psyche stirred long-suppressed emotions that begged now for release.

"Have you heard anything about the blood tests?" asked Jenny, changing the subject.

"No. They can take several days, sometimes weeks. I just sent them off today."

"I stopped by our local police station this morning. The chief, Chief Nick Carlson, doesn't believe we're in any future danger. He sees Jason's abduction as an isolated incident. I'd sure like to believe that."

"He's probably right, Jenny."

"Just in case, he's placing our home on his patrol."

"That all sounds good. Just don't let your guard down completely. Right now, everyone is guessing. We need more information."

"I won't. Thanks for reminding me. It's all beginning to seem so unreal." Jenny looked at her watch. It was ten minutes past noon. She had a couple of hours before Christian and Jason would tire of fishing. "You'll call then when you get the tapes?"

"Yes. But like I said, it'll take a few days. I'll call." Jenny heard the click before she could say good-bye.

Sharon could not help but hear the conversation, and when Jenny became quiet asked, "Well, is he coming out here?"

"I'm not sure. He referred to you as a pretty lady." Jenny couldn't resist the comment. Sharon squealed and appeared at Jenny's door.

"Looks like your visitor dropped his cap. Down there, beside the chair." She began to retrieve it, but Jenny stopped her.

"Don't bother. I'm leaving. I'll drop it at his office on my way out the back." That suited Sharon who turned, clutched her bundle for the courier, and headed down the hall. The plant would not shut down on her account.

Jenny quickly stashed a few remaining files in her desk, retrieved Bill's cap from her desk, called the switchboard, and checked out and followed Bill's route down the back stairs. When she reached his office, his door was closed, but behind it, she heard voices.

Chapter 29

"What do *you* want from me?" Bill Wilson spit the word *you* from his mouth; his anger directed at Jordan Green, who stopped by to talk after completing his routine tour of the plant.

It was Bill's lunch hour; his crew busily serving the food he had prepared. He scowled to show his anger at Jordan's seduction and his own unwitting participation in the abduction of Jason Poole. He had agreed to assist with the requisition of the truck but had not thought to ask what the truck would be used for. It was, he had been told, a matter of company security. That seemed sufficient.

"We have to talk! Now!" Jordan grabbed one of the two industrial style chairs in front of Bill's desk and sat down, resting his crossed arms on the chair's back. "You didn't call last night. I really thought you would."

"I have nothing to say to you. I don't care if I ever see you again," said Bill and abruptly stood and walked toward his closed door where he turned. "I can't believe we did what we did." He swore and shook his head. "Jordan…Jordan. I can't believe you got me involved in a…a kidnapping. That's a federal offense. If we still had the death penalty…" His voice trailed off.

Jordan craned his neck to answer. "I'm sorry, Bill. I really am. There's much more to this than I can talk about. It involves corporate security, like I said."

"But someone as nice as Jennifer Poole? Come on, Jordan. It just can't be." With the mention of Jennifer's name, Bill realized he was speaking loudly, and looking at the closed door behind him, toned it down to a loud whisper. "What will we do if we're caught? Jordan, we're accomplices in a kidnapping. You took Jennifer's Poole's son. How could we be so dumb! Jordan, I just can't believe it."

"I didn't take her son, Bill."

"No, you're right there. We took her son. I'm an accomplice to a kidnapping."

"I know, Bill. We took a great risk. We did it for the company. The cause was right," Jordan pleaded.

"Bull. It's all bull, and you know it." Bill paced back to his desk and stood behind his chair. "You didn't do it only for the company. Come on. There's more to it. What did they offer you? How much?"

When Jordan didn't answer, Bill continued, "You did it for money. It's always for money, isn't it, Jordan? Well, I did it for you, Jordan. I did it because you asked me. I trusted you. I figured you knew what you were doing."

"And the five hundred bucks you're going to get paid too. Admit it. You did it for money too," accused Jordan angrily. "And now, thanks to me, that measly five hundred bucks has grown to one thousand dollars, hard US."

"Well, golly gee! All that money and prison too. Thanks a lot. Yes, I wanted the money. But that wasn't important. You asked for help. You lied to me, and I said yes. That was long before you said anything about money." His voice had grown loud again. He continued nonetheless, "But never again, Jordan. You're unbelievable! Never again! And…And…You can roast in hell. In fact, you probably will. That was probably determined long before this. And now me right along with you." With nothing more to say, Bill silently pulled his chair back from his desk, plopped into it, folded his arms across his chest, and stared into a corner of the ceiling in the opposite direction of Jordan.

"Bill, I've asked for even more money," declared Jordan after a brief silence. "Someone is going to pay us for the trouble we're in, for the risk we took."

JENNY

"Your thirty pieces of silver wasn't enough?" Bill asked.

Jordan suffered through a long silence and said finally, "The plan was to scare the girl. Like I told you, it was a matter of company security."

"Scare Jennifer Poole? What on earth for? I'm sure you succeeded. How about her son Jason? Don't you suppose you scared him a little? An innocent kid. What is he, eight years old?"

"Ten. He's ten. And he wasn't frightened. He was given something. He didn't even know what was happening, didn't know enough to be frightened. He wasn't harmed in any way. And he won't remember anything."

"You know that? For fact, you know that? You drugged the kid? As if kidnapping isn't enough! You gave Jason Poole drugs?"

"Not me. Quit saying me. Look, Bill, there's much more to this than I can tell you. You've got to believe that. I wouldn't have brought you in if it weren't important. You just gotta believe that, Bill. We're family."

Frustrated, Bill shook his head. "Don't remind me. I don't know how I could've been so stupid. I can't believe that I believed you!"

"It's done, Bill, we can't change that. There are important people in this company who…Bill, I just can't say more. I can't."

"Jordan. Jordan," he said again, cursing.

"Well, that's the truth. Now we have to make it work out for us, you and me. Some good can come of this. We have to think this through and be smart about it."

"What good can come of it? What good?" He turned in his chair and lowered his eyes to glare at Jordan. "Jordan, how about you tell me what good can come of this?"

"Money, Bill. Money. That's what's good."

"I told you I don't care for your kind of money. It's bad money. There's no way your dirty money will ever be good."

"What if it's lots of money, Bill? More money than you or I have ever had at one time." Jordan paused to let the thought settle in Bill's mind. "With a lot of money, you could do some good. We could do some good. You…You could help Gary with his college. You've always said you'd like to see your son go to college because you couldn't. You could help him."

Jordan could see Bill beginning to process his words and pressed on. "We could buy a good bass boat. Just like we've always talked. One with a big engine, live well, the works. Enter tournaments. And Martha has always wanted to take a Caribbean cruise. That would be good to do for your wife."

"Don't be ridiculous. How much did you ask for?"

"I didn't give an amount yet. That's why I'm here to talk about it. Just told him we wanted more for our trouble."

"Him? Who's him, Jordan? Who's the *him* whose going to give us all this money?"

"The way I see it, we've got a couple of sources."

"Him and someone else?" Bill asked sarcastically.

Jordan struggled with his thoughts for a moment before deciding how much he dared to share with Bill. He didn't want to lose him; he needed to tell him enough to prevent that. "Bill, I can't reveal my source. I'm sworn to secrecy. But you can appreciate that I wouldn't have done all this if I weren't close to the top, really close to the top. There's money there. You can believe it."

He studied Bill's face. All he saw was anger, misguided for sure; after all, he had meant only the best for Bill. Had he not given Bill an opportunity to serve his company, to be recognized by the important people in the company, to be rewarded for his loyal service?

"I've been thinking about it. The other potential source is Jennifer Poole's people," he offered.

"Her people? What people would that be? Her people, like hell! She's struggling like the rest of us. What kind of people?"

"Bill, you just don't see it. She's a nice person, yes. Struggling? She probably is. That's also why she is vulnerable. She's being used." Jordan paused for emphasis and placed his head in his hands. After a moment, he looked up again. "Listen to me, Bill. There's just more going on here than you can see. I wish I could tell you, but I can't."

JENNY

Bill looked at his pathetic brother-in-law, this man who had been his best friend for more than twenty years, now pleading again for his help. When would he ever learn? Maybe Jordan did know more than he could reveal. Maybe good could come of it all.

"How much money, Jordan?" inquired Bill, his voice now subdued, compassionate.

"Forty or fifty thousand. I don't know. That's why I'm here. Thought we should talk about it."

"Jordan, you're crazy. You're just plum crazy. First, you get me involved in kidnapping the son of a company executive, one of their best people. Then you accuse her of something too secret to tell me. Now you're talking, what is it called, extortion, blackmail."

"Bill, these people have money. You better believe it. They were probably pleased as Cheshire cats when we agreed to do their work for so little."

"I didn't agree to nothing!" Bill corrected.

"They took us for suckers. They're expecting us to ask for more. We'd be suckers for sure if we didn't."

"You're going to get us both killed. That's what will happen, Jordan. Someone is going to get real pissed with you, not that I could blame them, and we're going to get killed. I know it sure as hell."

"No they won't. They're not that kind of people. I know them, Bill. You've got to trust me on that! I know them. They're not into killing people. They're into saving our company. Believe it, Bill! Believe it!"

"You're not believable, not any more. I swore never again to believe you. We're gonna get caught, or we're gonna get killed just as sure as—"

"We won't get caught," interrupted Jordan. "I stopped by the station yesterday. So far, the police are thinking it's part of a conspiracy. They're all looking for terrorists, like the press is talking about."

"Jenny said they told her it was an isolated incident."

Jordan's face reddened with surprise and anger. "What do you mean Jenny said? You talked to her?"

"I...I stopped by to tell her how sorry I was her boy had been kidnapped, and how happy Martha and I are that he was returned."

"You did what? Are you out of your gourd?"

"It was the natural thing to do. Jordan, she works in the same building as me. It would draw more attention if I just ignored it."

"You better be right! Don't do anything stupid like that again."

For several minutes, the two men glared at one another, fighting emotions they had not experienced before. Jordan was the first to break time to leave. Without saying a word, he turned his chair around and with great precision placed it in front of Bill's desk and announced, "I'm going to ask for fifty-thousand. We'll get twenty-five apiece. They'll pay. It's not too much to ask. There's money, like I said."

He reached for the door and pulled it open. As it swung inward, a white chef's cap fell from the door handle. Both men noticed it at the same time. Bill fumbled with his belt in search of the cap he had worn to Jenny's office.

"That wasn't there when I came in," said Jordan, concerned.

"Someone must have found it and placed it there while we were talking with the door closed," ventured Bill with great conviction. He knew Jenny had probably placed it there, but he wasn't about to create anymore trouble for her than he already had.

"Let's hope, whoever it was, didn't hear anything."

"The door was closed, Jordan. What could anyone hear?" reasoned Bill. He wanted Jordan to leave.

"You're probably right," said Jordan as he exited. After a few steps, he turned again toward Bill, a big grin was on his face. "Martha deserves a cruise. You've never taken my sister anyplace. Tell her business has been good, and you're expecting a good bonus." Then Jordan turned, heading toward the parking lot.

Chapter 30

"Sadler here." Gary sat alone in his office, thinking about his weekend that would begin any minute as soon as he would decide to get up and leave.

"Gary, this is Dan Sheridan. Have a minute?" Earlier, to take her mind off the subject for a while, Dan had told Jenny the blood analysis would take a couple of weeks. Gary had promised to put a rush on it.

"Just one or two. I'd like to get out of here early. Weather is supposed to be nice for a couple of days; heading for the cabin."

"Jennifer Poole is about to do the same thing, kinda."

"What?"

"Nothing. You're fortunate to have someplace to go."

"Try it sometime, no television, no telephone, no people, just the smell of pine. And if I'm lucky, fresh fish over a crackling fire."

"A fire in August?" interrupted Dan.

"Sure. That's what a cabin is for. It's the ambiance, the smell of pine smoke, and my own shore lunch inside the cabin."

"No phone? How do you get by with that? Can they run the district without you?"

"Sure. And if they really can't, I mean really can't, my secretary knows how to reach me. I've got a cell phone. I told the director they don't have telephone service in remote Minnesota. He didn't question it, and he knows better. Hell, he has his getaway too. You have to in this business. And it's not gotten any better since you turned in your shield. So what can I do for you before I disappear into the wilderness?"

"Did the blood samples get off?" asked Dan.

"Yesterday. I put a rush on it. Should have something early in the week."

"Any of your people at the Pooles during the news telecast? You knew the media wanted to go live from the Poole's living room."

"Yeah, we heard. And no. We had no one there. Why do you ask?"

"She saw a man on her deck in a flash of lightning at the height of the storm."

"Well, some of my people don't know enough to come in from the rain, but not this time. Whoever it was, wasn't one of mine."

Dan let it drop. "Anything with the truck?"

"Nothing definite. Lots of prints, but nothing identifiable, however. Employees were all over the vehicle, preparing it for the morning delivery. I'm not too hopeful there."

"So how did two men get into the plant with good security and drive away with a truck?"

"Well, from the police report and the one eyewitness, we're assuming two men. Our witness is mentally challenged, a ward of the town—something like that."

"How credible is that witness?"

"Can't rule out his story. Could be smarter than anyone knows."

"Probably is. He's not working for a living. Just walking the streets of a sleepy lake town. Not a bad life if you ask me."

"Doesn't sound like you've got much to show for the taxpayers' dollars."

"We did get surveillance tapes from Abel. We're going over them now."

"Does Abel have anything to say about what's on them? Did they notice anything unusual?"

"Not that they've told us. But they didn't have much time to review. You see, when we could have been standing on the Poole's deck, we were at Abel getting the tapes. Actually doing our job. Any other questions?"

"How about Bartlett? Any connection? This international theory the media is putting out?"

"Nothing. Still in a coma. It's not looking good. But we've located his apartment, and we're going through every inch."

"Can I get in to see Bartlett if he comes to?"

"On what grounds?" Gary Sadler had great respect for Dan Sheridan and would like nothing more than to involve him. Still, he thought it necessary to remind Dan he was a civilian."

"My grounds. It happened on my grounds." Dan understood. "Mall security is my job. We were lucky yesterday. I'd like to talk with him, Gary, ask him a few questions. Who knows, I might just learn something that could help you solve this case."

"You might at that. Come in on Monday. I'll make sure you get all the clearances you need."

"Not until Monday? I've got two days on my hands."

"Aren't weekends your busiest times? Your public needs you, Dan. See you Monday. We'll take a look at the surveillance footage then too. Anything else? The lake is calling. Until then, I'm going fishing. Bye."

Gary Sadler hung up the phone before Dan could respond.

"Good fishing," Dan said quietly to a dead line.

The instant Dan set down his telephone, it rang. He picked it up.

"Dan, it's Gary again. There is something I forgot to ask you. We can talk about this too on Monday. But I need something to think about while I'm watching the little red and white bobber."

"Which is?" Dan asked.

"When you left the bureau, weren't you running background on subversive groups running white slavery across our borders?" Sadler had read Sheridan's file, sent up at his request after Dan's initial contact.

"Yes. Why?"

"Ever hear of Random Enterprises?"

"Not that I recall. Should I know them?" Dan asked.

"Not necessarily. We've been trying to track the funding behind some of these low-budget groups. Random is an organization that keeps bubbling to the surface. It's a money pool. Sometimes it acquires stocks in companies for any number of reasons not always obvious. Sometimes it funds organizations, whose activities may benefit the pool's benefactors. One of those organizations is Senator Willard Malovich's campaign fund."

"And Willard Malovich chairs the Senate committee pushing the Mexican trade treaty. Probably more influential than the president himself," commented Dan, adding, "You see, I'm up on current events."

"I'm impressed. But there's more. We've been able to trace RANDOM to Creighton Leonard, the CEO of WYCO Toys," said Gary, dropping a bombshell.

"And that says there is something to this international conspiracy theory?"

"We're not saying so. The evidence doesn't support that. Maybe you'll learn more when you question Bartlett. But we believe for instance that RANDOM provides more than funding."

"I'm afraid you're losing me, Gary."

"This may not be an international conspiracy, but it certainly appears to be international. You know there is a Senate probe into the affairs of the good Senator Malovich."

"Yeah, it's all over the press."

"He was scheduled to come before a Senate panel in closed-door session, where he was to be confronted by a key witness, one of his boyfriends with a bitter spirit as far as the senator is concerned. That probe would put the treaty and its supporters into a tailspin from which they'd never recover."

"And?" asked Dan, still not understanding the connection.

"Not *and*, Dan. *But*. *But* it won't happen, at least not yet. The probe has been postponed. The key witness was found shot to death on the steps of a Boston church. First reports say a jealous lover did him in."

"The senator?"

"He's not that dumb."

"You don't think so?"

"You never believe the obvious. You know that."

"So where does that leave you?"

"Asking whose got the most to gain from a hold on the probe."

"The treaty advocates?"

"That's 50 percent of the businesses in the US. They can't all be bad. In fact, a deal with Mexico could be a good thing for the country." Sadler was getting off track, and he knew it. "The people who are investing the most in Malovich's efforts probably have the most to gain. That sounds logical, right? Well, way up near the top is Creighton Leonard if our RANDOM information is correct."

"And you think Creighton Leonard is involved in the death of the lad with a misguided sexual preference to keep Malovich's efforts moving? Sounds to me like you're really stretched out on this one."

"I'm not making accusations. It happens to be one of those not-too obvious leads. You happen to be in a position to help my investigation. I'd like your help."

"And Jennifer Poole is your link."

"Could be. You want to help find the people who took her kid. I'll give you the full investigator status you need to get into the right places. In return, I'd like you to keep an eye open for my investigation."

"How would I do that? I quit that business."

"As a special investigator reporting only to me. An independent contractor. They'll know at the top, of course."

Dan wanted to ask what all Gary knew, but didn't. He'd do that later if he agreed to help.

The line was quiet while Sadler waited for a response.

He could wait a little longer, thought Dan. "Gary, you were going fishing. We'll talk Monday. In the meantime, you've thrown some interesting bait my way."

"I could use your help, Dan. I need it. You're good."

"This fish is not ready to bite. Give me the weekend. I need to think it over. See you Monday." This time, Dan left Sadler with a dial tone.

Chapter 31

A car horn sounded as Dan darted through heavy mid-block traffic outside the federal building in downtown Minneapolis. He smiled back to a one-finger wave and entered the building's sterile lobby, took the elevator to the third floor, and quickly located the regional office of the FBI. Since it was Gary who had suggested the morning meeting, Dan had not bothered to call ahead. Entering through a large glass door, he was greeted by an attractive receptionist wearing a friendly, gracious smile.

"You must be Dan Sheridan. Mr. Sadler is expecting you. Please follow me." She was a trim five-six and probably a jogger, thought Dan, eying her slender, well-muscled legs. They would be approximately the same age. Her hips gyrated in a sensuous manner, obviously intended to impress him. He followed six paces behind until they came to a large solid wood door.

Gary stood as Dan entered and smiled for obvious reasons; the door held open by the left hip of the receptionist who smiled seductively and winked as she allowed it to close. "A field agent in disguise?" asked Dan.

"Not exactly. Though she does make a man my age wish he were young again. My wife died two years ago. Thought I could use the stimulation to keep my heart beating. Purely visual," he said, extending his hand to Dan while herding him to a corner of the medium-size office where a television monitor and a VCR were waiting.

"Coffee?" he asked. A silver thermos pitcher sat beside the VCR with a tray, two ceramic mugs, creamer, and a bowl of sugar cubes.

"Yes," said Dan with a smile.

Gary picked up the monitor's remote control and pushed "On." "These are second-generation security surveillance tapes, courtesy of Stan Girard, head of security at Abel Food," Gary began. "The now famous truck, number 622, was taken from stall 19."

"Abel has surveillance cameras placed throughout their three-acre production facility they operate 24-7. They go through as much Mylar as the Pentagon…In time there won't be a warehouse large enough to store his cassettes. But give this guy Girard credit. He's good. He's isolated the tapes from cameras located in the vehicle access area for the period two hours before and after the truck was believed stolen. More specifically, all truck activity from 3:30 a.m. to 7:30 a.m. Company records confirm the last order was processed and placed on board at approximately 5:30 a.m. All total, we have some eight tapes to evaluate, each approximately six hours in length. Tapes are changed at 8:30 a.m. each and every morning. To coincide with security shift changes."

"That's tight surveillance. Seems extreme. Serving something extra with their meals, are they?" asked Dan.

"No. That's the point. They serve most of the businesses in the Twin Cities, including the airlines. Several clients top the list of Who's Who in high technology. A malcontent could royally screw things up by gaining access to that food source and contaminating it in some way. It was just a year ago that…but that's another story. They have cause to be careful. And they are careful. As I said, this guy, Girard, is good."

"So we have forty-eight hours of videotapes to review," Dan said, looking at his watch. "And we've got about two hours to do it. Is that what I'm hearing?"

"Not quite. We have a team reviewing each minute of tape. You'll view an edited composite. For our purposes, we've isolated the tapes from only three cameras and have concentrated on the time period from 5:30 a.m. to 6:00 a.m., the approximate time when truck 622 was scheduled to depart on its morning route. We know it left on schedule because it made its first delivery at WYCO Toys at its regular time. That's according to Bill Wilson, their food services manager."

"And the rest of the tapes?" asked Dan.

"You're welcome to them when you've got the time. In the meantime, the viewing team will scrutinize every second of time. They're a breed of their own and will identify any irregularity, not just those relating to this specific case. They'll see it all, sexual abuse, clandestine romances, loafing, pilfering, you name it. These are things that are going on under the nose of management all the time in businesses all over the country, but they go undiscovered because of the lack of dollar resources allocated to this kind of Big Brother surveillance."

"Some would say it's invasion of privacy."

"Whose privacy? Look, it's happening on private company property. Businesses have a right to know what's going on with the property they own. Particularly companies like Abel food. Just think what someone could do with a little poison or a virus. Let's face it, this kind of surveillance is acceptable Big Brother activity."

"Maybe necessary, not acceptable. There is a difference," responded Dan as a chill coursed his spine.

"Well, don't lose sleep worrying about it. Most businesses can't afford Abel's thoroughness. And most tapes are boring as hell. If you don't have reason to watch 'em, you'd fall asleep. Tapes like these are often not watched because they're tediously boring."

"Okay, let's get bored," quipped Dan, again looking at his watch.

"I'm sorry," responded Gary, "My soapbox maybe not yours. I enjoy freedom, but not for just a few, at the expense of many. Sorry," he said, picking up a cassette and placing it in the player.

"Why make the one delivery? Why make any at all?" asked Dan as Gary pushed "Play."

"Presumably, someone didn't want the truck's disappearance to be discovered too early. It was the second delivery that never occurred. By then, discovery didn't mean anything. When the truck failed to show, that customer eventually called in. It was too late."

"And we have, for what it's worth, the testimony of the one witness, Old Mike. He places an Abel truck in Excelsior at the time of the abduction. Truck 622 that we discovered in your mall parking ramp. You wouldn't believe it would be all that difficult to ID the perpetrators on the tapes, but so far, we've seen nothing conclusive."

"Any proof Jason was on board the truck?"

"Nothing conclusive there either. It's pretty clean." Gary retrieved a report from his desk. "The usual dirt fragments on the floor, gravel, and sand from the parking area. Two strands of hair. Oh, and some fingernail pieces on the passenger side. Lab is running DNA now. So far, no ID."

A series of identifying numbers and subtitles flashed across the screen. "We have further edited out most of the nonevent footage, that period of time when nothing changed in the camera's surveillance radius. Most of what you and I will see will be movement, activity that actually occurred, but not in such rapid succession."

As Dan watched, the tape revealed employees entering and leaving the building through the employee entrance. In the lower right of the viewing screen was imprinted the exact time each segment was recorded. The sequencing was irregular due to the editing.

"It's not at all uncommon, according to Stan Girard, for unrecognized parties to be entering and leaving. Abel employs hundreds of people. Of course, some get sick from time to time. Their replacements are most often part-time people, some of whom are full-time, part-time, and on-call. Many are complete strangers brought in by *personnel*. They show up at their appointed time, work one shift and are never hired back. For our viewing pleasure, these 'strangers' have been highlighted or enhanced."

"What's Girard's take on these?"

"He hasn't seen this composite. Yours is the first viewing. He'll get a copy today. But he has qualified the strangers based upon *personnel's* records. Girard is truly ticked. Someone breached his security. Claims this is the first time ever a vehicle has been taken without authorization."

"Isn't that the point? The truck usage had been authorized but switched?"

"Right. Anyway, Girard is convinced the answer is in this footage. The man's been spending evenings searching his own version. But he hasn't seen the enhanced version." Both men watched in silence for several minutes. Gary broke the monotony. "We began with the most probable and are working down in time, and we're following the route the two men would most likely have taken. Again, we've concentrated on footage from just three cameras."

Gary pushed "Pause" when two highlighted subjects appeared in the employee entrance corridor. "Now here. These two appear in all three tapes. Two men. They entered the building at approximately 5:45. One younger appears to be darker skinned, hard to say, lighting isn't the best. The older man is probably in his forties. They don't fit our description." Dan found the lighting was bad even when enhanced.

Gary activated "Play" on his remote until a man and a woman appeared on the screen and paused again. "These two appear to be leaving, probably coming off their shift. They would have passed the two men in the corridor," observed Gary.

"Has anyone talked to them yet?" Dan asked.

"Not yet." Gary answered, fast-forwarding the tape to its conclusion.

The second segment began with a view of the company security guard at his command station. The camera was positioned behind the command console and rotated slowly to view down each corridor. Again, people came and went, some stopping at the console, leaving keys and reports, picking up their passes. After a few minutes, the guard stood, made a quick scan of his monitors, and exited down the entrance hall.

"He's gone for coffee," Gary explained. "He leaves every morning at the same time according to Girard. Goes to the cafeteria for coffee and a roll and returns within minutes." After another several minutes of silent viewing, Gary continued, "Now the same two men approach the command station. The swing of the camera doesn't help us. They remain pretty much out of the camera's view. You can see the guard station is empty. They continue toward the staging area where the trucks are loaded. By this time, number 622 has been loaded and is ready."

"Look," Dan said, "here's where the other couple, the man and the woman, pass them." Dan pointed to the screen. "Seems a good place to start. They weren't enhanced. They're regular employees?"

"That's right," said Gary, running fast-forward to the conclusion of the tape. "We'll return this tape to Girard to see if we can put names to all the faces. Remember he has his own tapes and apparently has not determined these two to be out of the ordinary. We can assume these two have every reason to be there."

"Can I have a set?" Dan asked. "The boy's parents may be able to identify someone. Could give us a lead."

"Us?" asked Sadler. "Does *us* mean you're back on the team? Or was that some Freudian slip?"

"Probably both," confessed Dan. "But, first, what are you really after?"

"I want him brought down, Dan. Whatever it takes."

"Him?" puzzled Dan.

"Creighton Leonard, CEO of WYCO Toys," answered Gary.

"Come now. Just because he's financing some hate groups to promote his own cause…? Are you tracking other lobbyists on the hill as well? And those who just might employ them? Or is Creighton Leonard just that special to you?"

That question brought a change in Gary's demeanor. His grandfatherly face darkened, and veins at his temples pulsed. Creighton Leonard was special!

"Does the name Lewis Wentworth mean anything to you?" Gary asked, turning from the now blank video screen.

"No. Should it?"

"Probably not. He was before your time. I forget what a kid you are…How old I am and that I'd like to forget," Gary mused. "Then

Lewis Wentworth didn't make the national news either." Gary leaned forward in his chair, elbows on each knee massaging his thumbs, his gaze somewhere in space, and the pulsing vein at his temples less prominent. "My sister's kid, Lewis Wentworth, was young, bright, intelligent, good-looking. I mean, the world was his for the asking.

"My wife and I couldn't have children. We knew that going into marriage. Fine with me at the time. You know how it is at the bureau, never home, calls in the middle of the night. Children wouldn't have been good for us. Not then. So Lewis became like our own. My sister's husband had died of cancer. She was alone and needed help, wanted a male figure in Lewis's life. She was eager to share her son with us, with me. It was great…Better than great.

"Her husband had been a lobbyist before he died. The man had a million connections. Politics and power manipulation were his life, and he was a true artisan at his craft. Man, he was good. And he made a bundle of money legitimately. He was not without temptation, but my sister kept him honest. Her love and the fact that I'd bust his sorry ass good and ruin his career if I ever found out otherwise.

"As an only child, Lewis was my sister's life. After Jim died, he became the absolute center of her universe. I mean, he became the focal point of her very existence. She was the best mother any kid could have. And he was the best son any mother could have. She wanted only the best for him. And because their lives had revolved around politics for so many years, and her and Jim's experience had been good, she wanted to see him learn the system, the political system. Her hope was that in time, Lewis would become a respected politician, a senator, congressman, an honest politician who could resist the temptations served up by lobbyists like…like her husband. Even though he had gone about it honestly.

"For Lewis's sake, she developed her own skills as a lobbyist. Then she made sure Lewis attended the right schools, joined the right clubs, and met all the right people. And while he was working his butt off to be everything she wanted, she was doing everything she could to assure a good outcome. Since money was never an issue—

Jim had left a sizable estate—she insisted he attend Harvard. When he graduated with a master's degree in political science, she made sure he secured a position as a page on the hill. He was on his way.

"Before long, Lewis was making his own contacts. His mother was right, politics was his forte. It was in his genes, just like it had been in his father's genes. Before long, he was assisting some pretty powerful people. And like his father before him, he was becoming a master of the system. He knew things about people that I could not even imagine, things it was my job to investigate. But I respected his honesty and never attempted to use him. And I am certain that through it all, he remained as pure as ivory. He would have been a remarkable senator or congressman, one of the few honest ones. I think that's what killed him or got him killed."

"Killed?" asked Dan. "Any proof of that?"

"They found his body in his apartment. Shot in the head. Police ruled it a suicide. A self-inflicted gunshot wound is what the medical examiner claimed. There was a note. His prints were on the gun. Everything checked out. Everything but a valid motive."

"And you're not convinced. You're thinking cover up?" asked Dan.

"Not that I've been able to prove. But I knew the kid. Really well. Lewis was a surrogate son. And the note he supposedly left behind never made sense. It simply wasn't Lewis. It had been printed on a dot matrix printer. It was Lewis's printer. It was a match. He had his own computer. Remember this is early '80s. It was an Apple of some kind…I don't know anything about computers. And Lewis was good with computers. Like everything else he set his mind to. The suicide note had been saved to a floppy disk. His computer also had a hard drive, but it was clean. There was no note there.

"The note was short and sweet. Too short and way too sweet. It read: 'I'm so sorry, Mom. I've compromised my career, everything we believe in. There are no honest politicians. I could never be one. Now there's no turning back. I'm sorry. I love you, Mom.'" Sadler's face flushed red, a spot on his left cheek just below the eye began to quiver as he held back his emotion and fought the memory of the crime photos showing Lewis sprawled beside his desk in a pool of blood. They appeared as though it were yesterday. There was a long silence. Sheridan felt compassion for this hardened bureau chief and waited. There could be nothing worse than losing a son, no matter what his age.

"Lewis was no prude. He understood very well what was going on in Washington. He had had two of the world's best teachers. He was also idealistic. And in that regard, he truly believed he could make a difference. It was not just a pious thought that some would have. No, Lewis knew inside he would make a difference. Thinking you can and knowing you will are worlds apart. It's what separates those that do from those that don't. You know what I mean, Dan. Anyway, compromise his career and everything he believed in just didn't make sense. Didn't then and still doesn't."

"And Creighton Leonard? Where does he fit in?" asked Dan.

"Bear with me. Compromise is a political doctrine. It's what moves Washington. But compromise in a negative sense? Lewis compromised his values…? It could never happen. There was a rumor that surfaced during the investigation, but no substance. None! Lewis supposedly had found a lover. The problem was the lover was gay, not a pretty young girl. A name was never offered, and no one ever surfaced. No one ever identified anyone. No one ever proved a thing.

"Lewis liked girls. He was attracted to them, and they were attracted to him, just like God intended it, right? But he was driven. He used to tell me, 'Later, Gary, when the right one comes along, I'll know, and so will the rest of the world. A successful politician needs a strong wife, not just a woman. A wife!' He knew that. He believed that. He had no reason not to, having had grown up with two of the world's best role models. But he just didn't have the time to find the right one.

"Those closest to Lewis were shocked beyond belief. They knew it was a lie. But the authorities wouldn't hear the truth. Lewis had been working with a congressman from New Hampshire on a committee to safeguard corporate America from hostile takeovers. It was complicated legislation. Anyway, one result that didn't sit well with some 'big money' was a provision that would prevent the dumping of assets after such a takeover. I mean, liquidation could take place but in an orderly fashion. Businesses must do what they need to do to stay in business. Anyway, in theory, the law would have weakened the incentive that attracted so many 'raiders' to their prey. The '70s and early '80s were the decades of corporate raiding.

"One of the strong opponents to the legislation was a senator from Rhode Island, Broderick Smith. He's no longer in office, died of some immune system deficiency, probably AIDS, as we know it today. He had been openly hostile to all members of Lewis's committee, where Lewis was working as an aid. I sound like my sister, 'Lewis's committee.' His congressman's committee. The fact is Lewis did all the work. He ran the show. Others got the glory.

"Broderick was a politician on a string. At the other end of his string was Creighton Leonard. They had been undergrads together at Harvard, a fearless twosome of sorts. They remained close friends through graduate school, but the ties were becoming less obvious, partially because Broderick's sexual habits were becoming too well-known in their circles, and Leonard sought to distance himself.

"Early in his career, Broderick showed great political cunning. But like so many politicians, he lacked money, a commodity that seemed to come easily to Leonard. They were a natural pair, Broderick and Leonard. Broderick provided political contacts and beneficial legislation where possible, and Leonard provided fuel to keep the home fires burning and the passion red-hot. Fuel came in the form of money, lots of it, and later sex was added. Lots of that as well. Whatever his subjects desired, he was, is, able to furnish. Leonard is a parasite feeding on the weaknesses of others."

"You believe Creighton Leonard murdered your nephew, Lewis?" asked Dan.

"Not personally. He's above that. But he arranged it. I'm sure of it. I just can't prove it. Not yet, anyway. Creighton Leonard is well connected. His parents are wealthy. He married a wealthy woman. He's charming in person, charismatic. He has his following. He moves in and out of the shadows of the world's corrupt—money laundering, pornography—doesn't deal directly in drugs, actually finds them offensive and too low-life, but even drugs are often found on the periphery.

"And he is a shrewd businessman. Wall Street loves him. He has a magic touch. But I believe Lewis got in his way. It was easier to kill him than to deal with him. Again, Lewis was sort of a white knight, a champion of good who, in his youthful zeal, would not give up. He would only become more difficult in the future. His death was expedient. So…bam." Gary raised the index finger of his left hand, pointed it to his left temple, and with the word *bam* dropped his thumb like the hammer of a pistol. "The gun was a small caliber revolver. It was still in his left hand when they found him. Here's where the clean laundry is full of holes. Lewis was right-handed."

Gary stood, arched his back, and continued, "I'm too old for this. The fact that Lewis was left-handed came up in the investigation but didn't go anywhere. His friends claimed he was ambidextrous."

"And was he?" asked Dan.

"I don't know. When he was a kid, we'd play ball. He threw with his right arm. I don't know. Someone claimed he'd broken his right arm and learned to use the other. I couldn't prove otherwise. Guess he had broken his arm. So that's it. Made it difficult to prove my case or generate enough interest to begin an investigation. But I've never given up. And I won't quit, can't quit until Creighton Leonard is history. But I'm running out of time. I'm retired and out of here in a couple years. That's why you're important. You're possibly my man of the hour." Pausing, he focused his attention on Dan and smiled, willing him to say yes. "What do you say? Are you in or out?

"First, another question. What is the link with Jennifer and Jason Poole? From all that I've learned, Jennifer Poole is one of WYCO's best people. Leonard is the majority shareholder, and she's his golden goose."

Dan stood to face Gary. "What are you not telling me?"

"You've got it all. Call it instinct? Something inside me screams Leonard is involved. The facts seem to deny that, but the facts are all too strange. Just don't add up. The Pooles are victims as in Lewis's case." Gary moved back to his desk and opened a drawer to retrieve a wallet-sized case. "This is yours. Unofficially, of course. I was able to retrieve it. It will open all the doors you need. Should anyone question you, they can call me. Dan, I can use your help." He extended his hand to Dan, revealing a small leather case and dropped open its leather flap to expose Dan's badge. "It's your old one, never reassigned." He paused to let his words sink in. "I need your help. You're new blood. Me? I'm an old horse with an attitude and a strong obsession that's more personal than I would allow in others. My objectivity could get blurred. I could make a mistake, and Creighton Leonard could get away. And that is one thing I could not endure.

"On the other hand, you were considered one of the best, and I believe you still are. You can be more objective than me." Gary eyed Dan. "You can be objective, can't you?" he asked finally. "I understand Jennifer Poole is a bright and attractive young woman, with a husband who's never around and a young boy who could use some guidance. Something you can relate to. Right?"

Dan felt a sting in Gary's words. "He's a good, bright boy. My son would be about the same age." He thought for a moment. "I'll do what I can. If the Poole family is in danger, I'd like to help. I'll keep you in the loop, and if it impacts your case, I'll let you know." He offered finally.

"And Jason's mother?" Gary persisted.

"Look. She's married. From all I know, happily so and out of bounds, off limits. You're out of bounds if you're implying otherwise."

"I'm not implying anything. I'm concerned about objectivity. That's all. I'm concerned about getting Lewis's killer once and for all. I'm sorry for the loss of your son and your marriage. But I need to know what effect those wounds may have as you get closer to Jennifer and Jason Poole, and Creighton Leonard with his House of Toys. It's a fine line that you'll walk."

"Gary, I won't use Jennifer or Jason to placate your obsession, as you call it. Even if I could, I wouldn't. Jennifer is too bright not to recognize feigned concern."

"Did I say *play* at concern? It's your legitimate concern that will gain you insights with clarity I could only dream of. I'm not suggesting that you use Jennifer Poole and her son, Jason. I'm suggesting that you help them. I know your gut instincts are telling you there's more to all this than we can nail down. You know there's something wrong, something missing. I want you to follow those instincts. I want you to protect the Pooles and prevent anything further from happening when the evidence will not allow me to take certain actions. I want you to help me put Creighton Leonard away for good. Whatever it takes."

Then out of the blue, Sadler asked, "Is she is as cute as they say?"

"Cute, yes. Charming, yes. Intelligent, yes. Guilty as charged. And I'm afraid she's determined enough to get into real trouble if she attempts to solve this puzzle on her own. And you're right, I think there is something very sinister here that is not going to go away." Dan paused. "You went fishing, and I guess I'm hooked. How can I say no? I can't. Now what?"

"You wanted to speak with Fred Bartlett. Sorry, it doesn't look like he's going to make it. We've gone through his apartment. Pretty sterile. What little we did find leads us to believe Creighton Leonard was his target, not the senator. You recall he sought revenge for the death of his wife and child. We don't know if that was his motivation, and maybe never will." Gary started toward his office door to show Dan out.

"Does my employer know?" asked Dan. "The people who are paying my very lucrative salary?"

"Only if you tell them. And why would you? Anything in your contract about moonlighting?"

"Moonlighting without pay?" asked Dan.

"What can I say? You know how it is with budgets."

Chapter 32

Jennifer Stewart reached into her jean pocket, pulled out a wrinkled dollar bill to pay for a glazed doughnut, and gave it to the clerk who smiled from under gauze netting covering her curly gray hair.

"Coffee or change?" asked the older woman. "Coffee is only a quarter. With the doughnut, it's fifty cents. Bottomless cup too."

Jennifer faced the bakery display case. Beyond the case was a small work area and a mirrored wall from which she could view any activity on the street. Her gaze swept from side to side, as far as the small bakery's walls would allow, searching for the man wearing a cowboy hat who had followed her down the street. Must have stopped. He was nowhere in sight.

"Miss?" said the older woman.

"Oh, I'm sorry. You were saying?" responded Jennifer.

"Coffee or change. Coffee's just a quarter with your doughnut…Miss, you're okay?"

"Yes. Coffee please. And that doughnut. Thank you." She pointed to her selection.

"Coffee's right behind you, sweetie. Help yourself."

It was midmorning in the small Nebraska town and coffee break time. Again, her eyes surveyed the sidewalk reflected in the mirror behind the counter. Two or three people passed by the window. An older man entered and stood in line behind her.

"Is there anything wrong, dear?" asked the motherly woman from behind the counter.

JENNY

"No. No thank you. I'm fine. The coffee?"

"Behind you, sweetie. Cup size doesn't matter. Please help yourself."

Jenny turned and walked slowly toward a steaming pot on a back counter, selected a large Styrofoam cup, and filled it nearly to the top. She had not really wanted a doughnut or coffee when she entered the bakery, but the smell of fresh baked bread whetted her appetite, and the coffee smelled delightful.

She took a bite of her doughnut and stepped aside to allow a man to squeeze past her. "Sorry," she said. A sip of coffee gave her the courage to step outside.

Halfway up the block to her right, she saw him, pretending not to see her as he looked in the hardware store's window. Turning quickly, she considered stepping back into the safety of the bakery, but two women with small children blocked her way. He began moving in her direction, the hair on her neck said he was getting closer. Ahead was the drugstore. She began walking toward it. *There'll be people in there and a phone on the wall. She'd be safe. She'd call her brother. And if necessary, she'd call the police.*

She walked slowly at first, afraid to look back. Then sensing him closing the distance, she picked up her pace. Coffee splashed from her open cup.

The drugstore, thirty yards more! She could hear heavy footsteps behind her and strained to listen over her own heartbeat. Suddenly, the footsteps stopped. She continued faster, refusing to look back. When she reached the drugstore, she flung open the screen door and rushed inside. The small store was filled with display counters and neatly stacked shelves with the pharmacy in the back. Standing behind the counter, dressed in a white smock, was the pharmacist. She ignored his look and, stooping low, ducked behind a high-display case in the first aisle pretending to look for something. The pharmacist watched silently as he continued to work behind the counter until she emerged from behind a display case and walked toward him, trying to appear normal.

"Excuse me. Do you have a telephone?" she asked.

"Pay phone. On the wall up front."

"Thank you," she said and reached her hand into her jean pocket and withdrew a crinkled dollar bill. "I'm sorry. Would you have change? For the phone?"

"Four quarters, okay?" He dropped the quarters into her waiting hand and watched her deposit one quarter into the slot of the old rotary dial phone.

She quickly dialed Stewart's Pork. Still morning, her brother Jim would be in his office. If not, the phone would ring in each of the five farrowing buildings and the birthing barns.

"Stewart's Pork." It was Jim's voice.

"It's Jenny. I think they've found me." She cautiously turned her head to look out the window.

"Where are you? And what do you mean they've found you?" Jim asked, concerned.

"In town, at the drugstore. I'm being followed."

"Jenny, I thought we settled that. No one, I mean, no one could find you here."

"Jim, they have. I'm being followed. A man in blue jeans and a cowboy hat."

"Jenny, what are you wearing?" Jim's voice was stern.

"Blue jeans."

"Like ninety percent of Green Bend, Nebraska. Lord, Jenny. You haven't been gone that long."

As Jenny listened, a Cadillac drove slowly down Green Bend's main street. Her heart banged in her chest as she watched the car come into view from the direction of the bakery and then slow as it approached the drugstore. She had stopped talking. She also stopped breathing. The driver was a man in his fifties wearing a black cowboy hat. From his open window, he surveyed the drugstore.

"Jim, what'll I do?" Jennifer felt panic. "He knows I'm in here. He just parked across the street." She froze. "Jim! Jim! He's coming in. He knows I'm here." She turned to hide her face, and he walked past

JENNY

her not more than twenty feet away. She took a breath and watched him walk directly to the pharmacist. She could only whisper, "Jim… He's inside. I'm going to run for it, Jim."

"Jenny, don't leave. Stay where you are! Jenny! Jenny! Do you hear me?" Jim shouted into the phone.

"What'll I do?" she whispered again.

"Jenny, is it a white car? A white Cadillac?"

"It's white. Can't tell the make."

"Do you see a woman inside?"

Jennifer strained to peer inside the window. "Yes, I think it's a woman."

"Jenny, that's Reed and Phyllis Baker."

"Who?" Jenny asked.

"It's Mom and Dad's old neighbors, Reed and Phyllis Baker. You remember them? They ran the dairy farm next door."

"The Bakers?" repeated Jenny. "I thought—"

"Yes, they sold the cows and moved to Florida ten years ago. They're passing through on their way to Los Angeles. I told them you'd gone to town. That's who's been following you. I sent them after you, Jenny. No one has followed you from Minneapolis. You just need to forget that idea."

Jenny turned to see the pharmacist point in her direction. The man under the black cowboy hat slowly pushed the hat back on his head to reveal wavy salt-and-pepper hair, and a grin formed on his chiseled face. "Jenny. Jenny Stewart," he yelled and walked quickly toward her through the maze of shelves and racks.

Jenny replaced the receiver on the wall phone in time for the man's outstretched arms to close around her in a bear hug. Tears filled her eyes. She felt so embarrassed. She felt so relieved. She took a step back and looked into the face of her father's best friend, Reed Baker. He had been more than a good friend; he had been like a second father to her.

"Wow, Jenny. It's good to see you again. It's really good."

On the other side of the small store, the pharmacist watched and smiled.

Chapter 33

At the east end of Main Street, an old rust-colored pickup turned into the Chevron station and pulled beside a self-service pump. A dark-skinned man wearing a plaid shirt, jeans, and cowboy hat covering a head of long black hair stepped from the cab. He removed his hat to block the sun and read the instructions on the pump, inserted the nozzle into his filler pipe, locked the catch, looked around the drive, and walked slowly to the public telephone beyond a stack of old tires.

A battered telephone book hung loosely from a chain below the black box etched with a decade of graffiti. The cowboy's muscular hands hauled the book to waist level and leafed through its pages. He stopped at the S, pushed his hat back on his head, and ran his finger down the column of names.

Four Stewarts were listed. Below James W was the name Stewart Pork and the address, RFD 23, County Route 30. He tore out the page, folded it, and poked it into the shirt pocket.

He paid the attendant and drove the rusty truck back onto Main Street, heading north into town, driving slowly, checking the storefronts as he passed by. A woman in a white Cadillac watched as the old truck rolled by. *A migrant,* she thought and turned to watch her husband, Reed, leave the drugstore hand in hand with Jenny Stewart.

At the north end of town, the pickup turned into the sandy parking lot of the Coop Feed Store, pulling up close to the wooden steps leading to a worn plank walkway and two screened doors. He climbed the steps and entered the busy room that smelled of grain, molasses, and stale cigarette smoke.

A hayseed of a kid in his late teens looked up from a pile of pink receipts as the cowboy approached his counter beyond a display of galvanized buckets. "Dirk" was the name embroidered on his dusty blue shirt. A beaming smile said he liked people.

"Delivery for Stewart Pork leave yet?" the cowboy asked in broken English.

The hayseed half-turned toward a glass cubicle behind which sat a curly haired woman with an oversized bright-yellow bow in her hair. "Anything for Stewarts today?" he yelled.

"Nope," came the response.

"Sorry," said the hayseed as he turned again to face the cowboy. "Are you sure you're at the right place? You're new here. You might ask at Randall's, half a mile or so on your right. Stewart's been feeding their Farmway brand for the past year. It'd be their delivery, not ours."

"Gracious, my mistake," he said politely and headed back out the door. His odds had been fifty-fifty. Where Jim Stewart purchased feed didn't matter as much as the name Dirk, the cowboy, could use as a reference. And Dirk had just confirmed he had found the Stewart Pork he had been instructed to find.

Inside his rusty cab, the cowboy glanced at a map that lay open on the seat. He would pick up County Route 30 a few miles south of town. Double clutching, he shifted into first gear and chugged slowly toward the blacktop in the direction of Randall's Feed Store.

Passing Randall's with only a casual glance, he continued a few miles until a narrow blacktop road appeared on his right where he turned and followed it to County Route 30 and continued for several miles until the blacktop again gave way to gravel. Dust and sand soon filled the cab as he continued without a clue as to where he was, driving between large mounds of sand rising twenty feet or so from the sandy prairie on either side of the narrow road and covered with tall grass and weeds. *Storage bunkers,* he guessed, and then the road turned due east.

He had driven for several miles when a large sign for Stewart's Pork appeared on his left, painted in bright-red letters with the logo for Stewart's Pork, the bust of a grinning pig wearing a chef's hat.

Downshifting, he turned into the drive and crossed over a ribbed livestock barrier that could have served as an early warning of his arrival for the way it shook his seat and every piece of loose metal. A couple hundred yards farther, he rounded another strange mound and found himself in a large parking area about the size of a football field, its perimeter lined with neat white buildings. One had a large white sign that read "OFFICE."

Twenty feet from the office door, he stopped, stepped down from the dusty cab, removed his hat, and used it to beat the dust from his clothes. When the air cleared, he replaced the hat and walked with authority toward the vault-like office door with a sign in bold letters that warned "WARNING—CONFINEMENT AREA. All visitors must register." He entered.

The interior of the office was tidy, consisting of a small waiting area with half-dozen reasonably comfortable chairs. Extending from the middle was a hallway connecting the main office to other offices in the back of the building. To the left of the hall was a glass partition similar to a cashier's booth one might see in some ancient country bank. Behind the glass, a slight woman wearing a white tissue hat, like worn by a surgical nurse, stood at the open drawer of a filing cabinet. She smiled at the cowboy as he approached the glass partition and stooped to speak through a small opening in the glass.

"Dirk, at the coop said you were hiring." It was a guess; hog farms were always hiring cheap migrants. His odds were nine to one. His English was now nearly perfect.

"Yup," replied the woman, who shoved a large leather-bound book under the glass partition. "Sign in, please," she said and walked to an empty desk where she pushed a button near the telephone.

Seconds later, the sound of country music stopped, and Jim Stewart's hearty voice echoed from a speaker on the wall. "Be right there." His words sent the woman back to the glass window where she retrieved the registration book.

"Juan?" she asked, reading what he had written.

"Ma'am?" he responded through the hole in the glass.

"Do you have a last name?" she asked pleasantly.

"Smith. Juan Smith."

"Driver's license? Identification?" she asked as she looked at him through the glass. "Sorry. It's the rule around here."

The cowboy reached into his back pocket and produced a gold-bound leather wallet. Inside, he thumbed through Air Travel card, American Express gold card, Gold Mastercard, and a Platinum Visa card, locating his credit card-sized driver's license at the bottom of the pile. On it was his picture, absent one cowboy hat, some numbers, and the name Juan Smith.

"Thanks," she said. "Have a seat if you like. Jim won't be but a minute." As she spoke, she returned to her filing cabinet, but not until she had made a notation in the book beside Juan's name: New Mexico, the state named on the card.

Jim Stewart's hog business was one of the largest in Western Nebraska. Behind the doors of his ten-million-dollar facility were thousands of genetically selected sows, whose sole function on the planet was to produce offspring, most of which would be raised on location and eventually slaughtered for markets around the world. Some would be sold as future breeding stock, expanding production of the hybrid reduced-fat pork that Jim had spent the last ten years developing.

Jim's farrowing houses, or birthing barns, were as sophisticated as the newest maternity wards of any big urban hospital and, aside from the odor that permeated the air for miles around the complex, were spotlessly clean and free of bacteria. "As sterile as a computer chip assembly plant," Jim would explain to any and all visitors willing to strip down to nothing, shower with a disinfecting liquid, and dawn sterile uniforms and booties before venturing beyond the air-locking doors leading to the heart of each production unit. There were twenty units on the bank's mortgage records.

The "houses" were contained in large earthen structures, remnants of a bygone military-driven era when large bunkers were used for storing munitions and other military paraphernalia. While other pork-producing farms utilized the obsolete bunkers, none did so with the efficiency and sophistication of Stewart Pork. As a result, his business was profitable and growing. This meant that Stewart Pork was, in fact, always hiring. But Jennifer Stewart's brother, Jim, was picky. He relied on no one but himself to interview and confirm a new employee, who, like every member of his team, needed to be the best in the business.

Jim was a perfectionist, and good help had been in short supply of late. He was happy Jennifer had come home to join him. He could use her help, and he could trust her if he could only get her to forget what had happened in Minnesota and get on with her life.

After Jenny's earlier telephone call, he had stayed in his home office finishing up paperwork when, as if an answer to prayer, the potential helper appeared. Five minutes later, he stepped down from his pickup truck and entered his on-site production office. Extending his hand, he looked into the deep dark eyes of Juan Smith. "So you're looking for work?" he asked hopefully.

Chapter 34

"Ya, ya, ya, ya, ya, ya, ya, ya, ya, ya."

The staccato banshee yell caused Dan to jump instinctively as he passed through the revolving door of the domed Minnetonka ice hockey practice arena. His mind had been on the report he held in his hand. *How much would he share with Jenny?* The scream startled him back to the present.

On either side of the door, bleachers rose fifteen steps to the edge of the vinyl bubble that covered the ice arena. He found an opening among the bystanders standing inside and walked toward the four-foot-high wood wall—the boards—defining the perimeter of the skating area.

Again, the yell muffled in the cold air. Its source was a portly man in his thirties wearing a down-filled jacket and a long dangling stocking cap with a tassel on its end, a sight that seemed out-of-place on a hot August day.

The cap made him aware of the cold, and soon his teeth began to chatter—something he could not remember having happened to him before. He wore a short-sleeved shirt and had left his sport jacket locked in his car—a long walk away. Jason's game was in progress, so he decided to ignore the cold and watch.

Glancing about, he spotted Jenny standing one row behind the man in the stocking cap. He thought she looked uncharacteristically solemn-faced, her hands inside the pockets of her fur-lined jacket. *She's beautiful, a most beautiful Eskimo,* thought Dan as he stared at her. Sensing his gaze, she turned toward him and smiled.

He suspected she was quietly laughing at him as she wrapped her arms around herself and shook her body in a mock shiver and nodded her head in lighthearted admonition for his poor choice in clothes.

Weaving his way through the small group of spectators, he walked up the bleachers toward her when suddenly everyone stood to better watch some action on the ice. "Your secretary, Shirley, told me I could find you here," he said, extending his hand. "She didn't warn me about the cold."

They shook hands, and everyone resumed sitting. "It's winter in here. Is it always this cold?"

"Only in the summer," she answered and motioned for him to sit beside her. "It's even colder in the winter. But you dress for it. Then you try to stand beneath one of the heaters." She paused briefly and drew his attention to the long fluorescent-like heaters high above their heads. "And her name is Sharon. My assistant's name is Sharon."

"Oh," he said, his eyes following her upward "They don't appear to be on?" he remarked.

"Don't need them in the summer," said Jenny, smiling at his introduction to Minnesota summer hockey.

"Speak for yourself," he said, a noticeable chatter to his voice. "Next time, I'll bring my jacket." He waved his papers in front of her. "These came today. Can we…?"

"Session's almost over. We can talk outside in a couple of minutes."

Dan nodded then, like everyone else, turned to face the ice. *Don't need the heater in the summer? Who says?* Stoically, he placed his hands inside his pants pockets and tightened every muscle in his body to energize his system in a sorry attempt to keep warm. He had never been to a hockey game, let alone been inside a bubbled ice arena—a fact he found strange having attended college in Syracuse, where hockey was a popular sport.

"Jason is number 11, blue and white, forward position on the left side," Jenny offered, her eyes fixed on the action in front of them.

JENNY

Dan spotted number 11 driving hard in pursuit of a big kid with the puck. His body tensed as he watched number 11 brace himself for impact. But there was no hit. Surprisingly, Jason was alone, racing toward the net, the puck nestled against the curve of his stick with nothing but ice between him and the goal. Dan shook his head in amazement. He had no idea how *11* managed such a maneuver.

Jenny was on her feet, screaming, "Yes! That a boy, Jason." Rising to the moment, the stocking capped banshee popped up into Dan's vision, thrust his fist into the air, and let loose. Dan was grateful he stood behind him.

Also in the moment and no longer conscious of the cold, Dan jumped to his feet. "He's gonna do it! He's gonna do it!" he shouted loud enough that Jenny heard him and smiled. "He's good. Really good," marveled Dan, turning excitedly toward Jenny, stopping short of giving her a hug.

Before Jason could get off a shot, a red silhouette streaked past, bringing a frown to Jenny's face. Following the action, Dan turned to see Jason trip over the red skater's stick and slide headlong into the boards. Someone yelled obscenities at the referee, who stopped play and skated after the red skater who was chasing after the stick he had thrown under Jason's skates. When he picked it up, the referee was waiting for him and, with a wave of his arm, sent the red skater to a door in the perimeter of the wall that was open and waiting for him. "Penalty box," explained Jenny as Jason and his four teammates skated off the ice.

Jenny turned to Dan and spoke into his ear so he could hear. He looked confused. "There's only a few seconds left in the game. Jason won't see another line change. We can talk outside now. Jason will find us. The coach will keep the kids for a while. No need to wait here in the cold."

With Dan leading the way, they made their way through the crowd. Outside, the sun brought welcomed warmth. He crossed the drive, stopping on a grassy knoll. His teeth stopped chattering. Jenny peeled off her parka.

September would arrive in two days, but the waning days of summer had not affected Jenny's tan. She wore Levi's and tennis shoes and a colorful sleeveless blouse that exposed her golden-brown skin. Her hair was pulled back into a ponytail, which swished from side to side as she walked. *She could pass for one of the kids*, thought Dan. *Or someone's older sister. Certainly not the mother of a ten-year-old.*

Dan was genuinely excited to see her again. She had an aura about her, a spirit, a visible zest for life. She seemed different from other women he had known, including his "ex." He felt a gnawing in his heart. *What is this? Get over it, Dan.*

He realized he had been staring at her. But that didn't seem to bother Jenny as she stood two feet from him, squinting into the afternoon sun. He smelled her cologne, and he thought of the movie *Scent of a Woman*.

It was Jenny who broke the silence, "Today was hockey tryouts. Jason is trying out for a traveling team."

"I'm sorry. What?" said Dan, slipping back into reality.

"Today was for preseason traveling team tryouts," she repeated. "The pressure will be on Jason for the next week or so. Today was a scrimmage, not an actual game. It's a time when the coaches make their selections for the coming year. Big stuff here in Minnesota."

Dan struggled for something intelligent to say. "Don't know much about the game, but I'd say he looked pretty good in there. That was some move. I don't know how he got that puck."

"Brains, not brawn. He has great instincts. And that's good because he doesn't have the weight yet. Some of these kids seem bred for muscle. Jason can outskate the big kids, but he can't outmuscle them. Like his dad, he takes the game seriously. Skates like his father too, fast with good moves."

"Your husband, is he here?"

"No," she answered ruefully. "Another corporate acquisition. This one in Washington."

It was obvious to Dan that he had not chosen a good topic to begin his conversation with Jenny.

"How's Jason doing? His tryouts?" Dan asked, changing course.

"Oh, he'll do fine. He shouldn't have any trouble making the team." She paused. "Listen to the proud mother here. But he is one of the better hockey players. We'll have another busy season." In her own mind, she pictured herself standing alone in the arena, supporting Jason as a single parent—driving, watching, waiting while she maintained a career.

There was a brief silence, and Dan asked, "Jason's memory. Anything yet?"

"Actually, he doesn't talk about it. Not anymore. At first, his buddies wouldn't let him forget. He was their celebrity, and he played it really cool. That was before hockey. Now he's a bit preoccupied, working hard, not taking anything for granted. Actually, it's a good diversion…for both of us. Making the team is his only concern right now. You can see, he's good. He'll make it, don't you think?"

"He's in if it's up to me." They both laughed.

"You'll have to take in one of his games. The season starts in November."

"I'd like that. I'd like to watch him play."

"I know Jason would love to have you come."

Sensing their conversation was becoming awkward, Jenny asked, "You said you had a report? Good news or bad?"

"Neither. But it does confirm that Jason was given a drug."

"It's what you expected?" she questioned.

"Yes. I saw something similar used in the Caribbean a few years ago. There it was called Devil's Brew."

"Deranged!" said Jenny.

"Well, so are the people who use it."

"You said there were no lasting side effects. Right?"

"None that we know of. Just short-term memory loss. And that's true only while the drug is in his system. He's acting okay? Nothing strange?"

"Yes, he's acting okay, and no, we've seen nothing strange." She paused. "But you're saying his short-term memory loss will improve now that the drug is out of his system? He will eventually remember what happened to him?"

"Not exactly. He will not experience ongoing short-term memory loss. But he may never remember details of his ordeal while under the influence of the drug." Having said that, Dan noticed a concerned look on Jenny's face.

"So…you're saying we have nothing more to fear because Jason won't remember anything to upset his kidnappers?"

"That's possible. His kidnappers probably know the effects of the drug. But that's not a sure thing."

"So what are you saying?"

"I'm saying remain cautious and alert. We're dealing with really bad people here. They destroy lives. They should be feared. They also need to be stopped." Dan was thinking about Sadler's request for help and Jenny's link to Creighton Leonard, but this wasn't the time to ask. "That's all, just caution."

The arena's entrance was a revolving door to minimize the loss of cold air inside the arena when people came and went. It was now spinning, spitting out sweaty kids laden with gear in baggy hockey shorts (breezers). Jason was one of the kids swinging an oversized duffel bag at his side. He spotted his mom and smiled when he recognized Dan.

"I'm sorry. I thought we'd have more time," said Jenny as Jason approached. "Oh, the videos? Were you able to get the news videos from the networks?"

"They're still promised. They should come any time. Stone will come through. In the meanwhile, we do have some security footage to examine, if you're up to that?"

"I don't understand," Jenny questioned.

"We have the tapes from Abel's security cameras taken about the time the truck was stolen. You may recognize someone or something. You and your husband could come to my office. If he's in town."

"He returns Friday. Leaves again on Monday." She embraced Jason, who approached all smiles. "Chris gets in about noon, Friday.

How about for dinner at our home? That might be the only way to catch Chris. He's anxious to see the tapes. So is Jason. Bring your wife or a friend if you'd like. I know it's rather awkward, but really, it might be the only way to include Christian."

"Thanks. Dinner sounds good. Getting out of my world at Mall of America is always a welcome change. And I'm not married. Not seeing anyone either currently. So I'll be solo. Friday would be fine."

Jason smiled at his words but remained silent.

"Great play, Jason," said Dan. "You would have scored. Where'd that kid come from? The one that tripped you."

"Cheap shot!" responded Jason. `

Jenny ran her hands through Jason's sweaty hair, not thinking. "Yuck!" she exclaimed. "Jason, Dan is going to join us for dinner on Friday. Have any other plans?"

Jason shrugged. She turned to Dan. "Five o'clock, okay?"

"Fine," he answered and added apologetically, "now I've got to run." He began to slowly back away and asked, "Jason, how about that boat ride?"

"Mom?" Jason asked as he looked at his mother.

"Sure. You and your dad…Don't see why not," Jenny spoke loud enough that Dan could hear. He gave one last wave, turned and continued his long walk to his car.

Chapter 35

On Friday, Jenny stood at her kitchen window. Small puffy clouds moving lazily in a gentle breeze dotted the deep-blue fall sky. In the distance, Jason was busily cleaning up *Little Red*, as he anxiously awaited the arrival of his father and his new hero, Dan. From her vantage point, she could see the area on the deck where Nicki had found the diamond tiepin. Her eyes moved to that spot, and suddenly the events of that formidable day played back in a foggy collage as she began preparing dinner and looked at the clock, *where was Chris?*

Nicki had called earlier and reported that unforeseen problems had surfaced in Seattle, and Chris's firm was obliged to *fix it,* a task that became Chris's to accomplish. This was an all-too-familiar scenario as far as Jenny was concerned, but Chris had given her his word—almost promised—he'd move heaven and earth and meet Dan Sheridan personally to thank him for all he had done. As always, Jenny would honor his good intentions and trust him to show up on time, but believed it when it happens. This was not the day for it not to happen.

She was eager for Christian and Dan to meet; they had similar personalities. Perhaps that's why she found Dan attractive, not only because of his handsome features, but from what little she knew of him he possessed character qualities that attracted her to certain men, beginning with her father: aggressive, strong-willed, determined, devoted to their work, and devoted to family, if Dan had one. She didn't know about Dan's spiritual side, but she'd discover that as the evening progressed. Christian would draw that out of him. She believed with all her heart a personal relationship with Jesus Christ was the most important quality of all, and that determined the depth and strength of the others. She smiled as she considered their similarities.

Chris loved steak—thick, lightly seasoned, and warm red in the middle—and she suspected Dan's taste was the same. Like an artist, she added a final layer of seasoning to three thick slabs of meat the butcher had selected and glanced again at the clock when the phone rang. It better be Chris calling from the airport; it had to be.

"Mrs. Poole? This is Peter. Peter Webster. Is Jason home?" said the small voice.

On the dock, Jason heard the phone ring and turned toward the kitchen as Jenny tapped the window to get his attention. He quickly sprinted from the dock to the patio phone. Peter was having a tough time with his parent's separation. And with school starting soon and prospects bleak for the two boys spending much time together, the calls were becoming frequent. Her heart ached for Peter. So did Jason's.

Within minutes, Jason appeared outside her window mouthing his plea, "Say yes." To what, she wondered. When the phone rang again, she understood. It was Susan Webster. As Jenny expected, Peter was having a particularly bad day, and his mother was hoping Jason could spend the night to keep his mind off the divorce. Jason was good for Peter, his best remedy for the blues. "I can pick him up," she pleaded.

Outside her window, Jason was patiently waiting. His ordeal of the last couple weeks seemed to be fading. Why bring it up again? With Jason away for the evening, the three adults could better discuss any action they should take, and either allay her fears or create greater concern for Chris, who seemed to be adjusting better than she.

"He's welcome for dinner," Susan pleaded again.

"It's not that." Jenny needed to think it through. "We have a dinner guest and a boat ride planned. He probably could care less about dinner." She paused. "All right. We can do the boat ride first." Another pause. "Chris will drop Jason at the Gordon's dock. Five-thirty or so?"

Jenny smiled at Jason through the window and gave him a thumbs-up and hung up the phone. Jason understood and bounded for the door. "Well?" Jason gasped out of breath at the kitchen's entrance.

"You set me up," responded Jenny and pulled him close, giving him a hug. "How about this FBI stuff? Lost interest already?"

"No. Not really. You'll make me leave for the good part anyway. Besides, you'll just sit around after dinner and talk. Boring. Peter's got a new radio-controlled car. You know, his dad. Sounds more fun to me. We're going on the boat still?"

"You men can take the boat out. Dad will drop you off at the Gordon's dock. You're going for dinner too. Peter's mom will bring you home tomorrow. You'll leave as soon as your dad gets home. Peter's mom is holding dinner. She can't wait too long."

"We're going by boat? Dan too?"

"It'll be one fast ride. Think you can handle it?"

"Cool…Full throttle. No problem, Mom."

Jenny sent Jason to pack his duffle bag for an overnight when she heard a knock at the front door. It was Dan holding a paper bag. He surprised her when she opened the door by planting a friendly peck on her cheek like they were old friends, or cousins, or something. *Similar personalities?* She wondered. *Would Chris kiss another strange woman so freely? What could he be thinking?* It would be an interesting evening. *Where was Chris?*

"Come in. Chris should be here any minute." She relieved him of his bag—it contained two bottles of wine, she could tell by its feel. "Jason is going to a friend's for the evening. He's gathering his stuff and will be down in a moment. He's been very excited to see you again." Jenny led the way into the kitchen.

"There's one red and one white. Didn't know what you were serving. You do drink wine?" Dan asked with some hesitation.

JENNY

"On special occasions. This is one of those," she offered with a smile. "You chose well," she said, stripping off the paper bag and setting the bottles on the center island. "A Merlot and a Chardonnay. The menu tonight is steak. How do you like yours?"

"Not fussy, but prefer it on the rare side. Guess you'd say red-center and warm."

Why did I ask? Jenny asked herself, smiling.

"Hi, Dan." It was Jason. He entered the kitchen carrying his overnight bag, set it down in the doorway as the telephone rang. Jenny picked up the portable and headed for the quiet of the laundry room.

Chris's voice brought an anguished sigh. "Jenny, we've got big problems here." That was it. Not even a "hi, honey." Chris was stressed.

"Where's here. Chris, where are you? Did the airline lose your bags?" Jenny asked, knowing too well his answer.

"No. Jenny, I never got on the plane."

"Chris. No! You can't do this. Not again. Not tonight! Jason and Dan Sheridan are both waiting for you. Steaks are ready. The tapes. That was the purpose for tonight. You promised."

"He'll leave the tapes, won't he? We can watch them anytime?"

"Anytime? Another time? We could be running out of time and not know it. Chris, we were going to do this together. Remember?"

"I'm sorry, Jenny. There was no other way to play it. All hell has broken loose here. We've got one side yelling 'foul,' while the other side's yelling 'lawsuit.' Believe me, this was not my set agenda either."

"I know, honey. Nicki briefed me. It's just…it's just that I need you here. Now, not later! So when…?"

"Probably two or three days. At least we attorneys have agreed to work through the weekend. This is happening because some lowlife steward is posturing for more power. Jen, I'm sorry," Chris said meekly, offering his olive branch one last time.

"I know…I know." She knew only too well. "Peter's mom is expecting Jason for dinner and to spend the night. You three guys were going to deliver Jason by boat." While she talked, she headed back into the kitchen and spied Jason and Dan heading toward the dock. "Two of you three guys are already waiting on the dock. I've got to go, Chris. Peter is waiting. His mom is waiting with dinner. Three days? Got to go. Bye, Chris."

"Wait! Jason won't be there?" asked Chris, suddenly wishing more than ever that he had walked out of the negotiations and caught his plane, an act that no doubt would have earned him considerable more time at home while he searched for a new job. "Reschedule!"

"Too late! We'll talk later. The puck is in play across the blue line. Chris, I have to go. Bye," she said in the vernacular she knew Chris would understand.

Chris wanted to continue the conversation but spoke to a dead line. "Play...Blue line?"

Chapter 36

It had been years since Dan had been onboard a boat of any kind. He remembered the days on Florida's Lake Okeechobee, a brief period in his life filled with true happiness. How life can change. A vision of racing across Lake Okeechobee with his wife Gale came and went like a soap bubble in the wind.

Back in the moment, he watched Jason take the keys from his mother and ignite *Little Red's* sturdy engine while his mother untied the ropes, setting the boat free to move slowly down the long channel toward the main lake. *Yes, how life can change.* For a few moments, he processed the turbulent events that had brought them together, the purpose for his coming for dinner.

Jenny sat between Dan and Jason, with Jason at the controls, a position to which she grudgingly acquiesced so her eager son could show off his boating skill. And more than once, Dan caught himself staring at her; his eyes tracing her soft, youthful features, catching the subtle scent of her cologne, watching wisps of hair dance across her face, driven by the wind from the boat's forward motion. He had not anticipated the games his mind would play and the feeling of loneliness those games would bring. The pain of the past had not changed.

The last thing he had expected was to be alone with Jennifer Poole, the woman he had privately committed to protect, the woman he was becoming dangerously attracted to. In fact, as much as he would enjoy the companionship, had he known of her husband's absence, he would have suggested they reschedule, if only to protect her from himself.

With such a last-minute change in plans, Jenny's only comment had come when she appeared on the dock. "Chris can't make it. He's stuck in Seattle. Let's see if *Little Red* still runs." She then instructed Dan where to sit to give her access to the kill cord. He knew the kill cord was to shut down the boat's engine, but he wondered if kill cord could have a double meaning, and if her husband could be the one doing the killing—his. Obviously not. But also obvious was her anger toward her husband. Without saying a word, he did as he was told.

Jason maneuvered *Little Red* around a large branch that had blown in from last night's storm and made his way down the channel bordered by tall reeds and soft tubular cattails waving in the disturbed waters. Trees on the shore hinted of orange, yellow, and auburn fall colors. It was beautiful.

No one spoke. When they reached open water, Jenny pointed south toward Excelsior, the course they followed on most Thursdays, the course they had taken the day Jason was kidnapped, the day he couldn't remember. Jason smiled and pushed the throttle forward.

Traffic on the lake was light for a Friday, made so by the lateness of the season—summer's end, shorter days and cool evenings. But tonight was warm, warmer than average for the time of year, and delightful. Dan had no idea where they were or where they were going as he watched the stately lake homes and cabins parade slowly by. He lowered his hand into the water and relaxed in its warm motion. He could see the town of Excelsior in the distance and wondered if that was their destination. Then as he turned to ask Jenny, he caught a glimmer in Jason's eye.

Jenny caught it too and knowingly nodded her approval. This was the moment Jason was waiting for. He turned toward Dan, smiled excitedly, gave him a thumbs-up and pushed the throttle forward. Dan was surprised by the sudden thrust and the force pushing him back against his seat as *Little Red* jumped out of the water and onto plane. A minute later, Jason eased up on the throttle, and *Little Red* settled into a fast cruise. They headed south toward Excelsior for half a mile and then began a sweeping turn to the east toward Woodland five miles away.

Jason glanced at Dan, whose expression said he was impressed. They were cruising now at fifty miles per hour. Short fall days brought the autumn sun close to the horizon, coloring the sky in shades of pink and yellow that reflected off passing windows as sheets of gold. The sight was impressive and brought a smile to Dan's windblown face.

It seemed only minutes before Jason nosed *Little Red* toward Woodland's shore on the east end of the lake. Dan looked at Jason, waiting for him to reduce speed, alarmed at their fast approach. Jenny showed no concern, but then she held the kill cord. As he considered their pending doom, Jason pulled back on the throttle and coasted the hundred feet to the dock, where he cranked the wheel, pulled the throttle into reverse, and magically swung the stern to the dock's edge.

"Wow!" shouted Dan, applauding enthusiastically as *Little Red* gently kissed the dock. Jenny smiled proudly, hiding her surprise.

"Thanks," Jason responded, beaming wide and pulling himself out from behind the wheel. Peter Webster was on the shore. Jason grabbed his overnight bag and deftly jumped to the dock. He would join Peter for a short walk to the Webster home.

Jenny and Dan watched them disappear across the Gordon's lawn and up the road. "We've got some good sun left," said Jenny finally and asked, "Care to see more of the lake?"

"Why not," responded Dan.

He watched Jenny slide behind the wheel, fasten the kill cord to a belt loop and smile furtively. The ride over had been exhilarating with Jason behind the wheel; what now, he wondered, with Jason's mother at the wheel as she eased the throttle forward.

They pulled slowly from the dock. Dan looked at Jenny. He was beginning to understand Jenny's love for the lake. Clearly, she had forgotten her disappointment with Chris. The lake had performed its magic. Dan could read it in her expression. This was Jenny's passion.

"This is Maplewood," said Jenny. "A small community, home of a couple hundred families. Actually, a neighborhood in the city of Woodland. It's where I was raised." Jenny maneuvered slowly along the shoreline, the sun sinking behind them.

"It's all very nice. Very nice. I can see you weren't exactly a ghetto child," kidded Dan. Jenny hit a switch on the dash to turn on the boat's navigation lights.

"No." Jenny chuckled. "It's true the families here are affluent, but they're also very real. I enjoyed a wonderful childhood. I realize now how much I took for granted."

"What money can't buy," quipped Dan.

"Not happiness. And I was a happy child. I had love, discipline, but not a lot of things."

Neither spoke for several minutes. Finally, Dan remembered the reason for their getting together. "This is the kind of wealth that attracts a kidnapper. Have you thought much more about that possibility?"

A reality check. "Yes, some. But there was no ransom demand."

"Possibly something went wrong before the ransom call, forcing a change in plans." He paused. "Then there was that man on your deck."

After motoring slowly for several minutes, Jenny pointed in the direction of the lake town of Wayzata. "Pretty, isn't it?" The sinking sun reflected of the windows painting the town gold—a heavenly confirmation of the community's wealth. Dan nodded agreement.

"Did you get the tapes?" asked Jenny.

"They came today. Compliments of Donald Stone and Gary Sadler's prodding."

"The FBI chief?" asked Jenny, surprised by the FBI chief's intervention on her behalf. "He knows I've asked for the tapes?"

"He knows. He carries more weight with Stone than I do. I asked him to pressure Stone, and he did. Stone seemed to be dragging his feet, and I wanted to bring them tonight. He's hoping you'll see something to help his investigation. They're in the car."

"So now you're working with the FBI?" she asked, sarcasm intended. "Do you report back to him what we talk about if it may help him?"

"No…And yes. Sadler's a friend. Not a bad friend to have, by the way. For you either. Isn't that what we're all about? Catching the people who took Jason? Before they can do it again? To anyone? You had asked the other day whether Sadler would continue his investigation. He is. And he's keeping me in the loop. It's give and take." This was not the time to tell her of Sadler's interest in her employer, Creighton Leonard, so he changed the subject. "Why do you ask?"

"Why am I concerned about your working for the FBI?" asked Jenny, a little bewildered.

"Yes. When you know we need their help."

"I'm not really. I mean, I know we need their help. I guess I need to know if I should be on guard with you and watch what I say. Not that I'd say anything I'd be concerned about getting back to Mr. Sadler. It's just that possibly I could do something the police would not like. He is the police."

"You may be surprised there. He's a realist," he said, considering Sadler's request. "But then, it depends on what you have in mind." He paused. "Jenny, what do you have in mind?"

"Nothing. But no one has been able to tell me why this has happened to me, to my son. That bothers me. That bothers me a lot. I don't think I can rest until I know why and the person behind it has been caught."

"Finding that answer will take time, Jenny. Why was he abducted? Why was he returned? Let's face it, someone put forth a great deal of effort to choreograph stealing the truck and kidnapping Jason. As it is, they took only Jason. Is that because at the time he was all that was available? What would have happened if you both had left together? Have you thought of that?"

"No. I guess I haven't."

"So they had Jason and released him where he would be quickly found. Remember the man who called me told me Jason's name and exactly where to find him? He could have told anyone in my office, yet he made sure he was speaking with me. In retrospect, I'd say he wanted to make sure Jason was found. What changed their plans? Or was that the plan all along. I'd doubt that. So who would want him as badly as these people and then have a change in heart? These are difficult questions to answer. We learn these answers, and we hit the winning home run. But I don't think this game will end quickly."

Jenny could only agree. Finding answers would be difficult. Chris promised to be home to help. But once again, well-intended or not, he was *unavailable* because the firm had changed his priorities. If she had to find the answers on her own, she would. She had known that from the beginning. Nothing's changed.

For the moment, the sun was setting, and she had miles of shoreline to meander. Dan was the one person who could help her find her answers. Who better to protect her and her son if she dug too deep. He was God's provision in her time of need.

"Hang on," she said. Dan grabbed the sissy bar in front of him. He had seen the sun sink to the horizon and understood the ride home would be fast. Jenny pushed the throttle full forward, kicking it harder and faster than Jason had. The sudden acceleration threw him back into his seat. A buoy appeared quickly. Clearing it, Jenny cranked the wheel into a sharp right turn that lifted Dan from his seat, centrifugal force pulling at him. He locked his knees under the dash to stop from flying out of the cockpit. When their course straightened, Jenny accelerated to maximum speed, sending the speedometer needle to seventy.

She followed the shoreline. Stately homes, docks, and boats under colorful canopies blurred by. "Spirit Knob," Jenny yelled, referring to the point of distant land. Dan strained to hear over the loud whine of the engine. "Once sacred to the Indians, who kept the lake's whereabouts hidden from the white man."

She turned sharply to port, keeping the shore at a safe distance, forcing Dan to slide across the seat toward her. Turning again, shoreline on her right disappeared and slammed him against the side of the boat. Jenny looked at him and smiled. Turns became more gradual as they cruised the eastern shore of Wayzata Bay and finally turned toward the west. The sun was a ball of fire sinking below the tree-lined shore seven miles ahead. Jenny was in her element, skimming the lake's calm surface on two inches of transom, riding a cushion of air passing under the boat's unique tunnel hull.

Passing Spirit Island, Jenny pointed the boat toward Big Island's north shore. Tears formed in Dan's eyes from the wind's assault as Jenny tweaked the propeller depth and coaxed the boat to the full limit of its hull design as *Little Red* screamed into the open water of Lower Lake Minnetonka.

Neither Dan nor Jenny spoke until Jenny pulled back the throttle and eased *Little Red* into the entrance of her reed-lined channel. "That was some ride," Dan said finally.

"A good way to unwind," Jenny responded and continued in silence until they reached the dock. The sky was a beautiful muted gold, silhouetting the towering cottonwoods, willows, and maples that dotted the distant channel's edge. Cars moving along the road perpendicular to the end of the channel already had their headlights on. Nights were coming early, summer would soon be a memory, and winter a harsh reality. But until then, fall. Dan had learned that fall in Minnesota was the most beautiful season of all.

At the dock, he jumped off. Jenny tossed him the stern line and watched with interest as he secured the boat with a half hitch. Satisfied that he could tie a secure knot, she walked to the front of the boat, grabbed the bowline, and jumped to the dock.

Dan extended his hand. "Allow me," he said with a smile. She smiled back and handed him the line, which he promptly secured to the dock post and took a step backward to admire his work. "It all comes back to you."

"Not too shabby. You've been around boats?" she noted and headed toward the town house.

"Some boats. One similar to this actually. Not as fast or high-tech, but the fish didn't mind. I was in school then. I would spend a good portion of my summers fishing on weekends. One summer, I trailered my boat through the South, hitting every bass tournament I could find."

"Well, I don't fish," declared Jenny. "Not for real anyway. I leave that to Jason and Chris." She climbed the steps to her deck and motioned for Dan to enter the living room through the sliding glass doors.

"Please, after you," he replied. Jenny smiled and stepped inside.

Dan followed her in and said, "It is a beautiful lake, Jenny. I can see that once Minnetonka gets into your blood you can't stay away. Certainly not for long. I appreciate the ride...and the racy tour," he said and jokingly wiped his brow in mock relief.

"You must have had a wonderful childhood growing up in this environment. I've always loved the water, rivers, lakes, oceans." He followed her into the kitchen where she checked the machine for messages. Finding none, she turned his way and smiled. *Off limits*, he said to his aching heart.

"About tonight...dinner? I can come back another time when your husband is home."

"Don't be silly. Who knows when that might happen? There's nothing certain with his career right now. Besides, we've got work to do. I'll fill Chris in later," assured Jenny without hesitation.

"Okay. What can I do to help? I used to be a wizard with a grill. Just direct me to the charcoal, I'll take care of the rest."

"It's a gas grill," she corrected. "You said the tapes were in your car. While you get them, I'll get you the igniter so you can play Boy Scout." She went to the cupboard and returned a moment later with a butane igniter in hand.

Chapter 37

Like most working farms in the United States, Stewart Pork knew no time clock and operated seven days a week. But this was Friday, and for employees who did keep the clock, the weekend was a time to unwind, which most did, wherever one could, through whatever means was convenient, even if not appropriate.

A major component of Jim Stewart's success was Jim's appreciation and respect for his employees' needs, which he honored above his own convenience, even corporate profits, which grew steadily, nonetheless. He looked out for his employees; they looked out for him, and somehow all the work got done. It was a fact emulated by competitors and neighboring farms. But weekends presented some unique problems because shift personnel were reduced in number. This Friday was no exception. At the stroke of 5:00 p.m., Jim's employees went to the time clock and punched out for their needed time off, time away from Jim's pigs.

Jim is impressively industrious by nature, a quality he nurtured by keeping his life as free from distraction as possible. For the next forty-eight hours, Jim would become a one-man band with limited help from a handful of trusted and dedicated staff who obviously loved him, their jobs, and their paychecks. He had never married. He didn't drink. He was social, but only to a point. He thrived on hard work, and on any given weekend, worked harder than anyone knew. When speaking before civic groups and high school seniors, his mantra was "profitability begins with hard work." Stewart Pork was a sterling example of hard work's reward.

Jim was also quick to point out that true success resulted from the contribution of others who shared the vision, exercised their knowledge, and cared about the result. Jenny Stewart was one such person who cared. His sister hated his pigs but loved him dearly. However, for the moment, she was concerned for her own well-being. She had invaded her brother's life by storm, beginning with a telephone call in the middle of the night. Stricken with fear, she sought Jim's protection. She had no place else to go, no place else to hide.

Fear of a lonely existence in obscurity had driven her from the family farm three years earlier; now fear of her discovery and her need for obscurity drew her back, back to Green Bend, Nebraska. Someone was chasing her; she needed a place to hide. What better place could there be than a solitary farm, miles from town, where security was nearly as effective as Fort Knox?

Visiting briefly with the Bakers had helped stem her apparent paranoia. And while the events, which prompted her hasty departure from WYCO Toys, were not entirely forgotten, they had diminished, proving to be not all she had imagined—*imagined* being the operative word. She was beginning to relax and accept Jim's assurance that she could remain invisible in Green Bend. After all, no one at WYCO Toys knew her background. Not even her boyfriend, Ted, who had been eagerly looking forward to a weekend of camping—and anything else Jenny might offer. *What do you do alone in the woods?* She would not take the chance to call him. She never did intend for Ted to be long-term. Her life would go on.

She had left Green Bend for a career away from the farm. Jim was her only family. Their parents had died a few years earlier, mostly the result of too much work, work they loved. But it was work that consumed them and eventually killed them. Yes, the pigs were to blame, although she couldn't prove it. Living for so long, working in such foul air just wasn't healthy.

Farm life was a solitary life, too solitary for Jenny. She had friends in Green Bend, but no deep ties, ties she would gladly sever for a real career in Minnesota and greater rewards. She had attended a junior college in Lincoln but found class work as tedious as tending the pigs. That meant she could move on or return home to the work she sought to escape. That's what her friends had done. The boys who went away to school, and there were some keepers in the bunch, either stayed away or returned to a life of slopping pigs. From her point of view, the keepers had all moved on. All but Jim.

Jim too had gone away to college and armed with new vision returned to the hogs. Jenny admired him greatly and had watched with family pride the adaptation of his vision to drudgery she longed to escape. She knew that soon, Jim would have no other life. He insisted he had learned that farm life could be different with new ideas, new technology. Maybe it was for him, not so for her. "What's different?" she had asked repeatedly. "The work hasn't changed the long hours. You have no more life than Mom and Dad." That's when the conversation usually ended.

"You'll be back too," he would say. And here she was, but she didn't plan to stay. However, as brief as her stay may be, she owed it to the brother she loved to help out any way possible. She would not be a burden; she would try not to distract him from his work.

He had introduced her to Juan Smith, whom he hired the day she reunited with the Bakers. He had worked a hog farm in New Mexico, not as big as Jim's, but the breeding and farrowing operations were similar in technology. He had all the right answers to Jim's questions.

He was a migrant, but legal and well-educated, claiming a degree in animal husbandry. He boasted being a father of six kids, whose mother would follow if the job worked out. He was taciturn, still friendly once you got him talking. And he was a good worker who didn't need to be told what to do because he loved pigs with a passion—Jim liked his passion. The New Mexico operation simply had been too small to utilize his talents.

Juan had shared these tidbits of his life while they worked the aisles in the houses, tending to the new mothers and their offspring. At first, she found it strange that he ignored other migrants who worked quietly around him. But he really was not one of them, considering his education and background. His clunky diamond ring said that much.

Jim had placed a call to Juan's previous employer after first calling information to confirm the telephone number Juan had provided. Speaking to an answering machine, he left a message requesting that someone—anyone—return his call. That was three days ago. Jim would call again when he got the chance. In the meantime, Juan's work spoke for itself. He was willing, eager, and able. He also requested to work over the weekend—a request Jim honored without hesitation.

Jenny was tending to a nine-hundred-pound mother of sixteen, when she heard the large metal door open and close at the far end of the long confinement building. She was kneeling beside the cage-like structure of a farrowing pen, out of the line of sight of whoever had entered.

"Jenny, are you in here?" It was Juan's voice. "Are you in here, Jenny?" the voice asked again. "There is a matter we must discuss."

"What is it, Juan?" Jenny yelled back as she stopped what she was doing and stood to address him. "We're not working together today. Jim needs you to work barn 10."

"This will not take long, Jenny. We must talk." He too was yelling to be heard over the loud whir of a dozen large exhaust fans and began to walk toward her. He was dressed like Jenny in white coveralls that had been sanitized and stored outside the showers within each barn complex, where everyone sterilized their body before entering the confinement area. Over his white coveralls, he wore long oversized white rubber boots that sloshed as he walked.

Jenny was about to scold him for following her into the barn. She knew he had not had time to shower. Such a breach of Jim's rules could be disastrous. Coming directly from another barn could introduce foreign bacteria and contaminate, even devastate, Jim's production. Knowing Juan knew better sounded an alarm that suddenly loaded her adrenaline. Something was different. She knelt down again to give the impression she was working, but as she did, she raised her head to peer over the cage. He was different. A menacing scowl distorted his usually smiling face. In his hand was a strand of coiled wire. Instinct said, *Run*!

"You almost got away, Jenny. But we went to your apartment," he told her. His voice had become a growl, no longer melodic and gentle. "We would not have found you. But we found your notepad. Right there by the phone. Your notepad with a little piggy with its curly tail. The piggy with a chef's hat. On the hat was the name Stewart Pork. It was too much of a coincidence to be a coincidence, Jenny. I am sorry. You saw too much. You were, as they say, in the wrong place at the right time."

She knew why he had come. "But I didn't see anything," she yelled. "Some people in a lighted room. What's that to see? Please, I didn't see anything. I swear," she pleaded, her eyes darting about the room, looking for…escape. When she looked down at her feet, she saw her answer, the pail of disinfectant she had been using to scrub down the new mother.

Juan blocked her only exit. If he were only closer, she could beat him back to the door; she was younger, faster. She bent even lower, pretending to hide as though she were overcome with fear, powerless to move, paralyzed by the realization that her life was about to end. Like one of Jim's pig in the slaughterhouse, the soon-to-be-executed waiting for the executioner.

The stainless-steel pail of disinfectant was too heavy for her to pick up and throw. It sat on a low cart that contained every item she might need to provide immediate postnatal care for Jim's expensive sows and their equally valuable offspring. She had been working her way down a long aisle of birthing cages to a crossway connecting similar aisles on her right and left. Juan's sloshing boots were no more than thirty feet away, moving toward her down an adjacent aisle.

On the service cart was a large vat of liquid nursing formula. Hanging from the vat's curved handle was a dipper used to pour the liquid milk into baby bottles that would be used to feed each piglet. Cautiously, Jenny grasped the dipper and quietly placed it into the pail of disinfectant and in one seamless movement slid the pail behind her to keep her hand out of Juan's sight, as his boots sloshed closer, now only steps away. He had uncoiled the wire, which now dangled from his hand inches above the damp concrete floor. There was a handle on each end, which she knew had only one purpose.

She gauged her timing. Her eyes on the loose handle. At the instant the handle began to raise, she jumped to her feet and thrust the dipper of disinfectant into Juan's face. He jumped backward, but too late, spitting and wiping his eyes, holding back screams of pain. It was a purple liquid containing a dye that enabled the attendant to identify the treated sows. It was now a purple uniform that pursued Jenny; the person inside disciplined and trained to deal with pain, which blurred his vision and slowed his pace—thank God.

Jenny's tighter fitting boots provided better traction than Juan's on the wet concrete. Twice he slipped, falling to his knees, giving her precious seconds longer to live. At the far end of the barn, she turned toward the center aisle and to the door leading to the outside corridor. Rounding the last corner, she too slipped on the wet concrete, where a hose had been left running to wash away urine and feces. She landed in the trough with two inches of liquid; the seconds she had gained now lost.

Instantly, she was back on her feet. She could hear Juan's sloshing boots but refused to look back. He was close. Too close.

A second cart with nursing bottles sat crosswise in the aisle. She hurdled it, but her ankle caught, knocking over the warm vat of liquefied formula. Milk covered the path in front of her; the stainless-steel vat clanged like a fire bell as it rolled down the aisle and careened off the metal bars of the birthing cages.

At the door, her wet slimy hands slipped on the knob. It refused to open. She kicked at the bottom, struggling with the knob and yelled for help. More precious seconds lost.

Finally, it gave, and the knob turned, and the heavy metal door yielded to her weight. As it swung open, she found the light switch and pushed the large black button to the fresh sound of a metal vat clanging down the aisle behind her. Once outside, she pushed the door closed, leaving Juan on the other side groping in total darkness.

There was no lock. Neither was there anything in the corridor that she could wedge against the door. She turned and ran down the long corridor to the office. The office shimmered gold from the setting autumn sun. Suddenly, one very bright light, activated by a motion detector, switched on as she passed. Darting into the reception area, she stopped, looked back, and swore at the door she had just passed through then quickly threw open the office door.

Jim's truck was visible in the yard, but there was no sign of Jim. She yelled his name. After the third time, she ran toward the mechanic's barn, fifty yards across the drive. The doors were open. She ran inside.

The back of the barn was dark. She ran into the darkness to seek a place to hide. But, like the farrowing barn, a halogen security lamp was activated by a motion detector. As she passed its sensors, light exploded around her. Dazed by the sudden brilliance, she moved in circles, forcing her eyes to focus and to find a way of escape.

A weapon. A weapon. The barn held tractors, service carts, stainless buckets, and other contraptions she couldn't imagine. Everything tidy, there was nothing loose that she could grab and use to defend herself. At the far end of the barn was a large tool chest. She ran toward it. She knew Juan would not be far behind. Lifting the lid, she grabbed the closest tool, a large heavy wrench.

But where to hide? Beside one of the tractors stood a tall locker with several doors spread along its face. She turned, ran to it, and tried one of the doors. It was unlocked and squeaked as she pulled it open. Small enough to stand inside, she stepped in, closed the door behind her, and listened.

In the noiseless compartment, she wondered if Juan had seen the lights flick on and had gone to one of the other barns. She waited for a minute, maybe two, hearing only the beating of her own heart. What had she stumbled upon after hours that would cause anyone to chase her all the way to Nebraska? Who were the people being filmed in the corporate conference room without their clothes? They were not filming a commercial. Whoever it was, was making a pornographic movie. That had to be the case. But was that so serious that someone would want her dead? There was more to it, perhaps that one familiar face? It had not been Juan's, who was about to kill her.

What was that? A muffled sound? Barely audible was the sound of Juan's oversized rubber boots. He had entered the barn, moving slowly, listening, searching, and growing closer. Her hand tightened on the wrench. Then she heard Jim's voice in the distance, calling her name.

"I'm here. I'm here," she wanted to yell. But the sloshing boots were too close. In her mind, she pictured Juan moving slowly toward the back of the barn. Soon he was directly in front of her. He was there. She knew it. She could sense his presence. He was studying the cabinet. She found it strange that she could know what he was doing, but she knew. He was inching his way toward her. She could smell him. The odor of disinfectant drifted through the ventilation cracks above her. It was time to act. She wouldn't just wait to die.

With every ounce of strength, she thrust the door open. She was right; Juan stood only inches in front of the door that slammed toward him, catching him squarely on the nose. He jumped backward, his hands to his face. Jenny leaped from the cabinet and swung at him awkwardly with the wrench. She missed but succeeded in pushing him to the ground with her free hand and the weight of her body as the wrench dropped to the floor.

She attempted to jump over Juan's sprawled body, but his hands clasped tightly around her ankle, immobilizing her. He rolled to one side, jerked, and then twisted her leg, sending a shooting pain to her knee, bringing her quickly to the ground beside him.

In an instant, he was on top of her, pulling her by the hair, jerking her head off the floor. She felt the wire sliding under her neck and slid her hand upward and under the thin wire, feeling it cut her skin as he pulled it tightly closed. All she could do was look up at the purple mass above her. Juan's nose was bleeding profusely from being struck by the door. His cheek had an open gash, probably from a fall in the dark. He reeked of urine and manure, only faintly masked by the strong odor of disinfectant. *What a sight to remember on your way to heaven or hell. Which would it be?* she wondered and closed her eyes.

Neither. As she waited, tension on the wire slackened, and she heard *thunk* before Juan's body went limp and crumpled on top of her. It seemed like an eternity before she rolled slowly from under the stinking body of her would-be executioner. Above her stood Jim. In his hand was a very large wrench. Gasping for air, she struggled to her feet and, after a long moment, wrapped her arms around her brother's neck and wept.

"I heard it all, Jenny. Saw some of it on the monitors."

"Thank God for the cameras?" she sobbed.

"No one knows about the hidden cameras but you. I can't be everyplace at once, but with the cameras I can see where I'm needed and go." Jim held her close and stroked her hair. "Something just didn't seem right. I don't know…Where he worked before, in New Mexico, they didn't call back. I had just gone to the office to call them. Juan didn't go to barn 10. He wasn't on the monitor. There were no sounds. When I switched to your monitor, I could hear him screaming at you. I don't know…I seemed powerless to move. Like I was watching a movie or something. I watched until the lights went out."

"Jim!" she exclaimed.

"I know. I'm sorry."

"He was going to kill me!" declared Jenny in amazement.

"I know. I just couldn't believe it," Jim said slowly, emotionally.

"Now we know they've found me. They know I'm here."

"He was alone. We don't know if there are others," Jim said, knowing better.

"There's more than him, Jim. Can't you see that? He said *they* went through my room and found one of your notepads. You heard him. He said, 'We found…' What have I done, Jim? What did I see?"

"What did you see, Jenny? Think!" Jim urged as he gently pushed her away, straightening her with a hand on each shoulder. You'd think she hadn't told him, but she had several times over. He simply had not listened.

"Nothing. That's just it. Nothing to get killed for."

"Sounds like someone was filming a porn movie," Jim said, thinking back to Jenny's telephone call from the freeway gas station. "But it must be more than that."

"Yes, I agree." Jenny turned, shaking her head, wringing her hands in disbelief. "Now you're in danger," she said and began to weep again. "I never should have come! Jim! I never should have come!"

"Cool it, Jenny. We'll deal with it. You're safer here with me than any place else alone." Jim bent down and pressed two fingers against Juan's jugular. "He's dead."

"Thank God he's dead," said Jenny. "Now what?"

"We call the sheriff."

"Jim, no one but you and me and…them…knows he's here. Right? If you call the sheriff, the press, an investigation, the whole world, will know where I am. But, Jim, if I leave, they'll leave too and try to find me someplace else." Jenny was thinking out loud, walking in circles as she did, each time stepping over the body as though it were just a thing on the floor.

"And Juan here?" asked Jim, watching her.

"Feed the bastard to the pigs. Then no one will know."

"What?" Jim asked.

"Feed him to the pigs. Just like Reed Baker did with his dead calves when he couldn't get the renderer to come out. He'd be gone in a matter of hours. Disappear!"

"And then we get them to think you've gone?" he asked. "How do we do that?"

"I do go. Jim, I have to go. You're not safe—"

"I said cool that idea!" Jim admonished.

"It's not just me and you, Jim. Don't you see…?" She thought for an instant. "No, you don't see. You didn't see…On television last Thursday. The networks carried a story about an assassination attempt on the life of Creighton Leonard, who is WYCO's CEO, and some senator. I interrupted something…that porno movie. Whatever…something perverted. A week later, an attempt is made on Creighton's life."

"And?" Jim asked, confused. "I don't see—"

"Well, neither do I. But that same day, someone kidnapped the son of a WYCO executive who also just happens to work at the same plant location as I do. The WYCO executive is a woman. Her name is similar to mine, Jennifer, Jennifer Poole. Her boy was returned the same day. Unharmed. You get it? Her name is the same as mine. Jennifer."

"So the names are the same. And you see a connection?"

"No, I don't see it. I know there's a connection. There has to be. People have said we look alike. Not really…up close, but from a distance…Suppose *they* only had a name and a sketchy description. Suppose they went after her by mistake thinking she was me? Just to frighten her…me?"

Jenny stopped circling. "I saw it on TV at Danny's Bar. I was still shaking from what happened to me. I tried to call her. It was late…very late. I don't know the time. She answered. She started asking me these questions. I couldn't answer. I…finally hung up."

She looked again at the body on the floor. Finally, she added insightfully, "I believe her son was kidnapped because of me."

"You don't know that. You said he was returned home. He's safe now. Right?" blurted Jim.

"I know it doesn't make sense. They let him go and then try to kill me?" She paused, her gaze scanning the lifeless body of her would-be assassin, his blood a crimson pool beneath him on the concrete floor. "We're not safe. None of us are safe," she said reflectively. "They'll keep coming until we're all dead. Unless someone can stop them first. Jennifer Poole needs to know why her son was taken." Her quiet voice echoed a new resolve.

"It's all conjecture," said Jim when he understood his sister's intentions.

"No, it's not. It makes sense. She needs to know. She's in real danger. So is her son."

Jim's eyes followed his sister's gaze to the corpse beneath his feet. "Back to Juan here. I'm going to call the sheriff."

"And bring on the investigation? I want to talk with Jennifer Poole first, without the police. Jim, we have to keep her out of the picture."

"The sheriff is a friend. He knows me. We went to school together. I'll tell him someone was trying to rape you…this migrant…I hit him to protect you. He'll believe that. Things like that happen around here. We don't have to mention Jenny Poole for now. He'll ask you some questions for the record. Nothing more. Come on." He took one last look at Juan, grabbed Jenny's hand, and tugged her toward the golden sky. "We'll talk later about your going back to Minnesota."

Ben Foley, Morgan County sheriff, arrived within thirty minutes of the call. After listening to the story, he asked Jim why he just didn't throw him to the hogs and save the county the burial fee. Jim wished now he had listened to his sister; he wished that for many reasons.

Ben would conduct an investigation, try to locate next of kin—doubting there were any—and as much as possible, try to keep the press zipped up. This kind of thing was bad on local morale. He didn't want self-proclaimed vigilantes going off harassing innocent migrants over one bad one.

By the time the questions were over, the local medical examiner had arrived and removed Juan's body to the county morgue. Jim would tell the other migrants who worked in the barns that Juan had moved on. Not an unusual event. Other than a few trusted officials, the world would not be the wiser. Juan Smith did not exist. At least not in Green Bend, Nebraska.

Chapter 38

"Compliments to the Boy Scout chef. The steak was great," praised Jenny as she and Dan Sheridan sipped their merlot on her patio, the last remnant of the day's light only a faint glow on the western horizon. Several times during the course of the early evening, she had thought of Chris, wishing he were here. She had convinced herself that Chris would have wanted her to continue with her scheduled dinner meeting with Sheridan and to learn whatever it was she hoped to learn from him. But into her second glass of wine, she began to wish Chris would be just a little jealous. Then Dan poured her third glass, and she was quite sure he would. *He could have come home. He could have made a greater effort. He simply didn't!*

"No bugs," observed Dan.

"Cooler evenings with a slight breeze. They don't like that. The bugs don't," Jenny explained, ignoring a growing thickness to her tongue.

"Is this typical Minnesota? I didn't know fall could come so quickly?"

"Yes. Overnight. The seasons change...overnight. One night summer, one nightfall, one night, it snows, and soon it's spring. That's Minnesota."

Off-limits! Off-limits! thought Dan as he listened to Jenny and watched her delicate lips form her words. The wine had brought a soft redness to her tanned face. In the flickering candlelight, she was radiant, absolutely beautiful. The scent of citronella mingled with her light perfume in a strange combination, producing a sublimely sensual aroma. The ponytail she had worn earlier had been undone by the windy ride home and hung delicately, slightly windblown, over her ears. Dan could tell that she had brushed her hair lightly, though he didn't know when. Gary Sadler knew this would happen, didn't he? Quietly, Dan cursed Sadler. There was a reason he had come here tonight. "Jenny," he said gently.

"Yes, Mr. Sheridan," she answered slowly. "I mean, Dan." She smiled and waited.

"The afternoon that I returned Jason to you, we met on this deck. Your mother was here." Dan began, feeling a little guilty for having poured Jenny a third glass of wine. She had undoubtedly compromised her values.

"Yes. My mother," repeated Jenny.

"We discussed the possible danger to Jason and to you if Jason should suddenly remember his abduction and be able to identify his captors."

"Yes. His captors," she repeated.

"Later, there was the storm that disrupted the newscast and Jason's interview."

"Tore the boat canopy. See over there." Jenny pointed toward *Little Red* without looking in its direction.

"You said on the telephone that during the storm, you thought you saw a man watching you as he stood here on the deck."

"I don't just think I saw him. I know I saw him. In a flash of lightning. Here one minute, gone the next. Just like the seasons…in Minnesota."

The sparkle in Jenny's eyes held Dan captive. In the candle's flicker, he watched her smile. So beautiful, so accessible, so vulnerable…so off-limits.

"Jenny, Jenny. Do you know what you're doing?" he asked compassionately, a two-edged question.

"Answering your questions, Mr. Policeman."

"Yes, I'm a policeman. A champion, protector of the innocent," he said loudly enough to startle Jenny, making her flinch slightly.

"A protector of innocence," he said again, softly, exasperated. "Your innocence," he whispered.

"I'm sorry, what? You're whispering." Jenny leaned over the table as she spoke, smiling and admonishing him. "Speak up, Mr. Policeman." Then she sat back into her chair and looked at her empty glass of wine, her third, and pushed it toward the center of the table. "No more of that, thank you."

Jenny shook her head to stop the spinning inside and to regain her composure. "Would you like a cup of coffee? I believe I'm ready for one." She took a deep breath and stood slowly, pushing her chair back under the table as she steadied herself. Feeling her legs securely under her, she said, "Ready," and took another deep breath and walked quickly through the patio door to the kitchen, hoping the line she walked was straight enough for her watching, admiring policeman.

When Dan heard the whine of the coffee grinder, he stacked up the dishes and carried them inside. Jenny had just filled the coffeemaker with water and flicked on the switch, then watched admiringly as Dan entered and set the dishes in the sink. *Such a handsome protector*, she observed.

"Jenny, I placed the videos on your living-room coffee table. Do you still want to view them?" he questioned.

"Please," she answered, avoiding more words, afraid she had already said too much with a thick tongue.

Dan headed into the living room, and Jenny turned to the coffeemaker, willing it to work faster. As it popped and sputtered, she looked out the kitchen window, beyond the deck to the torn canopy and *Little Red* shimmering in the light of the fall moon. *How dumb! Stupid!* she scolded herself and bit her lip to test her senses and her response to pain. It hurt.

Minutes later, Dan returned, a plastic shopping bag swinging from his hand. Jenny had already emptied the first few drops of very strong coffee into her cup and gulped them down as he entered. "The VCR is in there," she said and pointed to the large-screen television in the room he had just left.

Dan followed the line of her finger and emptied the contents of the bag onto the coffee table. It contained three videocassettes. Two were from Channel 6 News. With the promise of an additional story, Donald Stone had furnished one edited version of the noon news conference, which had been shown on the late-evening news the day of the conference, and one unedited version of the entire conference, as captured on tape by his cameraman. The final tape was the composite tape given to him by Gary Sadler of footage obtained from Abel Food's security cameras.

Dan's watch read 9:30 p.m., later than he had realized. Quickly, he selected the shorter Channel 6 tape, inserted it into the VCR, picked up the TV remote, and quickly pushed "On." After setting the tape to the beginning of the newscast, he shut off everything and looked toward the kitchen.

Jenny had just stepped through the patio door onto the deck. He watched her through the window as she walked toward the dock. The moon was already high in the cloudless night sky and cast shadows that obscured Jenny's approach to the shoreline. He walked to the kitchen, poured a full cup of coffee in the mug Jenny had set for him, and followed her out the door into a perfect fall evening.

Brilliant stars flickered overhead. Jenny stood on the dock, staring dreamily into the heavens. The candle on the patio table gave one last flicker and died as Dan stepped onto the dew-dampened grass and walked toward the dock.

"Thank you for a wonderful evening," he said and stepped onto the dock beside her. "I haven't...," he began but stopped suddenly, catching himself before he became too friendly. Caught up in the moment, he longed to touch her. "You've shown me life does exist outside the mall."

"Can you smell it?" she asked and drew a deep breath. "It's the smell of fall, early fall. Every season has its own distinct smell." Dan took a deep breath. She continued, "Another couple of weeks, and the smell will change again, when the trees begin to shed their leaves."

Feeling the warmth of the cup in his hand, Dan took a sip of coffee and felt a caffeine glow surge through his veins. It was unbelievably strong. "I like strong coffee," said Jenny, offering no apology.

"I see that."

"Especially after too many glasses of wine," Jenny added.

Dan walked out to the end of the dock and stared into the night. "Jenny, it's late," he said at last, reluctantly. "I really should be going. I set up the tape of the newscast on your VCR. There are two other tapes that I'd like you to watch. One is an unedited tape of the news conference. It's long, but if the man you saw was in the audience, you may spot him."

Jenny joined Dan on the end of the dock. "I'm sorry it got to be so late…but if you must go," she said, concentrating on each word.

Dan turned to face her. "The other tape is—"

"If I do spot him, then what?" interrupted Jenny. "I really don't know what to do next. I just feel…The man that I saw is involved. I just know it. I know he'll be on the tape, then what? Christian would know what to do. You know what to do. I'm confused."

Dan understood her confusion; she was frightened by the unknown dangers she would unleash. *Jenny was right, Chris should be home to protect her, his family.* He longed to hold her, to tell her all would be well. But he resisted and cursed Sadler under his breath.

"First, he needs to be identified," instructed Dan. "Once we know who he is, we'll understand more about motive. There's no evidence linking this person to Jason's abduction. He could simply have been a curious neighbor. It's like we're dealing with straws blown in the wind, and we need a handful to see the complete picture."

He considered Sadler's words. Sadler's interest in Creighton Leonard was such a straw, and he had a haunting feeling that Gary Sadler was right. As the straws are gathered, Creighton Leonard would be in the haystack. Still he didn't feel comfortable in mentioning Sadler's interest to Jenny. It would only frighten her and possibly compromise her work at WYCO, draw attention to her, and accelerate her danger. If Creighton Leonard had killed once, he would kill again. But Dan wouldn't let that happen to Jenny. He'd protect her from a distance; his feelings for her were becoming too intense, and that was not good for anyone.

"I have his tiepin," said Jenny. "Does that help? I don't believe it belongs to a neighbor." She took a step backward to retrieve the pin from her pants pocket but failed to see the mooring rope coiled behind her. It rolled under her foot throwing her off-balance.

"Whoa…Whoa! Whoa!" she yelled with both arms flailing in large arcs. Suddenly, with eyes wide as saucers, she teetered backward, beyond the point of recovery, and splashed flat on her back into the moon-rippled, shoulder-deep water.

It was comfortably warm from the ninety-degree days of the past week. When her feet found the bottom, she thrust herself upward, breaking the surface in a gurgling spray and instantly broke out into laughter.

She pulled her hair back from her face as Dan reached down to help her. When her hand was firmly in his, she gave a good yank and pulled him over the top of her, headlong into the water. When he righted himself and broke the surface sputtering and spitting out lake water, she couldn't tell if it was surprise or anger on his face. Whatever, it was too much for Jenny who laughed all the harder. Wearing a surprised look, he gave one last sputter, then saw the look on her face and smiled. What could he do but laugh too?

In the distance, a patio flood lamp snapped on. Dan and Jenny quickly ducked into the shadow of the dock, while Mel the neighbor came to his patio door to survey the shoreline. A moment later, unable to identify the source of the noise, he snapped off his light pulled his curtains closed.

Dan rubbed the water from his face, took a deep breath and looked at Jenny. *Jenny should not have done that.* She was dripping wet and beautiful in the moonlight. He struggled with his emotions, fighting the desire to grab Jenny, hold her close, push her wet hair from her face, and feel her firm body next to his as he and Gail had done so many times so long ago. *Sadler, Sadler.*

JENNY

Dan was the first to hear the telephone through the screened patio doors. *Saved by the bell.* "It's probably Chris," said Jenny, who heard it too. She moved quickly through the water and scrambled onto the shore with disregard for the splashing noise that would bring Mel back to his patio door. She ran to the deck and entered the kitchen to the phone's last ring, but when she picked up the receiver, she heard only the dial tone and angrily slammed it back onto its cradle while glancing at the answering machine lifeless and quiet on the kitchen counter. She had turned it off and had forgotten to reset it.

Standing in chest-deep water, Dan watched Jenny through the kitchen window allowing the water to cool his emotions, grateful for the interruption. He watched her walk through the living room and climb the stairs to the second-floor landing. It was time for him to leave.

A movement in the neighbor's townhome caught his eye—Mel returning to his patio door to peer into the darkness. Unable to move fast enough, Dan waived in Mel's direction and emerged from the water and walked slowly toward the Jenny's open patio door, hoping the neighbor would mistake him for Chris.

He slid the door open and stepped inside. A moment later, Jenny returned barefoot, wearing a terry cloth robe, and carrying a large bath towel. She smiled as she handed it to Dan; his wet clothing giving up its water to a growing puddle on the tile beneath his feet.

"I'm sorry. I couldn't resist," she laughed without remorse. "You're welcome to borrow some of Chris's clothes. You're about the same size."

Jenny! Jenny! Jenny! Sadler! He cursed silently and reached for the towel, praying the phone would ring again. She was so beautiful, even more so dripping wet. "I really should go." He paused, then blurted, "Do you love him?" he blurted out finally. "Chris?"

Taken off guard by his question, Jenny was suddenly very sober. "Yes. Very much." Their eyes met. "I do love my husband…very much. Why would you ask?"

It was a stupid question, Dan realized. "Sorry. I just…" Poorly timed, he looked into her eyes for an eternity and said finally, "I've got leather interior." "I'll be okay. I'll be dry by the time I reach the Interstate." This made Jenny smile. "Besides, I don't want to take liberty with another man's… things. Your husband may not appreciate another man wearing his clothes."

Jenny laughed again, and soon Dan joined in. "You're probably right," she confessed. She had never done anything to test Chris's trust; they had never given the other any reason to doubt their commitment to their marriage. She trusted that fact. She would explain her falling into the lake, and Chris would understand. It was all so innocent. Or was it?

"This is the tiepin," she said and produced the jeweled tiepin from her robe pocket. "I know it belongs to the man on the deck. I can't think of another reason for it being there."

"Looks expensive," observed Dan, inspecting it in her hand. Then he looked at her and instructed, "Look, view the tapes. If he was in the audience, you'll spot him. We can talk tomorrow. I really must go."

He used the towel to pat himself down until the dripping stopped and handed it back to Jenny, leaned against the side of the patio door, and removed his soggy shoes and socks. Stepping through the patio door, he wrung out his sock, tucked them into his shoes, and stepped back inside heading to the front entry. Jenny followed.

The air outside was fresh and cool as he stood in his wet clothes and turned to face Jenny. "On the security video, you'll see two men. It's a long shot, but you may recognize one or both. Don't look just for the obvious. Something you may see could trigger a memory. I'll call you tomorrow." Then with shoes in hand, he turned and walked to the drive.

Jenny watched his taillights disappeared from view, closed the door and locked it, and returned to the kitchen turning off lights as she went. In the living room, she picked up the plastic case for the video Dan had readied in the VCR. Printed on the cover were the

JENNY

words "Property of Channel 6." She set it back on the coffee table, hit the light switch, and headed for the stairs. *Morning would come soon enough.* Then she would satisfy her growing obsession with the stranger on the deck.

Chapter 39

Jenny's heart pounded in her chest as she shot upright in bed, her body drenched with perspiration. Her blanket lay beside her in a knotted heap. Outside the full moon shined brilliantly a few degrees above the horizon. *It was the wine. Too much, too late.*

She looked at the clock. She had been in bed only four hours. Yet she was wide-awake, energized by a nightmare receding into her consciousness like a lizard at the onset of daylight. She shook her head, demanded her mind to retrieve the dreamy imagery. Did it have meaning? She really didn't believe in dreams. *What was it? What was it?* Turning sideways, she dropped her legs off the side of the bed and closed her eyes, forcing her mind to search the nocturnal fog.

She had been with Dan Sheridan. Were they about to embrace? She couldn't tell. They were on a sandy beach. Whatever they were about to do was interrupted when suddenly Jason appeared, watching, crying. Then he was gone, and standing in his place was Christian holding a suitcase; he'd been traveling. He smiled as he approached, but with each step, his smile gave way to an angry sneer, the muscles in his cheeks began to throb. In the background, a small voice whimpered, "Dad, don't. It's Mom." But he continued. Then suddenly, the case Dan had been holding became a gun, disproportionate in size, big, requiring two hands to point it.

The only sound was Jason whimpering. But the gun didn't go off but, instead, morphed suddenly to…what? A Bible? Jenny watched in disbelief; it was her Bible. Then a shot rang out, and the Bible fell to the ground. Seconds later, Christian crumbled to the ground. Beside her, Dan smiled menacingly, a smoking gun in his hand. "Chris, what have I done?" she shouted, looked down at the twisted, lifeless body and wept. She woke suddenly. *That didn't happen, not really; it was a dream*, she realized as the dream gave way to reality like a wave dashed upon a rocky shore. In its place came fear. Was God speaking to her?

Walking to her bathroom, she turned on the light and stood looking into her mirror at eyes that stared back. She turned on the water and let it to flow across her hand, feeling it warm before splashing a handful gently on her face. It was calming. "Would you cheat on your husband? Could you really, Jenny?" she asked into the mirror. "What if Dan were less honorable?" She didn't want to go there and turned on the cold water, filled her cupped hands, and splashed her face. "You fool!" she said to the face in the mirror. "Fool!" she repeated and splashed more water at her face. Even the thought of infidelity was repugnant. She was furiously angry at the fool she knew she was and the hypocrite she had nearly become.

After Dan left, she went directly to bed. She was too upset with her behavior toward Dan to view the videotapes. Aided by the wine, sleep came instantly. Then came the dream—too real, too vivid.

Now awake, viewing the videos seemed like a good idea. Moonlight beamed through the large patio window as she made her way slowly to the kitchen. She was soon basking in the aroma of a fresh pot of coffee. She filled an oversized mug, walked into the living room, found the TV's remote, got cozy on the sofa, and pushed "On." She was ready.

Janet Spalding appeared presenting the noon news. Since Jason's kidnapping, Jenny had had little time to consider all that had transpired. Now she relived every moment and had to remind herself that she was watching the story of her son's abduction. She was more than a casual observer; this was her story. She took a deep breath and tempered her emotions with her knowledge of a good outcome. Jason was safe. It was like reading a book after first skipping ahead to read the last chapter. Was Jason truly safe? She wondered. What was their future?

Creighton Leonard appeared next in the video: a man of mystery and intrigue, suave and polished. There were rumors of a shaded past, ruthlessness, but nothing supported by fact. She had made inquiries but learned little other than a trail of one success after another. Creighton Leonard was a man of contacts, a man of means, a man of power. The fact remained: the man was brilliant, successful and rich. Other than that, she knew very little about him. Since taking over the company, he stayed to himself, appearing indifferent to those who did his bidding. Watching now, she learned nothing new.

Twice the camera panned the audience and zoomed back to Donald Stone standing at the forefront of the spectators, microphone in hand. With each pan, Jenny strained to spot the tall stranger. He was there somewhere. Finally, she spotted him; a quick glimpse. She allowed the tape to continue. He appeared again, another quick glimpse, standing two rows behind the man in the red sweatshirt, the would-be assassin.

She watched him draw his gun. And with her heart beating rapidly, she watched a man tackle him, sending him to the ground and causing the gun to go off and a pool of blood to appear under the red sweater. When the camera panned the audience, she strained to see the tall stranger. Twice he appeared. Excitedly she rewound the tape and replayed the segments. Yes, it was him. She played it again in slow motion. With the action slowed, his features were even less discernible, but there was enough to show to Dan. Maybe he could make something of it, offer some reason why the man came to her home. After viewing the videos, Chris would take it all more seriously. Take her more seriously.

Watching it in stop frame, she studied the blurred features of the man who had visited her deck during the storm and, with each sweep of the camera, felt a strange sense of déjà vu. *I know him. From where?*

Dan had said she might recognize two men on the security tape. She inserted the second tape and pushed "Play." The scene was the end of a long dimly lit hallway with people coming and going. Most wore uniforms, men and women reporting for their shift change. Occasionally, one or more persons of particular interest were highlighted by a halo of light added for the viewers' benefit during an edit.

Two men entered who had appeared before. A halo followed them down the hall. They turned their heads as they passed the camera and disappeared out of view. More scenes played. A man sat at a large circular desk where he watched several monitors. Recessed lights in the ceiling illuminated the entire area. An oscillating camera covered the junction of several corridors. After several minutes, the guard stood and exited down the hall. Soon the two subjects of interest reappeared, again turning their faces from the camera, deliberately obscuring their features in the shadows.

Time rolled by. Finally, Jenny yawned. She had no idea what time it was or how long she had been sitting in the dark. She was determined to watch to the end rubbed her eyes to relieve the tension in her eyelids from the strain of the flickering light and hypnotic effect of the video.

Outside, the moon had dropped below the horizon. In the darkness, she could no longer distinguish the dock in the distance. As people paraded across her television screen, her mind wandered. *What was Christian doing? He'd be asleep, of course. Was he upset that she had not reached the phone in time?* Soon, only disjointed thoughts trained through her consciousness like a slow-moving ticker tape until sleep came for the second time that evening.

Chapter 40

The ringing phone pulled Jenny into the new day. Slowly she pushed herself up from the sofa and shuffled toward the kitchen, yawning and rubbing her eyes. But the ringing stopped as she drew near. With her eyes fixed on the answering machine, she waited for the voice she knew would be Chris. But there was nothing. Walking closer, she could see she had forgotten again to turn on the answering machine.

Coffee. A light on the coffee maker said it was still on, so she walked toward it, and smelling the acrid odor of hours of old coffee decided to make a fresh pot. She worked in a daze, moving about the kitchen, habit dictating her actions. Minutes passed before the machine spit and sputtered and filled the air with the aroma of fresh brewed Colombian. She went to the sink and splashed her face with cold water to wash away the remnant of too much wine, shook her head slowly. No headache. That was good.

The phone rang again. She answered on the third ring; her tone more a question than a greeting. "Good morning?"

"Jenny? Is that you?" Chris asked from Seattle.

"Mmm, I think so."

"I called a few minutes ago."

"I thought it was you."

"Thought you'd be in the shower—"

"Not yet," said Jenny.

"Are you awake, Jenny?" Chris asked.

"Getting there. Keep talking. It's helping," she answered, sipping her coffee between words.

"Come on, Jenny. It's Saturday morning. Time to be up and about. Have a late night?" Chris's tone suddenly serious.

"Not really. A wet one," said Jenny, not sensing the bewildered look on the other end of the line. She spotted the clock; it read 7:10, making it 5:10 in Seattle. "You're up early."

"Apparently, you're not," quipped Chris. "Did it rain last night?" he asked, seeking the meaning of *wet one*. "I watched the late news. They said it was clear in the Midwest."

"It was. Wish you had been here," Jenny chided.

"So do I. Believe me. What did you mean by wet one?" he asked, finally, angrily.

"You remember Dan was here with the videos. He came for dinner. Well…Dan fell in," answered Jenny.

"In the lake?" Chris asked as an attorney would seek clarification from a hostile witness.

"Yes, Christian. In the lake."

There was silence in Seattle. Jenny continued, "Actually I fell in. Then he fell in. Silly really. We were standing at the end of the dock enjoying a cup of coffee when I tripped on a rope and fell in, pulling him in after me. Then the telephone rang. I ran to get it, thinking it was you, but got there too late. That was the evening"

"I didn't call," said Chris finally.

"What?"

"I didn't call last night. I went to dinner with our team. It was late when we got back. I didn't call."

"I thought you'd call to ask about the videotapes," she scolded. "You know, show some interest in this investigation we're doing together."

"Jenny, it couldn't be helped. We've gone through that. I'm sorry. Did you watch them, the tapes? Learn anything you didn't know? Found the 'one-armed' man?"

"He has two arms. Tall. Very tall. Could say kind of good-looking. Not handsome like you. And he was there in the audience."

"Did Dan?"

"He'd already gone. I went right to bed after he left, woke up in the middle of the night—"

"Too much red wine?" asked Chris lightly, knowing that red wine always interrupted Jenny's sleep.

"And watched the tapes until I fell asleep on the sofa," continued Jenny, ignoring Chris's remark. "Chris, the man on the deck, it was him. I know it was. The picture isn't the best, but he was also there in the audience. And there's more. I can't put my finger on it. A feeling. There's something familiar about him. I might know him. Maybe I've met him. I don't know. It'll come to me. But, you know, that kind of feeling."

There was a brief silence. "Tripped on a rope?" Chris asked jokingly. "Red wine? Jenny, I'm beginning to get the picture. And Dan fell in after you? That's how it went?" Chris couldn't resist the jibe. He was, after all, the attorney and trained to drill people, trained to recognize the truth camouflaged by many words. He loved Jenny with unfailing trust. That would never change, but a little teasing seemed appropriate.

"You had your chance to be a part of it, you know. But you chose to do something else. See what you missed?" she teased in return.

They spoke a few more words and said their good-byes. Through the open window, she could hear the distant call of geese. She filled her cup and returned to the living room, turned off the television, and settled into the sofa, her legs curled beneath her. The taste of fresh coffee was better than good. Some mornings were like that, the coffee tasting almost as good as it smelled.

Chapter 41

Mildred Knowles had allowed sufficient time for Sharon Miller to settle into her normal Monday routine. It would not be good to intrude too soon. She had seen Sharon come onto the floor fifteen minutes earlier and now walked down the long hallway past Jennifer Poole's office and entered Sharon's office.

The early morning sun reflected upon the lake's surface beyond Sharon's large window. The distant shoreline showing the first hint of fall colors, a soft-red and yellow glow adorning the distant towering maples, brought a smile to Mildred's face. She stood for a moment and reflected on the decision she had made years earlier to leave the city for the suburbs. She loved her work. Her mood was bright. It most always was. This morning, the scene before her made her especially buoyant.

"Good morning, Sharon," she said at last. "Can you ever tire of such beauty?" Mildred's voice startled Sharon, whose back had been to the door. One of the files she had been working on dropped onto the floor.

"I'm sorry. Didn't mean to startle you, dear," she said. "Will Jennifer be in today?"

"As far as I know," answered Sharon as she knelt to retrieve the papers. "Later today, we're scheduled at the store."

"You might want to change your plans. The telephones went on the blink over the weekend. All the voice mail messages for the entire floor rolled over to my message center. Thank goodness there weren't too many calls. It was repaired Sunday. I'm delivering them personally. Don't know if I trust the repair yet. Anyway, Jennifer got a call from Creighton Leonard himself. He'd like to see her in his office today. He said late morning or early afternoon."

"Mmm, that's interesting. I don't think they've spoken since the incident at the mall." Sharon placed the file in the file drawer and stood, her head cocked inquisitively.

"Second message was from a young woman. She said she'd tried calling Jennifer at home Friday evening but didn't get an answer. She wanted Jennifer to know she was coming into town with some very important information. Said she'd call when she got in and set a place to meet."

"Give a reason?" asked Sharon.

"No. Didn't leave a name either. That's odd, isn't it?" Mildred walked closer to the large window and gazed for a moment at the distant shimmering surface of Lake Minnetonka like a field of diamonds stirred gently by the light morning breeze. "Anyway," she continued finally, "I wanted Jenny to get her messages first thing. She wouldn't want to disappoint Mr. Leonard."

"Thanks, Mildred. I'll make sure she gets them. I'm expecting her anytime."

Mildred turned and walked toward the door, pausing in the entrance. "Does Jenny know Jennifer Stewart?" she asked.

"Should she?" answered Sharon.

"She could. Miss Stewart started work here not long ago. Bright girl. Full of enthusiasm. She worked late one night a couple weeks back. Had a long weekend planned with her boyfriend, wanted to take an extra day, and needed to get her work done. Well, she never came back. *Personnel* hasn't heard from her. The voice on the phone sounded like hers. Over the years, I've become pretty good at recognizing voices. Leonard's staff man…Oh, what's his name? Barons, I think. He had a mix up with the office calendar and thought Miss Stewart could help. He wanted me to call him if she called in. I'd better call him and let him know. The voice sure sounded like hers."

JENNY

"Like I said, I'll give Jenny the messages. If she's not here soon, I'll call her at home."

Sharon took her position at her desk, ready to begin a busy day. Mildred smiled and continued out the door. Her heels clicking on the granite floor as she walked back to her station; her burden now shared.

Moments later, Jenny stepped off the elevator. Passing the reception area, she greeted Mildred who was standing next to her station passing along messages to one of the secretaries who had just arrived. She gestured to Jenny but continued talking.

"Hi, Sharon," said Jenny as she entered her office and spotted Sharon at her desk in the adjacent room. "Any calls this morning?"

Sharon got up from her desk and joined Jenny in her office. "None that I've taken. Mildred said you're wanted at corporate today. Creighton Leonard would like to see you." She paused. "Has he said anything to you since the assassination attempt? I mean about Jason. Anything?"

"He went on to Washington. Almost immediately. Doubt he's had time."

"But even a telephone call." Complained Sharon.

Jenny shrugged her shoulders and set her briefcase on the edge of her clean desk. She looked very much the executive wearing a handsomely tailored suit with a short midthigh skirt. Three weeks had passed since Jason's abduction. On this Monday morning, Jenny felt a strong determination to get on with her life. She'd find the answers she wanted in the course of time. Fear for the safety of her family was still present but now under control. Three weeks had done that.

"Please call corporate and schedule Creighton for eleven. And… call mall security and see if Dan Sheridan will be available this afternoon," directed Jenny.

"Done. Do you know Jennifer Stewart?" asked Sharon on her way to her office.

"Isn't she the new girl? Started here a couple of months ago. I thought maybe she'd quit. I haven't seen her this past couple of weeks."

"A message rolled over onto Mildred's phone. Mildred said it sounded like Jennifer Stewart. She said she tried to reach you Friday evening. Didn't get an answer at your home, so she left a message here. She's coming into town and has important information for you."

"Interesting. Did she give a time?" asked Jenny.

"Apparently she'll call when she gets in."

Chapter 42

Jenny left her office at 10:30 and followed Shoreline Drive along the north shore of Lake Minnetonka to Wayzata. Always a beautiful drive, this morning was no different.

Across the lake, in her parents' neighborhood of Maplewood, she could see the maples already beginning to change. Coots were beginning to gather on the calm water of Brown's Bay. Soon they would raft by the thousands before moving south.

She parked in the ramp outside Wayzata Office Towers and took the covered walkway to the tower home of WYCO's corporate offices. Inside the large atrium, a piano played. *Nice touch*, she thought as she listened momentarily. She was very at home in the corporate environment but viewed headquarters much in the way she viewed New York City—a fun place to visit briefly.

There had been talk of moving her marketing division to the towers after the success of House of Toys, but her insistence that she needed to be physically close to production had prevailed. There she could keep her eye on scheduling and head off problems before they angered her large corporate clients. Besides, she much preferred being near the lake where the lake's serenity helped her maintain peace of mind. And it was closer to home.

JB Barons sat across the coffee table from Creighton Leonard, both engaged in their routine Monday morning review. Creighton's secretary entered after a quiet knock at his door. She entered with a fresh thermos of coffee and a plate of bagels from the building's cafeteria.

"Mr. Leonard, Jennifer Poole can meet with you at eleven as you requested," she said, placing the thermos on the highly polished table."

"Thank you, Kathy," Creighton answered, stopping her just before she was to leave the room. "Reserve a table downstairs."

"A private room?" Kathy inquired.

"No. It's not private." On the contrary, he wanted his lunch with Jennifer Poole to be public. The entire company knew of her son's abduction. It was time for a public display of his concern and generosity.

"Care to join us, JB?" asked Creighton.

Creighton had not confided to JB his intentions to meet personally with Jenny and thought he noticed him flinch ever so slightly.

"Can't. The Piper conference, remember?" came a quick response.

"That's tomorrow."

"Yes. But I'm deep in the numbers today." JB picked up a bagel to disguise his growing tension.

"Have you ever met this woman? Jennifer Poole? She's your heroine, as I recall."

"WYCO's heroine, actually," JB rebutted, resisting Creighton's trap. "And, no, I've not officially met her."

"Unofficially?" asked Creighton, sparring with JB.

"We may have met at a company function," JB lied. For what reason, he wasn't sure. The first he knew of Jenny Ward Pool's association with the company was when she left Millie's cafe in search of Jason. Had he seen Jenny earlier, he would have recognized her, and the abduction never would have been ordered.

He longed to see her to let her know he would protect her. *Protect her from what?* he thought. From the dangers he himself had instigated and engineered. He couldn't see what good would come of seeing her so soon after…after the fiasco. The entire subject made him uneasy.

"It's your call, Crey. You say lunch, and I'm there. It's just that Piper's investors need good numbers."

"They're better than ever," said Creighton.

"Stock's up because the market perceives long-term strength. Piper has issued a 'buy' recommendation. That's so much our own hype. Reality is much more fragile. You know that."

"All right, do the numbers," said Creighton reluctantly.

JB had guessed Creighton would yield. His fortune depended upon good reports, an appeased and confident constituency. His fortune was linked to JB Barons' ability to tell a good story. But this morning, JB had come to Creighton's office with another agenda. He removed a small tabloid from his case and set it on the table before Creighton.

"We need that treaty, Crey. No one knows that better than you. We need good press to pull off support. Then we get this! This fodder for the enemy cannon," said JB dramatically, stabbing at the paper in his hand. Creighton tilted his head to read the name on the tabloid.

"*The Chamber*? Isn't that the underground rag from Harvard? Haven't seen one in years. They're still around?" Creighton mused.

"Not the conservative press we knew back then. It's undergone a sex change. It's now the champion of gay rights. Anything perverted you'll find it in there."

"The sexual preference of some has served us well," Creighton reminded.

"Until now!" JB picked up the paper, opening it to page two and a bold headline, "Politician Murders Lover on Eve of Sex Probe."

"Similar articles have appeared in the *Wall Street Journal, the Post*. They've all cast their stones."

"But this one mentions your name. That's a first," said JB, his voice sounding alarm.

Creighton picked up the underground paper and scanned the article while JB continued, "Someone's done their homework. Seems they can prove Creighton Leonard is a power broker in the world of illicit sex. Your name has always been linked to the treaty and our good Senator Malovich, but never in this context."

"I agree. It doesn't sound good. But there's no proof. Besides, this is just some forgotten underground paper, and those are just shallow words. And you see a problem here?" Creighton made a sweeping gesture with his arms.

"This kind of thing can destroy us," JB said, waiting for his words to take effect. "If there's substance here, we're dead. The senator won't survive the probe. That's a given. If by some miracle he does survive, the allegations associated with this kind of crap will stall the treaty proceedings forever. Either case, we're dead. We need that treaty now."

"So do half the businesses in the US. WYCO's not alone here. There's considerable money pushing for this. Washington would be crazy to deny confirmation. Politics aside, regardless of which side of the aisle the power rests, they all need good times to continue. It will pass," Creighton insisted.

"This sex thing? It doesn't come at a good time, that's all. I know we've addressed the senator's perversion. I was there, remember? I was the one who discovered his…his weakness." JB treaded lightly, exploring new ground with Creighton. As the mastermind behind Creighton's financial manipulations, he had not openly questioned the methods Creighton might employ behind the scenes to accomplish his goals, methods well in place long before JB became a player in the action.

He looked out the floor-to-ceiling windows toward the Minneapolis skyline. For the most part, the abduction of Jason Poole had been his plan from the beginning. Reasonably innocuous at the time, the plan was intended to frighten an unwitting witness into remaining quiet about management's immorality. Send a message to compel silence. It was a perverse sort of blackmail for sure. But no one was to get hurt. The witness would be compensated for remaining quiet. But, then, Jennifer Poole was just a name, a name he didn't recognize. How was he to know she and Jenny Ward, for whom his heart still beat, were one and the same.

When he considered it, the whole scenario brought him out of his element. To devise such a scheme in the first place was so totally atypical of JB but seemed to be demanded by the moment. Creighton's challenge for him to "fix the problem" appeared so necessary. So he had played into the side of Creighton Leonard that he had previously ignored, a side that left him uneasy for the first time. Was it fear?

"You knew the senator was gay. You knew it all along, didn't you?" JB asked. "You led me to that discovery. That was your plan all along," he probed on. Creighton remained silent. His attentions focused on JB as he picked up a bagel and began spreading cream cheese on it. "When the senator called for more money, you said you had handled it. By that, did you mean the murder of his lover?" The word *murder* had an ominous ring. Creighton glared at JB, who waited for a response.

None came. JB turned and walked half the distance back to Creighton. He was treading on dangerous ground. He knew that, but Jennifer Ward Poole was worth the risk. "What would have become of young Jason Poole?" he asked, surprised by his own boldness. "My God! His mother wasn't even the right woman! We had the wrong Jennifer!"

Creighton stood with his hands in his pockets, controlled; his steely eyes glared at JB. "You're becoming too distraught over pure conjecture." Creighton's voice was firm yet strained. He fought to be reassuring. "I suggest you concentrate on the Piper meeting. You're right about our investors. They need reassurance. You do your thing with the numbers, JB. You're truly good at that. Don't waste your time on this speculation."

"I'm not sure distraught is the correct word, Crey." JB walked to the coffee table and picked up his case. "Mildred Knowles called this morning. Jennifer Stewart is returning to Minneapolis. She didn't know when. I presume it's imminent," JB said and turned toward the door to return to his office.

Moments later, the elevator stopped at floor 33, and Jennifer Poole stepped into the large atrium reception area and briefly admired the lavish surroundings. *Nicer digs than the executive floor at plant 1. Creighton Leonard's touch,* she thought. *He does have an eye for art.* She was pleased she had not dressed casually.

Kathleen Warren stood at the reception area laughing with the young receptionist. She recognized Jenny as she stepped off the elevator and held out her hand as she approached. "Hello, Mrs. Poole." Kathleen introduced Jenny to the receptionist and moved off toward Creighton's office suite, fully expecting Jenny to follow.

Forgetting something, JB had started back to Creighton's office to speak with Kathleen when he spotted Kathleen shaking the hand of a most attractive woman with long auburn hair. His heart thundered. Most certainly it was Jenny. Quickly he ducked back into his office and watched through the crack in his partially open door. Perspiration formed on his brow. Taking a handkerchief from his pocket, he swathed his forehead until Jenny and Kathleen disappeared inside Creighton's suite.

The receptionist had alerted Creighton of Jenny's arrival. He stood to greet her. He sensed only a vague recognition, recalled having seen Jenny at recent staff work sessions, but then he had not paid her much attention, his thoughts absorbed by Mikado Industries.

During his first six months as WYCO's chief executive, he had seldom mingled with staff or employees. For that, he had his inner circle of senior executives. Better to avoid getting too close. When JB had suggested his abduction scheme, Jennifer Poole had been only name, a nonperson. There was the mistake. No longer. Here she was, very real, very attractive—he could not help but notice. *The wrong Jenny* echoed in his mind.

"Mrs. Poole. Shall I call you, Jennifer? Or is it Jenny?" he asked, offering her his hand.

"My friends, call me Jenny," she answered truthfully.

"Thank you for coming over on short notice." He led the way to a sitting area and a coffee table resupplied with fresh coffee, fresh bagels, and packaged spreads from the cafeteria. "Before I forget, would you please join me at lunch today? Nothing formal. In the cafeteria. I've asked some of my staff to join us along with Kohl and Moore. Burt is traveling, as you know. This meeting is long overdue," he said. "It's time we get better acquainted."

Creighton nodded to Kathleen, dutifully standing by. She left immediately to search out the other guests for lunch, the first she had heard of the event, hoping they were still in the building. She'd make a phone call and cancel her noon run to Wayzata. She understood "staff" to include JB and her as well.

Creighton directed Jenny to the chair that JB had occupied moments before. "I regret my schedule has denied me the opportunity to really get to know my people such as yourself. It's people like you who have made this company the great company it is today. These past six months have been horrendous. I'm sorry to be remiss. Our activities in Mexico have been my priority. That and Washington, lobbying for LAIPT. You know it as the Latin America Industrial Partnership Treaty."

Jenny, her hands folded gracefully in her lap, was nearly biting her tongue. *Was he aware of her involvement?* she wondered. Despite her work on the treaty, she had never been invited to meet personally with Creighton.

"Jenny, I've asked you here for two reasons. Unfortunately, because of the near tragedies, yours and mine, you did not receive the public recognition you deserve the day you were to join me at the press conference. I'm truly sorry for that. And, of course, the LAIPT group is indebted to you for your contribution."

Maybe not a big jerk after all. Jenny smiled without comment.

"Burt Lehr has gone on record to say the agreement with Mikado would not have been possible without you. And, JB...I think you've met my personal advisor...insists you are the embodiment of the true spirit of WYCO Toys, the image we should portray to the world." He smiled when he spoke, every bit the charmer.

"Kind words, Mr. Leonard. I'm sure exaggerated," said Jenny, honored but uncomfortable with the praise.

"It's far too easy for a person in my position to overlook the significance of the company's unsung heroes. I don't want that to be the case here. I've asked you here to extend appreciation. I wish this could be more public. I promise to take care of that at a future time."

Jenny responded with a modest smile but said nothing. Creighton continued, "Secondly, I wish to offer you my personal assistance in the wake of your son's abduction, Jason, isn't it? My resources are at your disposal. I regret that your work for this company has in any way put you or your family at risk. If there is anything at all I can do—"

"Mr. Leonard, I accept your thanks and appreciate your concern. I don't feel my work here has placed my family or me at risk. Jason is safe now. He wasn't harmed. He has absolutely no recollection of the incident. He has no suppressed fears that could scar him emotionally. Our lives have pretty much returned to normal. The authorities believe it an isolated incident, whatever the motive. I accept that. I do appreciate the concern. Thank you. This does provide the closure I guess I've needed."

"Are you sure about your son? His experience was very traumatic. I'd be more than happy to provide counseling. A therapist?" said Creighton.

"Really, Mr. Leonard. I believe he'll be fine. I mean it's been weeks, and he never mentions it. He's into hockey, school, and a thousand other things that demand his attention. He's already on with his life," she assured.

"Then you don't believe as time goes on, he might be able to identify the men who took him?"

"What men?" asked Jenny innocently.

"Well…the press has said," stammered Creighton, taken slightly off guard.

Jenny didn't seem to notice. "I haven't been reading the paper," said Jenny. "As far as Jason is concerned, they could have been camel drivers or cowboys on wild horses. It's as though his memory has been completely purged. Believe me, there's nothing there. Apparently, they gave him some kind of a drug that blocks out all short-term memory. I'm told there will be no long-term problems, just no memory of the incident."

Creighton and Jenny sat quietly for a moment, each studying the other. Finally, Jenny broke the silence. "And how are you, Mr. Leonard? Someone was trying to kill you. It seems we're both targets."

"Yes. Some kook. A member of a radical group called STUFFIT masquerading as a security guard, Students Truly Unified For Free International Trade. We don't know his true motive. He's still comatose at Hennepin County Medical."

"You believe the two events are related?" Jenny asked.

"That seems to be the conclusion of the national press. They could be right." Creighton was delighted that the two incidents coincided. He could not have planned it better himself. The press was leading the way down a logical, but false, trail. He'd be safe as long as Jason could not remember. And the other Jenny—was it Jennifer Stewart?—didn't talk.

"But why me? Why my son?"

"To embarrass me. To draw attention to their cause, perhaps."

"And then make an attempt on your life or Senator Malovich? That doesn't make sense to me."

"Because you're rational. These people are not rational people. Believe me, Jenny. I know. They're radicals marching to a different drum."

A light knock at his door caused Creighton to stand as Kathleen entered with Wendell Moore and Daryl Kohl in tow. Jenny rose to greet them. "Jennifer, it's good to see you. You don't get over here often enough." Wendell was the first to speak, "How's your son? Doing okay, is he?"

"Yes. He's fine." Jenny admired Wendell, his decisive manner that somehow reminded her of her father. Daryl Kohl was another matter. She accepted his hand. It felt cold and limp. He looked at her with a condescending smile.

After a few awkward moments, Creighton led the group to the elevators and their table waiting in the building's cafeteria. It was just inside the large glassed dining room where a hundred tables were prepared and waiting for the noon crowd beginning to file in.

Jenny caught the eye of a man who had already started through the food line as she and Creighton's party moved from their reserved table to the first food station. Jenny led the way, unaware that she was being observed, as the man moved slowly along the display of prepared foods. At one point, when their paths crossed, Jenny recognized him and smiled. He smiled back and moved on.

He smiled again when he caught the eye of Wendell Moore, who turned and said something to Creighton, causing both to turn his way. Jordan Green acknowledged Creighton, seated himself at a table on the opposite side of the dining room from the executive party, nibbled at his food, and watched as the executives socialized.

When only empty food trays remained for the cafeteria staff to clean up, he picked up his and carried it to the conveyor moving dirty dishes to the waiting kitchen crew. Setting it down, he made his decision. He would not return to his office and the nuisance work that awaited him. He didn't belong in an office.

Instead, he'd make his plant rounds. At the end of the day, he'd stop by the station to see how the investigation was progressing. He and Bill had taken great risk for the company. Their risk deserved greater compensation than he had previously suggested. It was time to ask for more. Ask? It was time to demand. *How much would be fair? The hell with fair! Tolerated?* He had told Bill fifty thousand. The answer would come to him as he made his rounds.

Chapter 43

Jenny enjoyed the impromptu lunch and the recognition. As she sped down Interstate 494 toward Mall of America and the House of Toys, Creighton Leonard's smile played through her memory. He had been on his best behavior, she realized, obviously intending to impress her. That was okay. He possibly was less of a jerk than she had made him out to be. In fact, she was beginning to like him. Sometimes she was too quick to make judgments.

He was a complex person, surely a man of contrast, a man who controlled how his image was presented to the world. Obviously, she was now an instrument in that public persona, if only for the moment. That was okay too. Corporate life was not her life's ambition. She'd rather be a good wife and mother, roles that promised longer-lasting gratification.

Ahead, a sign announced her exit. She moved into the right lane and felt a chill. What was it? She couldn't shake a growing uneasiness. Was it an intuitive warning? Of what? Was it an overactive imagination? Was it something about Creighton's demeanor at lunch? It was more than premonition. It was more like watching shadowed footsteps move in an ominous dim glow, faintly visible under a locked door in the back recesses of a darkened basement. She knew too little about the man Creighton Leonard. Everyone knew too little.

The House of Toys had been only a marketing blueprint when rumors began to spread that WYCO's Asian manufacturing operations were in trouble—more from neglect than for any other reason. Harold Benner, then WYCO's CEO, had been discovered having an affair with a New York fashion model. In time, that led to a very nasty divorce that took Harold to the cleaners. There was also a series of bad investments involving company money and stock.

When the news broke, Harold disappeared, leaving his attorneys to plead his case, and the company's auditors frantically charging off all of management's fiscal errors to the wayward Benner. A few weeks later, the beleaguered Harold Benner committed suicide; his body found in his swank New York apartment by a girlfriend.

The company's board of directors immediately began its search for a new CEO. An interim management team was appointed to run day-to-day activities under the leadership of Burt Lehr, VP of marketing, and Jenny's boss. Although a capable manager, new pressures soon proved overwhelming for Lehr. The struggle to maintain respectability and present a pure public image in the mounting wake of a highly publicized scandal gave rise to Jenny's promotion to marketing director. Her responsibilities were expanded to include development of the now-renowned lavish in-store displays, themes intended to lure and captivate the anticipated throng of daily visitors to Mall of America.

Jenny quickly immersed herself in the challenge. That task and caring for her family left her little time to become embroiled in company politics. She successfully remained above all controversy; no doubt the reason she had lasted as long as she had. Even to insiders, each jockeying for position in the changing corporate structure, she was apolitical and perceived as little danger to anyone desiring ascension toward corporate control. Simply stated, she did an exceptionally good job, an accolade frequently uttered by her boss, Burt Lehr. What could be better?

Jenny found the parking ramp unusually empty for a Monday at Mall of America and took a spot close to the skyway door and grabbed the small bag of videos from the seat beside her. Confident that Dan had access to a VCR, she would identify for him her tall stranger. She had told Creighton she had the closure she needed and had put the previous week's turmoil behind her—words spoken from the heart, but the man on her deck was an annoying detail, leaving a haunting feeling that something remained amiss.

She'd present her tall stranger to Dan if only to prove she wasn't imagining things and welcome any advice he may offer. Christian's confidence in her sanity would also be renewed. She would soon get on with her life.

Inside the store, she was in her element—a good feeling. She sighed as she passed one of her displays in need of a seasonal change, a reminder that she had not set foot in the store for weeks. Having not set foot inside the store for a couple of weeks made everything inside the store ever more fanciful. These were her displays, stirring childlike wonderment, just the way she had envisioned.

After briefly pausing to hear the remarks of some wide-eyed children, she started down the pathway that would take her through the Island Jungle and to the escalator to her office, where she hoped her assistant would be waiting. The white sandy beach seemed too familiar with its swaying palm trees and assorted animals looking on. *Déjà vu.* Before crossing the swinging river bridge, she stopped to look back at that favorite display. *What was it?* She shook her head and moved on through the next display and to the moving stairway.

"How was Creighton?" asked Sharon, as Jenny entered her in-store executive office.

"Quite charming, really."

"Well? Tell me about it. You're one of the company's most important people. He's been here for more than six months, and he's hardly given you the time of day. Until now. Come on. Tell me about it," Sharon persisted.

Jenny set the video bag in the middle of her desk. "There are a lot of important people in this company. I just happen to be one of the luckier ones. This is a fun place to be," she revealed honestly.

"Jenny. The meeting."

"Let me finish. I thought about it on the way in. I'm glad, truly glad I didn't make the move to corporate. You know, I don't think I could function there. Too much fantasy…arrogance."

"You don't think all this is fantasy?" Sharon asked, sweeping her arm about the room.

"The difference is we understand that. At corporate, they don't seem to have a clue. They live their fantasy. Too much game playing."

"Must have been some meeting."

"Good meeting, actually. These thoughts came later."

"Well?" Sharon asked again.

"The meeting with Creighton alone was very brief. He apologized for his absence and apparent lack of concern. The treaty, LAIPT, has been his obsession, as he put it. But he did express his appreciation for my contribution. That was nice. He also offered to pay for Jason's counseling or therapy—"

"But Jason's okay. Right?" interrupted Sharon, her concern genuine.

"He's fine. I declined the offer. But it's nice to know Creighton cares. His concern seemed real enough."

Nelsen Field, the store's manager, popped his head through the open door. "Hello, Jenny, Sharon. I expected you earlier. The crew is reworking the *country* scene. Have time to take a look at it?"

"Sorry. Had an unexpected meeting at corporate. Give me ten minutes. Okay?" Jenny looked at her watch.

"Sure thing," responded Nelsen and vanished down the hall.

"That's it?" asked Sharon. "Creighton offered to help. But no raise? Promotion? Praise for your very capable assistant?"

"We had lunch in the cafeteria. Kind of a staff thing, I guess. It didn't seem preplanned. Wendell Moore joined us. Nice guy. Daryl Kohl joined us too." Sharon shook her hand as though she were shaking off germs.

Jenny smiled. "I know. The man really is a fish. Cold and clammy. Those beady eyes. Another reason for staying away from corporate. Kathy Warren, Creighton's secretary, was there. His assistant, JB, was busy and declined lunch. Everyone else was out of the office already."

"So you're having lunch in the cafeteria. And?" prodded Sharon.

JENNY

"Small talk, mostly. Very little business. Creighton talked about his Harvard days, his wife Virginia."

"Heard he was divorced. He lives alone in that big house. Doesn't he?"

"His wife, Virginia, lives in Louisville. He made it a point to say they are happily married. Her family's there. Her family home. Evidently quite wealthy. They see each other from time to time, but of necessity, live independent lives. She comes here to Minneapolis occasionally. She's visited the store. We've probably waited on her ourselves and never knew it."

"Some relationship," Sharon observed. "He discussed all that at lunch?"

"He was quite open about it. Probably wanted to put an end to the divorce speculation. I somehow thought the conversation was more for my benefit. Maybe that's what lunch was about, to reveal his lighter side, his humanity."

"His wife owns more of the company than he does," continued Jenny. "She's a woman of strong faith. A born-again Baptist. She likes the company for its wholesomeness. I'd like to meet her someday."

"Dan Sheridan will drop by about 2:30," said Sharon, changing the subject, looking at her watch. "Any minute now."

For the first time, Jenny noticed what Sharon was wearing. She looked "business," but her short light-brown skirt revealed legs that guys at the plant would talk about for weeks. "You look ready," Jenny said with a smile. "Very nice!"

"I wasn't very nice when we met the first time. I'm hoping to improve my impression."

"Didn't think you cared that much about men? This one in particular?" said Jenny.

"You know better than that. I just don't like most men. Most are jerks. You know what I mean." Sharon stepped into the center of the room like a model on a runway. "What do you think?" she asked.

"I don't think you're being very considerate," said Jenny with a big grin. "Dan doesn't have a chance."

Memory snatches of Friday's dinner with Dan—the wine, his inviting look, falling into the lake—flooded Jenny's mind only to be interrupted by a light knock at the open office door.

"Ladies," said Dan as he stepped inside. "I'm not interrupting anything? My secretary said 2:30." He looked at his watch.

Jenny picked up the bag containing the videotape. "I watched the tapes. He was in the audience. Would you have time to take a look? Is there someplace we could go to play this?" She swung the bag in her hand. "I wasn't imagining things."

"My office," answered Dan and withdrew his "hand-held" from its belt clip to buzz his secretary, turned and walked toward the window while speaking into its microphone. His office also had a view of the large indoor amusement area from where he could watch the crowds. He held the walkie-talkie to his ear. A moment later, static barked, and he turned again to Jenny. "Fifteen minutes. I'll meet you there."

"Make it thirty. Our display crew is waiting for me. I won't be long. I'd like Sharon to join us. She may recognize him."

"Good idea," Dan said and turned to the door. "Thirty minutes." He stopped midway, returned to Jenny, and held out his hand for the video bag. "I'll set it up. It'll be ready to go when you get there."

Sharon waited for Dan to disappear and then said, "Thanks."

"For?" asked Jenny, knowing the answer. Sharon only smiled.

"Bring the clipboard. The crew is waiting," directed Jenny and headed out the door. Sharon caught up with her where the press conference had taken place.

"This is where it all happened?" Jenny asked as she walked past small product displays that had replaced the gallery of onlookers.

"Who were they after? Creighton or Malovich?" Sharon asked.

"Don't think anyone knows for sure. It probably didn't matter who the target was. Some radical group wanted to draw attention to their cause."

"And Jason?" asked Sharon.

"Probably targeted for the same reason."

"But they released him."

"Could have been their plan all along. I just thank God he's safe."

Jenny and Sharon took the escalator to the second floor and headed for the corner of the store. There, inside large sheets of plastic suspended from wooden frames, a carpenter crew was building a miniature farmyard, the future toy animal petting zoo where children would come to play with WYCO's lifelike animals. They found an opening in the plastic and entered.

Inside, heads turned as Jenny and Sharon picked their way around power tools, electrical cords, and lighting equipment. A muscular man, straight out of a beer commercial, emerged from one of the several little barns, shaking sawdust from his curly brown hair. He shook hands with Jenny and walked to a large table where several blueprints were unrolled and taped down to the surface. It became noticeably quiet as the crew of virile young men stopped what they were doing to take in the pleasant change in scenery. One scruffy kid, whose hair swung in a ponytail, excitedly took a step backward, stepping into a bucket of scrap wood, knocking it over with a domino effect on tools, sawhorses, and assorted stuff too light to stay put.

After the dust settled, Jenny approved the plans and, with Sharon, left the construction site. "Well, you got their attention," Jenny said once outside the curtain.

"More than I got from Dan Sheridan," said Sharon with a pout. "I think he prefers you."

"I'm not available. Besides, it's really Jason he's attracted to."

"You mean, he's…?"

"No! Don't be stupid. He misses his own son who was killed years ago. Run over by a car. He would be Jason's age."

"Where's his wife?"

"Divorced. She went crazy after the accident. Booze, drugs, prostitution. Dan doesn't know where she is now. Or even if she's alive."

"That's sad," reflected Sharon as she processed the new insights.

"Yes. Sad," Jenny repeated thoughtfully.

Chapter 44

Outside the store, the two women walked past shops, movie theaters, arcades, and restaurants. With little traffic, the click of their heels echoed down the hall. Not a good day for business. Dan's office was on the opposite side of the mall, a couple football fields away. They walked quickly, in unison, amplifying the echo to a sharp staccato cadence.

"What do you think of him?" Sharon asked as they entered the perimeter walkway. Jenny, wearing a puzzled expression, turned to face her. "Dan. What do you think of him? Didn't he come for dinner last week?" Sharon repeated.

"Last Friday. Sharp, good-looking. In every way, a gentleman." A fact for which she was profoundly grateful. "Knows his business. Hardworking. I think he's hurting from his divorce. Seems to be a loner. Said as much himself. Probably needs a friend. Like you."

"You mean needs a friend like I need a friend? Or he needs a friend? Somebody fun like me?"

Jenny frowned and shook her head. "Like you. He needs a friend. And, yes, someone fun like you."

"You think I'm fun?" Sharon asked.

"You said you're fun. I didn't."

"I guess. I seem to chase the good ones away. Maybe I'm not fun."

"Maybe you're too much fun for the good ones," commented Jenny insightfully.

"Do you think so?" she asked, drawing another frown from Jenny. "Think we're the same type? You know. Could we get along?"

"You don't have a type," said Jenny with a smile. "As far as I can tell, neither does Dan. He seems to be a person of character, conviction. You're both nontypes. You'd get along."

"A man of conviction. That's pretty good for a cop," Sharon teased with the play on words.

"How's it going, Jenny. Everything okay?" shouted a woman from behind the counter of a gourmet coffee stand Jenny frequented on her "store" days.

Today she kept walking but half-turned to answer, "Back to normal. Thanks. I'll be back."

The shops gave way to a row of offices behind a glass door, marking the end of the public area. Jenny and Sharon entered, continuing through a set of double glass doors identified by a large brass plate as "Mall Security/Executive Office."

On the alert, the receptionist stood to greet them and led them directly to Dan's office. "Mr. Sheridan is expecting you in here," she said and pushed open Dan's door. The office lacked the grandeur of Creighton's lavish suite, but it was, nonetheless, very elegant for a *cop*. Sharon's jaw dropped in awe. "Wow," she mouthed.

A large television with built-in VCR player sat perched on one end of a mahogany coffee table. Dan moved two chairs closer to the table before he spoke. "We're all set." He removed the *remote* from the top of the television and handed it to Jenny when she was comfortably seated. "Okay, Jenny, let's see your elusive stranger."

Jenny pushed "On" and "Fast Forward" displaying the scenes of the newscast in rapid animation. After the opening of the news conference passed, she pushed "Play" and returned the action to normal play. "Here he comes," Jenny said as the camera angle panned to the audience. "There. In the background. The tall man." She rewound the tape and replayed the portion in slow motion.

"What are we looking for?" asked Sharon.

"I'm sorry. I didn't tell you. I think the tall man on this tape appeared later the same day at my home, on my deck during the storm. Do you recognize him?" asked Jenny. Not getting an answer, she let the tape play on for several minutes.

"There's our would-be assassin. One Frederick Bartlett." Dan identified the man in the red sweatshirt.

Jenny pushed "Stop Frame" leaving the image of the tall stranger and the would-be assassin, who stood a couple people in front of him. "There he is. That's the man who appeared on my deck. I know they're one and the same. Do you think Bartlett knew him? Are they together, or are both there by chance?"

"Not ruled out, but it seems Bartlett acted alone," said Dan. "I'll pass this on to Sadler. He'll find a connection if there is one. Here he is again." Jenny again stopped the video.

"Wearing a red sweatshirt?" observed Sharon.

Dan answered, "He wanted to be seen on television. It was his mission."

"For what reason?" Sharon asked.

"I'd call it a death wish. According to Sadler, Bartlett's target was Creighton Leonard. A search of Bartlett's apartment reveals Bartlett was stalking Leonard with the intent of killing him. STUFFIT is something the media has picked up on. Bartlett had nothing to do with STUFFIT."

"I don't understand," said Sharon.

"It appears that Bartlett intended for his life to end with his assignation of Creighton Leonard."

"But why?" persisted Sharon.

"I'm sorry I can't get into the details. It's an ongoing investigation. I've already said more than I should. So I must add that what I have disclosed is highly confidential and should not leave this room. Understood?"

Both Jenny and Sharon nodded.

After a long pause, Sharon spoke, pointing again to the television screen. "I recall Jason was giving a blood sample when this was going on."

"At the mall clinic," he continued after a brief pause. "Sadler has pretty much ruled out a connection between the two incidents. The one possible thread could be the intent to somehow draw attention to the trade negotiations in Washington and strike out at the Japanese," said Dan.

"Am I blind? I don't see how Jason fits in," declared Sharon.

"Jenny had a role in the negotiations with Mikado. Jason was a way to get to her," Dan responded.

"But LAIPT will expand trade in South America, Mexico, Latin America. Isn't that what they want?" countered Sharon.

"Yes, but according to the media, STUFFIT wants to stop Japan from competing altogether. There's enough anti-American sentiment in Japan to hurt this Mikado partnership if their people get mad enough. Killing a leader like Mikado would do just that: a new round of hate America. In theory, kidnapping Jason would stir the emotion on this side of the Pacific," Dan continued.

"Who would get mad at Jason's abduction? If you thought STUFFIT did it, wouldn't you just want to kill them all? Pardon my French. I just don't see it," said Sharon in frustration.

"That could be the reason why Jason was released. A backlash is obvious or was to some in the organization. STUFFIT is radical, but not all their people are stupid. What you just said may have finally come home to someone in the organization, and the order was given to abort the kidnapping. Again, in theory. STUFFIT is denying any association with Bartlett. According to them, he was acting on his own."

"Come on. Would they ever do anything but deny it?" Sharon persisted.

"Look, it's not my theory," exclaimed Dan, feeling the heat. "It's the media's. Jason just doesn't fit in. But they have nowhere else to nail it. They're self-proclaimed experts, the press, television, and the politicians. Given any issue, they have divinely inspired answers."

"Maybe he's the link to Jason," Sharon said as she pointed again at the tall man whose image continued to flicker in "stop frame" on the television screen. "I mean, it could be. He's in the audience during the assassination attempt. Yes, maybe completely innocent. Just there like a hundred or so other people, spectators watching. But he also goes to Jenny's for the newscast. The reason seems less important than the fact he was at both places. He's the one common thread."

As Sharon spoke, her eyes were drawn to the pager vibrating on her waist and excused herself.

Dan turned to Jenny. "What do you think, Jenny?"

"I know I saw that man on my deck during the storm. Why? I have no idea. And if he was there? What does that prove…he has good taste in tiepins? I don't know that his being there proves anything. You know, I find myself caring less about finding a reason for all of this. At first, I needed to know why Jason was the victim. Now, I…I'm losing interest, I guess. He's safe. The police say it's an isolated incident and doubt he's in any further danger. I'm beginning to question if I really want to know why."

Dan didn't push, deciding instead to change the subject. "Jenny, how well do you know Creighton Leonard? How long has he been at WYCO? Six months?"

"About that. I can't say I know the man. A management team, put in place after Harold Benner's suicide, runs WYCO. Creighton has left the team intact, concentrating on the trade agreement and LAIPT. Had lunch with him today though. Why?" asked Jenny.

"Creighton Leonard is very well-connected on both sides of the ocean. An enviable position, as most would see it. He's the one person who wins regardless of who's mad at who, and the dust finally clears. He has strong ties with the US Senate. He's a strong supporter of the Clinton administration and Senator Malovich, Chair of the LAIPT trade committee. Did you know Creighton plans to move your production south of the border?" Dan looked at Jenny.

"To my knowledge, that's not a sure thing. Mostly plant rumors picked up by the press. Although, at my level, we've discussed contingency plans. We're always evaluating alternatives. If the treaty is enacted, we expect to see a shift toward Mexico. But at this time, there's nothing definite." Jenny paused for a moment, studying Dan. "You know a lot about my business. WYCO doesn't seem a logical concern for mall security."

"I could have cared less thirty days ago. Then I received this phone call, and suddenly Jason was my concern. And…I met you. You work at WYCO. You're both my concern. My list of concerns continues to grow."

"And Creighton Leonard? Mikado? Senator Malovich? How concerned are you for them?" asked Sharon from across the room.

"Personally, very little. They're Gary Sadler's concern."

"And Jason, isn't?" asked Sharon, a hint of anger in her voice.

"As part of the bigger picture. Like Jenny said, Jason's now home. He's safe. Sadler's team will continue to poke around but in the context of the broader investigation." Dan was feeling Sharon's growing hostility and hoped it was directed at the system, not at him.

Finished retrieving her messages, Sharon returned to her seat in front of the television.

"What was so urgent?" Jenny asked.

"It was a call for you. A Jim Stewart. I had your calls forwarded to my pager. This morning, Mildred Knowles said you had received a call from Jennifer Stewart. That call came in over the weekend." Jenny nodded. Sharon continued, "Jim Stewart is her brother. He called from Nebraska. He'd like his sister to call him when she gets in. He left his number. You could call him."

"Maybe I should," Jenny commented absentmindedly.

"What is it Jenny? You look concerned," observed Dan.

"It's probably nothing." Jenny's mind was churning, and it was obvious to everyone. "I really don't know Jennifer Stewart. Why is she coming to see me?"

"Just who is Jennifer Stewart?" asked Dan.

Sharon answered, "She worked on our floor. Newly employed, a *gofer*. You know, *gofer* this, *gofer* that. Started a couple of months ago. A young woman—"

"Woman? As in there's a difference between a girl and a woman?" asked Dan. "Age? Is that it?" he asked.

"Age? Yes. Also behavioral. During the week, I dress up, go to a nice office, earn an income. I'm a woman," explained Sharon, tossing her hair back, straightening her posture.

"I've noticed," observed Dan with a look that was not wasted on Sharon, who squealed inside.

"But sometimes in the evening, usually on the weekends, I become a girl again and a little more fun," continued Sharon, slightly flushed and sensing she was making progress.

"And Jennifer Stewart?" asked Dan. "She was like that?"

"I really didn't know her well. We spoke only a couple of times. She had just started. Young. Pretty. She had some college and wanted to get into marketing, so she took the job at WYCO to see what marketing in a major corporation was all about. She had an innocence about her, eager to help. She didn't seem to be into the games that adults play. All this information is compliments of Mildred Knowles."

"And what became of this Jennifer Stewart?" Dan asked, returning to the subject.

"I assumed she quit, as I think back, but vanished is more like it. It was one of those things. You know. You don't realize someone is gone until you become aware that you haven't seen them for awhile."

"That was about the time that Jason was kidnapped, maybe a little before," added Jenny, stirring in her chair. "Now she has called me over the weekend. She called me and left a message on my voicemail about returning to Minneapolis with some information for me. What could that mean? Like I said, I didn't know her. I don't know what information she could have that would be of interest to me," Jenny puzzled.

"Possibly her brother knows. The phone's on the desk. Call him," prompted Dan.

Jenny walked to Dan's desk, dropping herself slowly into his chair and reached for the phone, like a person wanting to pet a sleeping dog that could suddenly awake and bite while Dan and Sharon looked on, exchanging glances as Jenny dialed Jim Stewart's telephone number.

"Jenny tells me that you were with the CIA and the FBI. Both?" Sharon asked Dan as they waited.

"Yes," answered Dan matter-of-factly.

"So what attracted you to Min-nee-so-ta?" she asked with as much Swedish accent as she could muster.

"Needed a change," said Dan.

"Something tame, like the world's largest shopping center?" Sharon asked.

"Something like that." He became silent, noticing Jenny slowly return his phone to its cradle.

"Tell me, Mr. Sheridan, are you always this reticent?" Sharon asked in her most pleasant voice.

"Reticent?" Dan asked absentmindedly, as Jenny approached them.

"Jim Stewart was out for the moment. The girl who answered didn't know anything about Jennifer other than she supposedly returned to Minneapolis early this morning."

Dan noticed from Jenny's changing expression the impact Jennifer Stewart had on her and made a mental note. Then sensing their meeting was over, stood to rewind the videotape, and placed it back in its bag, which he handed to Jenny. "Here," he said. "I'll get with Sadler and see what he can find on the tall stranger. Is there anything else you'd like me to do?"

"You've done enough. More than enough. I'm ready to let all this become history," Jenny said. "After I introduce Chris to the tall stranger." Jenny looked at her watch. "His flight is due within the hour. He's expecting me to pick him up at the airport." She turned to address Sharon. "Are you coming?"

"Actually, as long as I've got the ear of the mall's security chief, I'd like to talk with him about our store security. You go on. You'll be in tomorrow? Lake office?"

"As far as I know. See you then." Jenny turned, let herself out of Dan's office, and closed the door behind her, leaving Sharon alone with Dan to discuss the store's hypothetical security problems.

Sharon got right to the point. "Now, Mr. Sheridan, could I ask you a few questions about our security?"

"Be my guest," answered Dan.

"Actually, I was hoping you'd be my guest," Sharon said matter-a-factly, bringing a surprised look to Dan's face. "Dinner at six. Italian. A glass or three of a nice red wine. You can pick the spot. You know this place much better than I. We can talk about…security. At six?"

Dan looked at her quizzically. She looked up at him, a twinkle in her eye that he had not noticed at their press conference meeting and a beckoning smile. "Are you asking me for a date?" he asked.

Sharon straightened her tight skirt but didn't answer, allowing her smile and puppy-dog look to do its work. Jenny was right; she was not being considerate of Dan; she had him, and she knew it.

"Is this the girl in you wanting to escape?" he asked at last.

"It is," she confessed.

"Seeking adventure? Something new, uninhibited?"

"Within reason," she agreed.

"And security?" he asked.

"We'll get to that. This little girl is looking for that little boy in you that cared enough about Jason Poole to take him on the mall's log ride."

"Jason can do that to you."

"I know," Sharon agreed. "So can his mother." A smile swept across Dan's face. He got her point. "You really do care for her, don't you?" she pined, a new softness to her voice.

"I care. I find her to be one of the most remarkable women I've ever known. She's intelligent, very attractive," confessed Dan, surprised by his openness.

"And sexy?" Sharon offered.

"I can't say I don't agree. She certainly is that. But then…so are you," Dan continued, "Yet she has a quality I can't seem to describe.

She seems to have an inner strength. I don't know…a simple serenity. A way about her that says she vulnerable but confident that everything is under control."

"And besides, she's married," reminded Sharon.

"To a very fortunate man," Dan responded, adding, "and she has one remarkable son."

"Which brings us back to dinner. Does the little boy want to come out and play? And meet a nice little girl. You'd like her. Guaranteed." Sharon stood as she spoke and looked Dan squarely in the eye. "Camp Snoopy at six. At the base of Snoopy."

Chapter 45

Jenny parked in "short-term" parking and entered the airport terminal on the baggage claim level. For some reason, she enjoyed the airport with its milling people and echoed sounds. She enjoyed travel, the anticipation of a new adventure. On this Monday afternoon, most of the travelers would be businessmen and women beginning another work week.

The escalator took her to the departure level. She checked her watch at the security checkpoint. Five minutes before touchdown, time enough to buy some breath mints and hide the garlic from her lunchtime salad. A blinking monitor announced that Christian's flight had already touched down and was at the gate.

Running the rest of the way to the shop, she handed the cashier two dollar bills, retrieved a tin of mints, popped three tablets into her mouth, and darted back to the checkpoint. A small procession of travelers had begun heading toward her up the long corridor from the concourse. She moved closer to the terminal doors, sure that Chris could spot her as he headed up the ramp.

"The time in Minneapolis is 4:05 p.m. Thank you for flying United. On behalf of Chief Leighton and the entire flight crew, we wish you a pleasant stay in the beautiful Twin Cities or wherever your final destination might be."

Jennifer Stewart, sitting in a window seat, watched as the plane taxied to the terminal and the long jet-way swung into place. While the final words from the flight attendant droned from above, passengers began to stand and open the overhead compartments to gather their belongings.

She had driven herself to the Omaha airport, intending to return within the week, after having met with Jennifer Poole to determine what course of action they should take. Her brother Jim had been prevented from seeing her off; one of the farm's ventilation systems had gone awry.

Mechanical problems on board the aircraft in Omaha created an unwanted delay, while Minneapolis-bound passengers waited for another aircraft to be flown in from Denver. She had checked other flights but found them booked full of Monday commuters. Jim would be wondering why she had not called. His would be the first call she would make as she waited for her bag at the carousel. Her mind began cranking again.

It was all so logical, so obvious; the attempt to kidnap Jason Poole was an attempt to get at her. Someone had made a mistake, most likely confused by their similar names. How many Jennifers could there be in the world? Both used the nickname Jenny. Both worked on the same floor at WYCO Toys.

But she, not Jennifer Poole, had been witness to the strange gathering of people in the plant conference room. The light behind the door had attracted her. There had been a man and a boy, both nude. Curiosity killed the cat; it nearly killed her. Killed because of a porno shoot? Was that reason for murder? If it wasn't a promotional shoot, then what? Whose face was that in the shadows?

Had Juan Smith really intended to kill her? Of course, he did. She had seen the wire dangling from his fist. It was meant for her. It was all so vivid in her mind—the dampness of the farrowing barn. The smell of the disinfectant she had flung into his eyes. Her escape to the equipment barn. Juan on top of her, the muffled thud as Jim's wrench found Juan's skull. The sight of Juan's body lying in a growing puddle of blood. Too bad Jim had not fed him to the hogs. *What sweet justice that would have been!*

A hand on her shoulder startled her. She jerked her body around, and quickly the hand retreated. She was ready to fight; her face contorted. "Miss, are you all right? I'm sorry to startle you. The cleaning crew is here....I'm afraid you must leave the aircraft." The flight attendant looked surprised but in control.

Jenny looked around. Clearly, she was the only passenger still onboard. "How long...?"

"Six or seven minutes. This aircraft is scheduled for a quick turnaround. I thought you'd fallen asleep."

The small backpack Jenny had brought onboard was under the seat in front of her. She grabbed it, stood to leave, and offered a conciliatory smile to the attendant. Outside the jet-way, a flood of people from other arriving aircraft filled the concourse. Unfamiliar with the terminal, she didn't know which way to go and fought a sudden rush of panic, then decided to follow the crowd. Quickly she made her way up the concourse. Ahead, a sign directed her to the escalator and the baggage claim where she would retrieve the one small suitcase she had checked in Omaha. She wondered now why she had even checked the bag. It would have fit in the overhead compartment. But, then, it didn't matter. She wasn't pressed for time. She had not called ahead for anyone to meet her. She would have tried harder to reach Jennifer Poole by telephone but thought it better to meet with Jennifer in person, and that could best be arranged once on the ground in Minneapolis.

Juan said *they* had been to her apartment. Who were *they*? She imagined her room ravaged with drawers pulled out of her dressers, things overturned, everything a complete mess as *they* searched for any evidence of where she had gone. How long had *they* looked before *they* found the notepad by the telephone that gave the address of Stewart Pork?

Her first stop would be her apartment. She'd have to be careful, of course. There, she would find a change of clothes and a quick shower. *Yes, a shower would be nice.* If it was a mess, so be it. *They* had not gotten her; that's what mattered. *They* had discovered her whereabouts weeks ago; she presumed and doubted *they* had continued surveillance. After all, *they* expected her to be dead by now, not to return. But what if Juan was to report to someone? He had certainly not reported his success. Whoever was behind the attempt on her life must know she was still alive but would not expect her to return to Minneapolis. That hope comforted her.

To be safe, she would take a taxi to the apartment. If someone were watching, they'd probably be looking for her car. She'd enter the front door and walk to the back of the building and take the stairs to her floor. If she saw anyone at all, she'd keep on going. She'd knock at Mrs. Strasberg's door. She was always home. From there, she could call the police. It was a good plan if she suspected she was being followed.

She stepped off the escalator and with the flow of travelers herded to claim area 6. Several minutes passed before the turntable began to revolve and fill with luggage. Ten minutes later, she was alone and without her bag. Soon she realized she had carelessly followed the passengers from another flight. She had gone to the wrong carousel!

Scolding herself to be more careful and conscious of her surroundings, she retraced her steps through the turnstile and walked to a bank of monitors she remembered seeing along the way. They would lead her to her suitcase; she should have looked there in the first place.

Sure enough. Her suitcase had been sent to carousel 12. She set out in its direction at the other end of the building. By now, the crowd had thinned considerably. A man dressed in a business suit stood alone outside the gate of a distant baggage claim. He watched her approach, she noticed.

He stood outside the entrance to carousel 12 and smiled as she passed. Inside the claim area, a small suitcase rested on a nearly empty baggage rack for unclaimed baggage. It was hers. Either an attendant had removed her bag to clear the carousel or…? She rejected any further thought and walked to her bag.

"Allow me," offered the voice from behind Jennifer, startling her. She turned slowly. It was the man who had been standing outside the claim area. He had followed her in. In his early thirties, he was very handsome, about six feet tall and muscular with wavy black hair. His eyes were hidden behind dark sunglasses. Not giving her time to respond, he reached for the suitcase with one hand and, with the other, brandished a small leather case and a badge. She saw it clearly: FBI.

"Miss Stewart, Jennifer Stewart?" he asked politely. She looked at him, her shoulders relaxing slightly and, feeling relieved, waited for his instructions. *The FBI?*

"I'm Agent *Gomez*. Your brother, Jim, contacted us. He told us about the attempt on your life. You were very lucky. Local police confirmed his story. We were concerned when you did not come for your baggage with the rest of the passengers from your flight."

"How did you know I had a suitcase?" she asked, feeling the need to test him.

"Your brother told us to look for a beautiful young woman dressed in Levi's and a plaid shirt with a suitcase such as this." He held it out to her and began to move from the claim area.

"Miss Stewart, you may be in considerable danger. We have arranged a safe place for you. I wish you to follow me. Please." He walked quickly now toward the terminal door.

"Wait. I have to call my brother," she said as she stopped to look for the closest telephone.

By now, the agent had already moved ten steps ahead of her. He stopped short. "Miss Stewart, he is expecting your call. But we must hurry. You may use the phone in the car." He instructed as he walked back, prepared to take her by the hand.

"Agent Gomez, where are you taking me? I need to go to my apartment. My clothes are there."

"Your apartment is not safe. We will send someone for your things. Please, Miss Stewart, I am here to keep you safe." He began to take her hand, but she brushed him away and took two steps toward the terminal door.

"I will take you to your apartment. Only for now, it is important that no one knows of your return. Perhaps in a day or two. Have you called anyone to tell them you are coming?"

"No. No one. I…" She was about to say something about Jenny Poole but changed her mind.

"Yes, Miss Stewart."

"Nothing. Can we stop to get something to eat? I missed lunch. They didn't serve anything on the flight."

"Anything you would like. Compliments of Uncle Sam." The man smiled at his own humor.

"Oh, yes. That Uncle Sam. Sorry. I'm tired as well as hungry. You would be Uncle Sam, wouldn't you?"

He led her through the terminal doors into the cool-afternoon air. Even in the shade of the buildings, the light appeared golden, like the sky the day she fled the farrowing barn. It was a fall sky; its light, a beautiful muted glow. For an instant, at least, the beauty touched her spirit. Then she moved on.

The airport terminal was undergoing extensive renovation. Barricades were everywhere, as well as large canvas drapes, which hung suspended from scaffolding high above to isolate specific construction areas to protect the public. The agent led the way through the maze. Jenny followed two steps behind; her backpack draped over one shoulder. Quickly they walked through the building and exited through doors at the base of the escalator that she had descended to the baggage claim level. A driverless sedan waited for them at the curb.

As they approached the car, a man and a woman, each with a carry-on stepped off the escalator, exited the same door, and headed to the short-term parking ramp across the drive, passing them only feet away. Jennifer Stewart didn't recognize either the man or the woman, although her agent did a double take. She had, after all, only met Jennifer Poole briefly and had never met her husband.

She did notice a small gold earring in Gómez's left ear as he opened the trunk and placed her suitcase inside. When Gomez opened the passenger door, Jennifer Stewart stepped in and sighed as she settled into the rich leather upholstery. Relaxed, she turned and looked about the airport drive one last time before Gomez closed the door behind her.

An earring? She smiled at the thought. True to his campaign promise, the president was bringing the departments of the federal government into the twenty-first Century. This agent was living proof. He really seemed to be with-it, she reflected.

Dutifully she buckled her seat belt and caught a brief sparkle from a little gold cross dangling from the driver's earring. *With-it*, she mused again. She had an escort. She would be safe. It was a good thing that Jim had called the FBI. She had not thought of that. Yes, a good thing. "A quarter pounder with cheese would be just fine," she said to the watching eyes in the rearview mirror.

"Anything you say, ma'am," said the handsome smiling agent.

Chapter 46

Christian and Jennifer Poole made the commute from the airport to Tonka Bay in just less than one hour in normal rush-hour traffic. Jason had gone directly from school to hockey practice. And because he had another scheduled practice early the next morning, he would have dinner and spend the night at a teammate's home. Chris loved his son and missed him more than words could say, but tonight he relished the thought of being alone with Jenny and an evening to themselves.

The ride home had been filled with conversation, mostly Chris's, as he vented after a long weekend of nearly disastrous negotiations. He was like that whenever he returned home. Jenny let him ramble while she listened. Occasionally, she interjected her own observations, her opinions of the finer points of Chris's weekend—comments Chris welcomed and often found useful. As the car pulled into the drive, Chris was sufficiently unwound. The rest of the evening belonged to Jenny.

Chris grabbed his two carry-ons from the trunk and carried them into the house. Jenny brought Chris's briefcase and the plastic bag containing the newscast videos from the rear seat. On her way through the house, she deposited the briefcase in the front hall and dropped the videos on the coffee table in front of the television.

A blinking light on the answering machine told her only one message was waiting. She thought of Jim Stewart and wondered if Jenny had arrived in Minneapolis and had called her at home. Pushing "Play," she heard her mother's voice calling for no reason other than to check in. She listened to the message as Chris chugged up the stairs.

Jenny slid open the patio door and stepped onto the deck. She had not planned anything for dinner and eyed *Little Red*, wondering if it would be a good night to go by boat to the club for an evening out. The scene before her was beautiful to behold, the sun low in the western sky sent shadowy spears piercing earthward from small puffy clouds wearing crimson halos. It seemed only seconds before Chris joined her, coming up behind her quietly, placing his strong arms around her, hugging her gently. "I missed you," Jenny purred.

"Me too," Chris said, squeezing a little harder.

"You were quick. Unpacked?"

"Just don't look in the bedroom. It's not a pretty sight."

"Your suits?"

"On the floor. They need the cleaners."

"I was thinking of the club for dinner. We won't have many evenings like this."

"By boat?"

"What do you think?"

"Today's Monday?"

"All day."

"Club's closed on Monday."

"Mmm."

"I'm tired of people anyway. Besides, you need to bring me up to date. How about a fire in the fireplace, a glass of wine? A little talk…and…?"

"And watch the videos?" Jenny provided. "Living proof that the one-armed man exists."

"Proof? That's lawyer talk. Have I ever doubted?"

Jenny couldn't believe he'd said that, turned in his grasp, and smiled. "Not doubt. Just disbelief."

"How so?" he asked. Jenny didn't answer; instead, she pushed him away and headed back through the patio door. "I wouldn't call it disbelief either. More like insufficient knowledge due to a lack of credible evidence," he pleaded his case.

"I've got proof positive. Get your fire started. I've got to get into something more comfortable." Jenny's voice faded as she disappeared up the stairs to their bedroom.

Chris walked to the side of the town house to retrieve some aged oak logs left over from last winter's fire season. Not much there, he observed. With fall approaching, he'd have to order another load. Somewhere in his dresser was a card from the "Paul Bunyan" who had delivered last year's *cord*.

Jenny quickly pulled on her favorite jeans, went directly to the kitchen, and opened the fridge. "Not much here," Jenny informed Chris when he entered with an armload of split oak.

"Fish?" he offered. On the coffee table, he spied the plastic bag containing the videos, which he picked up and carried into the kitchen.

"Gone," she confessed when she heard his footsteps; she'd been thinking fish.

"These are your proof?" he asked, holding the bag out to her as though it were a dirty diaper and poked his head into the refrigerator.

"Well, they're proof that the "one armed" man exists. I can't say they prove much else." Jenny reached past his nose to retrieve a package. "Steak? The one you missed on Friday."

"Sounds good. Is the steak all I missed?"

There was seriousness to his question. It was good she was the one who had told him about falling into the lake. He had not heard it first from the neighbor, Mel. She had nothing to hide. But out of her own frustration that evening, she had let down her guard. That would not happen again. "Well," she said, "You missed the moonlight swim." Then she offered Chris her most seductive smile. "Now you can start the grill and set up the VCR. You're going to watch my evidence," Jenny ordered, changing the subject.

Jenny quickly assembled a salad, grabbed the leftover merlot, gathered plates and silverware, placed them all on a tray, and joined

Chris, who was sitting on the living room floor as one of the videotapes raced fast-forward on the VCR.

"Stop it right there. There he is! My proof positive. I rest my case."

A tall thin man, his face barely distinguishable in the poor light, stood in the crowd. "That's him?" Chris stopped the action and studied the picture for a full minute. "Now what?"

"I guess there is no what. But admit it, I've proven my point. I haven't a clue who he is. And want to know something I don't seem to care anymore? So I'll tell you what. Here's where it gets exciting. I'll do the steak. You watch the rest of the tape."

"So where is Dan Sheridan?" Chris asked a few minutes later as the video played on, and she entered with his steak, pan fried, pink center. "I'd really like to meet him." For Chris, Dan's obvious interest in his family had not registered until now. "You think of security for Mall of America, and you see somebody in a posh job."

"So just what do you expect?" Jenny asked somewhat defensively. She had placed the plate of steak on the coffee table and stood above him with her arms folded in front of her.

"I don't know."

"You'd like him, Chris. We probably won't have another dinner with him, so why not come to the mall and meet him? I know he'd like to meet you. He was disappointed Friday when you didn't show."

"I bet he was," Chris said sarcastically.

"And just what is that supposed to mean?" Jenny asked, her tone hinting of anger.

"I'm sorry. Nothing really. I was out of line."

"Yes, you were. Your son gets kidnapped. He is rescued by a good-looking cop who takes an interest in him and seems to be the only person willing to find out some answers, answers that just possibly could help us protect Jason from further harm. And you get jealous because you couldn't break away from your meetings, which you knew about well ahead of time. We had planned the dinner together, remember?" Then, surprised by how quickly the emotions of the past weeks resurfaced and gushed from her, Jenny stopped abruptly, rotated in place, and stared into space to collect herself.

"I said I was sorry. I didn't mean—"

"Yes you did."

"Time out. Change the subject here. What are we watching?"

Jenny turned again to face him, grabbed the remote from his hand, snapped off the television and lowered herself, legs crossed onto the floor. "I'm through watching," she announced. "Chris, I've made a decision. Nearly four weeks ago, Jason was kidnapped. Had he been hurt and not returned, I wouldn't be able to live with myself. Now, even though that's not the case, I'm frightened. I'm angry, I mean really angry, that something like that could happen to us. You've been gone most of time. I feel so alone. I feel that I've been facing this by myself, trying to reconcile what happened with my own understanding of reality."

Chris interrupted. "Honey, I wouldn't be able to live with myself either if something tragic had happened. I'd be here with you. I am now."

"That's not my point. The last few weeks have been a blur. What happened is more like a bad dream, like it really didn't happen. Or it happened to someone else. I can't answer all the questions, and I've been unwilling to let go."

"You see that now. That's good, Jenny! The answers are for the police, for Dan Sheridan to discover."

"I know that now. I really don't want to think about it anymore at all. I don't want to watch any more tapes. And that's my decision: to let it rest."

Chris gently stroked his wife's hair. "I haven't been much help. I'm really sorry. I didn't realize this was eating you up so." For several minutes, they sat silently and watched the fire's flicker when the kitchen telephone rang, bringing Jenny to attention.

"The answering machine is on," Chris assured, and Jenny settled back against him. "'The events of the day are not as you suppose, when you let them go in quiet repose.' Author unknown," said Chris smugly, proud of his quick composition.

"Sounds like author, Christian Poole," remarked Jenny, smiling again.

"Wise words, regardless. Care for more wine?"

"No. Your steak is cold," observed Jenny. "Tell you what. You 'nuke' your dinner. I'll fill the Jacuzzi. 'Let the bubbles soothe the troubles,' author, Jennifer Poole." With that, Jenny sprinted up the stairs to the master bedroom. Chris walked to the kitchen, placed dinner into the microwave for ninety seconds, noticed the answering machine was blinking, and pushed "Play."

"Hello," the voice said. "This is Jim Stewart calling for Jennifer Poole. Mrs. Poole, would you please call me." Chris jotted the number on Jenny's notepad. It was long distance. He assumed a customer calling. Whoever Jim Stewart was, he could wait. Jenny deserved a break. They'd not had an evening alone for weeks.

He placed the notepad beside the phone and rewound the answering machine before returning to the living room, steak in hand. His heart skipped a beat when Jenny entered, her robe hung loosely about her, exposing just enough to appear decent as if at the moment his thoughts were on decency. "Did you check the machine?" Jenny asked.

"For you, a business call. The number is on the pad," responded Chris, eager to finish his steak and retire to the bubbling Jacuzzi. "It didn't sound important."

Chapter 47

Outside Jenny's office window, silver-dollar-sized snowflakes filled the air, while intermittent sunshine exploded through the overcast, bringing brilliant contrast to the snow-covered white shoreline of Lake Minnetonka and the blue water just beginning to ice over at the water's edge. In spite of freezing temperatures, persistent fall winds had kept the lake open. That would change during the next two weeks as winter settled in for real. For today, however, the beauty was unsurpassed, framed in the stillness of a near-windless day.

Sharon Miller entered her boss's office and walked directly to the window behind Jenny to observe a brief break in the clouds where she spoke. "It's so peaceful," she said barely audible. When the clouds returned, she stepped beside Jenny.

"Here. Finished," said Jenny and handed Sharon a pile of papers. "I'll need six copies." She looked at her watch. "I'll deliver corporate's three copies myself. The rest can go in the *overnight* to Nelsen's attention."

Sharon turned from the window. "So you're going to do it?" she said.

"With the personal blessings of the CEO's wife, Virginia Leonard. How about that?"

"She's involved in this marketing decision?" Sharon was surprised.

"It's more than rumor, you know. She does own more of WYCO than Creighton does. She's got more to say about what goes on around here than most realize."

"Don't say that too loud around Creighton."

"He's the one who told me. Creighton is in town this week. He called me personally when Burt told him about my proposal. His wife shares my concern that for too long we've watered down the true meaning of Christmas. He gave me free rein to change the displays on the floor to depict the birth of Jesus Christ. My proposals are in your hand. Treat them with care," she joked.

As though divinely symbolic, sunlight exploded again over the lake, flooding light into her office. She turned to watch shadowy patterns dance on the ground below. "It is pretty…The snow and the water." After a brief pause, she added, "Looks like we'll have a white Christmas. A busy one too. Hard to believe it's only a month away. There's never enough time to get it all done. Chris is in town this week. Jason's first hockey tournament starts this afternoon. I'm meeting with Burt at his office. Still hope to catch an early dinner with Chris before the game."

"You'll do it, Jenny. You always do. Oh, I almost forgot. Anne Graham called for you."

Concern swept across her face as she remembered an assignment she had accepted months earlier. "Oh, Sharon, I forgot all about my high school cheerleader's reunion," she said in frustration. "And I'm supposed to be in charge. Can you believe it? What did she say? She's coming into town for the occasion."

"Well, she's here in town. Staying with her parents."

"Yes. Police chief, Nick Carlson. That's all?"

"She was just checking in." She paused. "Anything I can do? You look a bit harried."

"I made reservations at The Minstrels months ago. We'd skip class and go there for lunch. It's downtown in the warehouse district. Couldn't believe it was still there. Totally cool place to go back then. And were we cool. Can't believe how cool we thought we were. It's sure to rekindle some good memories. You could call and confirm our reservation. Eighteen on Thursday, three o'clock."

"I know the place. I took Dan Sheridan there."

"My! My! You and Dan Sheridan? I leave the two of you alone in his office, and the next thing you know, it's a budding relationship. Well? Are you going steady?" Jenny saw Sharon's bewildered look. "Now there's a term from the fifties. Today you don't go steady. You go to bed." Instantly, Sharon's expression changed to a "can't believe you said that" kind of expression. Jenny backpedaled quickly, "Sorry, didn't mean that. I mean, I wasn't insinuating anything about you and…Dan. So is this relationship serious? I haven't heard from him in weeks."

"Well, you know me, always the aggressor," Sharon responded lightheartedly. "So far, I'm the only one going steady. I'm the one who's serious. But he's enjoying being chased. And for your information, there's been no sex. Going to bed has never been suggested—by either one of us. He has stopped by the store a couple times to see how you're doing. He's asked about you."

"He's wanted to see Jason play hockey—or did. This whole thing with Jason…Not him. I've been the problem trying to put reason to Jason's kidnapping. With Chris traveling, it's been a little overwhelming. Well, I've decided to get on with life. Let happen what will. If he asks again, tell him everything has been fine. In fact, do tell him that. Everything is fine. Jason has not mentioned the subject in weeks…months, as a matter of fact, and I haven't reminded him."

"That's what you want, isn't it? No recollection?"

"It's what's best for Jason."

Sharon studied the face of the women who was more than her boss, the face of a caring and compassionate friend, who usually wore her emotions on her sleeve with a bold confidence that said the world could not hurt her regardless of how exposed and vulnerable she might be. But today, she saw a mask. It was the mask speaking, hiding real or imagined concern. For weeks, Jenny has seemed aloof, distant. Sharon couldn't put her finger on it, but she knew something was eating at Jenny from the inside; it was more than the season's heavy workload or changing the store's Christmas displays. It had to be the kidnapping, despite the fact that Jenny had not mentioned the subject in weeks. It began the day they had gone to Dan Sheridan's office together.

"Okay," Sharon said finally. "Eighteen for cocktails and dinner at The Minstrels, Thursday, 3:00. Will you be back?" she asked, turning toward her office.

"No. If I've got the time, I've got some shopping to do."

Jenny faced her window as she waited for her proposal copies. On the street below, a police car turned into the company parking lot and stopped at the front entrance.

"Have you taken any calls from Jim Stewart?" Jenny asked when Sharon returned with her stack of copies, neatly bound in their presentation covers.

"No. He's Jennifer Stewart's brother, right? You tried to reach him from Dan Sheridan's office. You never connected?"

"No. We haven't...I sort of forgot about him...And his sister. I think he tried to reach me at home. This morning, I came across a note saying he had called. I don't know when. Maybe weeks ago. It was Chris's writing. He must have taken the call."

"More than likely, she turned up someplace. He hasn't called here."

"You're probably right. Remind me to call him. Would you?" Jenny took three of the bound presentations and placed them into her leather portfolio. "I hope she's all right." Smiling absentmindedly, she grabbed her coat off a nearby chair and headed out the door.

Chapter 48

JB watched Jenny from behind his partially opened door as she left Burt Lehr's office and headed for the elevator. He had not been aware of her visit to the corporate tower, nor her meeting with Burt. She almost spotted him. They almost met in the hall.

Several times during the past couple months, he had wanted to stop by the old campus and surprise Jenny—he wondered if she remembered him. But each time, fear of being caught in an awkward situation, not knowing what to say, how to explain why he'd waited so long to come forward, deterred him. He couldn't quite do it.

She had always had that effect on him, left him speechless, tongue-tied. That hadn't changed since high school. He had changed, changed a lot as a matter of fact—she may even like him now as a friend—but her effect on him had not changed. He wasn't the beanpole she would remember, either. He had filled out his nearly seven-foot frame rather nicely, he thought. As the years passed, he found himself more pleased with the man he met in the mirror each morning. That was on the outside, but on the inside, his love-crazed schoolboy heart left him ill at ease when it came to Jenny.

When he was absolutely sure the elevator had closed, he walked quickly down the hall to Burt Lehr's office, his long stride covering the distance in seconds. He ignored the secretary who looked up at him in surprise as he swept by, his words directed to Burt.

"Wasn't that Jennifer Poole?"

"Yes, JB, she reports to me. She brought in some proposals," Burt answered sarcastically, surprised by JB's sudden and apparent interest in his department head. JB stammered to say something, but Burt wouldn't let him finish. "You're out of breath. She did that to you?" he asked, teasing, not knowing how close to home his words hit. "I admit she's very attractive. By the way, have you two even met? You should, you know. She's proposing a display change at the store. You're welcome to read it through. Interesting really," he said, waving the proposals in the air. "She has some strong arguments for emphasizing the historical significance of Christ in Christmas. Makes good marketing sense in my book. What do you think, JB, have we gone too far in watering it down? You know, Christ in Christmas?"

"That's not my thing, Burt."

"It's not? It should be," suggested Burt half-seriously, realizing he had found a tender spot. "You're the fiscal watchdog. Too much religion could offend some people: customers, consumers, the like. Could hurt sales…profits. That's your thing."

"This is Christmas for Christ's sake, Burt. What's Christmas if it's not religious?"

"An event. Like the Super Bowl."

JB shook his head in mock disgust. Of all the company's department heads, he got along best with Burt. Burt always knew the right button to push. That's why he kept his job. He knew how to get inside a person's head. He understood his market and what made buyer's tick, what made them buy. In marketing's forever tug-of-war with production, Burt most often emerged victorious. An ardent watchdog of quality goods, he had argued long and hard against the "junk" that overseas operations wanted to force on the US population. But on that account, he had lost.

Publicly, Burt supported the expected treaty with Mexico. That, after all, was the company position. He knew a corporate move south of the border was inevitable to bolster lagging profits. But privately, he believed WYCO was at the top of a long slide downward. Its descent would only increase with each piece of junk they introduced. As he saw it, Mexico would only hasten the fall. It was the move of last resort. He'd go down with the sinking ship though. A job change at his age was out of the question, something he wouldn't consider even for a minute. WYCO was his life. There had never been a finer toy company. Never would be again.

"Here. See what you think." Burt handed two of Jenny's bound copies to JB. "The concept is already approved by Virginia."

"Virginia Leonard?" JB was surprised.

"I'd say she's got more sense than her husband." His words came too easily. "You didn't hear me say that, JB. But it's true. You know, I haven't met the women, but I dare say I like her. These are Creighton's copies. Do me a favor and drop them off. He's expecting them, and I've got another meeting."

"Sure," agreed JB "And you may be right…About Virginia." JB turned and left Burt smiling after him.

He didn't go directly to Creighton's office. Instead, he walked to the secretarial area, found a copy machine where he disassembled one bound edition, and made a copy for himself, which he placed on his desk before continuing to Creighton's office. He was eager to read it through later when he had more time. It represented *her* work, and that made it worth his while to read. Anything to do with Jenny was worthwhile. He couldn't wait to study it, knowing it would reveal the very essence of who Jenny had become since high school. *Better than a photograph*, he thought to himself. The "Christ of Christmas"? Jenny hadn't changed much after all. Maybe more bold.

Creighton was on the telephone when JB entered his office and walked to the window looking out to the penthouse patio, now covered with three inches of fresh white snow. A sudden vortex of wind trapped by the building's walls swirled snow wildly across the open space. Still early afternoon, traffic on the Interstate below was beginning to snarl as motorists reacquainted themselves with slippery roads and other drivers. But this was lost on JB. He saw only the hypnotic cascade of white and, in his mind, the love of his life.

Reality came when Creighton's telephone conversation ended, and he sensed Creighton watching him. "Burt had a meeting and asked me to bring these to you. A display change at the store?" he asked and handed over the two bound proposals.

"Yes. Christmas displays. Jennifer Poole's contribution to Christmas. Virginia's too. This should be interesting. Tell me, how do you portray a baby as God? A topic my parents are still trying to resolve. Probably why they're still together after all these years. Each one trying to win over the other."

"Crey, that's not my thing," said JB, reflecting on Creighton's interfaith parents. It was the same with Creighton and his wife. He claimed to be Jewish, and Virginia an Evangelical Christian, whatever that meant. She was religious. But unlike Creighton's parents, Creighton and Virginia didn't live together. At least not often.

"It's not my thing either. You know that. Virginia insists that we have at least one display portraying the real Christ of Christmas. You get that, don't you, the real Christ?"

"Well, it is Christmas."

"I'm much more comfortable with Santa Claus."

"So whose idea was this, Virginia's or Jennifer Poole's?"

"Both, I guess. I've learned Jennifer Poole shares some of Virginia's convictions. By the way, Virginia is coming up for the office party. Thanks to Jennifer, she'll tour the store and see that her money is well invested."

A knock on the door announced Kathleen Warren, who entered with a concerned look. "Mildred Knowles just called. She said the police are on their way over here."

"The police?" Creighton echoed. "Over here? Did she say why?"

"Apparently, it's the Mound police with a detective from Minneapolis. Following up on a missing-person complaint. A Jennifer Stewart. She was an employee. She's been missing for several weeks."

Creighton's eyes met JB's. He saw more than surprise. "They probably need to see her file," he said matter-of-factly. "Better alert, Kohl. He can deal with them." Kathleen promptly turned, hiding a scowl, and left the room.

For several minutes of awkward silence, JB and Creighton looked at each other, neither knowing what to say, each wondering of the other's knowledge of the affair. "You told me this Stewart girl was returning to Minneapolis," Creighton said at last. "Does her disappearance mean you found her and decided to do something about it?" Creighton took the offensive, choosing the higher ground, leaving JB on the defensive. He didn't want a retake of his last *morality* discussion with JB.

"Don't be absurd. I let the issue drop. I thought she'd return for her back pay and be gone. I had assumed she had until now."

"Well, apparently someone's come looking for her. Now what do you propose we do?" Creighton sat back in his chair, his hands folded in his lap to make a steeple. His smug look said what he hoped: he had capped the ferocious geyser, at least for the moment. JB would worry the subject away and make every effort to right the wrong, keeping order in his world, even if denial of fact was the only way order could come.

"Let the blundering Kohl deal with it. You're right. They probably need to verify employment. She should have stayed in Nebraska. I don't suppose you had a hand in her disappearance?" He intended his sarcasm to hide true concern.

"For what purpose?" Creighton asked with steely eyes. Perhaps the geyser was not capped after all—an unfortunate reality.

"Perhaps she knew too much."

"I see. And what might that be?"

"Our involvement with Senator Malovich, for starters. Or your private film enterprise." JB had begun pacing, his eyes fixed on the Persian rug beneath his feet. He had not come to confront Creighton, but he couldn't help himself. It had started.

"Your highly rated productions. I know the senator likes young boys. And that was no infomercial being filmed in the conference suite. Where do you find them Crey, the boys? Or is that what the Martinez group does?" He didn't wait for answer. "And the only witness was Jennifer Stewart. How convenient. Now she's disappeared. For good, I suspect. Another function of your Martinez Group?"

"You're assuming too much." Creighton tried to hide his anger. "Martinez is a consulting firm on foreign operations."

"On failed operation, you mean. I'm not blind, Crey. I know you too well. I know what's going on." He had never before spoken to Creighton in such a manner, so accusing.

"Do you? Do you know me, JB?" Creighton's tone turned ice-cold. He studied JB, the only person alive beside Miguel Alverez that he had allowed to get close to him. The fact that he had tried to hide his darker side to protect JB from too much knowledge was for JB's own good, but it was obvious now that had been a wasted effort.

Creighton saw himself a victim of his own wishful thinking, for his young wizard had a conscience after all. What did that mean? A brilliant young mind, too important, too useful to discard.

"If you believe that, shouldn't you be a bit more cautious? Or are your accusations just the outflow of your impetuous nature? After all, if what you are insinuating is true, I would be a dangerous man. Dangerous, indeed."

"Are you threatening me, Crey? You can't make everyone disappear."

"That's hardly a threat. I've always been concerned for your well-being. You know that. I have made you a wealthy man."

"As it has suited your purpose. I'm not ungrateful."

"Stop that pacing!" Creighton ordered. JB had paced his way across the room to the coffee table and the small sitting area. He stopped short and dropped into one of the chairs. Creighton continued, "Why the sudden sensitivity over details that don't concern you? We have been good for each other. That is the essence of a good relationship: mutual value. You do what you do best, and I do what I have to do."

"Even murder?"

"Don't assume that. What's going on here? What's with you all of a sudden? A woman has disappeared, and you point your finger at me? When there is no proof, no evidence that can incriminate me?"

His lack of denial was not lost on JB. "You've made sure of that. Jennifer Stewart was the proof. Tell me. What will you do with our other Jennifer, Jennifer Poole and her son, Jason? More living proof."

The sound of Jenny's name coming from his own lips in such an impossible context, the possibility of exposing her to further danger, made JB shudder. He knew Creighton was capable of extreme measures, a callous ruthlessness lurking beneath his polished demeanor. Now, for the first time, he believed that included the ability to commit murder, and he shuddered at what he had just said.

For years, he had ignored his suspicions. As Creighton said, he did what he had to do. And Creighton was right; he had made him a wealthy man. But somehow, the importance of that fact was waning. Now there was Jennifer.

"Will they have an accident? Will they suddenly disappear for real? How will you dispose of that incriminating evidence?" JB was up and pacing again, his eyes fixed on one intricate pattern woven into the carpet beneath him. Why was he beleaguering Creighton, stepping in danger's path? He asked himself. Instinct. Expose the problem so you could deal with it; that's what he did.

"I don't like what you're saying. You're preposterous!" Creighton refused to be drawn in. His steepled fingers rotated around each other. "Anyway, they pose no threat," he said calmly. "According to his mother, the boy doesn't remember a thing and has no desire to do so," assured Creighton.

"Not yet. How about later? Six months from now? A year? Two?"

"He won't remember. The drug worked. And if he does suddenly, what would he remember? A ride to Mall of America in a truck with two strangers? Nothing too incriminating there."

JB breathed easier. Creighton's lack of concern seemed genuine. If he had the slightest fear that Jason and his mother were becoming a threat, he'd be more agitated, more hostile. He would be ordering her execution. Then, maybe, he already had?

"You were right about Jennifer Poole. She's attractive, bright, and she is an asset. And now she has become Virginia's property."

"How do you mean?"

"Virginia's financial backing does have its price. She sees WYCO as her company. You know that. And in Jennifer Poole, she has found a…a spiritual ally. A sort of stronghold in our midst."

"They haven't met."

"Not yet. But they will. At her *old Kentucky home*, she has built quite a file on WYCO. She reads every word of every report sent to her. That's good. Virginia is very astute. You know that too. She could run any company better than most men. The wholesomeness of toys, children's dreams, everything about this business is especially attractive to her. It appeals to her motherly instincts. The children we never had…couldn't have.

"Somewhere in our reports, she has discovered Jennifer Poole. She's the reason Virginia is pushing for a staff Christmas party. She intends to meet Jennifer Poole."

Creighton seldom spoke of his wife, a violation of privacy. JB suspected the reason the two did not live together was the inconvenience that posed to Creighton's lifestyle, which obviously ran crosscurrent to Virginia's Baptist's values. It had never seemed appropriate to question either one concerning their relationship—and it was none of his business. Aside from the distance between their bedrooms, she in Kentucky and he in Minnesota, they appeared to be the everyday husband and wife.

Relieved that Jenny had a place under Virginia's protective wing, the air between JB and Creighton became lighter, friendlier.

"You'll be here for the party?" It was more of a command than a question. He didn't wait for JB to answer. "Malovich won't make it."

"The last I heard, he was looking forward to Christmas in Minnesota, and a chance to get away from the investigation back home."

"I discouraged his coming. We need more distance between us. I'm afraid the 'dead lover' problem is going to stick. We don't need that kind of attention. The Senate ethics and moral practices probe is on hold until the first of the year. Everyone is expecting a criminal indictment when they come back."

The exploitation of the senator's homosexuality and the murder of his gay lover was ground they had already covered, JB remembered only too well. That discussion led nowhere. Creighton had unabashedly dismissed it like a week-old journal. But even now, JB was plagued by Creighton's possible involvement and the suspected role of the Martinez Group. But today, he wouldn't push it further. He would defer to a future time, which he knew would come as surely as a hangover from cheap booze.

"I'll miss the party," said JB, seating himself again in the high back chair.

While his words surprised Creighton, Creighton didn't become angry. JB had seldom missed an opportunity to take his place beside him at large functions, always eager to display his personal power and position, a game Creighton understood well. In fact, with JB, it was encouraged. *Why the sudden change?* He mused for an instant. *Another side to his young wizard?*

"My folks have asked me to come home."

"Really? Where is home?"

The question surprised JB. "I guess this is home. At any rate, they've asked me to be with them this year in Florida at their home. I've agreed. It's been three years. I've got some vacation time coming…I'll be gone ten days or so."

"What do you mean vacation time?" Creighton asked indignantly. "Since when do you keep track of vacation time? Take as much time as you need. Give my regards to your father."

"I will, Crey. I will." JB's voice became softer as his composure returned. He studied the enigma opposite him. How could a man, who at times was capable of great compassion, stoop to murder? The contrast was more than JB could comprehend, more than he wanted to think about.

Both heads turned as Daryl Kohl stormed into their meeting without knocking. His face was white with concern. "Sorry," he blurted when he realized his indiscretion. "The police are here investigating a Jennifer Stewart. She's been reported missing. Who the hell is this Jennifer Stewart? They're asking for her file."

"Is that so serious? Meet with them, Daryl. Give it to them." Creighton's voice did not hide his irritation. JB was right. Kohl was an idiot. The file contained only Jennifer's work history, two progress reports, and her job application. Kohl was an idiot.

Chapter 49

The next two days passed quickly for Jennifer Poole. Nelsen Field worked his crews overtime to complete the new display as Jenny had directed depicting the Christ child. Work, hockey, family had managed to preempt all thoughts of her cheerleading squad's reunion that she had organized months earlier. However, despite her preoccupation, the day had arrived. A most pleasing smile brightened her face as she drove east down Interstate 394. Outside temperature made one think of spring. Overhead, the sky was clear with only scattered clouds on the horizon. The daunting workload that had earlier threatened her week had been delegated away. She was ready.

Assisted by a committee of two, she had located the entire cheerleader squad, sixteen girls and two guys. All had agreed to attend. Still, she doubted Mark Stevens or Kent Simons, the only males on the squad, would be comfortable in a room full of gabbing women. But then, why not? That had not bothered them during their three years at Minnetonka High School. But she had not seen either Mark or Kent since graduation. They had gone off to college, and neither had attended their ten-year class reunion. She'd be delighted to see them and hoped they would attend.

Kathy was the only squad member she had actually seen since their tenth. Locating the squad was coordinated over the telephone. The tenth reunion had been held at the Lafayette Club on the shores of Lake Minnetonka. It was there one of the girls suggested they meet again in five years to maintain closer contact. She welcomed today's distraction, a day not centered on Jason's abduction.

She drove into a parking lot a half a block away from The Minstrels, grabbed her Skipper yearbook from the seat beside her, locked the car as the attendant walked up, handed him a five-dollar bill, and waited for her change.

The day had been unseasonably warm for the first week in December. All that remained of the season's first snowfall were occasional piles of melting ooze—obstacles she stepped over—as she put the change and her car keys in her trench coat pocket and set off to the Minstrels. Her eyes adjusted slowly to the dim ambiance inside, but with the help of a hostess, she found her way to the back room, already filled with conversation.

In the center of the room was a long rectangular table with eighteen place settings and an array of canapés. The back wall displayed squad photographs, some recent, but most were from high school years taken at events where the squad had performed. A large banner containing larger-than-life senior class pictures hung suspended from the ceiling. Each portrait displayed the never-to-be-forgotten phrase created by some yearbook staffer that characterized the stand-out quality of each member and deemed appropriate at the time. Included amongst these were "Best Dressed," "Muscles," "Steady Eddie," "Studious," "Always Early," "Never Late," and others, which may have forever haunted those whom they described.

Jenny located her picture, "Deep Like A River," and smiled. A yearbook staffer had participated in an after-school Bible study, where Jenny had been its leader and determined to expose the more serious side of one of the school's most popular girls and had changed the moniker from "Always Happy," just before press time. If those were the traits she had worn so openly fifteen years earlier, they had only intensified with the passing of time.

Her life had been good, but marrying young had not made it easy. Her values had sustained her through some very difficult times, and throughout, she had been *always happy* because she had a strong *deep-as-a-river* faith, which directed, protected, and controlled her life. For three years, she had been wife, mother, and sole breadwinner, while her husband pursued his education and a career in law. After Chris passed the bar and began work at the firm, her breadwinner role changed to that of contributor, but her contribution remained the lion's share. That had continued for two more years. Then growing affluence allowed a move to the suburbs.

It had been those early values that made her what she was today, good or bad; she had no regrets. She knew she had not changed all that much on the inside, and as she looked about the room, she realized that unlike most of her squad, she had changed very little on the outside—she could still wear her prom dress, an accomplishment others in the room could not claim.

"Jenny. Jenny Ward?" "Best Dressed" was still a knockout. Undoubtedly, she could still wear her prom dress. *Maybe she is*, Jenny thought to herself as she watched the beautiful woman approach from across the room, a glass of wine in hand. "So nice of you to arrange this. I can't believe it. We're all here. Mark and Kent too."

Jenny looked around the room, taking stock of who had arrived. She had been the last to appear. "I know now why we all felt so comfortable with Kent," declared "Best Dressed" as she sipped at her wine. "Looks like he's gone public. Can you believe it, Jenny? He's gay." She directed Jenny's eyes to a corner of the room where a small group was engaged in conversation. Kent stood to the right of the group and looked up when Jenny looked his way. He wore a well-tailored gray suit over a light-colored T-shirt. It all looked expensive. His hair was cut short and bleached, contrasting with his unseasonably tanned skin. Jenny smiled at him. He smiled back and mouthed a hello.

"Gay? Are you sure?" Jenny asked as Kent's attention returned to his small cluster of friends.

"He'll tell you he is. Wait and see for yourself." She savored another sip of wine and changed gears. "So how have you been?"

"Great. You know, mother, bus driver, coach, that sort of great. And busy. Always busy." It was a line she knew she'd repeat many times over as the evening progressed.

"And you're a director of marketing at WYCO Toys?"

"Yes, though I consider it a full-time, part-time position. Somehow, career responsibilities don't measure up to those of mother and coach. And you?"

"Single again. And looking. One of these times, it'll stick."

"How many? Marriages I mean. Sounds like more than one."

"Three. The last one left me for one of those." "Best Dressed" nodded toward Kent. "Best Dressed" was a label Karen had worked hard to earn, an obsession particularly during her junior and senior years, Jenny recalled. Her mother had died when Karen was seven years old. Her father was a kind man, who held various sales positions but produced only a meager income. There had been little left over to provide his daughter the "nice" things her classmates took for granted, like clothes.

By the time Karen reached high school, she was working three jobs after school and had taken up sewing. Soon she was the envy of every girl in school, owning as extensive a wardrobe as any Hollywood starlet, all her own creations. Physically endowed, she also had a body on which to display her creations, a noteworthy asset in a teenaged society where popularity was everything. Eventually, she attracted the studs, which became her personal entourage, and earned her another nickname she truly didn't deserve, slut.

While her classmates chose college, she selected a trade school to sharpen her fashion design skills followed by an apprenticeship with a New York fashion shop. There she met "Number 1," a successful trader with Goldman Sachs. After a brief courtship, they married and began a tumultuous relationship that ended six months later with dashed dreams of "happily ever after" and a substantial cash settlement that was sufficient to fund her own design studio and the beginning of a successful career.

"Tell me," said Jenny as she eyed "Best Dressed" strapless gown. "Is that…?"

JENNY

"Sure is. Designed it fifteen years ago and still wear it. Today it put me in the mood for all this," she declared, swinging her arm around the room for emphasis. "It took me years to shed Minnesota, but it's still a good place to come back to."

"Barbie" left a conversation with "Young and Foolish" and strolled over to Karen and Jenny. Unlike "Best Dressed," she wore a simple print dress that failed to hide the extra fifteen pounds she had been carrying around for the past ten years. Long blonde hair hung nearly to her waist, giving the impression she had not had it cut or styled since graduation. But reflecting an inner joy was a happy face, pudgy cheeks, and a beaming smile.

"Jenny. Karen. So good to see you. So who do we thank for all this?" "Barbie's" delight was genuine and obvious. Jenny felt "Barbie's" body quiver with excitement as she pulled Jenny close in a Minnesota hug. "I guess it's you, isn't it?" declared "Barbie." As they separated, she looked into Jenny's eyes and smiled before she muscled her close again for another embrace.

"Oh! I didn't know I missed everyone so much. And the both of you look so…goodness so unchanged for fifteen years. Me? Four kids later, all boys, this is what you get." She spun a pirouette, displaying her changed body and declared, "Wouldn't change a minute of it either."

"Life has its rewards," said Karen sarcastically. While inside, she envied the life she would never have: kids, house with a picket fence in the suburbs, normalcy she chose to forego years earlier. "Just think you could have had Kent."

"Barbie's" eyes followed Karen's to the other side of the room to where Kent remained engaged in conversation. "Some people do change. Don't they?" "Barbie" said thoughtfully. "What a surprise." She noticed the yearbook in Jenny's hand. "May I?"

She quickly thumbed through its pages, stopped at the page she wanted, shook her head, and smiled. Then she thumped the page with the back of her hand and gave the open book back to Jenny. "That's us, 'Ken and Barbie.' Made for each other." She chuckled to herself. "Actually, we knew otherwise. But the names made sense, and we pretended a relationship. You know, the Barbie era. He hadn't discovered his other self back then. Gosh, do you think I did that to him?" Both Jenny and Karen laughed and exchanged questioning looks as "Barbie" continued, "You know, sex wasn't my thing back then. I was afraid I wouldn't be very good at it. I got pretty good later on, though. Got me four boys to prove it."

"Evidently Kenny boy wasn't very good at it either," snipped Karen before she downed her glass of wine and headed to the bar for another.

For the next forty minutes, Jenny toured the room, speaking briefly to everyone except Kent Simons and Mark Stevens. Once her path crossed Mark's, and she felt a long-forgotten pat on her butt, but Kent remained out of earshot as he circulated, causing Jenny to wonder if he was avoiding her.

Finally, as two waitresses entered with trays of salad, Mark sneaked up behind Jenny, placed his big hands around her waist like he had done at every high school sports event during their high school years, and lifted her gently and slowly off the floor. "I was five pounds lighter then," said Jenny when her feet touched the floor, and she turned to look up into Mark's smiling eyes.

"So what's five pounds to old friends? Thank you for arranging this."

"You say that as though you're about to leave," observed Jenny, disappointed.

"I'm really sorry. I promised my kids, way back then that tonight we'd go to Mall of America and Christmas shop. It's a family tradition. The rule is: I can't change the date."

"*Steady Eddie* hasn't changed,"

"No. I'm afraid not. Commitments are commitments. And my three girls need me. But before I go, how's your son, Jason? My wife, Jo, works at Channel 6, in their newsroom. We couldn't believe it was you that made the national news. What a scare! Wow! Kidnapped. I understand he was returned safely?"

"Yes, and Jason is fine. He doesn't remember anything about it. He probably never will." She didn't add, "And if he did, she'd never tell."

"And they never found the guys that did it, or figured out why?"

"No. It's one of those unsolved mysteries."

"There you go. Sell it to the movies."

"Thanks, but no thanks. We're moving on with our lives. I'll probably never know who or why. I'm resigned to that."

Mark looked at his watch. "Really must go. Let's do this again. I promise to clear the slate next time."

"Okay, 'Steady Eddie,' that's a commitment. I'll hold you to it. You don't show up, and you'll be on the national news." Jenny closed her fist and shook it in his face.

She watched Mark leave without looking back when she felt a tap her on her shoulder. Turning, she looked in Kent's deep-blue eyes whose sparkle had dimmed from what she remembered, and she saw for the first time deep stress lines that etched his boyish face. Jenny had never known anyone who had done drugs and wondered if she was seeing their effect in her friend's appearance. "I hope you're not leaving too," she said, hoping her voice didn't betray her concern. "The party's just beginning."

"Oh, heavens, no. I've been looking forward to this for months. Wow, time flies. Actually, I'm meeting someone here later. I come here a lot when I'm in town. It's still one great place."

"You travel? Tell me, what have you been up to?"

"Acting, commercials, film. A little playhouse here and there."

"We have a star in our midst," she teased.

"Oh, don't I wish. No, nothing like that. I was introduced to acting at Boston College, made a career change my senior year, and began attending acting classes wherever I could. Mostly Boston and New York City. I've done some Off Broadway, community theater gigs. I just love it. Been looking for that big break ever since. And one of these days…Well, it could happen right here in Minneapolis. I've done commercials, infomercials, that sort of thing. Quite a bit of film actually. Mostly for businesses. Lot of that originated here.

"I have a meeting here later with a…Ricardo Burns about a film project. He's a front man for Martinez Enterprises out of Miami. I've worked with them before. They specialize in industrial productions, training, promotional pieces." Martinez rang a bell; Jenny knew of a Martinez Group that did corporate consulting. She recalled they'd used the conference suite in her building, but she had never met any of their people.

"Porn!" Karen's voice boomed from several steps away. "Best Dressed," who had been eavesdropping on Jenny and Kent, left a group of girls and stepped closer as heads turned her way. "It's porn!" she said again without shame.

"Tell us the truth, Kent. You're among friends here. You'll do it anyway before the night is over. We'll all confess what we've been doing with our lives. Why, you probably know my last husband, Tim Richards. That's tiny Tim Richards, although nothing, nothing at all, was tiny about Tim."

Jenny noticed Kent's face flushed red. He started to say something but could only sputter. Karen continued, "Can you believe it? The guy was gay. We dated for six months, and I didn't have a clue. I even married the guy. Talk about Minnesota dumb. I'm number one on that list. You'd better believe it."

Jenny felt Kent's embarrassment but, caught off guard by Karen's sudden viciousness, didn't say anything. She could not help wonder at his obvious shame when others in the room had reported that he seemed openly comfortable with his homosexuality. Had Karen's accusations hit too close to home? She doubted Karen had any prior knowledge of Kent's lifestyle.

Curiosity prevented her intervention. Karen continued, "Here was this big 'hunk' of a guy." Karen waved her arms about to describe his enormity. Fortunately, her wine glass—one of the many emptied during the course of the late afternoon—was again empty. "I mean he could have played for the Vikings. And handsome? A face made for film. Which he did, a lot of, I found out later. But unsuspecting me, Miss Minnesota Dumb, missed it all. I didn't have a clue. Not one single clue. I'd seen it all too. Fashion is my world, right? I've worked with them all, gays, lesbians, you name it."

"We were doing a fashion spread for some magazine and needed a good-looking male model. Enter Tiny Tim. He swept me off my feet. We did the shoot. It took two solid weeks. During that time, he never left my side. Gracious, well-mannered, masculine, attentive. For those two solid weeks, we practically lived together. We worked together, took breaks together, ate together. And he paid the tab. We did everything but sleep together. That just isn't me. It never has been."

Suddenly, Karen addressed Jenny, "Do you know, in school, with all those guys hanging around, I never once had sex? Not once. Oh, they tried often enough. My dad always said, 'Save yourself for the man you marry.' And that's what I did. I loved my dad. I stayed a virgin. He was always right. I always did what he said. It was some prissy girls from home-making class that called me a slut. And everyone believed it." She spoke matter-of-factly; she had long since buried that hurt. "Bet those girls, as jealous as they were then, are ugly and fat today, sitting at home with a dozen kids apiece, while big-bellied husbands suck on beers and flip channels for the week's big game."

"Anyway," Karen continued, "we seemed to have much in common, liked all the same things. Well, not all the same things, but I didn't know it at the time. For the first time in years, I was having fun in a relationship. We talked about it—our relationship. Our getting married seemed the right thing to do. It was to be a continuation of all the fun. Right?"

A waitress walked up, plucked the empty glass from Karen's hand, replacing it with a refill. Karen swirled the glass and sniffed its bouquet, then resumed her story. "After a month, I began intercepting Tim's calls from an escort service. He was doing very well as a model, and although I couldn't understand why he'd want to work for an escort service, I was okay with it. It paid well. He had his work to do, and I had mine. We were married, and that was that. Right? Wrong!"

Karen's tone turned caustic. "One day, I listened in on the phone. The slime! It wasn't an escort service. It was porn. He was into porn. Hardcore. Not just looking at it. He was doing it! Making the films. I asked him to bring one of his films…videos…home. We watched one together. God, it was awful. I absolutely couldn't believe it. To see my husband, the man I had promised to spend the rest of my life with, doing it with other women…Doing it with other men or whatever they are." She pointed a finger at Kent. "Perverts like you!"

"Look. I understand. I really do," said Kent compassionately—Jenny expected anger. "You lost someone you loved. But you never really knew him. You couldn't have. He didn't know himself. It wasn't right, and I don't defend his actions. But I do understand his dilemma." Feeling suddenly bold, Kent sought common ground in Karen's pain. "Look, I was the same way. Even in high school. Then I found myself. I was like Tim, confused. I've been there. It wasn't you. You weren't the problem. But it took you to help him see who he really was. You helped set him free. Good came of it."

"You left him?" Jenny asked.

"Not right away. I loved the guy. You know, I thought it could be made okay. But it couldn't. Finally, he left. I don't know. I suppose I had already severed the relationship emotionally. He replaced me with some guy." She pointed to Kent again as to say "like him."

Kent reached over to touch her shoulder in a comforting gesture. Angrily, Karen jumped backward to avoid him and, in so doing, emptied her burgundy wine over his expensive gray suit. Kent was horrified and raised his arms to examine the damage. A classmate, who had been speaking with Anne Graham only a few feet away, witnessed the accident and came to Kent's rescue. "Try some soda," she suggested. "It works on my carpet every time." She grabbed Kent's hand and began pulling him toward the door leading to the bar. He threw one last disturbed look at Karen and followed the tugging hand from the room.

There was a ringing sound from a corner of the room. Jenny turned. Kathy was tapping her glass to get everyone's attention. When quiet prevailed, she announced dinner was about to be served. Obediently the group settled into chairs around the rectangular table beneath the banner of beauties they once were. Jenny took a seat next to Anne Graham and set her yearbook on the floor between them.

Sandra, Kent's rescuer, returned alone and stood for a moment in the doorway. Her eyes met Jenny's; she winked and walked to a chair at the end of the table. Kent reappeared a minute later wearing a large bulky sweater five sizes too big that covered him like a painter's drop cloth. Mark's chair had been removed, leaving him no choice but to sit next to "Best Dressed."

The entree was chicken à la king. Entertainment came from two large televisions connected in-line placed at either end of the room so that all could see. For the next hour, they displayed scenes of the squad in action, many that would have made Mark blush, but which Kent enjoyed as one of the girls. At its conclusion, Kathy requested everyone open a yearbook to reminisce how life was once upon a time in 1979.

"May I?" asked Anne, reaching down to pick up Jenny's yearbook. "What a great idea. I haven't looked at mine since graduation." After thumbing through a few pages, she chuckled. "Boy, this brings back memories." Anne chuckled as her mind recalled the final bittersweet days of May 1979, when she was a high school junior bidding good-bye to her friends, many she would never see again. She looked up as a waiter's hand whisked away her untouched salad plate. She barely noticed.

After a few minutes, she sensed Jenny's uneasiness. "I'm sorry. I hope you don't mind," she said apologetically. "I just love reading what people have written. Yours is so full of good stuff."

"I don't mind. But what have you found that's so interesting?"

The question brought silence as Anne considered her answer. "You've always been different."

Jenny's eyes lit up. "My! How's that?" she asked.

"Oh!" she exclaimed, realizing what she'd said. "Only in a good sense. How do I say it? There's no one I respected more in high school than I respected you. And it's not that you were an upperclassman. You just seemed to have a better compass than most of us; your life always seemed so well-defined. You always had a purpose…direction. People, kids, teachers really admired you." Jenny was beginning to blush slightly. "I read what people said about you, what they wrote, and I'm honored that you'd let me read it. There's a lot of admiration and love in this book."

"I guess I've forgotten much of what's there. But thank you. I didn't try to be different really."

"Well, just look at…" Her voice trailed off. She thumbed several pages, found some tender notes written by friends and teachers fifteen years earlier, and read them to Jenny. Finally, embarrassed, Jenny reached in protest for the book. Anne only pulled it back and relentlessly continued.

"Look at this one. I mean, wow! This person really had a thing for you. It's not signed." Anne quickly thumbed through several pages until she located a large photo of Jenny standing by a school locker and pointed to a small heart drawn in the margin. She read aloud what was written inside the heart, 'Whatever you do, wherever you go, I will always love you. Always. Forever'." Anne feigned light-headedness.

"That? I remember it just suddenly appeared. I never learned who wrote it and always thought someone did it just to put me on."

"Oh, come on. I bet some guy really got turned on and was too shy to admit it."

"Yeah. Right," Jenny said incredulously.

"Well, maybe this one is not a good example."

Anne thumbed through more pages reciting other writings, all sincere accolades from teachers and friends.

"Okay. That's enough." Jenny tugged on the book until Anne released it. "You gave up your salad. You don't want to miss this. It's what you came all the way from Las Vegas for."

JENNY

"What is it?" Anne stared at the plate the waiter had placed in front of her.

"Chicken à la king. Don't you remember?"

"Never! See, that's what I mean about you. Great ideas always coming up with something different." Anne pierced the French pastry shell smothered with chicken and cream sauce, and then as Jenny watched a smile cross her face, she exclaimed excitedly, "Jerry Barons!" Her chicken-laden fork was now poised in midair as she further considered the revelation.

"Who's Jerry Barons?" Jenny asked.

"You probably didn't know he existed. He was so much younger," Anne said jokingly. "He was, after all, a year behind me, the class of '81. He wrote the note. I'm sure it was him. He was head over heels in love with you, Jennifer Ward. Tall, skinny kid. He had moved up from Kentucky or someplace south. We called him Jeb because he looked and acted like a young Jeb Clampett. You know the *Beverly Hillbillies*. The poor guy came to every game, every event, just to watch you. You didn't know?"

"No. You say a tall, skinny guy?"

"Yeah. I mean really tall. Really skinny. It was him. I'm sure it was. You really did a number on him," Anne continued. "Nice guy. Smart. He was in one of my study halls, and we'd sit in the corner and talk. I loved his accent. He joked about it...About how he felt toward you. But he used almost those exact words. He would never love another *woman*, his words, *again as long as he lived*. You weren't just another girl. You were a *woman*."

"I had no idea. I don't think I ever spoke to him."

"Apparently, you didn't have to. He fell in love all by himself. That's what you did to people, Jenny. See what I mean? JB Barons, Jeb Barons, southern drawl like you couldn't believe. Last I heard he went on to Harvard."

Jenny toyed with the food on her plate. "JB?"

"He preferred JB. Jeb was a label that made fun of him. He accepted that, but he preferred to be called JB."

"We have a JB at work. Personal assistant to our CEO."

Anne stopped eating and pulled her yearbook from under her chair. She thumbed through the pages. "Here"—pointing to a picture—"Jeb Barons. Kind of a geek but a nice guy. Same person?"

"I don't know." Jenny took the book from Anne and studied the picture. The face was smiling, looking directly at the lens. His short hair combed back and parted on the side. It was a familiar face. "We haven't met actually. We work at different buildings. He came with our CEO, Creighton Leonard. Been onboard for about a year."

Jenny returned Anne's book and began thumbing through her own, looking for a picture of Jerry Barons.

"Try Chess Club. That sounds geeky." Anne thrashed through several pages. "Here he is. Chess Club, second row, third from the left."

"May I see that?"

Again, Anne handed her the book. "What is it?"

"I don't know. There's just something about him. His height?"

"Well?" Anne noticed Jenny's composure change as her interest in the old photograph went from mild to shock.

"It can't be." Jenny turned the book to better see the face in the chandelier's light.

"Whenever you say it can't be, it is. What is it?"

"He's the man on my deck," she said slowly, almost in a whisper. "The face in the crowd."

"What's that supposed to mean?"

"It's him. He's heavier now. His hair was blowing…"

"What on earth are you talking about?"

"When my son was kidnapped. I was to do a televised interview from my home. It was cut short by a bad storm. Anyway, there was a flash of lightning. In that instant, standing on my deck…was this tall man, dripping wet, windblown."

"And?"

"And…It's him. This is him." Jenny paused, took two deep breaths. "I'm sorry. You wouldn't know? You weren't there."

JENNY

"Oh? And my dad's the cop? What don't I know?"

Jenny brought the chief's daughter up-to-date on all that had happened that fateful day. Their plates were still full when two waiters appeared. During the time it took to clear the table, Anne heard it all from the storm-drenched visitor to finding the diamond tiepin on the deck.

"And you think that JB, if that was him, had something to do with Jason's kidnapping? I don't know. You're talking about a man who, at one time, was crazy about you. It was more than some school kid's crush. He was crazy in love with you."

"That's just it, I don't know. He was there. That's all. I don't think the police, even your father, thought it too important. I reported the incident to him."

"Well, that's my father. All business. I'm sure he was more interested than he appeared," Anne said somewhat defensively. "That's just the way he is. Look, I sat next to JB for almost the whole year. I learned things about him his mother didn't know. He just would not do anything to hurt you. At least the JB I knew wouldn't."

Jenny continued, "I really didn't know him at all. But suppose this obsession with me could have grown out of control. Maybe, in some perverted way, he saw Jason as some sort of bait to lure me to him. I know that's far-fetched, but could it be?"

Anne looked again at Kent before answering. "This is the '90s. Anything can happen. But I don't think so. It was too planned. Too many people involved. Stalkers are loners, usually act on their own. My dad doesn't talk about his work, especially when cases are pending. Not even with me. But he has said there are leads in this case. Some cases take longer than others to resolve. This is one of those cases, but he says there is progress."

Anne thought for a moment. "It should be easy enough to determine if your stranger and JB are one in the same," she observed.

Jenny considered Anne's words. "I never would have made the connection. Actually, I'd about given up. If it is him, what does that mean? Your father's point: the man's presence at either place doesn't prove anything. If it were JB, he would have had plenty of reason to be at the press conference. And being on my deck later....? He could have realized who I was and came around for a look. If he felt the way you said, wouldn't he want to make sure?"

"But you say you hadn't met. It's not like he recognized you. You weren't at the press conference."

"No. But the fact that Jason was the grandson of Matthew Ward was all over the news. There's only one Matthew Ward, and he had only one daughter."

"Well, you will look him up. Won't you?"

Jenny didn't answer immediately. "If I don't?"

"It'll haunt you forever. It'll haunt me. You have to."

"I will then."

"Soon. For sure? Promise?"

"For sure."

Chapter 50

A little before nine o'clock, Jenny stood in the doorway saying her final good-byes to the cheerleader squad of 1979. She could not help but wonder what changes would impact their lives before they came together again. A cold chill grabbed her as a young man and a woman passed through the front door into the night air now filled with BB sized sleet pellets, a precursor of an approaching winter storm that had not been a part of the morning's forecast.

Kathy was speaking with The Minstrel's owner when Jenny caught her eye and smiled her "good night," turned on her heel, and began her cold walk to the parking lot.

"Jenny. Jenny." The voice came from behind her as she paused to put on her coat in the darkened dining room. Turning, she watched Kent slip off the barstool where he had been sitting. He trotted in her direction; his baggy sweater replaced by his suit coat, no longer spotted burgundy but visibly splotchy wet from the club soda.

"Do you have just a minute?" he asked with a pleading sort of look in his eyes.

"Sure."

"Maybe we could sit? Just for a moment." Kent pulled a chair from under the table and offered it to Jenny, then seated himself next to her. "This was a good evening. I hope I didn't make a fool of myself." The smile on his face said he didn't really care. He had come preprogrammed to speak out for gay activism and had done so. "Thank you for doing all this."

Jenny looked into his eyes and saw the handsome, *blonde*, good-looking high school senior, the one she had known fifteen years earlier with the laughing eyes and constant smile. For a moment, they just stared at each other; his haunting eyes carried a message Jenny could not interpret.

"Jenny, I am what I am. Like I explained to everyone in there, we all live by choices we make along life's way."

"And die by them," Jenny added. A remark that did not go unnoticed, but Kent refused to acknowledge that.

"You've never been judgmental, Jenny. I want you to know how I appreciate that."

"Kent, you're a friend. That will not change, ever. You know my view on your sexual preference, so I'll be quiet on that subject. Besides, you didn't stop me for a sermon," she said with a smile.

"No." He looked into her eyes. "Though I believe you could deliver a good one."

"So what did you want?"

Kent paused before answering. "Jenny, I wasn't aware of your son's kidnapping."

"Nor was half the room. I thought the whole world knew," said Jenny.

"I travel a lot and must have been on the road when it happened." He had difficulty finding the right words; Pandora's box was about to open. "You work at WYCO Toys. I guess I had heard that somewhere. But that doesn't matter. I mean that I knew. I never made the connection until now. Until tonight."

"Connection?" Jenny had not a clue to what he was talking about. She shifted uneasily on her chair.

"Well…I'm concerned for you," he began, clasping his hands on the table as though seeking some inner strength.

"That's nice. But…why?"

"For your safety, I guess. Jenny, this is…so awkward. I just feel that I should warn you. I want you to be careful."

"Kent? You're not making a bit of sense. What are you saying? Careful at what? I'm in no danger. If it's my son's abduction, that danger has passed. Even the police believe it was one isolated incident." She'd already dealt with the fear for herself, for Jason, and she had pushed it aside. She was getting on with her life. She didn't need this.

"Perhaps." Kent shifted uneasily. Jenny shot a glance at the person sitting on the barstool next to where he had been. His back was turned. His wavy black hair curled over the collar of an Armani suit. He wore a small gold earring on one ear, a fact that didn't register with Jenny.

"He's the agent I mentioned, the talent scout. I really should…" He started to leave.

"Not until you explain what you just said." Jenny grabbed his arm, not about to let him leave. "You can't just announce that I'm in danger and not tell me from what. Now finish what you started."

Kent shifted again in his chair, obviously cautioned by his surroundings. Jenny looked again in the agent's direction. "He's okay. He's not paying us any attention," she assured. The agent toyed with his drink as he studied Jenny in the mirror behind the bar. Jenny didn't notice. Kent had said her name Jenny. She was no stranger to him, nor was her son, Jason. He knew them both well—in his mind.

Kent took a deep breath forcing himself to relax before he continued in self-resignation. "It's not your job, Jenny. It's not what you do. It's where you work," he said at last.

"Kent? I work at WYCO Toys. The big toy company on the lake, remember? I'm just one marketing manager. We make toys. It's not the Pentagon. Not a high-security position, although you might think so with all the talk of international treaties. Kent, I appreciate your concern, I really do, but I don't understand it. What is it about where I work that could possibly put me in danger?" The nagging feeling of pending doom, which she'd been fighting for the past weeks, moved center stage with a throb in her shoulders. She tried to shake it off but couldn't. Her fears were real.

"This isn't the right place...I really can't say more," he said almost in a whisper and fumbled in his pocket for a business card. "I'll be in town for two days. I'm at the Hyatt. Any chance of getting together?"

"I've got a meeting at Mall of America tomorrow. Could you come out there? Say, lunch at eleven-thirty? You know where to find me at the House of Toys."

"I'll be there." He handed her the wrinkled business card. "This is my apartment in Boston. My answering machine is always on. If, for some reason, we miss each other, call and leave a message and suggest a time when we can talk. I pass through here quite often."

"Now you said yes to lunch tomorrow?" asked Jenny, seeking confirmation. "That's a promise?" Kent nodded and rose from the table. When she stood, he reached again for Jenny's hand and held it gently. She didn't pull back.

"Jenny, someone at WYCO is into more than toys. What Karen said earlier is true, although she didn't know it. She was just guessing."

"You mean pornography?" Jenny's eyes narrowed as she processed what he was saying? "That's the kind of films you make?"

Kent nodded. "I'm not proud of everything I've done. One thing leads to another. I go where the work is, where the money is. There's tons of money in sex these days. That work has brought me here to Minneapolis on more than one occasion during the past year. Your executive conference room makes for a great film set after-hours."

After he said it, he wished he hadn't and hoped he was the only one in the room who saw the change in Jenny's expression. Suddenly, he was uneasy speaking to her, strangely fearful but quickly dismissed the feeling. He needed to warn Jenny, and true friendship demanded risk. He only hoped he hadn't put Jenny in greater danger. Then how could he? Who would know they had talked?

"Kent, what are you saying? Someone is making pornographic films in my company's conference center?"

"I don't know the details, but I expect there's more to it than that. I wish I could say more, but I can't. Not here. Jenny, just know it's true, and you need to know. Please be careful. What's going on involves some very powerful people…dangerous people."

Jenny shifted her stance and nervously adjusted her coat. "Kent—"

"I know. We need to talk…Tomorrow…We'll talk then." His soft hands slowly pulled back from Jenny's. "Ciao," he said, turned and headed back toward the bar where his agent waited.

"Come to the store," she reminded as he stepped away. "Third floor entrance. The House of Toys." The hunched-over agent cocked his head ever so slightly. He knew the "House of Toys." This Jenny was more than just another pretty girl who had attended high school with Kent Simons.

Chapter 51

Greeted outside by the sting of wind-propelled sleet against her warm cheek, Jenny pulled up her collar and snuggled deeper into her coat. Ahead, a halogen lamp illuminated the nearly empty parking lot. The attendant's shack stood dark in the shadow of a granite-walled building undergoing rehab. Swirls of large snowflakes were covering the drab city gray with a blanket of white. She wasn't leaving any too soon. Jenny knew her homeward trek could become treacherous as she wound around the lake.

Her late model Jeep Cherokee stood near the sidewalk. Beside it, a black Mercedes had pulled in close to her driver's side door preventing her slender shape from slithering past. She walked quickly to the other side and inserted the key into the lock when a hand touched her shoulder. Instinctively, she jerked sideways, turned abruptly and looked into Kathy's surprised face, who had raised her hand to ward off the defensive blow she was certain would connect with her nose. Jenny corrected in time.

When both hearts returned to normal, they agreed to caravan home; Jenny would lead because she had four-wheel drive. Soon Kathy flashed her headlights to signal her readiness, and Jenny maneuvered her Cherokee out onto the street. Three blocks later, they turned down the entrance ramp to the Interstate and the fifteen-mile run to Wayzata.

They saw few cars, but road crews were already busy clearing the highway surface and laying down a fine layer of salt, the kind that would turn their cars white before they reached home. Approaching

Ridgedale Shopping Mall, the dashboard clock read 9:05. Here the still-full parking lot told her Christmas shopping had begun in earnest, and shoppers preferred the suburban malls. Jenny imagined the House of Toys and Mall of America had attracted its fair share of business.

Passing under Interstate 494, she located her cell phone and called home. Chris would be worried about her driving alone at night into the face of the growing storm. He'd been waiting for her call after seeing Jason to bed, early and exhausted from a hard practice, and started a crackling fire in the master bedroom fireplace before picking up the latest Tom Clancy novel, ignoring piles of paperwork he had lugged home with every intention of reading. With a little luck, the heavy snow would provide him an excuse to stay home tomorrow and enjoy quality time with his family—something he had not done in a long while. Early weather reports had predicted six to eight inches of fresh snow before the surprise storm abated midday tomorrow. Already three inches of snow had accumulated.

At Highway 101, headlights flashed in Jenny's rearview mirror, Kathy's signal that she was turning south, her Minnetonka home only a couple of miles further down the road. Jenny took the bypass around the town of Wayzata to exit west onto Shoreline Drive along the still unfrozen waters of Lake Minnetonka. She was six miles from home.

Fortunately, the storm had not produced any wind, but the heavy snowfall was accumulating at a rate of three inches per hour and increasing by the minute. Visibility was difficult in near-whiteout conditions. She followed fresh tire tracks on the unplowed roadway left moments earlier by another stubborn Minnesotan caught by the sudden change in the weather. Soon she was traveling only inches at a time, both hands on the wheel as she stared into the hypnotic cascade of white.

Suddenly, a road sign at the edge of her peripheral vision announced the Lafayette Country Club turnoff. *Strange!* She couldn't remember passing the boatyard at Tanager Lake. She must have dozed off. She shook her head and cracked her window. Cold air flooded in and felt good against the side of her face. She relaxed her grip on the steering wheel and realized her fingernails had penetrated its leather covering. She had only three miles to go.

She guessed her memory lapse had been two miles, roughly fifteen minutes at the speed she was traveling. Jason's memory lapse had been drug-induced and had lasted for months, blocking his memory of that dreadful summer day. To keep from dozing again, she forced her mind to recall the events of that Thursday in August and summoned images she had blocked from her mind. There was so much conjecture by family and friends, and assurances from local authorities, that all would be well. Her own husband had seemed the least concerned as he avoided the unwanted interruption to his career.

Only Dan Sheridan seemed interested. She wondered now if his interest had been motivated by his attraction to her. She could not deny her attraction to him. But she had only acted out of the emotion of the moment, fear of the unknown, anger with her husband, and the pleasure of a new friend. That combination was dangerous. A liaison would have never happened; she would not have allowed it. Would she? Too much wine had nearly undone her once.

Jason really liked him. Dan's concern seemed genuine enough. Part of her frustration had been avoiding him, for emotional reasons, while knowing he was the best source of help. She presumed he was still following the investigation, although they had barely spoken since she had introduced him to Sharon. He had initiated all contacts, each time following up some detail, and to inquire about Jason's memory loss. She knew he was more than mildly concerned that Jason's memory would return. And if his abductors shared the same concern, what then? That had been his warning all along. But so far, that had not happened, and even Dan had become silent.

His silence must mean there was nothing new. In the meantime, Sharon and Dan had dated some. She had avoided pressing Sharon to learn more of their relationship, not wanting Sharon to draw the wrong conclusions from her interest.

JENNY

A deer appeared suddenly at the side of the road but stopped short of crossing in front of her. Her musing continued. With Sharon in hot pursuit of Dan, his attraction to her would diminish over time. That's what she had wanted. It had been good for her to minimize contact. They would continue as friends. Now she needed to call him.

She'd do that in the morning and ask him to join her meeting with Kent Simons. He was no threat to Kent; he was no longer a cop—officially. Kent would understand. Dan would know what to do with the information. She hoped Kent felt strong enough about her safety that he would tell Dan what he had told her, even more, for there was obviously more.

Where did JB fit in? What was going on at WYCO? Little had changed since the takeover by Creighton Leonard. He had brought in his people, but the management group had been left intact. From her perspective, the company seemed poised for growth and expansion. All that seemed positive and good. The only negative were rumors of WYCO's plans to move much of its production to Mexico. Was that it, after all? Had her involvement in the negotiations triggered her danger, as the media speculated? But why just her?

What did any of it have to do with Kent and his sordid film career? The conference room, a pornographic film set? Why? What gall! Who? Any number of people had access. The idea seemed absurd. Still, he had warned her. He had been to the conference center more than once during the past year. *One year? That seemed important.* Whoever was responsible would have come with the new management or since—*within one year. So who was new?* JB? He was new. Creighton Leonard was new.

Ahead, a yellow blinking light signaled her turn south. Home was less than one mile away.

Wait! There was Jennifer Stewart! What had become of Jennifer Stewart? Did Kent know of her whereabouts? The snow had let up, and plant 1 was less than two miles farther. It seemed to be such a safe place to work, where she and Jenny Stewart worked—had worked—and where Kent supposedly had performed. It could have been on a quiet night such as this that Kent and someone very sick entered the conference room unnoticed? *Unnoticed?* She considered that probability.

Chris had intercepted the telephone call from Jim Stewart, probably weeks earlier for all she knew; it wasn't dated. And Jim had called only once. Had it been important, wouldn't he have tried again? Jenny must have reappeared. That was another call she would make in the morning, she promised herself, then slowly pulled into the familiar WYCO parking lot.

Until recently this had been the corporate home of WYCO. It was where it all began, years earlier, when farmers' kids seeking a better life left the farm for the factory and began making the country's greatest toys. Caught now in her headlights were the old buildings, WYCO's original offices. Tonight they were quiet, awaiting another week's production. She loved the place, possibly because she had grown up in its shadow. Here were the friendly offices she preferred. What caused the change?

By now, four inches of snow had fallen. A maintenance van, preceding her into the lot, had left tire tracks in the snow. She could see the darkened van in her headlights, its top covered with less than an inch of white fluff. She guessed the crew had been working inside for thirty minutes. She drove slowly along the old building, finding humorous pleasure in making her own marks in the deep snow. Behind old walls in the darkened corridors and offices, security lights emitted a soft muted glow.

She had grown up on Lake Minnetonka's opposite south shore when WYCO was legend for the work it afforded the lake community for the durable toys it produced. Then its towering offices and vast, sprawling warehouses were a symbol of the community's success and prosperity. In those days, lights blazed round the clock every day but Sunday.

She continued to the middle of the lot and turned off her lights. The company she admired as a child had changed. Its people had changed. The building was the same, but inside…change. Now much of the manufacturing took place elsewhere, mostly in the orient. And soon in Mexico if rumors were correct. They were more than rumors, she knew. She had had her part in changing the grand old company.

Since those early years, the company had grown to international proportions to dominate the world's toy industry. At what price? She wondered. Fewer than half the original workforce still worked inside its walls. Labor was cheaper elsewhere. And Burt was right—the toys showed it. That was a big factor in the company's recent decline, Jenny suspected. That is what opened the door to Creighton Leonard. The company had lost its competitive edge under the bungling leadership of Harold Benner. He had blamed the unions, called them greedy, while he was living aboard his luxury yacht.

There had been only a few managerial changes following the takeover, but it was working. Profits and stock prices were improving, if for no other reason than a change in leadership and Creighton's reputation.

Benner had moved senior management to the new plush quarters at the Wayzata Towers, where Jenny also would have gone, had she not argued her need to stay close to production. Besides remaining close to home—only three miles away—the old but spacious fourth-floor executive suite, one time home of the company's board of directors and retired conference center, had been recently refurbished. It would have been a shame and a waste of company dollars not to utilize the space. According to Kent Simons, they were being utilized, utilized in ways she would never have imagined. *An after-hours pornographic film set?*

Jenny stopped her car and watched lights on the executive level turn on and off as the cleaning crew made its way, room to room, causing muted shadows with exaggerated shapes to glide about like ghosts. *A cleaning crew?* Yesterday she would not have given it a second thought. Now she wondered: is this how Kent had come undetected, in some sort of service van? Tonight she had left him in Minneapolis. Tomorrow she would see him again, and she'd ask him.

Moving again, she pulled slowly out the drive into the storm's new energy. A face looked down at her from above, from behind a curtain discreetly pulled to one side. She didn't notice. From across the lake, a warm south wind blowing now with intensity was driving the snow into drifts. A snowplow appeared from the west and cleared her eastbound lane, passing in a halo of flashing yellow swirls of snow. She moved into its wake. Her thoughts turned again to Chris, her home, and a warm fire, a safer world. *Was it a safe world?*

Chapter 52

Sleep had not come easy. And morning came far too soon. Her scheduled meeting with Kent Simons was the only reason she would leave her safe world today. Everything else would be rescheduled because of the unexpected snow holiday.

Chris had read himself to sleep by the time she got home and didn't feel Jenny crawl in beside him. For an hour, she lay quietly, listening to him breathe, watching shadows dance across an amber ceiling, the death dance of the fire's slowly dying coals.

What she had feared was becoming reality. Their ordeal that began that Thursday in August was not over. Her resolve to make it so and put it behind her meant nothing. Time had not been an element of healing as she had prayed it would. Rather, it allowed the continued slow burning fuse of an uncertain future, a powder keg for which Kent had given warning.

She rose early. The smell of freshly ground coffee helped clear her mind. She was curiously excited to hear Kent Simons's entire story but felt unprepared for all the new day might bring. She glanced at the clock. It was 6:30 a.m. She wondered, *What would be too early for Jim Stewart?*

Upstairs she heard Chris running his morning shower. She refreshed her coffee, grabbed the portable phone, and found the note containing Jim Stewart's telephone number. Outside, the wind had abated, but large flakes still cascaded earthward. She turned on the yard light to pierce the early morning darkness. Fourteen inches of snow covered the ground. Only the hardy would venture out today.

She heard Jason turn on his radio to listen for the day's school closings. She knew his would make the list.

Ready, she took a deep breath and punched in the number for Jim Stewart. A woman answered on the second ring. It was a recording. "Stewart Pork," said the voice. Then the call transferred, evidenced by several clicks on the line.

"This is Jim," said a man's voice.

"My name is Jennifer Poole. I'm sorry about the time."

"No problem. We start early here. Your name again?"

"Jennifer Poole. You called weeks ago. I'm sorry, I just found your message," said Jenny apologetically.

There was silence on the other end. Jenny continued, "I believe it concerned your sister, Jennifer. We work, or did work, at the same company, WYCO Toys."

"Yes," Jim said at last. "I know who you are. I'd given up hope that you'd call. I tried a couple different times to reach you. I didn't know if my calling you would put you in danger."

Jenny wasn't sure she heard that correctly—*danger?* "I'm sorry. What danger?"

After a moment of silence, Jim answered in a choking voice. "When I called you, my sister Jenny was on her way to Minneapolis to warn you. She was concerned for you and your son…Jason."

"Mr. Stewart, that was weeks ago."

"Yes. I know. Like I said, I…I didn't try further because I didn't want to put you in any danger."

"I don't understand."

"She's disappeared. She left here with information concerning your son, Jason. She thought she knew why he was kidnapped. She boarded a flight to Minneapolis. I haven't spoken to her since."

"Has she ever done this before? Disappeared?"

"Once in Europe for nearly three months. But never like this." Jim's voice cracked, filled with emotion. "Mrs. Poole, I believe…she's been murdered."

His words struck Jenny like a shotgun blast before trailing off again. She was suddenly very much awake, and shocked, unable to speak and picturing him clutching the phone, holding back tears. She waited. Upstairs, the shower continued to run reassuringly. Her family was safe.

It took several minutes for Jim Stewart to regain his composure. When she heard his voice again, it was filled with resolve. For the next twenty minutes, Jenny sat in somber silence, numbed by his words as he recounted what he believed were his sister's last days, her midnight call as she fled Minneapolis, her fear that she would be followed, the attempt on her life, the assassin Jim killed defending her, her resolve to return to Minneapolis in an effort to protect Jenny and her son, and to expose those who would cause them harm.

Several times, Jenny's eyes filled with tears. She anguished for the girl she didn't really know. The fact that they shared the same name only made it worse and very frightening. It could have been her. Upstairs was now quiet. Chris would be down any minute for his morning coffee, expecting a day of family fun, a snow holiday.

"And the police?" Jenny asked finally.

"They've declared Jennifer missing."

"That's all?"

"There's no evidence. Until they find evidence of foul play, she's only missing."

"But the attempt on her life?"

"I've told them what I heard…saw. But, you see, that conflicts with my original statement that it was attempted rape. They're checking out both stories, but again, there's no hard evidence."

"But your surveillance? You said you had cameras—"

"Only my monitors were running. This is a hog farm. I need to know what's going on. I don't need to have a record of it. Tapes are expensive. The recorders were off."

There was silence while Jenny organized her thoughts. Finally, "Mr. Stewart."

"Please. It's Jim."

"Jim, why wouldn't you call me? Try again to reach me? I mean, possibly, I could have helped."

"Because I didn't think Jenny wanted me to." Jenny shuddered when she heard the name. "Late on the day that she left, long after she would have arrived in Minneapolis, Jenny called. I wasn't close to the phone, so she left a message on my answering machine. She sounded confused, said she was going to go into hiding for a while to think things through, and insisted that no one go looking for her. She would call me when she was ready."

"And you believed her. That's why you didn't call?"

"Not exactly. Her voice sounded forced, like it wasn't her. Yet I knew it was her. I learned many years ago that I couldn't win going against Jennifer. She is very strong-willed. It was entirely possible that she was rethinking what she should do and did go someplace to be alone."

"But you don't really believe that?"

"No. I listened to the message over and over." Jim lost it again but quickly recovered. "Then it dawned on me, she never mentioned your name. I mean, why wouldn't she say your name on the telephone in a message for me. After all, that's why she was going to Minneapolis. Then it became clear. She didn't say your name because she wanted to protect you. I believe that her killer…" his voice broke again. It took him longer to regain control. "She probably had tricked whoever had taken her into letting her place the call. That person was probably listening to her every word. She knew that if I didn't hear from her, I would immediately go to the police. That's what she didn't want me to do, even to her own peril. My doing so would have involved you. I really believe she was warning me to do nothing because she didn't want to involve you and put you in greater danger. That's the kind of person she was."

"But you eventually went to the police?" Jenny asked, puzzled.

"Yes. And I gave them the answering machine tape."

"When?"

"Weeks ago."

JENNY

"You'd think they would have contacted the Minneapolis police, and they would have contacted me."

"Not necessarily. I haven't gone into this detail with the police. Remember, I've already given them a false story. In their eyes, I may not be too credible."

"But it's your sister."

"It's because she's my sister." Jim broke down again but forced himself to continue. "I loved my sister. I'd do anything for her. Anything. She was killed—if she was killed—while trying to protect you. How could I go against her and expose you if that's the very thing she gave her life to prevent. It would have all been...It would have been for nothing. I'm so glad you called. I doubt I could have lived with this much longer."

Jim continued a few more minutes and expressed his surprise that Minneapolis police had not contacted her after they received a police report from Nebraska, a fact that reinforced his belief that for some unknown reason the authorities didn't care. And that thought undid him. Jenny waited until he'd recovered and agreed to contact him as soon as she learned anything helpful.

As the phone went dead, she sat on the edge of her living-room sofa, the phone clutched in her hands, her face paled from shock. The police believed Jenny Stewart was *only missing. Was Jim overreacting? Maybe his sister was holed up somewhere. She had disappeared before for three months. But Christmas was only weeks away. Wouldn't this be her time to surface?*

What really had she seen? Who had she seen? Was it Kent and his sordid friends? Whoever those *powerful* people were, they were serious enough for someone to kidnap Jason, albeit by mistake, then attempt to kill someone to keep from being exposed. The corpse of Stewart's would-be assassin was proof of that. Still, murder was incomprehensible. Jenny Stewart had to be alive. She must be out there somewhere, frightened for her own safety and the safety of Jason's family, struggling with what to do next. In time, she would come forward. It's possible the authorities had placed her in safe custody while they launched their investigation, a reason she had not been contacted. And now two people concerned for her safety had placed themselves at risk to warn her. Because of where she worked? That didn't make any sense.

"Honey, are you okay?" Chris asked from behind her on the stairs. "Is everything okay? Is it your dad?" As he spoke, he moved to the sofa and slowly sat down beside her and waited for her answer.

Shocked by Jim Stewart's words, Jenny did her best to relate all that Jim Stewart revealed of his sister's last days on the farm, her own discovery of the identity of the stranger on the deck, Kent Simons's revelation, and Kent's warning. When she'd finished, they sat in silence for several minutes, each reflecting on what it all meant.

"Do we have enough go to the police?" she finally asked her lawyer-husband.

"Sounds like they're already on it. I don't believe we'll be much help."

"Why would you say that? And why haven't they contacted us?"

"I'm not a criminal attorney, but it's possible they have her in protective custody while they gather evidence. This kind of thing could be far-reaching. Who knows who might be involved?"

Jenny thought for a moment. "But you don't think they have enough evidence? Is that it?"

"Jenny, I don't know. I know we don't have enough. And I know where this is heading. Believe me, we are safer leaving the investigation with the police, the FBI, or whoever is investigating this case. We're better off not getting involved. Understand?"

Silence. A couple minutes passed, and Jenny asked, "Don't you see? We're in danger. The police need to know what we know?"

"Which is nothing. Think about it, Jenny, any notoriety could place us in even greater danger. The police must be on the case. They'll contact us when the time is right. Let's not rush it."

"So they're gathering evidence. If it's evidence they need, I can get it for them."

"What are you saying, Jenny?"

"Chris. I can't just sit here and wait for the axe to fall. We need to get our own…evidence. I need to learn what Jenny Stewart was afraid of. Where she is now. I can get the police their evidence. Chris, think about it. I know I can learn the truth here, who took Jason, and who wants Jennifer Stewart dead."

"You can't be serious. Tell me you're not. Jason's mother, yes, my lovely wife, will end up like Jenny Stewart. Dead, if that's what happened. I don't think so. I won't allow it."

"How can you stop it? We're in danger. That's what these innocent—well, maybe not so innocent—people are telling us. Could it even occur to you that God has allowed this situation for a reason?"

"I forbid it…That's how you stop it. As head of this—"

"Yeah, right. Your job makes me the surrogate head of this family. Like it or not, 90 percent of the time, that's reality. Besides, it's only a matter of time. We're in the middle of this, like that or not. Something like this is not just going to go away."

Chris stammered, but no intelligible words came out.

"Don't you see? Whether Jason says something, even innocently, or someone at work hears something, the police begin asking too many questions. Whoever is behind this will eventually have to declare me one big liability. I was once, accidentally. The next time their coming for me won't be a case of mistaken identity.

"Chris, you're the attorney, the logical one here. What can we do? We can't leave here…pull up stakes and vanish. Run and hide somewhere, like Jennifer Stewart. And we can't ignore what we know. If the police need more evidence, I'm the one person on the inside of WYCO who can get it."

"You were ready to wash your hands of all this. That's still a good idea. Jenny that is still our best course of action. Please, believe it." Chris reached for her hand and rubbed it.

"I didn't know what all this meant. I couldn't comprehend Jason's kidnapping. Now we know why. Now I know. Jenny Stewart was on to something. Someone wanted to scare her."

"They've done that all right! We should take that as some kind of sign. Jenny, we don't need this."

"Now listen. She saw something. Something she wasn't supposed to see. Someone she wasn't supposed to see. We have the same name and work in the same location. Someone mixes us up. They think I'm the Jenny they want. So...so they go after Jason to frighten me into remaining quiet. Jason was an accident...One big mistake. That's why they released him. Chris, can't you see?"

"But murder? If that's what happened? The attempt was certainly made. Why would they release Jason if they are willing to commit murder?"

"I don't know. That's what we have to find out. This is escalating. Look, whoever is behind this probably feels safe now that Jennifer Stewart is no longer a threat and remains *only missing*. But somewhere, sometime, someone along the line is going to mess up. It has to happen. When it does happen, Jennifer Poole will take one giant step up their list."

Chris was looking into the palms of Jenny's hands as though the lines etched by chance held the answer. "What you've told me just doesn't make sense. If Jenny Stewart was the person these people were after and she was coming here to expose them, and her brother knew about it, tell me again, why he didn't contact you himself when she didn't report in."

"He did, Chris. He did. He left a message on my office machine the day she left the farm. He later called here." Jenny handed Chris the note with the telephone number for Stewart Pork. "This is your handwriting. Is it not? You took the message."

Jim examined the note. "It is. I'm sorry, Jenny, I just don't remember it. Plain and simple." He handed it back. "So why didn't Jim try again? That call must have come in weeks ago, or I would remember it."

"Weren't you listening? Jim believed Jenny was concerned for my safety, and he honored that concern by not contacting me again. He didn't want to draw attention to me. I don't know, maybe he thought our phone is being tapped. If someone grabbed her when she got off the plane, they would have known when she was arriving. Someone is tapped into this. According to Jim, I would have been the only person Jenny would have contacted. If someone were listening, he didn't want us to be identified. He was quiet for our sakes."

"So she's missing, maybe dead. What does that mean? I'm sorry. I'm having difficulty believing that."

"We don't know that she's dead. She can't be dead. But we just don't know. We need more information. We need more evidence. I'm going to meet with Kent Simons."

"Wait a minute. Who's Kent Simons again?"

"One of the nicest guys in the world—or was—who's now filming pornographic movies in WYCO's conference room." Her words evoked a questioning look from Chris, which she ignored. "He was on my high school cheerleading squad. We met at the reunion last night and agreed to meet again today at the House of Toys. Actually, I insisted. There was something he wanted me to know. He couldn't tell me last night. I'll have Dan Sheridan join us. Maybe he can make some sense of all this."

Chris knew he'd get no further information for the moment. "There's something else, Jenny," Chris said softly after a moment of silence. "And this is good news. We have more to think about."

Jenny didn't have a clue as to what he was talking about. What could be more important? *Had he been listening?*

"WYCO Toys is changing counsel. Nothing is final. But it's more than just conversation. It's close. Really close."

Jenny pulled her hand away from Chris's grasp. "So?" she asked. Under different circumstances, she would have jumped for joy. They're facing possible grave danger, and he's talking business? Jenny was dumfounded.

"Johnson, Carlson, Shapiro and Nord is the firm to be named."

"So?" Jenny asked again, her voice a decibel louder.

"Yours truly, Christian Poole, is the top candidate for lead counsel."

Jenny jumped up. She looked down at Chris. "I can't believe it!" She exploded and bolted to her feet. Her anger shocked Chris, as she had intended. "The gall," she shouted for effect.

She stepped away, bringing Chris to his feet, following Jenny to the patio door, nearly tripping over a large ottoman. "Wait just a minute. Hear me out."

"I don't need to," she answered, "Can't you see what's happening here? Are you blind? You want evidence. You are the evidence…I'm higher up on their list than I imagined. Who's Minnesota Dumb here? Someone wants to take me out of circulation. I'm being put on a leash, just in case, to keep me under control, keep me from looking where I might do some good. And they're using you to do it."

"In light of what you're telling me, that could be so. While it's all impossible to believe, there's too much here to deny that. But look! Is the outcome all that bad? It makes good business sense. I'm the best candidate for the job. More importantly, it's good for us!" Chris placed his hands on her shoulders and gently turned her until he was looking into her eyes. "Besides, keeping you on a leash just might keep you alive. That would suit Jason and me just fine. You know! Talk about what's important. We're important. Aren't we what's important, Jenny?"

"I know." She ducked under his extended arms and returned to the couch. "It's just…just too obvious. I mean, to do this now. You'll be made partner?" she said sarcastically.

"That's automatic."

"No more traveling?"

"Some, but less. WYCO's international, you know that. There will be some travel."

"Your son gets a father?"

"Yes. And your son keeps his mother. Don't minimize that. Honey, it's what we've been waiting for. No more surrogate head of the family."

He sat down beside Jenny and pulled her close, and she looked deep into his eyes. He looked into hers and saw more anger than love. "Despicable is what they are."

Chapter 53

Minnesota businesses rarely shut down because of snow. WYCO Toys was no exception. Nonetheless, fourteen inches of new snow accumulation left employees wondering if they should show up for work? Vikings at heart most did. Those who refused paid the price: the loss of a day's wage, a hit against sick days or vacation time, and more often than not, an angry boss who showed up because that was expected of management. As Sharon Miller's boss, Jenny knew what to expect as she dialed Sharon's home phone.

"Yes," answered a sleepy voice.

"Sharon. Jenny. Going in today?"

"It's a snow day. Right?" she asked.

"For some," answered Jenny and smiled at the image of Sharon rolling out of the covers and cursing the phone.

"Last night's weather said we were getting dumped on," Sharon's retorted. "Did we? I mean, is it as bad as they predicted?"

"When have we ever…?"

"There's always the first time."

"Right. When they play hockey in hell or something like that. You know, winter has only begun."

"Yes. Isn't it nice?" said Sharon groggily.

"Sorry to bother you on your snow day. Do you have my appointment book with you?"

"As always. I go to bed with it under my pillow. You know that."

"Good. Enjoy your day off, but first, do me a favor and clear my calendar. Reach who you can. Blame the weather like everyone else. Earn your keep."

"What's up?"

"I've spoken with Jim Stewart."

"Jennifer Stewart's brother? Learn anything?"

"Nothing good. Jennifer has vanished, totally disappeared. Can't tell you more. But it could be related to Jason's abduction. Now, I said, could be."

Before Sharon could comment, Jenny added, "One more thing, please call Dan Sheridan, have him make lunch reservations for three. Suggest Italiano's, but it's his choice. Let me know where on my voice mail. And please don't mention anything about what I just said."

"You mean to Dan?"

"Dan or anyone else. It's important. I want to meet with him first. Understood? I can't go into it now."

"Right, boss," answered Sharon as she rolled out of her covers.

Chris kissed Jenny good-bye as she headed out the door, sending her off with his blessing after she promised to enlist Sheridan's help. He prayed for her safety and that she would do nothing to change what appeared at last to be a very promising future. His appointment as WYCO's lead counsel was still a long way off.

Dressed in her favorite Levi's and wearing a short fur-lined jacket, she headed for the mall. The weather would not stop her from hearing Kent Simons's sordid story, every last repulsive word. First, she'd stop at the store, check her voice mail for Sharon's restaurant confirmation, kill some time, and later bring unsuspecting Kent Simons to his meeting with Dan.

Snow clouds had given way to a few white puffs, like cotton balls dancing on blue silk in nonexistent wind. It felt like a spring day, and Jenny loved it. At twenty degrees, the air was heavy and crisp. Under different circumstances, she would have stayed home to enjoy it with her family. But at last, she had some concrete evidence to pursue. Buoyed by the day's beauty, even the threat of danger seemed invigorating. Jason wasn't any safer now, not really. But his abduction had been an accident. That meant something and lifted her spirit even more. She parked in the ramp's third level and headed directly to the office of mall security. The meeting with Kent Simons was scheduled for eleven-thirty. She had ample time to prepare Dan. Besides, she had ignored him for weeks and looked forward to seeing him again.

In his surrealistic world of consumption and fantasy, Dan reigned as king. His secretary showed Jenny to his office where he was surveying his domain from the vantage of a large window overlooking the theme park. The glass was decorated with artificial snow to give the illusion of winter in a world where the temperature was always warm, always the same.

"Long time no see," he said when his secretary closed his door. "Where've you been? I've looked for you at the store."

"It's that busy time of the year." She knew that was a stupid thing to say. The Christmas season was no less busy for Dan. From the look on his face, he also thought it was stupid, more specifically, not the truth.

"Truth is…I'm embarrassed. I made a fool of myself that night we had dinner. Something I don't often do. I'm sorry," she said sheepishly in a tone that pleaded forgiveness. "Was I really bad?" she asked finally and took a chair opposite Dan's desk. He smiled devilishly.

"Really, quite good," he sparred after a few awkward seconds.

She gasped. For an instant, her heart stopped. That evening was only a blur in her memory. "You mean we…?" Maybe she had more wine than she remembered, and she did remember being very angry with Chris. But even then…

Dan smiled. "No, Jenny, you were good, as in wife and mother. No reason to be embarrassed. How's the 'one-armed' man?"

"I know who he is. At least, I think I know," she answered excitedly and proceeded to explain how she'd discovered JB's picture in the school yearbook, his position at WYCO, and all that Anne Graham had told her.

"So it looks like he had good reason to be in the audience," Dan said smugly after hearing her out.

"I know...he probably learned about the interview with me and showed up on my deck because he was curious. You were right. A lot to do over nothing."

"That's the way I see it. Now what? Give him back his tiepin?"

"I'll find out if it's his first. It probably is. So I guess I'll give it back. On the other hand, I'd like to see Renee get her car fixed."

Dan shook his head, puzzled. "Renee?"

"It's a long story."

Dan pushed his big leather chair back from his desk and placed his hands behind his head. "So what's up?" he asked. "I made reservations for lunch. Sharon called."

"Right. Italiano's?"

"Yup. What's the occasion? Why a table for three? She's not joining us?"

"I'd like you to meet someone."

"Then this is more than a social lunch. Who's your guest?"

"A guy. Someone I knew once...in high school...thought I knew."

"I'm not following you."

"Well, there's more. Something terrible is going on, and I find myself in the middle of it. Something sordid and big. I need your perspective. Maybe you can make sense of it."

"You mean something more than Jason's abduction?" She wasn't telling him anything he didn't already know.

She considered telling him about the call from Jim Stewart but decided to hold that back for now. Possibly over lunch. "It's all related. Anyway, you need to meet this guy, name's Kent, Kent Simons."

"Sure thing. I'll be there." Italiano's was a pizza and pasta restaurant opposite the entrance to Camp Snoopy. He loved Italian and was obviously curious what Jenny had been up to. How could he refuse? Of course, he'd be there. Besides, he detected her concern. He watched her smile and walked out the door swinging her fur-lined jacket over her shoulder. When she was gone, he reached for his phone.

Back at her office, Jenny sighed at the work piled high on her desk and decided to ignore it. She covered the mountain of papers with her jacket, closed her office door, and headed for Camp Snoopy, thinking through what she hoped to accomplish with Kent.

In her Levi's, she blended with the crowd wandering the park, kids and tourists who had come by the busload from nearby hotels with cameras and large shopping bags. It was a sizable group considering the weather. Most had been lured to the mall by one of many incentive packages offering free rides in the theme park, discounts at shops, and the promise of world-class shopping for everything imaginable. Marketing statistics proved the schemes worked; visitors joyfully parted with their cash—on average, several hundred dollars per person. Last evening's snowfall provided a true Minnesota setting, a winter wonderland today's visitors could view from the comfort of a warm bus, another winter tourist attraction.

She strolled along the familiar cobblestone walkway meandering through Camp Snoopy. A young girl walking with her mother sparked a smile as she nibbled a bulbous pink cloud of cotton candy. Jenny hadn't had one of those in a decade; she'd not kept her cheerleader's figure by eating sweets. Today the sweet aroma proved too much to resist and lost out to her emotional need for self-gratification, chasing her after the vendor, barely aware of the tourists wandering the serpentine pathway. Did she appear as carefree as those she passed by? She wondered. Appearance can be so deceptive.

Never would she have guessed what Kent had become. An actor in porn! And under her nose in the executive conference suite, only steps from her office. It was beyond comprehension. She had been deceived by her own her naivety. And now, perhaps a young woman was dead, a witness to the harsh reality of just how rotten and insane parts of the world had become. Jim Stewart's fears pulsed through her mind. True, Jason's abduction was the result of mistaken identity, but believing Jason was safe was self-deception of the worst kind. But what was she to do? She quickened her pace.

She longed for a more innocent time, cotton candy and things long buried in memories of her childhood, her favorite: the circus. She'd stand with her nose to the candymaker's glassed enclosure, while in the distance, a calliope played its piped notes, and she'd watch the candy man spin his sweet smelling pink-and-white stock of cotton. Even now, she could smell it.

Seeing her coming, the female attendant turned from her machine, reached to the back of her small booth to her inventory rack of prepared treats and offered one to Jenny. Jenny shook her head. "No. Fresh please." It was important to watch the magic. A moment later, she held in her hand a fluffy, sticky pink cotton cloud, spun atop its cardboard cone. Such fond memories!

She spied a bench close by, walked to it, and seated herself Indian style, legs crossed beneath her, and watched the passersby, who, if they noticed her at all, would take her for just another high school girl enjoying a day off from school.

But for all her trying, the candy's sweetness could not diffuse the reality of Jim's words. Poor Jennifer Stewart. Jim seemed so certain she had been murdered. Could that be? "God, don't let it be," she prayed quietly. "Oh, God," she said, suddenly feeling guilt. Jennifer Stewart had returned to Minnesota to warn her. Because of that, an innocent woman was missing without a trace, possibly dead. She pinched off a final bite of candy and restlessly trashed the rest into a nearby barrel.

She must do something! But what? Her mind was a whirlwind of confusion. Then there was Chris. Despite his gallant words, she knew he would be of little help. She didn't blame him. He had his career. Suddenly anxious and frustrated, she stood and continued her meandering.

Direction would come eventually. It always did. All things had a divine purpose, and as that purpose became known, so too came direction. This series of events was no different; it had its purpose.

JENNY

She knew that deep inside, that's the way God worked. God's divine purpose would be revealed in time. Then she'd understand her role and how to proceed. But until then, she couldn't sit idly by, knowing it was only a matter of time before attention would again focus on her. She must learn what Jennifer Stewart had seen, who she had seen, who could have taken her life—if that were the grim reality. It was impossible to believe that Jennifer Stewart was dead. She couldn't allow that fate to be hers as well. It seemed her role was to find evidence. She could work on the inside. And who would be the wiser. If she had a role to play, certainly that was it. She could do it quietly, without compromising Christian's promotion. She wouldn't knuckle under, either.

Kent was the beginning. Someone very sick was accessing WYCO's offices. He'd tell her who. Wouldn't he? But there seemed to be much more. Something more sinister than pornography, as despicable as that was. Why else would Kent warn her? Why else would someone resort to murder to keep from being exposed, someone powerful with much to lose. Could it be one of Creighton's inner circle, someone close to the top acting freely under Creighton's nose, even possessing sufficient influence to bring about a change in lead counsel? She felt certain about that. Chris was good; she had no doubt of that, but who in the company would know that? No one, at least not yet. His appointment was too soon, too contrived. Someone was watching her. Who would have such power, such freedom? JB Barons would, she thought. And then there was Creighton Leonard.

Of course! Chris's appointment would require Creighton's approval. Was it possible he directed the appointment? She pondered the idea. Kidnapping Jason? Murder? All things considered, nothing made sense. Creighton had turned the company around. Kidnapping, pornography, murder, a link to him would destroy him and the company along with him. *Oh, God*, she pleaded quietly. *Where do I begin?*

Up ahead was the fun park. Beyond that, she could see Italiano's empty courtyard, and beyond that, an open area filled with kiosks and vendors selling sweatshirts, T-shirts, coffee mugs, pet rocks, items convenient for a large shopping bag. Had Dan arrived early, he would be sitting at a table in the courtyard where he could maintain casual surveillance of the surrounding area. She hoped he'd be on time as she looked at her watch. She had only five minutes to connect with Kent.

Crossing the open area, she sprinted to the elevators, punched button 3, and through glass walls watched the floor drop away as the car ascended. When the door opened, she dashed the short distance to the store's third-floor entrance, hoping Kent had not arrived early. There was no sign of him, and for a moment, she wished she had been more specific in her directions. He could have arrived early, waiting at another entrance. Well, if he didn't show, she'd go looking for him. What would he be wearing? She wondered. Last night, he had dressed to make a statement.

The store was decorated to the T for the holiday season. She was particularly fond of the entrance display intended to entice shoppers inside where they would be met by greeters and treated like royalty for the shopping experience of their life. As she approached, it was obvious her greeters had taken advantage of the unexpected snow. She saw no one.

Large imitation boulders interspersed with real gravel, imitation grass and leafy trees, the setting of a modern-day construction site marked the entrance. Arranged on the set were road graders, trucks, spaceships, and lifelike animals. With a sense of pride, she walked to a bench under an imitation tree and sat down to wait.

Five minutes, that seemed more like thirty passed. She recognized a sales clerk heading her way and flagged him down. When he failed to recognize her, she produced her corporate ID and instructed him to wait there for Kent. "You'll know him when you see him. He's different," she said with no further explanation. He gave a funny look but asked no more questions as she dashed into the store to a telephone.

Kent was staying at the Hyatt. The information operator dialed the number that rang a thousand times before the room clerk answered. It took another five minutes for the clerk to confirm that Kent had checked out at 10:05, leaving no messages and no forwarding address. "Just gone. Sorry," said the clerk, sensing Jenny's irritation. She hung up the phone hoping "gone" meant Kent was on his way to meet her.

By now, Dan would have been cooling his heels at Italiano's for twenty minutes and would be wondering if she had stood him up. Concerned she might miss Kent if she ran downstairs, she entered the store, found a phone close inside, and rang Dan's secretary. She confirmed he had left his office a few minutes earlier without his cell phone or walkie-talkie. While Jenny waited, Dan's secretary called the restaurant only to report there had been no answer. With no way to reach Dan, Jenny returned to the store entrance. "Sorry," said the sentry. "No one has passed by. No one."

Deciding it more important to meet Kent Simons and reconnect with Dan later, Jenny dismissed the clerk and took up position outside the entrance. Ten minutes later, Dan came looking for her. He found her sitting like a forlorn high school girl, cross-legged between a giraffe and a fire truck, her elbows resting on her knees, her chin nestled in cupped hands.

For the past few weeks, he had missed her more than he had been willing to admit, pretty, cute, sexy, vulnerable—a magnetic inner quality he found impossible to describe or resist. He watched admiringly at a distance until she sensed his presence, looked up, and her eyes met his. They exchanged smiles. Smiling and shaking his head, he strolled slowly toward her. *O Jenny*, he thought, *you're too special.* In her absence the past few weeks, he found himself falling for Sharon Miller in a big way. But now seeing Jenny again—*Jenny,* she was special.

"You seem to have a tough time meeting people," he said when he reached her.

"I'm sorry." She made no effort to get up. "He promised to be here. The hotel said he checked out. Gone. I guess gone meant "out of here," not gone to Mall of America."

"You know, you really could use a bench or something here, a place for people to sit while they wait for people who never show up."

She ignored him and gestured to the bench beneath the tree. "Not very comfortable. It made my seat itch." Her openness made him smile. Today he was dressed professionally, like one of the president's men, in a dark-blue tailored suit, conservative blue tie, and wingtip shoes. He towered over her momentarily, then slowly lowered himself to sit cross-legged on the stones beside her and began making circles in the loose gravel with his finger.

"Care to tell me about him, this illusive friend of yours? And while you're at it, what are you up to, Jenny? What's this all about?"

"His name is Kent Simons. We went to high school together and met again last night at a reunion."

"And he was going to meet us here today? For what purpose?"

"Well, he didn't know about you. He was coming here to meet with me. You were my idea. Maybe he guessed something was up and that's why he didn't show. He had some very interesting…no, I should say disturbing, information about my employer WYCO Toys. He inferred I might be in danger because of my job. Not because of what I do but because of where I work. He couldn't go into it last night. Some guy, he said his agent, was waiting for him at the bar. Today, he was going to explain it to me. So much for old friends."

She picked up a handful of gravel and released it slowly as she waited for Dan to say something. When he didn't, she continued, "It turns out he's an actor, and he's gay. He's been making pornographic films. And you want to hear the kicker? Some of those films were shot at WYCO's offices after hours. Dan, he said he's been in my building, in the conference area just down the hall from my office, not once, but on several occasions. Right under our noses. He said the conference suite area made a perfect film set because it's set up like a hotel suite."

"That was something he was proud of?"

"No. Not really," he said more as a statement of fact and sounding ashamed.

"Somebody must have known. Who'd have access to the executive conference center after hours?"

"Any number of people. Mildred Knowles keeps a log. She's the receptionist on our floor. She has no real authority, but she keeps it supplied and records who uses it."

"And you've seen that log?"

"Of course. It's no secret. And I know no one has ever signed in to make pornographic movies. If they did, probably half the plant would have been there to watch."

"I don't mean something that obvious. Who uses it the most?"

"Department heads, salespeople, advertising, marketing mostly. It's sometimes used as temporary living quarters. Like I said, it's very well appointed, has everything. Managers from out of town, consultants, and sometimes salespeople on a tight budget might stay there overnight, maybe for short periods."

"A suite?" Dan asked.

Jenny nodded confirmation.

"How convenient."

"Like Kent said, a great film set. But there's more," Jenny continued. "And what comes next is the scary part. A young *gofer*, a marketing assistant who worked on my floor, disappeared about the time Jason was kidnapped. According to her brother, she worked late one night and stumbled into one of those film sessions. She fled, showed up at his doorstep—a hog farm in Nebraska—stayed for awhile, and when an attempt was made on her life decided to return to Minnesota to warn me. She never showed. He believes she was murdered because of what she saw."

Dan looked at her incredulously. "Jennifer Stewart," he stated a moment later.

"The same. Ring a bell?"

"The day you and Sharon came to my office, her brother called. He had wanted his sister to call him when she got to town."

"She did call him. But they didn't speak directly. She only left a message on his machine. Said she was going to hide out for a while to think everything through. She told him not to attempt locating her. She'd call him later. That was weeks ago."

"And?"

"Nothing since. That's the last he heard. He thinks someone grabbed her and was with her when she placed that one call. Dan, she was coming here to warn me, and she had been adamant about exposing what she had seen. Her brother, Jim, believes her sudden change in attitude was a deliberate signal for him not to go to the police. He believes she was worried the police would make us all very public and put Jason and me in greater danger. After that, he tried to reach me but didn't try again. He was concerned too many calls would put us in greater danger."

Suddenly, Jenny began to cry. "Dan, if this man is right, his sister was murdered because of me. And he's lived with the loss, alone and not knowing, just to protect me. And…and…I go off and eat cotton candy. Dan, what can we do? If he's right and she's dead… we've got to do something. I could be next. Dan, I could be next."

She didn't resist when Dan drew her close. And resting her head on his shoulder, she cried for several minutes. When she stopped, she looked into his eyes. "Is she dead, Dan?" she asked, sniffling, "Could the FBI have her in protective custody while they investigate?"

"I don't know if she's dead, Jenny. I do know the authorities don't have her. I just spoke to Sadler. The sheriff in Green Bend, Nebraska, has asked his help in investigating the disappearance of Jennifer Stewart. He got the call a week or so ago. Sadler called me for my take on it because of you. I didn't get much more information, but it's certain they don't have Jennifer Stewart in protective custody."

As Dan held Jenny, he thought of Gary Sadler's nephew who, decades earlier, was found in a pool of blood, accused of being gay, and guilty of compromising his position as a Senate page. Killed reportedly with his own gun held in the *wrong* hand. He too had gotten in the way of Creighton Leonard. Now Jennifer Stewart was another victim? How many more would there be?

Dan didn't share his thoughts with Jenny. She was frightened enough, and rightfully so. But he didn't believe she was in greater immediate danger. For the present, Jennifer Stewart's killers would assume with her gone, they were safe. He needed to talk further with Sadler. It seemed odd that Sadler seemed only mildly interested in the connection between the Stewart girl's disappearance and his nemesis, Creighton Leonard. He thought Sadler would have taken the information and run with it straight to Creighton's House of Toys.

"And the connection with Jason?" asked Dan after a long silence.

"Jennifer Stewart and I share the same name. And we look alike, I'm told. According to Jim Stewart, it was a case of mistaken identity. Jenny told her brother she suspected taking Jason was an accident."

"An accident?"

"Don't you see, someone got us confused? Then, instead of going after Jennifer Stewart, they came after me, Jennifer Poole, and took Jason to frighten me, to show me just how vulnerable and accessible I was. When the mistake was discovered, Jason was released here, where he was sure to be quickly rescued. He probably would have been released anyway if Jennifer assumed correctly. The kidnappers' only motivation was to frighten her, believing Jason was her son. We probably will never know that for sure."

"After that, things got out of hand? And Jenny was murdered."

"It makes sense. They were safe when they were dealing with Jason. They'd given him the drug…What's it called?"

"Street name is Devils Brew," Dan interjected. "A contraband hybrid form of the commercial drug, Rohypnol, known as the date rape drug. It's a prescription drug available outside the United States but highly illegal here in any form. The version, Devil's Brew, is more refined and can be better controlled. And it can be administered by inhaling, as it was in Jason's case. It's effective, producing, most often, complete amnesia with fewer side effects. And the victim recovers sooner."

"You didn't tell me all that before," Jenny scolded.

"It didn't seem necessary. Jason was safe at home."

A moment passed before Jenny continued, "You said it could be more controlled. What does that mean?" she asked and wondered what else he had not told her.

"To the extent that loss of short-term memory may not be total—contrary to their reason for using the drug in this case. Memory could improve. That's why I wanted you to watch Jason's behavior."

"Well, he still shows no signs of remembering."

"Considering the time that's passed...Well, you can't be certain."

Jenny resumed digging in the display gravel. "Anyway, because of the drug, they felt safe with Jason. But Jennifer Stewart running loose created a big problem for whoever was present in that conference center."

"You say they merely wanted to frighten Jennifer Stewart into remaining quiet? What changed? Why kill her?"

"Jennifer not only knew about the filming session. She now knew about the kidnapping. She'd figured it out and, in doing so, became a real threat. Furthermore, in the room during the filming was someone she recognized, a familiar face, someone whose name she couldn't recall. Someone important. Possibly very important. She was certain. That someone must be at the center of this and doesn't want to be known."

"Interesting theory," he said, noting a vague similarity to Sadler's story. "How important?" he asked, considering the possibility of a political connection.

"I don't know. Just important. Anyway, she escaped the building and left town. They got us confused and came after me through Jason. Eventually, they realized their mistake, searched her apartment, found her brother's Nebraska address, and tracked her there."

"You say you look alike?"

"Maybe hair, weight, stature. I really don't know. Friends would say the difference was night and day."

"But close enough to add to the confusion caused by the name. The conference room was on your floor in the building?" Jenny nodded confirmation. "Your office was close by. You were known to work late on projects. Someone probably came up with the name Jenny and didn't know there were two Jennys working on the same floor."

"Does that mean anything now?"

"You never know. These are all pieces to the puzzle. So how'd they get onto the farm without being noticed? That's ranch country. Strangers aren't generally trusted."

"Hired on."

"An assassin who knows about pigs?"

"The perfect employee. According to her brother. Very knowledgeable, knew everything about pigs. Used a hog farm in Arizona as a reference."

"Interesting. Should be easy enough to check. Hmmm…Didn't know they had hog farms in Arizona?"

"Jim thought he knew the farm. He was never able to verify the employment and sensed something wasn't right. The guy was too good. Too well-educated. A Latino. And dressed like money. He could have hawked his Rolex and lived for a whole year."

"Interesting," Dan said again, processing the details.

"It took about a week. When the time was right, he cornered Jennifer in one of the barns, but she got away. He caught her again and was about to finish her with a wire cord when Jim came to her rescue and hit him on the head with a big wrench. Killed him instantly. Jim called the sheriff. Claimed he found the migrant raping his sister, hit him, killed him."

"Why didn't he tell the truth?"

"To protect his sister. He hoped whoever was behind it would think she was dead and go away."

"Wishful thinking. They should have fed the bastard to the pigs. Wouldn't take long, and there'd be nothing to prove the killer had ever existed." Jenny gave him a curious look. "We had pigs in Virginia too. I saw the remains of one hog farmer who had fallen unconscious into a hogpen. Had he not been discovered when he was, there wouldn't have been anything to find."

A minute passed before Jenny continued, "With the attempt on her life, Jennifer decided to come here and face it head-on."

"But she never made it."

"No. Jim believes she was grabbed when she got off the plane. The airlines confirmed her departure from Omaha, and someone, presumably Jennifer, retrieved her bags."

"They knew she was coming and were waiting for her. But her brother is the only one who knew her plans."

"Not so," declared Jenny. "She left a message for me that she was coming to see me. That message could have been intercepted."

Dan stood, extended his hand to Jenny pulling her up beside him. "Now what?" he asked.

"I finish what Jennifer Stewart started. I need to find out what happened to her and why."

Dan led Jenny to the railing overlooking the theme park, leaned against it, his expression all business. "What Jennifer Stewart knew may have cost her life."

"That's what Chris keeps reminding me of."

"And he's okay with this? Your involvement, snooping around?"

"No."

"But you'll do what you want anyway." He played back what he was hearing.

"I have no choice. Chris knows that too deep down. Besides, I don't know if he's convinced we're in any real danger. He certainly doesn't believe he's in danger."

Dan began to say something, but Jenny cut him short.

"I know. I know. He's the attorney. I don't know what it will take to convince him. Possibly he feels responsible and is in denial. I just don't know."

Dan didn't respond. Jenny continued, getting back on track, "Jim Stewart said the police had insufficient evidence to conduct a serious investigation, and officially, Jenny is only missing. They need more information. Dan, I know I can get the evidence the police need. If anyone at WYCO is involved, I'm probably the only person

JENNY

on the inside who can dig around without suspicion." She paused and said, "Right?"

"Right," he said. That's the way it had been since day one. "So where do you begin?"

"Maybe with Creighton Leonard. See just what he knows."

"How do you propose to do that? Just ask him?" Dan asked.

"Well?" She thought it a good idea. "It is his company."

"Not a good idea, Jenny," he said for obvious reasons that he withheld from her. "The less he knows of your involvement, the better. Believe me. Just assume he knows something and treat it for what it's worth."

"You mean Creighton…?" She didn't finish. Dan had just confirmed her gnawing suspicion. Creighton Leonard was most likely responsible for Chris's pending appointment. She hadn't previously shared her thoughts with Dan and decided to say nothing more for the time being. She could be jumping to the wrong conclusion too quickly.

"I'm just saying, be careful," he warned. "Don't assume anyone is safe, or not safe, for that matter. You've got two people, Jennifer Stewart and your friend Kent, warning you to be careful. Stay on your guard. I'll check with Sadler. He'll help. And keep me informed. Jenny, I mean that. I need to know what you're up to."

"I will. I promise." She turned to leave but stopped abruptly. "Thanks, Dan. I really need your help right now."

He watched her leave. "We need each other," he said to himself.

Chapter 54

With less than three weeks remaining until Christmas, the pianist began her repertoire of Christmas selections. Jenny entered the atrium at the Wayzata Towers and paused to take in a few bars of "Winter Wonderland," her favorite. The snow had given work-a-day-Joes an extra holiday and showed no sign of going away, as forecasters predicted temperatures would remain in the twenties. A white Christmas was a sure bet.

Jenny pushed the button for the executive penthouse, moved to the back of the elevator, and shot up to the thirty-fourth floor. Before leaving her office, she had placed one phone call to JB Barons. Speaking only to his secretary, she left neither a message nor her name. Surprise was the order of the day. She would present JB with the tiepin and see what he had to say. For effect, she had dressed as seductively as she could without being inappropriate.

She carried a pair of high-heeled pumps in a small bag and quickly changed when the elevator stopped at 34, tucking the bag behind the receptionist's desk on her way. "I won't be long," Jenny said with a smile and asked, "Is Burt in?" Burt would be her reason for the visit, should anyone ask. She'd wink at him on her way out, regardless.

"He's marked in. Would you like me to ring him, Mrs. Poole?"

"No. You know who I am?" Jenny asked curiously, wondering whether to be impressed or be concerned that she was the object of water-cooler conversation.

JENNY

"Of course," came the quick response with a smile, begging a pat on the head like a golden retriever who had just brought in the morning paper. *No insights there.* And no pat on the head.

She poked her head inside the first set of doors, entrance to the corporate board room and senior executive conference center. The cavernous room was richly paneled and held a large dark-wood table with matching chairs. Barely noticeable at intervals in the walls were three large paneled doors, each closed. Jenny wondered if one door might disguise a bedroom, as it did at plant 1. On the far side, a wall of glass overlooked a rooftop courtyard and the Minneapolis skyline in the distance.

Better not get caught snooping. She closed the door and continued down the corridor. JB's office came next. It adjoined the conference room. This was the corporate home of "Jeb, JB Barons, class of '81." The yearbook picture of a tall scrawny kid flashed before her. She smiled as she considered what she was about to do. It bordered on cruel, even sadistic.

A neat brass door plaque said "Baron." With the door half ajar, she popped her head in and quietly opened it the rest of the way. Disappointment swept over her; the room was empty. *No fun!* She should have checked again with Miss Efficiency.

The office was not as large or as well-appointed as Creighton's, but nice, nonetheless. She suspected the closed door to her left offered access to the *board* room. Behind a large desk, the drapes were pulled back to expose the rooftop courtyard and a panoramic skyline. *Nice!*

"Ouch!" boomed a voice from under the desk. Jenny moved closer to investigate. To the left and behind the desk hung a suit coat from a rattan coat rack. As she considered the piece of clothing, the large leather chair behind the desk moved backward to reveal a man's back. The head remained under the desk.

Beneath the desk, JB watched in shock as open-toed pumps came within inches of stepping on his fingers, groping in search of a missing pen. "Ouch!" His head once more banged the underside of the desk. For a moment, he admired graceful ankles, knowing what was above them had to be the equally beautiful contoured calves of an unannounced guest. A very pretty guest, he surmised.

Her perfume was one he didn't recognize. "Ouch!" he said again. Jenny watched his back move slowly out from under the desk. Then "Ouch," followed another thud. His voice was now a polite whisper. There was a flurry of activity as his legs became tangled in the base of his chair. Finally, he came upright in one fluid motion, overturned his chair behind him, and stood looking down into Jenny's smiling, amused face.

"Well, hello," he said, trying to control his embarrassment. "And you are...?" Of course, he knew. He had recognized Jenny instantly.

"Jennifer Poole," she answered politely, playing the game. He was tall indeed, but not the scrawny underclassman she remembered. His frame had filled out nicely. While obviously not athletic, he seemed solid and was more handsome than she remembered.

"Have we met? I don't re..." He struggled for words. That was the effect she had on him.

"A long time ago. We attended Minnetonka High School at the same time. You knew me then as Jennifer Ward."

"Of course," he exclaimed in feigned surprise. "Class of '79. You were a cheerleader, dance-line..." JB had never seen her more beautiful, more radiant, or more ravishing. He was gasping for breath. He had never seen her so close. Well, maybe once, the day in the school cafeteria when he grabbed her yearbook and wrote his secret message. No, he would not forget that day. Did she ever learn who wrote those loving words, he wondered suddenly, words straight from his heart?

He felt beads of perspiration forming on his brow and took a step backward to right his chair, hoping to calm his pounding heart. "Please. Please sit down, Jenny," he said, seating himself. "Or is it now, Jennifer?" *Not too familiar, Jeb,* his mind cautioned. He had not shaken her hand, a realization that caused a head-rush as his long body settled into the leather chair. "What brings you here? I mean after...how many years? Can I help you with something, or did you just pop in to say hello? Anyway...my goodness. Good to see you."

JENNY

He relaxed but was speechless as Jenny settled into the chair opposite him. His heart still pounded. He felt dizzy. There she was, bigger and better than life itself, sitting a desk-width away like a dream come true: beautiful face, auburn hair, and captivating brown eyes.

"Both names work," Jenny answered. "I'd heard you were here at WYCO. Creighton Leonard's assistant?"

"Yes. A position of honor, I feel. We met while I was at Harvard."

"Harvard?" she asked, struck by the obvious difference in age.

"Before Harvard, actually. My father worked for Creighton. They've been friends for many years. I began doing special projects for Mr. Leonard while in the business school there. Ah…I was. He wasn't…attending, I mean. One thing led to another, and eventually here."

"You came here with him, then?"

"Yes. I'm the one who actually turned him onto WYCO. You know, growing up here in the shadow of all this." He waved his arms in a sweeping gesture. "At one time, my father owned some stock. WYCO has made several millionaires. It's a great company. I don't need to tell you that, of course. And now Creighton's genius will make it even greater. He's very astute. Underrated and understated, just like the stock. Tell me about you. You've been here for awhile, I understand."

"You knew I was here, and you didn't look me up?" she toyed. He stuttered something unintelligible. "Going on seven years. A friend of my husband, Chris, suggested I develop a promotional program for his New York based company. I did. It was successful, and doors opened for me here."

"How so?" asked JB to keep her talking.

"I used WYCO's product line in the promotion. WYCO had a quality image, a corporate quality central to the promotion. My client prospered, and so did WYCO. We moved a ton of product. I had been working as a waitress with Chris in school and saw an opportunity here. I applied and was hired on the spot. No more waitressing!"

"That's some success story. And you've continued to impress people here. Not the least of whom is Virginia Leonard."

"How's that?" she asked, basking in the recognition.

"Your success with the House of Toys, for one. Comments from your good corporate customers like Davis and Throm, the firm that initiated your interview here. And this"—he patted the top file on the pile of portfolios on his desk—"your display design ideas for the Christmas season. A stroke of genius!"

His knowledge of her career gave her cause for question, but she didn't let it show. It was obvious he'd been checking up on her. She didn't know whether to be honored or fearful. *Was she still his obsession after all these years, an obsession that began in 1979? Thanks, Anne.*

"You've read it? My proposal?"

"More than once," he said, adding, "great concept. I hope you don't mind that I retained a copy. It could impact the company. Therefore, it's my domain. I am proud of you, Jenny."

He was one big smile, tongue-tied no longer. "Isn't life interesting, Jenny? Here we sit, two kids from Minnetonka High School, both now on the inside of one of the greatest little companies in America. First me, with Creighton, and now you with Virginia." As he spoke excitedly, he patted her "treatise" and noticed a subtle change had come over her. Possibly he was being too familiar. He'd be more careful.

"I'm looking forward to meeting Virginia. I understand we have some common interests."

"You do, indeed." JB acknowledged but dropped the subject. Their common interest, Christianity, was not his thing."

"She'll be attending the Christmas party, I understand."

"Both of them. You know there are two? The important one is the executive's and friend's dinner at the Leonard's. Virginia is expecting to see you there."

"I've received no notice of that."

"An oversight, I'm sure. It's one week from tonight. You'll be there, of course?"

"If you're sure I'm invited."

"Positive. You're one reason Virginia is attending."

"I don't understand, JB."

"Jenny, you couldn't be in a better position. Career wise." He was bubbling inside. Virginia was her safe haven. Jenny couldn't understand how important that fact was.

"I'm flattered. I didn't realize she—"

"You're too modest." JB patted the proposal again. "This excites her. Believe it, Jenny."

Caught off guard by talk of Virginia Leonard, Jenny nearly forgot her purpose in coming. "Well, I've got a meeting with Burt." She stood under the pretext of leaving and reached into her Gucci bag. "By the way?" she asked, digging deep to produce her mysterious treasure. "Do you recognize this?" She was sure he flinched ever so slightly. She reached over his desk and held out the jewel.

"No," he responded, but he had hesitated too long. "Looks expensive," he said and leaned back into his chair.

"If it's real. Could be just some cut glass. Maybe I should just toss it."

"I'm no expert," JB babbled. "But I'd say it looks real enough. Don't think I'd flush it or throw it away. But why do you ask? Why might I recognize it?" A ruse, he thought. A ruse.

"Thought perhaps you may know who lost it."

"Why would I? Sorry. Lucky find if you can't locate the owner. Where?"

"On my deck after a news interview, the day of Jason's kidnapping."

"Oh, during that storm…?" He'd nearly given himself away. "How about…what's his name, the news anchor? Stone? He could afford a trinket like that." He tried to cover his blunder and looked at Jenny for a sign that he'd been exposed. Jenny gave none. That had been too close.

She tossed the stone into the air, catching it again in the other hand. "Won't Renee be thrilled." She watched a puzzled look sweep over his face, waited a moment, returned *her* tiepin to *her* bag, and turned on her heel. Before she reached the door, she paused. "Does the name Jennifer Stewart mean anything to you?" She watched him flinch again; this time, it was definite. He attempted to mask it by standing, but she had caught him.

"Stewart? Doesn't ring a bell. You're the only Jennifer I know offhand. Why?"

"Just wondering. She was an employee here for a brief period. Just wondering."

They didn't exchange good-byes. She set off in the direction of Burt's office and wondered what she had learned. JB had lied twice. He as much as denied he'd been on her deck spying on her. She was sure he knew the name Jennifer Stewart. He could have told the truth but didn't. He was hiding something. What? Why? She was onto something. She just didn't know what.

JB watched her approach Burt's office. His thoughts were no longer on her gorgeous legs, her short skirt, her decisive sexy stride. He had just kissed *twenty thousand dollars* good-bye. Sure, his insurance company was already processing his claim. No money would be lost. But Jenny knew something. That was most disturbing. She had caught him in a lie, not once, but twice. She knew he was not telling the truth about Jennifer Stewart or the diamond tiepin.

His face turned ashen. Could she know Jennifer Stewart was murdered? Even he didn't know that for certain. If she were dead, it was not of his doing. But could this one-time love of his life suspect he was involved? Could she think of him as her killer? It was too much to bear. Exhausted, he closed his office door and collapsed with a swoosh into his chair.

The love of his life stepped into Burt's office.

Chapter 55

Dan found Sadler sitting alone at a table near the second-floor railing overlooking the theme park. "Hope you don't mind my getting started without you," the FBI boss said, swallowing a bite of pizza. "I didn't know how late you'd be."

"No. It's good you started. Got a last-minute phone call. You know how it works. Thanks for coming over."

Sadler took another bite and queried, "So I'm here. You said we needed to talk. What's up?"

"The girl that disappeared from Nebraska, Jennifer Stewart. Jenny just heard from her brother. He seems certain that his sister was murdered to keep her quiet. I guess you know all that already."

"Not about his phone call. I am aware of his suspicions, however. He took long enough to contact her."

"He didn't make the call. Jenny initiated it. She came across a note that he'd called. Evidently, shortly after his sister disappeared. Like his sister, he was concerned further contact would put the Pooles in danger and didn't try further."

Gary didn't respond immediately. "That's it?" he said finally. "That's all you've got for me? I guess the best I'm getting is…pizza. It was worth the trip, I guess."

Dan reached for a piece of Gary's pizza. "Jenny is serious about helping now. Thought you'd like to know that," he said and took a bite. "She doesn't know about Creighton."

"You didn't tell her? Somehow, I thought you would."

"I agree with you. For now, she's probably not in immediate danger. But, Gary, we're putting her smack in harm's way. Are you prepared to protect her?"

"She's already there. It was her son they took, remember?" Dan puzzled at the remark.

"That's not an answer."

Gary ignored him. "How's her husband?"

"In the dark. She thinks he's in denial. He's got his career. Oh, he's concerned. It's just that he's too focused to get it." Dan lowered the pizza, showing concern. "Jenny is one brave woman. And she's creative. Something tells me she'll find your answers. I want to make sure she's protected."

"We're alone on this," Gary answered slowly, his eyes directed away from Dan.

"Meaning?"

"We're on to other things."

"Maybe the bureau is. You're not. You know where this will lead. You need to follow this to its conclusion."

"I know. The last act of my career. I intend to see this through. But someone up top is getting ruffled. I've been told…advised to cool it…pull back." Frustration was written all over his face.

"How so?"

"They're going to nail your man Bartlett for the assassination attempt. That's if he recovers. It's pretty obvious at this point he's an independent. There's no one to defend him. I mean he did what he did on national television. They'll prove he took the Poole boy too."

From the expression on Dan's face, he didn't like what he was hearing. "It's a cover-up."

"Call it what you like."

Dan considered the idea for a moment and reached for another piece of Sadler's pizza. "You know, blaming him will work to Jenny's advantage for now. Turn down the heat a bit. Buy us all time." Sadler nodded, sipping his beverage. "And the funding scam?"

"Random Enterprises, Creighton Leonard's clandestine money pool. Real enough, but we don't have enough to nail him on that, either. As deep as I've been digging, we get only glimpses of his shirt tails."

"There's still the kidnapping. Any fool would know Bartlett could not have been involved, and you're saying they'll nail him for that? I can't believe you're okay with that."

"Look, for now I'm following orders. I didn't get this far by screwing up. And, like I said, they'll nail Bartlett for that too." Sadler pushed the pizza away. "Dan this is my last chance, I'm seeing this through. But it's you and me Dan. That's it."

"And Jenny and Jason Poole."

"Yes…And the Pooles."

"We still have the missing woman, another kidnapping and a possible murder."

"Possible collateral damage but so far not connected. Not close enough to help, anyway. Believe me, Dan. Without the girl's testimony or her body, one or the other."

"Gary, you're not making sense. You're not telling me everything," asserted Dan.

Sadler shrugged. "Dan, you're concerned for the Poole's safety, as you should be. My help is limited. I do know that if Jenny stumbles onto anything, anything at all, she'll be safer if no one suspects help is coming out of my office."

"You are still in the game?" asked Dan.

Gary gave Dan that "you've gotta be kidding" look. "Covertly. Keep me informed."

"And protection? Does she get any?"

"I've got my eye on her. My way. That's all you need to know."

Each man studied the other, and in the distance, a marching band played Christmas carols. Dan would rely on Gary's reputation; he was one of the best. He had no other choice, he convinced himself. They were alike in many ways, Sadler and Jenny. Each had a mission. He was only a voice in the wind. Sadler extended his hand as he stood. The meeting was over.

"Jennifer Stewart saw someone that night at the old corporate headquarters. That's what this is all about," said Dan, taking the hand.

"Similar to the problem my nephew faced."

"If you say so. Now before you go, how about the body in Nebraska?"

"We're looking at prints, dental records, DNA. The guy didn't exist. He's a nonperson."

"And who specializes in nonpersons?"

"You should know better than anyone. Your records indicate you enjoyed such status once."

"Enjoyed?" spat Dan.

"Not a good choice of words, sorry. The point is few people are nonpersons. Terrorists? He was no terrorist. An assassin, yes, but not a terrorist."

"You say he's CIA?" blurted Dan.

"Or was. I don't think he's FBI." Sadler waited for Dan's response.

"An independent contractor?"

"That's my guess. The kind only someone with well-placed contacts would know, say, someone high up in government or politically connected."

"Leonard?" asked Dan. "There's no chance you're reading too much into this?"

"Open your eyes, Dan. The guy is connected. And don't tell me things like this don't happen in today's Washington. Then hold the thought a little longer and suppose it is some sort of cover-up."

Dan pondered that thought for a moment and changed the subject. "What about the kidnappers? Anything? What did you learn before you quit looking?"

"Not much. The truck, as you know, was clean. Nothing incriminating. We have questioned the driver who was to have made the actual deliveries that morning. He states he received an anonymous phone call a day earlier with a promise that an envelope was in his mailbox with two thousand dollars in twenties for him if he called in sick that morning."

"And if he didn't."

"He would be made sick. Very sick."

"And you believe that?"

"Have to. He handed over the money as evidence. In his position, I don't know that many people would do that. No, he seems to be telling the truth."

"And the videos…the surveillance tapes?"

"Maybe something there, but nothing too concrete. The *perps* did a good job of staying in the shadows. We were working on various enhancements with Girard, he's the company's security chief, but that wheel is grinding ever so slowly. We know two employees, a man and woman, leaving after their shift encountered two men in the hall. All they remember, or the woman remembers, is that the two men were not regulars and did not have official uniforms with the company logo. The woman said there was something familiar about one of the men, but she can't say what it was."

"Neat," Dan said, hoping for more.

"Yeah. She has my card with my number. If she remembers anything, she'll call. I believe the two men she encountered were Jason's kidnappers. Any more questions? I've got to run." Gary started to turn but stopped himself. "Believe me, I understand Jenny's importance. I don't want anything to happen to her or her family. Right now, she's all I've got. I'll protect her as best I can. Just keep me informed." Sadler reached into his pocket for a tip, remembered he'd eaten fast-food and returned the change back into his pocket. "Well, are you going to thank me for lunch? It was on me," Gary said.

"On your expense account, you mean," corrected Dan.

"No way. Covert and unofficial, remember?" he said and walked away.

Their eyes met again as Gary stepped onto the escalator and disappeared slowly from view.

Chapter 56

Christmas, now less than two weeks away, brought an embossed envelope to the Poole's afternoon mail. Chris studied the "winged dove" on its face before handing it to Jenny. "Another Christmas card. Looks like this belongs to you."

Jenny took it, examined the face, turned it over, and read the calligraphic return address. It was from the Leonards, Mr. and Mrs. Creighton Leonard, Orono, Minnesota. She knew what it was and opened it as she stood at the kitchen counter. "It's our invitation to the Leonard's party. Sure you don't want to go?"

"Only if you'll go to my office party. You go to mine if I go to yours." They'd already discussed their calendars leading to Christmas. It was Jenny who was short on time and had opted out. Chris was not happy about attending solo; all the partners would be bringing their wives. It was tit for tat. So Chris declined the Leonard's social. Besides, it was the one night Jason would be at home—no hockey. Jenny approved of the father-and-son time, the only reason she had acquiesced.

"Could be good for business, you know. Yours, not mine." Jenny teased. I'm told there will be about three hundred people coming from all over the globe. Famous people, senators, congressmen, doctors, lawyers, and a few Indian chiefs. Who knows, maybe Bill and Hillary. You know…If you're going to be chief counsel…" she chided.

"I know your thoughts on that. It hasn't happened yet, and I don't want that to be an issue with us. Maybe you should skip out.

JENNY

Think about it, late night, bedside fire, Jacuzzi, a little Christmas cheer."

"And Jason?"

"Okay. Anyway, I won't even be missed." Chris was thinking. "You serious about Bill and Hillary?"

"They're friends with Creighton, I've been told. Close. You just never know," she said and unfolded a note from Virginia Leonard, a personal message.

> *Dear Jenny,*
> *I'm sorry for the mix-up. Please accept my apology. I do hope you will come. I want very much to meet you.*
> *In Christ's love,*
> *Virginia*

She turned the envelope in her hand. "I really have to go," she said slowly, thoughtfully and placed the invitation in a basket of Christmas cards.

The invitation had said formal attire. Considering that it was easier for a man to drive a car in formal wear than it was a woman, especially bundled for a Minnesota winter, she wished she had been more insistent that Chris join her for the party. Too late now.

Chris and Jason kissed her on the cheek as she set her party shoes on the passenger seat and climbed in, twisting herself in the full-length fox and drove out the drive. It was a twenty-minute drive around the lake to the Leonard's. The drive entrance was easy enough to find, ablaze with Christmas lights on ornamental pines that lined the long stately drive. A true storybook scene. She guessed it had to have been Virginia's doing.

She saw a sign that read "valet parking" and drove up the long drive, stopping beneath the portico. One prayer had been answered—no long walk in the cold. A young woman hidden beneath a fur-lined parka greeted her and gave her a piece of paper with a number, her car check. She quickly kicked off her boots and slipped into her heels. The young attendant helped her out of her SUV and steadied her as she navigated around the Cherokee to the home's palatial entrance. Inside, voices hummed, and her thoughts turned to Chris and Jason enjoying themselves. Maybe she'd leave early and catch the last few dying coals of Chris's fire. No, the dye is cast. *I'll have a good time*, she told herself.

Two young women dressed in formal black-and-white servant's clothes greeted her. One helped her out of her fox jacket and disappeared down a long hallway; the other, an attractive woman with short red hair, led her to the formal living room, already loud with conversation.

The home was beautifully festive with everything that was Christmas—smells, colored lights, and a string quartet playing softly in the background. Christmas had arrived at the Leonard's Lake Minnetonka palace. Fire crackled in a cavernous fireplace at the far end of the room. Above the mantle, ablaze with lights, was a large decorative wreath, festooned with wide red ribbons and brilliant glass ornaments.

Feeling strangely alone, Jenny stepped onto the plush carpet and looked for someone she might know. Where was JB? A bar had been set up in one corner of the room; she wandered in its direction, searching.

"May I have this dance?" A light tap on her shoulder accompanied the softly spoken words and, as she turned around, received a surprise peck on the cheek. It was Burt, smiling and holding a scotch. She wondered just how many he had downed. No one would be dancing on the carpet. Burt knew that.

"Having a merry Christmas so far?" he asked. No slurred words to match his strange behavior.

"Very merry and very busy. You?" Burt's wife usually accompanied him to company gatherings. Burt read her thoughts as she glanced about the room.

"The same. But the same this year, being merry and very busy, has Elizabeth a bit under the weather. You see we're going to be alone.

JENNY

The kids are staying with their own families this year. I think it's dampened her spirit a tad. She'll get over it. We're taking a month after all this is done." He waved his arms to take in the entire holiday season. "We'll spend time with each of our children to see if we've taught them right. Your family's all here. Lucky."

"Yes, but always a bit too busy. Too much running around. Your plan sounds good."

"Sounds like Chris will be spending more time in the cities."

"How's that?" she questioned, surprised by the comment. Chris had sworn her to secrecy until his appointment was confirmed, if and when—two big questions. That's what would keep Chris in town. "You know something I don't?" she asked.

"Not that you're not aware of, I'm sure. But when it comes from the lips of Virginia Leonard, you've got a sure bet."

So it was Virginia Leonard, not Creighton, pushing for the change in counsel. Why?

"Jenny, you're on a roll. I couldn't be more delighted if the good fortune were my own. You deserve it. I'm sure Christian does too. I'm very pleased for you both."

"Thank you, Burt. You're so kind." She gave him a peck on the cheek. "Merry Christmas, boss."

"Now don't get carried away, girl." He beamed. "I wouldn't want Elizabeth to hear what we've been up to."

This kind of gathering was very good for Burt's business, even though he claimed to be apolitical and immune from company politics. He was very astute, and other than being forced to accept junk product from the orient, things pretty much went the way he wanted. He strolled away when another object on his agenda entered the room.

Alone again, Jenny continued to the bar, confident someone she knew would eventually appear. She declined an offer of wine and ordered her usual ginger ale.

The living room was large, probably sixty by eighty feet. Jenny's entire residence could fit within its cubic space. It was a local landmark of sorts; Jenny was familiar with its history. By lake standards, it was a new home built in the 1970s by new money, intended to make a statement. However, before it could be completed, its owner had been tried and convicted of larceny and tax evasion, sentenced to ten years in federal prison, and all property confiscated. Creighton had purchased the home at a bargain price after negotiating directly with tax officials, added his own refinements, and showed off his success by entertaining the world's elite while maintaining modest cordiality with neighbors.

Waiting for her ginger ale, Jenny turned, adjusted her wrap over her shoulders, and surveyed the room. For this special occasion, she was dressed in a full-length green satin gown, modestly cut yet flattering to her well-proportioned size four. Heads had turned as she entered the room; her beautifully cut gown flowing across the floor like a ribbon in a gentle breeze. One onlooker, a tall sandy haired man, his athletic body tastefully evident in his Armani tuxedo, left a group of men and headed her way.

Jenny recognized Minnesota governor Tawny Johnson from a distance. He appeared to be alone. Not that she'd recognize his wife if she were standing beside her, but for the moment, not a woman in the room seemed an appropriate fit.

She watched several hands reach out to him as he passed. *That's what glad handing is,* she thought. It took five minutes for him to cross the room. With each admirer, he'd stop, take an outstretched hand, cover it with his other hand, squeeze it, and shake it politely while he smiled and said something flattering. Between stops, he'd glance her direction, then move to the next glad hand.

So fascinated was she by the process, she was unaware she was staring at the man. He saw a willing quarry. She couldn't turn away. She'd never been hit on by anyone important before and was curious what the governor's approach would be. *Got your Christmas shopping done yet,* flashed through her mind. Actually, she couldn't believe he was coming to speak to her and wondered if he mistook her for someone else. She turned and placed her hand on the bar so that her wedding band was clearly visible.

"Vodka tonic, please," he told the bartender as he pulled up beside Jenny. "Love coming to the lake. Such a lovely spot: this home. It's really beautiful in the summer." His voice was deep with a slight rasp; his manner, enthusiastic. "I'm sorry to barge right in here. Can I order something for you, miss...?"

The ring, the ring. You had to have seen it, her mind said to him. Let the fun begin. "It's Mrs.—Mrs. Poole. And thank you, but I have a drink." She produced hers, twirling the swizzle stick to blend the spirits. He'd never know.

"Shall I address you as Mrs. Poole? Or do you have a first name? My friends call me Tawny."

"My friends call me Jenny." Holding her drink in her right hand, she produced her ring hand to be "glad-handed." He took it; his thumb resting on her wedding band. She waited for him to say something, but he only smiled. He had made no reference to being governor, and he ignored her ring.

"Forgive me for appearing forward. I couldn't help but notice how beautiful you are in that gown. You seemed to float across the floor." He hesitated and smiled reflecting. "You're a fashion model or in the movies? What is it? I'm betting on the movies."

So this is how it's done, Jenny mused. "Thank you, but neither. I'm just one of Creighton Leonard's hired hands."

"That could still put you in the movies." It was a strange comment. Jenny wondered if the governor was just trying to be funny.

"I'm afraid not. I'm in marketing. If you've ever been to the House of Toys, you've seen my work. Among other things, I design the large displays so that people from around the world go home and tell all their friends to catch the next flight to Minnesota and Mall of America."

"Quick. I like that. You've heard my speeches. I like that," he said, sounding quite pleased with himself. The governor was known for his forays abroad, drumming up business for Minnesota commerce and industry, a major plank in his gubernatorial campaign. He was also known for his domestic forays and his love of pretty women, a fact difficult for wife number three to accept. "You ever tire of working for Creighton, stop by my office. We could talk about a staff position. I mean that. I can always use someone like you." The glint in his eyes said more than his words. It also said he knew Jenny caught what he meant.

And just what might that position be, Gov? she refrained from asking. His words sounded innocent, but his presentation, his stance, his look said she was being propositioned. By the governor! She couldn't wait to tell Chris.

Out of nowhere, another hand appeared. The governor, of course, took it gladly and turned to speak with an attractive woman in her early forties who could actually have been a model or an actress. By the time he turned to resume his conversation with Jenny, Jenny had vanished.

She had really come to meet Virginia Leonard. Having seen pictures of Virginia, she set off looking for her. Present were most of the company's senior management. She looked from face-to-face, becoming ever more conscious of her growing fear that someone in upper management, possibly someone in the very room, had either ordered the assassination attempt on Jennifer Stewart in Nebraska or had, in fact, now killed her. Or knew who did. She had to find out who.

"Excuse me," Jenny said to a uniformed server as she approached with a tray of canapés. "Is there a phone I could use? Someplace quiet and private, please. Like the study or library?"

"Sure, follow me," she instructed Jenny. "Let's try the library." Two hallways and three turns later, she stopped outside two large doors, put her weight against one that opened to a large paneled room. A massive table sat in the center of the room. Beyond it, along one wall, beneath a faded tapestry sat another massive ornate desk. From what Jenny could see, the other walls were a rogue's gallery of portraits and artwork whose value, Jenny guessed, ran into the millions. Statuary strategically placed throughout the room, either standing in lifelike poses or on pedestals of varying size, and an assortment of leather furniture, completed the room's décor. This was a library!

"I'll close the door; make it nice and private. Can you find your way back okay?" It was not an idle question. She waited until Jenny answered, then quietly left.

Jenny was awed. She'd been a guest in numerous old luxurious estates—there were many around the lake. Her parents' friends lived in some of them. But never had she been in a private home with such a magnificent room. This had to be Creighton's room, obviously an area of the home he had completed after his purchase to accommodate his own taste. He was everywhere. Every inch shouted his presence. She could see him in the statuary, the art, and the tastefully displayed mementos. It almost brought on a chill.

At the office, Creighton Leonard was something of an enigma, a man clearly misunderstood, either intentionally—he seemed to enjoy the mystery of his power—or innocently, a man too complex for others to appreciate. Since her aborted meeting with Kent Simons and her resolve to gather evidence—whatever that might be, she knew her actions required some divine inspiration—she had forced herself to view actions in and around the office in a more sinister light. But so far, she had found nothing of value, certainly nothing that could implicate a WYCO employee in any way, least of all their leader, Creighton Leonard.

Now what luck. She realized she was witness to a very private side of the mysterious Creighton Leonard. It was too good to be true. She felt like Jack who had climbed the beanstalk and found himself in the giant's haven. And the giant was off entertaining guests. But was he? She had not seen Creighton mingling with his guests, nor had she seen Virginia. Her need of a quiet room to use the phone had been a ruse. Now to be safe, she located a telephone: there were two, one on the large table in the center of the room, the second on the desk near the wall. Seating herself on the edge of the table, she picked up the receiver. There was no dial tone. She waited, soon she heard voices, and thoughtfully replaced the receiver.

When the line was clear, she'd call Chris, if only to support her reason for being in Creighton's library and the remote possibility that someone might want to check on her. There could be a monitoring device, a type of caller ID in reverse. The thought crossed her mind; she was jumpy, maybe too jumpy. She'd make the call just in case.

The room was rectangular with numerous alcoves where beautiful priceless works of bronze and marble statuary sat on display. A ceiling rose fifteen feet above her head and was bordered by massive, layered crown molding, also the work of a master craftsman. There was harmony in the room; everything in perfect balance. Creighton Leonard was a man of passion and order.

Jenny felt directed to the far wall. The intricate wood panels and crafted molding would be perfect to conceal a secret passageway. She imagined a labyrinth of tunnels beneath her, possibly a passageway leading to the lake, to a large wine cellar or a vault. Slowly she ran the palm of her hand over the fine wood, testing it here and there by applying pressure with her palm. But nothing moved; nothing gave.

She thought it odd that for a library, very few books were visible, and those were gathered on shelves along a portion of one wall, as though for eye appeal rather than storage. Looking up, she spotted a rail suspended just below the ceiling. Her eyes followed it around the perimeter of the room and discovered, attached to the rail, a long brass-and-wood ladder. For what, she wondered, and walked to the bookcase. No paperbacks here, not at all like her own living-room bookcase beside the fireplace, where Chris had stashed the videos of that fateful day in August.

It was not a small collection. She recognized one or two titles on the lowest levels and surmised they were contemporary authors, some she had read in paperback. Here the paper jackets had been removed, revealing the hard bindings. They appeared to be specially bound, special editions, she suspected, collector's versions. Nice, she thought.

Could a person as busy as Creighton Leonard be so well-read? she wondered. Pulling a Grisham novel from the shelf, she flipped through the first pages. Atop one page was a date, hand scribed. Beneath the date appeared to be the initials CL. She pulled a few more from the shelf, different authors and examined them. Also dates followed by the initials CL.

She walked to the next section of books and reached as high as she could reach to withdraw a book, worn in appearance, *The Fundamentals of Corporate Strategy*. A thick book, not light reading. It too had a hand-scribed date, 1957, and the initials CL. She counted back; Creighton would have been in high school. She was impressed.

Many bronze statues sat on pedestals, some in the alcoves, some in the open. They were intricate works depicting animals, cowboys, Indians. Then she noticed a modest-sized bronze on a pedestal in the corner of the room. She had not noticed it when she entered. A young boy sat alone in the desert gazing into the heavens, from his expression, seeming not to have a care. On the rocks before him stood a wolf, beautifully detailed. It was watching the boy, its body taut, and its fine-tuned muscles ready.

Also unnoticed when she entered, in the opposing corner, was a bust of the master of the castle himself, Creighton Leonard. She would not have noticed the statuary had she not made a tour of the room. *Interesting!* It was not displayed prominently as one would suspect of a man with considerable ego.

The wall behind the large ornate desk was covered with pictures, some large, some small, probably one hundred in all. They didn't seem to be in any particular order, each apparently placed for artistic balance as much as for any other reason. As a display designer, she could appreciate that.

The pictures were from all over the world, and all were of people. Some had captions, some had not. Some were obvious, those pictured Creighton at various stages in his career—she could tell by the age—shaking hands or conversing with the then-presidents of the United States. There was Ford, Reagan, Johnson, Kennedy, Nixon, Bush on a yacht, Bill and Hillary on a dock somewhere, she guessed the Ozarks.

There were congressmen and congresswomen, senators, heads of state from various countries. They went on and on—a veritable Who's Who known personally by Creighton Leonard. The photo with Senator Malovich looked like it could have been taken lakeside. The house in the background looked like the one she was in. It would have been recent.

She did a double take at a young man in the picture who looked like Kent Simons. For a moment, her heart skipped, but closer inspection revealed someone other than her cheerleader friend who had stood her up. She was reminded that she had called his apartment number to say they had to talk, but as yet, he had not called back.

The phone call. She had better make the phone call. Looking around the room, she decided it would be better to use the phone on the large bare table just in case someone were to come in. Stepping around the ornate desk, she spied a leather-bound case. It looked like a book, but she could see it was a case for something. It was partially open.

Quickly she picked it up. It was similar to some of the books she could see on the library shelves. There was an Old English title in gold leaf, *Tawny*. The case itself was empty but would hold a videocassette. She carefully set it back where she had found it and walked to the large center table.

This time, she got the dial tone and pushed in her number. Jason answered, "Hi, honey, it's Mom. Enjoying the night off?" she asked.

"Yes and no."

"What do you mean?"

"Dad wanted to go skating. He cleaned off the rink and everything."

"Oh. And you had something else in mind?"

"Well, not really. Just not skating."

"But you did it anyway? Your dad has missed a lot of that. I suppose he—"

"I know. And we had fun. I creamed him. Boy is he getting old."

"And so are you, Jason. So are you. Enjoy it all while you can."

"For sure, Mom. After all, I'll be eleven in another month."

"How time flies. Is your father still up and around? You didn't cream him too bad, did you?"

"He's here. You got a call," he added.

Jenny was distracted by a sudden light at the end of the room. The double doors were open. She wondered how long, as Jason continued speaking.

"It was some guy named Kent. Didn't leave a message. Said he'd call later. He said he was sorry. Mom, what's he sorry for?"

A figure moved closer, and the doors closed behind it.

"You go to bed when your father tells you. I'll peek in when I get home. But I'll see you in the morning." She spoke a couple decibels louder for the benefit of whoever had entered. "Love you. Bye."

The figure was Creighton. She wondered if he had seen her snooping. That would not be good.

"Is that you, Jennifer? Jenny Poole?" The voice was deep, controlled, with only a slight twinge of irritation. Maybe that was her imagination.

"Mr. Leonard, I didn't see you when I came in. So good to see you now. Yes. It's me Jennifer Poole." She was speaking too fast and knew it. Nervous. Caught? "Remember, my friends call me Jenny," she said, remembering their lunch together, her special lunch.

"And, as I recall, you were comfortable with my name, Creighton…remember. Might I ask, what are you doing in here?"

He could see I was on the phone. What else? "I needed to call home. One of the servers showed me in here where it would be quiet."

"Quiet, it is. That's why I like it so. This is my world. In here with these books, works of art." He seemed comfortable, unusually so. In his world. Not threatened.

"These works in bronze. They're absolutely beautiful. I don't know that I've ever seen their equal," she said truthfully.

"You haven't. I assure you. They are all one of a kind. All priceless. Each one commissioned for a purpose." He walked to a cowboy riding a bucking horse. "This one for instance. As a young man, I knew this wrangler personally. He could break and ride any horse in creation. He was perfection. I'll never forget him."

He walked to a recess in the bookcase and turned on a small light illuminating a bronze roadster and a man dangling some keys. Jenny had stood right there and had not seen it. "This was a prize I won. From a friend." Off went the light. He returned to the table.

"In this room is my perfect world—books, many special editions or commemoratives personally presented by their authors. Some very old, some new. I haven't read all, but most." He seemed to be pleased that she was there to see *his world*.

"I believe I could hide away in a room like this," she said whimsically but sincerely. "But Chris and Jason don't know how to cook. They'd starve."

Creighton liked a sense of humor; he appreciated the subtlety in hers.

"But if this were my room, I would have a secret passageway, maybe to run to the lake for brief reprieves," she tested.

Creighton gave a slight chuckle. "I see you're a romantic. Well, me too. This room does contain some secrets. He stepped to the ornate desk beside the wall, opened a drawer, and withdrew a remote-control device. As he pushed a button, a portion of a wood panel rose and disappeared into the molding high above. Beneath the panel were more bookshelves. From floor to ceiling were leather-bound cases, similar to the one she had spied on the desk.

"I enjoy film as well. This also is a collection beyond price. Many of these are one-of-a-kind from around the world or first-cut editions never seen by the public."

Jenny wondered if the case titled "Tawny" had come from those shelves. If so, why was the case empty? Such a strange title, perhaps a foreign film. Maybe an old film. Possibly the oversexed governor was named after its star; an amusing thought. She suddenly felt a chill. Perhaps Tawny Johnson was the star. He had asked her if she was in the movies. Creighton's movies?

Creighton pushed another button, and a portion of the wall gave way to reveal a large viewing screen.

"So, Jenny, you've seen some of my magic," he said a moment later as the screen and the film collection disappeared again behind the panel at the push of another button.

"I'm impressed. A room like this had to have secrets. I knew it. I can see you could spend considerable time in here. What a way to relax." Now she was not being completely honest.

"Yes, it does have secrets after all." He was not about to reveal the secret vault beneath the floor, where the original 35 mm films were stored. "And I do spend time here. Occasionally, I share it with friends."

Jenny remembered three hundred friends were in attendance tonight. How many of those had seen his films or even knew they existed? Were there names of other important "friends" on the many cases hidden behind the beautifully paneled wall? Were the films kept in the leather-bound cases the kind of films Kent Simons made? Was that the kind of filming Jennifer Stewart stumbled upon that later cost her life? Were these the films that led to Jason's abduction?

"Does Virginia share your interest in all this wonderful art?"

That drew another chuckle from Creighton. "Oh, she does appreciate art. However, we have different tastes. Speaking of Virginia, have you two met?"

"No. Not yet." Suddenly, she felt relieved that he had changed the subject.

"Well, let's fix that. She's dying to meet you."

He led her out the massive double doors and down the wide corridors to the living room, which now was filled with people and conversation. The governor stood beside a striking black woman, who, even from the distance, seemed annoyed as though she didn't quite know how to extricate herself. She obviously was not in the movies either.

A slender woman, very attractive, with short coal-black hair, saw them coming, excused herself from a small cluster of guests, and quickly joined Jenny and Creighton in the middle of the room.

"Virginia, I found her. I would like you to meet our rising star, Jennifer Poole." Virginia held out her hand and firmly but gently glad-handed Jenny, one hand on top of the other.

Creighton finished his introduction, "Jenny, if there's one thing we totally agree on, it's our gratitude for the talent and dedication you bring to the company."

Suddenly, Creighton had become his public persona, and she suspected his words were directed more toward Virginia's ears.

Jenny and Virginia exchanged a few casual words after which Creighton excused himself. Then unable to compete with the high level of voices and laughter, Virginia took Jenny's hand and led her to a sofa at one end of the room, the opposite end from the bar.

They stood about the same height. Virginia had beautiful skin, was slender, appeared athletic, and was about the same age as her mother. In many ways, she reminded Jenny of her mother. She sensed, had they known each other, they probably would be good friends.

Virginia sat down and patted a space beside her. "Jenny. Is it all right to call you Jenny?" she asked.

"Of course."

"I'm known for my directness," she began. "That's both good and bad. So if you don't mind, I'm just going to jump in with both feet."

Jenny was not sure just what to expect. She didn't need to answer. *Direct is good.*

"Jenny, first off, I need to know, you're a believer, right? I mean, Jesus is Lord in your life?" This time Virginia waited for an answer. Jenny didn't hesitate.

"Yes," she said flat-out. She could be direct too.

"I knew as much from your display plan. I mean I don't care if you like movies, have a glass of wine, or even something stronger now and then. What's important is what's going on in the inside, that you're heaven bound and know it. See these people out here? Most of 'm are good, decent people. But some are either buying or a being

JENNY

bought and have not a clue where their final destination might be or how to really help anyone along the way.

"Jenny, in the minute we have here together, I'm letting you see me the way I really am because I need to know if it scares you. Am I too forward? I mean this is it. This is Virginia Leonard, business tycoon."

"Refreshing. Perhaps my style is different. But I'd say refreshing."

"Well, Jenny. If you want to keep Jesus in Christmas, I say amen. WYCO Toys is one of the finest toy companies in the entire world. We have the opportunity to impact the lives of children and their families in a very positive way. We must hang in there, run the company the best we can. You've been with the company a lot longer than me. You know what it stood, for once, the respect it once commanded.

"This company can be truly great again. The leadership got sidetracked. Now we must sail through some pretty tough sea. We must do the things we know in our heart to be right. Even if sometimes, we must stand alone. Jenny, it's people like you that will make this company great again. You should know I am here to help you any way that I can."

She stopped. Having found her ally, she looked at Jenny and smiled. Jenny wondered if Virginia might have her own suspicions of activities in the company that were beyond her control. It seemed Virginia was asking for her help.

"There is one thing," Jenny said after a brief silence. "I am aware that WYCO Toys is changing legal counsel, and my husband's firm, Johnson, Carlson, Shapiro, and Nord is the successor. I'm also told Christian will become designated lead counsel. I guess I'd like to know if that's true."

"Yes. It's true," Virginia said matter-of-factly.

"May I ask, why?"

"Because he's the best person for the job. It wasn't my idea initially, although it may have been my desire to make a change. It was Creighton's idea. I've always given Creighton credit for being an astute judge of character. Creighton nominated Christian. He will bring his name before WYCO's board of directors. But know this. I am the board of directors. I am the majority shareholder.

"I've studied his qualifications. I believe he is the best candidate. Now there might be someone with more experience, but I don't think there'd be anyone better. Christian is young. It's a big challenge that lies ahead of him. I don't deny that. I have given that considerable thought. But I'm willing to accept Creighton's nomination.

"WYCO faces many challenges, union negotiations, labor contracts approaching their anniversaries. These are your husband's forte. With my money, I could find another attorney, someone tough, relentless, ruthless who'd win at any cost. And we'd win. But at the expense of others. That's not what this lady is about. I can be tough, but not at the expense of others.

"I intend to win but fairly. Chris will find it difficult, but when he's done, we'll all win. That's our future. As this lady sees it." That said, Virginia became silent again, and for a moment, they just looked at each other.

"Thank you, Virginia," Jenny said at last.

"Thank you, Jenny," said Virginia, adding, "Now I've got some mingling to do," Then she turned and rejoined her guests.

Chapter 57

Dan told his secretary he needed fresh air and a break from the holiday confusion. Twenty minutes later, he turned off Interstate 494 and headed westbound on State 7 to Excelsior.

There had been only one witness to Jason's abduction. Duly noted in the reports, he was a likable "mentally challenged" man who had somehow survived into middle age on the streets of Excelsior. "Old Mike" was the only name given, but from the description of the man, Dan thought he would recognize him if he were out and about, reportedly, his daily activity.

The kidnappers just seemed too *clean*. Somewhere, there was a fact overlooked or ignored, something that could balance the equation. Dan hoped Old Mike could provide that something. Reports left little doubt that Mike's testimony was not considered too credible. But it was worth a try. He had to do something if Jim Stewart's assumptions were accurate. Things could quickly turn ugly if Jenny's informal research threatened the wrong people.

Ten minutes later, he arrived in Excelsior. He drove down Water Street where reportedly Old Mike spent his days, strolling both sides of the street, greeting everyone he encountered, real and imagined.

Reports also said Mike liked his coffee and sweets. Dan spotted a bakery and pulled over to the curb across the street. For several minutes, he watched shoppers stroll in and out of the specialty shops. There was no one remotely resembling the description of the one witness who had seen Jason Poole being whisked from the sidewalk of the sleepy town.

Although Dan was confident his *number two* would keep things under control at Mall of America, he wasn't willing to waste the rest of the day waiting for Old Mike. He looked up and down Water Street one last time before opening his door and crossing the street for the bakery. When he returned to his car, he rested two doughnuts and two black coffees on the seat beside him and set off slowly in search of Old Mike.

Moving east, just beyond Milly's, he spotted a figure in a tattered coat and scraggly fur-lined cap moving at the slow shuffle described in the crime report. Beyond he could see the shoreline where Jenny had tied her boat on that fateful August day. Dan opened the car door, grabbed the doughnuts and coffee, and moved to overtake Old Mike. When Mike stopped on the icy shore, Dan stepped alongside.

"You're Mike," said Dan after a moment.

"Yes. Mike. I'm Mike. Nice day, isn't it? Little cold, but nice day, isn't it? Mike's my name."

"You're the Mike that saw the boy named Jason kidnapped last summer…near here, wasn't it?"

"Yes. Mike saw Jason. Jason is home now. Jason's a nice boy. We're friends, Mike and Jason."

"Here, I have an extra. Want it?" Dan handed a cup of coffee to Mike with a doughnut balanced on top. "Here, it's yours." Mike didn't argue, just stood for a moment, coffee and a well-chewed cigar in one hand, a sugary doughnut in the other. "Boy that was something, wasn't it? A boy like Jason kidnapped from here," said Dan, attempting to engage Mike in sensible conversation.

"He had an earring."

"Jason?"

"Didn't know him. Wasn't a regular. Jason…such a nice boy."

"Mike, who had the earring? Not Jason."

"The driver. A cross. Wasn't a regular. Wouldn't give me a cup of coffee. The regulars, they'd give me coffee and rolls, sometimes a cookie, whatever they are delivering to the boats."

"You didn't recognize the driver?"

"He wasn't right. Mike remembers what's not right."

"What else wasn't right that day, Mike?" asked Dan, sipping his own coffee.

"The other man…big man…took Jason. That wasn't right."

"No it wasn't. What else?"

"A green car."

"A green car wasn't right?" Dan had memorized the police report of that day, including the recollections of this one eyewitness. A green car. Yes, he remembered a green car had been mentioned. "What wasn't right, Mike? About the green car?"

"He was watching."

"Someone in the car watched Jason being taken?" quizzed Dan.

"That wasn't right. It just wasn't right. Just watching."

"What was he watching? Was he looking at the lake like we are now?"

"Watching Jason. I could tell. Jason is a friend. Mike and Jason are friends." Mike now devoured the doughnut in two quick bites and then washed it down with the coffee. "Thanks, mister," he said. Then before Dan could get in another word, Old Mike turned and began his stroll back up Water Street. The interview, over.

Dan started to follow, but thought better of it and returned to his car. Moments later, he was greeted at the local police station by a woman officer in a blue uniform. "Your chief in, Nick Carlson?" Dan asked.

"Gone for the day, making his rounds," reported Stella Kraemer. "And you are?"

"Dan Sheridan. From Mall of America."

"The one who found young Jason Poole. I remember. Thought you looked familiar. Watched you on TV. Boy, that was something."

"I was in the area and had a question for your chief about the case."

"Chief say's you're a friend of Gary Sadler…working some on the case. Helping, he said."

"Some," said Dan. "Not much time, I'm afraid. Tell the chief I stopped by."

"Sure thing," said Stella as Dan turned to leave. "Anything I can help with?" she asked in afterthought.

Dan stopped. "You know the case?"

"As well as anyone, I suppose. I file the reports. Read 'em too."

"The day Jason was taken, any reports of a green car in the vicinity?"

"Green's a popular color. Gotta be a hundred of 'em around the streets on any summer day. Don't recall one being mentioned. Jordan Green...WYCO security...drives one. New green Ford Explorer. Just one of the hundred."

"Green?"

"Just like his name."

"Thanks, Stella," said Dan, reading her name tag.

"You betcha, Mr. Sheridan."

Chapter 58

It was dark, the air crisp with an occasional snowflake making its way earthward when Jenny and Chris passed the massive fieldstone pillars and entered Jenny's childhood neighborhood of Maplewood. Fresh compressed snow squeaked beneath the Cherokee's tires. Christmas lights twinkled through the trees of the wooded landscape from brightly decorated residences. Five days remained until Christmas. Tonight, the entire neighborhood was gathered at Jenny's childhood home to celebrate. It was an annual event. Tonight D' and Matthew Ward were hosting the affair.

This was homecoming for Jenny and many of her childhood friends, home for the holidays. The evening promised to be full. Chris didn't wait for a parking attendant but found a parking space at the side of the roadway and pulled over. It would a be a short walk in the winter's night air.

"Honey, isn't this just…just Currier and Ives?" exclaimed Jenny. She and Chris had often talked of owning a home in the neighborhood. Virginia Leonard's support of Chris's appointment to lead counsel gave hope that someday soon her dream could be realized.

Chris read her thoughts. "Would moving here make you feel better about my being appointed lead counsel to WYCO? A full partnership would follow. This could become possible. We could have what's-his-name list our place on the lake, sell it for more than we think its worth, and buy it here for less than we know it's worth. Isn't that the way it works?"

"I guess. Well, I do feel better about it…the appointment, knowing that Virginia Leonard is one of your strong supporters. I like her. She's seems honest and sincere. But I still feel there's more to your appointment than appears on the surface. Virginia said the appointment was Creighton's idea?"

They continued walking in silence as Jenny's thoughts turned to her suspicions in the case. She didn't want that. This was too special a night. "So who is 'what's-his-name,'" she asked, changing the subject.

"That real estate agent…Stanchfield…I think. Didn't he do the deal for the Leonard's? He's the best, right?"

One of the parking attendants ran past them on his way back to the house. Jenny recognized him. He waved. "Know him?" Chris asked.

"Not really. He worked the Leonard's party. I guess he recognized me." Jenny's voice trailed off, a plan forming in her mind. She couldn't shake the reminders and for a moment gave in to her thoughts. She wondered if the inside staff were the same as those hired for the Leonard's party. That could prove helpful when the time was right.

D' Ward had seen them coming and greeted Jenny and Chris at the door. "Good! You're here! There's someone you must meet." Then she was gone. A uniformed attendant took their coats.

To the left of the foyer was a library and a glowing fireplace delightfully warming guests with glasses of wine already in hand. Jenny smiled at Chris and entered the crowded room. In a moment, her mother returned and motioned for her to join her. Jenny excused herself and followed.

She was led to a group of guests surrounding a slight, beautifully grayed woman. She seemed the center of attention and the cause of some uproarious laughter. When D' caught her eye, she excused herself and moved with her hand outstretched toward her host and Jenny.

"No need to tell me who this beautiful young woman is," she said as she approached. "You were just a baby when I saw you last."

JENNY

"Jenny, this is Leah Holcomb," said D'. "She's the speaker at this year's missions conference." A waving hand from the kitchen caught D's attention. She excused herself. "I'll let you get reacquainted," she said and moved toward the waving hand.

For several minutes, Leah reminisced about her holding Jenny as a baby. Then her expression turned serious. "Your mother told me about your ordeal with Jason. It sounds to me like a miracle… returned the same day, unharmed. You were certainly protected," Leah said after finding a sofa and motioning for Jenny to join her.

"Yes, I believe that. It was a miracle," admitted Jenny.

"Your mother said the kidnapping was some kind of mistake?"

"That seems to be the case. There's no way of knowing for sure." Jenny recalled her telephone conversation with Jim Stewart.

"And Jason is okay? No problems, nightmares, anything since?"

"He's fine. There's been nothing."

In another room, someone had begun playing Christmas carols on the piano. Leah paused to listen momentarily. "God never makes a mistake," she said finally and waited for Jenny to respond. Jenny nodded.

Leah seemed to be struggling with what she wanted to say. "Dear," she said at last, "may I make a strange request?" She didn't wait for an answer. "Many years ago, Warren and I were serving our second tour in a remote Mexican village. Tragedy suddenly struck a young mother in my care. Her name was Maria Alverez." Leah's expression became distant. "She had a son, Miguel. He would have been the age of Jason today. She now lives in Santa Fe, New Mexico." Leah reached for Jenny's hand. "Your mother says you travel?"

"Yes, my work requires some travel."

"Do you stop in Santa Fe?"

"Yes, on occasion."

Leah seemed relieved. "Marvelous! Would you mind paying my friend, Maria, a visit? You see, I have sworn never to tell her story, but I sense she would be willing to tell it to you herself. And I believe you will find it helpful."

"I don't see—"

"I know. I wish I could tell more, but…I can tell you only that I feel compelled to suggest you do this. I'll give you her address and telephone number before this delightful evening ends."

With growing curiosity, Jenny agreed.

Voices had joined with the piano in the other room. Her mission accomplished, Leah stopped to listen. "Do you sing?" she asked finally. With that, she stood and motioned for Jenny to accompany her to the other room, leading her to the mounting chorus. Along the way, Jenny introduced Leah to Chris, who had come looking for her.

Chapter 59

Light snow graced the shoulders of one of Boston's homeless as he worked his way along narrow streets winding through the affluent residential neighborhood of Beacon Hill. This was the season of plenty for the likes of him, those inclined to forage nightly in the neighborhoods of the wealthy. With the many elegant dinner parties given during the weeks preceding Christmas, there was abundant provision in discarded refuse, such abundance even this gleaner was beginning to take for granted.

This was the bastion of the fortunate, people of import, business leaders, politicians, congressmen, and senators—many whose wealth and heritage dated back to the Revolution. Long ago, for reasons he never understood, this urban nomad had lost everything, including the home where he had lived most of his adult years. It was torn down for lack of proper funding.

But life could be worse. The papers were filled with stories worse than his, of those not as fortunate as he to find such a Garden of Eden as this. Earlier, he had seen a trail of cars and taxis carrying well-dressed passengers along Charles Street. It was here he began to stir after resting during the warm sun of the day. Now it was time to move about, to glean, to stay warm, to survive another night.

He found the alley that would take him to the back of the opulent low-rise residences. Here his garden began; here his evening forage would begin. Looking up, he saw shadows passing draped windows, heard sounds of muted laughter and music. Not all windows showed light. Residents gone on holiday, he presumed. Something the wealthy did.

He stuck out his tongue to catch a snowflake. There was less light here in the alley. He looked heavenward. The sky was lightly overcast, and snow fell from slowly drifting low clouds. The moon had begun its ascent. He proceeded slowly as the evening sky brightened. He could feel it. Tonight would be a good night.

The wealthy dined at such ungodly hours, especially when they entertained. It would be a long evening. Ahead, a door opened, and a man dressed in black stepped into the cold as he struggled with a large bag. Stopping momentarily, he waited while his eyes adjusted to the darkness. Then the sky opened, and moonlight exploded in brilliance. He threw the bag over his shoulder and moved quickly to a dumpster. The nomad watched the servant deposit his bag and then run from the cold, back to the warmth of the brownstone. Tonight the garden would produce a harvest. He knew just where to begin.

The servant disappeared into an estate home, where soon the glow behind the alley door blinked off. It was time.

It was difficult to see inside the dumpster. Fortunately, the latest addition to its contents rested atop the putrescent refuse. Retrieving it, he dropped it onto the alley's brick floor, dexterously removing its tie. "Ugh," he grunted, fully aware of the potential for disease or poisoning from anything not one day fresh. The contents were not up to his standard. He resealed the bag, returned it to the dumpster and closed the lid. *There would be more. There would be more.*

Time meant little as he worked his way up the alleyway, moving to the shadows when the moon showed itself. A reward would come. He passed several darkened homes and carefully inspected each rusty old container, finding nothing fresh enough to trust.

In the distance came a dull thud. He smiled. Another container lid being closed? Perhaps? *Dinner,* he thought hopefully.

A cat brushed against his leg. "Kitty, hungry?" he asked, reaching down to pick it up. As his hands touched the tail, he heard a meow and felt the warm fur pass through his partially covered fingers. In the dim light, he watched the cat scurry ahead. "Don't be frightened." He cajoled and picked up his pace in pursuit. "Please, wait. It's only me." And the game commenced as it had so many nights before.

"Kitty, where are you?" he asked, stalking the darkened alley. "Meow, meow. I know you're here. It's only me," he assured, sensing the cat close by. Then he saw it, its back arched, walking back and forth on the top of a dumpster, only a few yards more. He shuffled faster. "There you are, my friend. Oh! Who's this?" he said to the cat as he drew near and could see more clearly. On the dumpster lay the crumpled body of a man, his head turned facing him. The cat walked around the lifeless form that lay half on and half off the rusty container.

The nomad cocked his head and peered into the face of the still form. *Was there life?* He waited for movement watching for any sign of life. Then he moved closer and gently, respectfully rested his head on the lifeless chest. The body was warm. *How long?* he wondered as he slowly moved his head along the chest. Nothing!

Brushing a bulge beneath his cheek, he reached under the man's coat. High above, a curtain flagged in the light of a door open to a small balcony. He heard the flutter and looked up. A dark form moved from the light. He feared he had been seen. For the longest time, he stood there listening, waiting for what he didn't know. Finally, blaming his imagination, he returned his attention to the corpse and carefully extracted a wallet from inside the chest pocket. The cat meowed and brushed against his hand.

When the clouds again gave way to the ascending moon, he read from the wallet's identification, "Wil.…Willard…Ma…Malo…vich. Willard Malovich. Willard Malovich." The cat strolled across the dumpster lid. "Poor kitty," he said. "Poor, Willard Malovich." Then, excitedly, he blew upon his fingers, warming them and reached inside the folds of the wallet, withdrawing a wad of bills.

In the light of the moon, he inspected his find and smiled. The harvest was good, very good indeed. Now he chuckled. He understood money. The cat meowed, brushing his sleeve, its back arched. "Poor, kitty," he said again. "Poor kitty. Kitty, come home with me."

Gently, the nomad dropped the wallet onto the alley floor. Then he placed the wad of bills inside a shirt pocket and picked up the cat, snuggling it carefully inside his ragged coat. They would each keep the other warm. Back down the alley, another dumpster top briefly creaked open and slammed shut. At last, *dinner,* he thought and slowly began moving back in the direction of the noise. Above, the moon shone brightly. Surely, tonight's was a harvest moon.

Chapter 60

A car was waiting at National Car Rental when Jenny's plane touched down in Santa Fe. In the past, she had visited clients in Santa Fe but had never taken time just to see the town. Leah Holcomb's insistence that she meet Maria Alverez offered the perfect reason, a reason she had not yet shared with Chris.

All Chris knew was that Jenny needed to make the rounds of her West Coast clients; it was that time of the year. He had encouraged her to take time away from the pressures at home. Jenny had told him only that she would stop in Santa Fe on her return but didn't tell him why. He suspected she planned to shop and had warned simply, *take it easy*, a plea for her not to abuse the budget. She wouldn't and was content to keep her real motivation to herself.

Seldom did Jason bring up his kidnapping. He showed no sign of emotional trauma. Nothing had surfaced with the passing of time. Chris, too, had gone on to other challenges. So it was that Jenny planned her stop in Santa Fe to visit the historic city and call upon Maria Alverez. Leah Holcomb had insisted Maria's story could provide insights into her own near tragedy with Jason.

But Leah had not gone into great detail. Nor did she explain what she meant by helpful. All this Jenny found intriguing, even compelling, as her rental car curved through the town's narrow streets. Maria's very private ordeal was a story known by only a few. A telephone call from Leah had prepared the way. Maria would share her story, whatever it might be.

First, she'd see the town. A map led Jenny to the center of town, Old Santa Fe. She found a single parking spot on the famed square after driving around for half an hour familiarizing herself with the area.

She discarded her purse in favor of a simple wallet and took a deep breath as she stretched at the curb. The crisp clear air even tasted good. Her eyes searched for her first destination. Finding nothing immediately irresistible, she tucked her hands into her pockets and struck off to see Old Santa Fe.

Of the first ten stores, only six were open, and they offered only trinkets or items too expensive for her discriminating budget. Two blocks from the square, shops definitely became more interesting, though now interspersed with other businesses. Here, there seemed to be more artists.

At the end of an alley, she discovered a large open courtyard with trees, fountains, and a garden path leading to various shops and restaurants, an oasis of sorts. Many shops had their own open courtyards, and in the distance, she spied empty tables and chairs already prepared for the lunch crowd. Continuing to an open area filled with old bentwood chairs, she stood for a moment in the warmth of the sun's rays, then located a table and chair, and sat down. *Old Santa Fe, where cattle used to wander the streets on their way to the railhead.*

Beautiful people, she thought as she tried to guess just who was a true native and who was not, who really belonged and who didn't. One beautiful girl whisked passed as she was about to leave. The girl in her twenties, had to be of Indian mix. She wore a cotton dress that gathered at the waist but otherwise was loose fitting and hung nearly to the ground, covering silver-toed cowboy boots.

Her hair was long, straight, and coal-black. It flowed nearly to her waist. Her skin was beautiful, naturally brown and flawless. She wore a brown leather cowboy hat, one that was flat on the top.

Unlike the tourists, who, like Jenny, had stumbled upon this remnant of the old west, the girl had a destination and moved gracefully down the garden paths. Curious, Jenny followed at a distance. They didn't go far.

Within fifty yards, she came to two floor-to-ceiling glass doors. She produced a key from somewhere and swung them open. Whatever was inside was now ready and accessible to the public.

Their eyes met as Jenny stood in the entrance. Then the girl turned and walked up a flight of stairs to an office overlooking the store's large two-story foyer. A minute later, she reappeared to greet Jenny who had stepped inside to take in the most beautiful works of art she had ever seen.

"Welcome to the Leonard Gallery," the girl said in perfect English. Jenny expected a Spanish accent. "Please make yourself comfortable. Stay as long as you wish. If you need anything, I will be here." She handed Jenny a small brochure and disappeared.

It was 12:10, and Jenny wondered if she should stay over. *Why is it the best is always what you find last?* she mused.

The gallery consisted of several rooms, each with its own treasures. There were paintings in every medium. There were works in glass, beautiful originals, multicolored pieces of varied shapes and sizes, all perfectly highlighted by small beaming lights hidden in the walls and ceiling. There were works of stone and woven fiber, all with a practical use, but whose intricate artistry defined their true value. Jenny picked up a ceramic vase: $1,780!

Refusing to look at her watch, Jenny meandered from treasure to treasure. She would not let a schedule limit her enjoyment. She would see Maria Alverez in due time. Leah had assured her that Maria would be waiting, so she had not called ahead to the little mission school where Maria watched over Indian children from a nearby reservation.

Time passed quickly. Southwestern art had never held much interest for Jenny. Now she scolded herself for being too critical, judgmental. Her exposure was more limited than she realized. Now she was fascinated.

Eventually, the tiled walkway brought her into a large vaulted room, which she surmised was a reproduction of a room in a Spanish hacienda. Here, on massive plastered walls, were displayed the largest of the Leonards collections.

One in particular drew her to it. She marveled at its size and wondered where in her small home could she display such a piece. She couldn't. She guessed it to be eight feet high and no less than twelve feet long, totally in white life-size relief. *Awesome.* It was lifelike, to say the least, as though someone had captured a moment in time, preserving forever in plaster a plains Indian and the antelope he had just slain.

The medium was a papery substance too delicate to touch, soft like cotton with feather-fine detail. She had never seen anything like it. She looked at the price tag engraved on a gold plaque attached to the lower right corner. It in itself was a work of art—$32,750. Jenny wondered if shipping was included. Would the Leonards discount it five hundred dollars for cash. She wasn't serious.

Who were the Leonards of Old Santa Fe to collect such works of art? Jenny assumed Creighton Leonard's parents lived on the East Coast. She dismissed the possibility that the two Leonard families could be related.

She continued on, her credit cards still in her pocket. Passing through the room, she realized she had seen it all. Someday, she'd like to return to shop in earnest. Maybe when Christian made partner. According to Virginia Leonard, it could happen sooner rather than later. WYCO was now his client. Good would come in time, she could feel it. There was not one piece of art in the Leonard Gallery she would not proudly own.

As she was about to leave, one last work caught her eye. She had missed it when she entered—a casting in bronze. It too was life-size. *El Lobo* was the title engraved on a small gold plaque attached to a base made of ironwood. It looked familiar. Was it the style?

She drew near. It wasn't a metal casting, after all, but the same papery substance as the wall hanging the Wolf. How could anything look so real? The wolf seemed to be watching her; its intense eyes piercing; its muscles tensed, ready to attack.

Odd, she thought. She had never thought much about wolves. Creighton Leonard. She remembered Creighton had a wolf in bronze.

JENNY

His wolf, watching a boy of the desert, stood sentry at the entrance to his very private library.

"It's a beautiful piece." It was the girl. She had come up quietly from behind as from nowhere.

"Is it for sale? There's no price," observed Jenny.

"It has no price." Her smile was born of pride. "It is not for sale at any price. The artist is my father."

"From South Dakota?" asked Jenny in total amazement. A small plaque beneath the other work in paper had given the artist's home address as South Dakota.

"No." The girl smiled. "You noticed the similarity," she stated matter-of-factly. Again, Jenny was struck by her natural beauty. She had a softness about her like the priceless works of art that had captivated Jenny's attention now far too long. For the first time since entering the shop, Jenny glanced nervously at her watch.

"The artist is my father, but he's not an artist in the normal sense. This is his only work in this medium. It's one-of-a-kind. That's why it will not be sold. It is here for display. The Leonards are lifelong friends."

"Then your father is an artist?"

"A very good artist. But he has a normal job, an executive, a consultant to big companies around the world. His business is based in Florida. Art is his hobby."

"And the Leonards, are they from here? From Santa Fe?"

"They have been here for many years. Many years. Longer than most. Long enough to be natives. But they came from the East Coast."

Before Jenny could ask more questions, a young Indian boy entered the room. The beautiful girl excused herself, addressed the boy in what sounded like Spanish, and disappeared with him beyond the foyer. After waiting for several minutes for her to return and looking at her watch several times, Jenny took one last look at the wonderful gallery she had discovered and stepped into the shadowed corridors, trying to recall which way she had come as she followed the girl she would not soon forget.

Chapter 61

Jenny left the gallery hoping someday to return with Chris and Jason, when Jason was old enough to appreciate all that she had seen. When she started her car and pulled from her curb, she realized she not only had missed breakfast, her preoccupation with the beautiful girl and the Leonard Gallery caused her to miss lunch as well. Her stomach growled in protest. She ached with hunger, but a glance at her watch excluded the option of now stopping to eat.

Two blocks from the square, she spotted the highway marker for her route out of town. The road wound south. She was glad she had taken the time to familiarize herself with the area earlier that morning. Falling in with traffic, her mind soon wandered back to the shop she had just left, the exquisite young girl, and the Leonards.

The Leonards? She had never looked in a phone book to see how many Leonards filled its pages. Yet, she personally knew of only one other family, Creighton and Virginia Leonard. He had come from the East Coast. She had simply assumed his parents resided there as well. Was it only coincidence? She now wondered. Then there was "El Lobo." More coincidence? Or were the two "El Lobos," each in the possession of a Leonard, merely captivating and interesting objects of art, nothing more? *Had the young woman referred to her father as El Lobo, the Wolf?* Or was her mind simply playing tricks because she was too hungry to think?

Following her map, she located the small historic mission. She didn't anticipate a long stay to hear Maria's story. And if Maria decided to keep her story private? Well, she still had something to report back to Leah Holcomb. She also had her plane to catch and wanted some mementos to bring home for Chris and Jason.

Driving down the now-abandoned highway on the edge of the desert was like taking a trip back in time. Broken, crumbling asphalt eventually gave way to gravel and desert floor. Gravel roads, not much more than wagon tracks, led occasionally from the dilapidated roadway into the surrounding hills. Soon the small trees disappeared, and she entered a small desert valley. Ahead was the only visible sign of life, a small compound of four or five adobe buildings.

When she reached the compound, she pulled off the old road and stepped from her rental car onto the dusty roadside apron, the approach to the small group of buildings that comprised the mission settlement. It was like stepping into a scene from the late 1800s. She crossed the parking area to an old boardwalk and made her way toward the entrance of the main building.

Inside was a sparsely furnished but meticulously kept great room. Seeing no one, she stood still and listened. Muffled sounds of children playing drifted down an adjoining hall. She stood in an open space about twelve feet square with a low ceiling. Along the walls were openings to small cubicles or rooms of some sort and at the end a very large open area.

"Hello," she said at last. "Is anyone here?"

Immediately, a dark-skinned woman approached through one of the small openings in the wall. "May I help you?" the woman asked graciously.

She appeared to be in her sixties or early seventies. Her smile was most welcoming, and her eyes sparkled. She matched Leah's description of her radiant Maria.

"My name is Jennifer Poole. Would you be Maria Alverez?"

"Yes, I would be. I've been expecting you. May I offer you something to drink? Iced tea, perhaps? That's Leah's favorite." It was as though she were a neighbor stopping by for a daily visit with an old friend.

"Leah insisted I stop to see you."

"I know. She has told me about you and your wonderful family."

"I hope I'm not keeping you from something."

"Goodness, no. Meeting you is what is important for the moment. And my children will enjoy seeing a new face."

Jenny followed Maria through the room where the children were playing with plastic toys. Their deep brown eyes tugged at Jenny as she passed.

"Those two"—she pointed at two children who seemed to want the same toy—"their mother works in Santa Fe. Their father is incarcerated. I believe Texas was what we heard last. They will survive." She spoke loud enough for the children to hear her confidence and smiled at them as she approached. "One may become the president of the United States. The other may become a television celebrity. We have some time to decide." The boy, about six, and the girl, about eight, giggled at her remarks.

The third child, another girl with the most haunting eyes, also seven or eight, grasped Maria's hand as she and Jenny entered a small kitchen area. The child didn't speak but gleefully produced a painting of an eagle soaring high over a barren rock projected from the desert floor.

Jenny was deeply impressed. Maria made the introduction, "And this is our artist. She and her mother will have a gallery of their own someday." Jenny believed it. Somehow, she could not resist bending down to touch the girl's beautiful silky black hair. Then with a tilt of her head and a smile, the child turned and rejoined her companions.

They moved on to a small verandah overlooking the expansive desert valley already radiant with signs of early-spring flowers in bloom. Stopping at a small table surrounded by wood chairs painted in pinks and yellows and soft muted blues, colors of a vibrant desert, Maria motioned for Jenny to sit then walked back to the kitchen to return a moment later with a tray of cookies, two large glasses, and a pitcher of iced tea.

"Your son, Jason, is ten," she stated matter-of-factly as she set the tray before Jenny. "Please tell me about him. As you can see, I love the little children."

"I'm not sure where to begin. How much did Leah tell you?"

"Leah said he is very good at sports. Hockey, I think she said. I don't know…this hockey."

For the next fifteen minutes, Jenny allowed herself to talk of her son's athletic prowess. Then fearful of boring Maria to death, she got to the meat of her story, Jason's abduction, which she explained in detail, including the narcotic Devil's Brew and its characteristic effect of forever preventing him from remembering—she hoped. By the time she concluded, desert shadows were longer and darker, and she felt emotionally drained. She couldn't believe she had carried on so with a complete stranger. She still had a plane to catch after an hour's drive in the slow Santa Fe traffic, and Maria had not yet told her "her" story. Although anxious, she avoided glancing at her watch.

"What he cannot remember is good," observed Maria, at last. "We should pray that God keeps it hidden. You see, some things are best forgotten. We must keep our minds set on good thoughts, not evil thoughts and bad memories. Young minds are so delicate. So quickly the devil can capture young minds and injure them forever. Bad memories too often become sores that will not heal, cancer that can harm the spirit." Jenny looked at her watch. *Where is the encouragement here?*

"Leah Holcomb, wonderful Leah and her husband, many years ago saved my life and that of my son, Miguel. He was the age of Jason when God allowed him to become a man. Much too soon, I am afraid. But who am I but clay in the potter's hands. He is, El Lobo. He was my life, my hope, my future. And he was but a boy with not-so-good memories because he cannot forget. Leah has asked me to share that story with you. That is why you came?"

Jenny nodded. *Wait! The name El Lobo. She called her son El Lobo.* "Excuse me," said Jenny. "You call your son, El Lobo. Is that a common name?"

"Some would say so. But it is a name I gave him. Even as a boy, he displayed much cunning and bravery. He was not like the other children. I will tell you."

Maria seemed to be very much the pleasant woman described by Leah. She lived alone in the desert with her God and the children in her care, all safely together in primitive but reasonable comfort. Still, Jenny sensed within her a troubled heart and deep pain. She was also beginning to understand Leah's motivation in suggesting they meet: each might gain from the other, strength from strength. "What I am about to tell you I have told to no one but Leah, and of course, her husband, Warren. You will understand. It would do no good for others now to know."

Jenny glanced at her watch. Her flight could be changed. "If you'd rather not—" suggested Jenny with one last thought of a timely return home.

"You must hear. This is why you came. Why Leah sent you. I know I can trust you to do what is right."

Jenny settled back into her chair. Whatever the secret, she could be trusted.

"When I was a young girl, no more than twelve, I lived in a small village in northern Mexico. Like most of Mexico, we were a poor village. Farmers mostly. But the soil did not want to produce. Not like the beauty you see here. There, it was rocky, and the patches of good ground, small and overworked.

"God had sent Leah and her husband, Warren, to our village to teach us His ways and to teach us to read. It was at their school that I met Miguel's father. He came from another village, some distance away because he had heard of the school, and he wanted to learn. He was older than me and very handsome, strong with big arms and hands. He had been raised in an orphanage in Mexico City but had left to live for himself on the streets. He did not know his mother and father. The priest at the orphanage would not tell him anything but that his father was an evil man from another country. He learned the country was Columbia."

Maria spoke now with a twinkle in her eye, Jenny noticed, but thought it unusual that she did not call her husband by name.

Maria continued, "I was pretty then, they tell me. Not so heavy, like now. Miguel's father thought so any way and was very attracted to me as I was to him. Leah would say I was the reason he came to the school. But I know otherwise. He wanted to learn. He dreamed that his father was a wealthy businessman who was forced to leave him with the priest. By getting an education, he could become like him, a man of power and great wealth.

"Leah warned me to be careful because he was wise in his ways and too much a man for a young girl. Of course, I would not listen. He made me feel so special. He would take me on long walks and tell me his dreams. He wanted me to be a part of those dreams. We were in love. Before long, I was with child. I had sinned greatly. We were not married. My own father and mother could not forgive me. They put me out. Leah and Warren took me in to work at the school.

"Miguel's father did not like to farm. He did not like the dirt and the sweat. But he was intelligent, and he was learning at the school. One day, Warren Holcomb took him on a journey to a city near the border. There he had a friend who owned a factory, a small maker of furniture that was sold to Americans who came to buy at the market. I did not know at the time that Warren and Leah had bargained with Miguel's father. They would continue to teach him to read and do math if he would earn money at the factory to pay for his wife and his child."

Maria had not mentioned that she had married. "Did the Holcomb's marry you? Were you husband and wife?" Jenny asked.

"No. They talked of him as though we were married. And I think they wanted us to marry in time. But they believed I was too young at thirteen. But, then, he began to change, and they stopped talking of him as my husband. He was of the devil, they would say."

Jenny watched Maria's expression change, the twinkle in her eye gone, her face suddenly hard, her lips tight. Turning sideways in her chair, she looked again toward the mountains.

"I'm sorry," said Maria at last. "I am not such a good hostess. I will get more ice." She picked up the pitcher, disappeared into the kitchen, returned minutes later with the pitcher filled with tea and fresh ice.

"Where was I?" she asked as she sat down, her composure regained.

"The Holcombs had struck a deal with Miguel's father to provide for you and Miguel in exchange for an education."

"Yes," she said, settling back. "And I think they did not want his influence in the village. As I learned later, they did not need the money but wanted me to have, what you say, a nest egg, when I became of age." The twinkle had returned as well as color to her face. Jenny suspected Maria's coming-of-age was not life as she knew in Minnesota, a protected daughter of an affluent mother and father.

Maria continued, "Miguel's father seemed to like his new job and the money it offered. He would work for a week or two at a time, return to the village with money he had earned, and give it to Leah and Warren as he had agreed to do. At times, he had even gone shopping on his own for new clothes and toys for his son, and he would return to the village with gifts, excited to be with me and his son. There was a time when we even talked of becoming husband and wife.

"But what did I know? I was still very young. I gave him what he wanted from me without a formal wedding. I saw us in love with a strong young son. I didn't need the Holcombs to tell me what I needed and did not need. I could not see that things change, that our life could change. Before long, we stopped talking of marriage. As we grew older, I recognized my wrong thinking and began to pray that God would put it in his heart to marry. By then, it was too late.

"Leah had strong faith and endured considerable hardship. She taught me that strength was in God's word and worked with me to hide it in my heart. I would wait for Miguel's father to return, eager to share God's love with him and all that I was learning. At first, he showed some interest, but eventually, he would leave me as soon as

I gave him what he wanted, sex. He did not want to hear anything of God. He didn't care. Before long, the love I had felt for him died away, and so did his sex. He would return to the village less frequently. Soon he did not even know his own son. He just didn't care."

"How was Miguel during this time?" Jenny asked.

"You mean, without a father?"

"Yes. Jason's father travels a lot. And I—"

"But does he feel loved? That would be a big difference."

"He has no doubt of that," answered Jenny.

"Miguel's father did not know his father, and Miguel did not know his father. At least not as a father. He stopped coming back to the village with any frequency when Miguel was so young. But he did come back." Maria grimaced ever so slightly, a painful nerve touched but quickly recovered.

"It was certain, the man I once loved so deeply had changed. Living in the border city, he eventually took to street life. With his good looks, his charm, he became very popular with the ladies and eventually was led to drugs. It was when he was high on his dope that he would return. Return to our village. Return for me. When I would fight him off, he would beat me. That is the man...no, the beast...Miguel came to know. And to hate. There was no love. Leah was right. He was of the devil. The drugs had made him so.

"One day when Miguel was nine, almost ten, he came home from school—by then, Leah and Warren had provided me a small cottage on the mission compound—only his father had returned some time earlier. He was taking his drugs and was very mean... beyond any reason. I fought him off, but he was very strong. I was no match for him. Miguel entered as he was on top of me, hitting me in the face. I was nearly unconscious.

"Like his father, Miguel was very strong and big for his age. And he had great cunning. Cunning like a wolf, El Lobo. Like other village boys, he would spend much of his days helping in the fields, then go to school, when the days were too hot, and back to the fields until darkness. Then we would eat. That was life in our village.

"On this day, when he entered our cottage, he was outraged at what he saw. And he was fearful for my sake. He, too often, had seen me bruised and swollen. His machete was beside the door where he kept it. His father did not see him come in. And I was too senseless to keep my eyes open. Miguel came up behind his father, and with all the strength in his body, he swung the big knife against the beast's back. He died instantly. His spine cut in two." Jenny expected to see the sadness she had seen earlier, but Maria's expression did not change. She was relating something far removed from all that she was today.

Silence prevailed for several minutes as both mothers considered what had just been said. "It was self-defense," Jenny said finally.

"So it was. But it was just the beginning." Maria held up her hand to discourage Jenny's further comments. She needed to continue. "Miguel's father had not sent money for many years. But Warren knew that 'the beast' had become very powerful in the drug trade and that he had much money. Still, he owed much to others. I don't understand, but others, very powerful in the city government associated with him, would avenge his death if only to show protection for those in their power. Leah and Warren knew they would come for me and my son. We would not be safe in our village."

"But where could you go?" asked Jenny, connecting with the mother's protective fear for her child.

"Here. But not at first. All we knew was that I could not stay there. God eventually brought me here."

"I believe all things happen for a reason. Perhaps the reason for your trial was to bring you and your son to safety. Here in a different country."

"It is as you say. But let me continue. You must know the entire story, and I must now tell it. Thank you for coming."

Unconsciously, Jenny looked at her watch. Above, the seamless sky was bright, but with the receding sunlight, merged with the darkened and obscured, the surrounding mountains. Catching the plane was no longer a reality. She'd call Chris later from a motel.

Maria noticed Jenny's quick glimpse at her watch and anticipated her concern. "I have help here with the children. One of the mothers will see that my children are fed and properly put to bed."

"Your children?" asked Jenny.

"My grandchildren. Yes, they are like my own. Allow me, for my story is just beginning."

"I'm sorry."

"Oh, don't be. It's just that it has been so long. So long forgotten…ignored," Maria continued. "When Leah and Warren sold their belongings and moved to my little village to follow God's call, their very good friends, Grace and William Stoddard, moved here to begin their work with the Indians. Even though I did not have the proper papers, Warren thought he could find a way to get me across the border and, somehow, with the Lord's help, here to the Stoddards.

"Warren took Miguel and me to the border city and to the factory where Miguel's father had worked. A family took us in and shared with us what little they had for two days. Then we were introduced to our contact, a *coyote*, that is, someone who takes immigrants across the border."

"Illegal immigrants," Jenny added.

"That is so. But did not Moses flee with his people from Egypt against the government's orders? Did not Joseph and Mary take their baby Jesus out of the country to protect him from the bad king's orders? God was providing a home for us, for Maria and Miguel. There was a reason for Warren Holcomb to know the people he knew, his contacts. Just as there is a reason that you have come here today. Yes?"

Momentarily, Jenny considered Maria's words. She shared Maria's faith in divine guidance. Furthermore, she had questioned the circumstances that led her to Santa Fe. But any divine reason eluded her. A fact that made Maria's tale no less interesting.

"After two days of waiting, we were told to get ready. We would leave the city that night and go north. We would travel by night and hide in the rocks during the day, out of the sight of border patrol airplanes. The crossing would take two to three days. Both Miguel and I were in good physical condition and believed we could make the crossing with God's help. Once on the other side, we would meet a contact who would take us further north and eventually to Santa Fe.

"We were just three. The coyote stayed by himself when we were not moving, always watching for the patrols...when he was not watching me. He was a strong but ugly man. Many of his teeth were missing. He had long black hair that hung to his shoulders, held in place by a leather band covered with pieces of pounded silver and agates. Warren had paid him in advance—I don't know how much— and for two days, he treated us well. We made good time.

"During the daylight hours on the second day, we stayed among several large boulders under a piece of canvass and slept mostly. Because we had made good time, we were not rushed to continue. The crossing was planned for that evening under a full moon, and we had another five miles to travel.

"When darkness came, we broke camp but could not find our coyote. We thought he was scouting the trail that would lead us to this country. When the moon was high, we were ready to leave and still he had not appeared. We were worried that he had left us. Miguel insisted that he could find the way. I too believed that. As I said, God gave him great cunning, and I believed what he said and was not worried. But first, I needed to relieve myself and walked over the hill where we had camped. It was there that he grabbed me—our guide, our coyote. He had been waiting for me. He smelled horrible. With all the waiting, he had been drinking. Sometimes, during the day, when it was too hot to sleep, I would see him watching me. But then he would be gone. I did not think anything of it, you know.

"He had waited until I was alone. I passed between two large boulders. Suddenly, he grabbed my wrist and turned me around until I was facing him. He smelled like the devil himself—his breath. He put his hand over by mouth and locked my arm behind my back. I did the only thing I could think of and kicked him in the privates with my knee just as hard as I could. He screamed at me but released his grip.

"I started to run but tripped on the loose stones. I felt his weight come down on top of me, knocking the wind from my lungs. I remember I could not move, but I knew I had to fight or he would certainly kill me. I was able to reach for a large stone and rolled beneath him. I was not strong enough to knock him off, and he grabbed my arm as I turned. I remember looking at his face. The moon was now bright. He smiled and grabbed the stone from my hand. I saw him raise it over his head. I closed my eyes, unable to resist further. I knew I was about to die. I turned my head, prayed, and waited.

"Then his weight dropped upon me, knocking the breath from me. I shall never forget that horrible face, his putrid mouth open wide as it slid down over my face, the devil's kiss of death. Instantly, I screamed and pushed him from me as I rolled over. But still I could not get away. We were caught between the two big rocks. His body's dead weight held me. In the moonlight, I could see Miguel standing. He held a large stone that dropped from his hand as he looked at what he had done and waited. He had no time to think of his actions, only to save me the second time. But in less than one week, he had killed twice. My lobo, my son, killed two men, both men very deserving of death."

Maria removed her hands from on top of the table and folded them serenely, contemplatively in her lap, a faraway look in her eyes, her mind obviously struggling. In the distance, a dog barked, or was it a coyote—the four-legged kind. On the horizon, shadows appeared, indistinguishable from the black sky. A light snapped on in the darkened kitchen, a helper moving about to prepare the evening meal for the children in Maria's care.

Before Maria could continue her story, a short portly woman appeared at the kitchen door and signaled to Maria. "Please, you'll stay for dinner?" insisted Maria. Jenny hesitated only briefly, then nodded agreement. "And you are welcome to spend the night. We have guest rooms. They are not big, but they are clean. Our visit has just begun." She stood as she spoke, then started toward the kitchen door.

Famished and desiring to hear the outcome of Maria's story, Jenny agreed, "There will be another flight tomorrow. May I use your phone?"

Chapter 62

Christmas was only a memory for Christy Slater. Weeks had passed. Each week, Christy Slater's mother sought a day to return Christmas gifts, mostly children's clothes from relatives who had forgotten kids did grow from year to year. Today was the long-awaited day. She would make the two-hour drive from their country home, just north of Andover and the Twin City's northern sprawl, to Mall of America. This was the first day of the New Year's parent-teachers conferences, and she had promised twelve-year-old Christy that she could sleep in.

Christy's dad worked in the cities and had left home at his usual six-thirty. Her mother left an hour later, taking Christy's six-year-old brother, Roy, to Gramma's house, fifteen miles away by road, five by snowmobile through the heavily wooded flat land that separated the Slater families.

The note placed on the kitchen table instructed Christy to clean her room and then retrieve Roy from Gramma's. She was to use one of the family's three snowmobiles and return home before dark without question.

She did her room. Then, as a special treat for her mother, tackled the rest of the house. By midday, she was ready for Roy. With the January sun still low in the winter sky, twilight would soon descend. Then the densely wooded tract of land separating the two families would be no place to become stranded should the snowmobile have a mechanical problem. At three o'clock, she fired up a sled and began her way down the drive to the county road.

She had plenty of time to follow the trail along the shoulder of the road. She sat back, loose at first, gliding catlike over the foot of snow that had fallen during the past week. The wooded trail was shorter, but the road trail was faster. She'd return through the woods.

She arrived at her grandparent's home at four o'clock, as promised and after a short visit was ready to leave with her brother. "Bye, kids," Gramma said as she hugged them and watched from the back door as the children started on their way.

"Grams, call Mom. Tell her I'm following the trail through Nelson's woods."

Christy doubted her mother would be home yet but didn't let on to Gramma. She'd only worry and lecture her about the perils of snowmobiling without her parents. She'd worry anyway when she got the answering machine. But by then, she and Roy would be long gone—no lecture and halfway home. If anything went wrong, her mother would at least know where to begin looking.

Christy checked Roy's helmet strap, then secured her own. Straddling the saddle, she turned the ignition and gave one last wave to Gramma before gliding slowly down the long drive as the western sky turned a soft pink.

A well-packed trail crossed the driveway at the edge of the road. There she turned east and accelerated to thirty mph before slowing to turn into the woods.

A canopy of towering hardwood marked the trail's entrance. It loomed dark and foreboding. Once inside, the trail widened, giving way to a large open expanse. In the middle was a bog. She doubted anyone had visited it during the past year.

"Scared?" she asked Roy when they entered the wooded tunnel of hardwood.

"Yes. Hurry!"

She did. Her headlamp illuminated the quarter-mile run, which she covered quickly on the trail's level surface; her speedometer pegged at forty. Ignoring the strange shadows beyond the passing trees, she raced toward the lighter sky marking the bog. Where meadow and bog met, the trail junctioned east and west, uniting again a half mile farther on. From there, it would be an easy and fast ride home, an additional two miles.

She chose the westerly trail used years earlier by loggers who had cleared the woodland and created the meadow. Darkness was settling in, and it would be the faster route. But here, the wetland didn't freeze solid even in the coldest of winters because of numerous springs that bubbled up from the aquifer deep below. She slowed her machine.

"What's that?" Roy asked, and they maneuvered around a fallen tree blocking their trail. Christy's eyes followed his pointing finger to the edge of the bog. Something glistened faintly silver in the last rays of setting sun.

"Wanna see?" she asked, stopping the sled.

"Maybe it's money or something," said Roy hopefully.

"Yeah, maybe." Christy stepped off her sled and walked to the edge of the bog. It was soft underfoot. She jumped once, then a second time, testing its strength. It held. She continued tenuously. Ten feet farther on, she reached the deadfall where they had seen the sparkle.

"Do you still see it?" she yelled back at Roy.

"To your right. It's there. Hurry! It's getting dark." He shivered from the cold.

Christy kicked at the snow and moved slowly to her right. Then she felt it with her foot. Something hard. She became still, forced her eyes to focus in the dimming light, then kicked more snow. Just beneath a downed decaying tree, she saw it. Reaching down, she felt a handle. "Found it," she reported and tugged. Caught or frozen, she tugged again. The ice released its grip, and their prize swung free.

"Well. What is it?" asked Roy. Christy turned and walked slowly toward him holding the object in front of her.

"Looks like a suitcase or something. Wonder what it's doing out here. Who would've—"

"Let's open it." In the excitement, Roy's chills stopped.

Christy balanced the case on a felled tree trunk and tried the lock. "It's won't open," she said in frustration. Quickly she placed it in Roy's lap. "We'll, let Dad open it. Let's get out of here."

"Yeahhhh," Roy responded through chattering teeth as he wrapped his arms around the suitcase, and his sister climbed on board the snowmobile to begin their ride home in the dark.

Chapter 63

The smell of wood burning in the adjoining room signaled Maria that time had come to complete her story. She addressed Jenny, "Please join me at the fire. It will take the chill from the night air." They sat together in large leather chairs facing the open hearth where a fire of mesquite wood flickered. Both focused on the hypnotic dance of the flame, as Maria picked up her story where she had left off, someplace on the Mexican desert, south of the US border. She was there frightened and alone with her young son who had just killed for the second time to defend her life.

"We buried our guide under a pile of rocks in the lean-to where we had spent much of the day. Now we were alone with only Miguel, El Lobo, to guide us with the help of God. We knew we were not far from the border where we were to meet a border patrol who had been paid with the money Warren Holcomb had provided. He would take us here to Santa Fe where we were to meet the Stoddards, and they would take us to this very place where you and I now enjoy a warming fire.

"We set out in the moonlight. We could clearly see our path that would lead us north along a wash carved out of the jagged hills. We did not know where the border would be, only that someone would meet us.

"As the day became brighter, we continued in the shadows of the deep wash. Suddenly, we came upon a truck. We could see markings on the doors. It was the US Border Patrol. But we could see no one as we approached slowly. Afraid to go farther, we stopped and waited for several minutes. We worked our way closer when a man came from behind us out of nowhere. He had his gun drawn and ordered us to his truck. I prayed quickly that we would see our freedom. I felt we had been trapped, and I expected we would either be sent back to our village or left to die in the desert.

"He asked us who we were. I said, 'Maria. We are alone.' Then he went to his truck and spoke into his radio. Miguel motioned that we should run, but there was no place to go. We would wait. The guard returned and asked if I had money for him and what had become of our coyote. I told him that he took our money and left us in the desert. He did not believe me and grabbed my bag. When he could not find any money there, he began to tear at my clothes, thinking that I had hidden it on my person.

"Then I heard a gunshot. All I could think of was we would go to jail. It happened so fast. The guard jerked at the shot, then went limp and fell to the ground. Miguel also had fallen backward to the ground. I knew he had been hit too, but I could not tell who had fired. It was then I saw the gun in Miguel's hand. When the guard attacked me, he did not know that Miguel had grabbed his gun from his holster. El Lobo would not allow anyone to harm his mother."

Jenny listened as Maria's story continued. Tears came to Maria's eyes each time she recalled Miguel's heroism. They dragged the border guard's body into the wash. Because he had spoken to someone on the radio, they could not take the time to bury him. Neither knew how to drive the truck, so they continued north on foot through the wash, at times running through flat areas to put as much distance between them and the border as they could.

Miguel led the way as though guided supernaturally. He had killed three men in defense of his mother and to secure their freedom. Finally, their trail converged on a well-traveled road where they flagged down a young man driving a pickup truck. He was an artist on his way to Santa Fe. Maria saw him as an angel from God sent to lead them to safety.

Jenny could not argue that point, but while finding the story most interesting and heartwarming, she was unable to see what Leah Holcomb saw as a connection to her and Jason's experience. Both boys were the same age, but there, the similarity ended. Jason had been a victim, left without a memory, safe and unharmed. Miguel had been a perpetrator, forced by circumstance to commit the most violent of acts. In a sense, he too was a victim, but one who would spend the rest of his life dealing with the fact that he had taken three lives. Yes, he acted to protect his mother. Nonetheless, he had killed, not once, but three times, including the taking of his own father's life. *What kind of boy could do such a thing and be considered normal?* Jenny wondered. *What kind of man had he become?*

"That is quite a story. Have you told it to others?" Jenny asked at last.

"No. Only Leah and Warren know the entire story."

"And the Stoddards who took you in. Did you tell them?"

"Not the complete story. Leah and Warren knew that William and Grace could not lie if ever they were questioned. So we determined not to tell them. And they never asked. They knew only why I had to leave my village. Of course, Leah and Warren had to tell them that much."

"Yet, you feel comfortable in telling me."

"Yes, I hope it is not too great a burden. Leah believes it is important. But I must ask that you keep it to yourself, as I have done."

"Of course. I have no reason to tell it to anyone…other than my husband, Chris. He is an attorney and lives with secrets. I have never withheld anything from him. He may ask." An inner voice suddenly shouted at the falsehood of her statement. She tried hard to dismiss it.

"Then you must do as you feel best. It is in God's hands anyway." Maria smiled reassuringly, then placed another log on the fire.

"And your son, Miguel, where is he today? How did the ordeal affect him?" Jenny asked. "Does he still live here in Santa Fe?"

Maria anticipated that obvious question. "He is a good son. He comes here to see me often. And to see his daughter. But that is more hard on him. He lives in Florida, mostly because of his work. He is a, how do you say…a business consultant and travels internationally."

Daughter…travels…Florida? Jenny struggled with the familiar ring.

"He does not know to be a good father. You see, his was not a good example. He is El Lobo, a man who loves his family but who is very much alone." Jenny could hear the pain in Maria's voice. "His daughter is the mother of our little artist."

Jenny had retained the little girl's delightful gift. Now, reminded, she studied the picture in her hand, amazed at the talent of such a young child. "I spent some time in a gallery, The Leonard Gallery."

"Then you have met my granddaughter. You would have met *his* daughter. She also is named Maria. Named after me. Her mother died when she was born. Miguel was hurt deeply. It made him hard inside. But here in this place, he has tasted of God's goodness. I want to believe the Spirit of Jesus will soften that hardness. But there are times…sometimes I feel his past, his memories, his father's blood corrupts the spirit." The fire spit out a glowing coal; Maria moved quickly to sweep it back into the fireplace. "There are times when I feel a strong sense of evil," Maria spoke cautiously. Deep inside, Jenny knew she was probably the only person other than, perhaps, Leah, to hear such an admission from Maria.

"So. You can see it is right that Jason's memories remain good," she said as though suddenly reminded of the purpose of Jenny's visit. "I do not encourage that you cause him to remember. He is fortunate, if we can say such a thing, that the drug he was given blocked his memory. But even if he does remember it in time, you must know it takes more than memories to make a man evil. Miguel did what he did because he had no choice. He killed to save me. But he killed, nonetheless. It was his actions." She paused for reflection. "I wonder how it would be if we had stayed in Mexico." She paused reflectively. "We would probably both be dead by now. And you and I would not have met." She stood now and smiled at Jenny. She had said what needed to be said. "You must be tired from your traveling. Now you may have your choice of rooms."

Before retiring, Jenny confirmed her reservations on Southwest flight 382 bound for Minneapolis at 7:25 the next morning, with one intermediate stop in Denver. She would arrive home a little before two o'clock and call Chris from the airport. Suddenly, she felt exhausted and eager to return home.

Jenny's sleeping room was clean but Spartan and smelled of old wood, not unpleasant, but cabiny. The bed, however, made up for any lack of decorating. The pillows were large and soft, and the mattress, firm, just the way she liked it. Jenny opened the small-paned window, turned off the light, took a deep breath of desert air. Amidst thoughts of Chris and Jason, she folded herself under the comforter as sleep overcame her.

Chapter 64

He appeared as a silhouette in the light of a full moon shining over the city of Minneapolis, thirty-five miles to his east. The Darth Vader-like creature surveyed the icy course that would take him northeast over the lake to his target. Moon dogs—moonlight refracted through ice crystals in the atmosphere appearing as small rainbows on either side of the moon—added chilling confirmation of the subzero temperatures.

During the daylight hours of the past two days, he had mastered his high-performance machine. How he loved fast machines. This was a racing-style snowmobile—a new experience. But now he knew it well, and equally as well, the many roadways and ice house villages that dotted the icy surface of Lake Minnetonka.

Even in the extreme February cold, his jet-black high-tech snowmobile suit had kept him warm as he coursed the icy surface, rehearsing and planning his attack. But now the cold of night penetrated the very core of his being, and his teeth began to chatter. He stood in silence, psyching himself for his mission. Soon, the flow of adrenaline would overcome the bone-chilling cold.

In the distance, a long point of land pierced his vision from the south. He would pass between that point and a small island. Enchanted Island was its name on his map. Before that, he would cross the expanse of Smithtown Bay on an icy roadway carved over the lake's surface by ice fishermen whose little shelters dotted the icescape.

An ice fog, growing by the minute, drifted in the heavy air beneath his hillside vantage point. Normally, a breeze would keep the air moving and prevent formation of the icy clouds. Not so tonight. He had not allowed for the fog that would soon obscure his trek over the lake's frozen surface. While it could hide him should he be pursued, it would also slow his approach and his escape, something he had not planned for. So far, the fog was spotty with patches here and there. With luck, it would not hide the little *fish house* village, his destination at the other end of the lake, a distance of nine miles.

His muscular body shivered involuntarily. Never before had he experienced such cold. To keep warm, he needed to be moving. Then that surge of adrenaline, that indescribable feeling he got from living on the edge just before a kill, would block the cold. On with it, the mission that had brought him back to Minnesota.

Slowly he walked toward the crest of the cliff and looked over the expanse of Smithtown Bay. Crusted snow broke into large angular pieces under his weight. Beneath the surface, knee-deep powder engulfed each step, making it hard to walk. It was a strange sensation. Carla would marvel when he told her about the snow and the cold.

He stopped beside a small oak, long denuded of its amber leaves, and peered over the edge to the ice forty feet below. Lazily the ice fog stirred beneath him until it finally obscured the surface of the lake. He thought it strange and waited to see if it would pass. Above him, stars dotted the sky.

He raised his arm and clumsily pushed back the sleeve of his suit to expose a watch. Its diamond-covered face reflected the rising moon. It was light enough to read the time, and it was time to move.

His mission began in a residential area of large estates at the west end of Lake Minnetonka. He would double back and return to the ice at the small frozen lagoon where he had seen the cigarette boat docked six months earlier. He would then follow the moon eastward beyond the long point of land onto the large main lake, then through the distant "Narrows" that divided the upper and lower lake.

He had memorized the route, noting every landmark, stately home, each *fish house* along the way. But now, there was fog. It could obscure the landmarks he needed to locate his target and return safely.

He cursed his stupidity and his luck and walked back to his waiting machine. It was a strange little sled but in many ways resembled the WaveRunner he had mastered in the Caribbean. That had been an easy kill, the man and his woman asleep on their yacht. Now the ride was different over waves of snow that did not move, waves frozen in time. The sensation was different, but he had adjusted quickly and now felt comfortable at the controls. The speed and rapid acceleration of the racing machine was exhilarating. Capable of speeds greater than 120 miles per hour, the high-performance engine and the sled's steel-spiked treads responded immediately to his slightest squeeze of the throttle. How he loved fast machines.

He raised the rear compartment lid and made a final check of its contents. The moon was sufficiently bright for him to see inside. Wrapped in a small towel to protect it during the rough ride rested a small automatic pistol with a silencer. The snowmobile suit he wore was too clumsy for him to conceal the bulky gun in one of the many pockets.

On his right hand, he wore an insulated glove, and on his left hand, he wore a mitten with a slit in the palm that allowed him to free his fingers. Working in such cold was a new experience; his fingers moved slowly. With his exposed bare hand, he unwound the towel and felt the cold weight of the weapon. He would not dare to hold it too long in the open air; the intense cold seemed to burn. He did not intend to use that gun unless he were forced to: a last resort. This would appear to be accidental death by asphyxiation.

He pulled his fingers back inside the protection of the mitten. Then he rewound the towel around the gun and returned it to the small compartment. Next, he withdrew a second towel-covered bundle. This was a special gun, one that would add a new dimension to his assignment. Delicately, he removed the fabric. This is the weapon he would use.

Gently he rested the gun on the open towel inside the compartment and unzipped his suit's right breast pocket. From inside, he retrieved a small dart and quickly inserted it into the chamber of the small pistol. Yes, he could work the mechanism in the cold. To be fast and effective, he needed to keep his fingers warm and nimble. Even a small delay could be critical in the cold; the small dart, with its hypnotic drug, would freeze. But it would stay sufficiently warm inside his pocket.

He was beginning to warm—the adrenaline. Ejecting the small dart, he returned it to the warmth of his pocket and replaced the small air gun with its protective towel inside the compartment. He felt along the inside wall. Attached by a small Velcro strap was a flashlight, which he quickly removed. The light came on as he rotated the lens and transferred it to his gloved hand to illuminate a small case, which he opened with his exposed fingers.

Inside and surrounded by foam packing was a clock device attached to a small battery. A digital timer lit up as he pushed a button on its side. He smiled; the cold feeling more distant. He tested several buttons, putting the device through its arm-disarm cycle. Satisfied, he pressed the button a second time, and the clock's face became black. Next, he examined three loose wires. He would insert these into the explosive he found wrapped in plastic beside the small timer. The explosives disquieted him, made him uncomfortable. He did not know how it would behave in the cold. Then, too, he could become numb and clumsy. He just didn't trust it. But it would not do to leave it on the ice. In the distance, a dog barked. He quickly closed the small box, reattached the flashlight in its Velcro holder, closed the small compartment, and raised his watch to the moon—7:30.

Thoughts of the mission brought the adrenaline rush he needed, warming his body. The forecast called for temperatures to reach minus twenty-eight degrees before a north wind increased to twenty miles per hour by midnight. But for now, he felt warm. He was ready.

Straddling his sled's seat, he pulled down the protective visor of his helmet. The machine responded instantly when he squeezed the throttle, and he made a sweeping turn, retracing his track back to the lake's surface. Fog obscured the point of land he needed for reference, but the trail remained visible under his halogen headlamp. If the fog didn't worsen, he'd be on his way to the airport within the hour and soon in the arms of Carla waiting for him in warm Miami.

Chapter 65

Jordan Green pulled a twenty from his billfold and handed it to the cashier. She asked, "Sure you two are going to be okay out there? Dave is forecasting record cold. Winds are supposed to pick up to thirty miles an hour by midnight." She was cute, stood about five-foot-three, with short golden blonde hair that nearly matched the gold-and-maroon Gopher sweatshirt she was wearing. Jordan was a regular at the "Muni," and her question was prompted by sincere concern.

"Oh, we'll be fine. But you're always welcome to stop by and warm us up. We'll be out there till Sunday. Good sports weekend."

"Hope you've got enough propane. No coming back for a fill. It'll be whiteout conditions out there."

"Full tank and enough food for a week. And, of course, all the fish we can eat."

"Fish? Is that what you guys do out there?"

Jordan smiled like the Cheshire cat, as though he knew something she didn't know and accepted his change. "Only one weekend left before the twenty-eighth, and the houses have to come off the ice." Jordan tucked his change into his pocket and grabbed his case of Miller Draft from the counter. "Thirty miles an hour? That's what Dave is saying now? I had heard twenty earlier," he asked as he headed for the door.

"Yeah. On the six-thirty news. Revised upward. You guys take care. Okay? Don't eat any yellow snow." Jordan turned and smiled, then stepped into the cold and the long-awaited weekend with Bill, his beer, the television, and all the fish they could catch, which they sometimes did.

Jordan climbed into the driver's seat of his Explorer and set the case of beer on the seat beside him. This was his second trip into town for supplies. He hoped now he had everything. Bill was supposed to bring the beer, but it had slipped his mind. Along with everything else lately, his thoughts seemed to be elsewhere. He had been after Bill for weeks to spend the weekend fishing on the ice, like they had done so many times over the years. Bill finally agreed only because Martha insisted he get out of the house.

Martha didn't know what had gotten into Bill. He just wasn't his old self lately. That would soon change. Earlier in the week, Jordan had met with JB in the cafeteria and informed him they needed more money. He had thought about it for weeks before finally insisting JB meet with him. Although Bill didn't know, Jordan was doing it as much for him as he was for himself. Bill just needed the money. And so did Jordan. Jordan was sure the money would put cheer back into Bill's life.

Jordan had left work early in the day and had made his usual stop at the police station for any news that might be brewing, anything new on the Poole investigation, now six months old. As had been the case for the past several months, he almost had to remind the police that the incident had even happened. That was a good sign. That's how cold the case had become. The case wouldn't be dropped altogether, but it certainly appeared to have slipped from the back burner to a place it could eventually be forgotten. Unless something new happened, some new evidence. Chief Nick insisted there was none.

The Explorer felt stiff to his touch. The temperature must be dropping like Dave said it would. Of all the TV weather people, Jordan liked Dave the best. He was the most accurate.

He hoped Dave was wrong about the thirty-mile-an-hour winds, though. After leaving the station, he had driven directly to the *fish house* located two hundred yards off the east tip of Big Island and had started the stove. Both propane tanks were full, but a stiff wind would certainly draw out the heat. It was for that purpose that he had reinsulated the little house. Even in the worst conditions, he had enough fuel for four, possibly five, days. That thought brought him comfort as he rounded the corner, headed north on Water Street, and descended the short ramp to the ice at the Excelsior docks.

At the base of the gravel ramp, a large area, half the size of a football field, had been cleared of snow for fishermen and snowmobilers to stage their gear and temporarily drop their trailers. Beyond the open area, a three-lane roadway cleared by fishermen with plows on their trucks, ran from Excelsior to Big Island, a distance of approximately one mile.

Like a river with many tributaries, the wide icy roadway fed many smaller car paths that eventually connected to other plowed trails or ended at small clusters of ice houses frozen into the ice over someone's favorite fishing spot.

Once on the ice, Jordan pulled into the parking area to make way for another four-by-four that had followed him onto the lake. He stopped the Explorer and watched as the truck sped off toward Big Island.

At 7:30, the night was very bright. Jordan turned off his headlights to test his vision in the light of the full moon and wondered if Dave was right about the approaching wind. He rolled down his window to allow the cold night air to invade his warm cab. So far, there was no wind. If Dave was right, windchills on the lake could reach seventy or eighty degrees below zero before sunrise. He had seen it happen before, winds that lasted for two or three days straight. He wondered about his propane.

Dave could be right about the wind. And he could be wrong about the insulation he had added to his ice house during the summer, wrong about how long his propane would last under conditions of extreme cold and wind. The accuracy of Dave's forecasts haunted him, as in the distance, a swarm of snowmobiles with their halogen headlamps bobbing over the frozen lake rounded the tip of Big Island from where Bill was waiting. Then, almost mystically, they disappeared into an icy fog.

The bait shop off Highway 7 remained open until midnight, and they sold propane. Believing it better to be safe than sorry, Jordan flicked on the Explorer's headlights and headed back out the ramp and south on Water Street. Bill would be all right by himself for another twenty-five minutes.

Chapter 66

Bill topped off the gas in the portable generator, put on his jacket, and stepped from the warmth of the large *fish house* into the cold February evening. The *fish house* was the last house in a cluster of about twelve such houses spread over an acre of ice off the eastern tip of Big Island. It was the end of the road, a single lane that snaked through three wintry villages beyond the wider access from Excelsior. There was nothing to the east but Wayzata three miles away.

In the southwest a halo of light, arching over the distant shore, identified Excelsior. Headlights appeared on the wide roadway from Excelsior's docks to Big Island. Bill stood for a moment and watched to see if they would turn his direction. Jordan had been gone for about half an hour, Bill guessed. The headlights continued northward beyond the west end of the island. It wasn't Jordan. Beginning to feel the cold through his down jacket, Bill closed the trunk of his car and walked back to the warmth of the fish house.

The little house was twelve feet square and eight feet high. Bill and Jordan had designed the oversized *fish house* with all the comforts of home, including bunk beds and electrical wiring, which they connected to the gasoline-powered generator to power the television.

Earlier, Bill had arrived to a warm but vacant *fish house*, stowed his gear, and set about to tidy the place when Jordan appeared with minnows and snacks, ready for his first beer of the night. The beer—picking up the beer had been the one task assigned to Bill. But like everything else of late, it had slipped his mind. Jordan hadn't said much, just grunted, and disappeared back into the cold, mumbling as he went.

Now, Bill cleared the ice from the three holes he had reopened and turned on his radio, scanning through stations until he found some light music and, for a moment, thought of Martha. Finally, he sat down at the small table against one wall and looked around the cubical shack. A smile came to his face. He was grateful Martha had insisted he go fishing with Jordan. In her wisdom, she knew what he needed. It was time to make up. As he waited, Bill knew they'd talk out their differences. They would become buddies again over the weekend. It was time.

He wouldn't set his lines. Not yet. He had two full days to do that. It was good just to sit and listen to the lake sounds and Kenny G. The forecast warned of record cold for the next two days, even the possibility of strong winds. For an instant, he thought about the propane. The stove was Jordan's responsibility, and Bill trusted him to do it right.

The ice protested the dramatic temperature change and cracked loudly in the still night. It was a deep-sounding crack with a sustained rumble that began at one end of the lake and knifed its way along the icy surface to the other side, sending reverberating shock waves through the ice like ricocheting lightning bolts.

It was such a strange sound. Nothing else like it. It needed to be experienced to be understood. It was impossible to describe to anyone who had never been on the frozen lake at night, when one's imagination seemed to magnify every sound. A Minnesota earthquake, another fishing buddy had called it. As Bill sat quietly, he knew it would be a noisy weekend. His body shivered with excitement. He could hear a distant noisy swarm of snowmobiles heading his way. He tried to count them as he listened for the sounds made by their different machines, different engines and, with eyes closed, could visualize a pack of riders speeding across the lake into the face of a howling wind. Bill didn't own a snowmobile, although he had come close to making the big purchase on more than one occasion.

But the good ones, the fast ones, like the one he wanted, were pricey. On each occasion, reason, and thoughts of Martha, prevailed, and the urge subsided.

The Coleman lantern hanging on the wall flickered, and shadows danced about the room. Bill walked to it and pumped in more air. When it responded with a burst of brilliant white glow, he reattached it to the hook on the wall and resumed his reflective position. Bill counted eight or ten machines as the snowmobiles passed. He could not imagine being outside and actually enjoying the cold, like some of his friends who coursed back and forth across the lake from one house to another, from one bar to another until they were too tired or too drunk to continue. They knew he was spending the weekend on the ice. He waited for them to stop to hear that friendly rap on the door. He hoped Jordan was picking up enough beer to satisfy his growing thirst with some extra for his buddies, who always came visiting.

He yearned for a cigarette. It always happened at times like this. Old habits died hard. Fishing, beer, old friends—the old associations brought thoughts of lighting up. *A dumb habit*, he reflected. A habit he had defeated several years ago. But quitting wasn't easy. In fact, near impossible. Restless, he stood and readjusted the perfect glow of the Coleman.

Over the music, he heard a single machine heading his way. Maybe one of the riders who had just passed was returning home, calling it quits for the night. He picked up his tackle box and placed it on the table, swung his legs over the chair, and began to take inventory of its contents, waiting again for the machine to stop out front and that friendly rap. *To hell with the cigarettes.* The machine drew closer. It was definitely a high-performance engine. Its wail stomped all over Kenny G as it rounded Big Island, then slowed and moved along the path to his house. Jordan wasn't back with the beer, and now one of his buddies was stopping for a Bud. *Oh, well!* Bill waited.

It stopped about twenty feet from the house. There followed a moment of silence, then snow squeaked under the boots of Bill's first visitor. No friendly rap. The door latch moved upward, and the door opened, filling the warm room with a sudden burst of cold. A person dressed in a black snowmobile suit with a black helmet stepped inside. Bill smiled in silence and watched the man close the door and take a quick look about. He was supposed to guess who the visitor was. That was it. A game some of his friends played. Somehow, it seemed more fun after a couple of beers. He decided not to play.

"You got me. I give up," he confessed. "Jordan went after the beer. Should be back any minute. Let's see. Who is it? I didn't recognize the machine. Got a new sled?" Bill continued to rummage through his tackle box, not willing to get suckered in. Out of the corner of his eye, he watched the black boots move toward him, and the person's arm raised as though the helmet was about to come off.

He heard it and felt it at the same time—a spit of air and a sudden sting on his neck. In an instant, he sprang from his chair reaching for the thing that bit him, flailing his arms involuntarily to brush away the strange bee. His rapid movement overturned the table, sending his tacklebox flying to the side of the house, leaving a trail of fishing lures, bobbers, plastic worms, and jigs. Behind him, his chair collapsed as he fell forcibly backward, landing on the lower of the bunks.

His head came to rest on his overnight duffel bag as numbness settled into his arms and legs. He moved his hand. It responded. But it felt different. Then he didn't want to move. He didn't care anymore. He looked up as the visitor stepped toward him and removed his helmet. The game was over.

Horror exploded upon him at the recognition. Then his bladder released as panic flooded his body for his last moment of consciousness, his last time. "Gómez?" He gasped, and his mind relinquished control of his body to a new master.

Gómez let Bill lie for a moment as he set his helmet on the top bunk and looked about the strange little house. He had never been in a fish house. In his home country, a family of six could call such a place "home." It was not unlike the home of his early childhood before he was taken to the man in the city.

"You have made a mess of your little house, William," Gómez addressed the form lying on the floor until he was sure the drug had taken effect. "Get up now and clean it before Jordan returns."

The body that was Bill's opened its eyes and began to move and untangled itself from the overturned chair and stood. It was a very different Bill who looked about the room to survey the mess. After a moment, he obediently returned the table to its position against the wall, picked up the chair, and slid it under the table, then stood and for a moment gazed at the fishing tackle strewn across the floor.

Gómez watched, grinning sadistically as Bill knelt beside the tackle box and haphazardly scraped its contents from the floor and placed them inside. "Now sit at the table," he commanded after Bill closed the tackle box. "Do you know me?" he asked.

"Yes." Bill uttered, his reply barely audible and resumed his position at the small table. Gómez smiled. He knew when they had first met and had sat in the truck together that this day would come. Loose ends always needed fixing. That was his life, fixing—no, call it "repairing" loose ends. He smiled.

Chapter 67

Jordan left Highway 7 and turned north again onto Water Street, a fresh propane tank was on the floor behind his seat. The attendant at the bait shop had just confirmed Dave's forecast of approaching high winds and record cold, just as he heard it straight from the regional forecasting office on his weather band radio. Tonight, the insulation would be put to the test. While his confidence was unshaken, the third tank was a wise choice, a good safety precaution.

He and Bill would not be alone on the ice. Two pickup trucks preceded him down the ramp and sped northward toward Big Island. He followed fifty yards behind. The wide roadway turned eastward at Gale's Island and continued for half a mile before ending abruptly at the edge of a small cluster of *fish houses*. He followed the two trucks as they turned northward toward another cluster of houses.

Eventually, Jordan was alone on the ice. The other *fisherman* stopped less than half a mile from his village. They were close enough for help if he and Bill encountered any trouble, and for some reason, his cell phone wouldn't work. He had not had time to shop for a new battery. That should not pose a problem as long as he kept it plugged into his Explorer's cigarette lighter.

Rounding the eastern point of the island, he could see the lights of Wayzata through breaks in the icy fog. He guessed the fog was now one hundred feet thick and moving to the southeast, just to the north of his house.

JENNY

The icy roadway was reduced to nothing more than icy ruts in the snow, soon to be refilled. Fortunately, the snowfall for the winter was below normal. No one who fished this spot had a vehicle that was rigged with a plow. After the last big snow, some eight inches, someone in the neighboring cluster traded a cleared pathway for a beer, but there had been several one-inch snowfalls since. With the wind intensifying, the ruts would vanish. They would have to blaze a new trail when it was time to head home. Instinctively, he checked to confirm he was in four-wheel drive.

He passed the first of a dozen houses that tracked the edge of a drop-off in the lake's bottom. Another hundred yards, and a glow in the encroaching fog announced he was home at the wintry house he and Bill had built and shared. They both needed this weekend alone, a time to repair their friendship. He could hardly wait to tell Bill that JB had agreed to more money. He was surprised JB had agreed so quickly. He wouldn't dare to ask again. If the past six months counted for anything, he was "inside" now, accepted into management's inner circle. That meant more opportunities for added income, special assignments with special incentives. He would share those incentives with Bill.

He didn't recognize the snowmobile that occupied his parking spot. It had to be one of Bill's friends from the plant. *Let the fun begin*, he thought as he maneuvered his Explorer until it was facing south on the leeward side of the house, protected from the wind, from where it would be easier to leave on Sunday. He would have Bill do the same with his car after his first beer.

He didn't feel a thing. The butt of the air pistol in Gómez's powerful hand came down like a hammer at the base of Jordan's skull as he stepped through the door. He collapsed in a pile on top of a case of Miller Draft. Bill sat unmoved by the disturbance, somewhere in thoughtless space, and waited for direction. It came now.

"Bill, your friend is tired. Help me place him the in bed." Gómez kicked at Jordan's legs to move them from blocking the open door. Obediently, Bill grabbed at Jordan's arms and helped Gómez drag him across the floor and swing him onto the lower bunk. "Now you join him. It's late. You are tired, and I must be going. On the top bed."

As Bill climbed onto the top bunk, Gómez withdrew two darts from inside his suit and inserted one into the air pistol. He then pointed it at the side of Jordan's neck and fired. Quickly he inserted the second dart, and when Bill was settled, shot him with the a narcotic that would keep both asleep until the carbon monoxide and the cold did its work. He waited ten seconds and then removed the darts from his victims, leaving nearly invisible puncture wounds in the sleeping bodies.

Next, he walked to the stove and closed the damper on the chimney stack, forcing the stove's exhaust back into the cubical house. Then he turned the thermostat to maximum and picked up the fuel canister to check the level of propane. It felt full, but he couldn't tell how much. Perhaps too much. They could wake up. No. The odorless carbon monoxide would end their lives before the cold.

The case of beer laid broken open on the floor. He swore at himself for not having Bill clean up the mess while still in his semiconscious drug-induced trance. He picked up as many cans as he could see and set them on the table. Opening several, he poured their contents into one of the fishing holes in one corner of the house and returned the empties to the table. Finally, he opened one last can and poured some of its contents over Bill and Jordan; the remainder he sprayed about the room.

After one last look about the little house, he retrieved his helmet and put it on. The explosives he had brought with him would destroy any evidence, but he chose not to use it. An explosion would be harder to explain than asphyxiation. There remained the risk that someone could find them before they were dead, but that was a risk he would have to take. Should they be found early and recover, Bill would not remember anything, and Jordan had not seen him.

Satisfied, the man they called Gómez retreated into the cold night to his waiting snowmobile. Outside, the wind gusted from the northwest. Stars twinkled in the otherwise black sky while the full moon illuminated the snow-covered lake. The ice fog had dissipated in the intensified wind. Now wisps of snow rode the Siberian clipper, sending sheets of white racing to the southern shore.

Even inside the insulated suit, with adrenaline surging, his body reacted to the cold. He quaked involuntarily as he started his sled.

Aided now by the moon, it was easier to make out land formations as he sped westward. Ahead was the Narrows Bridge. He slowed, checking his bearing, then turned to the southwest entering the mouth of a narrow channel. Passing occasional homes, he finally came to a small cluster of townhomes. He turned off his headlamp and continued slowly, watching smoke billow from chimneys as the families residing inside enjoyed a warmth he now longed for.

He knew the Poole home, having scoped it earlier. As he approached, he arced wide to the left until he faced the rear of the home now less than one hundred yards away. He released the throttle, and his sled sank slowly into the crusty snow. The draperies were pulled, covering most windows and doors, blocking the unwelcome intrusion of cold air. But beyond the drapes, there was light. Someone was home. As he waited, shadows passed the patio door—a man and a child. He knew that would be Jason and his father. He waited as long as he could bear the biting cold; there apparently was no woman.

Then a man's face appeared in a window. It peered out over the blowing snow and cold night air. Gómez remained motionless. He was a shadow, invisible. But he was cold, very cold. Their time would come. Of that he was certain. *Soon enough*, he thought as the face disappeared from the window. He applied pressure again to the hand throttle, taking the snowmobile once again out the narrow channel, then through the Narrows, then westward, and off the godforsaken lake.

Chapter 68

A knock on the door found Jenny tossing and turning again, a mind churning, processing its own secret thoughts. *Rap, rap, rap.* "I'm awake. Thank you," she responded and listened to receding footsteps, and outside, birds singing the sounds of a waking desert.

After a quick, refreshing shower, she dressed in yesterday's clothes, all that she had brought in from the car the evening before, tenderly folded the little artist's gift into her bag and set out after the source of coffee's magical smell, now mingled with the fragrance of freshly baked bread. The coffee was still gurgling as she passed through the kitchen to find Maria standing in her robe on the patio breathing in the crisp morning air.

"It smells so good, don't you think? The cool air this time of day?" Maria spoke as Jenny approached from behind. "Did you sleep well?"

"Yes, thank you. And thank you for getting up so early to see me off and for sharing your story last evening," Jenny said sincerely.

"Come, let's go back inside where it's warm." She took Jenny's arm and led her back inside to the small kitchen table. After showing Jenny to a chair, she withdrew a steaming pan of rolls from the oven, placing them on the center of the table.

Jenny spoke as Maria prepared a cup of tea for herself before sitting down. "You didn't say much about the Leonards. Are they still here in Santa Fe?"

JENNY

"The Leonards are very active in Santa Fe despite their progressing years. They are in their seventies now, although you would not know it by looking at them. The gallery keeps them young."

"Your granddaughter said the Leonards came from the East Coast."

"From Connecticut, in the 1950s. They are both very artistic, and Mr. Leonard did not like the corporate environment. They came here for a new start."

"I find it interesting that the man who heads up the company I work for in Minneapolis has the same last name, Leonard. It's not a common name in Minneapolis to my knowledge. He lived in New York before coming to Minneapolis. I suppose there are many Leonards there. Is it possible they are related?"

"I don't know their background before coming here. They do have a son. He and Miguel are near the same age. They grew up together here in this very place. The original Leonard's Gallery was located here. Long ago, they donated it to the school. Shortly after that, they sent their son to boarding school in the east."

Jenny had to ask, "Would his name be Creighton?"

Maria's answer made Jenny's heart skip a beat. It was as though she had uncovered a lost key to the most obscure puzzle of her recent life. "Yes, his name is Creighton. Our boys were teenagers then. The Leonards are very gifted, intelligent people. So is their son, Creighton. At the time, the Leonards did not believe the educational system here in Santa Fe could mold the brilliance in that young mind. That was in the '60s. He was sent to a special school in Connecticut. When school was not in session, he lived with Mrs. Leonard's sister and her husband, coming here to visit occasionally and then for only brief periods."

"Are they close? Creighton and his parents?" questioned Jenny.

"Not like me and my son. No."

"Are they estranged?" inquired Jenny.

"I'm sorry, I do not know the word *estranged*," Maria qualified.

"Do the Leonard's ever see their son? Does he ever come back to see them?"

"Not in many years. It is strange, for I believe they love one another in their own ways." Maria sighed. "You know that Creighton is Jewish. Or he claims such."

"Yes. But frankly, he is not known for being a practicing Jew. He does not seem religious. Not in the world's sense." Jenny reached for more coffee and nibbled on a roll. "His parents…?" Jenny asked with a mouth full.

"His father is a Jew. His mother is Irish and Catholic. They have been able to reconcile their own religious differences. But they wanted Creighton to discover his own values. Perhaps it was a compromise for each of them. As a result he, too, compromised. He rejected both faiths. He has no faith. That is most troublesome for his parents. They blame themselves. And they do not speak of him often. It is very unfortunate, wouldn't you say?"

"But Creighton's wife. She is…." puzzled Jenny.

"Yes, Virginia," supplied Maria. "A very strong woman. And an even stronger Christian. She believes as I do, and I understand, as do you, a Christian is one who has accepted God's forgiveness, because of the sacrifice of his Son, Jesus."

"We have met. She is very open about her faith." Reflected Jenny with a smile.

"She was not always so, not always so strong in her belief. Creighton is a brilliant man with considerable charm and gifted with words, persuasive. If you know him, you have never heard him use profanity. Is that not so?" She didn't give Jenny opportunity to answer. "He is not a vulgar man. That is something he learned from both parents. Profanity, vulgar speech is a sign of ignorance. He does not allow it from his associates, I am told."

"I'd say he sounds like a good son." Jenny speculated.

"His parents do not share everything with me, nor does Miguel who will see him from time to time," Maria offered.

"They are still friends then? After all these years?"

"Yes. I do not talk business with my son, Miguel, when he comes here to see me and his family. He is a business consultant. He also is brilliant. As I said yesterday, very cunning like a wolf. The Leonards paid his way to attend Stanford University. They believe strongly in education. There are times in his work when he undertakes projects for Creighton."

"What kind of project? Has he ever said?" asked Jenny, again digging.

"No, he doesn't say. And I do not ask. He lives in Miami. I know he travels a great deal. He often just stops here, unannounced, as he goes from here to there." The adoring mother extended her arms in resigned puzzlement. It was enough to see her son and encourage his return to care for his daughter and granddaughter. She did not want a quarrel.

"I didn't know Creighton was now in Minneapolis," said Maria, changing the subject.

"For a year now. They, the Leonards, Creighton and Virginia, own most of the stock in my company. WYCO Toys is a very large international toy company. He took over the management to safeguard their investment, as rumor has it. And he has done a good job. The company is growing again."

"I did not know," Maria said again, almost apologetically. "I know so little of business. But I can say Virginia Leonard is a very good person and a good one to be involved in a company such as yours, a toy company."

"They don't live together. She lives in Louisville, Kentucky. We met for the first time at a Christmas party. She seemed to be very involved, working in the background. She must have her reasons to live elsewhere."

"As I said, her faith was not always so strong, so defined. Now she does not believe in divorce. Divorce is something she would never do. She honors him, though she disagrees with his behavior. Someday he could change. Is not that a woman's hope that her husband will change?" observed Maria. "It was mine. Far too long. But it is what God wants too, that a man and woman should stay together," Maria added.

Jenny looked at her watch, thought of the Santa Fe traffic and said, "I'm afraid I must go. I thank you so much." Jenny gathered her bag. Maria rose to give her a hug. "What behavior does Virginia disapprove of? Can you say?"

"No. It is only what his parents have told me. They are private people and know my concern but only tell me what I need to know."

"I see," Jenny said, exhibiting a disappointed, if not a puzzled look as she reached for Maria's hand.

Maria appreciated Jenny's warmth. "It has been good for me to share my story with you. I hope it is not too great a burden. I now have another friend to carry it with me. I hope it does not cause you pain." Maria hugged Jenny the second time. Considering her words, Jenny wondered if there were some unknown meaning.

"Thank you again," said Jenny. Reluctant to ask further questions, she turned and walked away. Maria watched from the door as Jenny climbed into her car to begin her drive north toward Santa Fe. She felt relieved, somehow, and trusted that her story would be safe with her new friend.

A car approached from the north as Jenny drove to the higher elevation on the road that would take her to the interstate. It was the only car Jenny had seen since leaving the interstate highway the day before. But she was in too great a hurry and too deep in thought to give it much attention aside from pulling closer to the shoulder of the road to allow the car to pass. She considered what she now knew about her employer—more history than she had known twenty-four hours earlier, whatever that might be worth. Her God was still in charge, perhaps intending to help her career. She found it easier to turn over such situations to her greatest source of comfort. She believed God cared a lot about such things when His children's hearts were in the right place. She trusted hers was.

The oncoming car slowed as Jenny passed. Its dark-haired driver too was lost in thought, eager to see his mother and granddaughter. Perhaps, his daughter would not be working. He longed to see her too. They could not be a part of his sordid world. He sighed as the little mission came into view.

At the airport, Jenny checked her bag at the curb and tipped the skycap. The flight attendant was holding the door for her and slammed it shut as soon as Jenny boarded. In the air, Jenny caught a final glimpse of the little mission, a spot on the desert floor that quickly disappeared from view as her eyes, heavy from a busy day, closed. When the flight attendant nudged her and offered a pillow, she opened her eyes long enough to see an amber-gold horizon, setting the magnificent Rockies ablaze, and for a brief moment she thought of Maria, Maria the grandmother, Maria the young girl, Maria the mother of El Lobo. Then her body surrendered to sleep.

Chapter 69

"Sure it's safe out here?" Dan asked police chief Nick Carlson. "Plenty safe. The ice out here is two feet thick. Probably more in some areas." Chief Nick drove off the end of Water Street in the department's only four-wheel-drive vehicle and turned on his flashing red lights before continuing toward Big Island on the freshly plowed roadway.

"That's Big Island out there. Named that by the Indians who lived around the lake in the eighteen hundreds. Yesterday you wouldn't have been able to find it if you were ten feet from shore. It was a whiteout, a ground blizzard. I got one of the city trucks to plow a new roadway. It had all drifted shut. I appreciate your coming right out. Sunday's your busy day at the mall, I suspect."

"I appreciate the call. But why me?"

"Sadler told me to call you."

"Sadler, huh?"

"He said you were helping on the case. Actually, when you called two weeks ago about a green Explorer being seen in the Abel Food parking lot the morning of Jason Poole's abduction, I didn't make the connection. It's still only a long shot. Absurd in fact. Jordan Green is head of security for WYCO Toys. He drives a green Ford Explorer. Just like this one, only his is a fancier version. Jordan has been a friend of the department for several years and has managed to direct WYCO's corporate giving in our direction. He lobbied the company for this." Chief Nick took one hand off the wheel and waved it about the interior of the department's new Ford Explorer. "Sadler said you'd be able to establish a connection if there was one. Again, it's a long shot. I feel guilty just pointing the finger."

"What have you got going?"

"Jordan's sister, Martha Wilson, called me at home shortly after 1:00 p.m. She was concerned for her husband, Bill Wilson, who was spending the weekend fishing off Big Island with Jordan. Bill didn't call home like she expected Saturday night. When she couldn't raise Jordan on his cellular this morning, she called me."

Dan looked to the northeast. Already the sun was beginning to set with probably no more than one hour of daylight remaining. A flashing red glow was visible over the treetops of Big Island signifying other police cars had arrived and, by now, the county coroner as well. "Does Martha Wilson know?"

"Not yet. I talked with her about an hour ago and told her only that we were looking into it, that we needed to plow a road to get there."

"How did you get there?"

"Snowmobile. One of my officers has one. He knew the house. Jordan had reinsulated this past summer. Said he was going to eliminate the draft. It looks like he got it a little too tight. They apparently died of carbon monoxide poisoning. Now they're frozen solid. We're guessing the time of death was late Friday night. They had two fresh propane tanks. Both full. The one they were using probably ran out sometime Saturday."

"What makes you suspect Jordan Green was involved in the Poole affair?"

"Actually, I don't suspect him. But I do have questions. Some things just don't seem right. Know what I mean?"

"You've known him for how long?"

"Several years. He always wanted to be a cop. Was an MP in Nam. I always thought his lobbying for our cause was his way of buying membership into the club. Our club. Not that he needed to. The entire community appreciates what he was able to do. At first, his meddling and weekly visits were annoying. But after a while, he was accepted."

"Club membership?"

"Of sorts. But more than that. He grew on all of us."

"What changed?"

"He just couldn't let the Poole incident drop. Like it was a fixation. Every week since last August, he'd come in and ask what was new with the case. At first, it seemed normal, since he was head of security for the employer of the victim's mother. But every week reminding us? It just seemed odd."

"Like he knows something?"

"Like he knew something and needed reassurance that his secret was safe."

Near the southwest shore of Big Island, the new roadway turned directly east in a direct line toward Wayzata and the eastern tip of the island. Dan had never driven on the ice. Now he marveled as they drove past two *fish house* villages each consisting of a dozen small cubicle structures. To the south, he recognized the shoreline he had sped past months earlier with Jason at the controls of *Little Red*.

"You're sure the ice is safe? It can hold all of us?" Dan asked when the road turned north, and he saw the source of the flashing lights, several squad cars from different communities on the lake, a rescue squad from the Excelsior Fire Department, a paramedic team from North Memorial Hospital, and a van from the Hennepin County Coroner's office. Chief Nick nodded with a smile.

"Why so popular? Looks like a police convention. Is there any community not represented?" Dan asked as they drew near, and he could read the lettering on the squads.

"Interesting question. Who owns the case? Big Island is governed by the city of Orono. To the south is Deephaven, to the west is Wayzata, and of course South Minnetonka Police representing Excelsior and neighboring communities. Out here on the ice, it's Hennepin County and the sheriff's department. The victims reside in Excelsior and Shorewood, both my jurisdiction. It boils down to the county and me. The others came for a 'look see.'

"By the way. Bill Wilson also works at WYCO. He's in charge of the kitchen and the plant cafeteria at the company's main plant on the lake. Where Jennifer Poole also works. The truck that took Jason supposedly made only one stop that morning. At WYCO, Bill signed for the delivery."

"You said he managed the food service, yet he bought from outside?"

"For special functions, visiting dignitaries. Like the Japanese delegation. Remember? They had toured the plant before going to Mall of America."

The plow had cleared a small parking area to the west of Jordan Green's *fish house* where most of the vehicles were parked in random fashion. Stakes had been placed in the snow and the entire area marked off with yellow crime-scene ribbon. Inside the ribbon stood the *fish house* with an old car along one side and a green Ford Explorer on the other. Both were partially buried in drifted snow.

The wind had stopped, but the temperature had not risen above five below zero for two days. Now with the sun going down, the temperature was heading toward another record low. Officer Larry Randall popped his head out of the *fish house* door, spotted his chief, and sprinted in their direction as Nick rolled down his window.

"Join us where it's warm," he said. Larry opened the back door of the Explorer and stepped inside.

"They had to be crazy coming out here when they did. Bodies are frozen solid. Never seen anything like it," Larry said as he removed his fur-lined gloves and began to blow on his fingers.

"Larry, this is Dan Sheridan. You may have seen him on TV."

"Sure did. Pleasure to meet you, Mr. Sheridan."

"Dan, this is Officer Larry Randall. Larry discovered the bodies about 2:30 this afternoon. Larry was also the first on the scene when Jason Poole was abducted."

"Larry, you may remember that Dan here was with the CIA and the FBI before heading up security for the mall. He's here as a courtesy to the FBI on another matter, and I've asked him to come along.

No need to ID him to anyone else here, all right? Just act dumb. If anyone asks, you only know he came with me."

Chief Nick was watching Larry through the rearview mirror, as Larry blew on his fingers to warm them and nodded. "I see the county's here, the medical examiner. What are they saying?"

"They haven't been here long. So far, all indications are accidental death. Everything is frozen solid, but you can still smell the beer when you step inside. There are several empties on the table. It appears they were sipping beers, talking. Numbed by the beer, they didn't notice the effects of the carbon monoxide. Fell asleep, didn't wake up."

Nick watched Larry's eyes in the mirror as he spoke and could see the emotion coming through. Larry and Jordan had become good friends. When the chief wasn't around to visit with Jordan or too busy, Larry would take him in and make him feel appreciated. "You okay?" he asked.

"Yeah. Just can't believe that's him in there. Frozen solid. I mean, I've got stuff in my freezer at home that isn't that frozen. Friday, when he stopped by, he was all excited about spending the weekend fishing with Bill. He said Bill was ticked with him over something he'd said months ago, and they weren't getting along all that well. It's a long story."

Nick expected it was, but he knew Larry needed to get it out. "Go ahead. I'm listening. I can't believe it either."

"Apparently, Bill had developed an ulcer over it. Martha, his wife, Jordan's sister, was concerned and encouraged Bill to bury the hatchet and go fishing with Jordan. They'd been through Nam together. Jordan was always looking out for Bill. Always helping him. He really felt bad about their relationship. This weekend was make-up time." Larry sniffed. "It's so friggen cold, nose won't stop running."

In the mirror, Nick saw that the runny nose went with the steamy eyes. He felt it too. "Did he ever say what he had said to Bill to set him off?"

"Never. Just that it wasn't much."

JENNY

"It was 'much' to Bill." Nick observed. In the mirror, Larry nodded.

"You ready? Want to see what being a die-hard fisherman in Minnesota can do to ya?" Nick asked Dan. Larry shook his head in disbelief. He was sure the chief didn't realize what he had said, how he said it.

Dan was dressed for the cold but was not ready for the shock of stepping from a warm car into twenty-below. He pulled his own parka over his head and followed Nick under the yellow ribbon. Nick recognized the other officers from the neighboring communities and greeted them as he stepped through the door of the *fish house*. Once inside the cramped quarters, the other officers stepped out to make room for the newcomers.

Battery-powered lights had been placed at various locations in the house, illuminating the inside like a stage set. Heat from the lights warmed the air, making the work of the medical examiner almost tolerable. The medical examiner was Dr. Janet Welsh. Dan recognized her when she stood to see who had arrived. She looked at Dan but spoke to Chief Nick.

"I understand he was a friend of yours."

"Yes. Jordan Green. Not close friends. But we were friends."

"Sorry," offered Dr. Welsh. The chief nodded. She continued, "Asphyxiation. Definitely asphyxiation. Time of death…? Hard to say for sure until we can thaw'm out…late Friday night."

"Faulty stove?" Nick asked.

"I don't know that the stove is faulty. Look here!" Dr. Welsh walked over to the damper on the stove and turned it back and forth. "This was leftover from a wood stove. You wouldn't use it on this kind of setup. It was closed off. Your man Randall said they were experienced, used this house all the time. Dumb mistake having one of these. Someone probably bumped it shut. Simple as that."

"You'll do blood samples? It looks like they'd been drinking."

"I'll tell you what they had for dinner once we get'm warmed up. I'll know'm both, inside and out. Have the relatives been told?"

"Not yet. Jordan was divorced. I guess my crew is about as much family as he had beside the other guy's wife. Bill had a wife, Martha, who was Jordan's sister, and a son away at college."

"This is Sunday. I'll have'm zipped back up by Wednesday. Funeral could be Thursday."

"I'll tell Martha. It'll be a big funeral. Both were from the area. People don't move from here, from the lake. If they do, they come back. There'll be folks who haven't seen each other in years. People they went to grade school with."

"Martha will need that. It's tough." Dr. Welsh's human side came out. She was an expert in dealing with life's final passage. "Now if you'll excuse me. I've got to get them transported."

"Need help?" Nick asked.

"No. Does it look like I need help?" The doctor gestured to the half dozen people milling about the square room. "I came prepared."

Dan walked over to the gas generator and removed the cap from the fuel reservoir. Nick joined him. "Every fisherman have one of these?" asked Dan.

"No. Most don't, in fact. Jordan wanted all the comforts of home, including electricity. Radios are common, battery-powered. Not much need for a generator." As Nick spoke, light music playing in the background drew his attention to a shelf on the wall behind the table. Noting that the fuel reservoir was full, Dan replaced the cap and turned to watch Nick walk to the shelf and pick up the radio, still playing nonstoplight jazz.

"Gophers played Friday," said Nick. "The game started at 8:00. Jordan was a fanatic. He wouldn't miss a game. That's why he had the TV here and the generator." Nick looked puzzled.

"The generator hadn't been used. Tank was full," added Dan, his thoughts tracking with the chief.

"Janet said she thought death came late Friday. They would have been alive for the game."

"The carbon monoxide? It could have knocked them out early."

JENNY

"Maybe." Nick turned to the table and the empty beer cans. Turning to one of the examiner's team, he asked for a plastic bag and got one, placing two empty cans inside. Then he handed the bag to Dan. "This is for Sadler. Have him run prints."

"What are you thinking?" asked Dan as he accepted the bag, knowing the answer.

"There's more than a dozen empties on that table. They weren't watching the game that started at 8:00. That means they were dead or immobilized before then. They hadn't been here long enough to get soused. They had to be inhaling the stuff. Which could account for them falling asleep, perhaps. But both of them listening to dreamy music? Falling asleep?" The chief was thinking out loud.

Dan walked over to the tackle box sitting on the floor near the door. Bending over, he opened it and looked inside. There were layers of little trays for lures and paraphernalia, but nothing was in its place. Looking about the room, he spied a small blue envelope on the floor only a couple feet away. He reached for it and examined the slip of paper inside—Bill's fishing license. Obviously, the box had been emptied, and its contents replaced by someone other than Bill. Someone who didn't care about fishing.

Dan looked about the room again for any sign of a struggle. There was none. Larry had said Bill's and Jordan's relationship had been strained. They could have fought and then made up. Brothers did that. Brothers-in-law did that too.

He watched as Nick walked over to Dr. Welsh and spoke to her briefly. Janet reached to the top bunk and began patting Bill's clothing. Where he stood, Dan could see some of the fabric was hard, unpliable, frozen. Finally, Nick turned and approached him. "Seen enough?" he asked. Dan nodded as the door to the *fish house* opened behind him, and a woman in coveralls stepped through carrying two large body bags.

Outside, Larry Randall straddled his snowmobile. It was a sleek black model, obviously capable of high speeds. Larry noticed Dan's admiring glance and smiled while he pushed a switch on the instrument panel, and two red lights on either side of the halogen headlamp began blinking. He pushed another switch, and an electronic siren shouted *weep, weep, weep.*

Nick shook his head and gave Larry a half-hearted salute, to which Larry nodded good-bye, squeezed the throttle, and quickly disappeared toward a cherry-red sky. Before motioning for Dan to climb back into his 4 × 4, Nick took one last look at the *fish house* that had been the object of considerable jokes and discussion over the years as well as its owner, the man who now lay frozen solid inside. He would miss his friend. The department would miss him. What would he tell Martha? Janet Welsh was right, it would be tough. It would be tough times ahead for Martha.

"Dan, I haven't told anyone but you about my concerns and my questions with regards to Jordan. I don't know what all this means, but I would appreciate it if you would keep the lid on it as long as possible. Jordan had a lot of friends at the station," Nick spoke as he maneuvered his 4 × 4 around the small parking area.

"I'm not official, remember," Dan answered.

"Not according to Sadler. He wants you to know everything. He said talking to you is like talking to him."

"That's confidence. I work at Mall of America."

"Look, I don't know what's with the two of you. Right now, I don't really care. I've got two bodies, one a friend, frozen stiff, a very kind wife and sister of the deceased, who doesn't know what's happened to the two most important people in her life, and circumstances that I'm sure are not what they seem to be. Right now, I need all the help I can get, and you're a part of that help. And from what Sadler says, very capable help."

"The medical examiner?" Dan asked, letting the compliment pass.

"She has no doubt that death was caused my asphyxiation." He drove onto the freshly plowed path and continued. "Wilson's clothes appeared frozen. They were wet and then froze. Frozen solid at his groin. He wet his pants. Or at least that's what Janet surmised."

"Not an uncommon reflex at time of death."

Nick reflected quietly for a moment. "Jordan used to talk about his brother-in-law's weak bladder. Ever since childhood, anything frightened him, he'd pee in his pants. Couldn't help it."

"You think he was frightened?"

"Enough so that I asked county to bring in their forensics team. Sadler may want his team in as well."

"We'll have to act fast. It's not like this happened back in the woods someplace. Everyone on shore knows by now that something happened back there. I don't think that yellow ribbon will stop anyone from nosing around."

"Like I said earlier, what happens on the lake is Hennepin County's problem. They'll keep a watchful eye. You're right, the last thing we need is some curious snowmobiler ignoring the tape and going in for a look-see."

The drive to Excelsior took only a minute at sixty miles an hour. During the brief ride, Dan reflected on the boat ride with Jason and his mother months earlier when the lake was blue and the shoreline a lush green, dotted with colorful boat canopies. Then, Jenny seemed eager to discover why her family had been targeted, why Jason had been kidnapped. But as time passed, she became content to let it lie. It was prettier then, and life seemed much more forgiving.

The plowed road ended at the base of the short ramp leading to Water Street. "What do you make of it?" Dan asked. The Explorer rocked and lurched as the chief maneuvered through icy ruts to the top of the ramp.

"How's your time?" Nick asked.

"I'm yours. I've got my pager if anyone really needs me."

"Good. We can talk on the way to Martha's. I need to tell her in person, if you don't mind. I can't keep her waiting any longer."

Dan knew what it was to wait for the words you dreaded most to hear, the words that said someone you loved was dead. When his infant son was struck down by a runaway car, he knew there was no hope. But he didn't die instantly. During the ride in the ambulance, he had hope as his baby boy survived the first ten minutes. He remembered praying with Gale outside the emergency room—something he had never done before. He looked into her eyes and could see her anguish as she tensed and forced her faith to believe Cory would be spared. Pain, despair, hope—all three present in her gaze. That was the last time he looked into her eyes and saw anyone who resembled Gale. An instant later, two words of solace exploded their world: "I'm sorry!" That instant, their lives changed irreversibly forever.

Dan lost two loved ones that day. Today, Martha Wilson lost two loved ones. Suddenly, he felt his heart breaking again. Death was so final.

"So far, there is not a shred of evidence that Jordan Green has done anything wrong. Had you not called and asked about a green Explorer, I probably would not have made any connection at all. And I probably would have accepted his death as accidental. Mysterious, yes, but accidental."

Nick could see his voice startled Dan, dragged him back from wherever he was deep in thought. He continued. "You said an employee at Abel Foods spoke to the driver of a new green Explorer in the company parking lot on the morning of the kidnapping."

"Yes. A young man, late twenties, had a brand-new car, a red sports car, and was eager to show it off. He pulled in beside a green Ford Explorer and said good morning to the driver, hoping he had noticed the new car. When the driver of the Explorer commented on what a nice car he was driving, he asked if he was waiting for someone. The driver said he was waiting for his wife who was running late. Then he changed the subject. The young man thought he knew everyone on the night shift. You know, you work at a place for a couple of years, see the same people in the parking lot and the company lounge every day. You get to know everyone. He didn't know the driver of the Explorer.

"I had been reviewing notes from Stan Girard's interviews with his employees and came across the employee's comments. I called you to see if he had mentioned anything to you. You were Girard's first contact on the day of the kidnapping."

"If he did, I don't recall. When you called me on it, the only green Explorer I could think of, and you know there's got to be a million of them out there, was Jordan's. I thought about his persistent questions about the Poole investigation. Other than the time Jordan had an affair with a young divorcée, he had never been so focused. I got the impression that he knew more than he was telling and that he was hiding something, although I never confronted him.

"I don't have any knowledge of why he would be in Abel's parking lot the morning the truck was stolen and Jason Poole was kidnapped. His brother-in-law, Bill Wilson, had worked at Abel at one time. Jason Poole was the son of a supposedly highly paid executive with the company where both Wilson and Green were employed. Jason's mother came from money. Jordan was a kind of Sergeant Bilko. That's before your time. But he was always scheming, coming up with ways to make more money. As far-fetched as it sounded, I began to wonder if Jordan hadn't attempted to kidnap Jason for a ransom.

"I went so far as to ask the president of the local bank to check both their accounts to see if unusually large sums of money had been deposited. That was a week ago. Because my questions were unofficial, he couldn't tell me the amounts. But he did verify large deposits were made in both accounts within the last ninety days."

"Does Sadler know this?"

"No. It's all too circumstantial. And I'm still having a tough time coming to grips with it. But when Larry discovered the bodies, it made me wonder. That's when I called Gary Sadler, and he suggested I call you. That too is a bit unusual. But I know you're working with Sadler, and you're close to Jennifer and Jason Poole."

"Did Gary say in what capacity I'm working with him?" Dan asked, doubting Sadler had divulged his interest in Creighton Leonard, his real motivation for bringing him in.

"No. And I don't really care. That's between the two of you. None of my business."

"Well. I was…am…quite taken by Jason Poole. I lost a son who would have been his age. But that's another story. His kidnapping just didn't make sense. Still doesn't. We still don't have a plausible motive. It wasn't a botched attempt. He was theirs. They had him. For how long? And for what purpose? We don't know. It seems that whoever took Jason had a change of plans and released him. Or they released him earlier than they had planned."

"Unless that was their plan all along. Just borrow the kid for awhile. That's my guess. It's consistent with what I know of Jordan Green."

"How so?"

"Jordan was a schemer and not above stretching the law or breaking it. But he was also a kind man, a decent kind of guy. He's the kind that would have devised a grand scheme to kidnap a kid, like Jason, for a hefty ransom and later come to his senses and shut down the operation."

"But they got their money. The deposits?"

"Which means someone paid them."

"But who? Had it come from the Pooles, I would have discovered it. They'd have no reason to keep it quiet. Besides, Jason's mother was just too eager to find the perps. Her motivation was very real. So someone paid them. Someone paid them off."

"Well, I don't buy this international conspiracy theory. Jordan just wasn't connected that way. He was small town. Excelsior is just about as big as he could handle. And he wouldn't hurt a kid. If he did it or was involved, he didn't think Jason would be hurt."

"Someone in the company? WYCO? To make it look like an international conspiracy?"

"Not a bad place to start. I'd bet it was orchestrated from inside."

"Someone inside with pretty serious connections. The drug they gave Jason is not common up here. Or in the states, for that matter. It is common in Colombia among drug traffickers. Used in rape cases or abduction cases, where juveniles are taken from their poor families and used as prostitutes. It desensitizes the conscious mind. The victim becomes a slave, operating in a drug-induced, hypnotic state. When the drug wears off, there's no memory of what happened."

"That would fit with my thoughts on Jordan's better side. Jason wouldn't be hurt, and he wouldn't remember."

"And he probably could have been convinced he was doing it for the good of his employer?"

"That's Jordan Green."

"So they got paid once. Then what?"

"Blackmail? Jordan could do that. Perhaps they were going back to the well? Too many times. The *fish house* was payback, ending further discussion? You said they had to be pretty serious players, drug trafficking, prostitution, selling kids into slavery."

"This is all interesting conjecture. Very little facts." Dan turned to look out the window and could feel the cold of the glass next to his face. Snowdrifts were everywhere, but already most of the driveways they passed were clear, people were ready for another work week. A hardy lot, Minnesotans, the weather just didn't stop them.

He had not spoken with Jenny for several weeks. Sharon had assured him that all was well with both mother and son, who were enjoying a very successful hockey season and had little time for anything else. He missed seeing Jason. He'd call Jenny, maybe take in one of Jason's games. Possibly, Sharon would join them. Yes, Sharon. Jenny had allowed herself to get too close. That wouldn't happen again. Dan accepted that reality. Now there was Sharon—neat girl.

"So Jason reminded you of your son? That's why you got involved?" The chief's voice pulled him back to the present.

"You can say that. The combination of Jason, his mother being so vulnerable and needing help…I just wanted to help. Sadler needed help. Because Jason was safe at home, Sadler's priorities changed. He could no longer extend his resources in a way he knew he should. The complexion of the case had changed."

"You got sucked in."

"Yeah, I guess. I felt their family needed to be protected. No, preserved is more like it. Maybe this doesn't make sense, but they have something this world needs and can't find. A certain quality of life, of faith, of innocence. The Pooles are an endangered species that needs protection. Initially, I was concerned for Jason. Jason is a witness to his own kidnapping. Whoever had Jason had the power to kill him, but they didn't. They didn't because they knew he couldn't recognize them, and killing him never was in their plan. That's consistent with your Jordan Green theory."

"And now?" asked Chief Nick.

"But now Green and Wilson are dead. If this isn't an accident, it's murder. If they were killed to keep them quiet, why stop there? I'm back to my original fear: Jason is a witness. He was left alone because he couldn't remember anything. Even if he never remembers, his life, his family, are all in danger. Worse, someone now seems to be acting in haste, trying to erase any tracks."

Nick turned down a heavily wooded road, sparsely populated with mostly older homes on large lots. "She's religious," Nick said finally.

"What?"

"Jason's mother, she's religious. She attended school with my daughter. Anne has always said Jenny is different, set apart from everyone else. She's religious, has an inner strength. That's what you see. A kind of determination. Right will win out. That kind of thing. She came in a couple days after Jason was returned. Showed me the tiepin she found on her deck. She had seen a stranger on her deck while the media was taping a newscast the afternoon of Jason's abduction. I thought it might be her father's."

"She did see someone. We viewed the tapes of the newscast. The man she saw was in the gallery during the press conference. So far, it doesn't mean much." For now Dan would keep the identity of Jennifer Poole's stranger a secret. It would come out later if he were linked to Wilson and Green by anything more than employment at the same company.

"For awhile I kept a squad close by her home. Nothing full-time. Close by, just in case."

JENNY

"So you did believe her?"

"Like I said, just in case. I didn't want to see her hurt."

Nick entered a long driveway that, unlike most others, was still filled with drifted snow. At the end was an older Victorian farmhouse with lights in the windows filtered through lace curtains. A woman's face appeared on a frosted pane as the Explorer pulled alongside the house and stopped adjacent to the front porch. It was Martha, an attractive woman in her "forties." She reappeared at the front door, pulling back the lace curtain from the door's large oval glass panel before opening it and allowing Nick and Dan to step inside.

"Chief Carlson? When I saw the headlights, I thought it might be Jordan and Bill."

Nick didn't speak immediately but waited for the door to close behind them. Dan sensed the tension in the air, and instinct told him Martha was expecting the worst. Nick and Dan stepped through the door. Then Dan and Martha heard the words they both most dreaded to hear: "I'm sorry, Martha! I'm really sorry!"

Chapter 70

Even though traffic was light heading into town, it was unbearably slow as moist exhaust from slow moving cars condensed on the roadways, forming a thin sheet of treacherous and invisible black ice, something to which Dan was still unaccustomed.

Turning south on Interstate 494, he reached for his cell phone and dialed Gary Sadler's direct line, and a dozen car lengths later, Sadler answered.

"WYCO's chief of security and his brother-in-law are both dead," said Dan after a brief hello.

"That's supposed to mean something to me?" questioned Sadler, obviously forced to divert his thoughts away from the project at hand.

"Interesting coincidence. Both were on the fringe of the Poole kidnapping. Now they're dead, asphyxiated, and frozen stiff. Looks like an accident. But somehow, that's too convenient. Forensics, I'm sure, will discover it was murder. Look, we need to talk."

"You're right. We need to talk. This may be the break we need. If you're right, things seem to be popping with greater frequency. Someone's worried."

"I know. That's what concerns me. The Pooles are right in the middle of this. Look, we know they've moved higher on someone's hit list. I need to know you've got them covered. You do, don't you?"

For a moment, there was silence on the other end of the line. Dan thought his cell phone had gone dead. "Like you said, Dan. We need to talk. My place or yours?"

JENNY

"Yours. Tomorrow."

"I'll be here," said Sadler, as Dan's car passed through a transmission dead spot, and his phone died.

Several car lengths farther down the interstate, Dan's cell phone was active again. He dialed the Poole's residence. Christian answered, "Hello."

"Christian Poole?" inquired Dan.

"It is. Who wants to know?" asserted Chris.

"Chris, this is Dan Sheridan. And I'm sorry to say we have yet to meet."

"As am I. I recall you came for dinner when…late August, September, but I couldn't get away from work. Sorry about that. What can I do for you? Jenny's not home."

"Oh? Well, no matter. How's Jason? Everything fine?" Dan asked awkwardly.

"Oh, he's fine. He and I are about to head to the airport to pick up Jenny. She's been away on business. The flight's been delayed." Chris hesitated, then asked finally, "You have reason for concern?" Maybe there was something Jenny had not told him.

"Not really. But there are some facts in the case that have surfaced. Things that you should be aware of. Could the three of us get together this week?"

"I'm in all week. Jenny should be too. This was her one big seasonal trip. I don't know her schedule, but she'd probably want to do dinner here."

"Not necessary."

"Probably not. But I know Jenny. Can we get back to you?"

"Fine. Jenny has my number. Just call and leave word. Now some advice: if her plane is coming in anytime soon, you'd better start now. Roads are a mess."

"Thanks. We're on our way. We'll get back to you."

Chapter 71

Dan's talk with Gary Sadler the next day did not go as well as hoped. He suspected Sadler knew more than he was willing to share or could share. Yet, Dan understood the need-to-know policy to maintain secrecy on sensitive issues. *Not enough*, he thought. He needed to know everything. How else could he adequately protect the Pooles. Nonetheless, he came away with more information than he had before—information he intended to share with Jenny and Chris.

His mind slipped back to last September as he turned onto the long lane that would bring him to Jenny's door. It seemed like a lifetime had passed since he had last been in Jenny's home. Then he had left dripping wet, both disappointed and grateful that the evening had ended before their emotions had gotten out of hand.

Then Jason's abduction had led only to suspicions. Tonight, those suspicions would take on a new dimension. It was time for Jenny and Chris to know the truth about Creighton Leonard, and to understand their real danger. He would do this despite Sadler's caution not to say too much. Sadler needed to put closure on the incident that had fueled his work for twenty years: the cause of his nephew's death and his adversarial relations with Creighton Leonard. For the first time, the usually cool Creighton was knee-jerking to events that could bring about his downfall. He was, after all, capable of making mistakes. Sadler welcomed the change and now sought convincing evidence. To get it, Creighton must be provoked more now than ever. Dan had agreed.

JENNY

Jason greeted Dan with a smile. The table was set and waiting with a steaming bowl of spaghetti noodles. Chris opened a fresh bottle of merlot, filling the glasses before sitting down. Dan recognized the label and felt a rush of memories. Jenny followed with the meat sauce. He seemed to notice a private smile grace Jenny's face for an instant before she spoke.

"Chris will return thanks," Jenny said and closed her eyes. Dan followed suit—when in Rome. Chief Nick had said she was "religious." In their family setting, it was not uncomfortable. But he didn't know if grace was for Jason's training or for his.

At the "amen," Jenny spoke again, "Sorry for the rush. As you might guess, Jason has hockey."

"It's a scrimmage," added Jason. "Can you come to watch?" he asked Dan.

Dan felt the pressure when all eyes turned his direction. "I'm sorry, Jason. I have some things to discuss with your mom and dad."

"Maybe he can attend one of your playoff games at the Bloomington Arena," Jenny suggested. "Could you break away? You'd be close by," she said, nodding to Dan.

"I'll check my calendar," he answered, hoping to end the discussion. Since his evening dunking with Jenny, Jenny had distanced herself. Dan understood that. He didn't think it wise to reconnect. Sharon had warned him that Chris could be more sensitive to his presence than appeared on the surface.

"It's about me, isn't it?" asked Jason.

Dan glanced at Jenny and got an approving nod.

"Yes. Some of what we need to discuss is. You know, we never would have met had it not been for you. I need to update your mom and dad on what's going on with the case. Okay with you, Jason?"

Jason nodded.

"How about it, Jason? Do you remember anything more? Any new information could be helpful."

"Nothing. I don't think about it much anymore. Like it never really happened." Jason admitted. "Since this is about me, can I hear what's going on?" he added.

"You could, young man, if you didn't have hockey," interjected his mother. "We'll fill you in later. Now it's time to be off."

Jenny turned to look at her husband, then apologetically, to Dan. "I'll drive Jason. Should be back in about twenty minutes. One of the moms will bring him home after practice." Excusing herself, she disappeared into the foyer.

Jason gulped down a glass of milk before scurrying after his mother, already backing the car out of the garage.

"More wine?" offered Chris, listening as the garage door closed. Not waiting for Dan to answer, he refreshed Dan's glass. "I don't know that I have really thanked you for helping Jenny and Jason through this. So, officially, thanks. I really do mean that." Then followed a litany of gratitude, seemingly rehearsed long ago and delivered at last.

"Now having said that, if you're no closer to who did it, just why are you here?" asked Chris.

There was an edge to his voice that had not been there when Jenny was present. Sharon had been correct. Dan understood. "Because," he answered, "while we're no closer to the actual perpetrators, events have occurred that you need to be aware of." Raising his glass, Dan sipped his wine and watched Chris relax slightly. "But there's more. My friend Gary Sadler at the FBI has asked me to solicit your help. He needs more evidence. And it seems Jenny is the person who can get what we need, what he needs."

"I see," said Chris. "That's what Jenny keeps insisting. Jenny and I don't have many secrets. She really does share everything with me." Again, Dan thought back to the dinner and the evening Chris had missed and wondered what all had been shared. Chris continued, "My concern has always been Jason's well-being. The fact that he was at home and safe seemed sufficient. I'm afraid I've not taken all that Jenny has said too seriously. I deal in facts. Here, there aren't many, mostly conjecture, much is circumstantial. You know, I just can't accept this conspiracy theory. And now this thing with Jennifer Stewart...It just can't be happening to us."

JENNY

"What do you know about Jennifer Stewart?" quizzed Dan.

"Only what Jenny has told me. She had been employed for a short time at WYCO. Then she disappeared. Jenny had a conversation with Jennifer's brother. He believes his sister was murdered because she had seen something or someone in the company conference center. I don't know. I just have trouble believing it all."

"You don't see any facts there? We do have the body of one would-be assassin."

"Or rapist. Isn't that what the local police believe? I'd say it depends on your point of view, doesn't it?"

"More than a point of view," came Dan's retort. "We have evidence to support the notion that he was a hired assassin."

"Evidence?"

"The weapon, a garrote, the tool of an assassin. A trained assassin."

"Or a killer who's seen one too many movies?" Chris added.

"Yes, or even a serial killer."

"My point exactly." Chris smiled.

"We've traced him to the CIA where he seems to have been trained, operating in deep cover early in his career and later dismissed as a rogue but still used occasionally."

"Now this is interesting. You can't be serious. Does Jenny know?"

"Very serious, but we can't find his file. Officially, he doesn't exist. And I've not told Jenny."

"And how can all this involve Jenny and WYCO?"

"Not WYCO per se. Creighton Leonard. Currently he is WYCO."

Chris swirled his wine. "Before you go any further, you need to know something. I may have to excuse myself from this discussion. You see, I may soon have to defend against what you are about to allege. I'm WYCO's next chief counsel. I would certainly be involved in their defense should your investigation lead to charges. Didn't Jenny tell you? She's known for weeks."

"No. But I've not spoken to her in weeks."

"Furthermore. If your request for Jenny's help involves gaining evidence against my client, that would be deemed a conflict of interest. Would it not?"

"Now that does depend on one's point of view. Don't you think?" Chris sipped at his wine and glared at Dan. Dan continued, "You're the attorney. Who's hiring you? The corporation or the person?"

"The corporation. But like you said, Creighton is the corporation."

"We're talking about your wife and family here. Don't you want to know the truth?"

"Of course, I want to know the truth. Of course, I'm concerned. But there's a lot at stake here. My becoming partner depends on this account. It's what Jenny and I have been working for. It's why she served and waited tables and sacrificed so that I could get my degree and a partnership in a reputable law firm. That's suddenly all on the line here."

"And your responsibility to the shareholders? Does that carry any weight?"

"The Leonards own most of the company. They have control. They are the shareholders that concern me now."

"But they remain two separate people. I've checked the records. Virginia Leonard really owns control. Don't you think she wants the truth? They don't even live together."

"But destroy her company, which this could certainly do? Destroy her husband? Never. Regardless of how she feels about him, she's not that kind of person. Anyway, we've no cause to believe their relationship is not good."

"No. But you must admit it seems a strange relationship. From all I know about her, she's the kind of person that would want the truth. The truth to save her company, to save her husband. If need be, from himself."

Neither heard the garage door open again, then close. Jenny entered the foyer and hung her coat in the closet. "My, sounds pretty serious," she said as she stepped into the room.

"Jenny, you'd better come in and sit down. I believe Dan has information we need to consider. He needs our help. And we need his."

"What's this, *our* help?" she asked, emphasizing *our*. She resumed her place at the table, sensing Dan must have made a breakthrough with her stubborn husband. "I guess I haven't been a very good spy lately. Hardly anyone remembers Jennifer Stewart, and there's no record of anything out of the ordinary taking place in the conference center. Also, the center's log during that period has conveniently disappeared." Her words carried frustration and brought a questioning look from Dan.

"Now there's more. Have you listened to the news lately?" Jenny and Chris looked at each other, both puzzled. Dan enlightened them. "Two bodies were discovered yesterday in a fish house on Lake Minnetonka. Both worked for WYCO. Both have some association with events surrounding Jason's abduction. It is more than coincidence. Jenny, you should know them both."

"It's true then? Jordan Green and Bill Wilson? Sharon told me. Talk at work. I thought it was just rumor. You know I've been traveling."

Chris suddenly looked both puzzled and very much concerned. This was all news to him. He turned to face Jenny. "Why didn't you tell me?"

"Like I said, I thought it was only a rumor. The two have taken long weekends before to go fishing. Half the plant does that this time of the year. The same rumor said it was accidental, carbon monoxide from the heater." Jenny looked at Dan for confirmation.

"It was that," he agreed.

"But you don't think it was an accident?" Jenny asked.

"No. I was there with the coroner and the forensics team. The police chief called me in. I've never been in a *fish house*, but I have done some serious fishing. It just didn't look right. Something was wrong. The place was a mess, especially the tackle box. Not what you'd expect from two seasoned fishermen. It looked to me like a struggle took place, and the mess was cleaned up later. There will be blood work on both bodies. Something was used to knock them out before they were gassed. That's my guess. With the heat turned off, it wouldn't take long for them to die and freeze solid. What was the wind chill? Sixty, seventy below zero. The chief suspects something too."

"Nick Carlson? He was a good friend of Green."

"Yes. Nevertheless, he believes Green was capable of a kidnapping if enough money were involved. Or, if, in some weird way, he was led to believe it would help his employer. His job was important to him, a corporate cop. Carlson said Green possessed a warped sense of responsibility.

"Also, Green's car was seen in the parking lot of Abel Food the morning of the abduction. He had no reason to be there. And one of the men captured on Abel's security cameras resembled Bill Wilson. A woman worker who had come off duty can probably make a positive ID. We're looking for a recent photo of Bill. There are none."

"Ask Sharon for a company directory. It's not the most current, but it's updated every couple of years, and Bill's picture would be there."

"Thanks. I will. It was only a matter of time before enough evidence would surface to implicate them both in some way to the disappearance of the truck used in the kidnapping. Once arrested, they would have told all and most certainly implicated someone very high up at WYCO."

"As was the case with Jennifer Stewart?" asked Chris.

"Just like Jennifer Stewart," confirmed Dan as he eyed Chris, now sure that he had Chris's full attention. "We believe her assumptions were correct. Jason's abduction was a case of mistaken identity. Someone mistook Jenny Poole for Jennifer Stewart, and the abduction of her son, in reality, was an attempt to get to her, intended as a warning. By the way, her suitcase was just found near a preserve in a northern suburb. Andover, I believe. Kids on a snowmobile discovered it. No body has been found yet. But her brother has identified the case. It was hers. She must have been close by at one time. Probably still is, but I doubt there'd be much left of her by now. The place is nothing but brambles and bog. It was a late fall, the temperature mild…animals, who knows what."

Jenny shuddered at his words.

"Then there is the supposed suicide of Senator Malovich." Dan looked at Chris. "You're aware of his efforts in the Senate to pass the LAIPT bill to the overwhelming benefit of WYCO." Chris nodded. "You're also aware of the Senate's ethics probe into the senator's personal sexual misconduct."

Now Chris did respond, "That has nothing to do with WYCO."

"Not on the surface. But evidence was mounting to indict Malovich in the assassination of a male prostitute, an acquaintance, a known companion of the senator."

"Again, nothing to do with WYCO," defended Chris.

"But the prostitute had strong links to an international cartel whose supposed purpose is to exploit world leaders, political and business, through sex, pornography, drugs, you name it. More than once, we have seen a thread linking this unnamed cartel and Random Enterprises, a money conduit under the control of your Creighton Leonard. It's been used to discreetly funnel money to groups, organizations, and individuals to further Creighton's insatiable appetite for power and wealth. Coincidentally, the would-be assassin is also linked to the same cartel."

"How so?" asked Chris.

"Many of the prostitutes come from third-world countries. Many are orphans or come from very poor families."

"Children sold into slavery?" asked Jenny.

"In some cases. But often, the families may actually believe they are acting for the good of the child. They are promised an education, food, housing, money. That's more than most of the families could ever provide for themselves."

"But prostitution?" questioned Jenny.

Dan shrugged his shoulders. "Take the case of the Stewart girl's would-be assassin. He was well-educated, a degree in animal husbandry from UCLA. But then, he was probably unusually bright. Nonetheless, he was born in Ecuador. His parents were killed in an earthquake. He survived and was taken in by relatives. But they had nothing for themselves. A man from the city, probably Quito, came to them and promised to look after the boy. Eventually, he came to the US. His college was funded by Random Enterprises."

"And you have proof of all this? Or is this just mere conjecture?" asked Chris.

"As I said, we don't have the complete file on our assassin. Even Sadler has been stonewalled on that account. Don't know why, but that's the case.

"Sadler has years of information, but still not enough proof to directly implicate Creighton. That's why we need Jenny's help and yours, Chris.

"What Jennifer Stewart saw or thought she saw is as close as we've come to proving any association with Creighton. Now we want to put the pressure on him. For the first time, he seems to be acting in haste."

"And get my wife killed?" exploded Chris.

"She will be protected," answered Dan calmly.

"I hope better than that male prostitute. He had to have been offered the same kind of protection. You said he was a star witness," reminded Chris. Dan stirred uneasily in his chair and finally turned to Jenny.

"Coffee anyone while we discuss my fate?" she offered, as though reading his mind. Not waiting for an answer, she smiled a resigned smile and walked to the kitchen. Shrinking at the truth of Jenny's words and not liking the sound, Chris shook his head in concerned frustration.

Chapter 72

Working late on a draft of the corporate budget for the new year, JB was at last paging through files and memoranda left on his desk by his secretary earlier in the day. Halfway into the pile, a handwritten note brought a cold sweat to his brow. He couldn't believe his eyes. *Police Chief, Nicholas Carlson of the Lake Minnetonka Police called to confirm that the bodies of Jordan Green and Bill Wilson were found in a fish house on Lake Minnetonka. Their cause of death: asphyxiation.*

He hit his intercom button and waited. When there was no answer, he looked at his watch. It read 6:12 p.m. Kathleen would have gone long ago. Green and Wilson? These were his people. Why hadn't he been told? A slow rage surged through him. Or was it fear? He read the memo through again.

He stood, plucked his coat from the rack behind him, threw it on, grabbed the memo, and headed out his office door. The secretarial station was empty, as was the desk in the reception area. To the left most of the executive offices were dark; only an occasional light streamed into the wide corridor. To his right, Creighton's office door was closed; a small red light at the side of the double door suggested Creighton did not want to be disturbed. It also meant he was still in the building.

Clutching the memo, he walked past Kathleen's empty desk and stopped at Creighton's door, knocked lightly, and waited. When there was no response, he knocked again louder and let himself in. Creighton was at his desk, a large legal-sized brief lay open before him. He looked up at JB, motioning for him to come in and be seated. JB moved toward the guest chairs opposite Creighton as the door connecting Creighton's office with the adjacent conference room clicked shut.

JB stopped at the edge of the desk. Creighton leaned back in his chair and studied JB before speaking. "Will you sit? Please!" he requested authoritatively. Slowly, JB sank into one of the chairs and unfolded the memo clutched in his hand. "That's better," said Creighton in a friendly manner. "You don't look well."

"Did you know about this?" said JB, passing the memo across the desk to Creighton who read it slowly.

"I was told earlier today. Too bad. I understand Green was well-liked. And his brother-in-law from our food services at plant 1. A real shame. An accident, I understand. I spoke personally with the chief…Nick…?"

"Carlson," offered JB.

"Carlson," echoed Creighton. "An investigation is underway, but all indications are that the gas furnace was not vented properly. I don't see much sport in freezing to death for the joy of fishing."

"I suppose not," said JB as he stretched out his long legs, kicking over a briefcase beside Creighton's desk. Presuming it was left by whoever had exited the room as he entered, he reached over to pick it up. The initials were MA, and the company identification card, Martinez Group, Miami, Florida. When he looked up again, Creighton was studying him. JB knew the look.

Finally, "With all that is going on right now, our security is important, is it not?" tested Creighton.

"What's going on, Crey?" JB asked, hiding a growing uneasiness.

Crey smiled catlike. "Do we have a replacement for Green?"

"Of course not. This just happened. I suppose, personnel…" JB sputtered.

"They have no one," Creighton sat upright in his chair, pulling it closer to his desk to stare across at his lanky protégé. "I've taken the liberty to bring in Alverez. You know he's an expert in these kinds of matters. As of now, he's in charge of security until a permanent replacement for Green comes along." Creighton sank back into his chair, again studying JB and waited for a response.

"That may take a while, Crey."

"Good people are hard to find," admitted Creighton. "You'd better get looking. Bring in a search firm. You know better than Kohl the kind of person we need, what's really at stake here. But let it be his idea. You can do that, JB." It was not a question.

"Yes, Crey. But, like I said, it will take time."

"We'll manage. You've met Alverez's assistant. He'll be here full time beginning next week."

"*Gomez?*" guessed JB, knowing that was not his real name.

"Ricardo Burns is his legal name. We'll refer to him as Richard Burns. He won't need an office, although he will have complete access to Green's office and files. He'll be staying at my house in the guest quarters until business stabilizes."

JB knew better than to express his views. For the second time in as many months, he was seeing a sinister side of the man he once honored as his mentor. It was obvious Alverez was brought in to protect Creighton. That's what he did. It seemed equally obvious to JB that the placement of Ricardo Burns and the accidental death of the two amateurs, Green and Wilson, was less than coincidental.

After a moment of silent reflection, JB stood. Creighton did likewise. "How well do you know Jennifer Poole? More than you've let me believe," observed Creighton in his same sinister tone of voice.

"Not well," answered JB truthfully to his own chagrin.

"I want you to get to know her better, JB. Can you do that?"

"H...How?" JB sputtered. "We move in different circles. I don't—"

"You'll find a way, JB. Like we said, good people are hard to find. I'm concerned for her. As I know you are." The threat did not fall on deaf ears. *It was a threat, wasn't it? A warning?* JB perceived so and took a deep breath to hide his growing stress and to diffuse the glowing blush sweeping his face. Defensively he turned to the door.

"Talk with Lehr," said Creighton, his tone commanding. "I'd like to know any reason Ms. Poole would lay over in Santa Fe. Santa Fe, New Mexico. My parents run a gallery there. Ms. Poole paid a visit to the gallery then went on to an old mission, the home of Maria Alverez. Do you find that interesting, JB? If you didn't know already, Maria is Miguel's mother."

"I didn't know. I'm sure there's an explanation," he said defensively.

"Yes, an old friend of the family, I'm told. But see what you can learn. Good people are hard to find, JB."

JB walked slowly to the office door, exited, and quietly closed it behind him. The real reason for Miguel Alverez's presence now all too apparent.

Chapter 73

"So what kind of evidence are you talking about? What do you need to know?" asked Jenny as she entered the room carrying a tray with coffee and dessert; on her face, a look of renewed determination.

"Even more important than what we may learn and gain as evidence is forcing Creighton's hand, compel him to act out of fear, do something that could expose him. We need him to believe that you could expose him. But I'll explain that later."

Jenny began to place the tray on the dining table but changed her mind and motioned for Chris and Dan to follow her into the living room. Chris had previously prepared a set of dry wood. "Match?" he asked. "When you don't smoke, you can never find the matches." Finally, he went to the kitchen and returned with a box of old-style farmer matches. The dry kindling quickly ignited, and Creighton Leonard again became their focus.

"Creighton is never personally involved, or so it would seem. We need to tie him to the extortion, and that won't be easy. His victims seem to be willing participants. Proof could be in a collection of pornographic books, videos, something that he may keep close by. The kind of proof Jenny Stewart may have seen."

"You've been following him for years, and you have no evidence of that? Come on," said Chris derisively.

"Not me, it's Sadler at the FBI. It does seem obvious, but he's dealing with very influential people in very high places. No one is willing to come forward. You could call it a brotherhood of sorts. Creighton's being protected."

"Okay, what do we do?" asked Jenny. "I'm not coming up with anything. Other than what you've told us, there's nothing I've been able to discover remotely associating him with any kind of illicit behavior. I've asked questions. I've inspected the conference center…I've even snooped in his house and almost got caught."

"No one said it would be a cakewalk. Sadler is the best of the best. Had there been sufficient evidence to nail him, he'd be in prison, and maybe half of Washington with him, for all anyone knows."

"So what are you saying? What do you want from us?" There was an edge to Chris's voice.

"Sadler has never felt so close. He's…Creighton is acting nervous, like someone way out on the edge."

"So we push him off?" Jenny asked matter-of-factly.

"Yes. We push. That is, you push." Dan looked at Jenny, saw a sparkle in her eye, and caught a quick smile. Chris, on the other hand, put his hands to his face and shook his head in disbelief. This just couldn't be happening to his family—it couldn't.

"Creighton has had many victims—" began Dan.

Chris was indignant and interrupted, "And you'd like Jenny's name to the list? Is that it?"

"That won't happen," Dan said forcefully, seeking a thread of hope. "The pattern we see is that only those who are capable of directly implicating Creighton and bringing him down become his victims. It's like a game to him. He doesn't need more power or money. But he needs to win. It's a cat-and-mouse thing. He toys with everyone. The world is full of his toys. All who associate with him, even many who don't, are his playthings—his house of toys. All but a few, like his wife Virginia."

"To the point," insisted Chris.

"Creighton is very clever. And we know he's not threatened by accusation alone. In fact, he seems to thrive on controversy. That's all part of the game. But when he knows he's about to be had, he goes for the kill. Remember, he will not lose. It's against his very being. And when he's about to become the loser, he does away with the winner if you'd care to call his victims winners. I mean, most have already been victimized by him in some way."

"You're saying he enjoys living at the edge of exposure," offered Chris. Dan nodded agreement. Jenny simply listened, holding her coffee cup in both hands as though warming away some chill.

"That's where Creighton is most vulnerable. When everything is on the line."

"And you want me as bait," guessed Jenny accurately.

"Yes, that's pretty much it. Currently though, you're not a big enough threat. You simply don't know enough. But believe me, you are one of his toys, and one that may help him get at his wife Virginia, although that feature of his character seems less defined. He loves his wife and has been true to her. But you and Virginia share much in common. Or so I've been informed. And no matter how you look at it, as far as WYCO is concerned, Virginia Leonard seems to be in the driver's seat, a fact not totally lost on Creighton. You may be a very special toy because of Virginia's attachment to your virtuous character. You're protected for now but vulnerable when the time is right. Should his play with you move to the next level, he may see you as a way to strike at Virginia when he is incapable of attacking Virginia directly."

"You make it sound so clinical."

"Not clinical, simply predictable. He knows that to be true of you too. There are certain choices your moral character simply will not allow. That makes you predictable."

Deep in thought, Chris knelt at the fire, added some wood, and pushed it around with an iron until it crackled with fresh intensity. "Where do we push?" he asked without looking up.

"Well, we know he lives alone," began Dan as he looked at Jenny, who nodded in confirmation.

"When Virginia is in town, she stays at the house, but her life is really in Kentucky. That's where her family is from. Creighton does a lot of entertaining. Who knows, maybe he's lonely. He's known to have frequent houseguests. That maybe more rumor than fact. He's mysterious, and people like that seem to spawn lots of rumors. Anyway, who knows who's at the house with him when Virginia is away?"

Chris turned admiringly and looked at his strong-spirited wife. Somewhere in his mind, a light sparked on. Jenny had been right all along. He had simply blocked out reality; his law firm partnership clouded the real issues.

"Anyway of finding out who his guests are? Get a guest list?" asked Dan.

"Creighton has a staff assistant. Actually, his lapdog. The man on the deck, remember." Chris gave her a questioning look. She smiled back.

"Yes, Barons, wasn't it? You were going to confront him. You've never mentioned what happened," inquired Dan.

"I confronted him. He denied being there. Actually, he denied that the tiepin was his." Jenny smiled as she recalled teasing him with her sexuality. She had not told Chris. "I don't believe him," she added. "I think he's embarrassed because he has a crush on me. He has since our high school days."

"Can he be of help in this? Will he help? Can you get close to him? Get his cooperation?" pressed Dan.

Jenny smiled again; her mind churning. "That might be fun," she said. "I think I can." Chris didn't like the sound of that but didn't say anything. "What else?" she asked.

"We don't know the degree to which he entertains his other guests, those whose weaknesses he can exploit. It's a big house. If he is the consummate host, I'd suspect it has all sorts of attractions, a kind of Playboy mansion. We know his guests come from all over the world. I suspect the place is self-sustaining. Meaning, I doubt that he sends a runner to the local video store even for special needs if he's into the kind of movies Jennifer Stewart discovered being filmed. Or to the local brothel," he added with a grin.

JENNY

"I doubt he does," said Jenny. "I've seen some of his collection…films. No titles. The night of the company party, I went there to gather evidence. Well, what did I know? Didn't find anything but some nice pieces of art. Creighton came in, discovered me, and seemed satisfied when I told him I was calling home. He told me he collects first editions, books, films. What I saw was hidden in the library walls. Some kind of secret storage."

"You didn't tell me about that," rebuked Chris. Jenny shrugged, thinking she had; he just wasn't listening.

"The Leonards all seem to have exquisite taste when it comes to art."

"What do you mean?" questioned Dan. From the look in Chris's eyes, he too wanted an answer.

"Now you're supposed to know more about Creighton Leonard than I do. Like where's he from? What was his childhood?" Jenny asked smugly, teasing.

"He graduated from Harvard Business School with honors. Before that, he attended some posh junior college, a boarding school. Lived with an aunt, I understand." Dan smiled. Sadler had briefed him.

"I said his childhood," reminded Jenny.

"According to Sadler, his parents live in New Mexico."

"Santa Fe, where they own and operate the Leonards' Gallery." Dan nodded confirmation. Jenny continued, "I was just there. I've never seen such a beautiful and diverse collection of art. One piece was of a wolf and a young boy. It seems the Leonards like wolves. This piece was priceless and created by a friend of the family. A Miguel Alverez. His daughter works at the gallery. His mother runs a little mission south of the city. I spent the night there as her guest." Jenny spoke as though she were speaking directly to Chris. She had told him some details, but not all.

Suddenly, she realized she had said more than she should; she had promised Maria that her story was safe with her. It was time to shut up.

"And the drawing you said was done by a budding artist?" asked Chris.

"The granddaughter of Maria Alverez, the person I went to Santa Fe to meet. The friend of Leah Holcomb. You remember? We met her at my parents' holiday party."

"Jenny, I don't see the relevance of what you're saying. Where does she fit in?" Chris shook his head. "You'd be a poor witness. You don't remember what you've told me and what you haven't, do you?" he asked.

Jenny smiled and shrugged again, glancing alternately at both Chris and Dan, not wanting the discussion to go any further. Finally, she added, "I guess it started with the different renderings of wolves. I bet the bronze wolf in Creighton Leonard's library is the work of Maria's son, Miguel."

"El Lobo, the Wolf," said Dan in reflection.

"What did you say?" quizzed Jenny, now excited.

"El Lobo is the wolf," answered Dan. "It's nothing. I was reminded of something years ago. We were watching the drug trade in South America. A power struggle ensued. There were assassinations. People there in the area were steeped in superstition and referred to some mythical creature, a protector of sorts, El Lobo, the cunning wolf. Interesting," he mused.

"Very," agreed Jennifer before changing the subject. "If I can get into the house again, then what?"

"For starters, find his secret room, the place where he may hide his evidence, whatever it is he holds over the heads of his guests. Then collect what you can."

"Am I missing something here?" Jenny asked finally. "If he's blackmailing people, influential people, heads of state, whatever. Why doesn't someone just finish him?"

"Probably a couple of reasons. One, they must assume that he has protected himself against an untimely death, a letter someplace, instructions left with a friend, something that would be made public should he suddenly disappear. Second, he is a respected insider.

JENNY

He probably has never actually threatened any of his so-called subjects, the people on his list, his guest list. The fact that he could is a given. But the fact that he has never pushed his knowledge too far has earned him respect. He is an able provider of certain services and trusted like an old friend. That's the real source of his power. For his service, he is granted certain favors."

"He's a pimp?" qualified Chris to his own amazement.

"To the nth degree. What he does isn't new, and it has propelled him to untold power and success. And when he's gone, someone will replace him. It won't stop now. This has been going on since Adam and Eve. We're probably just seeing the tip of an iceberg."

"So why the interest now? If we can't make a difference."

"Because innocent people are getting killed. That's what we can stop. The killing."

"I think I know how to get it," Jenny said at last, adding, "where to begin." The other four eyes turned to her.

"So much for my being made partner," Chris said in exasperation, shaking his head.

"Look at it this way," said Dan. "We're right. I know we are. I'd gamble that once Creighton is stopped, all the shareholders will be so pleased, particularly Virginia, that you could write your own ticket with the company. You'll be the hero. You and Jenny."

"And if you're wrong, that ticket could be to another world. It would cost the firm their most profitable client. And me, my job… career. They've been trying for years to get WYCO as a client."

Jenny ignored Chris. "Like I said, I know where to begin."

Chris knew it was for real. A new scheme was in play.

Chapter 74

D' Ward found the business card in her kitchen desk and handed it to Jenny, who stood while enjoying the last of her mother's gourmet coffee. Then placing her cup on the table and the business card in her purse, she followed her mother through the kitchen to the front foyer.

"Who's giving the party?" D' asked. "Are you celebrating Chris's becoming partner?" She knew of the pending assignment and possible promotion.

"Hardly. Not yet, anyway. At your Christmas party, I thought I recognized one of the car parkers. Thought I'd check it out. May have some work for the catering service that employed them. That's all. You know…through the company, that sort of thing." Jenny saw no reason to share the whole truth with her mother. She'd only worry.

"You can keep the card. I've got more, several, actually. Thought I'd spread their name about. They were a nice group of kids." D' stretched her back and looked into the morning sky listening to a pair of crimson cardinals greeting them from a nearby tree.

"Mother, the hostesses were older than me."

"I know. Still a delightful group of kids. That's what you'll always be, you know."

Jenny gave her mother a hug and a peck on the cheek. "Yes, I suppose. Forever young," she said and walked to her car in the drive. Having been gone for nearly two weeks meant work had piled up at the office. Sharon, in her efficiency, had dispensed with much of it

JENNY

but still expected Jenny to make an appearance to finalize contracts awaiting her signature.

Approaching Excelsior, en route to her office, she left the highway and took the bridge route into Excelsior. The unseasonably warm weather excited her. Knowing several weeks of winter lay ahead, this single warm cloudless day brought thoughts of spring and adventure.

Water Street abutted Lake Street, where she pulled to the curb, stopped her engine, rolled down her windows, and breathed in the fresh air; her hands rested on the steering wheel. Kiddy corner was where the delivery vans had parked as she passed behind them with Jason, crossing into the parking lot to enter Milly's that fateful day in August. She had not been to Milly's or even to the area since.

Come to think of it, after that day, she had not had much time for *Little Red*, her last real outing, her speedy tour of the lower lake the evening Dan Sheridan had come for dinner. She smiled at the thought of pulling Dan into the water. What would she have done with one more glass of wine? She shook her head in renewed disgust with herself for losing self-control and for getting carried away. Dan could have taken advantage of her that night if he weren't so honorable! *Thank God.*

Across the street was the entrance ramp to the frozen surface of Lake Minnetonka, where cars and 4 × 4s left the city street for the icy highway leading to area *fish houses*. Today the ice was quiet and barren. The dock where she tied *Little Red* was snow-covered, anchored in the grip of two feet of ice.

Beyond the dock, the icy roadway ran to Big Island and points north. Her eyes followed it to the east end of the island, where, she had been told, Jordan Green and Bill Wilson had been found frozen inside their *fish house. So they had been involved; how unlikely a thought.* She recalled the day Bill had come to her office to express his concern and his personal delight that Jason had been found safe. His concern had seemed so genuine. He had dropped his hat, she recalled. Later, when she went to his office to return it, she had overheard Bill and Jordan arguing. *So genuine,* she thought. Down deep, she doubted Bill had been a willing conspirator. If Dan's assumptions were correct, Bill surely had paid the ultimate price for his unwitting involvement, leaving behind a widow and a fatherless son.

Suddenly, Old Mike appeared in the corner of her eye. She watched as he strolled his way toward the icy shore, stopping to peer through Milly's street-side window before ambling closer to the lake where he would stand and let his thoughts turn to spring.

Memories. She took a deep breath and thought back to that August morning. She dug deep, concentrating, trying to shake loose any suppressed memories. There was something else. She couldn't quite unearth it. It was something important. Buried deep, if only she could.

Out of frustration, she turned her key in the ignition, but before leaving the curb, she found the business card her mother had given her and punched the number for Party Partners. Three rings later, she was rewarded with an answer. "This is Linda. How may I help you?"

During a brief conversation with Linda, Jenny learned the red-haired woman who had greeted her at the Leonards' party and had showed her into Creighton's library was indeed the owner of Party Partners. She was "out" but expected to return momentarily. Her name was Mitzi Freeman.

She continued her cell phone conversation as she drove slowly up Water Street, past the theater and the craft shops that had replaced the thriving stores that, in the not-too-distant past, had lined the streets. Party Partners didn't office in Excelsior but in a small strip mall west of town. "Please tell Mitzi that Jennifer Poole called and that I'm on my way over. Shouldn't be more than ten minutes. I really need to speak with her." Then to pique Mitzi's interest, she added, "I'm a marketing director for WYCO toys with some potential business for her."

She hung up clueless as to what business she could possibly throw Mitzi's way, but confident her corporate position would provide something. And for that, Mitzi could help her access Creighton's library one more time.

JENNY

She located the small glass front office in a cluster of businesses in a small mall a couple miles west on County Road 19. Although she drove by it almost daily, she had never noticed it. Linda watched her approach and jumped to attention as she entered the tidy office. "You must be Jennifer Poole. We don't get many walk-ins here. You're in luck. She's in."

Linda turned and led the WYCO executive to Mitzi's well-appointed office in the rear. Mitzi smiled when Jenny entered, walked around her desk, and extended her right hand. Jenny couldn't say why, but instantly, she sensed good chemistry. Mitzi would be a good ally.

During a brief conversation, they learned they had many friends in common, a feature of living in an area from which people seldom moved, or if they did, eventually returned. Not the least of these was JB Barons. He had been Mitzi's initial contact and source of employment at the Leonards' numerous gigs.

Saying as little as she could, Jenny explained her purpose for stopping and was ready for Mitzi's questions. "I think I've got this clear. You want to be one of my hostesses at a party thrown by your employer Creighton Leonard? I'm not going to ask why, but you know I'm dying of curiosity." Her brown eyes sparkled with interest and the hope that Jenny would confide in her, but she didn't push it. Raising her eyebrows while shaking her head in the negative, Mitzi asked, "I don't suppose you could go to Mr. Leonard and just ask him?" Even as she asked, she knew the answer.

"No. Sorry. In fact, he can't know it's me. You might say it's a little surprise I've got planned for him."

"Are you two close? Birthday, prank, or…?"

"Nice try. It's the *or* answer. In time, he'll learn it's me, but for now, he just can't know. Neither can JB. Will you promise to keep my secret?"

"Till death," said the smiling redhead.

The word *death* startled Jenny. She had not considered the possibility that she could be placing Mitzi in harm's way. She looked at

Mitzi. *No, Mitzi can take care of herself.* Jenny felt sure of that. As for the surprise, she hoped Creighton would be mortified. That was the plan, wasn't it? She'd motivate him into action if she could convince him she had gathered enough evidence to expose him. A sample of his prized collection of films for starters. She only needed to grab the right one. If she could find them. That was the problem. But she'd worry about that once inside. And she'd reveal her plan to Chris and Dan at the right time and get Dan's assurance that Sadler was ready and able to provide protection.

She doubted Creighton would have time for hosting dignitaries or any of his sordid friends at his home in the immediate future because of the congressional hearings that could require his attendance. That was fine with her. She'd have more time to plan. Time was on her side. And JB would likely know Creighton's social calendar. She smiled as she considered JB's crush on her and how she might encourage him to share it with her. What luck! He'd prove useful after all.

"It's our secret, right?" stressed Jenny as she turned to leave.

"It is that, honey. It truly is. Not a soul…promise," agreed Mitzi.

They also agreed to keep in close touch, one alerting the other when a party might be scheduled, a party sufficiently large for Jenny to attend without being noticed. She'd become invisible as one of several hostess staff. Smiling at the thought of intrigue, she stepped from the elevator at her third-floor office level, pleased with the way her plan was developing. She had not waitressed three years for nothing.

"Welcome back," Mildred Knowles greeted Jenny when she passed through the reception area. "You were on the West Coast?" she asked. "Hope you had better weather than we did, cold as all get-out. But then helps us better enjoy a day like this, doesn't it? You know…the contrast. Gorgeous out there today, isn't it?" Jenny paused and reached over the small desk partition to collect call slips. Mildred continued, "You heard about Green and Wilson. Lordy, a sad affair. You just never know, do you? It's just…so hard to believe when tragedy strikes close to home. Know what I mean."

JENNY

Jenny continued to her office.

"JB called for you...And these need your signature first thing. The world is waiting," said Sharon in her usual manner when Jenny entered. Jenny held out her arms and received a six-inch pile of manila folders.

"What'd he want?" she asked, continuing to her adjoining office.

"He said it was both personal and business. Mumbled something about restoring old friendships. I didn't press him. Should I have?"

"No. It's just...Timing is always interesting. I was going to call him today, that's all. By the way, know of any costume shops?"

The curious inquiry brought Sharon from her desk into the doorway.

"I want a waitress outfit. You know, something sexy, sleazy, short, black, white frilly apron. I'd rather not buy one."

"You've got a second job? Spend too much in Old Santa Fe? A little moonlighting?"

"Something like that," she teased. "Would you see what you can find?"

"Sure thing." Sharon's voice faded as she ran to her desk to answer the phone. A few seconds later, Jenny's intercom squawked. "It's JB calling you again."

Jenny picked up her phone. "This is Jenny," she said politely.

"JB here," said the resonant voice on the other end. "I've had you on my mind. You know, for being old friends, we don't see much of each other...and I was..." Even as he spoke, he blushed for being so forward.

"It's old friends, is it?" chided Jenny.

"Presumptuous of me. I'm sorry. Can I begin over?"

"You may," answered Jenny with a smile, knowing she was turning him on. *Where had she placed his tiepin?* She wondered as he began again.

"Actually, since you came to my office, I've wanted to see you again. Businesslike and proper, all that," he stammered and changed the subject. "You've heard about Wilson and Green. Terrible thing. The company doesn't have a good candidate for Wilson's job in food services. His assistant...what's his name?"

"I haven't a clue," responded Jenny, now quite serious.

"Oh, I can't...At any rate, what's-his-name has indicated he wants the position. Because Creighton sometimes uses the company service, he wanted me to stop by to evaluate the guy. He's been filling in for the last couple of days. I was hoping you could help me test lunch. I need a good honest opinion. Besides, you know what it was like before...when Wilson ran the show. You'd have a better basis for comparison. How about it?"

"Sure, why not? You're coming here...what time?"

"It almost eleven now. Before noon. Say, ten minutes to noon. Okay?" He had no intentions of getting closer to Jenny just to satisfy Creighton's request he do so, but he did like the idea of getting to know her better. *Not bad duty*, he thought. Furthermore, if Creighton asked, he'd give him something factual, dreamed up if necessary, yet something that would protect Jenny. It was a curious thing Jenny visiting Maria Alverez. Old friends?

"I'll be waiting." He heard Jenny say as she hung up the phone. Feeling the warmth of the late morning sun beaming into her large window, she stood, stretched, walked to the window, and surveyed the white snow-covered lake. *Interesting coincidence, JB*, she thought.

At precisely 11:50, Sharon entered Jenny's office and announced that JB had arrived.

"Show him in, please," said Jenny. She had enough time to sweep her fingers through her hair and put on her most pleasant smile before JB entered her office.

Actually, quite handsome, she thought, approaching him from the far side of her desk. Her gaze focused on his long angular face. Then she saw it: his was the face in the rain. She was certain. His was the face that appeared in the flash of lightning and was gone. Such confirmation. It could be none other.

JENNY

"Are you all right?" JB asked, concerned. She seemed starstruck.

"It was you, wasn't it?" Her query didn't immediately register.

"I'm not sure I know what you mean, Jenny." He placed his coat over the back of a chair beside her desk.

"The day my son was kidnapped. The day of the assassination attempt on Creighton at the press conference. Later, at the news interview at my home, during the height of the storm, you were on my deck. It was you. It really was you, wasn't it?" Jenny stepped a mere two feet from him and glared upward, noting his now-crimson complexion. His mouth moved, yet no intelligible words could be heard. She had him nailed. Now he'd owe her for sure.

"Yes." The word finally escaped amidst more mumbling. "Jenny...can we please discuss this over lunch. I can explain." He pleaded with his eyes and silently prayed for time to collect his wits—if that were even possible. She had that effect on him.

Trying hard not to laugh, Jenny looked straight ahead as they rode the elevator down. After the door opened on main floor, she led the way to the large cafeteria, which had once served culinary masterpieces to the company's executives and their visiting dignitaries. That had been before the relocation, before JB, before Creighton Leonard. But the food had remained superb although less fancy. *Poor Wilson*, she thought.

They walked quickly from station to station, choosing their fare. Then, finding a table well in the back of the executive dining area, she waited as JB held her chair waiting for her to be seated. *Interesting old-fashioned custom,* she thought. After he sat down, she proclaimed, "I'm ready. I hope you are. Explain." She jabbed at her salad and waited.

"I was at the press conference. In the audience." He smiled, continuing, "Actually, as it turned out, just steps behind the shooter. Front row seat, so to speak." He continued, "Of course, I knew Jennifer Poole was to be on the platform. But I didn't know you were...I didn't know Jennifer Poole and Jennifer Ward, the girl I so vividly remembered from high school, were one and the same.

Then, when the story broke on your son's abduction, I recognized you. Jenny, I was devastated. Simply shocked and devastated. That words appropriate," he confessed truthfully. "When the networks announced the interview was to take place at your home, I simply couldn't stay away…seeing you after all these years. And under such extreme circumstances."

"So why lie to me? You denied it."

"I don't know. Embarrassment, I suppose. I must confess, you do that to me…" he mumbled self-consciously, hoping she would understand. He continued, "I arrived late. It was already beginning to rain. The front door was open, but the place appeared too packed for me to enter. I worked my way around to the back and onto your deck, just as the lights went out."

She considered his words, and for the next several minutes, neither spoke. "The tiepin," Jenny said finally. "That big expensive one that had to have cost a small fortune. It belongs to you, doesn't it?" She watched his face as he avoided eye contact.

Finally, he broke out laughing. "No, Jenny, I'd say it rightfully belongs to you. You know, finders keepers. You did find it."

"But the cost," she argued.

"A lot. Let me assure you. But the insurance company has already processed my claim."

"That's dishonest. I don't know that I could—"

"Please, Jenny. I didn't say it was mine. I mean—"

"JB," she said his name, sweetness to his ears.

"If it were mine, I'd want you to have it. Really, I would. All that you've gone through." He was right, Jenny did find it. He didn't say it was his. She didn't need to decide immediately. Then there was Chris's secretary, Nicki, and her hail-battered car.

"So how's the food?" he asked, changing the subject. Jenny smiled. "As good as ever?" he pressed. She gave two thumbs-up. "That's all I need to know for now. A good honest opinion. I recommend no changes." He knew it would all change anyway, someday, probably sooner than later if congress ratified the LAIPT agreement and the company's production moved south. Not a good move, he was beginning to think.

For the next thirty minutes, they talked on many subjects, including her western trip. She spoke of Santa Fe but said nothing of her visit to Maria Alverez's home. For his part, he could not very well indicate he knew of Jenny's visit without arousing strong suspicion, so he dropped the topic. He'd create his own report for Creighton.

Jenny, for her part, praised JB for his work in the company and expressed her admiration for his ability to associate with such celebrities as Creighton and the world's business giants. Somewhere in the conversation, JB confirmed Creighton would be kept very busy in Washington until the treaty came up for vote. He predicted that was at least four weeks away. While a date for a large social event to celebrate its passage was yet to be determined, one was planned for Creighton's residence. She'd have her opportunity in mid-April, some six weeks hence.

They chatted all the way back to Jenny's office, mostly about days spent at Minnetonka High School and the coincidence of the two working together so many years later at WYCO Toys. *Wonderful*, was JB's word for it all. Jenny smiled a bit too condescendingly.

They entered Jenny's office where he retrieved his coat, shook hands, and he left. After he disappeared from view, Jenny returned to the warming rays of her window and the still-brilliant blue sky. Below, JB exited the building, climbed into his little green sports car, and backed from the white-lined parking bay. "Well, I'll be," Jenny said suddenly, loud enough for Sharon to hear and causing her to pop her head into the office at Jenny's most rare use of profanity.

It must have been the way the sunlight struck the little green car. Or perhaps it was JB's profile behind the glass of the door. Whatever it was, she suddenly remembered the piece of information that had refused her mental purging: the green car idling across the street from Milly's. It was his car. JB had been a witness to Jason's abduction. He had watched it all from across the street in his parked car. When he left, he had passed closely by her. But why?

She jumped back to her desk quickly grabbing the telephone. Sheridan's number was set in memory. She pushed in the code for his direct line and waited. "Dan! Dan! Dan! Where are you?" she said.

Finally, she heard his familiar voice, "Sheridan."

"It's Jenny," she responded. "Isn't there something in the investigation report about a green car? Did you mention it? Or am I imagining things?" she asked excitedly.

"Jenny, slow down. Yes, it was me. After the fact, we've learned there was a green car. Seen twice. Once reported in the parking lot at Abel Foods the morning, the truck was stolen. And the one eyewitness, Mike, told me he had seen a green car. Jordan Green had such a green car. A green Ford Explorer. We know his was the car in the parking lot. The assumption is it was Green's car that was seen by Old Mike."

"No, Dan. There was a second green car. I'm sure of it. I've always had a nagging…there was something I wasn't remembering. Well, today I remembered. There was a green car parked across the street from the restaurant."

"That agrees with Old Mike's account," interjected Dan.

Jenny continued, "It was a sports car. I saw it again in the parking lot below my window just seconds ago. I'm sure it's the same only because I recognized the profile of the driver behind the closed window, my old friend JB Barons. Dan, what can this mean?" she begged. "Tell me, what does this mean! Today he admitted being on the deck, my one-armed man, as you put it. His was the face in the flash of lightning. What can it mean?"

"First. Are you sure? You're not just imagining…The car, I mean."

"Dan, I'm sure."

"Well then, his silence would say he was involved." Dan thought for moment. "Does he have a deep voice?"

"Yes. So do many men. Why do you ask?"

"When I found Jason in the restroom, I went there because of an anonymous telephone call telling me where I would find him. It was a man's voice. It was disguised. But it was undeniably a very deep voice. It could have been his. Or it could be coincidence. Do you have his voice recorded anywhere? On say, an answering machine, voice mail? If you did, we could analyze it. See if it's a match with the caller's. Even disguised, certain patterns would be the same. Enough similarities, and it's a possible match."

"I don't know…I don't think so."

"Call him, ask him something, and ask him to leave the answer on your voice mail. When he does, save it."

"Okay. So what does it mean if we can prove it was his voice?"

"Jenny, then you'll know why no harm came to Jason."

"I don't understand."

"Look! You said Jenny Stewart believed Jason's abduction was an accident."

"That's what her brother said."

"Then just assume for a moment that your friend, JB, was involved in the plot to frighten Stewart by taking Jason, whom he erroneously believed to be her son. That could place him in Excelsior that morning. Then assume he recognized you when you came out of the restaurant looking for Jason, who by this time had been grabbed."

"I'm assuming," assured Jenny.

"Now think this through. You said your Mr. Barons had a serious crush on you dating back to high school."

"Yes. I'm sure it was him who wrote love notes in my yearbook."

"Any reason to believe his feelings toward you have changed?"

"No. Not really. I sense they're probably stronger than ever."

"And I bet strong enough for him to not want to bring you harm in any way. He is probably the reason Jason was returned so quickly, unharmed. For all we know, he's still protecting you, and you don't know it. He's in position to do just that."

"Should I let him know we're on to him?"

"No. We won't know for certain until we analyze his voice patterns. Don't say anything. He might do something stupid. It could tip our hand too soon. Just record his voice."

"Okay." Jenny agreed. She was about to sign off when Dan came back, "Jenny, what is the hand we're playing here?" he quizzed, his tone serious. "You said you had a way to get into Creighton's house. I've been waiting for your call. You're supposed to keep me informed, remember. This is not a game. You could be in considerable danger. Keep me apprised, Jenny. Keep me apprised."

For the next five minutes, Jenny explained to Dan her plan to be a hostess at the next "big event." Surprisingly, he liked the idea and asked to be notified when the date was set so he could coordinate with Sadler. "Now tell your husband. You've made him a believer. Don't lose him now," he said in closing.

"I will. I will," she said then clicked her phone and pushed in the direct line code for JB Barons. He would not have had time to return yet to his office.

His voice mail answered. "JB, this is Jenny. Forgot to ask you at lunch. Could you give me the name of the caterers who will be serving at the Creighton's celebration? I may have some private work for them, a family party. I'll be out. Call my direct line and leave it on my voice mail. Thanks. Thanks too for lunch. We should do it again. Bye."

She hung up the telephone and leaned back into her chair. Dan's theory made sense. Could JB be her protector? She sat in contemplative silence for several minutes. When the phone rang, she let it go to her answering machine.

Chapter 75

Following the progress of the LAIPT bill as it worked its way through congress was easier for Jenny than most observers because of her position within the company that had helped framework the bill. However, the timing of specific passage remained largely unclear. But the controversial committee chairmanship once held by deceased Senator Malovich was now filled by a Democrat from Rhode Island, whose reports said was a school chum of Creighton Leonard. Ratification was expected by the third week of April. Jenny could not help but wonder how that particular friendship had developed. Interestingly, the new chairman was the son of a Pentecostal evangelist.

Most of her information was garnered through a growing relationship with JB, who remained eager to share his knowledge with the heartthrob of his youth. He was becoming more at ease in her presence, less tongue-tied. And while Jenny's intuition at times said there remained a passion for her, that passion seemed increasingly paternalistic and protective. After all, she was happily married, and JB remained very much the gentleman.

She had successfully taped JB's voice and had personally delivered the little cassette to Dan who in turn passed it to Sadler. The FBI analysis of the voice confirmed JB as the caller who had told Dan where to find Jason; his participation in the kidnapping, undeniable. Nonetheless, Jenny was beginning to feel remorse at having fingered him, a reality that most certainly meant arrest. Perhaps the courts would be lenient if his involvement were coerced. What did seem certain to Jenny was that JB had acted to protect her and her family.

For that reason, Sadler was content not to move on JB, preferring that first, the bigger fish, Creighton Leonard, the fish that had eluded him for years, be caught red-handed. For this, Sadler and his handpicked force were ready to move, a wholly independent action while Washington remained ignorant. There would be no leaks to startle the prize catch.

Jenny was in JB's office at Wayzata Towers when a call came from Creighton himself. At last count, LAIPT had enough votes to guarantee passage. Now, barring something unforeseen, the president could have the bill on his desk within days. JB had less than three weeks to orchestrate the celebration "Big Event" at Creighton's residence. The date was set for April 17.

Leaving JB's office, Jenny returned to plant 1 and was pleased to learn Sharon had indeed found the waitress's uniform she had requested. "Well now. Care to tell me what you've got planned?" Sharon asked as she followed Jenny to her desk where she had left the boxed uniform.

"Wish I could, really. I'm not intentionally keeping you in the dark, please know that. It's just that I'm sort of sworn to secrecy. It won't be long, and I can tell you all about it." Jenny knew Sharon suspected Dan Sheridan was in on the secret, though she never said so.

What Sharon didn't know was that it was Dan's growing fondness for her, Jenny's aide, that caused him to request Jenny not confide in Sharon. He did so for Sharon's own protection. The less she knew now, the better. He would tell her everything eventually. Maybe on their wedding day, as Sharon teased. A husband and wife should not have secrets.

"Just in time," said Jenny, opening the box to examine its contents. "You checked the size?"

"It's you. It's totally you. Should be a perfect fit."

"Why should I doubt? Thanks." Jenny closed the box and tucked it under her arm. "I'll be at home if I'm needed. Got some explaining to do. Chris."

Sharon, brimming with curiosity, smiled understandingly, and watched Jenny exit her office and head for home.

Chapter 76

Chris pushed his garage door remote as he approached his townhome. The winter's snow cover was all but gone. All that remained were piles of dirty white ice, the last vestige of winter to give way to spring.

For Chris, living on the lake with Jenny was a never-ending education. He marveled each spring that she knew instinctively the exact day when the ice would suddenly melt and disappear, allowing boats to again travel its seventeen-mile length. *Little Red* was usually one of the first boats to skim the lake's shimmering and still-frigid waters.

"Honey, I'm home," Chris yelled as he set his briefcase inside the foyer.

"In here." The voice drifted from the kitchen. What appeared to be a maid moved past the doorway, too quick for him to discern who it might be.

"What's up?" he questioned. "Someone special coming for dinner," thinking that the only possible reason for catering help. He looked at his watch, 5:45. He had been very busy of late preparing for his new role as WYCO's lead counsel, and as he moved hesitantly toward the kitchen, he wondered if he had forgotten any mention of a party.

"Is Jason home?" he asked cautiously, testing his memory.

"Nope. Susan's dropping him off later. He'll probably stay there for dinner. They've been playing all day." Chris couldn't hear anyone else. His mind raced. He must have forgotten a party, maybe a company thing. Food was being quietly prepared. That had to be it.

JENNY

Ready to be banished to the proverbial dog house because of a failing memory, Chris picked up his pace and entered the kitchen from the living room. Working at the stove was a woman in uniform, about Jenny's size, but with short pitch-black hair worn pixy style.

She wore a black servant's dress. It was short, sexy. Jenny never dressed like that. *Too bad!* he thought, Jenny also had very nice legs to show off. Standing motionless, he made his comparisons. *Not bad!* was his conclusion. Her waist was a mere handful, pulled tight by what he presumed was an apron; its tie gathered artistically into a big bow that complemented what he imagined was a very nice behind.

Suddenly, feeling awkward by his prolonged silence, he asked, "I'm sorry, I thought Mrs. Poole…my wife was in here. Her voice…"

"Yes," answered the shapely maid, keeping her back to him, continuing her work at the stove. "She'll be back soon. She has wine ready for you and asked that I keep you entertained. Would you like that?" she asked in a sensuously low voice, similar to Jenny's, but lower, definitely lower.

Chris smiled while his mind mulled what she meant by entertained.

"Hors d'oeuvres?" she asked. He had his answer.

"That would be fine," he answered politely, still wondering what he could have forgotten. Certainly not their anniversary. *Sure! Sure! Yes!* They had closed on their little townhome in April. Moved in one day in April. *Yes!* He tried to think, *Eight? Or was it nine years?* That was it. It had to be. *What a wife! How I love her,* he thought. *Always so thoughtful, so full of surprises. What a night that was.*

Just as Chris turned to leave the room, the shapely maid came toward him. In her hand was a silver tray of steaming delicacies, something stabbed with toothpicks. He recognized his favorite bacon-somethings.

"You said she'd be back shortly. Please bring them to the coffee table. I'll wait for her in the living room." Chris had not made eye contact, not wanting to appear too solicitous. Not the time for wrong impressions. Jenny would be back shortly. He didn't want to be flirtatious. He walked to the sofa and removed his suit coat.

A fire was set in the fireplace but not yet lit. He found a box of matches on the coffee table, removed one blue tipped stick, and struck it on the hearth. Dry kindling snapped into flame. When he was convinced it would remain lit, he stepped backward and seated himself on the sofa.

The bacon-somethings with crackers and various cheeses waited on the coffee table. He thought he saw the shapely server heading his way, but she disappeared suddenly out of sight somewhere behind him. Then he smelled her cologne, sensual, a bit heavy. While he considered the fragrance, he felt a gentle kiss on the base of his neck.

"What...?" he said, startled but not making a move, picturing red wine spilling over his new suit. Then he felt a wetter kiss, more aggressive, on the right side of his neck.

He reveled in his panic as he slowly turned to kneel on the sofa. First, he saw the glass of red wine. The server held it high to avoid spilling. He couldn't believe what he saw next. He looked at her with eyes like saucers and beheld Jenny's lovely smiling face."

"Is that you, Jen? Tell me it's you." Her face was beautiful, eyes heavy with makeup, eyelashes long and sensual, obviously fake. Her skin was fair with the proper amount of pink glow adorning her cheeks. Her lips were a deep burgundy red shining wet and sensual. Slowly, they formed to make a kiss that she planted tenderly on his lips.

"Got'ya," said Jenny the server as she planted another juicy kiss squarely on her husband's lips before he had time to recover.

"It is you," Chris said again, hopefully, reeling from shock. "What are you up to? What's with the outfit?"

"Oh, just a little surprise. Do you like it?"

"I certainly liked what it did...What she...you...did. Thank God, it was you...I didn't..."

"Actually, you did quite well, considering—"

"Considering what?" Chris asked, relieved he had passed the test—whatever it was.

"Considering my lusty beauty," she teased.

"So what are you doing? In that…outfit? Are we celebrating something? And please pardon me while my heart returns to normal."

She extended the glass of wine toward him, which he took without hesitation and sipped it slowly, gaining control. "Jenny, what is it that you're up to? Tell me…what are we doing?"

"I needed to know."

"What's that?"

"How convincing I am as a waitress with, what was it, four years of experience."

"Four years. And believe me, you never looked then like you do now. Thank God!"

"Thanks," she pouted. "Is that a compliment? Maybe I shouldn't ask."

"Well…Let's say…you look very…sexy? Is that an apt description?"

"Only for you, love. So how about professional?"

"Yeah, I'd add professional…"

"Good," she concluded, "I guess I'm ready."

"For what?"

"For gathering the information Dan…no, the FBI needs on our employer, Creighton Leonard."

"Dressed like that? Someone is likely to take you away. My Lord, what are you planning?"

"We need information. Right?"

"I guess. So we've been told."

"So…Dan suggested what he needs is in some secret room. Right?"

"The inference was there."

"I've been there, Chris. Or very close. I mean it's just not logical that his warehouse of artifacts, if that's what we can call it for now, is anyplace other than his library, where, if you were listening, he showed me his…some of his collectibles. Don't you see I need to get into his library? I was there once. That's where I need to be to get the evidence. So I've found a way."

"I'm listening," said Chris.

"With the treaty soon to be ratified, Creighton has planned a grand celebration at his residence. I'm going as one of the wait staff. It's perfect. I fooled you, didn't I?"

"Yes…" Chris was silent for a moment then asked, "When is this event?"

"The seventeenth."

"Jenny, the invitation came today. We're supposed to be there together."

"That's even better. You can cover for me. Run interference if need be."

"Meaning you won't appear as Jenny but as Genevieve? What's your excuse for your absence?"

Jenny didn't answer, so Chris added, "I really believe it would be best if we showed up together as Jenny and Chris." After a brief pause, he asked, "You're determined, aren't you?" Chris seldom won against his determined wife, but the potential danger was troubling.

"Chris, you know I'm known for avoiding politics. No one will suspect anything covert from me."

"Yes. So what artifacts are you searching for when you make this highly illegal search of his library? And what if you get caught?"

"Do we need to go through that again? You know Dan and Sadler need hard evidence. They're hoping I will find something to force Creighton out in the open, force him to do something truly incriminating."

"Evidence, like a porno tape? What is it that will link a video or a movie directly to him? There's a notable difference between having pornography in your possession and actually producing it."

"He won't know all that the authorities know or do not know. But fear of discovery may force him to act."

"You mean go after you?"

After a brief pause, Jenny admitted, "Yeah, that's the plan."

JENNY

"Okay, Jen. I understand this has to be done. And I did agree...I know. It's just that I don't want you hurt. You seem to be ignoring the danger here. I'm...I'm simply uncomfortable with this whole scenario." He reached for his wife's hand and gently stroked it. "I love you, Jen. I'm sorry I haven't been with you on this. I'm..."

"I know," said Jenny as she stood looking down at him. "So, now, I need your support. I know there's danger. But please...please don't remind me. I need to remain in denial on that point. Stopping Creighton Leonard helps me justify why in God's wisdom he allowed Jason to be taken in the first place. I need that. Chris, I need that."

He released her hand, and she withdrew it slowly. "So what does Dan believe you'll find that can be so incriminating?"

"A video or film is the best guess. You know, everyone wants to be in movies and become a star. Dan believes Creighton has filmed his clients in action. Trophies, in a way. Like a big game hunter collects physical reminders of his prowess. That's probably what Jennifer Stewart interrupted."

"A long shot, isn't it? You're not going to have time to be selective. What can you tell from a title if there is any identification on his collection?"

"Well, what I saw was titled. For example, one videocassette I happened to see was titled *Tawney*. Who do you know with that name?"

Chris raised his shoulders and his eyebrows while he shook his head in bewilderment.

"Our good governor, for one."

"Jenny, you can't be serious. This is just too far-fetched."

"Now wait a minute. Is it? Is it really? He's a frequent guest of Creighton's. He's a known womanizer. He certainly hit on me."

"You didn't mention that before. You..."

"If I remember, he said I should be in movies. I didn't think anything of it at the time. But now...What do you suppose he meant? I mean he could have..."

"So that's one video you'll grab. What else?"

"Dan has given me a list of possible titles, key names of dignitaries. Look, it's a place to start." Jenny began to back away slowly, a glimmer twinkling in her eye. "Who knows, maybe I'll find someone really famous. The president, maybe."

"And that title?"

"How about *Billy the Kid* or *Jack and Jill*, as in Capitol Hill?" offered Jenny as she disappeared into the kitchen.

Chris could only shake his head in dismay. When she returned, she had unbuttoned the top buttons of her uniform, and her swagger was slow and sensual. When she spoke, she used the "lower than Jenny's" voice that had tricked him earlier. "Now for the entertainment. We have two hours before Jason comes home. And that wife of yours…Let's just say she's gone for the evening."

Chris's heart skipped a beat, and when she collapsed on top of him, nibbling at his ear, he found himself ready to discover just what beside the hors d'oeuvres the sexy server had in mind.

Chapter 77

Chris spotted Jenny across the room, a small silver tray in her hand laden with several glasses of expensive wine as she worked her way through the throng of guests. Present were the world's Who's Who. Many had journeyed from far reaches of the globe to celebrate Creighton Leonard's good fortune and hopefully, by association, their own. He caught her eye and held his empty wine glass high signifying he needed a refill. She began to move his way slowly as guests quickly relieved her tray of its full glasses. By the time she reached Chris, she had only empties. "Too much wine is not good for you, anyway," she teased. He grinned and deposited his empty glass on her tray.

"Well?" he asked in too obvious a whisper.

"Nothing yet," she answered. "Creighton is in the library with some guests. So…how am I doing? You don't think anyone has recognized me, do you? I haven't seen JB anywhere, and I hope I don't. He'd see through this disguise."

"No. I'm being asked where my lovely wife is by everyone we know, but so far so good. They seem satisfied with the hockey excuse. If you pull this off, you'll deserve an Oscar. The real you has to be known by half the room."

"Less than that. Fortunately, most of the executives weren't considered 'insider' enough and weren't invited. Moore and Lehr were, of course, but both are traveling." As Jenny spoke, her eyes swept the room. She had come in under the guise of filling in for another server who had become suddenly ill. Because she was so last-minute, she slipped past the screening interviews with Creighton's corporate and personal security staff. While guests were required to present their invitations at the door, the help entered through the back of the house. Earlier, a dark-haired man wearing an earpiece had spotted her. She had sensed his scrutinizing stare. Instinct told her that person should be avoided.

Jenny had totally overlooked the possibility of tight security. It had crossed her mind. But considering it now as she stood in the middle of such a diverse crowd, she understood Creighton's concern. Some in the room could hate him sufficiently to make an attempt on his life. If not his, one or two of his guests, as was the case at Mall of America press conference.

Suddenly, Chris felt her body stiffen. She ducked her head and turned her back toward the hallway entrance.

"The man in the doorway. Is he looking this way?" she asked cautiously.

Chris looked over Jenny's shoulder and casually studied the dark-haired man standing broadside in the hall entry. "Yes, but not at us. Why?"

"Do you know him?" she quizzed, her body rigid.

"Never seen him before like most in the room. Do you? Jenny, you're frightened...tell me."

"I don't know...Don't think so. Yet, something about him looks strangely familiar. Is he wearing an earpiece?"

Chris squinted slightly to reduce the glare in the room. At age thirty-five, he was becoming more near-sighted. "I can't see for sure from here. No, wait. He's wearing an earring. Yes, in his other ear. I suppose it could be an earpiece."

"He's part of Creighton's security. He was watching me earlier. I don't know, he gives me the creeps. Strange. Scary." Jenny positioned Chris so his back was toward the door and cautiously looked beyond his shoulder to the entrance of the room. She had been standing still too long. Mitzi had warned her not to be seen fraternizing with guests, a very early rule laid down by JB.

JENNY

Beyond the doorway, camera lights flashed several times. The dark-haired security guard remained motionless; his eyes sweeping the room. Quickly she ducked behind Chris. The look in his eyes showed his concern.

"Jenny," he whispered. She ignored him, venturing a peek from his other shoulder. The glaring lights from video cameras, *some media*, she thought, were trained on the entrance.

The first to enter was a tall handsome man, dark wavy hair, dark-skinned, wearing a pin-striped suit. She watched as he paused briefly in the *doorway*, nodded—she thought—almost imperceptibly to the security agent and stepped slowly into the waiting crowd of guests who immediately began to make room for him.

Next came two men, obviously security agents of some sort, eyes hidden behind dark glasses. They walked slowly, each melding into the crowd, going to opposite sides of the large room. Guests near her and Chris began to stir, blocking her view of the doorway. She pulled Chris sideways a couple of steps to clear her field of vision. Suddenly, her eyes connected with the dark-haired, ear-ringed agent who entered and took up a position inside the room's entrance.

Chris felt her flinch and instinctively moved to block the field of vision. "Jenny? You okay?" he asked.

"He saw me. Honey, gotta go." That said, she again poked her head beyond Chris's shoulder. The agent's attention turned to the entry hall as camera flashes again popped from just inside the room. She recognized the next guest as the Mexican ambassador. He was followed by Creighton Leonard, who looked very much at ease and triumphant. *What favors had he fashioned to gain such a victory?* she wondered. Behind Creighton came JB Barons.

"Here I go, honey," she whispered and squeezed Chris's hand, her other hand balanced the tray of empty wine glasses. "Love you," she said with a parting smile. "See you at home."

Before releasing his hand, she turned to him one last time. He felt a final squeeze as she moved off behind him. *Lord, protect her. Please, protect her,* he implored.

Clutching the tray in both hands, she made her way to a back wall, her eyes surveying each face. They smiled at her as she passed. None appeared overly concerned or sinister. None was familiar. Finding a coffee table, she set the tray down, picked up two empty glasses that sat on the table and added them to those on the tray. For a moment, she collected her thoughts.

There was only one entrance to the room from the main part of the mansion. To pass through there now would bring her face-to-face with the security agent who, one quick glance told her, had not moved. She worked her way along the edge of waiting guests toward a large drape that covered double French doors and the exit to a verandah. "Lord, let it be unlocked," she prayed silently.

Behind the fabric of the heavy drape, she could feel the doorknob. She pushed back the material and tested it. The door was unlocked. Sighing relief, she glanced about the room one last time. All eyes were on Creighton and his entourage who stopped just inside the entrance.

She took a deep breath and held it as she quickly darted behind the curtain into the warm spring night air. The security agent caught the movement of the drape and began to move in her direction. He pulled up short when he heard a crash on the far side of the room. In the distance, a server bent over to pick up broken glass from a tray of wine glasses that had been sitting on a small table. Chris stood over the girl, mumbling his apologies for being so clumsy.

Outside and grateful that the curtains were closed to block her from searching eyes, Jenny sprinted across the verandah and onto the grass. Continuing to run, she rounded the corner of the house. The days were becoming longer, and since daylight savings time had begun, it was still quite light at 8:00 p.m. The air was warm and moist, bringing with it the fresh smell of lake and a hint of fish. She reveled in the smell as she approached the long drive, now lined with cars and limousines.

She ignored the stares of occasional drivers standing beside their cars as they puffed away on cigarettes. The course she had taken

JENNY

around the house was not what she hoped, and suddenly, she realized she must pass by the entrance of the mansion to enter the delivery drive where her car was parked and reenter the side entrance to the home. Slowing to a less conspicuous pace, she straightened her dress with its frilly white apron and walked confidently past the entrance to the home. Several young men who had been hired to park cars for the gala event looked at her admiringly.

Once on the delivery drive and anticipating the need for a quick and hasty exit, she stopped at her car to verify the door was open and the keys waiting out of sight in the ashtray. Everything was as she had left it. Finally, filling her lungs again with the warm spring air, she continued to the delivery entrance, then through a short hall and into the kitchen.

Mitzi greeted her with a smile as she readied a tray of canapés. Immediately, she sensed Jenny's growing tension. "You okay?" she inquired.

"I'm fine," Jenny replied and motioned for Mitzi to accompany her to a corner of the kitchen, beyond the ears of helping staff. "I need your help, Mitzi. And somehow I feel I don't have the right to ask."

"Come now, gal. Ask away."

"I need to get into the library without being seen."

"That shouldn't be too difficult. Mr. Leonard had a meeting in there earlier. We're expected to tidy the place. I was just about to go there myself. Come along if you like."

"A...I need to be in there alone...and I can't be interrupted for at least thirty minutes."

"I'm sure you have your reasons," speculated Mitzi. Jenny hiked her shoulders in response. "No, don't tell me. I'm not going to ask. In fact, I have a feeling if I did, I'd wish I hadn't."

Jenny nodded agreement. "It's really better that you don't know. Really."

"Okay. Thirty minutes is a long time. Don't know if I can guarantee that. What happens if you're found out?"

Jenny answered with an unknowing look sufficient to signify the consequence would be dire. "Well, we better not wait. You ready?"

Jenny again nodded. Starting for the door, she stopped short to grab a service cart and an empty tub for dishes. "Gawd, I'd forgotten, gone in empty-handed. Not very professional, huh?" remarked Mitzi, turning to lead the way to Creighton's library.

Two knocks on the heavy door brought no response. Prepared to meet someone, Mitzi slowly pushed the door open. Looking around the room, she calculated the time needed to remove the debris from the very private meeting to be less than five minutes. She looked at her watch. "It's sixteen after eight. At eight-thirty, we begin serving entrees in the ballroom. Mr. Leonard may bring a small group back here. Don't know for sure. He's playing that by ear." She looked concerned. "Look, about fourteen minutes is all I can give you. Beyond that…Well, I'll try." That said, she quickly exited, closing the door behind her.

Jenny didn't waste any time. Grateful that Creighton had interrupted her on her last visit to the room and had taken time to show off part of his collection, Jenny walked quickly past the bronze wolf standing sentry just inside the room to the library-style desk where she remembered Creighton had placed the remote control that would open the hidden panel and reveal at least a portion of Creighton's video collection. She doubted Creighton would be so cordial this time should he come upon her snooping. One minute had passed.

As she remembered, the electronic remote rested on the desk beside a laptop computer with its lid closed. She picked up the remote and pointed it in the direction of the ornate wall panel. *What button to push?* Selecting the remote's up-arrow button in the library's dim light, she pointed it at the wall panel and pushed. Nothing. She pushed it again. Then again. Frustrated, she pushed all the buttons on the remote. *Come on! Come on!* she whispered. Then she remembered. Creighton had done something with the computer before using the remote. *Sure!* There had to be a computer-controlled access code. *That's just great! Great, indeed!* she thought and considered her limited knowledge of computers.

There was a chair on the opposing side of the desk. She looked at her watch, walked to the chair, and pulled it out from beneath the table. Four more minutes had passed. She sat, ran her palms over her cheeks nervously, opened the lid of the computer. The screen remained blank. *Great! Great! This is just great. Jason, where are you when I need you? You could figure this out.* "Lord! Please," she uttered aloud.

Jason had told her every new command was to be followed by an *enter*. She pushed *enter*. Instantly the screen lit up, and several menus scrolled past. *That's better.* When the scrolling stopped, the screen asked for her access code. "Lord!" she pleaded once again. Forgetfully, she ran her fingers though her hair, hair that was not her own, and swore under her breath

Access code? She typed in WYCO and pushed enter. Nothing. *I could be anything.* She typed in the name VIRGINIA. The computer refused to respond. She stretched her fingers to ease her tension then typed in HOUSE OF TOYS followed by "enter." Nothing! Finally, she thought, *access code…short…quick…easy to remember.* HOT, an acronym for House of Toys; entering it did nothing to change the screen. She resisted looking at her watch and retyped H O T, allowing a space between the letters.

She was in. The screen scrolled through several graphics then opened to a window with more options. Whoever had programmed the access control believed in keeping it simple. The options were: Open panel 1, Open panel 2, Access safe. This list offered twelve options in total. She selected, Open panel 1, reached for the remote, and again pushed the up arrow. *Yes! Yes!* Across the room, a large portion of the wall began to rise until it completely disappeared in the ceiling of the ornate room. Now visible under recessed lights within the panel itself were rows of trays each laden with boxes, videocassettes.

Approaching the open panel, she glanced at her watch. She had only six minutes to make her selections, close the panel, and return the system to standby or risk someone entering the room. She could not stop now.

She selected one of the cassette cases and opened it. Inside, the large videocassette had no title. Unable to decide so early into her search, she replaced it in its slot. Her darting eyes skimmed from cassette to cassette seeking a title like one suggested by Dan Sheridan. She discovered most were titled with humorous phrases; at least a hundred to choose from. *Eenie...Meenie... Inside The Kremlin* had an interesting ring. She picked it out and continued. Her eyes lit up when she spied, *Jack and Jill, Fun on the Hill.* This was too good to be true. "This one's for you, Dan," she said and removed *Jack and Jill* from the shelf while thinking to herself. She wondered if Creighton had titled the tapes himself. Was he also the clever punster. The titles played on words; someone was very clever, very sick, or both. Probably both.

Suddenly, her defenses shouted an alert. Her heart stopped. Someone was at the door. Horrified, she watched it open a crack. Breathing stopped. Her watch read 8:34. She had two videocassettes in her hand. The remote that would close the panel was on the other side of the room, well beyond reach. It wouldn't be Mitzi; she would be serving in the ballroom. Calculating quickly, she moved toward the service cart and deposited the two cassettes inside the tub of soiled dishes. She had been sent to clean the room, after all, and found it the way it was, panel open. Hopefully, the intruder wouldn't be Creighton himself or JB.

In the hallway, there was conversation. She froze listening. The door opened further. Voices grew louder. Again, the door stopped. "There you are, Mr. Leonard." It was Mitzi's voice, louder than the others. "I'm sorry, Mr. Leonard, we may have a crisis in the kitchen, I'm afraid. Orono police are here. They'll speak only to you. Something about illegal parking. I'm sorry. I tried to tell him...Mr. Leonard, could you come with me please. We're in the middle of preparing food and..."

Only when Jenny heard the footsteps receding did she breathe. "Thank you, Lord...Mitzi," she said audibly.

JENNY

Walking quickly to the desk, she picked up the remote and closed panel 1. On the computer screen, she moved the cursor to open panel 3, pushed "enter" and then the "up" arrow. Another ornate panel rose into the recess of the ceiling. She ran to the opened storage vault, her eyes scanning titles. There it was, *Tawny*.

"Yes! Yes!" she said under her breath and triumphantly raised her arms heavenward. She grabbed her final selection and deposited it inside the dish tub with the others.

Mission accomplished, she returned to the computer and pushed the "down" arrow to lower the panel. She considered the twelve items listed on the menu screen. Tempted to push the "open safe" option, she decided against pushing her luck further—who said this had anything to do with luck?—and chose instead "Exit."

When she had closed the laptop and turned off the computer, the door again burst open. This time, it was Mitzi. "We have to hurry, kid, they're coming back," Mitzi blurted, obviously out of breath. She began gathering glasses, dishes with remnants of food, ashtrays, everything and anything that didn't belong permanently in Mr. Leonard's exquisite library. In her haste, she had not noticed the videocassettes in the bottom of the tub, for which Jenny was grateful. Thank goodness, each video had its own protective case, for each was now covered with spent drinks and sloppy refuse.

Both women took one last look around the room. Jenny ran back to the computer desk to return the chair to its original position and followed Mitzi through the door, closing it behind them. As Jenny pushed the service cart in the direction of the kitchen, Creighton and a small group of guests entered the hallway twenty paces ahead.

Jenny took a breath and held it, smiling courteously. "The room's ready for you, Mr. Leonard. Do you wish to be served in the library?" Mitzi asked with as much confidence as she could muster when the two groups met.

"Please," came Creighton's response.

Jenny sighed. "Thanks, Mitzi. I really thought it was over. I mean, I would have been caught with my hand in the till. Figuratively speaking, of course. I really thought it was over, only minutes ago. You said the Orono police...?"

"It really happened. Once, last year. Put up a real stink. The police did. Anyway, all I could think of at the time. Mr. Leonard is infuriated by incompetence in anyone. Doesn't matter who, subordinates, public officials, doesn't matter, just incompetence. Next is swearing, vulgar talk. He can't tolerate that either. You'd think he was God himself. Mr. Leonard was not surprised to see the police had left to avoid another confrontation. Well, let him glory in his power. Needless to say, the police had not come. But it worked." She smiled at Jenny. "Get what you came for?"

Jenny smiled in response.

Inside the kitchen, Mitzi filled the sink with hot soapy water and began emptying the dish tub. "What do we have here?" she asked in amazement, reaching to the bottom of the tub to retrieve one of the videocassettes. "I didn't pick up anything like this."

"No, you didn't. I did. And you didn't see that," said Jenny. She retrieved the other two videos and then extended her empty hand to Mitzi to be rewarded with the third case dripping and sticky. She found a garbage bag on the counter and placed the three items of critical evidence inside.

"You know me, I won't ask. I won't ask," Mitzi assured.

"Good. Because I can't talk to you about these. And remember, you didn't see them. Okay?"

Mitzi nodded. "Like I said, I'm not asking."

"Believe me, Mitzi. It's better that you don't know." Jenny stepped up to Mitzi and embraced her. "I can't thank you enough for your help. You don't know how many innocent people you've helped by your action."

"Wow. That important, huh?"

"If these contain what I think they do. Yes, important."

"Your secret is safe with me. Until death. Remember, I said it earlier."

"Please don't let it go that far. In fact, someone may question you about these. You've seen the security here tonight. If they do, you don't know anything about these." She held up the garbage bag. "But you can say that you left me in the room alone for a few minutes."

"Then tell me, who are you? Are you the woman who came to my office and works for WYCO with the name of Jennifer Poole?"

"Good question. Just tell them that I was a last-minute replacement. Someone you really didn't know."

"With a name? At least a name."

"A name…Yes. Jennifer Stewart. Yes, that name should create the desired effect."

"Jennifer Stewart it is then."

Now resolute, Jenny gave Mitzi a final hug, turned, and exited toward the delivery entrance and her waiting car.

Chapter 78

Daylight was well spent when Jenny turned into the drive leading to their townhome, feeling good, mission accomplished. Once again, Susan Webster had consented to take Jason for the evening. Jenny's mother would deposit him at school tomorrow where Chris would pick him up early, excused from classes to accompany his mother and father in their family tradition, their first boat outing of the year.

As she suspected, Chris had not preceded her home from the Leonard gala. She shut off her engine in the garage and entered the foyer of the darkened home. Feeling her way, she hit the light switch on the wall. Lights on, she took her prized evidence into the kitchen where she dampened a towel and cleaned off the three cases. When they were toweled dry, she took her evidence upstairs to her bedroom and, sitting on the edge of her bed, quietly read the titles for a second time. In the quiet of her bedroom, she found herself overcome by emotion, awed by her good fortune in securing the tapes, good fortune she believed was not an accident.

Viewing the tapes was out of the question. Disappointing, but probably a good thing. Each was a commercial grade master, not the smaller home video variety. She didn't really need to pollute her mind anyway. But now she would not know the complete success of her ploy until the FBI could confirm the content of the tapes. It was scheduled that Chris would deliver them the day after tomorrow. For some reason, Sadler was unable to receive them earlier.

She found an empty shoebox in the closet and placed the clean cassette cases inside, setting the box on her dresser for Chris to see when he returned home. As she prepared a bath and got ready for bed, she considered the next day's schedule. She didn't feel comfortable keeping the tapes in their home until Chris could personally deliver them to Sadler. She decided, instead, to bring them to the House of Toys early the next day and secure them in her office wall safe.

That done, she would return home where she would take delivery of *Little Red* from its winter storage and launch it with Chris's help. Chris would then pick Jason up at school for the traditional "first on the lake" outing, with dinner dockside at Sunsets. Because of the risk of someone discovering her deception and coming to look for them, she and Chris had considered forgoing the event; however, after much discussion, they concluded the risk minimal enough to proceed as planned. Being first on the lake was a family tradition. And tomorrow's forecast called for unseasonably warm temperatures with a light south wind. If they were being watched, a change in plans now could attract even more attention.

After dinner, they would return the boat to their dock. For the night, they'd take up residence in a "safe house" under the surveillance of Dan Sheridan and Gary Sadler's team. Come to think of it: the family's protection was the reason for the one-day delay in Sadler receiving the tapes. He could not have his select team in place before then. Secrecy remained paramount.

The next day, Chris would pick up the cassettes at the House of Toys and deliver them to Sadler and the FBI at the federal building. Later, he would meet Jenny and Jason at the entrance to Camp Snoopy. The three would attend a brief planning session at Dan's office, setting their course for the next several days. They would then meet up with Jenny's parents and say their good-byes to Jason as he embarked on a trip to Disney World with his grandparents.

With Jason and Jenny's parents safely out of the way, Jenny and Chris could proceed with the next phase of the trap to bring

Creighton into the open. A phone call to Mitzi would instruct her to place a nervous call to Creighton. She would report her discovery of Jenny's deception and Jenny's admission that she had confiscated very incriminating evidence from Creighton's library, including, amongst other things, various videotapes. Then they'd wait. Sadler's team was purported to be the very best; Creighton would not get away.

As Jenny stepped into a warm bath, she tried to shake a growing sense of insecurity. What if the tapes were insufficiently provocative to cause Creighton's panic? What if they were, as Creighton had claimed, simply a collection of film? She tried to reassure herself that the plan should work. After all, Creighton couldn't be sure of what Jenny had taken. He had to realize Jenny had penetrated his private store of pornography and extortion files. A search would find the three videos missing, but he couldn't be sure of what else she may have taken. He'd have to suspect the worst: Jenny could destroy him.

After her bath, Jenny turned off all but one small night-light for Chris's benefit upon his return home and walked to the bedroom balcony door. Venturing out onto the small deck, she listened to the new night sounds of spring. "About time!" She took a deep breath. Overhead, a pair of geese honked boisterously, one of several mating pairs that marked the big bird's return to her channel.

To the east, the skyline of Minneapolis cast a luminous arc over the horizon. She could not remember when she had last stood at her balcony to take it all in. So much had happened during the past nine months more than she could ever have imagined. Here she was, about to close the final chapter on Jason's abduction and experience the satisfaction of nailing the person who caused it. Creighton Leonard, an enigma, a charmer and a sick, perverted villain wrapped into one. Greed, power, position, whatever his motivation—lives had been ruined because of him. Add to that, murder, political extortion, blackmail, and a sordid list of other heinous crimes. Surely, her involvement was not of her doing. Nonetheless, here she was a key player in ending Creighton's perverse reign.

JENNY

To the north, the big dipper sparkled, its cup pointing deep into space marking its eternal path northward. Somewhere along it's earthly path could be the yet-undiscovered remains of Jennifer Stewart, her whereabouts, a nagging mystery to authorities. Nothing more had surfaced since her overnight case had been discovered in a deserted preserve despite an extensive search by local police, FBI, and National Guardsmen. There simply was nothing. Closing the sliding glass door to a single wind whistling crack, Jenny held on to the notion that Jennifer Stewart had to be alive somewhere. She had to be.

Chris didn't wake Jenny when he entered their bedroom nearly two hours later. Standing in the dim glow of the night-light, he thanked God she was safe and quietly bent over her and gently, lovingly kissed her forehead. How he loved her. He had been so selfish, so inconsiderate of her quiet brooding over Jason's ordeal and the reasons for it. So selfish, indeed. Now, the reality of her present danger brought home just how much she did mean to him.

He had stayed at Creighton's long after the rest of his firm's partners had called it quits. Most guests had either retired to their guest rooms in the mansion or to their limousines. But he had stayed to the bitter end, nursing a single glass of wine intending to remain alert. If there were the slightest hint of anything out of the ordinary, he wanted to be aware. He needed to be sure Jenny had not been found out. So he stayed until he was sure, dead sure, she had not been discovered. Happily, the evening went the way of most parties, drinks—lots of them—and conversation, well-seasoned with new expectations from those who had fought so vigorously for LAIPT's passage.

Before crawling into bed, he examined the contents of the shoebox Jenny had obviously left for him to see. Satisfied that Jenny's assignment had been successful, he slid under the covers and "spooned" until sleep overcame him.

Chapter 79

"Congratulations! Mission Accomplished. Gone to the office to clear the slate for this afternoon. It's going to be a great day. See you noonish," said the note fastened to Chris's pillow and discovered by Jenny upon waking at 9:00 a.m., a good ninety minutes later than she had intended. Even the geese, engaged as they were in their raucous morning exercise, had gone unnoticed. Suddenly, she found the day noticeably shorter than she had planned.

Running through the shower and dressing in her favorite jeans, she bolted downstairs and turned on the coffee maker that Chris had thoughtfully prepared for her. It spit and bubbled as she turned on the answering machine, blinking to announce a waiting message.

It was Mitzi, calling shortly after Chris left for the office. "Mitzi, here," said the voice, "just a heads-up. All went well after you left. Thank God. No one suspects anything. No one approached me about anything out of the ordinary. Whatever you did, you did it well. Seems you're in the clear. Call if you have any questions. See ya." The assurance brought a sigh from Jenny.

Spring break would officially begin for Jason in three days, although he would leave school one day early to join his grandparents and continue to Disney World. But spring break elsewhere was in full swing, evidenced by the bustling crowds at Mall of America, vacationers bumping through her displays at the House of Toys as she made her way to her office and deposited her box of evidence inside her wall safe.

Eager to return home, she stayed only long enough to make two telephone calls. The first was to Dan Sheridan, who was not in his office. His answering machine sufficed, "Mission accomplished. We're on schedule. The evidence is in my office safe," she reported, knowing he would be pleased and, as planned, would now schedule with Gary Sadler. Phase 2 was about to begin.

The second call was to their boat storage service to confirm *Little Red* would be serviced and delivered to their dock before 1:00 p.m. Delivery in the water was an afterthought but welcomed since the day was already half spent. She didn't want to further delay their family's traditional first outing.

She had hoped to speak with Dan but didn't want to wait. Later, she thought. Indications were her family would have a day to themselves, a day they needed. Too soon, their lives would fill with new tension. Tomorrow they'd start the clock, beginning with Mitzi's call to Creighton. Dan and Sadler would be ready. *Gone for the day*, she thought, quickly walking past her in-store displays and giggling kids.

Leaving the parking ramp, she rolled down her windows, "Let spring begin," she shouted, then exited on westbound 494. Home now twenty-five minutes away.

Chapter 80

"You're sure they're gone?" inquired Richard Burns, who had been summoned from Creighton Leonard's kitchen. He had been raiding the refrigerator for a late breakfast apart from Creighton's other houseguests who were enjoying a sumptuous buffet in the formal dining room.

As instructed, Richard located Creighton in his library. From the fire in his eyes, it was obvious, Creighton was livid.

"Don't question me! Of course, I'm sure. I would not have suspected anything, but my *safe open* alert appeared on the computer screen. I checked it, the lock was open, the door closed, but access was possible. And, no, I don't know if anything was taken from there. I do know that three videos are not in their place."

"But you have other guests…"

"None who have access to this." Creighton gestured wildly, thrusting his arms toward the now-opened panels in the library walls.

"May I ask, who does have access other than you?"

"No one but Miguel. But he would have no reason. Besides, he will not be back until tomorrow. You're my security now. I want this resolved. Now!"

"Yes, Mr. Leonard. I will—"

"I entertained in here last night. Nothing from my library, of course. Conversation mostly. There were women present. Everything was in order."

"Before, perhaps…"

"No…wait. The catering service. Two women were in here. Cleaned the room between gatherings. I met them in the hall."

"But why?"

"Your people checked them out?"

"Yes. Thoroughly. All but one—a last-minute replacement."

"Then find her."

"Again, I must ask, what would be her motive?"

"Find her, and we'll know. Find her! I don't care what you do. No one is to know about this!" stormed Creighton.

Chapter 81

Jason bounded around the corner of his family townhome and ran toward the dock where his mother stood waiting to greet him with a big smile. *Little Red* rested quietly at the dock, waiting for its first run of the season.

In the distance, the telephone rang as Chris strolled onto the yard in Jason's wake. He gestured questioningly to Jenny, his hands palm up as he stopped and waited for instructions.

"Let it go. The machine's on. We've got more important things to do. Right, Jason?" directed Jenny.

"Right, Mom," agreed Jason.

Chris waited until the ringing stopped and the answering machine picked up the call before joining his wife and son on the dock. Jason scurried to release the lines.

"My God, please be home," summoned the female caller to the answering machine, "Please pick it up. Please pick it up." The Poole family was well beyond range to hear the message from the anxious caller.

"Jenny, Jenny, this is Mitzi. They know! They know it was you! They know, and I'm scared. What have you done? This guy…He was at the party…Creighton's security, I think. He came to my office just before noon. Barged right in. Linda was at lunch. Anyway, barged in, steamed as could be and demanded to know where the girls were that had cleaned Creighton's library.

"I told him it was none of his business. That didn't set very well. I demanded to know what was wrong. He calmed down and told me some things of considerable value were missing from the library. He didn't elaborate but insisted that the only persons who could have taken the items were the catering staff, and two of them had had access.

"I told him he was crazy. My staff wouldn't do such a thing. Besides, I was one of those girls he was referring to, and I didn't take anything. I thought he was going to come over the desk for me, but he didn't. Then I told him what you told me to say, that I had left you alone in the room to clean it up. He seemed satisfied with that.

"When he demanded to know your name, I gave him the name you told me, Jennifer Stewart. I don't know who Jennifer Stewart is, but the name sure set him off. I could just see all kinds of rage in his eyes. I mean it was just such…a look. He demanded an address. I told him I didn't have one and that you had come in to apply for a job when I needed a last-minute replacement for someone who called in sick.

"He stormed out. I followed. He climbed into his black Mercedes and left. I didn't give him your name. But, honey, I have this feeling he knows it was you. I'd bet on it. I'd suggest you get out of town. Go someplace, like to the police if you can. I've been calling everyplace for you. I know I'm taking a chance just leaving this message. I mean he could be at your home right now listening. But, honey, you gotta know. You gotta know." Mitzi hung up. *Little Red* with its cargo of three glided quietly up the channel to open water.

Chapter 82

The boat ride was exhilarating, to say the least. After a slow start moving slowly and methodically to be sure that Jason was capable at the controls, Chris smiled at Jenny and told Jason to "hit it." He knew the meaning and pushed the throttle to full. *Little Red* shot up on plane, instantly skimming the water at a comfortable sixty miles per hour.

They took the south route toward Excelsior through Echo Bay. Beyond Gale's Island, Jason turned eastward to Wayzata. Buoys had not yet been positioned to mark sandbars, points, and other hazardous areas, but Jenny knew the lake like none other and smiled smugly as her son brought *Little Red* onto a straight course equidistant from either shore, straight to Wayzata bay, flat out, slightly airborne, just the way she liked it.

"Look at that," shouted Jason, pointing toward Sunset's dock, their final destination, now less than a thousand yards in front of them.

"Well, we're obviously not the first," declared Chris, eyeing the oversized cigarette boat moored at one of Sunset's slips.

Jason pulled back on the throttle. *Little Red* slowed and settled into the water. To show his stuff, Jason approached an outer slip on his port side, turning the boat sharply just as they were inches away. As the boat swung to port, he cranked the wheel, pulling the throttle to reverse. The boat stopped instantly and swung gently against the dock, bow out. They had arrived. Chris and Jenny looked at one another and broke into applause.

"Yes!" shouted Jason, jubilantly giving two thumbs-up. He had obviously rehearsed the maneuver in his mind for days and timed it perfectly. Smiling, he jumped to the dock and secured both bow and stern lines before his proud parents could think twice of the matter.

"We're fast, but I doubt we could beat this," Chris speculated as they walked past the larger-than-life *Miami Vice* styled ocean racer, a "cigarette." "Bet, she'd do a hundred easily. What's the speed limit on this lake anyway? Forty, forty-five?"

"Didn't bother us either, did it?" teased Jenny.

"No, but this is overkill." Chris took one last look at the unfair competition and led the way to Sunset's waiting patio, already beginning to bustle with sun-hungry lake lovers. A table in one corner looked inviting; a young couple had just left. The Pooles walked to the table and seated themselves as a waitress came, gathered glass debris onto a tray, and swished the table with a damp rag.

Jenny watched the tray-laden server push open the glass door into the main restaurant and disappear inside. "She could have taken our drink order. I am ready for…for this time-honored family tradition. I am ready," declared Jenny, waiting for the server to return.

"Look! Isn't that JB? Creighton's assistant," asked Chris.

Jenny turned her head to look again at the doorway the server had entered. "It is. Say, the two of you have never met. It's about time, don't you think? He can join us. And don't let on we know of his involvement in all this." Jenny began to stir, changing position to catch JB's attention. "And don't mention the tiepin," she admonished. Bewilderment swept over Jason. He had no idea what his parents were talking about.

Jenny began to stand just as JB recognized her. His face turned ashen at the sight of her. He began to shake his head in the negative, and he brought a finger to his lips as if to shush her. She stopped, confused. The door opened behind him. He mouthed the word "Go! Go!" His eyes said he meant it. Jenny understood.

Quickly, she turned her back to the door and JB and reached across the table to grasp Jason's hand, then Chris's. "Don't say anything! Don't do anything! Don't even move!" she demanded in a loud whisper. The dramatic instruction produced its effect; Chris and Jason froze in their chairs.

"Something is wrong. Something is dangerously wrong. Chris, look at JB."

Chris turned nonchalantly. Standing beside JB was the security agent he had seen in the doorway at Creighton's party. He recognized the small gold cross dangling from his pierced ear. Towering over the agent, JB mouthed again, "Go! You must leave!"

Chris turned to hide his face. Only Jason now faced the doorway.

"I see what you mean," cautioned Chris. "It's the guy from the party. The guy who gave you the creeps."

"That means they know." Jenny hunched down to make herself less visible.

"It appears so," Chris agreed. Cautiously and calmly, he pushed his chair back from the table. "We better leave," he whispered. JB and Ricardo Burns stood no more than fifteen or twenty feet behind them, not much of a head start. "When I say go, move quickly."

Chris looked at Jason as he spoke. Jason shook his head in affirmation. His eyes were riveted on the two men standing in the doorway, one, the tallest person he had never seen close up; the other, a handsome muscular man with dark hair and a single gold cross dangling from one ear. The dark man was looking directly at Jason, at first innocently enough, but his mind churned, processing, seeking.

A gentle breeze brushed the back of Jenny's neck. Gone was the light odor of food replaced by the subtle sweet fragrance of a man's cologne. It was an odor Jason recognized, or thought he did, as he searched his memory. His eyes riveted on the man who had driven the van that had taken him from the street outside Milly's Lakeside Cafe.

Jason watched the door open behind the two men when a server laden with a tray of giant burgers and baskets of fries excused herself and crossed in front of JB. "Ready! Go!" said Chris the very instant they were blocked from Ricardo's view.

"To the boat," snapped Jenny.

Neither Jason nor Chris needed to be told. Jason led the way in a dead run. With the youthful agility of a gifted hockey forward, he twisted and turned, sprinting through packed tables as surprised eyes followed his finesse. Chris, slightly more encumbered, followed, nearly knocking down a waitress who had turned to watch Jason and had stepped in his path. Jenny chose a different course, sprinting past a table just emptied of its six diners but accidently hit a table sending plates, glasses, napkins, and baskets crashing and rolling over the patio.

She hurdled a small spring planting and descended the path to the lake and their waiting boat. She was only ten feet behind Chris. She reached inside her jean pocket, confirming she still had the boat key and picked up her pace without looking at the chaos behind her.

Jason reached the dock first and loosed the bow line. Seconds later, Chris did the same with the stern line. Both held their lines and waited for Jenny now running onto the dock to the confused looks of Sunset's diners pointing and screaming in their direction. JB was moving slowly, politely toward them, taking his time. But moving quickly and not so politely, Richard Burns burst through the throng, pushing two women over as he bolted for the dock.

"Keys," Chris yelled to Jenny, his male hormones demanding that he protect his family and deliver them to safety. Jenny handed them over and took the rope from Chris's hand.

Instantly, Chris was in the driver's position and inserted the key into the ignition, turning it hard until the high-performance engine awoke with a whine. "Let go the front," Jenny ordered Jason. He released his line and jumped on to the boat's front platform, quickly taking a seat on one of the small storage locker seats in front of the bulkhead. *Little Red* bounced in the water as Jenny shoved off and jumped aboard to join him on the cockpit seat. They'd made it. They'd be safe in open water.

Jason and Jenny held tight the "sissy bars" as Chris pushed the throttle full forward, immediately bringing *Little Red* to plane.

Instantly, the sixty-plus miles per hour rush of air made their eyes water. Jason faced the stern, his hair waving in the wind when suddenly he raised an arm and pointed toward shore at the dock they had just left.

Objects on shore grew smaller by the second as they quickly distanced themselves from those in pursuit. Jenny turned to follow Jason's point and watched the muscular security agent jump into the ocean racer and then quickly jumped back onto the dock. No keys. He yelled to JB running slowly toward him.

"Good!" shouted Jenny; they gained a few extra seconds.

When Ricardo reached JB, JB obediently fumbled in his pocket, eventually producing the keys to the high-powered craft. He then followed Ricardo onto the boat and took a position in the port side bucket seat.

Two swirls of cold exhaust clouded the rear of the "cigarette" boat as it sprang to life. While the two 350-horsepowered engines warmed, Ricardo released the lines, tossing them haphazardly onto the boat's surface before jumping back behind the console and backing the boat from its slip.

Free from the dock, he skillfully counterrotated the engines. He knew the boat. Knew it well. The large craft spun in its own length. He pushed the throttles, and the engines surged with an explosive roar. Instantly, the large tube-like boat lumbered to plane. He had his orders. His targets would not escape. He was in his element, power, speed, open water.

Jenny estimated a half mile separated *Little Red* from the pursuit boat, but it was capable of a far greater speed and gaining on *Little Red*. They were heading west. Jenny turned to get her bearings. On her left was *Spirit Knob* and *Woodland*, her parent's home. Ahead on her right was Spirit Island. Beyond was the open water of Minnetonka's main lower lake.

While the cigarette had speed, *Little Red* had maneuverability. Big Island lay ahead where they could outmaneuver the cigarette in its small bays and a channel that opened to Excelsior Bay. But then

JENNY

what? Reach the city dock and run to town? Unlikely, the cigarette was too fast. They'd never make it.

She looked aft again. The cigarette would be on top of them before they could reach the small cuts through Big Island. That was obviously the route Chris intended to take. But she could see they would never make it.

Moving at a speed much faster than theirs, the ocean racer was quickly gaining. She prayed, *Now what, Lord!*

"Chris!" she shouted in the wind to get his attention. "Chris!" she shouted again, tugging on his shirt. She had an idea. "Go that way!" she barked when he turned toward her. She pointed to the northern route, past Brackett's point and the Pillsbury mansion, toward the Arcola Bridge and Crystal Bay.

Chris shook his head and turned his face resolutely into the wind. Instinct told him the south was a better way. To the north were rocks, several reefs, unseen and as yet unmarked for the summer boating season. He didn't know the lake well enough to avoid them. He hunkered down. He was in control.

Ahead, Jenny could see a floating marker where Jordan Green's ice house had stood only weeks ago. Authorities had removed it prior to ice out returning it to Bill Wilson's home where it sat outside Martha's bedroom window, a grim reminder of her loss. Jenny had to do something. She and her family were next on the assassin's list.

"Chris!" she shouted again and slugged his shoulder. "Look! Look!" she shouted, pointing aft. The cigarette was gaining on them. "Give me the controls. We'll never make it."

He slid from under the wheel allowing Jenny to take his place at the controls. *She was right. Again. As always.* Looking back, he thought he saw a gun in the driver's hand. Or was it his imagination? He ducked down to make as small a target as he could and shouted to Jenny to do the same.

At the controls, Jenny shot a glance aft and cranked the wheel sharp to starboard. Ricardo reacted quickly and turned to reduce his angle of approach even more. They wouldn't get away. His gun now rested in his lap. He didn't need it. Not yet, anyway. He looked at JB who was facing forward, his arms helplessly crossed in front of him. He'd deal with him later. Those orders would eventually come. He knew they would. But for now, he was exhilarated by the boat's power and speed. He loved the chase and stood suddenly to raise his head above the windscreen and smiled into the nearly ninety-miles-per-hour wind.

Less than four hundred yards separated the two boats. Jenny held her course northward toward the western tip of Brackett's Point. One hundred yards from the point, she began a shallow arcing turn to the left, shallow enough that the larger boat could not gain any distance on them by cutting the angle. She was heading into Crystal Bay, separated only by an unmarked channel and the Arcola Bridge. She had two options. If they could make it beyond the bridge, there were several small bays and channels where she had a chance to outmaneuver the "cigarette."

But she had a better option.

Another glance aft. They'd never make the bridge. She marveled how quickly her mind was working, as though she was living in slow motion. Nanoseconds seemed like seconds, seconds seemed like minutes, yet time was passing in a heartbeat. And with each beat, the pursuer was gaining.

For one of those nanoseconds, she thought of JB and wondered, *Would he survive? Please save him, Lord.*

She glanced at her family, holding on tightly, their attention directed to the unmarked water ahead. Her family's lives were in her hands.

To her starboard was the shallow reaches of the bay and not a good place to maneuver. But to her port were rocks, big ones, a reef covering an area the size of a baseball diamond and hidden only inches below the surface, unmarked because the buoy markers had not yet been placed.

Her mind worked quickly. At her speed, only two inches of transom touched the lake's surface. The outboard engine shaft and propeller extended another eighteen inches into the water. But when properly trimmed for maximum speed, that depth diminished to six inches or less. Furthermore, the lake's level was usually at its highest level in the spring, after the ice thaw. She estimated twelve to eighteen inches of water covered the submerged rocky reef.

Glancing aft again, she could see the grinning face of Ricardo Burns. He was close. Too Close. Yet, perfectly close.

"Hang on!" she yelled. Chris and Jason tightened their grip. Chris was looking forward and praying that Jenny knew what she was doing. Jason turned sideways in his seat to watch their pursuers, almost entertained by it all, confident his mom did know what she was doing.

Abruptly, Jenny turned to a new heading toward Huntington Point. "Jenny! Jenny!" yelled Chris, a look of horror on his face. "The rocks! You're heading straight for the rocks!"

"I know," she shouted as *Little Red* sped on, skimming the surface of a large area of open water, rapidly approaching the large boulder reef, the home of abundant walleye and remnants of shattered propellers and rudders.

Creighton be damned, she thought and felt for the engine trim control beneath her fingertips and pushed it upward, tilting the engine backward, raising it almost out of the water. Inches separated the boat's hull and propeller from the rocks below. They were nearly airborne, flying on a cushion of air, a feature of the boat's hull design. She knew the "cigarette" had no such design. It was an ocean boat, designed with a deep "V" hull for cutting through rough, choppy sea.

But with little hull and propeller in the water, steerage was difficult. Jenny fought to hold *Little Red* steady; her knuckles tight and white on the steering wheel. Chris prayed in earnest; his eyes closed. Jason, realizing what his mother had done, waited for what would come next.

He didn't wait long. The distance between boats had narrowed to mere yards when he watched the ocean racer turn to port about to pass them. It was high on plane but displacing a lot of water, spraying water twenty feet on either side. Behind followed a treacherous wake that would certainly capsize *Little Red* if the cigarette were to pass.

Then it happened. Like the Exxon tanker Valdez, the "cigarette" went aground; the impact was abrupt and damaging. The sudden stop shot JB forward and, over the windscreen, landing him on the forward deck. Ricardo was not so lucky; his forward motion was stopped by the steering wheel that broke upon impact, impaling Ricardo on the steering shaft. His head broke the windscreen into a mass of jagged class chards that severed his jugular.

Smoke billowed out of the engine holds. Jason waited for an explosion, but none came. The cigarette's forward momentum carried it well over the first pile of rocks into a deeper section of the reef where it was sinking, filling the luxurious lounge of imported leather furnishings with water.

Clear of the reef, Jenny pulled the throttle back to neutral. As *Little Red* settled in the water, she looked back at the disaster on the rocks. Chris opened his eyes and watched the pursuit boat sink as Jenny put *Little Red* in motion again and maneuvered *Little Red* back toward the reef. Shaken by the experience, Chris shook his head and uttered, "I can't believe it. Honey you did it." Never…never again would he question his wife's judgment.

So he asked, "Now what? We leave them here? We're certainly not going to help."

"What are you saying? We can't leave them. They're injured," said Jenny as she steered toward the wreckage.

At such a slow speed, *Little Red* sat deeper in the water than when they crossed the reef at high speed. Nudging the reef's edge, they careened softly from rock to rock seeking an entrance to the deep center. They were now close enough to see the extent of the damage. "Doesn't look good. The driver…I don't know…doesn't look good," said Chris.

Jenny retrieved her purse from a cubbyhole beneath her seat and grabbed her cell phone. "I'm calling 911." While she reported the boating accident, Chris jumped into the cold water, shoes and

JENNY

all. By leaning on, the front edge of *Little Red* sat higher in the water enabling him to direct the boat over the rocks and into the deeper pool.

"We don't have much time. A sheriff's boat is coming from Spring Park, probably thirty minutes. We don't want to be here when they arrive," warned Jenny.

Chris didn't argue. He was now pulling *Little Red* in waste-deep water. Ice-cold water and loosing feeling in his feet. Maneuvering alongside the cigarette, he nosed up to the boat's long forward deck where JB lay motionless, blood dribbling from a gash in his head where he careened off the boat's spotlight. "He's breathing," announced Chris.

"Get him on board," said Jenny.

"Jenny? We're already witnesses, in fact, participants, to an accident where one person is dead. What are you thinking?" asked the attorney-husband.

"We can't leave JB here to be arrested. He's been trying to protect us. He's not totally innocent. But…he's not totally guilty either."

Resigned, Chris reached for JB's leg and started pulling him toward *Little Red*'s front cockpit. Suddenly, JB kicked his leg free and raised up on an elbow, regaining consciousness and appearing groggy and disoriented.

"It's Jenny. JB, you've been in an accident. You can't stay here. The police are on their way. You need to come with us," explained Jenny. JB glanced back at the broken windscreen and the lifeless body of Ricardo Burns and slowly reached for Chris's hand as Chris helped him onto *Little Red*.

As soon as Chris pulled *Little Red* clear of the reef and jumped back on board, Jenny pushed the throttle forward. "Hang on," she said, bringing *Little Red* up on plane and steering a course to their townhome channel. She ignored the "closed throttle" sign at the opening of their channel and continued at sixty miles per hour, covering the distance to their dock in seconds. She'd always wanted to do that.

They quickly secured *Little Red* in its slip and passed through their home just long enough to grab suitcases they had previously prepared, called Dan Sheridan to tell them what had happened to learn the location of the "safe house" he had arranged for them for the evening. For the immediate future, they would be under the protection of Sadler and his FBI team. Chris would deliver the tapes in the morning as planned. Then they would draw Creighton into the open.

After deciding to drop JB at the corner drugstore in Excelsior, where he could call for a cab to take him wherever, she stopped in her tracks. Overcome by emotion and coming down from the biggest adrenaline high she had ever experienced, the reality of what she had just done was more than she could take. While the garage door opened, she waived JB forward and drew her husband and son close. While they hugged, she quietly wept.

Chapter 83

Creighton stood over Jenny's desk at the House of Toys looking for something to pry open the locked drawer. He had quickly rifled through her file drawers and found nothing, not the videotapes he was looking for. That Jenny had not been to the lake office was confirmed by Mildred and the night guard. Jenny's small office at the House of Toys was the only other place she could have left them. Or she had them with her and planned to give them to the FBI.

Beyond the closed office door, staff had arrived and were busily preparing for another day's business serving families excited by spring break and a visit to Mall of America. Creighton had arrived before them and had not considered encountering anyone.

He had spent a restless night in his office grabbing a couple hours of sleep on his couch between fitful hours searching files for any incriminating evidence that could aid investigators that he knew were closing in on his enterprises. JB had not checked in, and he had no knowledge of the whereabouts of Miguel and Ricardo Burns. He couldn't believe his world had come to this, his web of blackmail exposed, his sex trafficking, slavery, and corruption that reached most of the world's political regimes—all because one employee was found to be in the wrong place at the right time.

That employee had been dealt with, but not before she had unleashed events that were now spinning out of his control, leaving his fate in the hands of a young mother, another employee who had gained the attention of his wife—her sister in the faith—and was now her confidant in his personal House of Toys.

Mildred Knowles didn't know Jenny's exact whereabouts, but according to Jenny's assistant, Jenny planned to meet her husband at Mall of America by the entrance to Camp Snoopy. Creighton guessed they would have with them the evidence to destroy him and set the world politics in turmoil.

"I thought I'd find you here," said the resonant voice he had known since childhood. Creighton had not heard anyone enter. He looked up to see Miguel standing in the doorway.

"Good, you're here. And Ricardo?"

"Dead."

Creighton looked surprised.

"Killed on Lake Minnetonka in a boating accident. Apparently, he wanted to experience the boat's power and speed on your lake." Miguel paused for a moment and watched Creighton's face turn red with anger before continuing, "Unfortunately, he did not know where the rocks were. He died instantly."

Creighton stood in disbelief.

Miguel continued, "He carried no identification. It will take time to identify him. But the boat is licensed to Random Enterprises. That fact will cause many inquiries and turn up the heat. And eventually lead them to me and to you."

"The tapes? The Pooles must still have them?" It was more of a statement than a question as a new plan formed in his mind.

"I'm afraid so, amigo."

"And what of the Pooles?"

"I believe they are now in protective custody."

Silence followed. Two lifelong friends stared at each other. Each understood their relationship was about to change. Finally, Miguel let his eyes sweep Jenny's office. On the wall behind her desk was a framed picture of an eagle soaring high over a large rock formation protruding from the desert floor. It was the work of a child. He knew the child. The artist was his granddaughter.

JENNY

His mother had told him of Jenny's visit to the small mission and her gift.

He turned back to face Creighton. "It's over, my friend," said Miguel. "For me and...well, you decide for yourself."

"Not if I can stop the Pooles. The evidence so far is only circumstantial."

"And what do you propose?"

"I'm told they will be here today. They plan to meet at Camp Snoopy."

"And then what?"

"We stop them."

"And how do you propose we do that in such a crowded place?"

"We grab the boy and the tapes."

El Lobo stood in silence shaking his head slowly as he studied Creighton, his decision weighing heavily on his heart.

"No." Miguel held up his hand to stop Creighton from moving farther in his direction. "As I said, it's over, my friend. The killing must stop." He paused briefly. "I will no longer play a role in your war with Jennifer Poole. In fact, I want her safe. She will not be harmed further! Or her family. Do you understand?"

Creighton had never faced such firm opposition from his childhood friend. He glared at Miguel and mustered a response. "Why now?" was all that came to mind.

"I am reminded of another boy and his mother, forced to flee their home in fear." He paused, adding finally, "You see how life turns full circle. This family does not deserve such a burden."

"And now?" questioned Creighton timidly, for he understood El Lobo's fury.

"I leave. As should you. We will not see each other again, my very good friend."

"But—" Creighton gasped.

"That is how it must be. I am no longer safe in this country. I must go," said El Lobo and turned to leave. Halfway to the door, he stopped, "You understand, my friend, Jennifer Poole will not experience further harm? She and her family are to be left alone, yes?"

As his words registered with Creighton, El Lobo passed through the office door and disappeared beyond one of Jenny's lavish displays.

Creighton stood in disbelief. They had been through so much together. He felt sadness but did not know how to respond. He knew Miguel was right; he too must leave. And something told him he did not have much time.

After surveying the office one last time he stepped through the door and into the store. It was a short distance from the office to the store's third-floor entrance. A discreet glance confirmed that no one was close by. He walked quickly to the entrance, exited the store, and headed for the escalator. He knew what he must do.

Chapter 84

A light mist enveloped the Twin Cities shortly after a crimson sunrise. Dan Sheridan grabbed his umbrella from behind his driver's seat and sprinted to the covered portico of the Hilton Airport Inn. It was a short drive from Mall of America but too far to walk in the dismal weather. Besides, Dan needed his car for the drive downtown, where he would deliver the tapes Jenny had rescued from Creighton Leonard's residence to Gary Sadler.

Sheridan and Sadler had made a last-minute decision that the best place to hide the Poole family would be in plain sight and close by. The Hilton Airport Inn was the perfect hideaway. It was also a way to reward the Pooles with a brief luxurious holiday for the dangerous role Jenny had accepted to gather evidence. The cost of such a respite was beyond the standard per diem allowed by the bureau or mall security, so Sheridan and Sadler agreed to split the difference. Sadler, in particular, was delighted to provide such a reward and was already reveling in the soon-to-be concluded quest to see Creighton Leonard behind bars.

Plans had changed with the death of Ricardo Burns. The threat to the Poole family remained very real, but Sadler believed danger was no longer imminent. With a lower threat, there was no need for the Pooles to join the meeting with Sadler and Sheridan; plans were already set and in play. If the tapes implicated Creighton sufficiently to warrant his arrest, as they suspected they would, a manhunt would soon become official. Already, one of Sadler's team was on its way to Leonard's Lake Minnetonka residence.

Inside, Dan walked to the front desk, asked to use the house phone, and requested a call be placed to the Poole family in the "executive suite."

"Sir, are you Dan Sheridan?" asked the attendant. Dan nodded. "The Pooles have asked me to direct you to the restaurant where they are having breakfast."

The restaurant was only a few steps away. Dan entered and found the Poole family seated at a table against the back wall. They smiled as Dan approached, and Chris retrieved a shoebox from beneath the table.

"Everyone okay?" asked Dan.

"We are now," answered Chris. "Thanks to *Little Red* and Jenny's skill behind the wheel."

Dan recalled Jenny's guided tour of Lake Minnetonka and smiled. "You're very fortunate."

Chris handed Dan the shoebox containing the rescued videotapes and motioned for Dan to take a seat beside him. "Time for a coffee?" he asked. "You now have the evidence to shut down Creighton's empire."

Dan raised the box in the air. "Thanks for these. That comes from Sadler as well." With that said, he placed the box on the edge of the table and took a seat beside Chris. "Coffee sounds good. Haven't had any yet this morning. Sadler has been waiting for this evidence for half his life. A few more minutes won't hurt. Besides, I'd like to hear how you outmaneuvered that cigarette boat."

He paused for a moment and added, "If you didn't know, the driver of that boat was the assassin Ricardo Burns. He didn't survive. Some witnesses said there was a second passenger in that boat, but a second body has not been found." He paused again as the waiter delivered a cup of coffee. "You called 911. Did you get close enough to the wreckage to notice another body?"

It was Jason who answered. "We wanted to get home as fast as we could and left. We didn't see another body." Jason smiled discreetly at his mom, hoping she would not scold him later. It was the truth. They didn't see another body, as in dead body.

Dan smiled at Jason. "Well, if there was a second person, we suspect that person was Creighton's assistant JB Barons. Sadler has been unable to locate him. It's very possible that a second person could have been thrown out along the way, swam to shore, or drowned. The county is combing the waters.

"Now, how did you outmaneuver that ocean racer?"

Chapter 85

Creighton methodically closed the hidden door in his library wall, just another sculptured panel in the meticulously finished library. Next, he replaced the portrait of his mother, Ann, painted so many years ago by his father, Raymond. With emotion sweeping over him, he lingered for a moment and ran the back of his index finger over the textured face. Remorse coursed through his body. *Enough!* Turning abruptly, he checked his emotions and stepped back to his desk, picked up a leather-bound directory, and placed it into his opened briefcase. He had a plane to catch.

Suddenly a movement in the shadow of the library door caught his attention. He had not heard anyone enter. Whoever it was must have come in while he was in his concealed vault. Nonchalantly, he placed his hand over the pistol he kept in his desk drawer, pushed his chair to the side with his knee, and waited.

"I thought I'd catch you here." It was JB's voice. "I received a call at the office. The plane's ready. The flight plan is filed for Bogota. Sudden, isn't it?" He remained in the shadows, only faintly visible to Creighton in the dim light of his gracious library.

Creighton withdrew the pistol and nonchalantly placed it in his briefcase with his directory. He would not need to use it against his young protégé.

"It's over," he said, impatiently turning to JB. He had no time to waste. "Ricardo is dead. Miguel wants out. I will soon be linked to this entire affair. Now, if you'll excuse me, I have a plane to catch. The same goes for you, by the way. I suggest you join me. There's nothing here for either of us. We can live comfortably anyplace in the world but here."

"So we can start again and ruin even more lives?" JB moved from the shadows toward Creighton, passing through a shaft of light from a small recessed lamp in the ceiling that reflected on the pistol clutched in JB's hand. Creighton wished he had not closed his briefcase.

Creighton slid the briefcase off the desk and stepped toward JB. "Do you plan to use that, JB? It's just not you. Really, it isn't," Creighton said with confidence.

JB gestured with the pistol, stopping Creighton. "I'm afraid I never understood the true source of your power over others. I know about your vault, your library. You have a trail of influence from the House of Toys, to DC, and to almost every center of power around the world." He paused and then said, "I'm sure you're aware Jennifer Poole has sufficient incriminating evidence to end it all."

With a look of resignation, Creighton shrugged and said, "I'm afraid so. My secure vault was not secure enough, was it? Now I must be going."

JB gestured again with his gun, causing Creighton to take a step backward.

"Like it or not, JB, were in this together, you and me," he said nervously. "Face reality. There's room for you. We need each other, now more than ever. You'll be safe with me."

"Someone has to stop you, Crey. You're an evil man," said JB, resolutely blocking Creighton's path.

"It's an evil world. And when did you become the saint? Now get out of my way," Creighton said angrily. Determined to hold his ground, JB took one step back and nervously gestured again with the pistol.

Creighton decided not to test him further. "What is it you want? Money? More money? It must be money. Today's world runs on money and sex. You're no different. Not really."

"I have enough money, Crey. I want my life. And you've pretty much ruined that."

"I've ruined it?" screamed Creighton indignantly. "You've acted on your own. Like the rest, you went along for the money. It certainly wasn't for sex."

"The money, yes, but not murder. Tell me, would you have killed Jennifer? Would you have killed the entire Poole family if they'd not gotten away? Killed them like Jennifer Stewart?"

"That was not my doing, believe it or not. In fact, believe what you will. You seem to have made up your mind as to my guilt or innocence. Now use that thing or get out of my way. You know you really should join me," he spoke through his teeth. "Now I must be going." He lurched forward and swung his briefcase at JB's hand.

Surprise filled his face as the gun exploded, and he felt a searing pain in his chest. Then his legs suddenly would no longer support his weight. He slumped to the floor, half propped in a sitting position against the back of his desk. Blood gurgled from his lips.

JB looked at the gun in his hand. Disbelieving and disgusted by what he had done, he flung it to the far corner of the room and stooped down next to his onetime mentor. Creighton's glazing eyes met his. "Don't you see?" said the dying man in a faint whisper as he weakly grasped JB's shoulder. "It's not just me. You were like...like a son. Safe. I kept you...safe. Now—"

Before he could finish, he winced in pain, blood bubbled from his drooping mouth, and his eyes closed for the last time.

Slowly JB stood, aghast, his eyes focused on Creighton as though expecting life to return. It had happened so suddenly. But that was why he purchased the gun—to *stop Creighton for good.*

What did Creighton mean by "it's not just me?" *Of course!* Suddenly it came to him. *It had to be.* Quickly, he reached down and released death's grip on the leather case. He had seen the small book Creighton had placed inside. He withdrew it and thumbed through its pages. Names, dates, numbers, notations. It had to be the names. The book was the source of Creighton's power, the names of those he served.

Earlier, he had let himself in through the servants' door. Now he raced through the elegant halls, back through the kitchen, and to the back pantry and garage. He ruled out the Porsche parked in the far stall and ready to go. That would have been Creighton's escape, another of his toys. Only those closest to Creighton even knew he owned one. But bright red, it was too easy to spot, even in traffic.

Cautiously, JB peered through a small window in the garage door. Satisfied no one was near, he found the garage-door opener, pushed its button, and darted to his car. In the distance, he heard the wail of sirens. Packing his lanky frame behind the wheel, he sped down the long drive, stopping briefly at the roadway before turning west, away from town, the opposite direction from which the police would come. He was free. The thought was invigorating. Confidence engulfed him. Jennifer would be safe; he'd see to that. He too would be safe. His fingers caressed the small book on the seat beside him. The plane was waiting.

Epilogue

Colorful maples held their colors of crimson red and brilliant yellows a week longer than normal before a heavy, gusty rain washed the branches clean. Coot were rafting by the thousands on Minnetonka's bays, a prelude to their southern migration. Next, the geese would follow. With the onset of fall and winter approaching, life for the Poole family had taken on greater normalcy.

School for Jason had begun in earnest, and any spare time was filled again with traveling hockey. Christian made good on his promise to become more involved and signed on as assistant coach for Jason's team, a flexible position to accommodate his occasional travels. As a full partner in the law firm of Johnson, Carlson, Shapiro, & Nord, stints out of town were now less frequent. Duly encouraged by Chris's participation, Jenny became even more involved, serving now on the parents' committee as cochair.

Jenny considered those activities as she strolled slowly under soft gray puffy clouds, sailing quickly overhead, carried by a twenty-mile-per-hour wind from the northwest, so typical of a Minnesota fall. The thermometer read sixty degrees, but the wind made it feel much colder.

The Pooles' mailbox stood on the country road at the end of a quiet lane. As Jenny approached it, she pulled the drawstring on her down jacket to retain more heat and studied the leafless trees, skeletons that allowed the chilling wind even greater freedom. With the leaves gone, she had an unobstructed view of the upper lake to the west and the lower lake to the east.

She had come home early today. She was pregnant again. Experience told her morning sickness would soon end; then she'd get big—she hoped not too big. Her baby was due in May. She was betting on a girl. She had always wanted one of each. She had been an only child and did not wish to be the mother of only one. Even with an eleven-year spread in age, Jason also looked forward to a sibling.

She and Chris decided this would be their last winter on the channel. Perhaps their last winter living on the lake, what with lakeshore prices ever rising. They simply needed more room. Just the week before, she had found the business card of their real estate agent who had helped them locate their townhome five years earlier.

Following his advice, they would put their home on the market early next spring. First things first, he had advised. Once the house was sold, they'd find just what a partner's pay could get them.

But she had a dinner to prepare. Chris would come home early. They would be joined later by Dan Sheridan and Sharon Miller. Their relationship had blossomed recently, so much so that Jenny was expecting an announcement would come at dinner. She smiled as she reached inside the mailbox. She was so very happy for both of them.

Inside the box was a sizable stack of mostly junk mail. She retrieved it all and glanced at the last envelope, another sweepstakes. She'd sort it later.

Clutching the pile in one hand, she snapped the door close just as a gust of wind whisked away an envelope, blowing it five or six feet before it was snagged by a leafless clump of lilac. She rescued it, and turning it over, she looked at the return address. *What is so special about this envelope? Things happen for a reason. Is it worth saving?*

There was no return address, but several stamps she didn't recognize were accompanied by a postmark that read *Argentina*. She knew no one in Argentina. Bemused, she tapped the envelope on her forehead. Savoring the suspense, she placed the mysterious letter back in the pile and began a leisurely stroll home.

Dan Sheridan had been prophetic in his speculation that Chris would become the hero in the Leonard investigation and be able to write his own ticket with the company and his firm. The affair certainly accelerated his becoming partner. And with Virginia Leonard actively directing in the background and a new management team running day-to-day activities, Christian Poole's position was secure. He was Virginia's man.

The brush with danger increased Chris's awareness of each passing day and proved the compelling force behind his increased involvement in his son's life.

The affair had its effect on Jenny too and her realignment of priorities. She had been offered a vice-presidency but, after due consideration, had turned it down in favor of motherhood. She continued to work at WYCO, where she would have a job as long as Virginia owned the company. But she knew that would not last forever. Virginia was a shrewd Christian businesswoman, and if she could not pursue her evangelistic ideals and still run a profitable business, she'd forego the business.

Additionally, a decision had been made to move 80 percent of the company's US production to Mexico. It was only a matter of time before the corporate offices would also relocate somewhere closer to the transplanted operations, a relocation Jenny would not make.

The lake was too much of her life. Besides, Chris's income would continue to grow. And...already it seemed more than enough, although not yet sufficient to buy a home on the lake. But she believed that would change in time. In the meantime nothing was more important than her family, each member a true gift from God.

A 'V' formation of honking geese passed overhead, playing in the wind on their way south. In the spring they flew in pairs, sometimes small formations of four or something under ten. But in the fall, they'd gather into larger formations of fifty or more. Jenny didn't know the reasons for it, but recognized the signs of the pending migration. She watched them swoop low, skimming the water before climbing and turning to take the wind head on.

Jenny passed the front door and continued beyond the garage, around the house and into the rear yard, where just a week ago *Little Red* had waited at the shore for one last ride. *Little Red* had saved her life. But she knew even it had seen its best days. Next year she'd push for a larger, safer boat that even a new baby could enjoy. She looked at the empty slip. *Little Red* now sat in winter storage.

A tidy pile of wood sat ready at the patio door. They'd need it, she thought, the weather was changing. A sudden chill caused her to shiver as she entered her living room through the sliding glass door, the same door where Jeb Barons had sought a glimpse of her as he was pummeled by rain and hail. The costly tiepin still resided safely in her night stand jewelry box. Where was he? she wondered. He had never been captured. Dan would have known and told her. She hoped he was safe somewhere. But where? Argentina, perhaps? She glanced, again at the pile of mail as she set it down on the coffee table.

Virginia had turned over Creighton's entire collection of master films and videos to the FBI. She had never imagined the extent of her husband's perverse involvement. Seeing them carried out by the truckload seemed a grim mockery of her own rebellious years when she refused to heed her own parents' warnings and fell in love with Creighton. At the time, he seemed everything she wanted in a man. She just didn't know his darker side; she was blind to it. Over the years, they had grown distant, for sure. But to his credit, he had remained faithful to his wedding vows. As she had expressed to Jenny at the funeral service, he was a person of great contrast.

Jenny had waited for indictments to follow confiscation of the tapes. Dan had viewed several with Gary Sadler before all the evidence was ultimately moved to some archive deep in a secret location. He had confided to Jenny the delicate nature of the videos and contradictory lifestyles and morals of the many known public figures they portrayed. But even he didn't mention names. He understood the need-to-know philosophy and believed it best that Jenny didn't know. With knowledge came danger, danger she didn't need.

She would ask about them again, tonight at dinner, but she knew the response she would get. At least her family was intact and safe. One very immoral man had been taken down, and who knows how many lives had been protected? What a year it had been.

She glanced at her watch. Jason would arrive home within the hour. Coffee brewed while she fetched the mail. Its strong, enticing aroma filled the air. She poured a cup, returned to the living room, and set the coffee next to the mail. Thinking of Chris, she retrieved several pieces of split wood from the neat pile beside the patio door and, with the help of two matches, heard the fire's friendly crackle.

She made herself comfortable on the sofa where she could see the fire and the channel beyond the patio. Finally, she was ready. She picked up the mysterious envelope, mused over it momentarily, and then methodically tore it open. Outside, a small flock of geese splashed down just beyond the empty dock.

The envelope contained a card, its face hand-painted. It was beautiful, a solitary crimson rose on a pale-yellow background. She smelled to see if it was scented as well. The paper was soft and delicate. It brought to mind the exquisite work of art displayed in the Leonard's Santa Fe gallery, the rendering of a Plains Indian and the antelope he had just slain. Someday she'd write to Maria and inquire about her granddaughter.

When she could bear her curiosity no longer, she took a breath and slowly opened the delicate card. Inscribed inside in beautiful penmanship were three words: "Forever! Jenny. Forever!" Instantly, her eyes moistened, and emotion overwhelmed her. Only one person on earth would understand the significance of those words: the boy who had loved her, the man who had protected her.

There was no signature. Like the note in her yearbook, he knew she would understand. At least he was safe. She sighed. But how long could he remain on the run? she wondered. Was he beginning a new life somewhere? In Argentina?

Outside, a gaggle of Canadian geese dashed across the calm surface of the channel until finally their big bodies lifted into the north wind. She watched and wondered, *It's spring in Argentina. Would they fly that far? Mmm…a new beginning.*

Cast of Characters

Jennifer Ward Poole…heroine
Christian Leighton Poole…husband of Jennifer
Jason Poole…son of Jennifer & Christian
Jennifer Stewart…WYCO gopher, missing witness
Jim Stewart…Jennifer Stewarts's brother, Nebraska hog farmer
Creighton Aldon Leonard (51). New CEO Wyco Toys, villain, BEGAN Feb. 94
Miguel Alverez… El Lobo, (51) Creighton's childhood companion, villain, "The Wolfe"
Gomez… The assassin, alias Richard Burns
Maria Alverez…Miguel's mother
Virginia Leonard…Creighton's estranged wife
Raymond Leonard…Creighton's famous artsy father
Ann Leonard…Creighton's mother, famous interior designer to the stars
Matthew Ward…Jennifer's father, Executive businessman
"D" Ward…Jennifer's mother
Johnson, Carlson, Shipiro, & Nord… Christian Poole's law firm
Dan Sheridan (35) …head of Mall Security, former FBI
Cory Sheridan… deceased son, would have been 10. Struck by car at 18 months.
Gale Stearn Sheridan… Dan's estranged wife, whereabouts unknown
Jordan Green… (45) head of Wyco security
Bill Wilson… (44) Green's BIL, Wyco food service
Martha Wilson… (43) Bill Wilson's wife, Jordan Green's sister

"Old Mike" ... Excelsior's character, only witness
Kirt Fenton... Christian's New York contact, Jennie's inspiration
William & Grace Stoddard...NM reservation missionaries
Warren & Leah Holcomb... Missionaries from Minnesota in Mexico, helped Maria
Sharon Miller...Jennifer's admin. Mgr., secretary
Renee Nichols (Nicki)...Christian's secretary
Susan Ewing...The Ward's neighbor, Peter's mother
Chief Nickolas Carlson... Minnetonka Police Chief
Anne Carlson Graham... (32) Chief Nick's daughter
Ramon (Ken Edwards) ...Anne's first husband and father of her children
Nick (12) & Donny (11) ...Anne's Children
Terry Graham...Anne's 2nd Husband
Officer Larry Randall...Mtka policeman
Officer Stella Kraemer...Mtka policewoman
Stanley Girard... Abel security head
Gary Sadler...Local FBI head
Lewis Wentworth...Sadler's nephew believed to have been killed by C. Reynolds
Lilly Turner...Mall security woman, good with kids
Shirley Jones...Attractive, FBI rookie
Donald Stone...Channel 6 news anchor
Janet Spalding...Channel 6 co-anchor
Helen...Dan Sheridan's secretary, girl Friday
Dr. Jim Clark...Attending Mall physician
Tawny Johnson...Governor, State of Minnesota
Willard Mallovich...Senator from New York
J.B., Jerry (Jeb Clampett) Barrons...Jenn's secret admirer, Leonard's assistant
Lester Barrons...J.B. Barron's father and one-time employee of Creighton Leonard
Kathleene Warren...Secretary to Creighton and J.B. (45), Attractive, efficient

Mildred Knowles…Plant #1 executive receptionist
Martinez Group… Int'l consulting firm, front for Maquelle, drugs, prostitution, etc
Ricardo Burns… young killers alias, Gomez, alias, Richard
Juan…Assassin #2
Fredrich Bartlett… would-be assassin…member of STUFFIT
STUFFIT… Students Truly Unified for Free International Trade
LAIPT… (Latin America Industrial Partnership Treaty)
Wendal Moore… WYCO, VP of Operations
Burton Lehr… WYCO, VP of Marketing
Harold Benner…Past WYCO President, embezzled funds, committed suicide
Mr. Makido…Japanese Business, object of assassination attempt
Daryl Kohl…VP of personnel
Random Enterprises…Money pool used by Creighton to fund questionable org
Reed & Phylis Baker… Old farm friends of the Stewart family
Dr. Janet Welch…County medical examiner
Nelson Field…Store Manager "House of Toys"
Mark Stevens…Male cheerleader, married three kids
Kent Simons… Male cheerleader, Gay, Actor in Porno flics
Tiny Tim Richards…Karen Walker's third husband, divorced, he
Sandra Klempken…Cheerleader, "Barbie," mother of four
Christy Slayder…girl on snowmobile (12) who finds Jenny S suitcase
Roy Slayder…Boy on snowmobile. Christy Slayder's 6 yr. old brother

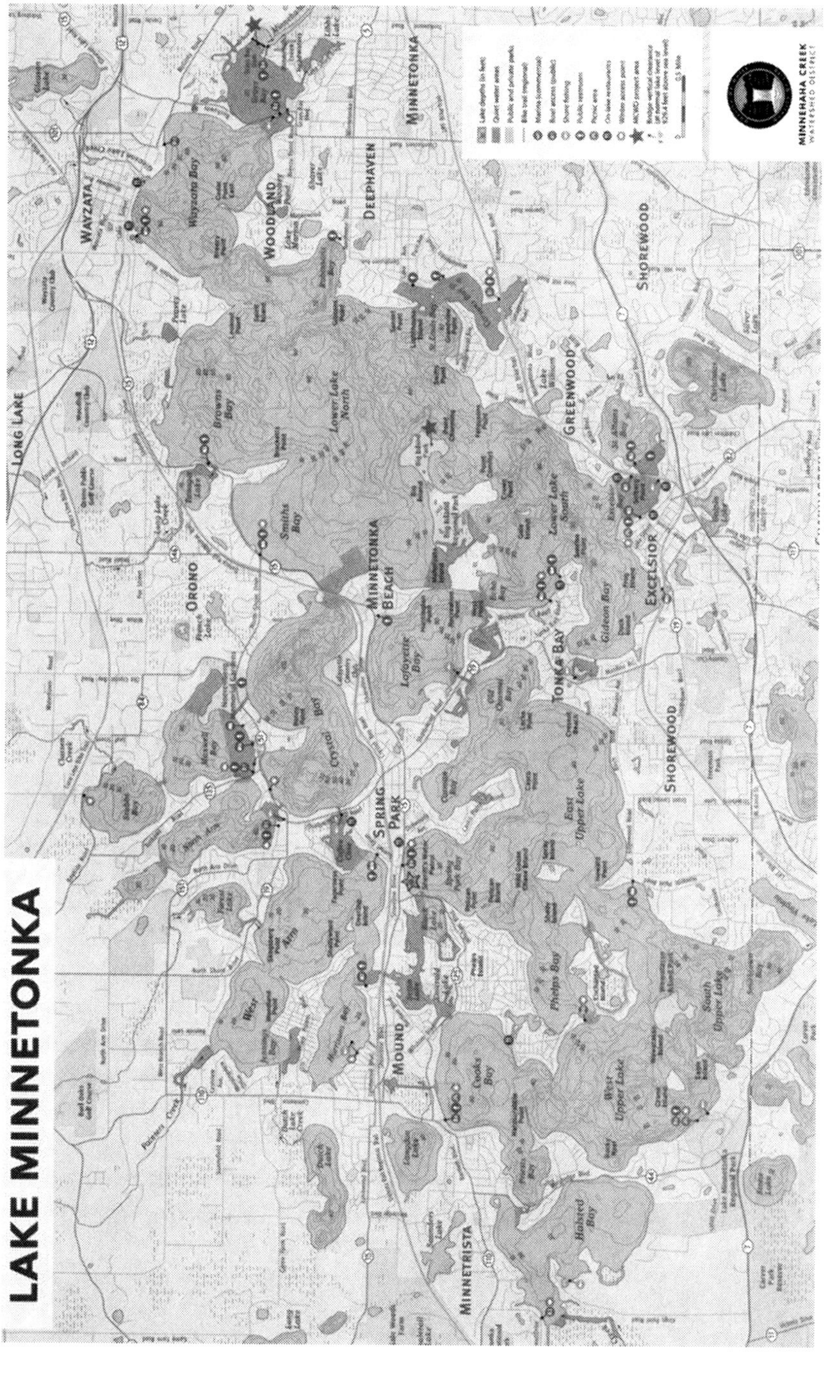
LAKE MINNETONKA
WAYZATA
LONG LAKE
ORONO
WOODLAND
DEEPHAVEN
MINNETONKA
GREENWOOD
SHOREWOOD
EXCELSIOR
TONKA BAY
MINNETONKA BEACH
SPRING PARK
MOUND
MINNETRISTA
MINNEHAHA CREEK
WATERSHED DISTRICT

About the Author

Inspired by a junior high school English teacher who loved his writings and discovered his writer's heart, Ronald Stanchfield became a lifelong writer of stories, biographies, and poetry, mostly for private consumption. Growing up in the corporate environment of a family business, Ronald and his identical twin worked their way to board-level management before selling the business. Rewards of this corporate lifestyle offered extensive US travel and provided fodder for his writing in a style rich in vivid detail that draws readers into the moment and bystanders to the scenes parading in written word.

This style is evident in Ronald's first novel, *Jenny*, his second book. His first book, *Good-bye, Mitch*—coauthored with his daughter, Rebecca Chepokas, and written after the death from cancer of Rebecca's son, Mitch—serves as an inspirational guide for readers experiencing similar tragedy.

Now brimming with suspense, the novel *Jenny* rewards its readers with delightful imagery of scenes and events, fueled by reflections of Ronald's life experiences as Jenny journeys into the unknown with the conviction that all things happen for a reason.

CPSIA information can be obtained
at www.ICGtesting.com
Printed in the USA
FFOW03n1918230118
44601702-44495FF